The Aviator's Apprentice

The Aviator's Apprentice

Will Turner's Flight Logs
Part One

Chris Davey

Lucky Press
126 S. Maple Street
Lancaster, OH 43130 USA

Publisher's e-mail: books@luckypress.com
Book website: www.luckypress.com/willturnersflightlogs
Series/aviation-related website: www.turnerlogs.com

Cover Design: Peri Poloni, through indypub
Editing, Illustrations & Interior Book Design: Janice Phelps
Proofreading: Sonja Beal
The cover photograph is from the Hulton Getty Collection.

The Aviator's Apprentice and subsequent titles in the series "Will Turner's Flight Logs" are available at your local bookstore, at www.luckypress.com and other online booksellers, and through Lucky Press, 800-345-6665. For information on wholesale purchases for pilots associations, veterans organizations, military libraries and bookstores, book clubs or other non-bookstore special markets, or for purchases outside the U.S. and Canada, contact Lucky Press.

Publisher's Cataloging-in-Publication

Davey, Christopher
The aviator's apprentice. Will Turner's flight logs: part one / Chris Davey ; illustrations by Janice Phelps. -- 1st ed.
p. cm. -- (Will Turner's flight logs)
ISBN: 0-9679050-3-2
Library of Congress Card Number: 00-106579
1. Aeronautics--History--Fiction. 2. Air pilots--Fiction. 3. World War, 1914–1918--Fiction. I. Title

PR6054.A95D38 2001 823.92
QBI00-304

To
Peggy Grace Adair

Will leaned forward and shouted in good humor, "Matrett, I think it's important you should know, just in case we're killed, that you are a complete and utter asshole. You should know that before you die." To Will's surprise, Matrett ignored his provocation. He just pointed. "Take us down and follow the line of that river."

Will shrugged. Perhaps he knows, he thought. He eased the throttle a fraction, and the Farman sagged gratefully into a shallow dive. Will held them at seven hundred feet. Matrett pointed down with another angry jab of his finger. "If we go lower we'll be in range of every rifle an' machine gun in the German army—if they are down there," Will shouted.

Matrett twisted in his seat. He pushed up his goggles. "That's the idea. If they start shooting at us we'll see the flashes. Scared, Turner?" he sneered.

Without replying, Will pushed firmly on the stick and felt the weightless sensation as the Farman pitched into a dive. At four hundred feet they trundled steadily across the plains to the east of Paris in search of the elusive German army. After half an hour, which put them almost to the northwest of the capital, and still with no sign of their quarry, they swung south and east.

Ten minutes later Matrett pointed excitedly, "Bloody hell, Turner! There they are! Take us over that wood." Matrett indicated a forest north of the river. They crawled toward it at three hundred feet. Will looked in disbelief as hundreds of gray-clad figures rushed from the edge of the trees. Even at this height he could see the flashes from hundreds of rifles aimed at them. Simultaneously, he felt the controls jerk in his hands as bullets crashed through the wings and tail surfaces. Matrett turned to him, a look of fierce triumph in his eyes. "Found 'em, by gad! The top brass will have to be—," he paused for a second and turned to look down as Will forced the controls over, trading height for speed to take them away, "—lieve us now."

Will stared at him, horrified. As Matrett spoke the last words, bright blood burst through his lips to blow back over Will's shoulder. "You damn fool, Matrett, you're hit."

Matrett had collapsed in his seat, moving feebly. Will tried to gauge how far they needed to fly. It had to be twenty miles to the British lines, but he could put down as soon as he saw friendly troops. He looked longingly to the south, but even as he did the motor coughed, hesitated and then ran on. It might as well be twenty thousand miles, he thought bitterly. Why the hell had he allowed Matrett to taunt him into such a stupid stunt once they knew the position of the cavalry? He struggled on, coaxing the Farman through the air.

Looking ahead, Will saw another enemy formation camped by the edge of a field. From two hundred feet he could easily see vehicles and horses and even upturned faces. He flinched, expecting another fusillade of bullets and tried to ease the biplane away. What insignia is that? he thought dumbly—a big red cross on a white circle.

Matrett stirred himself to look at Will as he heard him cut the switches to stop the motor. "What the hell are you doing?"

Will could not hear the words, he just saw Matrett's lips moving in pooled blood. "Saving your fool life," he bellowed. He concentrated on an inevitable crash landing. The Farman, once so reluctant to fly, now seemed bent on prolonging its life. They were in danger of overshooting the field. Will thrust his right foot hard against the rudder and pushed the stick to the left while pulling back. The big machine staggered in a sideslip, hanging for a moment almost stationary before subsiding gracefully to the ground. Will let go of the controls as they hit and put his arms over his head. He expected an impact but there was none—just a splintering, shattering, screeching crash that went on for what seemed like minutes. The noise stopped. He looked around. He almost laughed. They sat, still strapped in their seats, on the ground in what looked like the makings of a bonfire. "Christ!" he swore. "A bonfire." He unbuckled his seat belt and then tugged his observer clear of the wreck.

Matrett was still conscious. Glaring at Will, he found enough strength for words. "You treacherous bastard...you cowardly swine. You've surrendered."

Characters:

In America—

Will Turner ....Graduate of MIT in mechanical engineering.
John Turner ....Will's father. Wealthy businessman, engineer, inventor.
Charlotte Turner ....Will's mother. An Englishwoman, known as "Charley" to her friends.
Victoria Turner ....Will's sister. Looking for direction and adventure.
Nathan Walker..............Civil War veteran. Self-taught engineer.
Cordelia Walker............Nathan's wife. Previously Will and Vicky's nurse.
Henry Walker...............Their son. Graduate of Florida Agricultural and Mechanical University.
Roscoe Vandersand.......New arrival in town. Son of prominent politician.
Jeff Vandersand............Roscoe's older brother.
Walter Julien ....A neighbor and friend. Involved in real estate.
Emily Julien ....Walter's wife.
Marie Julien ....Their daughter.

In England—

Frank Penrose ....Charlotte's brother. A career army officer.
Constance Burnett ....Frank and Charlotte's older sister. Suffragette. A widow.
Rupert Penrose.............Frank's son, an officer in the Royal Flying Corps.
Kate Penrose ....Frank's daughter. Rupert's younger sister.
Tom Armstrong.............Will's employer. Pioneer airplane pilot, engineer.
Archie Carstairs ....Rupert's best friend. Cavalry officer.
Sophie Pellew ....Rupert's fiancé.
Marjorie Pritt-Allison .....Friend of the family and social climber.

Chapter One

FROM THE ALLIGATOR'S ADMITTEDLY LOW PERSPECTIVE, WILL Turner made for real irritation. Will's sister, Victoria, would agree. For an artist the scene was perfect: sparkling water, old growth crowding the bank, and light her Yankee aunt, Audrey, once described as "sunshine filtered through orange-blossom honey." But Will, standing in the river, spoiled the picture she was trying to paint. She pushed up the brim of her wide, straw hat with the chewed end of her paintbrush and sighed. She knew there was nothing to be done about his looks—hair like straw, nose too big and bent, scar on his eyebrow—but for goodness sake, she thought, surely he doesn't have to keep waving his arms around!

"Will! How do you expect me to capture this scene if you insist on wavin' that rod 'round your head?"

"I'm wavin' this rod so I can cast. That's what you do when you catch fish."

"Brother, you couldn't catch cold. I'm better with rod an' line than you'll ever be."

Will knew Victoria was right, but had no intention of admitting it. He was still working on his witty reply when she sat bolt upright in their little skiff.

"Will! There's the biggest damn gator I've ever seen about ten yards yonder!" She spoke softly.

Will was standing closer to Victoria than he was to the bank. One careful step at a time he started to move toward the boat. He raised one foot, balanced on the other, stretched and stepped down carefully onto the firm sand. He leaned forward, balanced...

"Run Will!"

The young man needed no extra encouragement. The plop and gurgle as the old reptile slid into the lake told him the time for stealth had gone. The water came up to his knees, and the harder he pushed the harder the resistance, but blind panic gave him the strength he needed. Arms flailing, legs rotating like a windmill to escape the drag of the river, Will did a credible imitation of a man running on water. With a clumsy joining of a leap to a dive he fell into the boat.

Victoria rolled off the seat into the bottom of the boat as it rocked wildly, dropping the oar she was about to use as a spear to fend off the alligator. She seized the oar again and raised it above her head grasping it in both hands. "Come on you old son of a—," she stopped, peered into the water, and then looked further out.

"He's gone! Buggered off! He's way over there." She pointed down river.

Will struggled to get his breath, then rolled over on his back. "Vic, I don't think that's at all polite," he admonished his sister, knowing full well there was no taming her.

"Aunt Connie says it."

"That's just the point, she's *not* polite—an' *she's* English."

Will's sister plopped down with a bump and put the end of her brush in her mouth. She sprawled like a boy, dressed in faded dungarees and an old worn shirt. Resting one bare foot on the gunwale, an elbow on her knee, Victoria relaxed into teasing her brother, "Nobody here even knows it's a cuss word."

Still waiting for his heart rate to slow down, Will let his head fall back and studied his sister through half-closed eyes. He admired rare beauty. Victoria's recent skirmish with a deadly fever had pared away the youthful softness in her face to reveal the features that stopped men in their tracks: wide blue eyes, high cheekbones, slightly prominent chin and nose, a mouth permanently on the edge of a smile. Her friends never called her pretty; that did not do her justice. Victoria's rivals comforted themselves by calling her the "Indian" behind her back. The young men just called, often as they dared. Her lustrous black hair was, indeed, inherited from her great-grandmother. The Creek nation often was blamed for her spirited nature, too. A precocious skill for cultivating the blooms that graced her family's formal gardens may have been an inheritance from those native cultivators, but Victoria Turner's independent nature was hers, alone.

Will Turner's looks favored his mother's. Tall, with blond hair running to red, Will's features were more accurately described as strong, rather than handsome.

"What are we goin' to do with you, Sister?" he asked.

"Send me away to New York or Paris—to study."

"Nah! Too tame for you."

"Then teach me to drive, Will."

"Aw...come on, Vic, you know women can't drive." Will expected nothing less than a spirited response, and his sister did not disappoint him. Her eyes narrowed, Victoria took the brush from her mouth and applied the pointed end vigorously to his ribs.

"Ow, that hurts!"

"It's meant to, Pig Face." She said, giving him another prod to emphasize the point.

"Okay, Okay! I give in. Women *can* drive."

She smiled at him sweetly, then lunged forward, pretending to pin him to the bottom boards with her knee on his chest. "So when you gonna teach me, Brother?" She introduced the brush handle to his left nostril.

Will's eyes crossed as he struggled to focus on his nose, "Soon as Daddy says it's all right."

"Promise?"

"My word as a gentleman."

"Ha! That don't mean much. We can start tomorrow."

"What! You mean to say he's already said yes?"

"He surely did." She took the brush out of his nose and sat back on the seat. "Daddy reckons you might as well teach me before I try it for myself, 'cause then he'd have to thrash me for disobedience."

Will laughed,"That'll be the day."

❧ ♦♦♦ ☙

Will knew the real reason their father would give in to Victoria's request. He had come perilously close to losing his sister to a vicious fever just a week before, and grew up more in a matter of days than in all his previous twenty-two years. He had seen his capable, confident father reduced to a stricken wreck, and his mother worn helpless. Even Cordelia, their childhood nurse, behaved with quiet concern, instead of displaying her usual cheerful contempt of sickness. But Cordelia's husband, Nathan, saved Victoria the night her fever reached its crisis.

Even Will, who recognized the bond between Nathan, the old engineer, and Victoria, his wilful sister, could not say from where the mutual respect and affection originated. He guessed they were very similar characters. When Victoria's needle-sharp wit made her go too far in polite society, it needed no more than a disapproving look from Nathan Walker to bring her back to what he considered proper behavior for a young lady. The night the fever reached its crisis Nathan pulled her back in a way no one else could.

Will had sat beside Victoria's bed all night long. Her father and mother lay exhausted in the room next door when Nathan, who had never been far away, arrived for his turn in watching over her. Will had mistakenly thought that his sister was sleeping peacefully after hours of delirium, but Nathan instantly recognized a crisis. Her pulse fluttered, she breathed shallow and ragged. Nathan could see they were losing her. With tears streaming down his face he had taken Victoria's shoulders in his big hands and shook her firmly while whispering fiercely in her ear. "You ain't goin' no place child, 'til I give the order an' I *ain't* givin' the order. Now come back here! Get back I say!"

They had seen no miraculous return to consciousness. Nathan told Will to massage her hands and feet while he applied still more cold towels to her face and trickled water on her parched lips. They had no need to call Cordelia, she knew she was needed and appeared at their side. For once she didn't chide them for not keeping the girl decently covered.

Not long after dawn, Victoria had opened her eyes and asked for water. In a weak voice she told them about her strange dream. She saw herself trying to wade through a river. Nathan stood on the bank behind her in his fancy Federal uniform yelling orders to her to "Get back here!"

She smiled at him. "Can't even go to sleep without you bossin' me, Nathan." She had looked around the room, puzzled. "Good to see you, but why're ya'll in my room, boys?"

That was too much for the pair of them. They staggered out to the veranda where Will found his eyes filled with tears. Nathan put an arm around Will's shoulders and squeezed him hard. When Nathan spoke, his voice seemed strained through gravel. "Close, William. Too damn close." He had turned to the rising sun and made a sound between a laugh and a sigh, " 'Why you in my room, boys?'!" He shook his head and took Will by the arm. "Let's go find a drink." By noon Will was in worse shape than his sister, who was already making a sound recovery. His mother and father woke to find their daughter fully conscious and sensible for the first time in three days, while their son lay peacefully unconscious in the big wicker swing on the front porch.

Cordelia had worried because neither she nor Doc Rogers knew for sure what had hit Victoria so hard.

A week later, the morning of Will and Victoria's painting expedition, Cordelia sat at the kitchen table, poring over books. "Wasn't no yaller fever, that's for sure," she grumbled. Will looked over her shoulder at the tight print in the well-thumbed medical textbook. "Does it matter what ailed her?" he asked innocently.

She twisted in her seat and treated him to one of her "idiot-boy" looks over her spectacles. She could suffer fools, with a certain grace, although not gladly, but she made no excuse for his relative youth. "Surely does," she said glaring at him. "What if it comes back? What if it's a new contagion in these parts? Seemed like some kind of brain fever to me so at least you'll be safe, hon'."

Will's attention was diverted. Newly baked moon pies cooled on a tray on the far side of the table, the sweet chocolate scent making him reckless; he timed his move and lunged. Without raising her eyes from the page, Cordelia's hand shot out and seized his wrist. He felt as if an iron band clamped on him.

"Slow, much too slow," she scolded mildly. "Take those, put them in the basket with the other stuff an' carry yourself down to the lake with your sister. She's bad off for air an' gentle exercise."

Will had chosen not to argue with Cordelia.

❧ ♦♦♦ ☙

Now, he found himself alternately assaulted by one of nature's most fearsome creatures and by his sister on this beautiful afternoon.

Will suddenly looked to the shore from where a voice hailed them. Nathan stood beside his heavy wagon on the path beside the water. "What in tarnation do you think you're doin', boy?"

"Doin' what, Nathan?" Will called back.

"Foolin' around tryin' to walk on water. That's like to blasphemy in my book, 'sides you'll frighten the gators and moccasins." Nathan's laughter floated down the smooth flowing river and drifted out into the lake.

Will looked suitably chastised. "I think old Jackson was fixin' on me for supper." He pulled on the line secured to the bow of their boat. The rope sprang dripping from the water, being fastened at the other end to a post on the bank.

Nathan bent down, took a firm grip and hauled them in, his strength undiminished by seventy years. "Talking of supper, you're both off the hook," he said. They stared at him, willing him to go on.

Pausing for a moment, he relented, "Well come on children, tote your stuff in the wagon. Okay, I told your mother that *you*, William, would need scrubbin' with kerosene to come clean after this morning's work, and Victoria would never be able to take rich food so soon after her bout. She said this once you could miss formal dinner. Anyways, there's Christian folk dining tonight; you young devils might frighten 'em."

Will grinned, "Not crazy Preacher Flint?!"

"The same. Alleluia!"

"Praise the Lord!" added Victoria.

"An' pass the ammunition!" intoned Will.

Flint was a local institution. Will wondered if the preacher should be in one. Wild of eye and beard, ferocious in sermon, prone to making up the scriptures as he went along, he commanded a remarkable following. People came from miles around to hear him preach, to hear the gospel, to marvel at his loquacity, to lay bets on who he would slander next in his fury.

"An' Father Morgan?" Will asked.

Nathan nodded. "I think he's there to referee."

Victoria's mouth dropped open. "Oh no! The Reverend McAllister is goin' to be there as well?"

Nathan nodded gravely, "Yep."

Victoria stopped, bent slightly forward at the waist, hands on her hips, alternating looks of horror and glee on her face. Glee won. She gave a little skip then took Nathan's arm. "It'll be a riot."

She was right. Tradition had it that an Irishman should be the Catholic priest, but McAllister was an Ulsterman and a Protestant to his bones. Will felt it even more ironic that the town's Catholic priest was an urbane Englishman, Father Peter Morgan. Nobody knew what had spawned the mutual dislike shared between McAllister and Flint, but they detested each other. Only two weeks before, Flint had announced to his rural congregation that McAllister was a practicing heterosexual. Skillfully combined with a sermon involving the beasts of the field, Flint was delighted that his unsophisticated audience, unfamiliar with the word, had drawn their own mistaken conclusions, just as he had gleefully intended.

"Mother must need her head examined!" Will exclaimed in disbelief.

Nathan jerked his head back to focus clearly on the young man before him. "Hell no, William! She feels strong about bringin' Christian folk together, you know that. 'Sides, there's Reverend Tucker and Mr. Calacott, as well. Between them they'll keep the peace."

Will looked doubtful, "Hope you're right, Nathan."

Victoria giggled, "Hope you're wrong, Nathan."

He glared at her. "You, Missy, will go without dessert and eat all your greens for that." She made a face at Nathan, then skipped back to the boat to get her painting box. Nathan took Will's arm. "Your sister's on the mend, but her manners ain't improved one bit."

"Nathan, you'd hate it if they did."

Smiling, the old man heaved the picnic basket into the bed of the wagon, then seized the still-giggling Victoria and lifted her onto the box before climbing up himself.

Will swung himself into the driver's seat, took the reins loosely and called, "Home, General." The horse set off, broad back swaying in perfect rhythm.

Within minutes Victoria leaned against her brother, straw hat tilted over her face. The late afternoon sun sprinkled shafts of light across the road and through the cool tunnels formed by towering live oak and cedar. The treetops leaned in toward each other, exchanging confidences whispered to them by the soft breeze.

Nathan pulled his pipe from the pocket of his vest. He stuffed the bowl with tobacco from an old leather pouch, then struck a long match on the sole of his boot. Fragrant clouds jetted from the corner of his mouth. He smiled as he watched the smoke drifting into the air. "Will, we have to talk 'bout this flyin' machine of yours. How long since you started tryin' to make a hop?"

Will counted off the numbers on his fingers. "We had the *Flyer* all together by the end of January, so I guess about six or seven weeks. Since then we've been chargin' up an' down the field without much result, to tell the truth.

Nathan paused, puffing gently on his pipe, "Do you think ~ *puff* ~ you might could have overdone the strong ~ *puff* ~ and underdone ~ *puff, puff* ~ the light?"

The engineer in Nathan had watched with a mixture of pride and trepidation as Will and his own son, Henry, made rough sketches of their idea of a flying machine. Then, they turned those drawings into well-drafted plans, and finally turned those first ideas into solid reality: a wood and canvas airplane they proudly named the *Florida Flyer*.

Will wiped the sweat from around the collar of his shirt. "I don't know, Nathan, I feel we're fixin' to fly, I've seen daylight under the wheels. One time I felt that motor pickin' up right smart with the wind on the nose. If I could just find another fifty revolutions or get shed a few pounds I can get her up, I know I can."

"Two ways you can do it, Brother." The two men turned with surprise.

"Thought you were sleepin', Sister," said Will.

She pushed up the brim of her hat and squinted at him. "Nah, just restin' my eyes, listenin' to you missin' the obvious."

Will and Nathan exchanged knowing, resigned looks. "Let on," Will offered.

His sister smiled. "Two ways to lose a few pounds: number one, throw out the silverware in the dining car."

Will raised his eyes skyward, and Nathan chuckled. "Number two?" Will winced as he said it.

"Fly nekked!"

Will shook his head and put his face in his hands. Nathan laughed so hard he dropped his pipe and had to scrabble on the footboard to retrieve it. He sat up, writing an imaginary headline in the air. "I can see it now in *The Democrat*," he said, "Tallahassee *baredevil* sets height record." He fell back dabbing his eyes with a grubby handkerchief.

Victoria squirmed back to a sitting position. "I'm serious."

"You don't say?" said Will, trying not to join in the hilarity.

She pushed back her hat and nudged Nathan. "Well, not complete, but just think, how much do your boots weigh? Pants, shirt, vest, that silly cap you wear? You want to fly, Brother, you have to make a sacrifice or two, unless you want to rename it the "Florida Possum." Of course what you're standin' in need of is a lighter aviator, an' I'm your girl."

"Aha! Thought that might come into it," Will leaned back.

Nathan looked at her seriously. "You mean that, don't you, girl?"

She nodded firmly. "You bet I do, but I know it's Will's baby an' only he gets to fly it. But when he gets a mess o' them revolutions of his, I'm gonna be his first passenger." She turned to her brother; they looked at each other steadily. The mood changed. "Deal?" she asked.

He looked at her squarely and nodded. "Deal." She kissed him lightly on the cheek and tipped his cap over his eyes.

"Still think you should try it nekked."

Their laughter attracted the attention of an elderly lady tending her front yard as they rolled slowly past her property. She nodded curtly as Nathan and Will raised their hats to her. She watched the two young, white people laughing with the old, black man as the wagon rumbled slowly away from her—looked around to make sure nobody saw—then spat.

Even though it was fourteen years into the new century, no hard-surfaced road served Leon County (even in Tallahassee, the state capital), but the road improved as it turned down into the business district. The Walker's home and business premises stood, quite literally, on the other side of the tracks, but that did not have the same connotation as in many towns. Nathan crossed good steel rails when he went home, not an unbridgeable social divide. That dubious distinction went to French Town, to the northwest of the downtown district.

A railroad track running into their yard before disappearing into a lofty, timber-built shed made the Walker property stand out. This was how Nathan made most of his substantial living. His forge and machine shop kept the wheels turning for the railroad. It was a hard business, and Will thought of Nathan as a hard man in the finest sense of the word. He was a member of a small, but significant, black middle class that flourished in spite of all the obstacles in Southern society, possibly even because of them.

Nathan often confided, tongue-in-cheek, to people who expressed candid surprise at finding he owned the business, "Work with rolling stock an' locomotives and you'll be black as me inside the hour." He was a proud man but a realist. While he chafed and bridled at the insults and casual bigotry, Nathan was the first to admit, "Florida ain't paradise, but there's worse places." He expressed a theory that the exotic mix of Spanish, French, English, and Indian culture, over the years, had made people just a little more tolerant of dark skin.

Will steered the wagon into the yard. The sturdy house that joined to the workshop was shaded by oak and decorated with the ever-present magnolia, the soft scent vying with the sharp tang of machine oil and hot steel. On this late Saturday afternoon the blossom held sway as the forge cooled. Victoria jumped down from the wagon and started to unhitch General McLellan. Nathan leaned over the side. "Victoria, leave that to your brother, it ain't fit work for a lady."

She ignored him but suddenly reappeared, a trace in her hand. "Nathan, I been meanin' to ask for a long time: Why did you name this beautiful, big horse after a man you told us was a nitwit?"

He jumped down and, taking the harness from her, spoke quietly, "Because he was the other horse's ass I followed for a long time—the name fit real well." Victoria was overtaken by a fit of the giggles that increased when a familiar voice boomed out from the kitchen door.

"Mister Walker, I heard that! How is that child ever goin' to be raised a lady when you use language like that in front of her? Quit cuttin' the fool an' get in here this instant!"

He grinned at Victoria. "Oops, I'm in trouble again."

" 'Pears so, Nathan." She buried a hand in the horse's mane and led him to his stall beside the shed.

In the wash house, Will worked with strong lye soap to rid himself of the morning's grime that the long day's sweat hadn't already dissipated. A familiar voice urged him to "budge up."

"Well, hello Henry! How you doin'?"

Nathan and Cordelia Walker's son caught the soap Will flipped to him. "Oh, 'bout one in a hill an' every other step. How about you? Catch anythin'?"

"Damn close to catching old Jackson's teeth in my rear," Henry stopped mid-scrub and whistled softly, envisioning the infamous alligator.

"That old boy still hangin' around then? Well, I'm glad you didn't get eat up, because...it's done."

Will paused, and his smile flashed in the cool gloom. "You mean done, finished, ready to roll?"

"Double-done, double-hitched, double-fastened, ready to slingshot you to glory!" Henry confirmed.

Will made a triumphant fist and punched his friend lightly on the chest. "You're a pal. Thank you."

"Well, let's hope you're sayin' that after we try it, I still think there must be a better way."

Will quickly dried himself; his reddened face appearing above the towel. "Let's try it soon as I get back from St. Pete. It'll work, trust me."

Henry pulled a face. "Ain't that what your Uncle Silas told his crew just before he pulled the 'down' lever?"

Will did not rise to the bait, "I do believe he did," he replied with a smile. "That's chicken an' dumplings I smell; let's get at 'em." The two boys clattered up the steps to the back door. A heavy wooden table—scrubbed so hard and so long nobody could tell what tree gave of its best—dominated the kitchen. Today it groaned under the weight of steaming dishes. In the corner, a fine, wood-burning stove supported simmering pots.

"Hands!" Cordelia barked. Will and Henry presented first their palms, then turned their hands over for a fingernail inspection. They passed. Will caught his sister grinning but knew better than to argue. Nathan lived the far side of seventy, but still had to pass the test. Will knew if you failed you went back and scrubbed until you passed. Cordelia insisted on hygiene in her kitchen, and if you wanted to eat, you had to meet her standards; Will and Henry always wanted to eat.

The easy familiarity shared by the Turner children and the Walker family seemed perplexing to some folks, in particular, Will and Victoria's "Yankee Aunt." The local townspeople found this quietly amusing. Aunt Audrey had lived away from Tallahassee for so long that her perspective had changed and she did not readily accept the fact that Will spent more time with Henry Walker than he did with his white friends. Neither did she find it easy to accept that Will and Victoria would often eat with the Walkers and even stay overnight with them.

"But where do they sleep?" Audrey timidly asked her sister-in-law, Charlotte.

"Well, Victoria has her own room and Will bunks down with Henry...where else?"

"You mean in the same bed?"

Charlotte had raised her eyes skyward. Tempting as it was to scandalize her prim sister-in-law, she liked her too much to make fun. "No, Audrey. What sort of town do you think we have here anyway?"

Audrey's small face had tightened as she sought the word, "Contradictory—that's how I'd describe it." She had been very definite about that in her nasal, Boston way, and she had, whether by acute perception or luck, hit the proverbial nail square on the head. "Contradictory" described it well. Henry and Will were more like brothers, which was hardly surprising as only a year separated them. They had grown up together.

Just as the rich in the North sent their sons away to school for someone else to raise, the wealthy in the southern states saw nothing strange in hiring a woman, invariably a black woman, to be responsible for the care and discipline of their sons—especially discipline. Many people, even then, would cheerfully admit the prized manners of the southern gentleman had often been imparted with a firm, black hand.

Will and Henry shared the same food, the same adventures, the same room without giving it a second thought, but in public they could not share the same church or school. Henry, however, never missed the opportunity to point out that his "Lincoln Academy" pre-dated Will's Leon County High School. The races did mix and co-operate away from the workplace, such as at the great exhibitions of floral displays that were the pride of the county. Even then, the citizens mingled happily, but would be served the same food from different tables.

The Turners and the Walkers lived in a society trying to come to terms with its past and cope with the future. The worst excesses of reconstruction were in the past, the real struggle for civil rights just beginning. In rural areas the Ku Klux Klan routinely terrorized. Most people, however, still spoke with pride of the open war that broke out in Calhoun County before the Civil War, when the friends of Jesse Durden, an anti-slavery farmer murdered by pro-slavery supporters, set out to avenge his death.

It was a society that would not admit its inequality in so many ways, yet, admired the stand against the ill treatment of black farm workers, made by Doctor William Hollingworth; a stand that cost him a near-fatal beating. The people took a perverse pride in their contrary nature. So much so that when the legislature introduced a law forbidding people to teach their workers reading and writing, it encouraged an immediate upsurge of literacy in the black population. One despairing member of the state government had declared, "If you pass a law telling these people to sit down, they'll politely stand up." Politeness, after all, was highly prized. They would tell their elected assembly to go to hell...in the nicest possible way.

Those who cared about appearances comforted themselves with the idea of Henry as Will's "colored man," imagining a master-servant relationship that fitted their prejudices. Those who really knew them were aware that Henry provided the common sense, the ballast, that usually kept Will from the worst consequences of his enthusiastic approach to life and engineering. Those same people hoped fervently that the engineering experiments created by Will and Henry took place at a safe distance from their own property and persons.

Nothing was contradictory, though, about the meal Will and Henry sat ready to devour that evening at the Walker's table. Cordelia rapped a serving spoon on the wood.

"Henry! Grace." They bowed their heads.

"ForwhatweareabouttoreceivemaytheLordmakeustrulygratefulAmen."

"*Again,*" Cordelia cautioned, "you are *not* auctioning tobacco." Henry repeated the ancient prayer at a suitably reverent pace. The instant he finished, the three men tried to pile whatever was nearest on Victoria's plate.

"Whoa boys! What are y'all tryin' to do to me?"

"Why...make sure you pick up some weight," Henry stated the obvious.

Victoria smiled, "So you can call me 'Jumbo,' I suppose."

Henry piled on more peas. "Say hello to the circus, Mizz Vicky. We can't bear to see you so thin."

Cordelia sighed. "My boy, talking sense; it's a strange and wonderful world." She laughed and the whole kitchen seemed to shake. She had a wonderful laugh—nothing held back—not a polite titter, not a giggle; she owned a laugh full of spirit, involving her entire being. Her laugh said, "Eat, my friends, this is the stuff of life and I love you." And eat they did: chicken and dumplings, fresh peas and butter beans, buttermilk fried okra, skillet fried corn. On the side was pone corn bread and sliced tomatoes. While the first onslaught gained ground, conversation was limited to "water please" and "pass the hell"—the bottled hot sauce guaranteed to strip paint. As they worked toward dessert, questions and answers were bantered back and forth.

"So how's this latest idea of yours goin' to get the *Flyer* off the ground, William?" Nathan asked.

"It's kind of a runway-come-catapult, Nathan."

The old man stopped, banana pudding halfway to his mouth, "Are you sure that's wise?" He pursed his lips and stared at Will.

"Well...the Wrights used the same method, and it worked for them."

Nathan grunted, carefully licked his spoon, then pointed it at Will and Henry in turn. "Remember what we agreed then, just like the Wrights: step-by-step, slow an' careful, prove each stage in turn. *Let's not run before we can walk, or sink before we can swim.*"

The two boys joined him in the chorus: "Just like Uncle Silas!" It was their private joke. Victoria looked pained. "Just what is so funny about Great Uncle Silas? Didn't he do most of the work inventin' the submarine?" They all turned to Nathan who regarded her kindly.

"You're old enough to know the true Turner history. He did do valuable work on underwater boats. The plain fact is he made the first underwater crossing of Boston Harbor. His vessel was *real* advanced for the time. The only boat in the war to be driven with an electrical motor, though the fumes from the accumulators nigh on choked him."

"Well, why do people make fun of him?" asked Victoria.

Nathan beamed at her. "Part because he was a big enough man to see the funny side, himself. The "Squid" submerged fine; though it moved pretty slow. It was the comin' up he hadn't given enough thought to. Lucky for him he fetched up on the mud at high tide, otherwise they were like to get drowned. When the tide went out, the top poked out the water an' the sailors could reach in an' pull him an' his crew out."

Victoria had been looking at him wide-eyed as this story unfolded. As he finished, her laughter bubbled up, "Poor old Silas, what did he do then?"

"What he should have done in the first place," said Nathan, "thought it out and experimented some more. He made it in the end. He had some fine patents by the time he died...a very old man, in his bed, I might add." He jabbed his spoon toward Will. "And make that your ambition, William." He shook his head. "I don't like the sound of this catapult idea one bit."

Cordelia jumped in to defend the boys. "Stop fussin', Nathan, they know what they're at. William has a de-gree in engineerin' after all."

"Yeah, but Henry don't have no degree in doctorin', an' if this hare-brain scheme goes haywire, a doctor will be what they're needin' ...at best!"

"Aw, shush now husband, you'll be tellin' us you never took a little gamble now an' then." She abruptly pushed her chair back, ending the debate. "Dishes now everyone, then time for some word games before bed. Church tomorrow, an' Victoria, don't forget the reception at Mrs. Adair's in the afternoon." Victoria groaned and lowered her head on her arms.

"Come on, Sis', you can play the 'Southern Belle' with the best of 'em. 'Sides...Ah do de-*clare,* you's the prettiest gal in town."

She stuck out her tongue at Will. He did a pretty fair impression of her friends.

Cordelia broke in firmly. "For once your brother is right. You *are* the prettiest girl in town. Why ain't you goin' in for May Queen?"

"Because a body ain't purdy if yah don' have nice yaller hay-uh."

Nathan looked puzzled. "Pretty yaller what?!" he asked, cupping a hand to his ear, "been here fifty years an' still can't understand you cracker girls."

Vicky grinned. "You know, hay-uh, on your hay-ed." Nathan fell in, laughing his booming laugh.

Victoria laughed with him, "It's true though, you look at the winners these past five years; all have hair like straw." Cordelia leaned over and whispered in her ear.

Vicky's eyes opened wide. "Really! Out of a bottle? But how do you know?" Cordelia leaned really close; Victoria's hands flew to her face again to cover her embarrassment. The older woman rounded on the men who were straining to hear.

"Girl talk! Git yourselves into those dishes. An' William—," He sat up straight, "you get your things ready for your trip down the coast. I want to see them boots shinin', a fine crease in your pants, an' I'm goin' to trim your hair before you get on that train. I don't want folk down there in St. Petersburg sayin' we breed a bunch of hooligans here in the capital. No sir!"

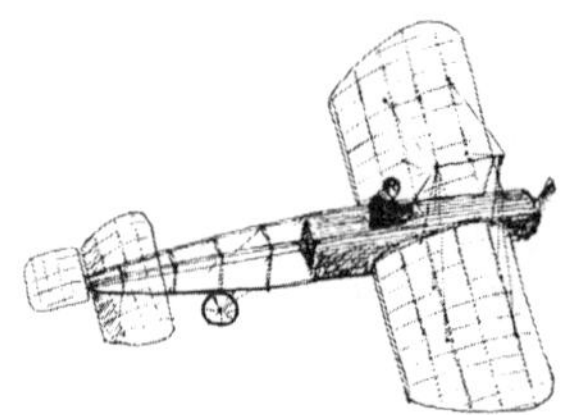

Chapter Two

WILL HAD TRAVELED FOR OVER A DAY TO REACH THE TERMINAL OF the Tampa-St. Petersburg Air Boat Service: a weather-beaten shed knocked together from bleached scrap timber, sagging into the sand just beyond the limits of St. Petersburg, on the Gulf coast of Florida. He ignored the premises and concentrated on the single machine comprising their entire fleet. Will concluded it looked like a happy marriage between a two-wing flying machine, already becoming known as a biplane, and one of the new sporting motor boats. The pilot and passenger sat side by side in a cockpit cut into the smooth line of the hull, or fuselage, depending on who described it. The lower of the two wings attached to the hull directly behind the cockpit. The upper wing fixed on a supporting structure of struts and wires almost seven feet above it.

Buried in the hull between the wings, with only the tops of the cylinders showing, rested the motor. This drove a two-bladed propeller, mounted behind the wings, to push the machine through the air. The shaft supporting this was carried forward, secured at its front end by a drilled horizontal beam fixed between two upright struts. These joined the forward, or leading edge, of the upper and lower wings. A long chain connected the motor to the propeller. This chain ran in front of a crude radiator filling half the space between the wings.

Behind the motor the hull narrowed to the point where it carried the tail surfaces. The horizontal stabilizer, a simple triangle with the point forward, sported a set of generous elevators. The vertical surface consisted of a simple, square rudder. To a critical eye, the lines of this Benoist flying boat, the entire fleet of the world's first scheduled airline, appeared workmanlike rather than innovative. Will thought the Benoist was perfect.

Steve, the mechanic, finished topping off the giant radiator, left, then reappeared with a small set of steps. "All aboard for Tampa!" He said as he motioned toward the steps placed beside the cockpit. "Just put your feet on the seat, hands there and sorta' slide down."

No sooner said and Will was settling himself in the comfortable wicker chair. He grinned up at the mechanic, "Fits nice."

Steve reached in and produced the ends of a stout, leather safety belt. "Just strap this 'round yourself so's you don't fall out. You don't want to go the same way as poor Harriet Quimby or Colonel Cody."

Memory of the fate of the two aviation pioneers, both flung from their machines for want of a simple restraining device, had Will cinching the belt tightly around his waist. Steve stood back, leaning his head to one side while rubbing his chin thoughtfully. Coming to a decision, he removed Will's cap, turning it around before planting it firmly back on his head. "Ever ride a motorcycle?" he asked.

"Sure have. I ride a Harley," said Will.

"Then you know the problem."

Will nodded, leaning forward and pulling a pair of green-tinted goggles from his shirt pocket. Steve nodded approval, stepped back and flung his right hand up into a comically exaggerated salute. "Ready Cap'n!" Tony Jannus, the world's first official commercial pilot, returned the salute and vaulted into the cockpit.

"Okay. Let's go—fuel's on—carb's primed—give her a swing," Tony called.

Steve was standing on an old crate and had to stretch to reach the prop, but it turned easily. The big motor sucked and gurgled, drawing fuel and air into the cylinders.

"Magneto switch is set and on," the pilot said as his hand went to a lever by his side. Tony eased it forward a fraction, "And the throttle is set. Let her go!"

Steve stretched further, then paused, feeling for the resistance that would tell him the pistons were compressing the fuel and air mixture into the cylinders, then almost casually pulled the prop through. The motor started, pulsing life into the airplane.

"It started right up! First time. Just like that!" Will said, raising his voice over the rumble of the exhausts.

"Yeah, no problem, always does. Good thing, prop being so high and all." Tony replied.

"It's not so loud, I can hear you fine."

"It's quiet enough just ticking over, but wait 'til I give her some revolutions...you'll love it, sounds like a real racer. Meantime, we let her warm up, and I'll run you through the controls."

Tony folded his long fingers lovingly around the polished wood rim of the big wheel in front of him and showed Will how the control surfaces moved as he pushed and pulled, at the same time rolling the wheel from left to right and back. He pointed into the gloom beneath the instrument panel, or "dash" as he called it, to show Will how the rudder bar moved the vertical tail surface, and he demonstrated the instruments. The rev counter, oil pressure, and coolant temperature were familiar enough to Will, but he watched carefully as Tony showed him how to adjust the altimeter to compensate for atmospheric pressure. "Just in case I fall asleep and you have to fly her back yourself," Tony said with a quick smile.

Steve stood at the wingtip, carefully checking the rigging. Tony looked at him, raising his thumb. The mechanic nodded, bent down and pulled a cord disappearing beneath the hull. With a jerk the flying boat started down the beach. It gained speed, the beaching trolley underneath rattling on the lightweight track leading down to the water's edge from the hangar doors. The Benoist moved like a startled duck waddling toward a pond, but it transformed at the water's edge; launching into its natural element like any other water bird. The light ripples of surf kissed the polished wood hull as the sea embraced it. They floated free.

Tony brought the revs up smartly and the motor took on a more urgent note. "We need a little breeze over the tail for steerage. See that buoy? That's our marker, we turn there to start our run. Sing out if you see anything floating. Give the boys a wave," said Tony.

Will turned to see the fishermen waving from the pier. He waved back as Tony asked, "Okay, you all set? "Let's go to Tampa!"

Before Will had a chance to reply, Tony pushed the throttle wide open. The subdued mutter of the exhausts swelled to a pulsating roar. The horizon swung past the nose as they turned to face open water, then abruptly steadied. A movement at the edge of Will's vision attracted his attention. Fixed to the struts at the end of each wing a faded Stars and Stripes streamed bravely in the gathering wind. A grin plastered itself to Will's face as the airplane increased speed. A glance over the side revealed a surging bow wave. The Beniost rode so low in the water that Will could have reached his hand to touch the surface. For a few seconds the hull strained to push the water aside, then Will felt a steady thrust from below his seat, as they began planing on their own wave; up on the step, he could feel the water beating on the planks under his feet.

The vibration increased, and the rushing air stung his eyes. Before he could pull his goggles down, the hammering abruptly stopped. A breathless pause, one more solid thump, then a sensation of incredible smoothness. They were in the air. The horizon quickly expanded on all sides, and even though the wind whipping his face spoke of speed, it felt as if they were slowing down. Will gazed around in wonder.

Past the pilot's shoulder, the beach stretched into a hazy, blue distance. Ahead the water sparkled and flashed. While looking over the side, Will could see clearly through the water to the bottom of the shallow bay. Suspended secure beneath the bridge-like structure of the wings, above a world revealing itself like a flower opening its petals, Will fell under the spell from which he would never be released. He twisted to see over his shoulder. The light caught the whirling propeller, spinning a shimmering line. Beyond it the pier receded in the distance. He laughed out loud. He was airborne; he was really flying at last.

Tony tapped Will's hand to get his attention. "See the altimeter there? We're at six hundred feet." He pointed to the nearest wing strut. A spring mounted pointer moved over a gauge scribed on a metal plate. "I must register a patent on that," he shouted. "My speed indicator...wind blows on that flat piece of metal on the pointer, moves it to show our speed against the gauge. We're doin' about sixty per, not bad, eh?"

Will looked at the primitive instrument. "It's incredible! Fastest I've ever been. Don't think even the 'Special' gets goin' that fast on the old iron rails in these parts. So it'll take us 'bout twenty minutes then?"

Tony had to shout over the combined roar of the slipstream and the exhausts sprouting just behind them, "Thereabouts, but on time."

Will peered over the nose, surprised to see the far shore of the bay fast approaching. Tampa was a sprawling town of mostly low, white buildings growing out of the morning haze. He could make out a line where clear water pushed up a thin beach. A towering building that reminded the young man of a giant wedding cake dominated the town. Behind it, green forest extended to the distant horizon.

Tony leaned toward him again. "Since you're in no particular rush, we'll make a circle over the town. This'll remind the good people we're still around." With that he eased back the throttle lever, and the nose dipped. As the motor sighed down to a restrained rumble with an occasional "pop" from the exhaust stubs, the altimeter adjusted its reading to five hundred feet.

Will felt as if he was hanging motionless in the air while the landscape moved around him. The plane rolled seamlessly into a wide turn. It felt so natural to Will, the balance already part of him. He gazed down on foreshortened buildings; flat roofs held pools of the previous evening's rain, brilliant awnings launched out over sidewalks. The streets were laid out for his inspection in a living map. Upturned faces and waving hands acknowledged their progress. The shadow of the wings fell over the cockpit as the Benoist swung back to the bay. The height was back down to four hundred feet.

"You ready for a little fun?" Tony asked pointing down while making a circular gesture. Will nodded eagerly. The power poured on, but Tony held the nose down as the Benoist tried to respond to the added thrust by climbing. The whispering wind that had meekly followed them over the town now chased them into the dive with a triumphant scream as it played in the taut rigging. For the first time, Will heard the banshee howl of a power dive. The surface that looked so smooth at five hundred feet became more sharply defined by the second. He knew he should be scared because they had to hit—right heeeere! But, faster than his mind could register the unfamiliar attitude, they whipped over into a near-vertical turn inches above the water.

Will likened his first encounter with G forces, generated by the violent change of direction, to being sat on by a horse while somebody else tried to push his head hard into his chest. At the same time the horizon, which previously always appeared to move more or less from side to side, if it seemed to move at all, now reeled past top to bottom. It was a steep and tight turn by any standard, and it had its effect. Will was hooked; from that day forward he would be quite happy to be stood on his ear.

He watched his pilot make broad, sweeping movements with the controls. The wings slashed back level, the turn checked, the power came off and the nose pitched up sharply as Tony hauled the control wheel back to his chest. The view ahead disappeared as spray blossomed up from the keel to slap back in his face. Will felt the safety belt cut into him as he pitched forward, then was pulled back in his seat as the Benoist decelerated sharply then surged forward on a wave of its own making. He sat blinking and gasping as the flying boat wallowed with the propeller idly swinging.

The spray cleared to reveal the waterfront buildings. Tony cut the switch to the magneto, and the motor hissed as it finally stopped. Two boys were splashing through the gentle surf to grab the wing-tip floats. They steered the plane toward a makeshift pier floating on empty oil barrels.

"Hey fellas! What d'you think of the show?" asked Tony.

The smaller boy beamed at him. "Pretty fine, Cap'n, but when you gonna give us one o' them loop de loops?"

"C'mon guys! Would that be respectable behavior for a scheduled passenger service?" Both boys nodded happily. Tony leaned toward Will. "Try that and you could forget the 'flying' part, this old girl converts to a sensible boat just as soon as the wings tear off. Anyways, how d'you like flying?"

Will looked slowly around, like a man waking from a trance. His answer was inadequate, colloquial, and heartfelt. "Gee-zuz, that was fun!" He eased himself out of the cockpit to stand with Tony on the rickety pier. Will stamped his feet on the boards and grinned. "Knees hardly knockin' at all."

Tony took his arm. "Boys here are well trained, they'll tie her up. C'mon I'll buy you a coffee."

Back home in Tallahassee the spring flowers were in full bloom, the air mild and soft. But here in Tampa the sun already had an edge that made them seek the shade of the awning in front of the café. Will sipped his first Cuban-style coffee: syrupy, sweet, and muscular.

Tony grinned, "I won't take more than one of those. Makes my hair stand on end, then the wind blows it off." He patted his thin patch.

"How's the lime pie?"

Will paused between mouthfuls. "Mmmmph—ver' nice, thank you."

"So tell me, Mr. William Turner, what makes you travel all this way just to fly from one side of Tampa Bay t'other? If you wanted to take a flip, Mrs. Law is giving rides off Daytona Beach. Don't tell me you're afraid of flying with a lady driver. Ruth's as good as or better than most men, and she don't charge as much to get you up in the sky."

Will took a sip of coffee to unstick his teeth. "You're makin' history." From many people it would have sounded over-dramatic, but Will's open face and transparent enthusiasm made it a statement of fact. He leaned forward, struggling to find the words. "The first passenger flying line in the...in the...well...in the *anywhere!*" His hands waved to indicate the "anywhere."

The waitress smiled at his gestures, then turned to speak rapidly to Tony who burst out laughing. She winked at Will and nudged his shoulder with her ample hip as she passed by. He stopped suddenly, not used to the rapid Spanish or being flirted with by a lady of his mother's age. "What did she say?"

"She says you talk with your hands like a Spanish gentleman, but you have such pretty yellow hair." Will blushed furiously, but Tony rescued him. "So I'm making history, eh? To tell the truth I had hoped to make some money, but history will do just as well. Besides, it's a good thing you came before the contract ends."

Will sat back with a bump. "Oh, I'm really sorry."

"Hey! Don't take it to heart so. We're doing okay, but when the vacationers go home so will the profits. The contract's only for three months. Our backers are not about to go into debt now that they've proved the point."

"What point is that?" Will asked.

"That an airplane can run reliably enough to offer a scheduled service. We're just a little ahead of our time. It is a practical proposition. You know, between us, my brother and I have taken over a *thousand* people flying."

Will's face brightened. "Yes, of course you have, makes it easier for me to get the idea across at home, as well."

Tony leaned back comfortably and smiled. "Let me guess. You tell your folks that one day, fleets of airplanes will ply the skies above our great nation, carrying people, freight and mail, just like the railroads do now."

Will almost jumped out of his seat, "That's right!"

"And they think you're plumb crazy," Tony guessed.

"That's right, too!" Will laughed, because it was true. Tony had the situation summed up perfectly. "How did you know that?"

"Heard the same story with variations at flying fields and air meets from here to New York City. It's been nigh on eleven years since the Wright Brothers dragged their airplane off the ground, and there are folk out there still think it's a conjuring trick. Mind though, same people will tell you the world is flat. Wouldn't give a fig for their opinion. Pay 'em no mind."

Will shook his head, "It's frustratin' though, 'specially when you see the progress they're making in Europe. In Russia they're flyin' a four-motor ship. They reckon it can carry ten passengers. They even have a promenade deck."

Tony stopped in the process of lighting a small cigar. He paused with the match flaring in mid-air. "It has a what?!"

Will delved inside his jacket. He produced a stout, brown envelope and fished around inside. "A promenade deck. Here it is, I've a picture of it." He flourished a newspaper clipping and passed it across.

Tony held it to the light, moved it away and brought it back close to his face. "Well I'll be..." The grainy photograph showed a vast, gothic machine: a huge biplane given scale by factory buildings in the background. Two excited figures ran below as it swept across a snow-covered plain. The machine itself was fantastic enough, but what really grabbed Tony's attention was the figure clearly visible on a walkway atop the fuselage, casually holding a safety rail.

Will explained, "It's called the *Ilya Mouremetz* and was designed by a Mr. Sikorsky. It mounts four one-hundred horse Argus motors an' spans nearly a hundred feet."

Tony shook his head, "Great Scott! I thought we had the niftiest airplane going."

Will rummaged inside his envelope again. "Well, what do you think of this?" He passed across a page torn from a magazine. It featured a beautifully drafted line drawing of a machine that could have flowed straight from the pen of H.G. Wells, the master science fiction writer. Every line shouted speed. The nose formed a blunt, bullet shape. The pilot sat deep in the fuselage with his head barely protruding into the slipstream. Behind the cockpit, the fuselage tapered to elegantly flared tail surfaces; carefully sculpted spats encasing the undercarriage legs showed something of the Art Nouveau style in their precise curves. The single wings were short and deep in chord (the dimension from the leading edge that meets the air to the scalloped trailing edge when seen in plan view).

"French?" asked Tony.

Will sat back eyes wide. "That's right, the Deperdussin, how did you know that?"

"It just looks French. Style, it has real style."

Will smiled, "It has speed as well, over one hundred and twenty miles per hour."

Tony stared at him, "I can barely make half that"!" He paused then said, "*De-per-dus-sin,*" rolling the word around with perfect pronunciation.

"Do you speak French?" Will asked.

"Not really. I courted a girl in New Orleans for a while. Do you think, based on that connection, they'd let me take this hot ship up?"

He looked a little wistful, but Will was not sure if it was for the speed or the mademoiselle from Louisiana. "Well, I surely would," said Will.

"I believe you," said Tony. "So, tell me how you come by this stuff; it's bang, up-to-the-minute news. Look at the date here, it's barely a month old and this is a British publication."

Will thought for a second then emptied the envelope, carefully brushing crumbs from their table before setting out the contents. There were two photographs: one showed a three-quarter front view of a tidy little two-wing machine, almost as clean in its lines as the French racer. The other was a larger print of superb quality, showing a young couple posed informally against the lower wing of a larger biplane. The young man, in uniform, had his arm around a girl. The camera caught her lively smile perfectly.

At first glance Tony thought she gazed at the young officer adoringly, but a closer look showed she laughed with him. Her clothes were fashionable, but worn almost carelessly. Her tumbling hair escaped from a formal, high style. Tony whistled approvingly, "Lucky dog! Quite a girl."

"He might not agree. That's his sister...they're my cousins," said Will.

"Yeah, I can see that now. It definitely looks as though they like each other too much to be a married couple." Will's eyebrows shot up, but Tony grinned, "Just kidding; that's a beautiful picture. What is he, a pirate?" He pointed to the cap badge the young man wore. It was possible to just make out the skull and crossbones.

Will laughed. "No, he belongs to the British Lancer regiment that was in the Charge of the Light Brigade; their motto's 'Death or Glory'."

"Remind me not to pick a fight with those guys, sounds like they take things pretty serious," said Tony.

"Not Rupert," laughed Will, "he doesn't seem to take anythin' very serious, except flyin'. He's had himself attached to the Royal Flying Corps."

Tony was impressed, "You must be pretty proud of a cousin like that."

Will felt no need to play it down. "You bet! He's flown the English Channel twice." He began to expand on that adventure but stopped short as he saw Tony smiling at him.

"Well, you will have flown Tampa Bay twice by the end of the day, and as I recall it's a similar distance," said Tony. "And—while I don't want to concern you for your safety—it has *sharks*." He added as an afterthought.

Will considered for a moment, then a slow smile spread across his face. "I guess you're right. But it's not the same, I'm not doin' the actual flyin', I'm just a passenger."

"Now, don't give me that 'just' line. We need people like you—where would a passenger line be without passengers?" Tony had a good point but knew he was wasting his breath. Will Turner either had the bug or the bug had him, and it was obvious—Will knew what he wanted.

"I have to fly, Mr. Jannus, it's all I've wanted to do since I can remember."

The pilot nodded, "And you're not getting much encouragement at home?"

Will narrowed his eyes against the glare as he looked past Tony out over the bay, easily visible from where they sat in front of the café. He shook his head wearily. "Don't take me wrong. My folks are the finest I could wish for, but in a way it's worse than not havin' any encouragement or even them tryin' to stop me." He leaned back for a moment, eyes closed, his exasperation obvious. "They won't take aviation seriously!"

"Surely with your cousin making a name for himself, they must know that aviation is here to stay."

Will inclined his head, conceding the point. "I think that may even have somethin' to do with it. My father thinks airplanes are only for the military. He reckons they'll never carry a useful load that can be made to pay. Fine for soldierin', observin' the enemy an' all that—he even reckons airplanes will fight each other in the air—but makin' money? 'Never.' He's a railroad man through and through, an' stubborn as a mule. He won't even budge on the idea that the highways need improvin'. He says the *railroads* are the only way forward." Will took a sip of coffee, put his cup carefully in the saucer, then rubbed his chin. "Then, of course, they think I'll break my damn, fool neck."

At this, Tony slapped his hand down on the table, threw back his head and roared with laughter. "Now we get to the bottom of it, Will! They care about what happens to their son. Can't blame 'em. Too many accidents have happened not to admit that there is some risk. I can say that to you because you're a flyer, but never say it to 'Joe Public,' that's your duty as an aviator," Tony cautioned.

Will fiddled with a toothpick. He studied the point for a moment then looked up. "In my case it goes further than just ordinary concern. My daddy has been described as a 'safety evangelist.' There's never been a fatal accident on his line. He spent thousands on safety guards for the machinery at our sawmill, designin' them himself. He even took my Harley away for a month when the sheriff complained I'd been speedin'."

"Had you?"

"Just a little...maybe."

Tony smiled. "Is there more to this than just a professional attitude?"

For the second time Will sat up straight and stared at the wiry little man. "Mr. Jannus, you have what my English teacher called 'rare perception'."

Tony Jannus laughed, "Nah. Just nosey. So, tell all."

"My father is one of four brothers. There's Uncle Bertie, who's the black sheep of the family, though I really like him."

Tony chuckled, "I've one like that. The kinda guy who used to give you a quarter when you were a kid and not tell you how to spend it."

"There's the oldest, Uncle Roy. He's a lawman out West, though he retires next year."

It was Tony's turn to be surprised. "Good Lord! Not Marshall *Roy* Turner, the man who shot Dan Savage?"

"The very same."

Tony let out a low whistle. "Savage by name, savage by nature, so I heard. If ever there was a man who deserved shootin' it was he. How about the other one?"

Will nodded, "The fourth brother, William, who I'm named after, was killed in a railroad accident two years before I was born."

Tony sighed, "I'm sorry to hear that, Will. I can understand why your daddy might feel the way he does."

"Yeah, particularly as the accident was of Uncle Will's own makin'."

"Hell, that sounds a mite harsh." Tony said.

"It is, but it's no use lookin' for somebody else to blame; he took risks and knew it. One day he pushed his luck too far. My pa made his money from one invention that he an' Uncle Will worked on for years. I won't burden you with the technical details, but it's a manner of steam injector that can boost the pullin' power of most locomotives. We collect royalties from all over the world now. When they perfected it, they had to demonstrate it. It's in the nature of steam, if you can boost the pressure in a locomotive boiler, you're goin' to show the modification in a better light still."

"But aren't there safety valves that limit how much pressure you can build, or have the railroads been lying to me all this time?"

"There surely are, but Uncle Will was a brilliant engineer, he knew how to lock them off without it bein' obvious what he'd done. But one day—"

Tony pointed at the sky. "Kerboom?"

Will nodded, his face grim. "Ever since then my pa, who always has been a cautious man, has grown downright fanatical about safety in transport, in all its forms. I guess that's why he's so against aviation. He can't see how it could ever be made safe enough for the payin' public."

"And you don't agree with him," Tony said.

"No, sir, I don't. It can be made as safe as we want it to be. This is what's really behind all this talk of his—that I'm wastin' my time an' education."

Tony had noted Will's work-hardened hands, but from the way he spoke and the clothes he wore he could see that Will Turner did not come from dirt poor farming stock. "What form did that education take?"

"I earned my degree in mechanical engineerin' at Massachusetts Institute of Technology; finished last year."

"My, oh my!" Tony said. "Only the best science and engineering school in the country." He leaned over the table, a mischievous smile on his face. "How did a cracker like you get by in Yankee land?"

Will's pensive look was replaced by a broad grin. "Good manners, an' my sister came visitin' often times. All those Yankee boys had to get past me for a date. They went crazy for her accent an' even I have to admit she's a handsome gal." He flipped open his wallet and showed Tony a recent picture of his sister.

"*You,* sir," said Tony, "have a gift for understatement. She's a beauty. Seems to run in your family; pity it don't extend to the male side.

But seriously, Will, aviation needs people like you. We need real, trained engineers at the drawing board if America is going to keep up."

"Mr. Jannus—"

"Tony, please call me Tony."

"Tony, I don't want to be chained to a drawin' board. Leastways not all the time. I want to learn to fly."

"Well, that's no problem," said Tony. "Build your own plane and fly it. Anyway, you still haven't told me how you get this stuff so quick." He leaned forward, looked around the other tables, "You can tell me, Will. Is your cousin secretly flying the Atlantic Ocean and mailing this stuff in New York?"

Will relaxed with the gentle kidding. "No, he was attached to what they call the military attaché in Washington D.C. a couple o' years back. He sends stuff to me through a guy at the embassy who mails it express. Keeps me right up to date."

"You're lucky. Sounds like your cousin's a real pal."

"He sure is, I only wish he was still here to see it fly." Will stopped, too late.

"To see what fly?" Tony was quick; he needed to be, in his precarious line of work. He had spotted the heavily folded drawing on the table. "Come on, show me." He looked eagerly at Will who now shifted awkwardly in his chair.

"Well, I don't know, it might look really amateurish to you."

The pilot brushed aside his protests and opened the drawing for close inspection. It took him about a minute studying the carefully drawn plan.

"That's just a rough sketch," Will muttered apologetically.

Tony looked up, "If this is a rough sketch, Rembrandt's a cartoonist. Who did this?"

"I did," Will admitted.

Tony smiled, "You better be careful, given enough power this will fly. Are you really going to build it?"

Will shrugged, "Already have, just need to find that power."

Tony thought for a moment. "I'm being serious now, this looks good to me. What's the motor you hung on it?"

"A JAP air-cooled V twin."

"That's a British motor surely? Where did it come from, did your cousin send it over?" Tony asked.

"No. My boss, Mr. Walker, bought it from a French guy who used it in a cycle he was tryin' to set a speed record on, at Daytona Beach."

It had been a gallant attempt. Monsieur Maigrot had not allowed chauvinism to influence his choice of power unit. The monstrous English engine propelled his *Moto*, as he called it, at phenomenal speed along the hard-packed sands. After three runs he briefly held the record. He admitted it was unfortunate to say the least, that while returning for a fourth run, the fluttering handkerchiefs of his bevy of newfound admirers distracted him. He had smiled his most rakish smile, he had waved his most debonair wave, and he had motored smoothly into the Atlantic.

Rescued and cooed over by his new and most solicitous friends, Maigrot quickly forgot about record breaking and returned to his first love. He opened a restaurant in St. Augustine, and enjoyed being a Frenchman, not caring for a moment that some people muttered the word "stereotype." That outrageous accent and waxed moustache were what his customers expected.

Will knew nothing of this, his only contact being a neatly hand-written note that came with the rusty remains of the world-beating motorcycle. In careful English it gave details of the specification of the motor and urged him to take "*the utmost carefulness with all this power.*" These details he now gave to Tony, who studied them carefully.

"What prop you using?"

"It's a big one, over six feet tip to tip with quite a twist to it," Will explained. "We bought it from a crazy, old guy who tried to fit it to a punt. He reckoned he could skim over the swamp grass with it. I don't know where it came from before then."

Tony took a quick draw on his cigar. He puffed a jet of smoke into the still air. "You might have a problem getting enough power out of this. Look what he says here about the modifications he made. Steep cams, high compression and aluminum pistons are good, but you're going to have to rev this motor hard to get full power."

"Can you give me any ideas?"

"Yeah, smaller prop with less of a pitch," Tony answered confidently. "That will lose you thrust though."

"Another idea is to give your machine a start so the prop has less work to do; that'll soon have motor spinning right up."

Will perched eagerly on the edge of his seat. "We're tryin' that!"

"How so?" Tony asked.

"The same method the Wrights used: a launch ramp with weights and pulleys to give a shove."

"Hmmm, you're on the right track," said Tony, "but, Will, please be careful. It's going to be hard to turn back if your system works well; it's all or nothing as a way of getting airborne! Call me over-cautious like your dad, but my advice would be to keep trying for a regular takeoff. I was thinking more in the way of finding a field with a decent slope to it."

Will thought for a moment, "I don't follow what you mean about the prop havin' less work to do."

Tony took a pencil from the pocket of his battered, leather jacket and sketched quickly on a napkin. "This is just a theory, mind you, but it's from an engineer friend of mine. Note that, Will, an engineer like you. He reckons that when a wing stops flying, when it 'stalls' as some call it, it goes through a period when it causes really massive drag. That's why it's so dangerous to fly too *slow.* That old drag just jumps up and pulls you down." He made an emphatic downward jab with his pencil, and looked at Will to see if he was following the explanation.

"Imagine that your prop is really a wing that goes 'round and lifts you along. Now, what if that prop has too much twist or pitch to it. It's like a wing that is permanently in a near-stall condition. Until it starts to move forward when the *relative* airflow is changed by the forward movement. Then it un-stalls. The drag all but disappears, the motor can spin up to give some power, and away you go." Tony finished with a triumphant upward sweep of his hand.

Will studied the drawing. "That makes sense...damn! Why didn't *I* think of that?"

"From what I hear of college, you might have been distracted by curves other than those on these power and drag graphs."

Will grinned, "Might could have been...just a little."

Tony stubbed out his cigar, twisting it firmly in the ashtray while fixing Will with a solemn stare. "You have to make me a promise. In return for all this useful knowledge, promise me you will go slow and careful, step by step. Try a few fast runs, then check your fittings; try a few more, get the feel of her. Don't even think about that launch ramp 'til you know it'll hold together. Better still, take some lessons, you must be able to afford it. I kinda get the impression you don't come from a poor family. You say your daddy's a railroadman? What exactly does he do for the railroad?

Will shifted awkwardly again, "Well, he sort of owns it, or a big part of it anyway."

"So where's the problem?"

"There's no problem. Pa just doesn't believe in handin' out cash without it bein' earned. An' he's made it plain, he won't spend one penny on anythin' to do with flyin'. That doesn't bother me; I'll just go an' earn what I need."

"No offense meant, Will, but I can't help but like your father's principles, even though he's wrong about aviation."

"Oh, no offense taken," Will said. "Sorry if I sounded a mite prickly. It's just that people make certain assumptions when they find out who my family is. You've heard people talk of playboys?"

"Oh sure," said Tony, "I read *The Playboy of the Western World.* J.M. Synge was the author as I recall.

"Yeah, well some guy back home called me a 'playboy'."

"What did you do?" Tony asked.

"Well, I felt like bustin' him on the nose, but a gentleman does not resort to fisticuffs so I told him to go play with himself; 'cause he surely was known for it."

"Then what happened?"

"He busted me on the nose an' we fell to fightin' outside Mr. Cohen's store, 'til he came out an' threw a bucket a' water over us." He stopped as he noticed Tony was shaking gently with barely-suppressed laughter.

"Well, I'm glad you're not too much of a gentleman, Will, otherwise you would've been pounded."

"Fact is, I was anyway, when Cordelia came by just at the wrong moment. Got my ears boxed, truly. She said I wasn't too old for a thrashin'."

"When was this?" Tony asked.

"Last week," replied Will. That was too much for the hard-pressed aviator. He rocked with happy laughter, and wiped a tear from the corner of his eye.

"I'm sorry, Will, you just have a way about you. I don't mean to make fun, just seems like things happen to you."

Will smiled, in no way offended. "It's funny you should say that, my mother says just the same. Maybe I'm a little prone to accidents. Not with machinery, mind, just seems like I find myself in situations by mistake."

"Well, you know the old saying, *a man who never made a mistake never made anything.* I'm not so different myself. Take this airboat service for an instance. It's shown me how we can make money."

Will's ears pricked up. "How so?" he asked eagerly.

"Well, I'm not going to pretend to you that we're really keeping to the schedule now. If some good soul wants to fly to St. Pete or back at a different time, we can't afford to say no. To run a schedule you need a ship like that Mr. Sikorsky's flying saloon, something that will take a good load of passengers, where you can at least break even with less than a full load. I fly fully loaded or empty; and if I'm forced to fly empty to stick to that damn schedule I lose out in a big way. If Joe Public wants to fly at half past the hour I gotta do it. I can't tell the customer when he should fly, to suit me. A tailor doesn't try to sell me a new shirt when I want a new pair of pants. No reason for me to try to sell him a flight at midday when he needs to be in St. Pete at half-past eleven."

"That's an interestin' way of putting it," Will said.

"It's more than a good way of telling it," Tony laughed, "I really do have a tailor who has to measure up some rich customer in St. Pete at half-past the hour, so I must fly! No pun intended Will. I'll be back for you 'bout four o'clock, say?"

Will pulled an ancient watch from his vest pocket. "Yes, please. That gives me time to look around the town. This is not like anywhere I ever saw in my life. What is that big pile we flew past on the way in?"

"That pile, William, is about the fanciest hotel in Florida, if not the South. Mr. Plant's Tampa Bay Hotel. Go take a look, but don't buy a beer, it will break your budget for this trip," Tony cautioned. "Take my advice, go stroll into Ybor City. You looking to buy something for the folks at home?"

"Have to do that," Will agreed.

"Then go buy your daddy some cigars. The area is named after Señor Ybor, the cigar manufacturer, but you can see your cigars being rolled if you buy from one of the buckeyes."

"Buckeyes?"

"Independents. They work out of storefronts. You get real good cigars for a few cents."

The waitress had moved back to their table, and she leaned over and spoke to Tony again. Will picked out the words "Fort Brooke." She looked at Will, wagged a cautioning finger then patted his head as she swayed back to the kitchen. He looked at Tony who grinned at him.

"She's saying stay away from Old Fort Brooke. There are bad women there still. The daughters of La Culebra, *the Serpent.*" Will's blank look showed he did not have a clue what his friend was talking about.

Tony lowered his voice, "Ladies of the night, *loose lilies.*"

Enlightenment dawned. "Oh! You mean *whores.*"

"Well, if you want to put it like that, yes—whores, pickpockets, and card sharks. She's right, you stay away. I want you in one piece when

I get back. One other thing young William, don't go smiling at any *señoritas* under the age of sixty. There's some fearsome, jealous guys amongst these Cubans. They make the best of friends and the worst of enemies.

"Now come and help me turn the ship around. You'll love my passenger—bravest guy I ever met—hates flying."

"You're kiddin' me again!"

Tony paid the bill and led Will back into the street with an arm around his shoulders. "Mr. Turner, believe it or not, there are those who do not share our enthusiasm."

Will shook his head and suddenly smiled, "We'll just have to persuade 'em, Cap'n."

"Indeed we will. We surely will," agreed the aviator.

Chapter Three

HER MOTHER'S INDULGENCE ALLOWED VICTORIA THE LUXURY OF occasionally wearing clothes suited to her activities. An old pair of her brother's dungarees and one of her father's shirts had covered her decently for the fishing and painting trip the week before. Even then, however, she was only allowed to dress comfortably because her mother knew no one from polite society would travel in that part of the county and see her. The impatient young woman chafed against these rules, but the very next Sunday, when she caught sight of herself in her best outfit in the long mirror near the front door, she smiled inwardly. Her calf-length, blue skirt was cut high enough from the floor to show off fashionable black ankle boots. The cream, silk blouse had just enough in the way of frills and ruffles to attract the eye without looking fussy and, by tying the ribbon of her hat behind her neck instead of under her chin, she had achieved a jaunty and daring angle.

Her brother, fresh back from his trip to St. Petersburg, walked up behind her and echoed her thoughts, "Not bad little sister, not bad at all."

"Why, thank you, Mr. Turner." She practiced a demure simper, then ruined the effect by linking her arm with his, using it to swing off the step. She dragged him quickly ahead.

"Are you givin' it a try this afternoon, Will?"

Will pretended not to hear, but his sister knew that he had. Will quickened his pace to get them out of earshot of their mother.

"Just a trial run down the ramp. We won't be flyin', don't worry about that. Not 'til I get those extra revolutions."

Their parents trailed some distance behind. But, as most mothers do,

Charlotte Turner, known as Charley to her many friends, had ears like a bat. "What's that you're discussing children?"

Will turned and walked backwards to answer his mother. "I was just sayin' the *Flyer* won't fly until I get some extra revolutions from the motor."

"Do slow down, William," Charley called, and Will and Victoria stopped to allow their mother a chance to catch up. Charley bustled up and took Will's free arm. "Does this flight mean the ruination of another shirt?"

Will gave it some thought. "I hope not. I promise I'll get changed before going out to the field."

"You make sure you do, those oil stains drive me to despair." Charley called back to her husband, John, who lagged behind, admiring an azalea in Walter Julien's front yard. "John, will you make haste? We're late already!"

Will's father lowered the bloom and loped after them. A tall, rangy man, John Turner looked as if he moved on springs, holding some kind of compressed energy inside his spare frame. He gave some people the impression of being permanently lost in thought, even absent-minded: a dangerous under-estimation for anybody doing business with him. "Excuse me, family. Am I missing some important discussion here?" John linked up to his wife's unoccupied arm and the Turner family swept up to the church in a wide formation.

Some members of the congregation assembled outside shot disapproving looks, exchanging glances with their friends. Something about the Turner's obvious affection for each other made them uneasy. There was even talk that John Turner discussed matters other than the running of the Turner home with his wife, an unusual practice in most families.

John Turner could not have cared less. He was a generous and modest man, without a trace of arrogance, and he felt no need to impress his neighbors or conform to the exclusive rules of male society. His emotional security was an established part of his character, though some said his self-confidence came from being wealthy. An invention, one that ended up earning handsome royalties, had made him rich.

Generations of Turners had bent over drawing boards, tinkered in workshops, nearly drowned, been blown up and knocked down. Their efforts met with varying degrees of success. Some ideas worked and made an impression; other ideas worked and made money. John Turner's steam injector had nearly doubled the power output of conventional railroad locomotives. It worked spectacularly and made him a fortune, primarily through investments. Investments chosen as carefully as he had once drafted the mechanical details of his inventions. John owned large segments of the railroad in Florida and Georgia, a sawmill and a good part of the land surrounding Tallahassee. He felt very comfortable with his life, but his daughter's recent illness had reminded him what a lucky man he was.

"Good morning John, Charlotte, children—how are y'all?" Their neighbor Walter Julien hailed the Turner family. John and Will raised their hats to Mrs. Julien and her daughter, Marie. Walter's pride in his distant French ancestry had led him to name his daughter after the last French queen. He tried to foster the impression of an aristocratic family history. Some of his acquaintances assumed he had a connection with the Marquis de Lafayette who had led an attempt to establish a utopian non-slave colony in North Florida with émigré French citizens in the early nineteenth century. Utopia had proven to be hot and dangerous. Instead, the practical French farmers had settled in Tallahassee, where they established the area known as "French Town." Walter was not descended from the Marquis but from a Huguenot family who tilled the fertile fields of Flanders before emigrating to Florida. He had inherited a green thumb, not a title, to his eternal regret.

"Is that an Indian Azalea, Walter?" John Turner asked.

"Why, yes, John. Did you see how it's changing to that deep shade of color? I call it magenta. I swear that flower is nearly half as pretty as my Marie."

"Oh! Daddy, you are so awful," Marie protested. Walter Julien smiled indulgently. Victoria turned away from the Juliens, muttering something under her breath, which brought a glare from her mother.

Marie and Victoria had been friends, yet rivals, their entire young lives, but their relationship blew hot and cold. This was a frosty period. Victoria thought Will paid far too much attention to Marie. She adored her brother, and while she knew that she should not feel possessive about him, she had admitted to Cordelia more than once in the past that she found it hard to share him with eligible females. She also had never found another young man as comfortable and fun to be around as her own brother.

◆◆◆

Cordelia and Victoria had sat together on the porch swing outside the Walker's house on the evening after Will had left for Tampa for his flight with Tony Jannus. Victoria found it easy to share confidences with Cordelia; thoughts and feelings that she somehow could never discuss with her mother.

"So what's so different about Will when you stand him against another gal's brothers?" Cordelia had asked. Victoria thought long and hard, then a slow smile lit her face. "I can tell you one thing. He teases, but he knows how far to take it. Enough to make me laugh, but not so far he makes it hurt."

The swing shook with Cordelia's hefty chuckle. "But you'd never admit it."

"Why, no! I love him dearly, but of course I *hate* him. That's what sisters have to do." She paused, her face serious again, "But I hate it when he flirts with other girls."

"So, you're sayin' our William is a flirt?"

"You bet! There's only one person worse than him an' that's Marie. She'd flirt with a chair leg given the chance. I reckon my brother's gonna get himself a reputation as a lady's man."

Cordelia looked at her carefully. "You're right. But only part right. He ain't no lady's man. Leastways not like some I know."

"What do you mean?"

"William likes ladies, and they like him."

"So, how's that different?"

Cordelia sighed. "I hope you never really get to know about this, but I guess you will. There's many men who hate women, or at least they're scared of us."

Victoria's eyes had opened wide. "You mean the love that dare not speak its name?"

"No girl! Those fellas won't do you no harm. I mean those snakes who pose as a gentleman an' then try to own you and use you. Trouble is, the only men *you* really know are too damn decent. It ain't given you no preparin' for life. You don't have no shell. No harm in developin' a little protection, like a turtle."

Victoria had crossed her arms and pushed the swing back with her heels. "I don't need any shell. I can take care of myself. An' if I can't, then Will can come and rescue me—"

"Who—that old flirt?"

❧ ♦♦♦ ☙

A grin slipped across Victoria's face as she recalled their raucous laughter that evening. Now she watched Marie playing up for Will's benefit.

The Episcopal Church before them suited Charlotte Turner. It reminded her of the Church of England she had left behind when John Turner brought her to Tallahassee soon after their marriage. Unlike most churches in the South that favored a white exterior over wood or stone, St. John's was an unashamed Gothic Revival in solid dark brick. It could have been dropped into any parish in the South of England without raising comment for its style. Built in 1880, the church boasted a 12-bell carillon and twenty Gothic-style windows. Walter Julien once described it as "the gentleman's path to heaven," referring to the prominent part played by many of its members in the community.

Charley Turner resorted to feigning a sneeze, at the time, to cover one of her infamous giggling fits. Walter made this remark at dinner while the Turner's butler, the lugubrious Jim Cobb, leaned past Charley's shoulder pouring wine. "Yes ma'am," he murmured. "If the devil cast his net when all the gennel'men comin' out St. John's, he'd have hisself good fishin', uh-hnn."

Even on this spring day the congregation welcomed the cool interior of the church, but a new arrival kept most lingering outside the church. The Turners stood staring like everyone else as Roscoe Vandersand made his entrance in a cloud of dust. The automobile he drove up in (or *piloted,* as John would call it, thinking that "driving" did not do justice to the behemoth Roscoe steered) was like nothing seen in the area before. Built of massive proportions and described as an "open sportster" in the manufacturer's catalogue, it towered over other cars. The driver sat exposed in a sumptuous, leather-upholstered throne, reminiscent of the furniture seen in a gentleman's club. A fold-down windshield gave some protection from the elements. The hood stretched away into the distance, flanked by sweeping mudguards flowing back into wide running boards alongside the driver. A barn door of a radiator gleaming with nickel plate dominated the front aspect, proudly flanked by driving lamps of searchlight proportions.

The whole machine gleamed in brilliant white; the paint setting off the polished brass instruments and levers. The wooden-spoked artillery wheels, sported what many considered to be the new-fangled pneumatic tires.

Charley gasped, "What has his daddy bought him now?"

Her husband's face twitched slightly as he controlled his glee at this acid remark. "Moby Dick, I think, my dear—the 'Great White Whale.'"

It would have been hard not to make an entrance in a car like this, but Roscoe Vandersand knew how to make the most of it. He yanked hard on the brake to induce a slight skid from the wheels as he pulled up. He allowed the motor to idle a few moments as he peeled off his gauntlets and goggles. It sounded like a drum being softly beaten at the far end of a drainage pipe, the bore of the exhaust being a similar diameter.

Roscoe turned his smile on the gathered audience. "Well, good morning ladies and gentlemen. What a splendid day for a drive if I do say so myself." It seemed Roscoe took personal credit for the perfect blue sky.

Will might have been envious, but he didn't know the meaning of jealousy. "*La France*—it's an *American La France.*" He announced with surprise, knowing it must be the only example south of Atlanta.

Roscoe turned his smile on Will. "It certainly is, William. What do you think of my little runabout?"

Will answered honestly, "It's a beauty Ros. You're a lucky guy."

"Oh, not so much lucky as discriminating, I hope, William," Roscoe paused to flick a speck of dust from his sleeve.

Will bit back a sharp reply and settled for, "That as well Roscoe," through gritted teeth.

Roscoe was not listening. He turned his attention on the crowd. "Walter, how are you? Emily, are you well?"

Mrs. Julien almost curtsied in her eagerness; she had very high hopes for Marie. "Oh yes, Roscoe, very well. What an absolutely splendid automobile... "

He was already turning his charm on the real object of his interest. "Marie, my dear, perhaps you and your mother would care to join me for a spin before the picnic this afternoon?"

Marie flushed pink, "Ooh! Yes, please, Roscoe!"

Victoria leaned close and whispered in her mother's ear, "That's right, girl, play hard to get."

Charley covered her laugh with a cough, "Ahem! Can't keep the Good Lord waiting, people. Hurry along now."

They walked quickly up the steps. Charley whispered to her husband, "How does he manage to keep that white suit so clean in that machine?"

John Turner smiled, "Like father, like son...no mud ever sticks to his daddy in Washington either." Charley looked sideways at her husband.

It was an atypical remark for John Turner, but accurate. Roscoe's father, Miller Vandersand, had prowled the political jungle for over thirty years; close enough to controversy to benefit from it's warmth, but never so close as to get burned. The mystery for John and others was why had the old rascal sent his son down to Florida? Many were flattered, but a few, like John Turner, puzzled over the choice for the son of an ambitious senator.

Honest men, and there were enough, admitted that, while not exactly a backwater compared to Washington, Tallahassee was almost an outpost. John had settled on two possibilities. It could be the old man knew something the rest of the country did not. Perhaps the son had been sent south to prepare the way for a grand enterprise based in that area of north Florida stretching along the Gulf coast, known as the "Panhandle." Or, for some reason not disclosed, Roscoe had been sent away to avoid a scandal. John had an uneasy feeling it was the latter.

The young man seemed pleasant enough, a little arrogant, but with those looks John allowed Roscoe could afford to be. He was what the ladies described as "dashingly handsome." His black hair shone almost blue with oil. It was thick and so careless in the way it flopped over his forehead that he clearly had it cut for that effect. He possessed striking blue eyes and features so regular they could have been mathematically calculated near perfection. His cleft chin seemed to have been arranged for the benefit of his female admirers; they went wild over it, or as wild as deemed polite anyway. There was something, however, about those beautiful blue eyes that bothered John Turner; he could never really fix them. Still, he reasoned, the man should have the benefit of the doubt until proven otherwise. Nevertheless, he was very pleased when his daughter declared she could not see what the fuss was about.

"Why's ever'body goin' crazy 'bout the man's chin?" she asked one day. "Looks like he's got two backsides when everyone else makes do with one!"

John was so pleased, he quite forgot to notice this was an indelicate remark for a young lady. He had merely murmured, "Quite so, my dear, don't repeat that in front of your mother."

Charley felt something in the air on this beautiful Sunday—not just spring. Attending church was the highlight of the week. The place to be seen, the place to flirt, to exchange gossip, the pause that gave the week a proper measured pace. For many like Charley, it was a time to take stock and pray. But today she felt uneasy. It was not just Victoria's illness; she felt changes coming. The day before, she had confided as much to her old friend Cordelia. The atmosphere of the big, airy kitchen at the Walker home soothed her in much the same way as the church. She had sat absentmindedly stirring her coffee at the big table.

Cordelia took her seriously, "Lawd sakes woman, peoples call me a witch, but when *you* get the heebies, I start to worry."

"I don't know my dear. Perhaps I'm getting old, but I've some uncomfortable feelings about the way the world is going," Charley said.

The older woman had tried to rationalize her fears. "Well, there's big problems with the cotton these days. They reckon there's some disease getting at the plants, but that won't trouble the Turners much, you're set up for life!"

Charley had swished her coffee around then stared gloomily at the grounds in her cup. "Maybe the news from home: they say there's going to be another European war."

Cordelia snorted, "Well, them Europeans stayed out of our war, so the polite thing to do will be for us to stay out of theirs." She paused, then a look of real concern came over her handsome, old face. She reached across and squeezed Charley's hand. "Oh lawd! I'm sorry hon', I'm forgettin' you have that fine young nephew, Rupert, an' he's a soldier ain't he?"

Charley shook off her gloom and squeezed in return. "Yes, and with fine young men like him, the old country should have nothing to worry about."

"There you go hon', nuthin' to fear." They had both laughed, neither fooling the other for a moment. Charley had felt a little better as she waved farewell to her friend, clutching a basket laden with preserves and two bottles of nicely maturing orange wine.

She thought about the previous day's conversation as they took their place in the family pew. Cordelia was probably right, but Charley still felt a sense of foreboding. The rest of the congregation did not share her unease, they sang their favorite hymns with gusto, and willed the sermon to its end. The girls peeped from under their hats, the boys stared and nudged each other, the adults tried to take it all in and look pious. It was not just the sunshine. They were looking forward to a new social event. Roscoe Vandersand was hosting a picnic.

It was styled an "informal afternoon reception," but these people knew a picnic when it was promised. The pleasingly elaborate printed invitations promised "victuals included." It was exciting to go to a picnic waiting for a surprise. Usually picnic baskets gave everyone a chance to savor, share and show off their best casual cooking, but "victuals included" provided enough mystery to heighten anticipation.

The setting was ideal and locally popular. Richmond Springs, named for the village near London, not the town in Virginia, was one of many places in the state where cool, clear water bubbled up from an underground source. Florida stands on a limestone base. When ancient caves collapsed, the resulting voids filled with water to form sink holes. A natural antidote for the fierce heat of summer, these springs provided recreation for everybody. Sometimes they were tiny: one even existed hidden from sight in the middle of a wood, forming a pool inside a cave, known only to the neighborhood.

Some formed natural swimming holes, where informal bathing was popular with the boys, depending on the time of day and who might be in the area. This activity also proved to be popular with Victoria and her friends, especially after Lucy Whiddon found her granddaddy's telescope and they found they could watch the boys unobserved. But swimming suits were worn at the Richmond Springs Resort Hotel. In the last few years mixed bathing had become acceptable, to most people. A few still huffed and puffed, all the while secretly wishing they could join in, but anyone with sense could see the bathing suits were as modest as anything worn at church on Sunday.

The hotel's developers, who included John Turner, had enlarged the natural pool, tiling the bottom and sides. They fed it through a terracotta pipe, artfully aimed to provide a constant waterfall at one end. The water flowed out over a spillway to cascade over artificial falls, before flowing into the nearby lake. Manicured lawns sloped up and away from the pool to the hotel itself, a mock colonial building nearly two hundred feet long. Tennis courts, fountains where tropical fish swam, even a croquet lawn added to the luxurious atmosphere. Suites of rooms available to rent, a resident band and a varied program of entertainment organized by the manager and part owner, Luther Powell, all contributed to a well-deserved popularity.

Roscoe could not have chosen a better venue for this part of his campaign to gain acceptance in his new hometown. Charlotte Turner, if asked, would have told him he need not try so hard. She had arrived at the end of the previous century to a welcome that surprised her with its warmth. John Turner had done an excellent job of "selling" her the idea of her new home. She would have followed him to the North Pole if he had asked, but she delighted in her new hometown. He had sent her a copy of Mr. George Barbour's *Florida for Tourists, Invalids, and Settlers.*

Barbour described Tallahassee as "One of the loveliest places in all America." The neatness of the homes and lawns really caught his attention, "...and gardens, almost all having quite ample grounds, well kept...and flowers, flowers, flowers!"

Arriving from England, a delighted Charlotte found Mr. Barbour had not exaggerated the charms of the state capital. She found the whole atmosphere unpretentious and her welcome generous. Plus, coming from a family of gardeners, Charley was happy to find the description of Tallahassee, as the "Floral City," perfectly accurate. It was as much like England as she could have wished. Even the summer heat did not trouble her; she had spent much of her childhood in India, where her father helped guard the frontiers of the British Empire.

Roscoe Vandersand did not do things in a half-hearted fashion. He had virtually taken over the hotel and its grounds. Nobody could take offense though, because he declared "open house." He planned this event as his debut into local society. With very few exceptions, everybody at the service that Sunday morning intended heading for the springs just as soon as they decently could.

One of those few exceptions was Will. He hoped to make his way there, to join his parents and sister, after a few aviation experiments. After all, he reasoned, his flying field, situated on the opposite shore of the lake, was only a mile away as the crow flies.

Lengthy conversations in the shade afforded by the porch and the towering oak trees next to the church usually kept friends behind after the service, but nobody lingered today, much to Will's relief. He ran home and through the door, taking the sweeping staircase two steps at a time before the others reached the steps leading to the imposing entrance. Two minutes later he threw himself back down the stairs.

His mother stopped him with a firm hand in his chest. "Just because you're in a hurry doesn't mean you can't eat. There's enough in here for you and Henry."

He opened the canvas bag his mother thrust into his hand, "Mother, there's enough in here for Henry, me, and the Seventh Cavalry."

She smiled sweetly, "Quite! So how will you feel if you have nothing to offer them if they turn up?" She presented her cheek; he kissed her. "And you take care!"

He swung the bag across his shoulder. "Mother, I *always* take care. See you later at the picnic." She raised her eyes heavenward as he crashed through the door.

Will ran to the back of the house where his motorcycle lived in the grandest of the many outbuildings. He had long since dispensed with the pedals meant to aid starting on the single-cylinder Harley. He was already running as he turned on the fuel valve, primed the carburetor and, in one flowing, practiced move, leapt aboard side-saddle. His weight overcame the resistance of the motor, spinning it barking into life. As the slim, gray machine accelerated toward the road, he swung his leg over the rear wheel and settled in a racing crouch.

In the dining room his mother paused in pouring a post-sermon coffee. Charley shook her head, "John, why are boys so noisy?"

He looked up from his newspaper. "I guess we just like it. Covers the sound of you ladies chatterin'."

She glared at him, "Men!"

Out on the highway Will urged his machine on. When the Model 5-35 first chuffed from the Harley-Davidson factory in 1909 it earned itself the nickname "The Silent Gray Fellow." Conservatively engineered with the luxury of sprung forks and the refinements of mechanically activated valves and adequate silencing, it earned itself a reputation for solid but uninspiring performance. Of course, in the hands of a skilled owner, that could be changed. Will's bike was still gray, but now—rattling like a Gatling gun—it was stripped to the bare essentials, benefiting from long, patient hours of work on the motor.

When Will's cousin Rupert had tried it the year before, he returned breathless from his ride to announce: "Will, it goes like stink!" From the faraway look in his cousin's eyes, Will guessed, correctly, this was British for "It's very fast indeed!"

Now he used all that hard-won speed to get to the flying field. He swung right onto East Tennessee, accelerated hard, chose his line, then swooped left at the big junction with Monroe. A few stragglers still wandered away from the church. They stopped to disapprove of the racket he made as he roared past, but returned his wave anyway.

Emily Julien sighed, "Such a charmin' boy, but so noisy!" She smiled at her daughter, "With good looks and a good family..." She left it hanging.

Marie wrinkled her nose, "Well, I s'pose he's kinda handsome...in a folksy sort of way."

Her father stopped, his walking cane poised in the air. "My dear! If by usin' this colloquial, somewhat vulgar expression, 'folksy,' you mean Will Turner is manly, intelligent an' athletic, with looks that suggest refinement, good taste an' breedin', I will accept it as a description."

Walter loved words; he had a good education and made sure everybody knew it. He was also a snob, a namedropper, and a social climber, but he genuinely liked Will. He too had high hopes, and they involved Will as a prospective son-in-law. He felt as uneasy about Roscoe Vandersand as John Turner did, and he would have been quite happy if young Roscoe turned his attentions elsewhere, family connections or no family connections.

Will blasted on, blissfully unaware of the debate he left in his wake. All he could see behind was dust and a haze of blue smoke. Ever since the law officers had put their own motorcycle into service, he had been obliged to check over his shoulder.

Will had complained to his father, "A brand new, sixty-one cubic inch, model 'J' V-twin for heaven's sakes! How am I supposed to keep the right side of the law?" His father, with impeccable logic, suggested he moderate his speed.

This was something Will found hard to do with an open road on a fresh spring day. He pushed the throttle lever harder, driving the bike on at nearly forty miles per hour. The Neoclassical and mock Queen Anne style mansions gave way to "vernacular" houses. These were sturdy homes with wide porches and immaculate paintwork. Before long, these gave way to nature. The forest grew close to the road, in some places even forming a canopy overhead, as the moss-draped oaks grew thick alongside the road. Sunlight flickered on his face, set with concentration as he dodged the worst of the ruts. Just beyond the city limit he eased back and bumped onto a narrow track, leading through the short fringe of forest into more open country.

Rail fences zigzagged around pastures. In a month or so, come May and June, briar berries would cover the fence jams. Henry would send their young helper, Winsy, collecting them. Winsy would return in triumph to Cordelia with his haul. She would set to making wine from them. Winsy was related to the Turners by blood. Will had once questioned exactly what kind of a cousin he was, "By marriage, mother?"

She had looked slightly pained, "Hmm, yes...something like that dear." He was a perceptive young man. He knew his father's brother, Uncle Bertie, had something to do with Winsy, so thought better of making an issue of it. "Something like that" was the explanation everybody else seemed to accept.

These thoughts were far from his mind as he crested the rise above their field. He throttled back sharply, stood on the brake and skidded through the gate, his bike rewarding him with a satisfying backfire. He pulled off his goggles and ran his fingers through his thatch of blond hair, hardly believing what he saw before him.

Will had not seen the shed since before his trip to St. Petersburg. Henry Walker had transformed it. Left to his own devices, but ably assisted by two of his father's mechanics and Winsy, Henry had transformed an idea sketched on the back of an envelope into hard fact.

The shed now had what appeared to be an elevated railroad track springing from its wide doorway. Starting at head height, a length of lightweight iron track extended away and down from the shed for a distance of almost one hundred feet. Supported on wood trestles, it effectively made a narrow gauge railroad with a distinct down gradient. This incline was enhanced by the field's descent toward the lake, at its southern boundary.

Will and Henry had borrowed the yard truck to drive to Thomasville, sixty miles to the north in Georgia, to collect the materials from a now-defunct logging operation. They had taken a day to get there, a day to load, and a day to get back over the rutted, muddy road. "Mud holes connected by short stretches of swamp," as Henry described the highway on their return, plastered from head to foot in thick, red clay. The truck weighed over four tons when empty. By the time they had overloaded it with iron and timber, they knew they would be bogged down a few times.

Will looked around for Henry and found him at the lower end of the track, sighting carefully along the rails, checking for signs of warping.

Henry straightened up, pushed a pencil stub back in his hair and replaced his old straw hat. "Well, what do you think?"

Will was speechless for a moment, then he put his arm around Henry's shoulders and squeezed him. "I think, Henry Walker, you're a genius."

Henry paused for a moment, checked up the track again, then grinned, "Okay, yeah, it's pretty damn good, if I do say so myself."

Will tipped Henry's hat forward over his eyes, "Yeah, you *can* say it yourself. Now how do we get the *Flyer* up on the track?"

Henry strode ahead, leading Will into the shed. He raised his arm in a sweeping gesture that took in the apparatus rigged just inside. "How's about that?"

His handiwork was elegant in its simplicity. He had reinforced the beams inside the old barn to take a sliding block and tackle. By working one chain, the machine could be lifted to the height needed, pulling another made it slide forward to rest its wheels on a "dolly"—not much more than a flat tray with recesses built in to restrain the airplane's wheels from pitching off. The dolly rolled smoothly on flanged wheels on the trackway itself. A smaller version accepted the tailskid.

Will gave a start as a small figure dropped from the roof beams to the floor in front of him; Winsy could never resist a climb. Few could resist Winsy, a boy small even for his ten years. He made up for his lack of stature with energy and enthusiasm.

He was chattering even as he hit the floor, "Will! You're back! Are we gonna fly today, Will? Are we? Are we?"

Will placed a hand firmly on Winsy's head to stop him bouncing up and down, but the child still had his arms stuck out, flapping them wildly to imitate a duck. Will regarded him kindly. He could not help noticing how, with the sunlight strong in the doorway behind the boy, he could see the light shining through Winsy's big, protruding ears. His hair was bleached almost white by the sun, and, despite the best efforts of his long-suffering mother, it looked just as Nathan had once described it—an explosion in a haystack.

Will tried to dampen the boy's enthusiasm, "We might just get a long glide today."

Winsy's little face fell, "Gee, Will, I was hopin' to see you loop the loop."

"Good grief boy! One thing at a time. But, tell you what, later on I'll take you on the Harley an' smuggle you into Roscoe's picnic, with those smart new Orr's overalls, you'll do, I reckon."

"Oh yeah!" Satisfied with that, Winsy scampered off.

Henry called after him, "An' you can cut me a piece of rope with that fancy new Barlow of your'n: six feet, not an inch more, not an inch less."

Will turned to Henry and asked him quietly, "New overalls? New pocket knife?"

Henry shrugged, "You know the score: overalls, your daddy—pocket knife, mine."

Winsy came back with the rope. Henry took it from him and tied a loop in the end. "Know what this is for young'un?" The boy shook his head. "Put this end 'round the tail skid. As we haul her up, you stop the tail from swingin' 'round, got it?"

Winsy's big ears almost flapped as he nodded, "Got it, chief!"

Will grinned at Henry, "Okay, *chief*, let's get her out." They hauled on the chain, raising their creation into the air for the first time. The system worked perfectly, albeit in a series of jerks. Within five minutes Tallahassee's first locally-built airplane stood on the launch ramp outside the barn. Will had been too modest with Tony Jannus back in St. Pete. His machine could stand alongside any factory built machine and compete in comparison of design and craftsmanship—it was the product of three years of hard work.

The *Flyer* lacked the curves of a French Morane or the almost ethereal grace of an Antoinette monoplane. Instead, the words *rugged, well proportioned,* even *handsome* described it. A monoplane, its single-wing finished in a flourish with rounded and slightly swept tips. The body, or fuselage, had an almost circular section that tapered toward the tail where the horizontal and vertical stabilizers reflected the shape of the wing. The pilot sat with head and shoulders exposed to the slipstream in a cockpit installed at a point ahead of where the trailing edge of the wing mated to the fuselage. Just ahead of the cockpit, function took over from form: a robust king post, often called a cabane by European aviators, formed a skeletal steel tube pyramid in front of the pilot's face. Strands of piano wire stretched from the apex of the pyramid to fix near the wing tips. These carried the weight of the wings when the airplane stood at ease on the big motorcycle wheels providing the landing gear.

With the *Flyer* settled into its launch system, Will scrambled up and took his place. Henry prowled around checking everything he could reach. Will waggled the single lever sprouting from the floor of the cockpit. It was fashioned from a baseball bat, turned down on a lathe to shave off a few more ounces. They had chosen the control system adopted by the British and French, which moved in the natural sense: a push forward lowered the nose, a pull raised it. A nudge to the left dropped the left wing; the other way lowered the right, initiating a turn to the low wing.

To prevent the airplane slipping into the turn or sliding out of it, pedals connected to the one vertical control surface. This rudder turned the nose left, or right, to balance the turn. Will knew the theory; now he had to prove it.

Henry worked his way underneath, between the trestles holding the track. He connected a cable to the bottom of the trolley supporting the airplane. This cable snaked forward thirty feet, circled a pulley, came back under the machine, returned to the barn end of the track, around another grooved wheel and went straight up into the roof of the barn. There it looped around another pulley, on the other side of which it suspended, amongst other items of scrap, an anvil.

The system worked on a simple principle: a pull on a rope released the weights, these dragged the cable over the pulley, and, in turn, this force traveled to the launch trolley via the pulley thirty feet forward down the track. Henry theorized that this would impart a steady thrust to the whole "shebang," as he put it. The *Flyer* would hopefully rise off the trolley before it even reached the end of the track.

Henry suddenly appeared alongside Will, a little breathless, cable hook still in his hand. "Will, is this wise? How about we just give you a trial push down the track by hand, engine running half speed; then you can just do a gentle glide and work up to the big one?" He looked at Will hopefully.

Will thought carefully. He polished his goggles, holding them up to the light to inspect them. "To be honest with you, Henry, I think you're a tad optimistic. I reckon with all the weights on the catapult, and the engine running full speed, we'll only get a glide anyway. I'm concerned that if I don't get enough speed right off, I won't be able to stop the wings floppin' one way or t'other when I roll off the end of the track. Then I'm twixt the devil an' the deep blue sea. Not goin' fast enough to control her, but goin' too fast to stop without diggin' in a wing and goin'—as Rupert would say— 'arse over tip!' "

Henry looked at his friend for a long moment, then down the track. "Okay, maybe you're right, but I've only put half the weights on."

Will grinned, "That'll do." He jumped in his seat as Winsy stuck his head over the other side of the cockpit.

The boy surveyed the sparse instrument board. He tapped the revolution counter with his knuckles, "Hey Will, if you go gittin' yo'sef kill't, can I have the Harley?" Henry and Will looked at him for a moment in disbelief, then took in the mischievous grin.

"Yeah! Okay it's yours, but on one condition."

"What's that?"

"You tell me what 'Winsy' is short for; I can't die without knowin'."

The little fellow struggled for a moment. "Winston—it's short for Winston."

"Well, hell, boy! That's a noble name. Now climb up behind Henry and make sure he doesn't fall in the propeller when he flips it over." Will's two assistants clambered to the nose of the machine, balancing themselves on the trestles between the track. Will switched on the fuel. Henry pulled the motor over a few times to suck gas into the cylinders, called, "ready," and, on Will's signal, expertly flicked the prop over. The motor caught and quickly settled down to its distinctive, offbeat rhythm. The ground crew jumped off the track and stood back.

Will settled himself into the seat and quickly checked the gauges. The sight glass on the crankcase of the motor showed oil pumping nicely. His revolution counter showed signs of life. This was it! He tightened his seat belt another hole, then paused to take in the scene. It was beautiful: a penetrating blue sky picked out perfectly by a few cotton-ball clouds, sailing on a gentle breeze. In front of him the pasture sloped toward the fringe of the lake, just visible between the line of trees that separated their field from the water. The big scimitar propeller rode around on the soft percussion of his motor; his hand rested on the throttle. He felt elation, anticipation, pride, and in no way afraid. He had discussed the mechanics of controlling an airplane for hours with Tony Jannus. He had been able to lean across the cockpit of the Benoist on the return journey over Tampa Bay and handle the controls. Even if he did achieve a prolonged glide when the *Flyer* left its track, he was confident he could control it.

Chapter Four

HENRY WALKER COULD WORK WITH ANY MATERIAL. RAISED WITH the acrid smell of the forge in his nose, he shaped and turned any metal then known. He could braze and had already mastered the new technique of gas welding. Henry cast a white-metal bearing shell before most boys could tie their own laces; but given the choice, he loved to work with wood. A carpenter's carpenter, he had a feel for timber—literally. He could run his hand over a rough hewn plank and tell what it would be good for, where it came from and how long it had seasoned in the yard. He created joins that left barely a trace in the surface of the finished article. Above all, he knew just how to create the maximum strength in a structure while keeping the weight to a minimum. To crown it all, his nature told him to build always with an eye for a beautiful line.

Henry was his own fiercest critic, but today he allowed himself a smile. The *Flyer* was his masterpiece. Henry and Will had seriously considered a metal structure for the fuselage but chose a conservative route. They did not know enough about the strength of welded joints. They wanted to fly, not pioneer new techniques. There would be plenty of time for that later. So they created a wooden wonder, with a frame of the finest spruce, braced by piano wire. It was not a first-time effort. They had previously built man-, or boy-carrying hang gliders after the style of the German pioneer, Otto Lilienthal. A lack of suitably high launching sites meant their efforts led to little danger, but a useful accumulation of knowledge and, of course, enormous fun.

Henry lived by the rule: *If it looks right, it usually works right.* It would have been easier to leave the *Flyer*'s wing tips as square-cut right angles, but he labored to finish the wings with a graceful curve. He felt it had to work better. They could have built the fuselage behind the pilot as an open framework, like Monsieur Bleriot's English Channel-hopping monoplane. When Will tentatively raised the suggestion the look of horror on Henry's face stalled the sentence on his lips. Their machine not only featured a covered fuselage; they fashioned it as a semi-monocoque, giving it strength from overlapping strips of birch veneer laid over a light frame, just like a racing skiff. The young men covered the wings and tail in finest Irish linen, hand-stitched to the ribs and drawn taut by the careful application of the lethally aromatic liquid called, simply, "dope."

In the strong light of the noonday sun, Henry could admire the spars and ribs through the fabric. But his nerves made his stomach churn. Building the airplane was one thing, watching his friend prepare to test it was quite another. He stood with his arms folded, his head to one side listening carefully to the beat of the motor. He looked steadily at Will who turned, beaming, toward him. Henry wiped the sweat from his forehead, replaced his hat, looked quickly around and called to his helper, "Winsy! Stand here where I can see you."

His hand went to the rope, fixed to the pin, that released the weights to send Will on his way. "Ready?" Nothing to gain from delay, thought Henry.

Will bellowed over the rattle of his motor, "Ready when you are!" Henry shut his eyes, muttered a brief prayer, and pulled hard. For the barest fraction nothing happened as the weights took the slack out of the system. Then *everything* seemed to take place in an instant. The *Flyer* shot forward, the ground shook as the weights crashed to the floor inside the barn. Henry just had time to register two other sounds: the motor rising quickly to a never before heard staccato roar; and a voice shouting, "*Whooooooa—*"

This was Will's reaction to the very unusual sensation taking him from behind. Their catapult launch pushed him so hard he felt himself thrown back in the seat. In any other situation that would have been no problem, but for a man with his left hand on a French-rigged throttle control and his right clutching a control column, it opened a whole new set of possibilities. His cousin's regiment would have been proud of him: the two main possibilities were death and glory. Instinctively he hung on; inertia did the rest. As he tried to keep his balance by holding onto throttle and stick, his backward momentum opened the throttle wide as his hand came back. In the same movement the control column came back to his stomach. His machine did exactly as they hoped. It pointed its nose to heaven and strove for the sky. Behind him Henry stared in disbelief. The

Flyer did not even reach the end of the ramp—it shot skyward like a game bird breaking cover. The angle looked impossible.

"Oh, Will!" Henry shut his eyes.

The crash did not come. Henry opened his eyes, and his jaw dropped. Winsy hung on his arm, jumping almost to his shoulder with excitement. It flew!

The *Florida Flyer* sailed quickly away: nose down now, motor humming, heading for the gap in the trees that led to the lake. "Okay—put her down! Get back on the ground! Quick, before you run out of roo—"

Henry felt helpless; even if Will could have heard him, he was too far down the field. From the air the meadow looked very small, limiting Will's options. He had reacted instinctively in the second it took to recognize the attitude his airplane had reached by thrusting the stick forward. For a heart-stopping moment he floundered on the edge of a stall: that moment when the wings lose their grip on the air. But the nose came down obediently—the *Flyer* stumbling forward into a shallow glide with the motor picking up like a good horse sensing a downhill run, leading the charge from the giddy height of their unintentional zoom.

Will felt completely calm. He could have frozen on the controls, but he had planned for this moment. Ever the optimist he had considered what to do in the event, the wonderful event, their plan worked. It was simple: He would steer through the gap in the trees, gain height over the lake, make a wide turn over the water, come back over the trees and make a perfect landing. Easy! he thought.

The first part worked well. The *Flyer* settled comfortably about twenty feet above the grass. Will noted that he barely had to move the stick. The gap in the trees grew bigger until he sailed through, the branches reeling back to give him his first indication of speed. Over the water now, the confident pilot hauled back on the stick. The *Flyer*'s nose lifted, the motor changed pitch and the tail hit the water with a resounding *thwack.*

For a moment Will was certain he was about to be pitched end-over-end as the tail rebounded into the air. For several seconds he looked at the surface of the water skating under the nose, which now pointed as far down as the tail had gone up. Then the *Flyer*'s natural stability balanced out the aerodynamic forces and set the plane back on an even keel—twenty feet up.

"Jesus H—," Will found himself talking to his machine. "What in tarnation—?" Then he remembered how Tony Jannus had explained what he called the "float trap."

"I'll be damned if I know why, Will," Jannus had said, shaking his head, "but every machine I ever flew, once you settle about a wingspan's height above the ground or water, will just float along nice an' easy on a light throttle 'til the cows come home. And believe me it's worse with a monoplane."

Damn cows better not be in my way, Will thought grimly, I'll not be able to climb above 'em. He realized that his motor at full power compared exactly to Tony's "light throttle."

For the moment he had time to think. The lake measured nearly a mile across at that point. The motor still pulled hard, but he was eating up the distance to the far shore. He could cut the power to splash down in the lake, or hit the trees. He chose the water, but even as he resigned himself to a soaking he saw salvation: if he could only get the nose around a few degrees he could make the shallow water by the Richmond Springs. There would be plenty of people to help him drag the *Flyer* to dry ground and save three years of hard work and expense from a watery end. With infinite care and the lightest pressure on stick and rudder bar Will nudged the airplane onto its new course. Then he saw a better option. He could clear the pool and fly straight onto the upsweep of the lawns. The gradient would stop him before he hit the trees. He saw only one difficulty to deal with—he had to steer through the lounging picnickers.

Just a few hundred yards away, and fast getting nearer, his mother remarked to Victoria, "Is that William's motorcycle, dear?" A few other guests turned toward the entrance to find the source of the unexpected racket.

Victoria shook her head. "I don't think so, Mother, that sounds like a two-cylinder machine to m—," her voice trailed away. Just catching a movement from the corner of her eye, Victoria clutched Charley's arm and pointed as a hundred other heads swiveled. Conversations stopped in mid-sentence. Teacups fell to the ground. Jaws dropped in astonishment.

Will, for his part, just realized a big problem was looming straight ahead. He recognized Mrs. Murray and Mrs. Foster and could tell they were deep in gossip. He knew that if they did not look up, it could be disastrous. He took his hand off the throttle and waved it from side-to-side in a frantic and useless gesture. "Get outta the way!"

Fortunately, they did look up. For one dreadful moment their ample bosoms locked together as they tried to run through each other. But panic prevailed, and they split apart to throw themselves out of the way.

Will cut the magneto switch with a decisive sweep of his hand. His wheels touched. They rebounded, but robbed of its propulsion the *Flyer* was content to give a little skip—the slope of the lawn being steep enough to slice away any attempt to gain a last flight. Will hauled the stick back to his stomach to plant the tail on the ground. His feet danced on the rudder bar to keep the *Flyer* steering straight along the path that had magically opened before him. The airplane swished through the astonished crowd, swung slightly toward a big marquee, then tripped itself gently on one of the guy ropes. The tail rose slowly, the big propeller taking the weight of the whole machine. It paused for a moment before the blade gave way, jerking the *Flyer* into a properly upended position, the tail pointing at the sky.

Absolute silence fell for a few moments, even the birds, stunned by the arrival of their noisy first cousin. Then all hell broke loose. Some people ran, others screamed, many did both. Will hung by his seat belt trying to steady his feet on the rudder bar. He felt strong hands under his elbows and heard an excited hubbub of voices.

Somebody pulled his goggles off.

"My God, it's Will Turner!"

"Good grief! He did it! He flew it!"

Will recognized excited faces, old classmates: Davie Brewer, Len Dumanion. They lifted him clear of the cockpit.

"Are you okay, Will?"

He felt solid ground under his feet but his knees felt as if they might disgrace him. He looked at the mass of faces crowding around. "I think so," he said, feeling a bit dazed.

Luckily for him someone else took over. Luther Powell, hotel manager and entrepreneur, hit the lawn at a dead run. He had seen the peaceful scene plunged into chaos from the dining room and burst through the doors contemplating homicide. As he gained the top of the steps Powell considered legal action. Halfway down he realized who had arrived and prayed his partner's son be in one piece. By the time he sprinted around the long trestle tables his antennae were picking up the swelling excitement. Always the opportunist, by the time he pushed through the crowd clamoring around Will, he saw the chance for more profit materialize like a mystical insight.

"Will, my boy!" Luther gasped, "You made it! May I be the first to congratulate you on behalf of your *backer*, The Richmond Springs Hotel." He grabbed Will's hand, pumping it hard.

Will was still trying to come to terms with being safely down without killing himself or anybody else. "My *what*, Mr. Powell?"

"Your backers! Ha ha! Always playing the silly goat, folks, that's Will Turner all over." He leaned close to Will, his grin firmly in place: "Follow my lead, son, and I'll cut you in," he hissed through his teeth.

Powell raised his voice over the rising babble of excited onlookers: "You boys, carry this hero up on your shoulders.

"Tom! Joshua! Get those ladies organized to bring two big bunches of flowers.

"Mayberry! George! Set me up some kind of a platform."

Powell had to compete against another voice more strident than his. Preacher Flint was in full flow. "And the Lord visited his wrath on the assembled host of sinners with a visitation of ang—," Flint broke off as somebody tapped him firmly on the shoulder and thrust a hip flask under his nose.

"Jack—shut up!"

"Hmm, don't mind if I do Peter." He took the proffered liquor from the ever-practical Father Morgan and took a deep draught. "Aaaah." Flint wiped his mouth on his sleeve and handed the flask back. "Shall we go assist the ladies?"

The priest took a quick pull himself and capped the flask: "It's our duty, Jack." As it happened, the ladies were sorting themselves out without help. Victoria had joined the rush to the wreck. Hitching up her skirt she climbed into the cockpit to release Will's belt before his enthusiastic friends pulled him in half. She pulled off his goggles and planted a kiss on his dazed face. Ignored by the crowd she had time to turn off the gas valve on the fuel tank, stopping the remaining fuel pouring over the hot cylinders. Face flushed with excitement she dashed back to her mother who stood to one side, hands partially covering her face.

"He did it Ma! He damn did it!"

Her mother slowly turned to her. Charley's mouth tried to form some words, but when they came out they didn't make a lot of sense. "That's not his best shirt is it?"

Victoria flung her arms around her mother's neck. "'Fraid it is, Ma." She suddenly recalled her conversation with Will the previous week, on the way home in Nathan's wagon, and broke into fits of laughter as she remembered her advice on how to lighten the load. "But believe me! It could have been a whole lot worse!"

Violet Foster and Lila Murray still sat on the grass surrounded by anxious and curious friends. Lila won her breath back. She straightened her hat, trying to regain some dignity. "Frank, what the hell was that?" She had her composure back, but the refinement refused to slip into place. Her husband had dashed along with the crowd, but now returned, shamefaced, to his wife.

Still, he could not contain his excitement. "It's John Turner's boy, Will, in his flying machine." He helped Lila to her feet, and she, in turn, extended her hand to her friend and helped her up.

"Hear that, Vi? We near been run down by young Will Turner."

Violet still blew from her lively sprint. "You don't say. There's me thinkin' it was the Angel Gabriel." Vi had an edge of irritation in her voice, but before she could go on, Luther Powell appeared at her side and took her arm.

"Dear ladies, please accept these as a token of our appreciation for your quick thinking in guiding our brave young aviator to a safe landing." He thrust a massive bouquet at each of the startled women.

Lila spoke for them both, "Why, thank you, Mr. Powell, so pleased to be of assistance."

He poured on the charm, "Won't you join us on the podium for the presentation ceremony?"

Violet took his arm, drawing him close. "Luther," she whispered, "this is a pile of horse pucky; but treat us right and we'll go along with it."

Powell's smile did not falter as he reflected on the old saying: You can take a girl out of the country...but you can't take the country out of the girl! In the less than five minutes since Will's landing he had already arranged a stage, won over the only people he thought likely to be upset by the precipitous arrival, and mentally rehearsed his speech.

He handed the ladies over to unflappable George, his headwaiter. Luther looked quickly around. "Tom! Where the hell is that damn fool Vandersand?"

The young porter skidded to a halt, "I just saw him drivin' away in his automobile, sir. He had a face on him like thunder!"

"He what?! Never mind, grab some men, put that machine back on its wheels, then drag it under the big tree." Tom dashed off on his mission. Luther shook his head, thoughtful for a moment, then strode toward the stage. "Ladeeez an' Gennelmen! By now you will have realized The Richmond Springs Hotel, with Mr. Roscoe Vandersand, has laid on a special demonstration of daring and downright courage for your pleasure—"

"Yeah! We noticed Luther!" The heckler earned a huge cheer and Luther loved it. Five years working the carnivals had taught him how to play a crowd.

"Glad you keep your eyes open, Bob," more cheers, "in the new science of aerial locomotion."

Powell turned slightly to one side and held out both hands toward the *Flyer,* now being wheeled into place, as if presenting a magic trick. "With the generous assistance of The Richmond Springs Hotel, Mr. Will Turner, inventor and engineer, has perfected his airplane and demonstrated it for your edification and delight by making his first flight to join us on this beautiful afternoon. Ladies and gentlemen, I give you our proud city's first home-grown aviator, Will Turner!"

The applause rose to a roar. Will sat on the edge of the stage, trying to put his thoughts together. Someone thrust a glass of lemonade into his hand, and he took a long drink.

Victoria grabbed his arm, "Come on, Will! On your feet, get up there." He staggered to his feet, visibly unsteady. The crowd loved him. A tall, shy young man with tousled hair and eyes outlined white by the goggles that had provided protection from the oil that blackened the rest of his face, Will stood as their very own hero.

Luther took his hand, holding his arm high like a victorious prizefighter. "A few words from the intrepid bird-man." He stood back, leaving Will centerstage.

"Well...er...thank you for being here folks," he struggled for something else to say. "Guess I won't lack witnesses when I tell the Aero

Club she flew—," his audience erupted into cheers and laughter again. He started to go on, but Luther stepped to his side again.

"Don't push it, Will, you're doin' fine, leave it to me." Will gratefully stepped back, and Luther addressed the crowd again. "And we have to thank Mrs. Foster and Mrs. Murray for their prompt action in bravely indicating the best landing path for Will." He motioned for the ladies to join them. They resisted for what seemed a polite pause, then hurried on stage. Luther quickly arranged them on either side of Will and indicated to his photographer to take his shot. The powder flashed and the camera fixed the moment for posterity.

"Now if you care to continue enjoying the hospitality of the Richmond Springs Hotel—"

Not bad, thought Victoria, he managed to work the name into one in every three sentences.

"The *Florida Flyer* will be exhibited inside the grand marquee. For twenty-five cents you can gaze on this marvel of modern engineering, for one dollar you can sit in the machine and relive Will's epic flight. All proceeds to the hospital fund." This announcement met with more applause. Tom, the porter, did not need direction; he had anticipated Luther's move and the *Flyer* had already been rolled into the big tent.

On the edge of the crowd, Charley stood between Preacher Flint and Father Morgan. Despite the fact that Flint appeared deranged on occasion, he was a kindly man. He offered her a cup of tea. "Steady your nerves, Charlotte, my dear?" He looked pointedly at the priest's pocket. Morgan smiled and added a generous measure from his trusty flask.

She drained her cup in one go. "Thank you, gentlemen, I needed that." She fixed a polite smile as Lila and Violet bustled up, slightly flushed, with matching oily marks where Will had gallantly kissed their cheeks.

Lila took her arm and squeezed it, "You must be so proud of your son, Charlotte."

Violet winked, "And he's just so *cute!*"

Charlotte smiled resignedly, "Yes, he is, thank you for being so understanding. He must have given you the fright of your lives." The two ladies took her hands in theirs.

Lila smiled, "Believe me, my dear, the *thrill* of my life. When you're married to Frank you need a little excitement." The two ladies burst into a fit of giggles and trotted off, hand-in-hand.

Peter Morgan smiled, "Your son seems to have taken years off them."

"But he's just put years on me." She frowned. "His daddy is not going to find this at all amusing, I fear."

Will's father remained blissfully unaware of the commotion his son had caused. Just before he was due to leave for the picnic, Nathan had appeared with the alarming news that a bridge to the east of town showed signs of collapse. Gratefully, he joined his friend on this urgent errand; afternoon receptions were not to his taste. Walter Julien had offered to drive Victoria and her mother to the Springs in his new Studebaker. He had plenty of space, as Roscoe had been good as his word, picking Walter's wife and daughter up in his shiny white tourer.

On the other side of the lake, Henry knew nothing of the outcome of the flight, but he knew their plans had gone seriously awry. He followed Winsy, sprinting across the field to the edge of the lake. From the moment Will disappeared through the gap in the trees Henry strained to hear the approaching roar marking the *Flyer*'s return. As he ran he abandoned that hope. The cracking bark of the motor faded before he even reached the shore.

"Winsy, shin up that tree, an' see if he's in the lake."

The boy scrambled high in the branches in the time it took to say it. "Can't see him, Henry."

"Well keep lookin', he can't be anywhere else."

"Could be right up in the sky," Winsy gazed hopefully into the blue.

"No, he must've sunk, but I can't understand why we don't see some of the *Flyer*. Come on down, we're takin' the boat." Henry quickly untied it and, by the time he grabbed the oars, Winsy had jumped in.

"Gators might have ate him up."

Henry glared at him. "Trust me, boy, if the *Flyer* plowed in, them old boys will have taken such a fright they'll be halfway to Jacksonville by now. We'll just go straight across, same way he did, then we'll find him swimmin'." He pulled on the oars, and the boat shot forward. Henry rowed like a machine, if anything his strokes grew more powerful as they surged the pair across the lake.

Winsy sat in the bow, shielding his eyes against the reflected glare. Henry wanted to scan the surface, but he had no choice but to face to the rear. "Henry, there's somethin' goin' on at the Springs."

"I know that, boy, just keep lookin'," he heaved on the oars even harder.

"No, I mean there's somethin' strange goin' on—everybody's runnin' 'round—Heck Henry, I can see him!" Winsy jumped up, nearly falling over the side in his excitement.

Henry sculled the boat around for a clear view. "Hellfire, Winsy boy! You're right! He made it." Winsy had seen Tom and his crew pulling the tail down and now, from their vantage point on the lake, they could clearly see the crowd gathered around the *Flyer*.

"God! I hope he's okay." Henry applied himself to the oars with renewed strength. They had to steer to one side of the artificial falls to avoid the strong flow of water. Winsy jumped over the side and dragged the boat to the shore. Henry tossed him the line and Winsy fastened it to a tree. They splashed to firm ground and started running up the sloped lawn.

"Miss Vicky! Miss Vicky! What's goin' on, is he all right?" Henry had spotted Will's sister near the edge of the crowd deep in conversation with Marie. Victoria let go of Marie's hand and dashed to Henry. Quite forgetting the proper protocol, she hugged him hard. In all the excitement nobody noticed; it was a day when nothing seemed quite as before.

"Oh, Henry, dear! You should'a seen it. He came cruisin' 'cross the lake easy as you please. Just missed two ladies over there, I was standin' here, with Mother...anyway, they ran clear an—"

He took her hands, looked her in the eye and repeated his question. "Miss Vicky, is your brother okay? Did he hurt himself?"

"Aw, hell no, Henry, he's fine!"

Henry closed his eyes and put his head back. His lips moved silently in prayer. "Thank you, Lord."

"Anyway, as I was sayin', I was standin' here with Mother an' he put his wheels down just there, an' he rolled on up the hill 'til he hit that rope an' she just sorta' went up on her nose an'—," she stopped in mid flow. "Aw, bad news, Henry, the propeller busted up."

He took her hand and squeezed, "Miss Vicky, I can make a new propeller. I can't make you a new brother!" When his words finally sank in, Vicky calmed down.

"Shoot! You're right H. I didn't think on it that way! Guess we're kinda lucky."

"You bet we are! Come on, better show me the damage." She took his hand to drag him to the marquee. He hardly stepped inside before

Luther Powell grabbed him.

"Henry! Just the man I wanted to see. Can you fix this propeller thing?"

"Not to fly again, Mr. Powell"

"Heaven forbid! Just to pretty it up to exhibit." He held up the broken blade for inspection. Luther really had taken charge. Henry examined the splintered end, then held it against the stub projecting from the hub.

"Got any tools here, Mr. Powell?

"Anything you want. Give Thomas a list. Joshua! Get Henry somethin' to drink." He hurried away, giving orders as he went.

Henry looked up from his examination of the broken parts. Vicky watched him with undisguised admiration. "You can fix just about anythin', can't you Henry?"

He smiled, "Do my best, Miss Vicky, but I can't fix things the way Mr. Powell does. He really knows how to *organize* people."

"What do you mean?"

Henry eased the propeller around to give himself a better angle to work. "What I mean is Mr. Powell may have saved us from gettin' into real bad trouble. There's some folks who would have been screamin' the place down. An' had Will arrested, me too on account of bein' his accomplice. 'Accessory after the fact' they calls it in law. 'Specially on account of me bein' a *black* accessory."

Victoria's face mixed disbelief and horror. "They wouldn't! They couldn't!"

"Henry is right. They could and they would." Vicky started at her mother's voice; she had not noticed her standing behind her. Charlotte was as perceptive as Henry. They both knew just how lucky Will had been. She preferred not to think of it, but her son could just as easily have killed somebody else as well as himself. "Mr. Powell is a very able man, and he may have some influence on your father but there is still the Sheriff to consider; and there is no telling what he will have to say about this."

He had a lot to say, but could do nothing about it. Sheriff Clarence Drew had an uncanny instinct for incident, accident or misdemeanour. His faithful Model T rolled up to the party within half an hour of Will's landing.

Luther saw him coming and quickly headed him off, drawing him to one side. "There's no harm done, Clarence."

The sheriff wagged a beefy finger under Luther's nose, "Mr. Powell," he intended to keep things formal, "there might be no harm done, but the law's been broken."

Luther switched from charm to firm in an instant. "What law, Sheriff? What law's been broken?"

Clarence drew breath to reply, then stopped for a second to think. "Reckless driving in a public place! That covers anythin' from a horse an' buggy to a motor truck, through motorcycles an' automobiles. It'll do for that flyin' buggy just as well!"

The sheriff sounded triumphant, but Luther was having none of it. "You *drive* a horse and buggy, a motor truck, motorcycle or automobile. Show me where any newspaper reports Mr. Orville Wright *drivin'* his airplane!"

"Now don't get smart with me, Luther Powell—"

"Well I guess I'm just goin' to have to! Because not only was he not *drivin'*, he was not doin' whatever he was doin' in a *public* place. He flew from his daddy's land to his daddy's land!"

The sheriff puffed himself up to his full height and wagged his finger again. He let out his breath, "Dammit—you're right, Luther! But I'm goin' to have words with the boy."

Luther relaxed, glad the confrontation had ended amicably. He steered the sheriff toward the refreshments. "Somethin' tells me you won't be the only one!"

Chapter Five

CORDELIA WALKER WAS BORN A SLAVE ON THE MURCHISON plantation, the year the War Between the States erupted. Still not old enough to know what it meant when freedom came, she did understand there seemed to be any amount of people coming and going. Sadly, among the going was her mother, dead from a fever. Her father had been killed, laboring in the earthworks before Vicksburg. The Confederacy never sent black men into combat, at least not with a gun, but the Union shell that blew him to bits made no distinctions based on race.

Annie Murchison lost her only child, Billy, to cholera while he was in camp at Richmond before he even saw the enemy. Her friends believed her husband died of a broken heart. It seemed everybody on the plantation grieved for somebody or something lost in the war. Annie dealt with her loss the only way she knew how. She worked. Now, as the sole owner of the property, she followed her Scots non-comformist conscience, and freed her slaves. When the war ended and the infamous carpetbaggers arrived, she saw them off. When neighbors told her it was immoral to teach her workers to read, she immediately set aside a room as a school. "You may be happy to employ field workers," she told other landowners in her Edinburgh drawl. "I employ staff."

The young Cordelia had been an exceptionally quick learner. At the age of twelve she read from the works of Shakespeare with confidence and enjoyment. She caused a stir with her obvious rapport with animals. It even led to dark mutterings: "Just ain't nat'rel!" some of the older folk would opine. They saw the fiercest yard dog following her around like a fawning puppy. The men who worked the big horse teams never worried, however, they just appreciated her talent. She grew into a sturdy young woman who they taught to harness, groom, and even drive the horses. Cordelia earned the task of caring for Doctor Rogers's horse when he made his frequent calls to the plantation. The animal was a brute, but in Cordelia's hands he was mild and obedient. Dr. Rogers and the "missus" would sit for hours on the porch, intent on a chessboard.

One fine spring day the doctor arrived in the late afternoon. He climbed painfully to the porch. His old chess partner looked him over carefully, "Hector, you're gettin' old."

"Thanks, Annie, so are you."

She laughed but took his hands carefully in hers. He winced. "You're the doctor, Hector, so this is your second opinion. That's not just the 'screws', that's what we call arthritis." She told him bluntly.

"Won't stop me pushin' pieces 'round the board or lifting a glass of that real Scotch whisky."

"True, but it is going to stop you from driving that stupid animal of yours. Good grief, man! I've seen a glass of water with more brains than that thing. He's done this to your hands. Let me shoot him for you."

"Only if you'll pull the buggy, I can't afford a new horse."

She snorted, "That's because you 'forget' to charge for your services, you old fool. Come on, get this down you for the pain, then you can borrow Cordelia to drive you for the next few days. She's the only one who can handle that beast."

It was a "lend" that was to last nearly twenty years. Cordelia quickly became indispensable to the ailing doctor. She soaked up knowledge like a sponge. Before long she was performing the role of nurse and midwife as well as driver. Her work with Hector Rogers exposed her to all aspects of life in the rural South. A black woman working on a cotton plantation could lead as sheltered a life as her white contemporary living in the polite society of a large provincial town. But Cordelia spent twenty years dealing with the medical consequences of human frailty, stupidity, cruelty, and injustice. She had spent days patiently removing tar from the victims of a "Klan" visit. She set bones for women brutally thrashed by drunken husbands. She had picked buckshot out of feuding farmers following idiotic disputes, the causes of which were lost at the back of the top shelf of local history. She knew frailty, stupidity, and fear when she heard it, and she believed she heard them all now as she sat facing her husband and John Turner the morning after Will's flight.

Anybody watching would have been struck by the similarity between the big woman and the kettle simmering on the range. They were both coming to the boil. "You are considerin' what?!" Her voice sounded all the more menacing for its even tone.

John Turner met her gaze, "I believe we should put an end to this flyin' nonsense now. That machine should be broken up before it kills somebody."

Cordelia struggled to keep the contempt out of her voice. Her mind raced as she marshaled her arguments. She knew she could bully most people with the force of her personality, but on this issue John Turner would not be swayed by scorn. They had crossed swords before and she knew what a stubborn man he could be; most mules were tractable by comparison. She honored him for that but meant to win this argument. He would need persuading; logic might succeed where anger was sure to fail. She flicked an imaginary speck from the table with her duster and looked steadily at the two men sitting opposite. Despite the warmth of the kitchen, the atmosphere was frosty. "Have you two old men...," she trailed the *old* a little, "considered how much you are to blame for this near accident?"

Their reaction told her they had not. They turned to look at each other, then back to her. Nathan spoke, "Just how do you fathom that?" He leaned forward, challenging his wife.

She looked at him steadily, then back to John: "You didn't take them serious."

Nathan sat back and folded his arms, "That is ridiculous, Wife. I spent hours making sure they were workin' right."

"Yeah—you did, but you didn't really want to see it fly."

Nathan slapped his palm down hard on the table. "That is *not* the case, Mrs. Walker, I wanted those boys to succeed."

Cordelia smiled. "*Mister* Walker, you wanted to see them succeed in making a little 'hop', so to speak—just enough to bring the reporters out to the field to see daylight under the wheels, and claim a flight. You didn't want it to *really* fly." She saw the quick glance between the men. Glory be, she thought, right on the nose, I got you! Cordelia tried to keep the triumph out of her voice when she spoke. "So you fixed 'em up with that old motorcycle engine knowing full well it'd never make enough power to take Will up to where he could hurt himself. You just try to tell me I'm wrong!" They could not. Instead they looked at her, speechless. "Well, go on then," she challenged. Nathan slumped back in his chair; he tossed the pencil he had been playing with onto the table.

Cordelia snatched it and jammed it into the jar where it belonged.

"Well, John, am I right?" she demanded.

For the first time that morning his face softened into a smile. "Pretty close, I'll admit. How did you work that out?"

Cordelia raised her eyes to the ceiling and sighed, "Honestly, John Turner, what do you think I do all day? This place is carpeted with engineerin' an' aviation journals. I don't need to be Orville Wright to work out that a motor built to do one job ain't necessarily goin' to do another. That heap of junk was never goin' to pull their airplane into the sky." He still did not understand. "I *read* the damn journals an' I married an engineer. I've gained a fair idea of what works, even if I don' get covered in oil an' filth."

He nodded, "Okay, but let me ask what you would now be saying to me if I'd bought him a real airplane motor that would have taken him up to where he could get himself killed?" He leaned forward, challenging her in turn.

Cordelia knew it was a fair question. And stubborn as he was, she respected him for this chance to speak up for "her boys." Most men would have just gone ahead and smashed up the airplane in their anger and fright, they would have felt no need for consultation with wives or mothers. "I'd have made sure he had proper trainin', and the machine had been checked out by a professional aviator, which is just what you should have done."

"But I don't want him to fly—dammit!" John surprised Cordelia with his passion.

She leaned toward him and smiled gently. "John, I know you don't, and neither do I. You're his father, an' I raised him near enough. But you might as well tell an eagle not to spread its wings. If you try to stop him, he'll just fly away and you won't have any say in how he does it." John looked into her eyes for an age. He knew she was right, but it was a truth he did not want to hear. Cordelia judged the time right to press her argument home. An appeal to fatherly pride might just work, "'Sides, have you considered what folk are goin' to think if you break up the *Flyer?* Will's their own hero. That airplane is public property—," she held up a hand to still John's protest, "I know, but they don't see it that way. You two will be about as popular as liquor salesmen at a prayer meetin'."

Nathan scratched his head. It was never easy, but he knew he would hear Cordelia's opinion whether he wanted it or not. "Well, what do you suggest?" he asked.

"Ground 'em, roast 'em, an' punish 'em hard," she spoke without hesitation. The two men looked at each other again, relieved to find they all agreed on something. Cordelia caught their looks, "Don't you worry, we're goin' to make sure they face up to the consequences of their rash behaviour. There can't be any doubt on *that* score."

John sighed, "Without breaking up the machine how do we do that?"

"'Sakes! Come on, John Turner, have you no imagination? Mr. Luther Powell already showed you. We make them work their tails off at the Springs for the next week, makin' charity dollars for the infirmary fund demonstratin' the *Flyer* in that big tent. Then, on top of that, they can give all their spendin' money to the fund."

"An' the roastin'?" asked John.

Cordelia smiled grimly, "John, you take yours, Nathan you take ours—then send 'em both to me."

Will and Henry were summoned from the workshop, nervously trying to rub their hands clean on cotton waste as they went. Henry received a military style dressing down from his father in the office. His obligations as an engineer, responsible for the safety of the traveling public and using equipment entrusted to his care, were hammered home. Henry stood to attention, facing front, as Nathan paced up and down in the small space available.

"You came this close—," Nathan pinched his forefinger and thumb together and pushed them under Henry's nose, "*This* close to being party to a fatal accident. Walkers ain't *never* been involved in a serious mishap! Why's that?" He snapped the question like slamming a steel trap shut.

"Because we check...double check...then check again—sir!" Henry added as a quick afterthought.

"So what went wrong this time?"

"I did all the checks...but I made a mistake," Henry admitted.

Nathan was shorter than his son was, but at this moment he appeared taller. Certainly he looked Henry straight in the eye. For a long moment they stood toe to toe. Then Nathan poked his son hard in the chest to emphasise each word.

"That—is—the—last—mistake—you—will—ever—make—when—dealing—with—an—airplane. Do you understand?"

Henry did understand, and for all the severity of the dressing down his heart leaped. This meant he might be allowed near an airplane again. "Yessir! You bet—I'll get it right in future."

"Damn right, you will," Nathan barked, "now go see your mother. She's goin' to have words with you. Dis—*missed*!" Henry turned smartly on his heel to leave; he paused at the door. "Sorry, Pa," he said.

"I know you are, son." Nathan's voice sounded more gruff than usual.

Will's interview with his father was conducted standing at the side of the ornate desk in Nathan's study. John Turner's words were delivered at a lower volume, but stung just as much. "Just what in God's name did you think you were doin'? Were all those years at school wasted? A freshman could have done the calculations needed to show the weights needed to keep that damn catapult contraption inside safe limits until you learned to control your machine."

"I guess I was too impatient, an' I suppose—"

"Impatient! What the hell would happen if our railroad engineers just happened to grow impatient? By God, William, if ever I needed proof that aviation is not safe for fare-payin' passengers, you just handed it to me."

Will leaned forward and placed his hands on his side of the desk so father and son confronted each other face to face. Even in his anger, Will recognized this was the first time he had truly argued with and stood up to John. "Father, I was not carryin' any passengers. It was my own damn neck—"

"So what about those innocent citizens you damn near ran down?"

Will had no answer and knew it. His thoughts kept returning to how close he came to hurting someone on the ground. He knew he should have dumped the *Flyer* in the water. "Okay, I admit it, it was stupid, but it won't happen again."

"Damn right it won't happen again." The stricken look on Will's face made John soften his tone. He went on quickly. "No, I'm not orderin' you to break up your machine. But I've already given orders to dismantle that stupid launching system."

"It worked," Will said quietly.

John drew breath, his deep set eyes bored into Will, his arms bent where he leaned on the desk so he looked like a big hound on the point of attack. Will did not flinch. They faced each other for a long moment. "Yes, it did." John said. As angry as he felt, John Turner the engineer could not deny the system succeeded. "Dammit, William, sit down." He slumped back in the big leather chair on his own side of the desk. Will perched uneasily on the chair facing him.

John put his head in his hands for a second and then rubbed his temples vigorously. Then he looked at his son. "Will, don't think I'm not proud of you. The whole town's proud of you. But I know, and *you* know it was luck that saved you from bein' a villain instead of a hero, an' bein' lucky is not enough for a Turner. I have the family name to think of."

"Yes, sir."

"I will wait until the end of the week before I decide what we are goin' to do about you an' your ambitions. We might both say things we regret if we carry on now. For the time bein' your machine will be exhibited at the Springs to raise money for the hospital fund."

"Yes, sir."

"We will see where we go from there. Now, Cordelia wants a word with you an' Henry together"

"Oh, hell, sir!"

"Indeed. Rather you than me."

Will's face was ashen at the end of the interview with Cordelia he shared with his friend and accomplice. Even Henry's rich ebony coloring faded in the heat of her tirade, delivered in the kitchen—her domain. John retreated to the office with Nathan as Cordelia thundered into their sons, closing the door quietly behind him and leaning his back against it. He accepted the whisky glass Nathan pressed into his hand despite the early hour.

"They tangled with gravity and Mrs. Walker all in the space of twenty-four hours. Nathan, I don't know which I would consider safer to deal with."

Nathan poured for him, "Gravity," he growled, "at least you know it obeys physical laws."

Will and Henry returned to the machine shop a lot happier than when they left it, even though their ears still rang from a catalog of their inadequacies and failings. Will leaned back against a lathe and wiped sweat from his brow, "That was close. I thought, for a minute or two, that we'd lost the *Flyer.*"

Henry grunted and scratched his chin, "We came pretty close, anyhow."

"What do you mean?"

"Remember I stitched that plate on the back of the propeller to make it look like it was in one piece?" Will nodded and Henry continued, "Well, I had my nose up against the motor an' I couldn't help but notice the broken tie-down studs on the left cylinder. If you'd been a second later switching off, that barrel was goin' to come right off an' seek employment somewhere's else where they don't work machinery so hard."

Will turned pale again, "Oh hell!" he muttered, "I could feel oil blowin' back in my face."

"No harm done, no way we could use that motor anyhow, not after this."

"I'm thinkin' 'bout what might have happened. Soon as I flew out over the lake I hauled back on the stick. Planned to make a circle and fly back, but I hadn't enough power. If there had been, it would have quit with me a hundred feet up over the trees, like as not."

Henry took a practical view, "Well, you didn't have enough power, it didn't quit on you, an' you got down safe...don't do to keep harkin' on about what might happen. Wings might have fallen off, trolley might have come off the track, whole shootin' match could have gone up in flames after you landed, but none of these things happened so don't worry on it."

"I s'pose you're right."

Henry suddenly pointed at him, "And! Mr. Pro-fesh-nal Aviator, do you know *why* it didn't go up in smoke after you went ass up?" It obviously had not occurred to Will who shook his head. "Because your little, pain-in-the-ass sister saw gas pourin' out the carburetor where the float had stuck an' had the sense to turn off the valve at the tank. You owe her, William. Looks like she was the only one who got it right yesterday."

Will brightened up, "My little sis? Well Lordy! I'm a lucky brother. Some boys get stuck with an idiot for a sister."

Henry let out a dismissive snort; he sounded like his mother. "Yeah! But some sisters get an idiot for a brother."

Will was heading for the door but stopped, regarding his friend with a rueful smile. "Point taken," he said quietly. "I really don't feel too proud about yesterday. I mean, it was fine while I was up there, but when I think on what could have happened...well, I'm just glad nobody was hurt. If I'd known how much upset this was goin' to cause—," he stopped, reflecting for a moment. "I ain't *ever* seen your daddy so mad, nor mine. And then it sounds like Cordelia chews 'em both out. An' my ma's upset, keeps burstin' into cryin' when she looks at me. Never thought what I was doin' could cause so much feelin' amongst so many people."

Henry had never seen him so thoughtful, it was a new side to his friend and he liked it, even if he did sound a bit down it was good to know the man had feelings. Nathan had a saying about "daredevils." His father had sayings about a lot of things, but it seemed very accurate: "They dare and the devil pays the consequences." Henry decided to draw a line under this and lighten Will's mood, "Well, everybody's let off steam now and all the hurt is out, so let's go back to work an' show 'em what model citizens we can be."

Though they had no choice in the matter, Will and Henry threw themselves into the task of exploiting the *Flyer*'s fame for charity fundraising with enthusiasm and good humor. They were surprised and gratified at the number of people who made the pilgrimage to the hotel each afternoon after working hours to marvel at the *Flyer*. Many paid the extra to sit in the cockpit while Will patiently explained the controls. He loved to see how some would grab the stick and waggle it around with enthusiasm while others cautiously took it between thumb and forefinger, as if fearful of finding it charged with electricity. They all showed plain delight, however, when they saw the control surfaces move at their command. Their pleasure made the effort very worthwhile for Will.

Instead of growing bored with the task, Will and his crew found ways of improving the show. The cash generated toward the provision of medical care for the poor pleased everybody involved. Will could now point out to his father that aviation could be made to pay but had the sense to keep that to himself. Sunday afternoon was to be the *Flyer*'s last show, and Will was determined to make it their best day yet. Will and Vicky were meeting the Julien family who were lunching at the hotel. Walter Julien felt genuinely proud of Will's achievement and basked happily in the reflected celebrity.

Marie had invited herself to help the fundraising and even Victoria had to admit she made herself very useful. Marie surprised them all with a gift for organization. She charmed the people waiting in line as she took their money and served lemonade, tasks considered unseemly for a young woman of good family when connected with commerce, but seen as noble in the cause of charitable works. Marie came up with their best fundraising idea yet. As the *Flyer* had flopped back on its wheels, following the undignified upending, the fabric under the left wing had been gashed by a steel stake driven into the ground as an anchor for the tent's guy rope. An "all in" price of a dollar fifty bought Will's autograph on a piece of genuine "*Flyer* fabric" taken from the damaged wing, and the privilege of sitting in the cockpit for Will's guided tour of the instruments and controls. This proved an irresistible deal for many people.

Henry had made wooden steps to give easy access to and from the cockpit. Will did his bit by wearing clothes considered appropriate for an aviator. He sweated in cavalry breeches, a tweed shooting jacket, riding boots and a leather flying cap, with goggles on his head. He had worn nothing like this on his flight, but everybody who saw it swore that was how he dressed on that day.

They drove up to the hotel on the Sunday morning in the Auto Wagon, the motorized buggy built by the International Harvester Company and the first gasoline-powered vehicle owned by the Turners or seen in the district when John bought it five years before. Will pulled on the handbrake and stared in surprise at the line already forming. Marie bustled around inside the tent, determined not to miss a moment in Will's company or any chance to impress him.

Inside the hotel, in the ladies lounge, Emily Julien leaned over the coffee table. She looked around before shielding her mouth with the back of her hand. She and Kathleen Powell, wife of Luther the manager, were alone and sharing the hottest gossip in town. "Gone!" Emily announced in a firm but quiet voice, "Disappeared as if spirited away."

Kathleen's eyes opened wide with surprise and pleasure at the prospect of real scandal, "You don't say!"

Emily sat back, primly placing her hands together. Her lips pursed as she made an elaborate little nod, "Ah do say! And to think—we even considered him a prospective beau for our daughter!" She had perfected the little shudder she now gave. "They say he was seen in Thomasville that evening, in a low chop house," she paused for effect, "the worse for drink!"

"You don't say!" Kathleen prompted.

"Ah do say! Then that vulgar automobile of his was seen headin' for At-lan-taah." She managed to stretch the name of the famous old city, especially the last syllable, in a way that conveyed what she really meant: Sodom and Gomorrah. She realized her own lips were moving in synchronization with Kathleen's so she pressed them together.

"You don't say!"

"Ah most certainly do! Oh to think of it. Alarmin'! They do say the boy is unbalanced."

"Who says that?" asked Kathleen.

Emily found herself caught off guard, about to make her standard reply, but Kathleen had tossed in a valid question. Emily recovered quickly, "Medical opinion," she stated firmly.

That was good enough for Kathleen. "Medical opinion" came from Cordelia, via Charley Turner, and everybody knew they could rely on her experience.

Kathleen had been one of the few people who saw Roscoe storm away from the hotel on the afternoon of Will's flight. "I'll let you into a little secret, Emily," she said. "Roscoe missed a golden opportunity last Sunday."

"Whatever do you mean?" Emily's eyes opened wide.

"Luther wanted him to share in Will's glory. Remember he announced that the Springs *and* Roscoe had sponsored Will's machine?"

"Now you mention it, he did."

"That was so he could share in the limelight. That way he could have achieved a higher standin' in the community. He would have looked good, the hotel would have looked good, an' havin' said that, Luther was hopin' Roscoe really would have put some money into Will's airplane experiments. All Roscoe had to do was stand there an' smile. Instead he threw that monstrous tantrum an' went roarin' off to Atlanta. When he went past our Obadiah he was drinkin' from a bottle of brandy."

Inside the tent, Will managed to swallow a mouthful of sandwich as he changed into his costume behind a screen at the back of the big marquee. "I tell you, Henry, I feel bad about Roscoe. I barged into his special show back last week and I have had no chance to apologize. Now they say he's gone off to Atlanta, where he's most likely gettin' into all kinds of trouble. I'm goin' to ask your daddy for time off so I can travel there tomorrow an' find him." Henry glanced over his shoulder, pausing in his attempt to knot a bright red bow tie around Will's neck. "Talkin' of trouble—here it comes."

Marie bustled up, "Henry, what are you doin' with that tie? You'll cut off the circulation to his head. Give it here." Henry happily stepped aside, stopping only to give Will a huge conspiratorial wink from behind Marie's back. Will glared at him as she set to work with nimble fingers. Henry found Vicky sitting at the table used to count the money and issue tickets. She glanced back over her shoulder at her brother, then turned to Henry with a grin.

"They do say, in parts of Africa, if a girl does that for a man then she's engaged."

Henry nodded sagely, "They do say, in parts of Florida, if a girl does that for a man, he's done for!" Henry sat down, shaking his head.

Vicky passed the sandwiches, "There you go H, ham with that hot English mustard Ma sent over. While you get yourself outside of them, check my figures." She pulled a pencil stub from his pocket, where she knew she could always rely on him to keep it. They both worked silently on separate sheets of paper, looked up together, then swapped them over without a word.

After a few more minutes, Henry wiped his mouth with the back of his hand. "Are you thinkin' what I'm thinkin', Miss Vicky?" he asked.

She leaned forward so she could see the queue forming outside. Her lips moved silently as she counted down the line, "Yeah, it's hard to believe, but you're right, we could crack the thousand dollar mark."

Henry stepped to the door. "Roll up, roll up, ladeez an' gennelemen, view the machine that made Tallahassee famous." Luther had given him lessons. The team worked hard all afternoon and into the evening. By the time the sun settled behind the magnificent oaks lining the boundary of the hotel's grounds, they had worked through the line and sent every customer away feeling they had shared in the adventure. They had collected a grand total of nine hundred and fifty one dollars since Will's landing.

Marie added up the figures once more. "Oh shoot! I thought we'd clear a thousand dollars."

Henry looked at the pile in front of them in wonderment. "I ain't gonna shed no tears, Miss Marie, we did awful good. The *Flyer* didn't cost nary a third this much to build."

"Be nice to make the thousand though, children." They turned to find Walter looking over their shoulders. He looked, well, a slight flush to his face, suggesting an afternoon in the sunshine drinking Luther's special "home brewed fruit punch." So called, Luther told them, because it was brewed at home in Kentucky, then carried in under a truckload of fruit to avoid Florida's recent alcohol prohibition, and packed quite a punch. Walter rocked gently, then added triumphantly, "And you will."

"We will?" they chorused.

Walter swayed again, pleased at their response. He took another long drag on the enormous cigar he held. Marie thought grimly how lucky it was he had something so substantial to hang onto. She knew only too well how embarrassing her father could be when he had too much to drink. He blew a stream of fragrant smoke over their heads, "Because Walter...," he paused to tap himself on the chest, "because Walter hasn't had his turn at the controls yet. An' I'm donatin' forty-nine dollars to the cause."

A ripple of applause ran through the tent. Will looked past Walter to where Nathan and his father had just pulled up in the yard truck, ready to help dismantle the *Flyer* to load it for the journey back to the barn.

He put a hand on Walter's shoulder to steady him, "Mr. Julien, for that size of a donation, we'll give you more 'n a sit in the cockpit. Mount up. We're goin' to simulate my flight. Okay boys?" Most of Luther's staff had joined them, they installed Walter in the pilot's seat by lifting him bodily. Will climbed up to perch behind him on the top decking. "Okay, start her up!"

Walter flipped the magneto switch to "run." That was easy, it worked in the same way on his car. Will pointed to the throttle control, "Now open her up." Walter slid the control to wide open, his imagination provided the noise and blast of air from the now stationary motor. "Now push the stick forward to bring the tail up." Will signaled his helpers who shouldered the tail into the flying attitude. "Now take her up!"

The airplane rolled from the marquee for the short journey to the front of the hotel, where Nathan and John Turner stood shaking their heads. The *Flyer* trundled across the grass at a brisk trot while Will gave instructions. "Put the stick over to the left and add a little rudder." The boys at the tail took their cue and turned to the left. They rolled onto the fine gravel drive. "Now close the throttle, ease right back on the stick and bring her in," Will instructed.

The crew gratefully lowered the tail to the ground. Just then Emily Julien arrived at the top of the steps, drawn by the laughter outside. "Husband! What in blue blazes do you think you're doin'?"

Walter stood up in the cockpit, Will steadied him with a hand on his back. "Emily my dear! We were simulatin' aviatin'!"

She studied him with her head slightly to one side, affection vying with exasperation. "Walter, when will you act your age?"

He took off his hat and bowed with the unsteady grace of the inebriated. "I have finally decided what I am goin' to be when I grow up. I am goin' to be an aviator."

Emily raised her eyes to the heavens then shook her head, "William, be a dear an' drive us home." They carefully lowered Walter to the ground and delivered him to the care of his wife. "Coffee for you, Mr. Julien, strong and black," she insisted as she led him away.

"Yes, my dear."

Within the hour the *Flyer* was dismantled and packed on the truck, its wings neatly stowed alongside.

John moved along the truck bed, checking his lashings. "Will, you better do as Mrs. Julien asked. It's gettin' late, we'll unload in the mornin'. You drive them home in the Studebaker. Victoria can take

Nathan in the Autowagon; she's been drivin' it for nigh on three months anyway."

Will and Henry broke the sudden silence that followed John's observation, "She what?"

Nathan looked at Vicky and shrugged, "We've been found out!"

John just smiled, "Children! Make a man old before his time."

Nathan smiled sheepishly, "You can say that again!"

The convoy set off for town. Luther and Kathleen stood on the steps to wave them off. "Y'all take care now!" Luther called after them. He turned to his wife, "Reckon we're gonna hear a lot more o' that Turner boy."

Kathleen turned her smile on him, "You don't say?"

He eyed her archly and primly pursed his lips. "Ah do say!"

Will lead the convoy on the way back to town. The night closed in, but Victoria had no trouble following him. Nathan sat beside her, the perfect driving instructor. He sat with his hands behind his head, contentedly puffing on his pipe; he knew how to instil confidence in his pupil. Behind them the yard truck swayed as John weaved through the potholes. He slipped the truck into top gear with an expert flick of his wrist, then used that hand to delve in the pocket of his jacket hanging behind him. "Put fire to the end o' these, Henry, me boy." He passed two of the big Cuban cigars Will had brought back from Tampa, "I think we earned them."

The Studebaker Will drove had been designed to accomodate a chauffeur. A sliding screen separated the well-upholstered passenger compartment from the front seat area, which Will now shared with Marie. Emily Julien discreetly left the screen closed, to allow them a little privacy. Will smiled at Marie, "Your folks seem happy tonight." His breath caught slightly in his throat as he felt her hand on his knee.

"Well, they should be." She leaned closer to him, breathing the words in his ear.

"Why?"

"You know."

"Oh yeah, sure," he bluffed. He had not a clue what she meant, but when she snuggled even closer he got the message it somehow involved him. For the second Sunday in a row, Will felt things getting away from him.

Darkness had seeped into town by the time they rolled past the capitol building, but evening strollers paused to wave a hand in greeting. A few knowing looks were exchanged at the sight of Marie with Will in the front of the Studebaker. She knew just what they were thinking and revelled in it. The little column of vehicles broke up as Will turned into North Gadsden to deliver the Julien family back to their impressive home. He swung off the road into the drive, taking the big car in a wide sweep to stop precisely in line with the ornate entrance. He jumped from the driver's seat and handed the ladies out before Samuel, the Julien's butler, reached the bottom of the steps.

"Evenin', Mister Will, how went the day?" he glanced inside the car at the now peacefully dozing Walter. He chuckled, "Ooh, yes! A good time!"

Emily sighed, "Don't encourage him, Samuel. Wake him up and take him up to bed please."

Will opened the door wide and took Walter gently by the arm. "Come on, Mr. Julien, sir. We're home." Walter came awake quickly; he stepped down from the car attempting to look alert, and failed. He swayed dangerously for a moment, Will caught him while Samuel took the other arm. He was drunker than they had realized.

Walter still clutched his cigar, now mercifully extinct so his expansive gesture did not produce the usual trail of sparks. "D'ya like my Palladian window Will? 'S lovely window. One day you could have a house with a window like that." He paused, swayed again then squeezed Will's shoulder fiercely, "Play your cards well, my boy, and you could have this very Palladian window!"

"Walter! You need a nice lie down." Emily spoke firmly, she knew they could be seen from the street.

"Yes, my dear," Walter meekly agreed. Will and Samuel guided him up the steps, the ladies following behind. Inside the double doors the butler took a firmer grip on his employer.

"Leave him to me, Mister Will. We've done this before." Will gratefully gave up his burden and turned to take his leave as Walter staggered uncomplaining to bed.

"Well, I better be goin' home now, Mrs. Julien, Marie. Thank y'all for your company."

Emily laid a hand firmly on his arm. He felt her fingers distinctly through the thick tweed material of his borrowed jacket.

"Oh no, William! You'll stay for supper." She made the command sound like an invitation.

He raised a feeble protest, "Oh no, I couldn't put you to the trouble. 'Sides, they'll be expectin' me at home."

"Nonsense William! Thanks to the wonder of Mr. Bell's telephone apparatus we can call and tell them. And I know your mother would not want to deprive us of some male company at supper." Her voice lost it's refined drawl for a moment as she shouted upstairs, "'Specially seein' as our usual male company is in no fit state." Marie had Will's other arm, drawing him steadily toward the dining room. He did not put up a fight, his stomach told him to give in. It was after all, he thought, at least a ten-minute walk home.

Emily followed them in, gesturing toward the table, "Just a little informal snack, William, now tuck in."

For an informal snack it was a grand spread, not just a few cold cuts of meat with pickles and relishes. He could choose between pork tenderloin grilled with rosemary—he detected the soft, almost woody tang of the herb—or there were ribs with mustard sauce and, to go with them: new potato salad, butter beans, fried sweet potatoes and stewed okra with tomato. Mae, the cook, had gone to a deal of trouble to fix this "informal snack." She watched him eat, through the narrow gap gained by not quite closing the door to the dining room. "Oh yes, Samuel, the boy has the prettiest table manners and can he eat! Makes it all worthwhile."

The butler grunted as he reached up to the cupboard for the dessert bowls, "I reckon' she's tryin' to fatten him up for the kill."

Mae giggled, making her chins quiver. "Hush your mouth, Sam Webster, you can't blame the girl for takin' an interest. 'Sides, he could do with fattenin'. I've seen more meat on a stray cat."

At the big table, Emily subtly guided the conversation. "Have you considered what you may do for a career now you have your qualifications, William? You cannot spend all your life in Mister Walker's workshop."

"Yes, ma'am. I am goin' to form my own company to develop passenger an' freight carryin' airplanes. Then maybe start a line to operate them."

"Oh! So you've not considered real estate then?" Walter had done very well in the property business, as their surroundings testified.

"No, ma'am, I'd say there's already one good property agent in town and I don't see myself as competin' against Mr. Julien."

"Oh no, William, I was not thinkin' so much of you settin' up against Mr. Julien, I was thinkin' along the lines of you workin' in the business. Learnin' the 'ins and outs' so to speak and then...well who knows what that might lead to?"

With a flash of inspiration Will suddenly saw exactly where she intended things to lead. The prospect of a partnership in a real estate business had never occurred to him as a possible career, but, as the Julien's had no son to pass the business on to, Walter's successor had to be found. He felt flattered she would even mention the idea but the answer seemed obvious. "Well, Mrs. Julien, that is a kind offer, but surely that position should go to—," he was on the point of suggesting Marie's future husband as the obvious successor, when the realization struck him. *That* was the position really under discussion. Will had been painfully slow on the uptake, but he made up for it by quick thinking when the situation revealed itself, "a man with real business acumen. 'Sides, Mr. Julien won't be retirin' for many a long year yet."

Emily smiled her most winning smile, "That is true, William, so there's plenty of time for you to see the sense of it. Please do not take this as any reflection on your family, but a gentleman of your refinement does not seem cut out for a career with his hands. I can't see how you could possibly make a business out of these airplanes of yours."

Will could see no point in making an issue of it but held his ground. "You agree with my daddy there, an' most other folk, but I'd at least like to give it a try. Then if it don't work, I'll have to find somethin' else to do."

"Well there you are then, William, that's settled. A piece of pie?" He wasn't at all sure what had been settled, but the pie smelled delicious. All through their supper he had been conscious of Marie's steady gaze. It made him nervous. His feeling of unease increased when he saw the family's pet retriever walk past the open door. If the dog was not under the table, he thought, what kept rubbing his leg? He turned to Marie, who returned his questioning look with an innocent smile.

"Coffee, Will?"

"Oh yes, thank you, Marie." She left the table and went to the kitchen.

Emily rose at the same time. "William, I do hope you won't consider me rude but I am feelin' rather weary. Would you excuse me? I feel the need to retire early. I am sure Marie can look after you and I just know you two must have lots to talk about without an old woman like me eavesdroppin' on your conversation."

"Oh no, I mean yes, of course, Mrs. Julien, goodnight." He stood up from the table, extending his hand. She took it, but, to his complete surprise, kissed him lightly on the cheek.

"Goodnight, William, be seein' you soon." He could have sworn she winked as she turned to leave the room, her skirts rustling. He needed to come to grips with this situation: Mrs. Julien acting so familiar and left almost alone with Marie. Mae, the cook, still clattered around in the kitchen, a reminder they were unobtrusively chaperoned, but people did not expect the run of the downstairs until they were engaged or at least "intended." He felt out of his depth again.

Marie returned, "Shall we take our coffee on the veranda, Will? It's such a beautiful evenin'." A wide platform ran the length of the house at the rear, set with cane furniture. It gave an elevated view of the ornate garden sweeping down to the boundary of Walter's property. Will sat back on a cane two-seat couch. He heard the creak and rustle of the structure as it took his weight. Then he wriggled forward until he perched on the edge as Marie sat down next to him, placing the coffee cups on the table in front of them.

She edged closer, "Will, I been meanin' to ask."

"Yeess?" He sounded cautious.

"Why can't you be my knight in shinin' armor for the May Queen ceremony?"

He laughed, relieved to be able to give a straight and uncompromising reply. "Because the shining armor won't fit me. The only guy who can squeeze into that old tin suit is little Lenny."

"But can't it be made to fit? Knights in shinin' armor should be tall."

"Well, maybe they should, but in the real olden times they were little fellas an' that is a real suit. Anyways, once we get him up on that big old horse of Nathan's, he's gonna be the tallest person there."

"But I gotta kiss him."

"Well you can if you must," Will answered thoughtfully, "but I'd just stroke his nose and scratch his ears. He likes that." She looked at him carefully, his face betraying nothing for a moment, then the tiniest grin tugged at the corners of his mouth.

She giggled and slapped his chest playfully, "Not the ho...silly...Lenny. But I want to kiss you," she had not meant to say that, it just slipped out, but once said there was only one thing she could do. It would not be fair to say she threw herself at him. She made more of an energetic roll. Will found himself being well and truly and expertly *kissed.* He understood the Beaufort scale for wind strength. Marie, he felt, kissed way beyond *force two,* "gentle stirrings." She kissed at hurricane force. Taken off balance and thrown back in his seat, even through the layers of cotton and linen, Will felt in contact with her whole body. He was delightfully aware she did not just tremble against him, she managed to undulate. He realized his hand had gone around her to stop her rolling off the couch, and now it firmly gripped her backside. He snatched his hand away as if it had been on a hot stove. She just as forcefully grabbed his wrist and put it back, without taking her mouth from his.

They stayed locked together for what seemed about a century to Will, or it could have been half a second. Marie suddenly disengaged, pulling her head back to focus on his face. He could see her perfect white teeth in the dim light as she grinned at him.

"I'll teach you to make fun of me, Will Turner."

He considered for a second, "Better teach me some more, I'm a slow learner." She obliged. The coffee went cold where she had left it on the table. A discreet outbreak of coughing ended the lesson. They split apart as Sam feigned a sudden bronchial attack to warn of his approach.

"S'cuse me Miss Marie, but it's time we was closin' up for the night." He poked his head around the door. She looked immaculate, if a little flushed.

"Oh yes, Sam...fine. We were just discussin' English literature."

"Yes, Miss Marie, haint tale was it?"

"Why?"

"Mr. Will's hair's standin' on end." The old man turned away to hide his smile. Will self-consciously patted his head as Marie took his other hand to lead him inside.

'Haint' was the word used by many to describe a ghost or spirit. If Will or Marie had looked out into the garden at that moment, they might have had their own story to tell. But they missed seeing the crouching figure moving silently from behind a magnolia, to merge with the shadows at the edge of the lawn.

Will and Marie paused at the front door. She held both his hands, reluctant to let him leave. "I have to go," Will said with genuine regret.

"Yeah, sure you do, but I'll see you real soon, won't I?"

It seemed a strange question to Will. He saw her nearly every day anyway, but he understood there might be a difference between seeing and *seeing*. He needed time to think, but heard himself saying, "Oh, yes, that's for sure!" She did not say anything else but squeezed his hands and stretched up to kiss him again, this time lightly. Will started down the steps, then turned to wave goodbye. He carried on walking backward. She did look wonderful with the light behind her like that he thought. He stumbled, nearly falling flat on his back and was rewarded with her laugh. Recovering, he swept off his cap to wave an extravagant farewell. She still stood at the door as he reached the end of the drive.

Will set off for the short walk home with his thoughts tumbling. His heart still thumping. He stopped to put his hand to his chest. He really could feel it pumping away. He had enjoyed a magical day with his closest friends, and Marie had brought it to a wonderful conclusion. Could he be in love? he asked himself. No! he decided. How could he fall in love in half an hour? Then again he had known Marie all his life, at least ever since he could remember. Maybe, he reasoned, it had crept up on him. He shook his head and whistled softly, more an exhalation of breath. Will decided this really needed some serious consideration.

He walked head down, so deep in thought, he missed seeing the big white car coast across the junction behind him. He looked up just as he heard the boom of its exhaust, but, seeing nothing, paid no mind to the sound floating away in the night as he vaulted the side gate to his own home.

Chapter Six

IN THE WALKER'S WORKSHOP, ALONGSIDE THE MASSIVE BULK OF A freight locomotive, Henry paused between swings of his sledgehammer. "Well, did you kiss her?"

Will checked the drift they were using to drive a steel pin out of a seized connecting rod. "Gennelmen don't discuss that," he grinned up at Henry.

Henry swung the hammer in a precise arc. "Gennelmen don't, I agree, but did you?" *Clang.* Will did not flinch; he held the drift straight and true, his fingers only an inch from the hammerhead hissing down to slam into the steel.

"Might have," he caught the look on Henry's face. "Okay, to tell the truth, *she* kissed *me*."

Clang. "Oh *really!*" Henry swung the hammer easily back; he somehow managed to make that look like a gesture of disbelief.

"Yeah, really. She took me by surprise, then took advantage of me."

Henry threw the next swing away, and the hammer fell with a thud into the hard-packed dirt floor. "An' you put up a hell of a fight I bet!"

Will grinned and scrutinized the progress of the drift with far more attention than it needed, "Of course...after all, ah have mah reputation to consider."

Henry paused to wipe the sweat out of his eyes with a grubby kerchief. He spat on his hands, picked up the hammer and swung it with ferocious pleasure, the pin gave a fraction. *Clang.* "Who won?"

Will lowered his voice, even though the shed rang to the sounds of hammering, "She did—a knockout. I'm tellin' you...I don't know where a girl could learn to kiss like that!"

Henry grunted, "I do...you can let go now, drift's in far enough."

Will straightened up; as tall as he stood, the driving wheel of the locomotive still towered over him. "You do? How'd you know that?"

Henry swung again. *Clang.* "Julien's girl, Essie, you know her?"

Will nodded agreement, "Sure do. Handsome gal. But what's she to do with it?"

Clang. Henry renewed his attack on the frozen pin. Now he didn't have to worry about hammering Will through the rod, he could put all his formidable power into the job. With a final triumphant blow the drift disappeared through the rod, pushing the pin free to fall clattering on the track below. He stood back, beaming: "William, you have a lot to learn."

"Alrighty, teacher, I'm all ears."

"Marie's an only child, ain't she?"

"Of course."

"Well, Essie's been like an older sister to her. Them gals get together in private, they get to talkin'. Mostways about us! No mind Essie's a servant gal; where women's concerned it's them an' us. They's more than just friends, they's all sisters under the skin. It's like a secretive society half the world belongs to, an' us men, we're excluded. Now that's not to say we don' join in the fun, but it's strictly 'invitation only', on their terms."

Will laughed, "Wise beyond your tender years, but what's this to do with kissin'?"

"My! You're slow, Will. Essie's a famous kisser, a *champeen* kisser, I reckon Marie's been havin' herself some expert tuition."

"So how come you know all about Essie?"

Henry smiled modestly. He polished his fingernails on his sleeve, making an exaggerated show of examining them in the light filtering through the soot-grimed windows. "Because...I help her practice."

Will slapped his friend on the back, "You're such a *helpful* feller. Come on, we have to finish early so we can fix Lenny's armor. Marie won't ever forgive me if her champion can't move when he arrives at the old oak."

For the rest of the day they drilled, reamed, measured, measured again and fitted. At the end of the afternoon they rolled the locomotive back from the shed to start the process of steaming up. They were free to begin what promised to be the trickiest job of the day: making the armor for the May Queen's knight fit Leonard Dumanion, high school scholar, and would-be medieval gentleman.

The aspect of life in Edwardian Tallahassee that intrigued Charley

Turner more than any other was the fascination her friends and neighbors had for the literary works of Sir Walter Scott. Her close friend, Willa Mae Sweeting, owned one of the better bookshops in town. She confirmed that only the Bible outsold Scott's novel *Ivanhoe.* Charley found, to her great surprise, that apart from London, the two English towns people knew of were York and Ashby-de-la-Zouch, both because they featured in Scott's novels.

This enthusiasm for a fictitious world encouraged the annual May Queen celebration when the whole town would gather for the crowning of the elected May Queen and her king. An amateur theatrical production with elaborate costumes and pageantry followed by speeches, parades, fireworks, eating and surreptitious drinking into the small hours. It was the social event of the year, and Len Dumanion was one of the stars: not because he was elected to the position, but because he would fit the only suit of armor available.

Will welcomed the task. It took his mind off the inevitable confrontation with his father. John had told him that they would discuss his future the following day. Will had decided there was nothing to discuss and did not look forward to his father's disappointment. The anger he could manage, the hurt he knew he would cause troubled him deeply.

Will and Henry had relied on the railroad locomotive to stay still when they levered, hammered and adjusted any part of it. Little Len, on the other hand, who had shown up at the shop at the appointed time and was promptly encased in the ceremonial suit, tended to bend and flinch when they applied the necessary force.

His muffled voice squeaked from deep inside the helmet, "Henry, why can't I just have the flap up all the time? It'll help me breathe, too."

Henry flipped up the helmet's visor to peer inside. "Len, can't you see? You have to be mysterious, that's the whole point." Len could not see much at all through the narrow gap, just Henry intent on the hinge and then Will's face behind him.

"The Unknown Knight," quoted Will, "who, clad in gleamin' armor, sits on a magnificent charger; his cap is on, his visor down...on every tongue is the question, 'Who can it be?'"

Len stayed stubbornly unimpressed. "Easy for you to say, Will, but you ain't sweatin' in this damn tin can. What happens if it sticks shut?"

Will tapped lightly on the steel with a wrench. "Quit frettin'...I'll be right behind you. It won't freeze up anyway, but just in case, one quick spin on our patented quick-release nut, an' off it comes. An' not only have we considered your safety, good Sir Knight, we're goin' to make you right comfortable as well with our patented coolin' system."

They could only see Len's eyes, but he looked doubtful. "This ain't nothin' like the ice cream maker you invented? The one that showered ever'body at the train depot with the makins when she blew up?"

"There you go again, exaggeratin'," Henry pointed out calmly, "It didn't blow up, just squirted a mite too powerful. This idea is a lot more *so-phis-tee-cated.* Go find the ice packs, Will, so we can show him."

Will picked up the breastplate that Cordelia had offered to polish and headed for the kitchen. He stopped in his tracks. The last thing he expected to see at Nathan Walker's engineering works was Roscoe Vandersand's magnificent white sportster, but there it came, tearing down the road, bounding over the railroad tracks before skidding to a halt a few yards away. Red Georgia clay plastered the paintwork. Roscoe clung to the wheel. He reflected the state of his car: hair wind-blown and matted, several days growth of black bristling beard clinging to his face like a stain. His suit looked as if he had slept in it. He said nothing. He just sat and stared at Will through red-rimmed eyes.

Will started walking toward the car. "Roscoe! Where have you been? We've all worried about you." He stopped in his tracks as Roscoe lurched awkwardly out of his seat, half onto the running board. He reached under the seat.

As Roscoe turned back to Will his face twisted, "You unholy swine, Turner. You dishonored mah fiancé!" His arm came up.

Henry stiffened. He was not too surprised to see a revolver in Roscoe's hand. "Oh shee-it!" he muttered. Although his mouth suddenly felt like sandpaper, he managed to shout to his friend, "Run, Will!"

Will could not bring himself to believe what Roscoe was so obviously pointing in his direction, even when he heard Henry's warning shout. The situation seemed surreal, yet it certainly looked like a pistol—a very big revolver—in Roscoe's hand. He knew he should be doing *something* because he could see Roscoe pulling the trigger. With the startling clarity given to those in great peril he could see the chamber turning. He even had time to relax when he first heard a light snapping sound; he recognized the sound of a percussion cap firing. By the second time he thought it was a joke—a bad joke—but a joke nevertheless. The fourth time the pistol clicked he started to experience a twinge of annoyance, but a cough accompanied the fifth snap, and a cloud of dense blue smoke from the muzzle. The final time Roscoe pulled the trigger there was no mistake, and Will saw nothing to joke about. The pistol fired with a flash of vivid orange flame through the smoke, and a flat report, like a baseball thudding into a barn door.

"What the—?" Will found himself addressing the peaceful blue sky. Why am I on my back? He asked himself. His ears rang from a metallic clang. His mind drifted, disorientated. He vaguely heard the kitchen door crash open and someone bellowing; he recognized Cordelia's voice. The feeling of unreality increased as a nightmarish face obscured his view of the sky. He closed his eyes. This was better he thought, but the voices were growing louder. He shut his eyes tight. An automobile engine roared, the sound receding.

"Ohmigod—he's been shot!" Henry's voice shouted in his ear.

Will's mind partly cleared. Who's been shot? he thought. I can't lie around here...sounds like an emergency. He opened his eyes. The nightmare head had disappeared and was replaced by Len's anxious face; he had taken the helmet off. Henry and Cordelia joined him peering anxiously down.

"Told you that wouldn't get stuck on your head, Len." Will heard himself say, heard himself as if he were far away.

"Don' worry about that now, hon', you just lie still," Cordelia said.

Ignoring her instructions, Will tried to raise himself up on his elbow as his mind began to clear. "Who's been shot?" he said weakly, looking at those gathered around him.

Cordelia gently pushed him down again. "You have, hon', now just lie easy while I find the damage."

"No, I ain't—"

"Oh, yes, you have," Cordelia insisted.

"Then why don't it hurt?"

"Yeah, an' why ain't he bleedin'?" Henry threw in.

Cordelia quickly examined Will. "Are you sure you ain't hurtin'? Can you feel any blood?"

"No."

Her face showed relief and suspicion in equal measure, "You sure?" He struggled to a sitting position, helped by Len and Henry.

"Positive. Just winded. What the hell happened?"

Henry suddenly pointed. "Hey! Looky here. Damn bullet bounced off this tin hide." He picked up the breastplate lying a few feet from where Will had fallen. He pointed at a clear dent that had not been there before, the center clearly defined by an indentation about half an inch in diameter, high up on the left side.

Will tottered to his feet, helped by Cordelia. He stood for a few seconds bent over with his hands on his knees, taking quick, shallow breaths, then stood up straight and brushed dust from the seat of his pants. Cordelia turned him all the way around carefully, raised his arms, took his chin and turned his head each way and stared intently into his eyes.

Will smiled weakly at her. "Is this horse fit for work, Doc?"

Her reaction took him by surprise. She took his head firmly in her big hands, squeezed gently then put her arms around him and hugged. There were tears in her eyes. "You's a damn lucky, stupid fool, Will. I thought we lost you then." She released him suddenly and stepped back. Her voice returned to its usual volume and laughter flowed with her relief. "Hellfire, boy! I swear I ain't never seen nothin' like that—you flew! I ain't kiddin' hon'. You saw it boys. You tell him what happened. He don't have the sense back yet."

Henry stood with Len, looking from the breastplate to Will and back again, shaking his head as he did. "Lawdy, Will, Ma's right, I'd wager you came two feet off the ground and traveled six feet back. Just as Roscoe fired that shot you moved the armor you had under your arm over your chest. Kinda held it up like a shield."

Will scratched his head. "I don't recall doin' that."

"Instinct, boy, for pure self-preservation," said Cordelia, "an' Roscoe Vandersand better have that in buckets, 'cause if I lay hands—," she did not finish the sentence, she stopped speaking as Nathan wheeled his big motor truck into the yard.

He swung down from the cab and looked from Will and Cordelia to his son and Len. "What the hell's goin' on here? I just near on been run off the road by that Vandersand boy—Jesus, Henry! What happened to that?" He took the breastplate and held it level to examine the dent.

"It appears young Roscoe tried to shoot me." Will coughed and turned away to spit.

"Good Lord, Will, are you okay? Did he miss?"

"In a manner. I was totin' the old breastplate there an' the ball hit that instead of me."

Nathan stared at him, mouth open. "Are you sure?"

Will walked over and picked the discarded pistol out of the dust. Roscoe had flung it wildly at Cordelia as she burst from her kitchen. He examined it briefly then handed it butt first to Nathan. "I'm sure."

Nathan took it, pointed the muzzle at the ground, eased back the hammer and spun the cylinder. "Look at this, an old smoke pole revolver. Must be fifty years old." He said nothing for a moment but stood shaking his head, then looked up sharply. "So what happened here?" He directed the question to his wife.

Cordelia shrugged, "Not much to tell. I heard Roscoe's big old car drive up, heard shoutin', looked out the window to see Roscoe pointin' that thing at William, I ran out the door, next thing I see is Will flyin' through the air. Roscoe takes one look at me, throws that at me an' then he takes off."

"You foolish old woman! You're only supposed to head for the sound of firin' when you have something to shoot back with!"

"Who the hell you callin' foolish?"

"Whoa! Hold it folks," Len broke in, "Shouldn't somebody call the sheriff?"

Cordelia glared at her husband. "Yeah. Shut up an' do somethin' sensible for a change."

"No need," said Henry pointing over the tracks. "Here he comes."

Clarence Drew's nose for trouble had not failed him. The Model T rattled to a stop. Clarence hauled on the brake and switched off. He sat with his hands on the wheel for a moment, then hauled himself out, hitching up his trousers as he did. "What'd you find there, Nathan?"

Nathan held the revolver by the muzzle and supported the butt with the end of his finger, displaying it for all to see. "Cap n' ball Colt. Mighty fancy piece for all its bein' old. Property of one Roscoe Vandersand."

The sheriff took it from him and expertly snapped the cylinder out of the frame. He sniffed it, turned it around, then pried the caps off with an ugly, split thumb nail. "All the caps fired, but only two loads discharged. I reckon this thing's been loaded so long, damp's in the powder." He paused, looking around the yard, "So who's shootin' an' why? There's rules about that sorta thing inside city limits."

Nathan grunted, "Roscoe Vandersand done the shootin'. As for why, looks like he was intendin' to kill our William here."

The sheriff's eyebrows shot up. "Did he now? That would explain why he went past the train depot doin' near on a hunnert mile an hour. I was collectin' a package an' heard the shot, then saw him go past like the devil hisself was on his tail."

Nathan looked grim, "Worse, Clarence...my wife was after him."

Cordelia smiled at the lopsided compliment. The sheriff chuckled, "Understan' why he was in such a' all-fired hurry." He looked over to where Henry knelt beside the big tan colored bloodhound that had jumped from the car, "What are you doin' Henry?"

"I'm showin' him the tracks of Roscoe's car, maybe he can follow it."

They all turned to look at him; embarrassment clouded Henry's face as he realized what he suggested.

"Not unless you're fixin' to teach him to ride a motor-sickle at the same time. Young Mr. Vandersand'll be halfway to Panama City by now. Use your telephone, Nathan? I'll put word out to get him stopped before he crosses the state line. He's some explainin' to do, even though no harm's been done."

Len spoke up. "No harm done?! He knocked Will flat. If he hadn't been holdin' that old piece of armor he'd be dead."

"What? You mean he was *aimin'?* I thought he was just tryin' to scare y'all."

"Well, he sure did that." Len confessed, "I near messed my pants."

Clarence fixed Will with a glare. "Can you give me any reason why he should want to do you in, Mr. Turner?"

"'Sakes, Sheriff, I expect he's all fired up about me bustin' into his party like that, but if he'd stayed around I would have apologized.

"Hmmmm...you never know what goes on in a hothead's mind, but I wouldn't have thought even a crazy man would want to kill you over that. Punch you maybe, you'd have deserved that."

Will shifted from one foot to the other, his face colored. "Maybe."

Clarence shook his head, "No, that don't make sense. Did he say anythin' before he started shootin?" He looked from one face to another.

Henry broke the silence. "Yeah. He shouted somethin' about dishonorin' his fiancé."

The sheriff's face broke into a wide smile, "Now we're gettin' somewhere. *Cherchez la femme.*" He mangled the pronunciation. "Look for the woman!" He snapped his fingers as if it all became clear to him. "Okay folks, here's what I want you to do: everybody write down what they saw. Write it clear an' don't miss any details. This here's what we law enforcement officers call a 'witness' statement an' it might be used in evidence." He turned to Will, "I'll be visitin' with the Juliens an' findin' out what their Marie has to say."

"Oh no, Sheriff, do you have to drag her into this? This is between Roscoe an' me." Will said.

"Like hell it is, son! This is between Roscoe Vandersand an' the law. Then I'll be callin' on you an' your pa. Tomorrow mornin." It was a command not a question.

Will shrugged, "Okay."

Henry went to the front of the car and cranked it to life. Sheriff Drew nodded to him, "Thank you, son." He turned to Will again, "First I have to lay hands on that idiot Vandersand, then I have to talk to Miss Marie. I have a feelin' she might be who he's all steamed over. Then I'll decide what to charge him with." He pointed to Len. "Need a ride, son?"

Len looked at Nathan. "Need me anymore, Mr. Walker?"

"No, son, I think we have the measurements we need."

Len vaulted into the car. Will suspected he eagerly anticipated fielding the questions as to why he was riding through town with the sheriff. They stood back as the Model T clattered away. Will shook his head, "Do I get the impression he ain't takin' this serious?

"Nathan pulled his pipe from his pocket and stuffed the bowl. He pointed the stem up the road toward the fast disappearing car, "That might be the look of it, son, but you'd be wrong; he's takin' this real serious, as you'll find out."

"How do you mean?"

"Well, for one thing, he's gonna be askin' you a lot of questions."

"Why me? I didn't try to shoot myself!"

Nathan could see Will working himself into a temper rare for him; it had been a bad scare and it showed. Nathan took his arm and pulled him back toward the house, "Easy, boy, nobody is sayin' this is your fault but you have to admit, the two big excitements around here in the last few weeks see you slap-bang in the middle. Come on, let's have ourselves a coffee stop an' a bite to eat, then we'll see if you're up to workin'."

"I'm okay," Will said. "No need for fussin'."

Back inside the kitchen, Cordelia slid a newly baked loaf of bread onto the wooden table. Nathan and Henry cut thick wedges from it and loaded them with ham and pickles. They sat around the table with the coffeepot between them.

Nathan pushed the loaf toward Will. "Get some food down you; it'll do you good." Cordelia glanced at her husband and quickly shook her head.

"No thanks, Nathan, I seem to have lost my appetite." Will said.

Nathan stood up from the table and went to the dresser. He took a bottle from the cupboard and poured a generous measure into Will's cup before sloshing coffee from the pot. Cordelia leaned across and spooned sugar into the mixture. Will smiled and picked up his cup. As it cleared the saucer a tiny ringing sound trembled in the air. The others pretended not to notice. He took the cup carefully with both hands and drank deeply. He paused and placed it firmly back in the saucer.

Nathan faced him, "Okay, boy, apart from nearly bein' shot, what's eatin' you?"

"It's the sheriff. Sometimes I think he's got it in for me."

Nathan blew across the top of his cup then put it down, "Sometimes he must think you've got it in for him. He likes things nice an' peaceful, an' jus' as he's dozin' off in his office, that old telephone takes to ringin'—," Nathan put an imaginary telephone to his ears and rolled his eyes, "an' there's some citizen: 'Will Turner's jus' come past my house doin' hunnert miles an hour, raisin' a ruckuss.' Or, 'Will Turner's jus' flown his airyplane into mah picnic.' Or, 'somebody's down the Walker place tryin' to murder Will Turner.' "

Will never could sustain a sulk, and a smile broke through. "Well it wasn't my fault I got shot at. 'Sides I can't understand why you're so friendly with that pompous old bigot, Clarence Drew."

Nathan, in turn, showed a flash of rare temper. "Oh! So you're lecturin' a seventy-year-old nigga boy on bigots."

"No, sir, I am not doin' any such thing but you have to admit, anythin' happens around here where there's any doubt an' old Clarence grabs the first black man he can find an' throws 'em in jail."

"Then what does he do?" demanded Nathan

"Well, I suppose most times he seems to find the right miscreant an' lets the first guy out." Will admitted.

"Even when the right miscreant is a white man?"

Will knew what Nathan had in mind. The previous year a rare murder made the headlines. A lady had been found battered to death, her money stolen. The finger pointed at the gardener, a new face in the town. Clarence duly arrested him and threw him in jail. Five days later he arrested her young husband and released the gardener. "Ten to one the husband's always done it," he told Nathan. The husband was now appealing against the death sentence handed down by the court. Will conceded the point, "Okay, that's true, but it wasn't fair Raymond Thomas spent five days in jail."

Nathan had calmed down as quickly as Will, "Maybe not, but it probably saved his life."

"What do you mean?" asked Will.

Henry joined in, "Aw, come on Will, where have you been? This is confederate country, not Alice's 'Wonderland'. Jim Crow's alive an' kickin'. Might be all charm an' good manners on top, but the Klan's behind many a respectable door in this town."

Will looked from son to father, "You don't mean he was like to get himself lynched? Nothin' like that happened for years 'round here."

Nathan and Henry nodded emphatically. Nathan speared himself another piece of ham, "Nothin' like a nice lady getting her head stove in happened for years either." Will still could not bring himself to believe such a thing could happen in his town, "But there's plenty o' good folk here would stop it."

Nathan nodded, "Sure is, but that's not how these things happen. Only takes half a dozen men to grab some poor Negro boy in the middle of the night, next mornin' we'd find him hangin' from a tree just outside o' town. All the good intentions in the world ain't gonna save him. 'Sides what did Ray say to your ma when she visited him in jail?"

"Yeah, he did tell her he would rather stay in jail."

Nathan laughed, "The boy has sense. More than can be said for your ma. That little visit ruffled a few feathers I can tell you."

Will puffed out his cheeks, "Whew! Ain't that the truth. I know there was a lot of whisperin' behind her back, but nobody said anythin' to her face. Lucky they didn't because they would have looked pretty damn foolish when Ray was released."

Nathan looked at him sharply, "They wouldn't have dared anyway."

"Why's that?" asked Will.

"Because your daddy's not a man to cross, an' if there's one thing more powerful than bigotry, it's cold, hard cash. An' John Turner will wield it like the sword of justice if he knows he's right, an' damn the expense to him."

"My daddy? Would he use his money to put something right?" He turned to see Henry smiling, "Is there something I don't know?"

Nathan looked at his son disapprovingly. "Well, we have to tell him now, with you grinnin' like a damn clown, he's goin' to pester the life out of me 'til he finds out."

"Tell me, tell me!" demanded Will.

Cordelia put her hand on Will's arm. "Don't you dare let him know we told you. Swear?"

"On the Bible." Will answered solemnly.

"You own a sawmill, c'rect?" Cordelia said.

"We do."

"Do you know why your Daddy bought it?" Cordelia asked.

Will shrugged, "Investment I s'pose."

"Wrong. About five years back I found out the manager was insistin' on a special payment from his employees. The sort of payment only their wives and daughters could make. If they didn't provide the service, their man was out of a job."

"What d'ya mean? Like sewin' an' laundry an' such?"

Cordelia glared at her son who gave a bark of laughter at Will's words. "This ain't no laughin' matter, son!"

Henry composed himself, "Sorry, Ma."

Cordelia turned back to Will, "No, William, not sewin' an' such," she explained patiently, "I'm talkin' about poon-tang!"

Will's eyes opened wide, "That's disgustin'!"

"That was your daddy's feelin' too, but he didn't rush in. Found himself a private investigator to check that it was true, an' not just a bad mouthin' rumor. When the Pinkerton confirmed it, your daddy bought the mill for near twice what it was worth an' fired that man. An' he didn't stop there, no sirree! Had the Pinkertons trail him through the country, and every time he tried to get hisself a position, your daddy wrote to the people an' told 'em as how he'd caught him with his hand in the till. That was true as well. Last I heard he had to leave the country an' get work on the loggin' camps in Canada. Let's see him try his dirty business on some big Canuck lumberjack."

Will stared at her open mouthed, "Goll-ee gee!"

Nathan stepped in, "So you see, when it comes to chivalry, it ain't dead. Just sneaks up on the bad guys wearin' a old black coat an' spectacles instead of shinin' armor." Will sat shaking his head. Nathan punched him lightly on the shoulder, "You've quite a name to live up to, William Turner, but you ain't doin' bad so far. Talkin' of armor, let's go shine some."

They worked on into the evening, sitting on the porch with Cordelia and Nathan. Normally Will would have enjoyed the task, but he was unusually subdued. Cordelia squeezed his shoulder as he stood to go. "Don't take on so, hon'. The sheriff will put an end to Mr. Roscoe Vandersand's foolishness, you see if he don't."

"That's kinda what concerns me. Maybe he's right: perhaps I have been the cause of a lot of trouble around here. Might not have been a good idea to come back after school."

"Now don't be a damn fool, Will," said Nathan, "Roscoe's the one causin' trouble; you're a hero in this town."

Will shrugged, "Oh well, what's done is done."

"That's right, Will," Cordelia said, "no sense in worryin' about what's done. Now you go home an' get a good night's sleep. That bang scrambled your thinkin'. You'll see things different in the mornin'."

Will hoped so but could not shake his black mood. He slept badly, his sleep punctuated by strange dreams. He rose early and shaved carefully. The sheriff was due at eight and he knew that whatever the outcome of that meeting, he could not put off the showdown with his father. Clarence Drew arrived punctual to the minute.

John Turner felt the meeting should best be kept informal and ushered him into the kitchen. It was in many ways the most handsome room in the house. The walls were tiled to head height in a pleasing white and blue pattern. The floor was cool stone. On one wall a massive Welsh dresser, an heirloom from Charley's family, carried an array of fine china. A coffeepot bubbled cheerfully on the range. John handed Sheriff Drew a cup and poured for him. "Are you sure about this Clarence? You really think Roscoe was tryin' to shoot Will? Could it just have been a prank that went a mite too far?"

Clarence eased himself into a chair behind the long kitchen table, next to Will. He put his coffee down and pulled the big Colt revolver from the burlap sack he had laid carefully on the table, the cylinder was still separate from the frame. He fished the caps out of his shirt pocket. "Exhibit A," Clarence announced, "as they say up in the courthouse. Look how all the caps have been struck but only two loads fired. From what you told me, Will, one of them was a misfire, but the last one went as it should. Even then, I guess the powder was so old it never threw the ball that hard. When that cartridge was new it would have put a hole straight through that piece of steel, an' you."

"Was he aimin' at you, Son?" John asked.

Will shook his head, "I can't say for sure. He was wavin' that old piece around an' shoutin' an' hollerin'. Tell the truth, I think he was so drunk he didn't know what he was doin'."

Clarence scratched his chin. "Booze an' firearms is always a dangerous mix. Maybe you're right, William, but I've no choice but to treat it as attempted murder at this stage, no question. But what you just said, John, about it bein' a prank could be how some people, includin' a jury, might see it. 'Beyond all reasonable doubt' is what the law says, there's no way we could make it stick in court."

"Well why bother in the first place?" Will asked. "If it was up to me I'd drop any charges. I just need to talk to the man an' clear this mess up, do you agree Pa? I reckon we can put this all behind us."

"Let's hear the sheriff out, Son," John said, inwardly pleased at the mature approach Will was taking.

"It's not up to you, William," the sheriff said reasonably. "You may be ready to call it quits, but him an' the law ain't. An' who's to say he won't try again?"

"Aw, Sheriff, I'm sure when he sobers up he'll come to his senses, we can work this out 'tween ourselves," Will said.

"Well now, if it's just a case of 'drunk an' disorderly' an' he gives himself up, we can settle this with a few days in the slammer an' a stiff fine for reckless discharge of a firearm. But it don't look like he's goin' to turn himself in, an' I need the serious charge to justify askin' other lawmen to track him down."

"How's that goin'?" John asked. He wanted to be fair to Roscoe, but his first concern was for Will.

"Well that's the damndest thing, it should have been easy to catch him. There's only two ways it made sense for him to go. He was headin' west when I saw him, so I called Quincy first. They sent a man down the road but he didn't come that way; no surprise as I was expectin' him to break north for the Georgia line, anyhow. We covered the roads to Bainbridge and Thomasville but unless he found a way to make himself invisible, he didn't go that way neither. That automobile of his needs a halfway decent highway to make progress."

John scratched the back of his neck, "Don' make any sense. If he doubled back through town he would have been seen, that only leaves—"

Clarence finished what John was about to say. "Yep...somehow he cut off south and west, no sign of him down around Wakulla so he must have gone down into the Appalachicola woods."

John shook his head, "That really is strange, if ever I saw a city boy it's Roscoe Vandersand. We better find him afore he gits eat up by somethin' wild."

Clarence sat back, teasing a piece of food from between his teeth with a stubby finger. He examined the morsel for a moment, "Yep. Stuck in a gator's teeth like these collard greens. Unless, of course, he found himself some help. That's what makes me so sure he planned this. Think on it: that automobile of his is the most conspicuous vee-hicle in the county, if not the state, but no one's seen hide nor hair of it since I saw Roscoe zoomin' by yesterday afternoon, two minutes after the shootin'. I reckin it's hid somewhere, not far from town, an' he's either lyin' low with some floozy, or he's a lot smarter 'n we give him credit for—an' he's got clean away in some other direction."

Will understood why Roscoe might want to run in the face of pending charges, but he struggled to fully accept the idea that the man had actually planned to kill him. "You really think this was what they call *premeditated*, Sheriff? You really think Roscoe came meaning to kill me?"

Clarence laughed, "You been readin' those trashy pulp crime dreadfuls? That's a helluva word."

Will smiled. He began to see Sheriff Clarence Drew in a different light. Their previous discussions revolved around Will's enthusiasm for speed, loud exhausts and mechanical inventions. The first two cost Will fines his father had refused to pay.

Clarence clapped a big paw on Will's shoulder, "Cheer up, son, any fool can go through life an' never raise a ripple. Plenty of fine men had others tryin' to kill 'em, look at your Uncle Roy! You're in good company."

John leaned back in his chair, hooked his thumbs behind his suspenders and pulled them away from his shirt. He let them snap back. "Clarence, no offense, but in a way, if he's just gone, flown the coop and disappeared from the area, it might just be the best thing for everybody. I understand you have to uphold the law, but as you said, it'll be hellish difficult to get any charges to stick. There again that's maybe just me bein' lazy...you have your duty an' I know you'll do it."

The sheriff gave a short laugh, "Thank you for that vote of confidence, John, but I'd be a liar if I said that thought hadn't crossed my mind too. If I could be certain I'd run the fool out o' town, we wouldn't worry too much about the legal aspect."

John regarded the sheriff carefully, "Then you ain't certain—"

"C'rect. I can't take the chance; for whatever reason I do not know. Roscoe's lit out from town usin' some plan he worked out before, an' that makes me think this was more than just a spur of the moment act of foolishness."

Will shook his head, "But why would he want to kill me? I've never done anythin' deliberate to upset Roscoe. I thought we were gettin' to be friends, maybe not bosom buddies but, you know, 'pals' at least. I fixed Roscoe a try-out for the baseball nine, for goodness sake."

Clarence shrugged his beefy shoulders, "There's many reasons for a man to go off the deep end, but from what I see, our Roscoe is not what you would call the most well *balanced* of men. I've been askin' 'round an' what I've found ain't what you'd call reassurin'."

"Such as what?" asked John.

"I'd rather not say at this stage...just rumours mostly...but you know the old sayin' about where there's smoke there's fire—"

He was just about to go on when Violet, the maid, put her head around the door. "Mister John, sir! You're wanted on the telephone," she paused, "a call from Washin'ton."

John went to the door, "Thank you, Violet." She shot Will a knowing look as she turned away. John strode through to the hall and picked up the mouthpiece, swinging from its wire. The sheriff and Will strained to hear the conversation. John returned a few minutes later.

"That's a turn-up for the books. The 'Old Fox', Senator Miller Vandersand, is sendin' Roscoe's older brother to discuss this 'unfortunate incident', as he says."

Sheriff Drew grunted, "Good, if I can't lay hands on one of his no good sons, I can give the other a good grillin'."

John smiled, "I'll take a guess Mr. Jefferson Vandersand is some hot-shot lawyer, an' he won't take kindly to a grillin', Clarence.

The sheriff''s bushy eyebrows reminded Will of exotic hairy caterpillars, even more so when they shot up in a show of innocent surprise as they did now.

"Oh, he won't know he's bein' grilled. I'll just be a simple country boy, aksin' a few simple questions." He chuckled, drained his coffee cup and stood to go. "When's he comin'?"

"Friday next." John said.

"Good. Maybe we'll have this sorted out by then." Clarence Drew settled his big Stetson hat and opened the door to go.

John held up his hand, "Just one thing, Clarence. Miller Vandersand asked if we could try to keep this discrete."

The sheriff threw back his head and roared. "Discrete! His halfwit son blazes away at the town's new hero shoutin' about dishonorin' his financee, an' he wants to keep it discrete? Lawd sakes, John, this is the most excitin' thing since Preacher Tibbles ran off with the Sunday school teacher." He held his hand to his ear. "You can hear the drums beatin' from here." They could see his shoulders still heaving with laughter as he drove away from the house with a cheery wave.

Will stood shaking his head. "Oh my Lord, he's right, Pa, this is just so embarrasin'." He looked at his father standing there in his shirt-sleeves with his neat string tie. His black hair only lightly shot through with silver streaks.

John looked at him steadily. "Can you imagine how your mother feels about all this?"

Will nodded. "I can guess, Pa, an' I'm truly sorry, but it's not of my makin'."

John shook his head. "I cannot agree with you on that, William. You set this chain of events in motion with that bloody flying circus of yours."

Will sucked in his breath, those words sounded like his mother's. "Is that what she thinks?"

"She does, and so do I."

"But, sir! That just isn't fair."

"Fair! What's fair got to do with anythin'? If you hadn't gone bargin' around in that infernal machine of yours, none of this would have happened." John had taken up the same stance as he had at their last confrontation. Fists balled on the table top, taking his weight as he leaned forward.

"Dammit, sir! That's not why Roscoe's all riled up."

"Of course it—," John stopped in mid sentence, "What did you say?"

Will walked quickly to the kitchen door, looked quickly out into the hall then closed the door. "I said, that's not why he's all riled up. Though I admit I don't suppose it helped."

John stood back from the table. He hooked his thumbs under his suspenders again and leaned forward in his familiar questioning pose, one only too familiar to Will as he grew up. "So what the dickens have you done? Pray tell."

The sarcastic tone was not lost on Will, but he kept his voice even. "I think he saw me kissin' Marie."

John straightened up, scratching his head vigorously as he did whenever he was baffled. "So what? Marie likes kissin', no disrespect to the child, but the whole town's kissed her, she even kisses our damn dog."

Will grimaced, "Well, Father, there's kissin' an' there's... "

"Smoochin'?" A trace of a smile played around his lips.

Will shrugged, "You could say that. I think he might have been spyin' on us. Remember I stayed for supper at the Julien's on Sunday night?"

"Yes, I thought you were late home."

"Well, Marie an' I took coffee on the back porch after Mrs. Julien had retired for the night. An' one thing led to another, an—"

"Will! You didn't!?"

"Oh no, sir! Not *that*, but we did do some serious...smoochin'."

John fiddled with the end of his mustache, his face serious again. "Will, there's no law against that. Why didn't you tell the sheriff?"

"Oh come on, sir! A gentleman could not do that. If Marie chooses to tell him, that's one thing, but wild horses wouldn't drag the story from me."

John nodded. "Point taken. But why do you think Roscoe was spyin' on you?"

"I never paid it no mind at the time, but as I walked home I heard a big powerful automobile driving fast away from the crossroads."

"And you're sure that was Roscoe?"

"I can't be sure, I didn't see it, but that car of his makes a real distinctive sound. He could easy have snuck into the Julien's property at the back."

"Okay, say it was Roscoe, what difference does it make? He's not engaged to Marie so why all this dishonorin' his fiancé nonsense? If she'd been engaged to him, her mother would be shoutin' it from the rooftops."

"Maybe he intended to ask her," Will offered, "maybe he's just a very jealous guy, either way, that's why he went off the deep end."

John sucked in his cheeks. "I'm sorry, Will. Though you are probably right, by your own admission your flyin' exploit is at least part responsible. You made him look a fool, then you made him jealous."

"Yes, sir."

"As I've said before, William, I have the family name to consider. You are involvin' us in all manner of wild goin's on, an' it all goes back to your flight. Your mother asks, quite rightly, what will people think?"

"Yes, sir."

"I'm sorry, but after this I have to forbid you carryin' out any more flyin' experiments. I'm not breakin' the *Flyer* but that machine will never take to the air again, and you will stop wasting your time with this aviation business."

"No, sir."

John stopped. "I beg your pardon?"

"No, sir. I will not give up this aviation business. I am over twenty-one and quite capable of making my own decisions. If you will not allow me to pursue an aviation career in my own hometown because it is causin' embarrassment, then I shall move elsewhere where our family honor is not an issue.

John looked hard at his son. "William, family honor is always an issue." Will said nothing. A fly buzzed against the window, then stopped. The silence sagged around them. Finally John spoke. "Very well, if you insist on wasting your time and education in this blind alley, that is your concern, I cannot try to stop you. But I shall have nothing to do with it. I will not contribute one penny toward this dangerous and expensive hobby."

"That is not a problem, sir, I will make my own way."

"You understand exactly what I am sayin', Will? Only son or not, you will not receive any allowance, or any consideration in my will."

"Yes, sir, you're cuttin' me off."

John felt a wave of nausea but dare not show it. "Only until you come to your senses and come back to work in a respectable branch of engineerin'."

"That will only happen when you accept my branch of engineerin' is respectable, sir. Now if you have nothin' more to say on the matter, I must go and pack."

John forced the words out. "I have nothin' to add. Good day to you." Will took his proffered hand and shook it, turned on his heel and walked out of the kitchen without looking back. John stood leaning on the table then collapsed into a chair, his head in his hands. He fought to keep the tears back. "Damn, damn, damn, damn..."

Chapter Seven

LATE ON THE FRIDAY AFTERNOON FOLLOWING THE SHOOTING, JOHN Turner stood waiting for the train from Jacksonville. He was pleased to see it easing into the depot precisely on time. With his world turned upside down, John felt in need of some reassuring reliability in his life.

The porters jumped down to place the steps the passengers used to alight from the train even before the locomotive hissed to a complete stop. A wayward jet of steam blasted from a relief valve, obscuring John's view. He was looking for an older version of Roscoe and hardly noticed the short, heavy-set young man standing nearby looking around with the slightly lost air people have when they expect to be met, but do not have a clue what their escort looks like.

John was surprised when the stranger approached him; he thought he was a traveling salesman and was about to brush him off.

"Mr. John Turner?" he asked.

"Mr. Jefferson Vandersand?" John recovered his manners, extending his hand.

"People call me Jeff," he grinned, shaking John's hand warmly. "Vandersand's enough of a mouthful as it is."

John took in Jefferson at a glance; he was nothing like his wayward brother. Where Roscoe was tall and very handsome, the elder brother registered as short and what people would politely describe as homely. His round, amiable face showed signs of the extra chins it would carry in later life. There's no doubt, thought John, he's a Jeff, not a Jefferson.

"Automobile's outside, can I take your bag?" John asked.

Jeff held up a single, small leather traveling bag and laughed, "I'll manage, lead on Mr. Turner." John led him through the depot into the bright afternoon sun. The Model T sat chuffing gently; as was typical of most people, John had left it running. Jeff Vandersand climbed into the seat next to him.

"Nice car, Mr. Turner."

John wondered if Jeff had a sarcastic wit. In Tallahassee people smiled at John's loyalty to the mass-produced Ford, when he could easily afford something far grander. Jeff's next words convinced John of his seriousness, and that he knew his automobiles. "Best cost-per-mile ratio of any automobile on the market, over forty percent better than its nearest rival."

"You know about autos, Mr. Vandersand?"

"Please, call me Jeff," he prompted before going on. "Don't know much about the engineering side but I do know about costs. It's my job."

"I thought you were a lawyer?"

"Oh lordy, no!" Jeff laughed. "I'm a bean counter—an accountant—you know, a fancy name for a bookkeeper." He fanned his hat in front of his face as the car moved off. "Goodness, that breeze feels good, it gets pretty warm here, I guess."

John laughed, "You can say that again, an' this is only springtime. Please call me John, everybody else does." What he had been expecting to be a difficult first meeting was turning out a pleasure. Roscoe always had to work at being charming, John thought, as if it was expected of him. Jeff, however, came across as just a naturally friendly soul.

Tallahassee did not let John down. Recent rain showers had laid the dust, allowing the early blooming flowers to flourish their dazzling colors for the benefit of his guest. The towering trees cast a benign shade for the many citizens strolling along their route, giving Jeff the impression the town had been planted in a forest, rather than the trees having been planted in the town. John slowed as they passed the recently completed capitol building, the late afternoon sun gilding its dome.

Jeff whistled appreciatively, "Some horse."

"Beg pardon?" John shouted over the clatter of the motor.

Jeff laughed, "My father has a legal advisor, a lawyer who, frankly, I do not get along with. He called your city a 'one-horse town.'"

"Does this lawyer know anything about Florida?"

"No, but he's often described as a horse's ass, maybe that's why he's so familiar with 'em." John laughed, he could see Jeff Vandersand did not mince words.

"Your family is descended from European nobility, ain't that right?"

John asked.

"Did Roscoe tell you that?"

"Well, he suggested it."

Jeff Vandersand laughed again, "Yeah, he would. 'Delusions of grandeur' I think it's called. We're an English family, too, John. At least since the seventeenth century, as far as I can make out from genealogical research. The original Mr. Vandersand was a Dutch sailor who had to leave Holland in a hurry. If he was nobility, he disguised it well by running a tavern in the English County of Norfolk. The only thing he passed down was a fine pewter drinking tankard. We keep it on the mantle shelf at home."

Jeff's description of his ancestor kept them occupied for the final few yards of their journey. Charley Turner waited at the entrance of their home to greet the guest.

Jeff shook hands with her, "Pleased to meet you, ma'am."

"Mr. Vandersand, you'll be staying with us of course," Charley said. It was a statement more than an offer. Nobody could accuse Charley Turner of being churlish. Just because this man's brother had tried to murder her son, she felt that was no reason to fall down on her obligation to live up to the high standards of hospitality expected.

"I don't want to be any trouble, ma'am, I could find a ho—," he saw Jim the butler taking his bag into the house. "I'd be honored," he conceded graciously.

"Would you like to wash up after your journey?" John asked.

"I surely would sir, it is a mite warmer than I expected." He was dressed well, but not comfortably, in a heavy wool suit. His stiff celluloid collar cut into his neck and his neatly knotted tie added to his discomfort.

Charley called to Violet who hovered in the background, "Show Mr. Vandersand the guest room, please, Violet." She turned back to him. "Take your time, we'll be in what we call the back dining room when you're ready." Jeff followed Violet inside.

"What do you make of our guest?"

"I like him."

"You've only known him ten minutes," Charley pointed out.

"I know, but you'll see what I mean."

When Jeff Vandersand rejoined the Turners, John saw the vest had disappeared and the stiff collar had been replaced by a less formal cotton number. Jeff was shown into the back dining room by Jim, who could not resist announcing him as if they were entering a grand ball.

Jim swung back the heavy oak doors, "Mis-tuh Jefferson Abraham Vandersand."

Jeff stepped through the door and looked around: "Good grief!" he gasped, "I'm sorry, didn't mean to be rude, but it's...it's..."

"Ridiculous?" Charley suggested.

"No, ma'am, begging your pardon. It's magnificent, in a..." he struggled for the word, "a *baroque* fashion."

The Turner home showed no sign from the front of its eccentric construction. A single room sprang at right angles from the rear of the house, like the nave of a cathedral. Its roof soared so high it merged with the top of the main structure. Built from imported stone, with a superb marble floor, it benefited from elaborate windows, almost as high as the eaves. The ventilators, adjusted by a system of gears and rods helped keep the temperature comfortable in the heat of summer.

John made the introductions. "Mr. Vandersand, may I introduce those of us who we feel can contribute to the proceedin's? This is Sheriff Clarence Drew who represents the law."

"How do," Clarence greeted him.

John continued, "Mr. Nathan Walker, his wife, Cordelia, and son, Henry, who both witnessed the incident. Mr. Walker is Will's employer."

If Jeff felt surprised he gave no sign of it; either of finding Will worked for a black man, or of the way the Walkers dressed. Nathan and Henry both wore dark suits. Henry, the more conservative, stuck to a matching vest, but his father, Nathan, sported a natty silk number. His collar was pinned discreetly under his tie by a gold clip. John noted Nathan wore his best boots, the ones he had made for him when he visited London a few years previously. Cordelia outshone them both. Taller than her husband or her son, she knew how to make an impression, without resorting to what she called "trashy." She wore a high-collared, long-sleeved cream silk blouse. At her throat rested an intricate cameo brooch. Her skirt was a rich, dark blue, cinched at the waist by a wide belt with a silver clasp. Her hair was pulled back in a tight bun, giving more emphasis to her broad forehead. Charley thought her friend looked gorgeous. Jeff was clearly impressed; he made a slight bow when he took her hand.

"Jefferson Abraham?" Nathan boomed.

"Pa wanted to cover both bases. You know politicians." Jeff replied without embarrassment. He was clearly at ease. A meeting involving not only black people, but women too, lay outside the experience of most men, but Jeff was all business.

"Take a chair, Mr. Vandersand," John prompted.

"And a glass of lemonade," Charley added.

Jeff impressed his hosts. Without a trace of arrogance or conceit, he took charge of the meeting. In a few minutes he established the facts of the shooting, heard Cordelia's and Henry's versions of events, and satisfied himself of their accuracy.

"I am sorry that Mr. Will Turner could not be here, after all, he is the victim of my brother's foolishness." Jeff looked around; he sensed the tension in the room. Nathan and Henry shifted uncomfortably, Cordelia and Charley glared at John.

"I very much regret that too, Jeff, but he was called away unexpectedly," John looked steadily at Charley. Her lips were compressed in a thin line but she added nothing. "He did, however, make a full statement about the incident and the events leading up to it. The sheriff has a copy for you."

Jeff took the thin file Clarence pushed across the table toward him, took a pair of reading glasses from his vest pocket and perched them on his nose. He glanced up and smiled, "Bear with me for a moment." He quickly scanned the pages, paused for a moment, then took off his spectacles. "Your son is very generous in this. He is trying to make excuses for Roscoe, but there's no point in beating around the bush. It's clear to me my brother is responsible. Whatever the provocation, Roscoe behaved like a complete fool." Jeff sat back, "Would it be possible for me to travel to where William is working, or for you to let me know when he will be visiting home? It is my duty to apologize, in person, for my brother."

"Oh, I don't think that's necessary, Jeff." John said.

Jeff smiled, "I think it is."

"You are most gracious, Jefferson," Charley said. "I will make sure that William returns home at a time convenient for you. I am sure *you* two will get along fine."

There was something in the way Charley stressed the *you* while shooting a fierce look at her husband that made Jeff quickly move the conversation on. "What about this business of my brother shouting about somebody dishonoring his fiancé?" He paused, turning to the ladies, "I feel quite sure nothing improper has happened, I would not be asking in front of you."

Cordelia laughed, "Appreciate your concern, Mr. Vandersand, but Charley an' me ain't no shrinking violets, ain't that right hon'?"

Charley smiled, "I'm from a British army family, Mr. Vandersand. I've seen most of it and heard the rest."

"Thank you, ladies, do you have any clues?"

Charley took the cue. "I have taken the liberty of questioning Marie, with her mother present, of course, and she assures me the question of marriage never arose. She was actually beginning to question your brother's motives because their friendship was not progressing according to the usual custom. Marie could not understand what he wanted from their relationship."

John detected a look of alarm on Jeff's face as she spoke. "What exactly do you mean by the 'usual custom', Mrs. Turner?" Jeff asked urgently.

"There's a certain protocol...," she paused. Jeff was clearly a straight talker who appreciated directness.

"S'cuse me hon'," Cordelia took over, "what Charlotte means is they never got past first base. You could even say they never got to the ballpark."

Jeff's head dropped, he rubbed his temples vigorously. "Oh, no—not again!" he groaned. "Let me guess; even though he knew Marie for months he never even tried to kiss her, never held her hand, but treated her like a queen. He sent her beautiful flowers, would do anything for her, but left her wondering what he did want?"

"New Haven all over again?" Clarence Drew asked quietly.

Everybody turned to stare at him. "How did you know about that?" Jeff demanded.

"It's my job," Clarence stated flatly. He passed another folder across the table to Jeff, who opened it and briefly scanned the contents.

"How did you come by this?" an edge of anger slipped into his voice.

"As I said, it's my job. I'm a peace officer, and I use anything I can to keep that peace."

Jeff looked at the sheriff carefully, sizing up the man behind the badge. He reached a decision. "You've read that report, Sheriff; what's your opinion?"

"At best, criminal stupidity, at worst I'd judge second degree murder."

Jeff silently congratulated himself for his good judgment. He sensed the man was straight. He had no alternative; the Turners were owed an explanation. "Last year my brother became involved in a duel."

"In a *WHAT!?*" it came out as a chorus.

"You mean with *pistols?*" John asked.

Jeff shook his head. "I wish—there probably would have been no harm done. No, I regret to say, with swords, sabres to be precise." He paused, "I am very sorry to say that a man died."

"Oh my goodness!" Cordelia spoke for all of them.

Jeff carried on. "The report Sheriff Drew obtained is by the investigating officer. He voiced the opinion that Roscoe should be tried for manslaughter; the coroner, however, declared the death a tragic accident."

"How much did that cost your daddy?" Clarence growled.

"Ten years of favors called in, a harder currency than dollars in Washington. What would you have done if it was your son, Sheriff?" Clarence shrugged, but said nothing.

"But what were they doin' fightin' with real swords?" John asked.

"In his wisdom, my father sent Roscoe to Heidelberg University in Germany for a year, to broaden his mind. He learned sword fighting there. I believe they have a tradition of dueling, though the authorities deny it. The object is to slash your opponent's cheek, the resulting scar being seen as a badge of honor."

"Sounds like a badge of *stupidity*," Cordelia said.

"Couldn't agree more, Mrs. Walker. The young man who died had fallen out with Roscoe over a young lady. He was a member of the fencing club at Yale, as was Roscoe. They fought with unguarded blades and without protective clothing at a site outside New Haven, at dawn of course. The witnesses' statements in the police report show they fought like wildcats. Roscoe's blade nicked the artery in the other man's neck. He died in seconds."

Charley felt herself turn pale, "Oh my God," she whispered.

"Quite properly the university authorities expelled Roscoe on the spot, even though criminal charges were not brought," Jeff said.

"An' that's why he was sent down here, to hide him out of the way while the dust settled?" John guessed.

"Exactly. Now he's managed to kick up a regular sandstorm, dammit! 'Scuse me ladies, but my brother's behavior has caused me a substantial amount of vexation over the years."

Charley put her hand on Jeff's arm. "Believe me, you're not alone," she looked at John who smiled ruefully.

"I have one of my own," John admitted. "There's more than one way they can get in trouble with the ladies," John said, thinking of his brother Bertie.

"Thank you, I really do appreciate your understanding over this matter, but I don't think the law can be quite so sympathetic, nor should it be," Jeff added firmly.

Sheriff Drew stared at him amazed, "I beg your pardon, sir, are you sayin' you want your brother charged?"

Jeff looked him straight in the eye, "Sheriff, I might as well tell you now, my father and I do not agree on this. He wants you to drop any charges, and is prepared to go to great lengths to persuade you to do it."

"Are you sayin' he'd try to bribe me?" Clarence asked, his voice dangerous.

"No sir, he doesn't know you well enough."

Clarence relaxed, Jeff's honesty appealed to him. "So what do you think I should do?" the sheriff asked, his eyes crinkling with a smile.

"If you want to throw him in jail, I'll hold the door open." Jeff soon realized everybody was looking at him with surprise. "I'm serious, I love him dearly, but my brother has been indulged all his life and now he thinks he can get away with anything. The best thing for him at this stage is to suffer the consequences of his actions. A spell in the cooler would do him good. Frankly, I'm tired of clearing up after him." He stopped suddenly, aware his frustration showed openly, but all he saw around him was agreement and sympathy.

"I'll cut you a deal, Mr. Vandersand," Sheriff Drew said.

"Go on," Jeff prompted.

"If we can catch him, I'll throw him in the county slammer for thirty days for 'attempted wounding,' then drop all other charges."

"And if we can't catch him?"

"You just make sure he never shows his face 'round here again."

Jeff stretched across the table and shook hands. "You have a deal, Sheriff. When do we start looking for him?"

"You want to go into the woods and swamps after him?" Clarence sounded surprised.

"Certainly do...will I see an alligator?

"That's fer certain," his hosts assured him.

The following morning John came down early for breakfast to find their guest sitting with Jim, the butler, on the back porch. He found the coffeepot on the stove and poured himself a cup before joining them. The predawn coolness felt delightful. The brighter stars still shone in the west, but the first wash of light blue tinted the eastern horizon.

"Jim was telling me about some of the wildlife we might find in the woods," Jeff said.

"Hope you haven't bin frightenin' Mr. Vandersand with tales of fifty-foot 'gators, cotton mouths, an' swamp monkeys," John said.

Jim laughed, "No sir, Mr. Jeff here *wants* to see wild things. 'Spect we can show him some good size 'gators an' such, but he'll be lucky if'n he sees a swamp monkey."

"Why's that, Jim?" Jeff asked.

The old man cast his coffee dregs into the bushes. "Because it don' exist 'ceptin' in some people's fevered or booze-sodden minds."

"Aw! come on, Jim, what about them mysterious screams in the night folk hear?" John asked.

Jim's grin shone white in the darkness, "'Tween you an' me, that's folk findin' that there's fire ants in the privy. Anyway, enough idleness if we're goin' to get a good start. What can I do you gennelmen for breakfast? We have eggs, grits, ham, toast, biscuits, English mammy-lade," he paused for breath.

"That'll be fine, thanks Jim...all of those," said John. "Thanks for offerin' to come with us."

He explained to Jeff, "Jim was raised in these woods, knows his way 'round like it was the backyard here. Kin to many folk an' friends with even more, he's our best chance of findin' Roscoe."

Vicky wandered into the kitchen, rubbing her eyes free of sleep, "What time we goin'?"

"As soon as you've eaten a proper breakfast young lady."

"Pile it on, Jim, it's goin' to be a long day." Vicky said.

They used the Autowagon because it managed the rutted dirt roads with ease. They had a clear plan based more on local intelligence than geography. Sheriff Drew had, as he put it, "leaned" on a few people and confirmed that Roscoe had indeed headed west on the trail to Blountstown. This road skirted the southern bank of the Ochlockonee River. They knew they had little chance of finding Roscoe, but if they could find his car, Clarence felt that would be a start.

They set off dressed for the country. A pair of high boots and some light-weight clothes that fitted Jeff, more or less, had been found. Most important, they provided Jeff with a decent size straw hat. The sun was scrambling into a clear blue sky when they picked Henry up. Nathan spread a map on the hood, and they gathered around. "I'm sorry I can't be joinin' you, but somebody has to keep the work movin'."

"Appreciate that, Nathan," John said.

Nathan chuckled, "An' I'm too old to be crawlin' 'round them woods. Now, you don' have to be Mr. Sherlock Holmes to figger out he most like got away from one of the landings on the south side of the Ochlockonee an' headed downriver." His finger traced a line. "My best guess is you'll find the automobile jus' off the trail somewhere between Huston Road an' Williams Landing. Find that an' Clarence can probably work out who took him, and where, by which landin' it's near."

The Autowagon rolled out of town. Jim sat up next to John in front, while Jeff sat lounging against the tailboard, facing Vicky and Henry in the back. "You look real comfortable Mr. Vandersand," Vicky said.

"I am, but I'd be more comfortable if you called me Jeff," he grinned at her.

She noticed he really did have exceptional teeth, and his eyes had a sparkle she had never noticed in his brother's. Why—she asked herself—did she find Jeff more attractive than his handsome brother? Perhaps because he didn't shoot at Will. The mischievous thought showed itself in her face.

"You seem pretty happy yourself, Vicky," Jeff observed.

"I just love bein' out in the woods," she replied.

"Same here," Jeff said.

"Are you serious?"

"Indeed I am. I love nature, I wanted to study botany and zoology at school but Pa insisted I study business and accounting, so I could finance Roscoe's political career when Pa's gone."

"You what!?" John had been listening to the conversation and this news made him haul on the brake and turn around so he could make sure he heard right.

Jeff grinned, "That's right! 'Roscoe for President.' That's Pa's long-term plan. He wants to found a political dynasty." He studied the faces staring at him, open mouthed, enjoying their reaction.

"I'm serious, that's his plan. He says the modern politician will need to have presence, by that I guess he means handsome. That's what'll win votes, Pa says. Roscoe should be on his way to the White House if that is the only qualification.

"What do you think of that idea, Jeff? What do *you* want to do?" Vicky asked.

"Me? I want to make pictures of our native animals in the wild...without getting eaten by a grizzly bear." Jeff replied.

Vicky let go a yell of laughter. "You're a hoot, Mr. Jefferson Abraham Vandersand."

"Thank you, ma'am, I'll take that as a compliment," he bowed to her.

John put the wagon back in gear and set them rolling again. He called back over his shoulder, "So what do you think of Roscoe's chances...as a politician I mean?"

"'Bout the same as a snowball down here. If I can keep him out of serious trouble I will have done better than Pa," he sounded melancholy but soon brightened up. "Do you think we can find my automobile at least?"

"You brought a car here?" Henry asked.

Jeff realized he was causing more confusion and quickly ended it. "The *La France* is mine, I just loaned it to Roscoe. I don't like to think of it in a swamp somewhere. Under this manly chest beats the heart of a bookkeeper."

"We'll find your automobile if we have to search 'til Christmas," John promised over his shoulder. They showed Jeff the woods in all their glory: live oaks, silver bays, cedar and pine. Vicky explained how the hammock land was rich in humus and pointed out how the undergrowth was either saw or palmetto, and how the Spanish Moss lived off its host tree. They scared up a big alligator for him and he heard a rattlesnake. Jeff marvelled at early butterflies with wings like illuminated soup plates, and wildflowers. They thought their visitor might burst into tears or write a poem on the spot when they first sighted an orchid. But they could find no sign of the big, white, American *La France* automobile. They searched thoroughly, on foot, down to the river on one side of the track and into the deep woods on the other. John moved the Autowagon a few hundred yards at a time as they slowly worked along the very rural highway.

Jim called a halt at midday, "I have a suggestion. I need to transact a little business with Mizz Lee. Mr. John an' Mr. Jeff, you check out Scott's Landing. I'll take the wagon with Henry an' Mizz Vicky, an' they can be checking out the track down to Seddon's Landin'. We'll all catch up with 'em there an' we can deal with that picnic Mrs. Walker provided. Sound good?"

"Fine by us," they all agreed. Jim slipped over to the driver's seat and the Autowagon chugged off down the track.

Jeff watched them go, "A little business...*here?*" He asked John. "I don't mean to pry, but what sort of business can you do in the middle of a jungle?"

John laughed and touched his finger to the side of his nose, "*Jungle* business, you'll see." Jeff shrugged and followed him into the trees.

Jim braked to a stop after a few hundred yards. "You want the shotgun Henry? Snakes'll be wakin' up now."

"Naw Jim, Miss Vicky's got a fine big stick to look after me with," Henry said. "See you in half hour or so?"

"I'll be quicker'n that," Jim laughed, "cain't see that food lasting long with you around." He let in the clutch and the wagon lurched off along the track. Henry and Vicky worked their way methodically down the path. The vegetation was so dense they knew the car could have been pushed off the track and easily camouflaged with branches and leaves. They were looking for traces of recent activity: wheel tracks, cigar butts, anything that would give a clue to where Roscoe had abandoned the car and met with his suspected collaborators.

They found nothing. The path, a few yards away from the main track, narrowed so that it was barely wide enough for a mule to be led down to Seddon's Landing. This was a strong, wooden landing stage, supported on piles driven into the riverbed. Projecting a few yards into the water, it allowed a shallow draught boat to tie up without grounding.

Henry squatted to unpack the wicker picnic basket while Vicky skimmed a stone over the water.

"One, two, three...and four! Did ya' see that Henry? Four strong skips."

"Mighty skillful, Miss Vicky."

I wish we'd brought a fishin' pole, this river is loaded." She sat down cross-legged. She was dressed much the same as Henry: dungarees, high boots, long-sleeved man's shirt, and a wide straw hat. "Damn it's hot! Wish I could just shuck off my clothes an' jump in!"

"Lordy, Miss Vicky," Henry sighed, "don' even think on that. Us men, we'd have to eat our dinner back in the woods an' the flies are gettin' fierce even—," he stopped abrubtly as a branch snapped behind them.

"That's right, nigger boy, don' even let her think on it. Where we come from we'd hang you for jus' lookin' at a white woman."

The voice came from behind them just back in the woods. Henry froze, but Vicky lacked his nose for trouble and whirled to face the stranger. "Where *you* come from, folk scrape their knuckles when they try to walk standin' up."

Henry slowly stood up and turned. His instinct had not let him down; there were two of them. The taller one had a face like a vulture. A beak of a nose seemed to almost touch his pointed chin, which was covered in stubble. A battered felt hat drooped over long, greasy hair, shading his eyes. The shorter man wore a hat with such a wide brim it put Henry in mind of a sombrero, his droopy moustache added to the Latin air, but when he spoke it was in a nasal whine with no trace of a Spanish accent.

"Reckin' we should do the decent thing, Mort, an' save this young lady from his evil attentions."

Vicky tried to dart past Henry. "Why you filthy mouthed little—," Henry gripped her arm, bringing her up short.

"Miss Vicky, let me deal with these," he couldn't think what to call them, "people." They were hardly gentlemen; their clothes looked disgusting. He recalled climbing from locomotive fireboxes looking cleaner than these two; he couldn't even tell what color their pants had ever been. He found a horrible fascination with the smaller one's pudgy face; it displayed the fiercest eruption of acne he had ever seen. What looked really ugly to Henry though, was the double-barrel shotgun the tall one had aimed, more or less, at his middle.

The one called Mort leered at him, one or two teeth shifted in the gloom of his mouth. "Nat'relly, if you was to look at a white woman, how you might say, au natural," he snickered at his choice of words. "I'd jus' have to shoot you to protect the young lady's honor, even in these parts." He licked his lips; it reminded Henry of a toad catching flies.

The small one piped up with his whine again, "Yeah, you're right, Mort." Henry felt his chest tighten, he had a nasty feeling he knew where this was going. Vicky stopped struggling against Henry's grip and fell quiet. "So why don't you go ahead an' shuck off those duds little lady, jus' like you said."

She glared at him but said nothing. Henry pushed her back and took a step forward. "Over my dead body, puss face," his voice came low and quiet.

Mort grinned, it looked like his face had ruptured, and when he spoke Henry could sense the anticipation, "Gettin' personal now are we? Well come on then handsome nigger boy, whatcha waiting fer?" He hefted the gun up and pulled back the hammers.

Henry smiled back, "I'm waitin' for the *ugly* old nigger boy to cut you in half with the twelve gauge aimed at your back. An' his *will* fire. You sure 'bout yours?"

Mort kept the gun pointed at Henry but spoke out of the corner of his mouth, "He's bluffin'. Ocky, tell me he's bluffin'."

Ocky turned slowly, paused, then turned back to face front. "He ain't bluffin'. There is an ugly old nigger six feet behind us, with the biggest damn scattergun you ever seed."

Jim spoke, "Ugly *and* twitchy...very, *very* twitchy."

"What should I do, Ocky?"

Jim answered for him, "Drop that piece afore I blow you to kingdom come!" Mort dropped the gun and thrust both hands straight in the air.

Vicky punched the air in triumph. "Attaboy, Jim! You got the drop on 'em!" Henry took off his hat and fanned his face. He had trouble breathing, let alone yelling. Now that the danger was over, his legs felt weak.

Vicky flung her arms around his neck, "Henry you were magnificent—you're my hero." She glared at the two strangers triumphantly.

"What in tarnation is goin' on here?" John asked, stepping out from the trees to find the strange scene confronting him.

Jim kept the twelve gauge at his shoulder, "These two scallywags were tryin' to persuade your daughter, at gunpoint, to divest herself of her clothin' for their amusement."

John stepped up to them. "Turn 'round," he rasped.

"Meet the young lady's father," Jim said.

Mort felt like a rabbit trapped by a snake as he looked up at John Turner. He could not look away from his eyes: slate gray and unblinking. "Give me one reason why I shouldn't beat you to a pulp an' throw you to the 'gators?" John's voice was so soft Mort could not be sure the words had been spoken. It was more as if they had been passed through those awful, implacable eyes straight into his frightened brain. He was relieved when Jeff spoke.

"John, excuse me, I've a good reason why we should delay killing them and throwing them to the 'gators."

"What's that, Jeff?" asked John, just as polite.

"They might have some useful information."

Mort could see a faint smile flickering at the corner of John's mouth; it did not extend to his eyes.

"That's a good point, Jeff, they might tell us something. Then would you like to kill one of 'em?"

"After what they tried to do to Vicky and Henry? I would like to kill both of them, thank you." His voice stayed mild. But Jim's was not. He had heard a faint noise from the small one.

"Oh my gawd! He's sh—I mean soiled hisself." There was no mistaking the stink, even though it competed with the general stench of their unwashed bodies.

It had a quicker effect on John than any pleading would have done, his anger diffused to disgust. "Fer Chrissake go stand over there, an' mind you don' try anythin'. Jim, march this one to the end of the pier."

Mort finally got his voice back, "Look, mister, I'm sorry for what we did. We was jus' funnin' an' didn't mean no harm. We was jus' tryin' to scare the n—," he thought better of it, "the colored boy. An' my gun wasn't even loaded, honest, it was just a joke..." His voice trailed off.

"Well, as jokes go that was about as funny as a toothache, you stupid sonofa—," Henry bit off his retort; Vicky had heard enough bad language for one day.

Jim picked up the ancient shotgun and glanced at the breech. No bright percussion caps sat poised to fire a powder charge. He snorted his disgust. "You really are as dumb as you look. You used an empty gun to threaten a man who could break you in half with one hand. You've got an unusual idea of funnin', stranger."

Mort spoke up again, "Well I said we're sorry, but there's no reason fer me to lie to you; we ain't done nuthin' wrong, ask anythin' you like, we'll help you." Fear made him desperate to make amends. He had recognized John and had enough wit to understand how much trouble he was in.

Jeff stepped up to him, polishing his spectacles. "What are you doing here?" he asked.

"Our boat's tied up at the next landin'. We run a little produce up the river from the Gulf."

Jeff put his glasses on and peered at Mort's ugly face. "What kind of produce? Booze?" Mort glanced at John, then nodded quickly.

"Did you run another piece of contraband down the river Monday night past? The two-legged kind?" Jeff asked. Mort looked puzzled.

"A man, you idiot."

"No, why would we do that?" Jeff calculated Mort was either cleverer than he looked or telling the truth.

"Okay, were you on the river Monday night and Tuesday morning?"

"Yeah, we was." Mort answered confidently.

"Did you see a boat going fast downstream, after dark?"

"Yeah, we did."

Jeff blinked, surprised to receive such quick answers. "Where?" He prompted.

"Just t'other side of Jackson Bluff, one o' they fancy sportin' gasoline motor boats with the special keel that climbs outta th' water. Went past us throwin' a big wake." Mort threw in the details to convince them he told the truth.

"Where had it come from?" Jeff demanded.

"Hell sir, I don' know for sure, there must be twenty landin's this side o' the river.

"Okay, one final question, do you know who owned the boat?

Mort shook his head. "Honest to God, sir, I don't. Nobody we know could afford such a fancy thing." He was desperate to convince them. His next words did. "But I guess it might be the same person as owns the big fancy automobile, can't be many people out in the woods with that sorta money." If he had not been so thoroughly nervous he might have enjoyed the reaction.

"WHAT fancy automobile!?"

Mort did not know who to answer first as everybody except Ocky had fired the question in chorus. His nervousness induced a stammer. "Th-th-th, b-b-big white one just back behind you in the trees." He pointed, "It's no more 'n twenty yards off the track. We found it under a pile of branches an' such. Looks like somebody was tryin' to hide it, but we knows these woods an' we saw somethin' different in there. We just found it when we heard Mr. Henry here and the young lady."

John stepped forward and thrust his face into Mort's. "You better be tellin' the truth."

"I am, sir, I got no reason to lie to you. It's in there, large as life."

Jeff turned to John, "Let 'em go, or turn 'em in to the sheriff?"

John shrugged, "What do you think, Henry? Vicky? It's your call."

Vicky spoke for both of them, "Let 'em go! They're stinkin' the place up."

Jeff jerked a thumb over his shoulder, "Take your friend and don't stop running 'til you reach the Gulf."

"Thank you, sir, yessir, on our way." Mort scampered back to the bank. Jim handed him his gun with a smirk. The two bootleggers did not look back. They could be heard for a few seconds crashing up the path.

Jeff clapped his hand on Jim's shoulder, "Thought you said there's no such thing as a swamp monkey." It broke the tension, everybody started talking and laughing at the same time.

"Sorry 'bout the *old,* Jim, but you're still ugly," Henry added.

"That took guts to face 'em down like that, Henry, yo' daddy's gonna be proud of you," Jim said.

"*I'm* proud of him," said Vicky, "I didn't feel one bit scared with Henry by my side."

Henry rolled his eyes, "I noticed that, girl. Just what does it take to scare you?"

"That was some timing, Jim," John said. "Everybody likes to think scallywags like those two get what's coming to them, but usually they get clean away."

"Uh huh, Mr. John," agreed Jim, "the smart ones often do. But the dumb ones get caught, an' if brains was dynamite them two couldn't blow their hats off. They was so easy to sneak up on."

Jeff was already plunging back into the woods and the rest followed him. Henry called after him. "Take care, Mr. Jeff, there might be snakes makin' a home in your automobile."

Jeff stopped to peer into the dense vegetation between the trees. "By Jimminy! Here it is." Jeff forced his way into a scrubby thicket of saplings, pushing branches aside as he did. They joined him hauling branches away from the *La France* that lay at a slight angle looking more than ever like a beached whale.

Henry seemed to be all over the stranded automobile in seconds, assessing likely damage, working out how to pull it from its boggy resting place. "No serious damage," he announced from underneath the chassis. "Biggest problem's how to drag it back on the road, it's a far piece to push." His hands appeared gripping the edge of the running board, followed shortly by his smiling face as he dragged himself from beneath the car. "So how we goin' to tackle it, Miss Vicky?"

"Ooh, ah do declare," she said striking a pose with one finger on her cheek, "you askin' a lady how to do a man's job?"

"Yep." Henry said.

"It's no use tryin' to pull it with the Autowagon, we'll never gain the traction. I'd say we fix a runnin' line to that tree yonder an use the block an' tackle we carried with us to drop the pullin' ratio so's we can haul it onto firm ground." She answered briskly. The others grinned at Jeff who stood, mouth open, staring at her. "Unless you've a better idea, Mr. Vandersand." She fluttered her eyelashes at him.

John slapped him on the back. "I've spent the last eighteen years tryin' to raise a genteel young lady, an' my son and Henry have spent as long raisin' the world's first lady engineer."

"Aw, come on, Daddy, it's just common sense."

"Well, maybe," John said, "but experience counts as well. You see, Jeff, when other young ladies were takin' dancin' classes an' learnin' to sew, Vicky was always hangin' around with William an' Henry makin' a nuisance of herself."

Vicky wrinkled her nose. "That lady stuff was never as interestin' as what the boys were doin'. Hey, Jeff, do you want to go for a ride in the steamboat we built?"

"Miss Vicky, that would be a real pleasure. I'll swap you for a drive of my automobile, when we have it back on the road and cleaned up." He was looking sadly at the shabby state of his car. The brasswork was faded, the paint grimy and stained while the leather upholstery already showed signs of mildew. Henry assured him that a few days in the workshop would soon have it looking like new.

"Hey people, let's eat," John said. "All this excitement's left me bad off for a good feed. An' we need to build our strength up for haulin' this beauty back to solid ground. He led the way back to the landing stage. Cordelia believed a picnic deserved as much care and respect as any other meal. The wicker basket she had packed held plates, silver wear, napkins; all the things needed to give a meal some class.

Jim and Henry moved to sit some distance away but Vicky noticed, "Where are you two goin'?"

Henry looked awkward but Jim spoke with quiet assurance, "'Pearances, Mizz Vicky, just 'cause we're in the woods don' mean standards can be allowed to fall."

"An' just whose standards are those? Mr. Crow's maybe?" she answered hotly. "You two just saved me from a fate worse than death, an' you're worried 'bout what Emily Julien might say?!"

"Vicky!" John interrupted angrily, "Just watch your mouth."

Jeff sized the situation up in an instant, he saw the older man felt this meal was a formal occasion and he should keep his distance, probably because Jeff himself was there. Henry had naturally moved with him to keep him company. Jeff spoke quickly, "I'd be honored if you gentlemen would join us."

Jim could not refuse the invitation. He may have been freed by law, but he was still bound by protocol in his own eyes. Jim smiled and bowed slightly, "Thank you, sir." He moved back to join the group, followed by Henry. They sat down and before they could stop her, Vicky started to serve them. Jim tried to look disapproving but his voice betrayed his admiration. "You always get the last word, don' you, Mizz Vicky?"

She grinned smugly, "Ice in your lemonade, Mr. Jim?"

"Seen one o' these Jeff?" John asked, grateful to him for heading off an awkward moment, "Vacuum flask, Will made it."

Jeff stared at the ice, "Miracles of modern science! Now *that's* what I call useful!"

Henry uncorked a clear glass bottle and held it out toward Jeff. "This is what Jim was collecting from our friend Miss Kathleen Lee. He winked, "This is what 'jungle business' is about." He poured a measure into Jeff's glass.

He took a sip. "Mmmmm, now *that's* what I call powerful."

Vicky sat cross-legged next to her father. "Daddy, I have never seen you so steamed. Would you really have tossed them to the 'gators?"

"Oh goodness no, child, I just meant to frighten them."

"That's the difference between you and Roscoe," Jeff said quietly. "I think he would have killed them for that." The group stopped talking among themselves and all turned to look at him.

"Are you serious?" John asked.

"'Fraid so." Jeff replied, suddenly grave, "I do believe my brother wants to live in the past. He's fixed these ideas of honor and chivalry in his head, and sometimes I believe he wants to find Camelot and recreate King Arthur's Court. This whole Walter Scott chivalry thing is what attracted him to your area in the first place."

"Well, I think that's kind of fine an' noble. Can't fault a body for wantin' to stand up for what's right." Vicky said.

"Oh, I agree, but he's lost all sense of proportion. It's fine until he shows up on his white horse—"

"Disguised as your automobile," Vicky suggested.

"Exactly," Jeff conceded, "to defend some young lady's honor and goes way too far." He shook his head and sighed, then brightened. "But at least we found my automobile, and for that I am most grateful to you all." He raised his glass to toast their success.

Chapter Eight

RICHARD LESESNE PEERED INTO THE VIEWFINDER OF HIS CAMERA. "Okay, Will, now!" The roar of the motor and thrashing of chains and propellers faded. Richard felt the familiar sag of the Wright biplane as the hard wooden seat seemed to drop from under him, but he concentrated intently on his work. His hands moved fast, exposing the plate.

"I don't want to hurry the artist at his work, Richard," Will could speak in normal conversational tones, the idling motor could barely be heard above the gentle sigh of the wind in the mass of wires holding the Wright biplane together, "but we're goin' to be wearin' those trees if I don't bring the power back on soon."

Richard jerked his head up from his camera. "Jesus Christ. Pull up, Will!" His knuckles turned white as he gripped the strut next to him. The fronds of the palm trees seemed to grope for him like broad, splayed fingers, but as they drew closer he saw them sweep past a hundred feet below as the Wright responded to the thrust of the big propellers whirring behind him.

Richard grinned sheepishly at Will who was sitting next to him at the controls, "Aw, sorry, Will," he said leaning closer. "That gets me every time. Things never look real through the camera, and when you look up you see just how real, and solid, the world is. I appreciate you being ready to cut the power though, it stops the camera from shaking. Ruth won't do that for me, and then all the pictures come out blurred."

Will pushed the big lever in his right hand firmly away and, at the same time, worked the top section of the lever with a turn of his wrist. The Wright model B biplane soared out over the sea in a wide turn. They sat completely exposed to the forty-mile-per-hour breeze on a

framework attached to the leading edge of the lower wing. Two long, curved skids projected forward on each side of them, supported by additional struts stretching back above their heads to the upper wing. At the angle formed between these struts and the skids, a fixed stretch of canvas like a miniature sail had the name "Ruth Law" painted in bright red. Their feet rested on a fixed bar. Will controlled the rudders with the small, jointed section on top of the stick. Pushing and pulling a separate lever with his left hand worked the elevators to raise or lower the nose.

The Wright brothers had clung to their original idea of a motor driving two pusher propellers, but had abandoned the elevator arrangement in front of the pilot. The tail assembly now carried the rudder and elevators while the machine was rolled from side to side by warping the complete wing structure. The lever in Will's right hand had to be long to give the purchase needed to do this. It was a crude arrangement, and in Will's opinion not worthy of his heroes.

He held a steady course for a few minutes, a hundred feet above the surf, flying north parallel with Daytona Beach. Behind the dunes they could see a few scattered buildings set in miles of featureless scrub. Richard leaned close again. "There's great potential here, Will, you ought to think about settling."

"I can see how you might attract a few tourists in the winter time, but who's goin' to want to be here in the summer?" Will asked. "I can't afford to sit around in the sunshine six months of the year."

Richard grabbed Will's arm and pointed ahead. A few cheap wooden buildings, two and three stories high, faced the beach. "There...there's the future, Will!"

"What? The Bretton Inn or Ormond Beach?"

Richard jabbed his finger, pointing beyond to where a stretch of land appeared greener than the surrounding area. Will circled the Wright above it. Figures, moving between strangely shaped depressions cut into the surface, waved up at them.

"Golf?" Will sounded doubtful. "Can't see it ever catchin' on. Anyway, why would anybody come all this way to play golf?" He leaned into the turn and then heaved the Wright in the opposite direction to bring them facing south, back toward Daytona Beach. "I suppose I can see it in winter. Must be hell lookin' for that little white ball in a snowdrift up north."

Richard laughed, "You can mock, but we're getting more and more tourists every year. There's plans to build hotels all along this frontage. If you want to set up this flying line of yours, you should be making plans now to bring in the visitors." He pointed ahead "After all, Will, how much more of a landing field do you want?" Will could not argue. Several aviation entrepreneurs had set up joyriding operations on the beach over the past five years, attracted by the endless expanse of hard, smooth white sand. A perfect runway stretched hundreds of miles along Florida's Atlantic coast.

The previous year, 1913, the owners of the Clarendon Hotel at Daytona Beach had decided that airplane rides were a valuable attraction and offered full-time employment with full material support for the season. The contract had been won by Mr. Charles Oliver, but not for himself. He acted as agent for his wife who flew under her maiden name of Law. This was their second season by the sea. It was to this couple that Will had presented himself a few weeks earlier. His offer of fifty dollars plus his skills as a mechanic, if they would teach him to fly, had been eagerly accepted. The season was drawing to a close, the queue to fly had dwindled and the Wright showed the scars of hundreds of pleasure flights. Will appeared as a gift to them.

The young man proved an exceptionally able student pilot and, in Ruth's eyes, some kind of an airplane engineering genius. Within three days of his arrival she had sent him off solo. Will had cruised above the beach for twenty minutes in a state of bliss, making lazy turns, climbing and swooping above the surf. The following day he carried his first passenger. Since that day he had given fifty people their first flight. Richard was the local photographer and a regular. He turned his aerial photographs into a line of successful picture postcards that more than paid for his flights, turning a handsome profit because of their novelty value.

The Clarendon Hotel was a handsome brick structure with eight floors, built as two rectangular towers with the narrow ends facing the ocean joined by a center section featuring a façade rising to a point above the main entrance. Standing completely isolated at the edge of the ocean it dominated the landscape. Will and Richard could see it clearly from altitude even as they swung out over the golf course at Ormond Beach.

Will smiled and pointed down. Richard looked past his feet, resting it seemed, almost in thin air on the open latticework. He could make out a figure mounted on a motorcycle speeding along the flat sands. The motorcyclist waved to them and then gestured ahead with an outstretched arm. "He wants to race." Will shouted, pushing the nose down. He flattened the Wright a few feet above the sand. The speed won in their dive put them ahead of the bike. They both sank low in their seats to reduce the drag but to no avail. The bike drew level; the rider crouched over his gas tank. For a minute they raced side by side along the deserted beach until, with a nonchalant wave, the motorcyclist forged ahead. Will laughed and hauled back on the stick. The Wright soared into the sky. "He has the speed, but we have the view."

They circled the Clarendon again, bringing the airplane into wind. Will cut the motor and glided down. He judged his height perfectly, holding the wheels just above the surface until he felt the gentle shudder telling him the wings were about to stall. He eased the elevator control back and the wheels sank to the surface. A burst of power kept them rolling up to the hangar built at the edge of the beach just south of the hotel. Richard unbuckled his safety belt, an innovation for this season, and stepped down between the wheel skids. Will handed him the camera in its sturdy wooden case.

A slim, dark woman wearing a loose white shirt, black riding breeches and outlandish French cavalier style boots appeared at the door of the hangar, holding a coffeepot aloft. "Do you have time, Richard?"

"Thanks, but no thanks, Ruth. I have to develop these plates and get them to the printers. I'll send you copies as soon as I have them back." Richard loaded his camera into his Model T and left them with a wave of his hand.

Ruth poured two mugs and handed one to Will as he stood carefully studying the Wright biplane. "Penny for them, Will?"

"I was thinkin' there are so many improvements I could make to this machine. I can't help wonderin' why the Wrights didn't build it differently in the first place. Take the propellers an' this bicycle chain arrangement. It's just so inefficient, must lose so much power dragging all this 'round, an' with this motor you can't afford to lose any."

Ruth smiled, her teeth showing white in her deeply and unfashionably tanned face. "Well, they were bicycle mechanics." She suddenly giggled, "Think yourself lucky you don't have to pedal and have a little bell on the handlebars to warn people you're coming." She looked sideways at Will. She was suddenly serious again. "Did you ever meet Orville or Wilbur?"

"Never had the pleasure."

"I have, and to be honest, Will, while I count it an honor, I could never say it was a pleasure."

"I have heard they can be hard going." Will said.

Ruth laughed again, "That's a gift for understatement you must have inherited from your English ma. They were the stiffest, most stuffy men I have ever met. Absolutely correct mind you, perfectly polite, but I don't think either one knew how to smile. I only spent a day around them, and not long after that Wilbur died, but I wish you could have been there, Will. It would be easier to explain what I mean about them."

Will stood with his chin in his hand. "Try anyway."

"Well, when you spent time listening to them, you could see how their character helped them achieve what people had been trying to do for centuries, but how it was also their character that made them keep building the *same* machine and not moving on." Ruth looked carefully at Will. "I'm not explaining this very well."

"Carry on, I think I catch your drift," Will said.

"It's as if they felt they invented *the* flying machine, and that was the only way to build it. For them to start building radically different machines incorporating all the improvements that are obvious would weaken their case. And, as you know, Orville is still pursuing patent infringement actions he doesn't have a hope of winning." She shook her head and sighed. "It's all very sad really."

Ruth reminded Will of a younger version of his Aunt Audrey, the "Yankee Aunt" as Vicky called her. She had the same slight build, the same slightly clipped New England accent, and the same analytical mind. But there the resemblance finished. Where Audrey was reserved and correct to the point of being described as prissy and humorless, Ruth Law was a lively and witty woman with a mischievous penchant to shock. She designed her own flying outfits. The one she wore now was one of her own creations. The cavalier boots had tops that flopped over just below her knees. Her riding breeches were tight enough to set men's pulses racing and the ladies at the hotel gossiping. The loose neckline of her shirts prompted even more comment.

Ruth sipped her coffee and pensively pushed the toe of her boot against a wheel. "The truth is, Will, much as I love the dear old thing, I need something with a lot more...*oomph* for exhibition flying."

Will's eyebrows went up. "If it's *oomph* you need, you'll have to write it into the specifications."

She punched him playfully in the chest. "You know what I mean. Horsepower, dammit, and a beefed up frame."

"Just what do you have in mind, Ruth?"

She looked around carefully and lowered her voice. "Don't you dare breathe a word to Charles, but I'm planning to *loop the loop.*"

"My word, that'll be something to see," Will said. "But make sure Charles doesn't know, he'll have a fit. He's nervous enough about you flyin' as it is."

Ruth's forehead furrowed. "You're right there, Will. He's a darling man and I don't want to cause him too much worry, but flying is my life."

"You're preachin' to the choir, Ruth. Trust me, I won't let on. But what I can see you need to do, is pay a visit to Mr. Curtiss. I bet he can build you the machine you need."

"I think he can, but I won't sell the Wright. You've worked wonders, and she's fine for flying passengers," Ruth said.

Will finished his coffee and picked up his toolbox. "There's always room for improvement. While we haven't any passengers I'll go take a look at the rigging."

Ruth nodded. "I'll lend a hand. Anyway, I've been meaning to ask—and talking of family has reminded me—how did your ma take it when you walked out?"

Will and Ruth had become fast friends and he found it easy to talk to her about personal matters. "That's the strangest thing, " he said." I expected a terrible scene, cryin' an' such, but she was calm as you like. She said it was for the best while things calmed down, and then she gave me a hundred bucks in an envelope. It was as if she had been expectin' it. I tried to tell her I did not want or need any money an' she came over quite steely. Told me this was not Turner money, this was *her* money an' she'd do what she liked with it."

Ruth gave a cheer. "Yay! Good for her."

"Then I had to go tell Nathan I was leavin' his employ, an' I wasn't lookin' forward to that. But he was just the same, told me it was for the best, that it was about time Henry took more responsibility, and then, blow me down, if he didn't give me twenty bucks in an envelope! Just like *he* was expectin' it."

Ruth grinned at him. "Sounds as if you were the only one not expecting to leave."

"You're probably right. Just me an' my sister. Now, Vicky broke real bad. We had floods of tears an' she wouldn't let go my arm. I did not expect that at all. It was downright embarrassin'."

"I can see how she wouldn't want to lose you." Ruth glanced at him and saw him blush. "She seemed to have cheered up when she came to visit with your friend Henry."

"Oh yeah, she got over it, an' now she's been flyin' with me she probably thinks it's all worthwhile."

Ruth bent to pick up a wrench from the toolbox and glanced under the wing as she did. A figure was walking toward them. "Good Lord. I do believe it's Wyatt Earp." She saw a tall man dressed in a long black coat, high boots and a wide-brimmed hat. He wore a heavy mustache accentuating his thin features.

Will stared. "No it ain't," he said quietly. "Talkin' of family, that's my pa." Ruth stared at the stranger approaching, and then back at Will.

John Turner walked around the wingtip, swept off his hat and offered his hand to Ruth. She felt the strangest desire to curtsey, but resisted it. "Miss Law, charmed to make your acquaintance." He flashed a dazzling smile. She stared at Will again and then back to John. "No, ma'am, there's not much of a family likeness."

Ruth recovered, "Except in that you are both very charming. Delighted to meet you, Mr. Turner. Have you come to fly with us?"

"Indeed I have, if that is convenient." John turned to Will and offered his hand, "Good afternoon, Son, are you willing to take me up?"

Will hesitated a moment then took his father's outstretched hand. "Of course, sir, every passenger is welcome. Let me just check her over."

John stood back saying nothing as Will and Ruth scurried around the machine checking the rigging and control wires. Without a word he stepped up into the passenger seat next to Will, and Ruth strapped him in. She took his hat. The motor started with Ruth's first swing on one of the two propellers. Will turned to his father. "Ready?" John nodded. The Wright bumped over the sand, quickly reaching flying speed. Will was too busy with the eccentric control system to take in his father's reactions at first, but once in the air he sneaked a glance. John's face was serious as he watched Will's hands on the controls. He gazed carefully around the machine and then concentrated on the view. As the Wright climbed and the beach and ocean revealed themselves, Will saw the beginning of a smile. He took them up to Ormond Beach, over the golf course and a mile inland. The sun blazed over the dazzling blue ocean and the white sand almost glowed in contrast. Will resisted the temptation to demonstrate any stunts to his father, instead he concentrated on making the smoothest flight and landing of his short career. He noticed Ruth was nowhere to be seen when he rolled the Wright up to the hangar. He switched off the engine and father and son sat in silence.

At last John spoke. "Are you an' Miss Law...you know...?"

Will was caught off guard. "Good Lord no, sir! She's a respectable married lady an' her husband is my good friend."

John allowed himself a smile. "Keep your hair on, Son, she's a damned attractive woman an' I guessed she was single as she styles herself 'Miss'."

"No, that's her professional name. She's really Mrs. Oliver." They sat in silence again before John finally spoke.

"William, this don't make one tiny bit of difference to my opinion, so don't go gettin' any ideas I'm changin' *my* position on financin' you."

"No, sir, an' I'm not changin' my position."

John's face twitched. "But I have to admit that was the best ride I ever had. The most fun I've had in years."

"Good. I'm glad, sir."

John looked at Will sharply. "Stuffy don't suit you, Son. Okay, I'll admit that as carnival rides go, this is the best. But that's all it is, a thrillin' experience. I still don't see how these things will ever carry revenue earnin' passengers in enough numbers to make it pay."

"I don't agree, sir. They will, given time."

"Well, I still say you're wastin' *your* time with them. You are possibly the finest young steam engineer in the country, an' I believe *that's* where your future lies." Will said nothing. John looked out to sea for a full minute. "Dammit, Will, this ain't easy for me."

"It's not easy for me either," Will's knuckles showed white where he gripped the control column, "I didn't want to fall out with you, Pa. I don't give a tuppeny damn about the family money or my inheritance. I just want you to respect what I'm doin'."

"I do respect you, Will. But I believe you are wrong. An' I don't want you wastin' your time." The uncomfortable silence descended again. At last John spoke. "Anyway, somethin's cropped up that might get us out of this jam." Will still said nothing. "Okay, I admit it," John said, raising his hands and letting them fall again. "My jam. Okay? Satisfied? *My* jam. I'm about as popular as termites in my own home. Your mother an' sister are puttin' me in a squeeze. Damn! I'm supposed to be head of the house."

Will shrugged, "Sorry, Pa, I mean it, but I am followin' a career in aviation, whatever you say."

John nodded, then pulled an envelope from his pocket. "Well, I never said there's no career to be had in aviation engineerin', I always have said that the airplane will be useful to the military. Read that."

Will took the envelope and turned it over suspiciously. "You want me to join the army?"

John just pointed. "Open it. I haven't read it but I know what it is."

Will ripped open the envelope and hastily unfolded the single sheet inside. He read:

Dear Mr. Turner,

I hope you will forgive this informal and hurried letter, but I must come straight to the point. I am in desperate need of an assistant. Your cousin, my friend, Rupert Penrose has told me of your accomplishments and your qualifications. We both feel you are the man to help with the work contracted to me by the Royal Aircraft Factory at Farnborough. You may be aware that tensions are rising in Europe, and it is felt that preparations must be made. Included in these are the provision of a standard engine to power the aeroplanes of the Royal Flying Corps. The motor selected is proving very troublesome. Can you help me solve the problems?

I can afford to pay a salary commensurate with your abilities. I can also assure you that there will be further projects involving both power plant and airframe improvements from Farnborough. My works are at the field close by your family home in Hertfordshire, to the north of London. Accommodation, therefore, will not be a problem.

Please cable your answer as soon as possible. I look forward to hearing from you very soon.

Yours Most Sincerely,
Tom Armstrong

Will looked at his father, then read the letter again. He looked up to see his John smiling. "How did you know about this?"

"It came with a letter from Rupert explaining Tom Armstrong's offer," John paused, he knew it was for dramatic effect.

"Will, it came by special courier, a young British officer in a fancy-pants uniform came down by train from the military attaché in Washington. They want you, and they want you bad."

Will stared at his father, "You're joshin' me!"

"I'm not, Son. That letter arrived yesterday mornin'. Of course Rupert did not know about our little difference, an' that you were down here. So I hopped one of our own freights to Jacksonville last night, an' caught Mr. Flagler's express to deliver that as quick as possible."

Will felt a lump growing in his throat. Tears pricked his eyes. "My lord, Pa, then you want me to take this up?"

"Of course I do! You...you...," he could not find a word. "This is a great opportunity. You'll be workin' for the Royal Aircraft Factory. Engineerin' is engineerin'. An' that will stand you in good stead for life. So when you do see sense an come back to the railroad, you'll be able to say, 'I worked for one of the great establishments in the world.' Who knows, I bet they have a Royal Locomotive Factory somewhere, an' you might be promoted to work there."

Will stared at his father. "You are jokin'."

John turned to look at him. He said nothing, but Will read his smile. "Yes, Will, I am. And I know I should not make fun of your ambition. This is a great opportunity. You will learn a lot from Tom Armstrong, I've heard he is very highly regarded in his field. Go. With my blessin'."

Will slowly climbed down from the wing of the Wright biplane. He suddenly felt lightheaded, yet helped his father to the ground. "Pa, I do respect your position. An' I don't expect you to change it. Mr. Armstrong says he can pay me a halfway decent salary, so money is not an issue. I will say, here an' now, I won't expect a cent from you until I prove airplanes can be commercially viable. And somehow I will."

"You really believe that, Son?"

"I do."

"Then we'll have to agree to disagree. An' that means you will have to grow used to watchin' your accounts because I'll live up to your expectations, I won't give you a penny."

To John's surprise Will smiled and shook his hand. "Pa, you have yourself a deal."

John laughed, "Some deal! In the meantime I would like to entertain you and the Oliver's to dinner this evening at the Clarendon. I guess the season is comin' to an end an' they won't be inconvenienced by your leavin?"

"They had hoped I might join them up north for the summer flyin' season, but I know they will understand."

"Good. We can send the cable to Mr. Armstrong from the hotel, and you can call your sister long distance an' tell her you will be home 'fore Friday."

"What's special about Friday?"

"Come on, Will, you haven't been away that long. It's May first, the big day. Marie's moment of fame an' your sister's as well."

"I don't understand. Vicky didn't even run for May Queen."

"She didn't. But she's ridin' in the *Flyer* with you, at the head of the parade."

"Good Lord, Pa, now you're joshin' me again."

John slapped him on the back. "Son, it's not just at home I'm bein' put under the thumb screw. The Chamber of Commerce insisted the *Flyer* is towed at the head of the parade right behind the royal coach, an' they insisted you be there with it."

"How we towin' it?"

"That's you all over, Will—trust you to think of the practicalities. I think you'll like this. Roscoe Vandersand's brother, Jefferson, is doin' the honors with his big American *La France.*"

"That's *his* car?"

"Indeed it is. I expect Vic told you how we went out in the woods an' found it pushed into the trees down by Seddon's Landin'?"

"She told me all about it. An' the little adventure with those two bootleggers. Man! If I'd been there I think I would have tossed 'em to the 'gators. Was that right—they threatened Vic an' Henry with an empty gun?"

"Sure did."

"Then it sounds as if you rescued *them.* If Henry had set about 'em there wouldn't have been much left. He's a hard man to aggravate, but when he blows—watch out!"

John nodded. "He's a good man our Henry. Did you know *The Democrat* featured him as the first black man to fly? Picture of him there with you an' this here airplane, with a big grin on his face."

Will laughed, "I suppose Tallahassee is claimin' that as a feather in the civic cap. He certainly enjoyed his flight when he came down with Vic. He was more nervous than I expected, but soon as we were in the air he was whoopin' an' hollerin'. He took the rudder an' elevator control an' flew just like a natural."

John walked slowly around the Wright biplane as they spoke. He pushed and pulled on the tail surfaces, ran his fingers over the wing covering and peered hard at the long chains running from the motor fixed between the wings to the propellers. He snapped a glance at Will. People who did not know him found it a disconcerting habit but Will knew that look. "William, it sounds like some kinda blasphemy, takin' account of who built this. But your machine is years ahead. This is...is...," John lowered his voice, "downright ramshackle. It's well put together, but it's about as streamlined as a barn."

"With a porch on the front?" A voice inquired from behind them.

John turned and bowed to Ruth who had appeared from inside the hangar. "Nicely put ma'am. Now, would you an' Mister Oliver do me the honor of joinin' Will an' myself for dinner at the hotel this evenin'?"

Ruth linked her arm through his. "It would be our pleasure, Mr. Turner." Will watched them stroll toward the hotel, chatting like old friends. He scratched his chin. And they say I'm a flirt! He thought to himself.

Dinner was a great success. Will realized how determined his father must have been to at least restore civilized relations between them. He had brought Will's evening clothes with him knowing they would dine together. John had taken a suite for the night, giving Will the chance to take a proper bath for the first time since his arrival. He had slept in the hangar and unofficially made use of the servant's washroom at the hotel, but that was no substitute for a decent wallow in hot water. The Clarendon might have been miles from anywhere considered fashionable, but it made up for it with a grand dining room with a fine view over the ocean. Glittering chandeliers hung from high ceilings spilling light over spotless tablecloths and shining silverware. In the intervals while the string quartet arranged their sheet music for the next piece, the sound of the surf sliding up the beach could be heard from the darkness beyond the open French windows. The cuisine tended more toward American tastes than contemporary European. The chef was a Frenchman who had quickly learned that if he wanted to keep his job, experimenting with exotic sauces was a quick way to lose it. Father and son dined on succulent steak with all the trimmings. The service was impeccable. Will's easy manners had endeared him to the staff, and he earned hero status when he took Henry flying. They vied to serve their table.

He was surprised and touched the next morning when most of them took time to shake his hand and wish him well when he loaded his tools and old leather bag into the cab taking him and his father to the railroad station. He was even more surprised when Ruth kissed him warmly and hugged him fiercely when she said goodbye. "Take care, Fly Guy."

He saw tears starting in her eyes. "Hey! You as well, nothin' risky now," he winked and she giggled as she took her husband's arm. They waved until the cab turned a corner. Ruth in her latest risqué flying outfit and her husband, Charles, elegant as ever in his white suit and Panama hat.

Will and John made the journey home in record time. The northbound express on Flagler's railroad connected with a westbound at Jacksonville with minutes to spare. Will had to admit it was an impressive demonstration of the efficiency of the railroad system. John gave him a smug smile as he snapped his watch closed after noting the time as they drew up to the house just after midnight. Will's hopes of a leisurely start were dashed at six the next morning by the sound of Henry hammering on his door. "Come on, Will, we've only one day to finish the stuff for the May Queen ceremony, drag you're lazy ass out of bed."

They snatched a quick breakfast in Cordelia's kitchen and then set to work. The following day was May Day, and the celebration of the May Queen Pageant. A long list of adjustments to costumes needed attention. Lennie Dumanion felt he was being altered to fit the repaired armor instead of the other way around. The Walker's ever-patient horse, General McLellan, now looked the part of a knight's charger with a vast cloth covering from his withers to his hooves and back to his tail. Charley told them it was properly called a "surcoat", although she was not actually sure, but this was accepted without question as she was held to be the expert on all things English.

The level of horsemanship required of Lennie was minimal, but his nervousness was apparent to everyone. This led to an important innovation for this year's ceremony. For the first time a black person would feature in the proceedings; Henry would have to lead the horse. The organizer of the event, Felicity Adair, decided no risks could be taken.

"You want me to dress as a what?" Henry's reaction came as no surprise to Will, and he agreed with his point of view.

"Mrs. Adair, you might just as well come out with it an' say Henry's gotta play a black slave." Will knew there was no point in beating around the bush with the organizer. "Why a Moorish page; why not a Saracen warrior?" he demanded.

Felicity Adair looked at Henry carefully, taking in his powerful build. "Oh yesss! I like that idea." The decision made, she gave orders to her friend Mildred Crossland. "Mildred, robes for Henry, somethin' grand...an' a turban...he must have a turban. Oh...an' a scimitar! That's a job for you, William, a big scimitar."

Mildred glared at Will as Felicity Adair strode off, clipboard held firmly in front of her as she ticked off another task accomplished. "Thanks William," Mildred said sarcastically, "just what I needed, a Saracen warrior's costume."

Will turned his most winning smile on her, "Thanks, Mrs. Crossland, I knew you could do it. I'll arrange the big scimitar."

Her irritation faded, "Now you know why we call her 'Fizz' Adair."

"Yes indeed, more fizz than a Co-Cola," Will turned back to Henry as Mildred scurried off to find the material she needed. "How about that then? You get to act heroic."

Henry scratched his head thoughtfully, "We-ell, it's surely an improvement, but do you mind if I ask why an English knight would be trailin' 'round with a Saracen warrior? I recall from my learnin' of the Crusades they were sworn enemies."

"Easy. The Saracen is a horse trader. The English knight is takin' this new steed for a trial run, but the Saracen ain't takin' his eyes off the horse—'til such times as the money's in his hand."

"Well, trust you to fix an inconvenient little thing like history! That'll do me," Henry agreed. "Now, let's run Lennie through his part again. I'm feared he's gonna have someone's eye out with that damn spear."

"Lance, Henry...it's a lance," Will corrected.

"Spear or lance, it's a' accident waitin' to happen."

Henry's fears were unfounded. The following day went like clockwork, even though it seemed they would never finish all the detailed preparations in time. May Day fell on a Friday that year, a good enough excuse to start the weekend early for most people. The ceremonies and celebrations started in the afternoon and centered on the old oak near the east end of Lewis Park, a small green area located near the big main street known as Monroe. This magnificent tree had been used as the focal point for the pageant for at least fifty years, probably longer. The script called for Marie to be crowned with her King, a smug-looking Curtis Piggott, and then for her champion, the Unknown Knight, to ride up to the platform to present the tip of his lance on which Marie would attach her "favor", a scarlet silk scarf.

Lennie's big moment arrived to the sound of surprised gasps—the

Saracen was a late entry. General McLellan, Nathan's horse, swaggered into the arena with Lennie encased in full armor perched on his back. Henry stalked alongside looking suitably fierce, in purple robes swinging a wickedly curved scimitar in his free hand. Having Will carve it from wood and paint it silver made it easier to handle. Henry led the General to exactly the spot he had marked earlier that morning. Lennie lowered the lance and held it steady long enough for Marie to tie on the scarf. Kindness balanced the flirtatious side of her character. She had practiced this small maneuver many times to keep the strain of holding the lance in place to a minimum for Lennie. He raised the long wooden pole triumphantly then prepared himself for his big challenge. Henry glanced up at him, "You ready, Len?" he hissed.

"As I ever will be," came the muffled reply from inside the helmet. Lennie leaned forward and grabbed the pommel of the Western saddle.

"Hup! General!" Henry commanded. The big horse performed his party piece to perfection, rearing on his hind legs and pawing the air to tumultuous applause, and sighs of relief as Lennie stayed aboard.

Curtis then launched into his lines from *Ivanhoe*, looking very surprised when his concluding question, "Who can it be?" was answered enthusiastically by Lennie's mother from the passenger seat of Jeff Vandersand's sportster.

"It's my Lennie!" she yelled to the crowd, her face a picture of devotion. Lennie could only hear the roar of approval through his armor and was saved the embarrassment. Henry led them off to the side where Will and Nathan stood waiting to lift Lennie safely back to the ground. They quickly removed his helmet to reveal his very red and excited face.

"I did it, fellas, I didn't screw up an' make a fool of myself in front of Marie." Adoration shone in his eyes as he spoke her name. Henry, the temporary Saracen, slapped him on the back, "You make a good champeen, Leonard, I reckon the May Queen's gonna kiss you hard enough to blow your socks off." He winked at Will as he said it.

The parade quickly assembled. Nathan's workshop had turned a common farm wagon into a credible imitation of an open royal carriage to lead the procession forming up behind the high school band. Jeff Vandersand had made a special journey from Washington ostensibly to collect his car now restored to its former glory by Henry and Nathan. He admitted to John, however, that he would not miss this show for the world and had volunteered to pull the *Flyer* in the parade. Victoria had awarded herself the honor of sitting in the cockpit, wearing a costume she had put together modeled on the outfit she had admired when she met Ruth Law on her visit to her brother during his sojourn in Daytona. Will, to everyone's delight, had been demoted to walking behind steering the *Flyer* as it was pulled along by Jeff's automobile. Vicky had pointed out to anybody who would listen that he had crashed the *Flyer* when he sat behind the controls himself so it was safer in her hands. He had fabricated a set of wheels that supported the tail while he steered them with a long handle from behind. This allowed him to swing the airplane through any curve.

The band was squeaking and thumping as the musicians tuned their instruments when Vicky climbed up to the cockpit. Charley stepped close and beckoned her daughter to bend down so she could speak to her. "My dear, try not to upstage Marie, this is the biggest day of her life."

Vicky grinned and pulled the goggles down that she had been wearing on her head. "I'll keep these on so I look funny instead of pretty...how's that?"

Charley squeezed her hand, "Perfect, sweetheart, she's no match for you anyway." The band performed with gusto and led the parade proudly on its route. Behind the *Flyer* every organization in the county marched or rode on wagons decorated for the occasion. When the parade finally wound back to its starting point at the park the crowd was treated to demonstrations of maypole dancing while different choirs serenaded the citizens with their favorites. Everybody enjoyed the food supplied by the Chamber of Commerce, while hip flasks made surreptitious rounds as the evening wore on. Ten years earlier, in 1904, Leon County had voted to go "dry" under what was known as the Local Option Law, but it had been a narrow victory for the temperance movement.

John and Charley Turner moved arm in arm through the crowds. They were considered to be one of the most influential couples in town, whether they liked it or not. Courted for their wealth by some and genuinely liked by many more, they made slow and stately progress, stopping to chat every few yards. Even though their movements may have appeared random to a casual observer, John felt himself being carefully maneuvered by his wife.

"Okay, I'm comin'," he protested at a particularly sharp tug on his arm. "Who you spyin' on, Mrs. Turner?"

"Observing John...I'm just observing," she answered quietly, nodding to where she could see Will and Marie sitting together on the edge of the bandstand. Marie had fulfilled her role as May Queen to perfection, but as the evening wore on she found herself able to link up with Will without causing offense. Many people already viewed them as as an "item", an impression Marie's mother Emily did nothing to discourage. Marie floated along on the arm of her real life hero, and Will sensed some of the turmoil she felt. It was in many ways the happiest day of her life. Attention was the electricity that made her shine. But Will's impending departure cast a long shadow.

Marie clutched his arm tight and looked up at him. "You're only goin' to be away for a few weeks, ain't that right?"

He stopped and turned her around to face him, taking her hands in his. "I have to go where the work is, an' Europe is where all the aviation work is really pushin' ahead. I may be gone for months." He saw her bite her lip to stop it quivering. "'Sides, I was away for months at a time when I was at school."

"That was only a train ride to come visit you. England's on the other side of the world," Marie pointed out firmly. Her geography may have left something to be desired, but Will understood her concern. He tried to lighten her mood.

"Maybe it is now—but within our lifetime you'll be able to fly there in a couple of days."

To his relief Marie giggled as she reached up to tweak his ear. "Aw, come on, Will, the *Flyer* barely carried you to the other side of the lake. Cain't see it crossin' the Atlantic Ocean."

"Well, she's standin' in need of a smidgin more power, maybe another motor...or three. An' a cabin. Folk won't stand for sittin' out in the breeze all that way; it's a tad airish over the ocean. But somebody's goin' make it, just you wait an' see. 'Specially as a British newspaper has offered a prize of fifty thousand dollars, near enough, for the first airplane to cross the ocean. I would dearly like to claim that prize. If that don't convince my daddy, nothin' will.

"You really are serious 'bout this, Will Turner."

"I'm serious," he said simply. "That's where the future of travel is goin', an' I'm goin' to be part of it."

Marie put her arm around his waist again, and they resumed their slow walk toward the crowd. "Then I'd better start takin' it serious, too," she said thoughtfully.

"I wish you would." Will said with feeling.

Saturday had been allocated for Will's packing, and it seemed to him that every woman in his life had an opinion on what was needed, and wanted a hand in it. He wanted to take his tools and a change of underwear; they wanted him to take a full wardrobe.

John interceded on Will's behalf, "His good wool suit, white tie an' tails, an' his Norfolk jacket in case he goes shootin' with Uncle Frank. He's not about to be presented at Court."

Sunday had been set as the day for his departure for England so dinner on Saturday evening had an atmosphere that combined sadness and excitement in equal measure in Will's view. This event had to be styled as formal. To his embarrassment Charley wanted to ensure Will's "table drill", as she called it, would not disgrace the family or his country. She knew just how snobbish society in England could be, and that certain people would be watching carefully for breaches of whatever was considered correct at the time. She had no need for concern: Cordelia had already checked to see if all the lessons she had given over the years had been absorbed. The correct glass, the appropriate cutlery for each course, what was considered a white tie occasion and how you knotted that infuriating item. Gentlemen might have been born, but they still needed polish in Cordelia's view. Everybody there voted Will's *bon voyage* meal a success. He worried that Marie could easily dampen the spirit of the evening, but she determined to show a brave face, and succeeded. Jeff Vandersand's ready wit soon raised her spirits. In the short time since they had met, Will had decided he liked Roscoe's brother very much indeed. He was not so involved in his own thoughts that he did not have time to notice with approval just how much attention his sister paid their guest.

Emily considered herself very modern sharing a table with the Walker family. Her husband, Walter, despite his "Old South" upbringing had never had a problem with this issue. He held his own philosophy: if a man would drink with him he could not see why he should not eat with him, and he had shared many a bottle with Nathan and John. The party broke up long after midnight. Marie planting a defiant kiss on Will in full view of Charley instead of shaking his proffered hand as they said farewell.

The same group assembled at the station the next morning to see him off, with the addition of half the town, or so it seemed to Will. News of his journey had spread with the general perception that he was going to teach the British how to build and fly an airplane. The Chamber of Commerce decided that the departure of the town's hero deserved a grand send off. Will was not altogether surprised when the band appeared playing their favorite Souza march, but he still blushed furiously. Henry pressed a package into his hand and told him to open it. He found a brand new Barlow pocketknife with his name inscribed on it. He had been holding up well to that point but tears welled up in his eyes.

Henry saved him, "Boys in the workshop clubbed together. You were always borrowin' someone's knife, an' as we ain't goin' to be around we thought you better have your own." Will surreptitiously wiped away a tear with his sleeve as he tipped Henry's hat over his eyes.

"Thank everyone for me, Henry," he said, his voice thick. Will's last view of those closest to him as the train pulled was his mother and Cordelia looking concerned, his father thoughtful, Henry and Nathan proud, and Marie sobbing in spite of her best efforts, leading Vicky to fall apart. The two girls smiling bravely through their tears and holding each other was the image he carried with him as the train rounded the bend.

An old lady in the opposite seat lowered her book. Her eyes twinkled, "Quite a send off young man. Goin' to be away for long?"

"A few months, I guess, but I'll be home for Christmas."

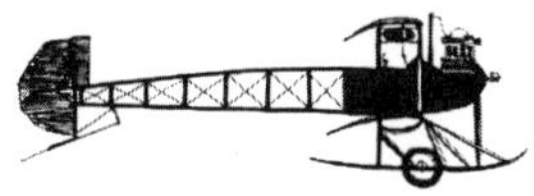

Chapter Nine

WILL HAD NO DIFFICULTY FINDING HIS UNCLE. FRANK PENROSE stood inches taller than the other people waiting by the barrier at London's Waterloo Station for the boat train from Southampton. Will half expected to see him in a uniform—he had noticed far more soldiers than he was used to seeing—but Frank wore a dark blue suit. There was nothing remarkable about his clothes, they were slightly old fashioned but immaculately cut. He attracted discrete looks from passersby, especially women. They would have found it hard to put an age to him. In fact, he was sixty years old but carried himself as a man years younger. His spare frame did not carry an ounce of excess flesh. For a soldier, his thick, iron gray hair was unusually long, swept back from a high forehead that served to make his face longer. Frank's firm, almost heavy jaw ended in a pointed chin that added to the impression. His skin was darkened by a lifetime in the open air, leathery and wrinkled, but it was his eyes that held attention. Dark and deep set, they drew people in willingly or reluctantly. They belied his oddly diffident bearing, so much so that when strangers guessed his occupation they would plump for university professor. He had none of the strut and swagger expected of a military man.

For Will those eyes shone with affection and the craggy features were wreathed in a huge smile. Frank took Will's hand in his and clasped it firmly. He placed his other hand on the younger man's shoulder. "Let me look at you, William. I have to say it. My, how you've grown!"

"I expect so, Uncle, it's been five years since you visited."

"Goodness, that long?" he sighed. "Five years too many. Is that your only luggage?" he pointed to Will's old leather bag.

"Yes sir, I had my trunk sent on to the house."

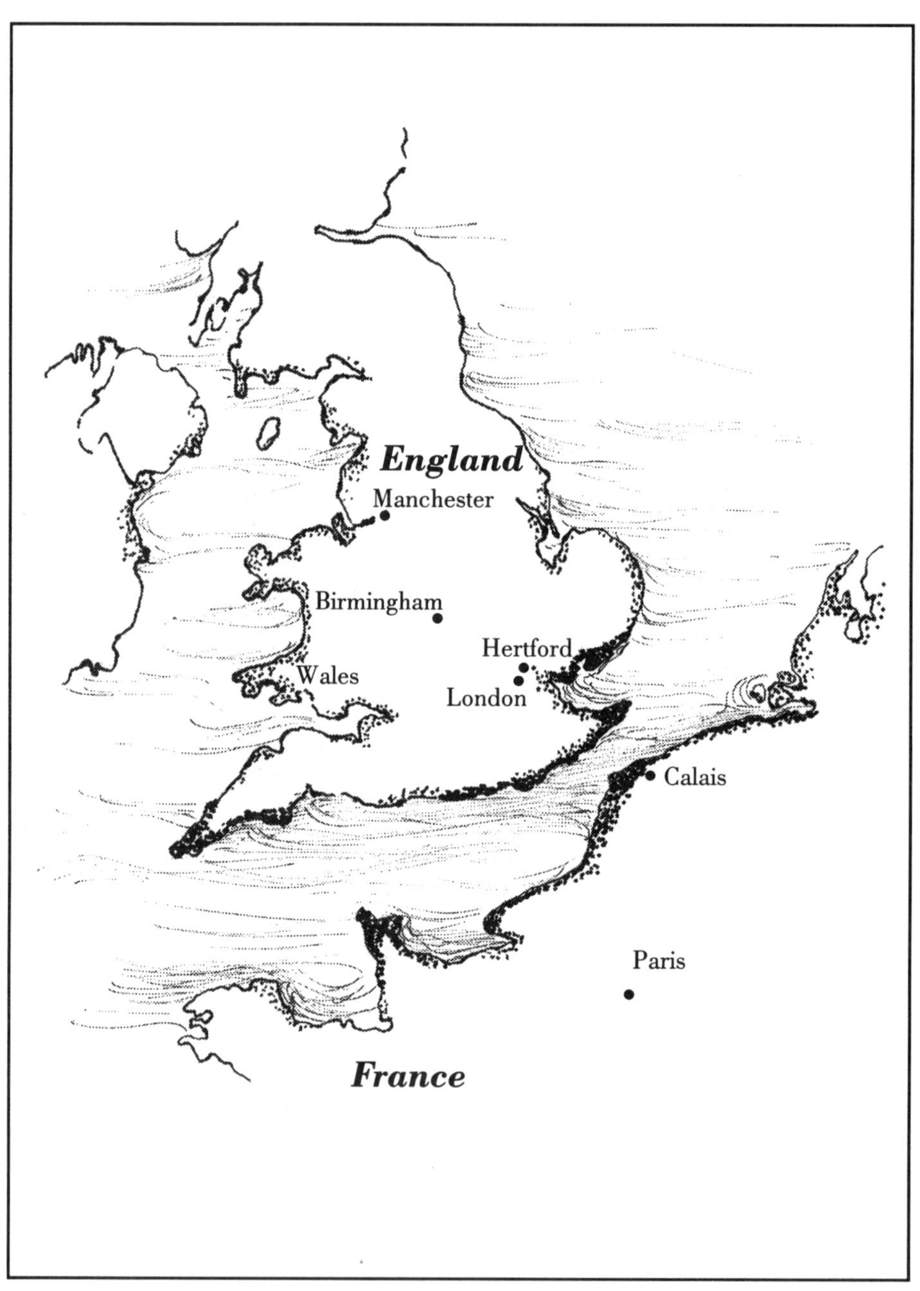
England
Manchester
Birmingham
Hertford
Wales
London
Calais
Paris
France

"Capital! It's so much easier to travel light. Come along, I have my car waiting." He linked his arm in Will's and led him through the crowd to the entrance. His car was more sporting than imposing. It was an open touring model with bodywork in a deep green. The radiator was tall and narrow with a distinctive sculpted indentation on either side of the filler, merging with long fluted cut outs tapering as they ran the length of the hood before disappearing at the base of the windshield. A folding roof stowed neatly behind the rear seats. Will whistled with admiration as the driver pulled up to the curb.

"What do you think of her then?" Frank asked, smiling, knowing he was fishing for compliments.

"She's a beauty," Will peered at the badge on the radiator. "It's a—how do you say that, Uncle?"

"A Vauxhall. Pronounce it the English way, '*Vox*-hall'." He opened the rear door for Will and ushered him aboard. Frank introduced his driver, "William, meet Sergeant Joe Thorpe—biggest rogue in the army."

The man who had that accolade to live up to turned in his seat to shake hands. "Pleased to meet you, Mr. William." He looked nothing like Will's idea of an army sergeant, not that he had met any. Joe Thorpe could have been a bank manager. He had a round face accentuated by circular wire framed spectacles. His thinning hair still had a reddish tint that matched his little toothbrush mustache. He wore a black suit with a stiff-collared shirt; he topped off this outfit with a bowler hat. "Where to first, sir?"

Frank thought for a moment, "It's a beautiful day Joe, let's take William for a sightseeing tour."

"Right you are, sir, Buck House, Palace of Westminster, Nelson's Column it is." Joe slipped the car into gear and slid smoothly into the afternoon traffic, on the wrong side of the road it seemed to Will.

"Have you eaten yet, Mr. William?" he asked over his shoulder.

"Well, not for a while, but I can last."

"No need to," Joe reached under his seat between shifting gears, "rations for two there, sir." He passed a heavy brown paper bag to Frank who looked inside.

"Oh splendid, Joe, what would I do without you?"

"Starve probably, sir."

Frank grinned at Will and passed him a fat cheese sandwich. "An army marches on its stomach, so Napoleon believed." Landmarks that had been part of Will's life through pictures and family anecdotes were presented for his inspection and pleasure as Joe Thorpe wheeled them through the busy streets. They were as imposing in reality as Will had hoped. He could not have wanted a better tour guide than Joe: a Londoner born and bred, he knew his city and provided a running commentary while handling the car with practiced ease. From the station he turned left to take them over Westminster Bridge so Will's first view of the Houses of Parliament and Big Ben was from the best vantagepoint.

"I'd describe the architectural style as 'gingerbread gothic'," Joe sounded faintly disapproving. "I'll show you some of Christopher Wren's work in a minute. Now, there was a handy bloke with bricks and mortar." He pointed up at the tower of Big Ben, "Lot of people think it's the clock, but it's the bell they named it after." And so he carried on, sharing with Will his knowledge and enthusiasm for the city. They cruised past Buckingham Palace where Will saw his first Guardsman in scarlet tunic and towering helmet. Joe made a very important point. "That thing on his head is a *bearskin.* It ain't a busby as a lot of people think. A busby is the hairy hat the cavalry wear." Joe did not speak with the guttural cockney accent, he pronounced the "h" sound at the beginning of a word but still ran them together in a way that made Will listen carefully to catch his meaning.

"Are you a Cockney, Joe?" Will asked.

"Bless you no, sir. To be a Cockney you have to have been born within the sound of Bow bells. I was born in Chiswick out to the west. We consider ourselves a cut above the East End." He swept around Hyde Park Corner, weaving through the horse drawn vehicles that made up the majority of traffic. They sped up Piccadilly with Joe pointing out the famous hotels. They dived down Haymarket into Trafalgar Square so Will could pay his respects to Admiral Nelson on his column. "They do say," Joe said, pulling the car to the curb, "they put his statue on the column so he could see the sea."

"Can he?" Will was peering up with his hand shading his eyes against the sun.

"No, that's bollocks," Joe replied bluntly. "I worked it out he would have to be five times higher, and he'd need a bleedin' good telescope."

"Trust you, Joe," Frank laughed. "I've been telling visitors he could see the masts from there."

"Oh, he can, sir, but only the ones just down the river." He slipped the car back into gear and dodged around a motor bus to launch them off down the Strand. Heading east they entered Fleet Street. "Home of British journalism, Mr. William, where the truth is rigorously sought out then knocked into the shape that suits the owner of the newspaper."

"Ouch!" Frank said. "That's rather caustic, Joe."

"Thank you, sir," he was unabashed. "Also home to some of the hardest drinkers in the land. If ever I take on a pub, this is where I want it to be."

Fleet Street led into Ludgate Hill, giving Will a superb view of St. Paul's Cathedral. "Now, as I said, that is a piece of real architecture." For the first time Will heard a note of reverence in Joe's voice. "When you take some time off, which I hope you can, I'll lay on a guided tour, the vicar's a mate of mine."

Frank saw the look of surprise on Will's face. "Joe and the dean of St. Paul's belong to the same chess society," Frank explained.

"You will be making sure he takes some time to see the sights properly, won't you, sir?"

"Absolutely, Joe." Frank took his watch out, "and now I think we had better be heading back to the club."

"Right you are, sir, but don't worry about coming back to the office, I've covered everything."

"Oh, I'm sorry, Uncle Frank," Will said, "I don't mean to be keepin' you. I could take one of these buses." He had seen the big, red, double-deck motor buses with the winding staircase to the upper deck exposed at the rear of the vehicle.

"Goodness no, Will, you've given me the best chance to bunk off for months."

Joe laughed, "Nice to have a chance to skive like this, Mr. William, we don't find an excuse very often."

"*Skive?*" It was yet another word Will had never heard before.

"I think it's known as 'playing hooky' in your part of the world, William," his uncle said. Joe knew the streets intimately. He drove them around the cathedral then north. Will swore to himself that he would no more come to London without a native guide, than he would attempt an expedition up the Amazon. The city seemed vast to him, an endless parade of magnificent buildings and history. Even New York, sprawling as it was, had some kind of logic in its street numbering system, but here he knew he would be lost in minutes.

As they drove Joe continued his commentary, "On your right, University College, on your left, University Hospital." They swung into Euston Road leading into Marylebone Road. "On your left, a fine example of a Nash terrace." Will admired the Georgian homes of Park Crescent. "On your right, Regent's Park." Joe braked sharply and swung the wheel hard left. "And this is Baker Street, famous for Sherlock Holmes. Please note, there is no 221b; a lot of people come looking for him, they take it hard when we tell them he's not real." He swung the wheel again to turn into one of several side streets leading off the main thoroughfare. Both sides of the street were lined with terraces of what looked like grand family houses. Identical black wrought iron railings prevented passers-by from plummeting into the basement areas separating the building from the sidewalk. The ornate front doors, all black with shining brass knockers and letter boxes, were reached by way of a short flight of scrubbed marble steps. As they pulled up in front of number seventeen, the door opened as if somebody had been watching for them. An elderly man, dressed in a black tailcoat descended the steps.

"Good afternoon, Colonel, this must be Mr. William." The old man spoke with the kind of voice usually associated with undertakers: deep, precise, and formal. He had long side whiskers that went well with his long hooked nose, the curve of which merged with his forehead as it sloped back to the point where a few strands of gray hair were ruthlessly plastered down.

Frank introduced Will, "Mr. Middleditch, this is my nephew, William Turner." Will shook hands. Frank explained that Mr. Middleditch held the post of club steward. Middleditch clicked his fingers and a much younger man scuttled down the steps and took his bag.

"Oh, that's all right, I can man—" Will spoke too late, the youth had grabbed it and sprinted back up the steps.

"No trouble, sir." He called over his shoulder as he disappeared through the door.

Frank shook his head. "Can't young Cyril ever forget he used to be a pickpocket, Mr. Middleditch?"

"No, sir, and I make sure he never forgets." He said grimly. Turning to Joe he smiled, revealing yellow teeth. "There you are, Joe," he passed him a slip of folded paper, "put that on for me."

Joe looked at the note, "Worth a flutter?"

Middleditch laid a bony finger against the side of his nose and winked. "From the horse's mouth."

Joe stuck it in his pocket. "Right you are, Albert. Do you need me anymore today, sir?"

Frank shook his head, "No, I'll see you in the morning here at 08:00; we'll drive William to the station then go on to the office." Joe drove off with a wave. Frank turned back to the steward. "Anything special on the menu this evening?"

"Oh indeed, sir. Mrs. Vigus has laid on something very traditional for the young American gentleman: brown Windsor soup, roast beef with all the trimmings including her horseradish sauce, Yorkshire pudding of course, with spotted dick and custard to follow." Will, if not familiar with everything mentioned, knew what each dish was, except "spotted dick and custard."

The club fascinated him. He had to stop himself gawking as he followed the steward inside. From the street it gave the impression of a tall, narrow family house. Beyond the door Will realized it was an illusion, the premises of his uncle's club extended into the houses on either side. Numbers sixteen and eighteen were all part of the same building. Cyril, the youth who had snatched his bag, stood behind a grand mahogany reception desk. He opened a leather bound register and spun it around to face Will.

"Would you like to put your moniker there, Mr. Turner?"

Frank translated for him, "Just sign there, Will," he laughed. "It will take a little while to learn the local lingo."

Will had a sudden thought, "Oh no, Uncle, I forgot! My evening clothes are in my trunk."

"Don't worry, we don't dress for dinner on weekdays; you can wear what you like. One of the members wears his kilt and an old sweater."

"Yes, Colonel Penrose, sir," Cyril chipped in. "Mr. MacPherson says it's healthy to get the air 'round your—"

"Quite! Cyril," Middleditch interrupted sharply. "I'm sure Mr. Turner will be treated to the benefit of Mr. Mac's theories soon enough. For the moment I expect he will prefer to, as I believe they say in his country, 'freshen up'."

Will acknowledged this unexpected but familiar expression with a slight bow. "Mr. Middleditch, I do believe we could learn each other's 'lingo'." The club was furnished in the manner of a comfortable hotel: that was, to a large extent, the role it fulfilled for its members. Will was impressed by the height of the ceilings and the extensive wood paneling. The furniture was much heavier than he was used to. When he sank into an armchair it seemed to fold around him. He pressed down on the bed in his room and it gave under the pressure. Softness equated to comfort. The member's dining room was a cozy and surprisingly small room. Despite the bright evening outside, a fire blazed in the grate beneath an ornate marble mantelpiece.

Frank advised on the choice of drink to go with dinner. "This is good plain food. You may prefer wine, but I think a robust meal deserves a robust drink. I like beer with beef. Stan, the wine steward, keeps an excellent pint of bitter, but it's an acquired taste. My favorite is India Pale Ale. It's a beer brewed for the army overseas, a little lighter, more akin to the lager beers you drink at home." Will found it went down very well with his roast beef, nicely extinguishing the fire in his mouth lit by the hot horseradish sauce. The spotted dick turned out to be a cylindrical pudding dotted with raisins and smothered in custard. It was a meal needing their full attention, but eventually they sat back with satisfied sighs.

Over coffee Frank explained something about his club, "You have to be voted into membership, but it tends to go through 'on the nod' in families. We usually have the members other clubs won't accept."

"Why's that, sir?" Will asked.

"They tend to be more eccentric than the famous St. James street clubs are prepared to accept. It's not a question of snobbery, we have men from all walks of life, including members of the aristocracy. Between you and me, though the official name for the club is 'Thetford's', we are known as 'The Odd Fellows', which is a bit of a cheek as that's also the real name of a perfectly respectable friendly society."

"But you're not eccentric, Uncle Frank."

"I have my moments, William, but, to be honest, I'm a member because my father, your grandfather, Hector, held membership all his life. I'm an easygoing sort of chap and the antics of some of the others don't bother me in the least."

As if to illustrate his point the door burst open. The man filling the frame might have just come off stage. Then again, Will thought, he might just as easily have walked off a Scottish mountainside.

"Frank!" the apparition roared. "Is this the laddie come to rescue Tom?"

"Mac, old boy, meet my nephew. He has indeed come to help our Tom conquer the heights." Frank was clearly delighted to see him. Will found his hand crushed in a giant paw. He did not need to be told this was Angus MacPherson, the legendary artist. It was the first time Will had ever met anybody wearing a kilt, but instead of the short jacket and frilled shirt seen with formal highland dress, Angus wore an old fisherman's sweater pockmarked by small holes with singed edges. His red hair grew long and unkempt merging with the beard that started just below his eyes and finally gave up halfway down his chest. This alone would have been enough to mark him as a man of unusual presence, but his sheer size made sure he dominated any gathering.

"Come on, you lads. Never mind that port, it's an old tart's drink, let's away to the bar for a dram." Frank grinned at Will and motioned for him to follow. The bar was a riot of mismatched styles. Old wood vied with new nickel plate on the beer pumps. A huge mirror covered the wall on one side of the room while heavy red wallpaper covered the rest. Some of the chairs were leather wing armchairs, while others were, incongruously, rattan cane. Trophies adorned any free wall space; Will instantly decided he liked the place.

"So, how's the portrait business?" Frank asked. Angus found his pipe in his sporran and lit up; Will could see where the holes in the sweater came from as glowing embers erupted from the bowl.

"No' bad, Frank, no' bad at all, but that Lady What's-her-name—she's a funny woman."

"Why's that, Angus?"

"She only asked me tae paint her in the *nude!*"

"Oh I say! That's a bit strong, old chap."

"I should bloody say it is," Angus replied. "When I told her it would be another fifty guineas, but I'd have tae keep my socks on for somewhere to put mah brushes, she went all huffy on me. Nae bloody sense o' humor these aristos."

That set the tone for the evening. The bar quickly filled and Will was introduced to a succession of members representing most of the professions to be found in London. The only thing they had in common were strong opinions and a willingness to express them, regardless of whether anybody else found them interesting.

Over breakfast the next morning Frank explained his fondness for his club. "It's the least stuffy gentleman's club in London. I think I would rather sleep on the embankment with the tramps than have to spend the week with the people who use the better known clubs."

The prospect of his uncle sleeping rough struck Will as bizarre. Frank wore his working uniform: immaculate khaki service jacket with the scarlet tabs of a staff officer on the collar. His breeches were made of a lighter material and tucked into high black boots, their glossy leather reflected in his Sam Brown belt. "I kind of expected to find you lived in a barracks, Uncle, you bein' in a manner of a soldier."

"What! Sleep over the shop? No thanks, Will, all that stamping and shouting, bugles blowing and drums beating, I've had enough of that."

When Joe Thorpe drove up to collect them he, too, looked every inch the soldier. Instead of the high boots he wore what were known as 'puttees', tightly wound strips of material spiraling from below the knee to meet the top of boots that shone like patent leather. His creases looked sharp enough to shave with. As he opened the car door he flung Will a salute.

"You don't need to salute me, Joe," Will protested.

Joe grinned, "When we're in costume we salute everybody, the punters expect it." He motioned toward the club staff watching from behind the dining room window, "And after all, they pay our wages."

On the way to Liverpool Street station Frank told Will why he had insisted on the overnight stay in London. "I wanted you well rested, Will, this is going to be hard work. They're all of a twitter at home about your arrival. Katie's friends will want to marry you, and your Aunt Connie will be waiting to challenge you in all manner of ways. She holds a poor regard for us chaps and military men in particular. You have the good fortune to only be a man and not compound the felony by being a soldier. I'll explain why one day."

"I declare I do not know what gives me most concern, Uncle, my aunt or my cousin's friends," he said as he climbed out of the car at the station.

Frank slapped him on the back, "Don't you worry about my sister Connie, just be ready to give as good as you get when she puts her debating hat on. No, you watch out for those girls. You're a catch in their eyes. You'll do well to listen to Kate, she'll look out for you."

Will enjoyed the journey out of London. For the first part of the run the suburban service stopped every few minutes at immaculate but small stations serving the towns now part of London's growing sprawl. But by the time he changed trains at the village of St. Margaret's in Hertfordshire the railroad had been running through unbroken countryside for nearly half an hour. The final part of his journey, on the tiny branch line train that took him into the heart of the countryside, provided him with a real treat.

Kate Penrose had been looking out for Will in the literal sense for over half an hour, when he tapped her on the shoulder. She knew the train was not due into Upper Bardfield station until just after eleven, but even though trying not to show her rising excitement, she still arrived long before the stubby little locomotive wheezed up to the platform dragging its tiny two-car train.

She spun around, "Oh! It's you, it must be, but how did you—"

Will took a pace back, swept off his cap and bowed, "Cousin Kate, I presume." He straightened up, "So do we say hello?" She stepped forward, took his hands in hers and kissed him on the cheek. She stepped back still holding his hands.

"Welcome to the country, William," she said breathlessly. He decided there and then if blushing ever became an international sport, his cousin could blush for England. It made her prettier than ever, and Will thought she started from a strong position on that count. When the most recent pictures of her had arrived in Tallahassee, his father had remarked that whenever people spoke of an "English rose" they must have had Cousin Kate in mind. She had the fair complexion, highlighted by her pink cheeks, that went with the auburn hair framing her face in a cascade of natural curls. Her big round eyes were so strikingly blue Will felt it almost indecent, or at least unfair on the rest of the human race who, depending on gender, would feel deeply jealous or hopelessly attracted.

"I beg your pardon if I startled you, Kate. I rode with the engineers." She looked over his shoulder to where the crew of the locomotive leaned out of the cab, grinning. She stuck her tongue out at them, which just made them laugh as they coaxed their train back into motion.

"I expected you in one of the carriages; that's why I looked the wrong way," she explained.

"It's my Indian blood," Will offered. "Can't stop myself from sneakin' up on folk."

She looked at his face carefully, then giggled, "You're making fun of me."

"I am," Will admitted solemnly. "When I arrived at St. Margaret's they seemed to be expectin' me, an' when the train came in, Sidney, the engineer, invited me to ride with them on the footplate. That's a great honor, Kate."

"Oh, I know, but I hope you were not patronizing about their little engine, comparing it to those great big things you run."

"Oh, lordy no. These little locos are quite somethin'. They're real powerful for their size. Did you know they call them 'gobblers'?" He paused, "An' I don't suppose you're real interested either."

She took his arm. "Just so long as they take me up to town, they can call them whatever they like," she said with a merry laugh. "Come on, Mr. William Turner, Aunt Connie is waiting to see you." They climbed into the lightweight two wheel carriage Kate had brought to collect him. She told him they called it a trap. She gathered the reins and called to the shaggy little pony in the shafts, "Home, Gladstone!" He snapped from his doze at the sound of her voice and stepped out brisk enough to jerk them back in their seats. "He's like that," Kate apologized. "He'll do anything for a woman, that's why we called him Gladstone."

"You mean after the serious old gent who used to be Prime Minister?" Will asked.

Kate gave him a sly smile, "The very same."

"Are you tellin' me he was a ladies man? That's surprisin'!"

She laughed gaily, "Oh yes, he loved the ladies, and the 'not so' ladies...if you follow my meaning. Aunt Connie can tell you all about him, she knew him well and thoroughly admired his views on reform. He is one of the few politicians she ever had time for."

Will shook his head. "Jeepers!" he muttered. At home it would be considered very "fast" for a young lady to discuss such matters. Will could see she knew how to break the ice.

The road climbed steeply away from the station then leveled, running between high grass banks topped with thick hedges. The weather remained fine with a few soft white clouds riding a gentle breeze. The smell of newly-mown hay, the first cut, drifted around them almost acid in its freshness. After a few hundred yards the road dipped into a sun dappled tunnel formed by an avenue of chestnut trees.

"This favors one of our canopied roads," Will said, arching back to admire them.

"That's the first time you've said anything in American," Kate said sounding pleased.

"Oh, you can't blame the Yankees for that, that's the South in me talkin'."

"Well I like it, whatever Marjorie Pritt-Allison says, you can 'y'all' or 'howdy-doody' me as much as you like." She nodded emphatically to press the point.

"I'm tryin' to mind my language an' not sound like a hick," he said. "Mother's been coachin' me in the King's English, but I'll 'howdy-doody' if you like. So tell me, what in tarnation is a Marjorie Pritt-Allison? Sounds like a new British *aer-o-plane*." Will stressed the English way of describing a flying machine.

Kate looked at him in mock surprise, "Well, Cousin, you're learning to speak properly already. A 'Marjorie P-A', is the biggest snob in the village. She thinks anybody from over the English Channel is barely civilized—and as for colonials, which you are, well, little better than savages."

"Hey!" he protested. "We're not colonials, Washington booted old King George back over the Atlantic."

"Aha! As far as Marjorie is concerned that's the proof. How could any nation in its right mind reject the benefits of rule by the British king? I can't wait to tell her your great grandmother was an Indian. Could you wear a feather and war paint when you meet her?"

"Whoa, hold up there, Kate, Gran'ma McLaughlin's people were some of the most civili—," he stopped. "Now you're makin' fun of me."

"I am," she said smugly. They had met only minutes before, but they were chatting and joking like lifetime friends. They turned on to the main road and rattled through the village at a brisk trot. Kate anxious to hear about far away, and to her, exotic Florida: Will anxious to learn everything about, to him, exotic Hertfordshire. He tried to take in the different styles of the houses lining the long village street. Some of the cottages seemed to have sprouted from among the towering oak and chestnut that stood behind them. They were entirely clad in blackened wood, except where brick chimney stacks climbed clear of their thatched roofs. Straight lines seemed an unknown concept; the structures sagged and leaned comfortably, having found their ease over the centuries. One house, larger than the rest, featured walls of small red bricks, but they still bulged and sagged where they had taken the load of the tiled roof. Its thick wood window frames followed the established trend away from the right angle and perpendicular, without affecting the way tiny lozenge shaped panes of glass nestled in the intricate internal lead frame.

In complete contrast, a row of neat houses, newly built, stood next to the post office. Their yellow brick was picked out with decorative patterns in red tiles, the roofs were gray slate with bright blue paint glossing the doors and window frames. The building Will found particularly interesting took pride of place in the middle of the village, opposite the lane leading to the church. It was long, with an unruly thatched roof; a brightly painted sign hung from an iron frame outside. "Is that a pub?" he asked hopefully.

"Yes, that's the 'Bull'. Mr. Haines is the landlord."

"What's it like inside?"

Kate tried to look prim. "Oh, ladies don't frequent public houses."

"So you've never been in a pub?"

"Oh yes," she laughed, "I just said *ladies* don't frequent them. Aunt Connie and I often stop for a lemonade if we are out on our bicycles or on a long walk. Mr. Haines keeps a very nice garden at the back."

A heavy farm wagon, painted in bright yellow with intricate pinstriping in red on the iron shod wheels stood outside the pub. The line of the body was a continuous swoop with the lowest point between the axles. Two massive black horses stood between the shafts, munching the contents of their nose bags. Their harness shone as bright as their coats. Two men sat at a bench in front of the pub, tankards on a table in front of them. They wore heavy corduroy trousers, that Will could see were tied just below the knee with twine, and open-neck, collarless shirts.

They both raised their hats as Kate and Will approached. "Mornin', Miss Katie, is this the American gent?" the older one asked. Kate drew Gladstone to a stop.

"Yes, Jack, this is Cousin Will, all the way from the State of Florida."

The two farm workers shook hands with Will, the younger one self consciously wiping his meaty fingers on his shirt first. He was eating an onion in the same way most people would eat an apple. "Welcome to Upper Bardfield, Mr. William. Do you play cricket?" he asked hopefully.

"Give him a chance, Arthur," Kate protested, "he's only just arrived."

"I know, miss, but we're still one man short for Sunday, and if we 'ave to field the vicar again, I reck'n it'll kill 'im." Will looked from one to the other, this was the first time he had heard the local dialect: rich and rolling with lengthened "a" sounds, the other vowels chopped short and "h" discarded completely.

"I think I'd like to try, Kate," Will suggested.

It was the right thing to say; the two men beamed at him. "Well, that's settled then," Arthur sounded pleased. "Mr. 'arris can teach 'un the rules, an' Mr. Rupert can find some spare kit."

Will grinned at the men, "That's a date then."

"He means he'll be there," Kate explained.

"Oh, right thee are then, moulder." Arthur agreed.

"*Moulder?*" Will asked Kate as they trotted on.

"My-old-dear," Kate explained. "People tend to run words together. They like you already."

"Well, they seem friendly fellows."

"Oh, they are, especially as you are now on the cricket team."

"It doesn't seem to be a difficult outfit to get into."

"Will, if you're warm and can hold a bat, you're in. It's the nearest thing to tribal warfare we have left," she added brightly. "Great fun if you don't get your head knocked off. Cricket balls are very hard." They turned off the main road just past the pub. Will was astonished to see a palatial residence standing back from the corner, complete with crowning bell tower glimpsed through the gate in a high brick wall.

"My goodness, Kate, what is that?"

"It used to be the country residence of the Bishops of London, but it's in private hands now. Rather vulgar don't you think?"

Will considered for a moment. "Sure has a gracious plenty o' frills in the buildin' I'd say."

"A gracious plenty," Kate tried the expression for size. "I see where you chaps earn your reputation for politeness."

A short and very steep hill climbed between towering earth banks at this point. Water trickled in a continuous stream in a gully beside the road, the air felt dank and cold. They jumped out of the trap to give Gladstone a chance on the gradient. Will tried not to, but could not avoid seeing how careless his cousin was with her skirts, he saw a flash of shapely calf above her boots. With a final twist the road flopped exhausted among the fields that reached to the brow of the hill. Will expected Kate to stop the pony to let them climb back aboard; instead she hitched up her skirt with one hand and vaulted back into her seat. He was so surprised he had to run to catch up, tumbling back into his seat beside Kate slightly breathless.

She nudged him hard, "That long sea voyage left you out of condition, Will. What was it like, sailing on the sister ship to the *Titanic*?"

"The *Olympic* is a beautiful ship, and fast. I made the whole journey in eleven days."

"My goodness, hardly time to become acquainted with the other passengers. They say it's like the London season compressed into a few days."

"Well, I'm not too familiar with the ways of high society, but it was pretty grand," Will said. "There were balls every night, tea dances in the afternoon, concerts and the most amazin' facilities. They even had a Turkish bath and a gymnasium."

"But what were the other passengers like?" Kate pressed him. "Did you meet anybody famous?"

"I don't know about famous, but there was a lady travelin' without her husband who was very nice to me. She was Lady somethin' or other, but she made me just call her Alice."

"How nice was she, Will?"

"Very nice, Kate," Will said, refusing to be drawn. "But the most excitin' part of the voyage was when we passed through an ice field in the night."

This had the effect he hoped on his cousin. "Goodness, Will! You saw icebergs? Weren't you afraid?"

"Maybe just a little nervous. The captain announced on the loudspeakers during the evenin' that we would be slowin' down in the night because icebergs had been reported. Alice insisted she wanted to see an' I escorted her on deck after midnight. I tell you Kate, it was eerie. The ship just coastin' along in a flat calm sea—"

"Oh my! Just like that night." Kate said.

"Almost, except we had a full moon. For a long while we just watched the stars an' all those strange lights thrown up in the ship's wake by phosphorescence. It was bitter cold, but so beautiful."

"Just you and Alice surrounded by a million stars. Oooh, how romantic, Will."

He shot her a disapproving frown. "Just Alice, me, an' about a thousand other people all checkin' out the lifeboats. Anyway, we were all thinkin' about turnin' in because there was nothin' to be seen, when the engines almost slowed to a dead stop. Man! It went so quiet, I swear everybody was holdin' their breath," he looked at his cousin to make sure his story was having an effect. She stared at him wide eyed. "So quiet we heard a telephone ringin' on the bridge. Then we felt the ship heelin' over as she turned. An' there it was..."

"An iceberg!"

"Big as an island, Kate. You never saw anythin' like it in your life. We nearly strained our necks lookin' for the top of it. It stood, I don't know, maybe four times higher than the ship, this big ghostly shape in the moonlight. We passed close enough we heard the wash of the ship splashin' against the base of it."

Kate shivered in spite of the warm day. "Our cook, Maisie, would call that a 'spooky' experience. You must have thought about all those poor drowned souls on *Titanic*."

"Couldn't but help to, Kate, we were just about where she went down. It made me feel queer to think of her wreck lyin' all those miles below us."

"And then what did you do?" Kate took hold of his arm and looked at him with a big grin.

"Why, I escorted Alice to her suite an' bid her goodnight of course."

She screwed up her face. "The perfect gentleman."

Will smiled. "I hope so."

He could see a set of six chimneys, made in an ornate spiral shape, rising above a line of dense evergreen trees on the bend of the road.

He felt growing excitement; this was his first sight of the family home. The house was far grander than he imagined. Penrose Cottage, he could see, was yet another family joke. To Will it fell somewhere between mansion and ancestral stately home. The house lay fifty yards back from the road, separated from it by a high red brick wall topped with a lighter stone. Two sturdy stone pillars stood wide apart at the entrance; from these, extensions of the wall curved inward to meet the supports for the black iron gates that stood permanently open. This arrangement allowed a carriage to turn in without swinging wide in the road. The pillars reminded Will of two broad shoulders with the curved walls forming two arms reaching in to hold the gate.

Kate hauled Gladstone to a stop in the gateway to give Will a chance to see the house in its entirety. "What do you think of your family 'pile' then, Cousin?

He paused for a moment to arrange his thoughts. "I honestly thought Grandfather's home was a cottage because of the name. I have never seen a picture that showed the whole property, though I should have realized from the stories Ma told."

She patted his hand, "I can see why you might have thought that. Calling it a 'cottage' was Grandfather Hector's way of cocking a snook at old Cheesman who bought that grand house you asked about, then named it the 'Bishop's Palace'. Our house is nicer and has more land, but Grandpa never could abide a show off." The Penrose family home was built with the same warm red brick Will had seen in houses in the village but on a much grander scale. There were two main floors with the roof space obviously used for extra accommodation. A dormer extension thrust out from the pitch of the roof to merge with the shape of the front of the house. This was not a plain flat wall. The big main entrance door, framed in stone and reached by a short flight of steps, stood proud as did the window above, giving the impression it had stepped forward to greet visitors. The paired windows on each floor flanked this extension.

"The main house was built in the last years of George the First's reign, about 1725 we think," Kate said. "It's a good example of the early Georgian style, see how everything is symmetrical, the windows matched in pairs either side of the door." Will pointed out the two-story extension against the right side of the house. "Oh, that's a much later addition, barely a hundred years old. Aunt Connie says it makes the house look like somebody leading a smaller friend home from the pub." Will was to learn that Aunt Connie had a gift for finding the appropriate simile; the extension leaned against the main part of the building as if seeking guidance and comfort. To Will the house appeared imposing but not daunting: as if meant to be grand, but the architect saw the joke before he finished. "Come on, Will, that's enough of the history lesson, lunch will be waiting."

She quickly drove the pony and trap to the side of the house. A boy, who Will guessed to be barely in his teens, ran out of the stables at the rear of the yard behind the extension. He wore a smart outfit of riding breeches with polished brown boots and gaiters; a yellow vest gave him a slightly rakish appearance. Kate introduced him, "Will, this is Peter, our groom. Be a dear and look after Gladstone for me." She threw him the reins.

He touched his cap, "Right you are, Miss Kate...pleased to meet you, Mr. William. They're in the kitchen," he added over his shoulder as he led Gladstone away. Kate took Will's hand to lead him through a side door. She stopped just inside.

"Aunt Connie, what on earth are you doing?" Constance Burnett stood on a chair holding a jug high in front of her.

"Hello children!" she called. "Wait a moment please, I'm teaching Maisie a lost art. Watch and learn Kate." She paused for a second then deftly tipped the jug to send a stream of liquid cascading into a stone bowl placed on the floor in front of the chair.

The young woman with her bent down, picked up the bowl and examined the contents. "It works!" she declared triumphantly. "It's all nice and fluffy."

"And that," announced Connie from her perch, "is what is meant by 'stoning' cream. The only way to put air into your confections." Will stepped forward to help her down. She leaned forward so he had to catch her around the waist; he found himself face to face with his aunt for the first time in five years. "My goodness, William! You grew up even more handsome than I thought." Will took his turn at blushing.

"It's wonderful to see you again Aunt Constance," he said with feeling. Recognition struck him forcefully. His aunt carried a striking resemblance to his sister. The same well defined features: firm jaw, high cheekbones, gray eyes. Her skin hardly betrayed her age though she made no attempt to disguise the tracery of fine lines at the corners of her eyes and mouth. Her hair, worn piled high in the modern style, though now silver, was highlighted by streaks of gold. "You have not changed one piece."

She kissed him and patted his cheek. "Flattery will get you everywhere. I'm seventy-two years old, William, but I still love to hear it. Now," she turned to the girl with her, "this is Maisie, our cook." Will offered his hand; Maisie took it shyly and bobbed a curtsey. She was dark, plump and pretty, her cheeks and forehead dusted with flour; the white making her brown eyes appear even darker.

"I hope you'll enjoy your stay with us, sir. I'll do my best to keep you fed proper."

"I know you will, Maisie, I'm give up to be a boy who likes his food an' I'll try to do your cookin' justice." She bobbed again and giggled at the unfamiliar accent and expression.

"Come on, William, we'll give Maisie her kitchen back. Let's show you the house and your room." Connie took Will's arm and lead him to the main part of the ground floor. With Kate following, she quickly familiarized him with the main features. The rest of the day passed with unpacking, a tour of the outbuildings and several meals: a lunch of cold cuts of meat with pickles, afternoon tea with an assortment of sandwiches and cakes, including scones, small sweet cakes cut in half and spread with preserves and cream. Finally dinner with steak and ale pie, mounds of spring vegetables and a steamed pudding for dessert. He coped manfully with everything Maisie could put before him, but he was grateful for the chance of a stroll in the grounds before bed. The formal gardens had been laid out by a student of the famous "Capability Brown", but he had left the walled kitchen garden intact. This was all that remained from the house that stood on the land before the existing building.

"Burned to the ground during the Civil War," Constance said, shaking her head sadly. "From all accounts it had been a beautiful timbered Elizabethan manor house."

"Did Cromwell attack it because our ancestors were cavaliers?" Will asked, hoping for a tale of family romance.

Constance made a sound between a laugh and a snort of disgust. "That's the official version," she said. "In truth the story is very different but typical of men, and soldiers in particular. We still have correspondence dating from the time. Your 'umpteenth' great grandfather blamed one of the local gentry for the events of that night, and claimed compensation from the Crown. Not that it would have got him very far because they chopped Charley's head off the next year."

"What happened?"

"Oh, the usual sort of thing," sighed Connie. "Our ancestor raised a local militia for the King. They would meet here for 'training'...*that* probably consisted of seeing who could drink the most. They all drank themselves absolutely legless one night, someone let off a musket for a jape in the main hall and set fire to the drapes they used in those days to try to keep the place warm. Nobody noticed and before long they found themselves warmer than they intended. According to the letter, they escaped the fire but were too sozzled to try to put it out."

"Poor old great, great, great...whatever."

"Probably served him right," Connie pointed out unsympathetically. "He was like as not leading the singing and carousing."

They were slowly walking toward the edge of the property when Kate suddenly grabbed Will's arm to stop him. He had not noticed the sharp drop into a grass covered ditch. The level of the fields was six feet lower than the lawns behind the house.

"Oh," he said, stepping back in surprise. "I didn't see that."

"That's the idea, to give an unbroken view over the countryside without a fence. It's to stop the cattle from wandering into the garden to eat the flowers. It's called a 'Haha', you can guess why," Kate prompted.

"Because that's how people go when they see somebody they don't like disappearing over the edge?" he guessed.

"Exactly." Connie agreed. "One day I'll lure Marjorie to the big drop."

"Oh come on, Auntie, you don't mean that." Kate said.

Connie just smiled. "Meeting Marjorie—that's a pleasure yet to come, William," she promised. "And speaking of pleasure, Kate, my dear, it's a beautiful evening, shall we partake of a 'snifter' while watching the sunset?" They settled in metal garden chairs, sipping sherry as the sky glowed through pink and gold.

"I could get used to these long evenings," said Will, pulling his watch from his pocket. "It would be dark at home by now."

"It's our northern position, Will," Kate pointed out. "Did you know we are on the same line of latitude as Halifax, Nova Scotia?"

"No, I did not," he looked at the lush countryside surrounding the house. "Thank the Lord we don't share their weather an' scenery."

Connie raised her glass to the glowing sky. "I'll drink to that."

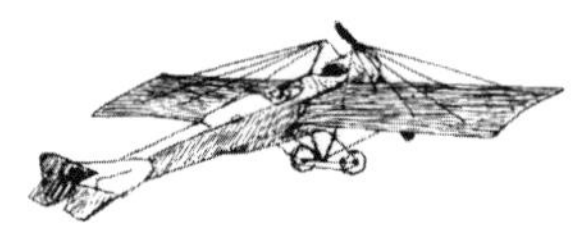

Chapter Ten

WILL HELD THE PISTON IN LINE WITH THE CONNECTING ROD, checked the clamp holding the rings in place, then nodded to Tom. "So what happened then?" he asked not taking his eyes off the cylinder barrel, as Tom Armstrong, his new boss, eased it over the piston. Will had started his new job a few days before.

"Then she dumped all the water ballast over the Inspector's head and they shot back up to five hundred feet," Tom pushed the barrel firmly into place and threaded the hold down bolts into position. He talked as he worked, quickly and precisely. He was describing how Will's Aunt Connie became the family's first aeronaut. Just as her nephews Will and Rupert sought technical advance, Constance pursued social progress. She was a suffragette: committed, fearless, and implacable. Her crusade for the right for women to vote began many years before, and she still campaigned with undiminished vigor. In the early years of the century she pioneered aerial propaganda by dumping leaflets from a balloon sailing over London. She quickly discovered the drawbacks of ballooning, as a posse of policemen followed her progress.

"Of course," Tom paused for a second to select a wrench, "before long there was a stonking great crowd following the balloon. When she eventually came down and the coppers tried to 'feel her collar' as they say, Aunt Connie had the mob on her side."

"I thought the suffragettes aren't popular," said Will.

"There are many people will try to tell you that, it's the line in the papers, but opinion is really very divided." Tom tightened the last nut and stood back to admire their work. "Anyway," he continued, "whether they agreed with her politics or not, the crowds love a balloon flight and they admire a sport. When the police tried to arrest her all hell broke loose."

"Is that when she had the scuffle with the police inspector?" Will asked innocently.

Tom stood up from lighting the spirit stove they used for boiling the teakettle. "She told you it was a 'scuffle'?" he sounded incredulous.

"Yes, she told me the police manhandled her. They put their hands in places where a gentleman should not, and when she protested to the inspector, he slapped her, so she slapped him back with her handbag. That sounds unfortunate," then he added, "but at least it's ladylike."

Tom laughed, "Not very ladylike when there's half a house brick hidden inside." He could see the confusion in Will's face. "She broke the blighter's jaw," Tom said with a satisfied smirk, "and he deserved it. Of course they threw the book at Connie: assaulting a police officer, incitement to riot, they even charged her with littering because her leaflets were scattered over half of London. Funny thing was that's the only charge they made stick, cost her a fine of a fiver. The police evidence was flawed because most of the coppers were wrestling with the crowd and the Inspector was too embarrassed to admit he was bested by a woman in a stand up, knock down fight."

Will sat down heavily on an upturned barrel; the revelations about his aunt's activities had come thick and fast. "Lordy, Tom!" he sighed. "I've been raised to think of England as the home of good manners, decorous behavior an' social order. Now I find there are policemen who abuse their power an' the workin' folk are like to bust out against authority."

Tom handed him his tea and pulled up another barrel. He patted Will's arm, "'Cheer up old son', some French chap once said, 'the mob is the last bastion of democracy.' As for bent coppers, I think that's just something you have to accept as part of becoming wordly wise. The important thing you have to realize is that these ladies are deadly serious, and so are the interests they are up against. Suffragettes have been beaten up, imprisoned, and indecently assaulted. A lady died last year when she threw herself in front of the King's horse at the races. Believe me, they mean *business.*" Tom dipped one of the round cookies in his tea that Will had learned was called a 'digestive' biscuit. "Anyway, where do you stand on women's suffrage?"

Will had quickly learned that his uncle's description of Tom as a man with a mind like a steel trap was well deserved. They took to each other instantly, but Will found he needed to think fast around his new employer. Tom's interests ranged far beyond engineering and flight, but unlike many with strong opinions, Tom was interested in what other people had to say. He waited expectantly for Will's reply.

"Ummm...well..." he stalled for time, "it seems very radical to me. I hadn't given it much thought, to tell the truth. It just isn't done...is it?

Tom rocked back and roared with laughter, "You'll have to do better than that, Will. Your aunt's going to chew you up if you get into an argument with her and her chums."

"Uncle Frank did warn me to brush up on my debatin' skills."

Tom blew across the top of his enamel mug to cool the dark brew of tea he had prepared. "You'd do well to. Where do you stand on universal suffrage in your own country? When your Mr. Walker visited a few years ago he told me about the trouble he had to vote, he said even now he can't vote in the, what are they...primary elections?"

Will felt himself on firmer ground, "I do think that's wrong. Nathan reads an' writes as well as anybody, owns property and pays taxes; he should have full votin' rights."

"So what about Mrs. Walker, why shouldn't she vote? Or your own mother for that matter? They read and write, own property and pay taxes, even if it is by proxy."

"By proxy?

"Perhaps I'm using the wrong word, Will. What I mean is they can own property, and they pay taxes indirectly through their husbands—Mr. Walker and your pa. It just isn't fair in my opinion. The best thing I can say is, 'How would you feel?'"

Tom swigged back the last of his tea and cast the dregs out on the grass in front of the hangar. "Enough putting the world to rights, Will, the Flying Corps needs this motor."

Will took their mugs to wash under the faucet outside the door, "You make me think about things I have never paid much mind to before, Tom."

Tom's teeth appeared in a broad smile from underneath his huge walrus mustache. "Glad to hear it, Will. The education comes free of charge, now let's heave this into the test stand." The object of all their hard work sat gleaming in a wooden cradle. The Royal Aircraft factory had developed their "1a" motor as a replacement for the popular French Renault of seventy horsepower. The British motor was designed to produce ninety but often fell short. Tom Armstrong had been contracted to find out why. His report had been uncompromising.

"The material in the exhaust valves is rubbish," he had told Mervyn O'Gorman, Director of the Royal Aircraft Factory at Farnborough.

"Well, find another supplier and redesign them if you have to, Tom."

O'Gorman was equally straightforward.

"And the overall design is hopeless." Tom had pressed on, "This exhaust-over-inlet valve layout is antiquated; it owes more to steam practice than petrol. I could give you another thirty horsepower if you would let me build it with an overhead valve set up."

"Regrettably we just don't have the time. Just do what you can," O'Gorman instructed. Tom replaced the telephone receiver in its cradle—and did what he could. That had been two weeks before Will's arrival. Tom was delighted with his new assistant; he felt more progress had been made in three days than in the previous three weeks. They worked hard, and fast.

Though Will needed no extra incentive to apply himself he did have one. Once Tom had satisfied himself their modified motor was reliable, they would embark on an intensive program of air testing. Will patted the wing of an airplane standing nearest the door of Tom's hangar. "I still can't believe my luck, gettin' to fly in a machine like this."

Tom grinned, "I can't believe my luck, having the army sell me two virtually brand new machines for fifty quid each. On the other hand it makes me livid they could be so stupid as to reject them. Imagine how poor old Howard Flanders must feel!" Tom could sympathize with the man who had designed and built the Flanders F.4 monoplanes now standing in his hangar. They had passed all tests, performed faultlessly, were reliable, safe and easy to fly. They reached nearly seventy miles per hour and climbed to two thousand feet in only eight minutes on the power of their Renault engines. The machine carried a crew of two, seated one behind the other. Sadly for the designer, Howard Flanders, the army had banned monoplanes following a series of accidents with the single wing layout.

"At least they paid him," Tom said, "but I doubt it was much consolation. Still, their loss is our gain."

Will fixed the lifting straps attached to the motor over the hook dangling from their lifting gantry. "What I do not quite follow," he said, "is Uncle Frank's part in this. I was give to understand he is in the Royal Engineers, not the Flying Corps.

Tom swung on the chain and the motor lifted out of the cradle it stood in for working purposes. "What do we engineers do?" he asked.

"Build things mostly, I guess," Will said.

"What else?"

Will thought for a moment, "Fix things I reckon."

"There you have it. Frank 'fixed' it for me to buy them off the military. The deal was that I removed the Renault engines and sent those back in the lorry that brought the new motor up here. They were going to scrap the airframes otherwise. The best part was bringing the aeroplanes back here. Rupert flew '422 and I took '439. What a flight! Perishing cold being November, but a perfectly clear blue sky."

Tom's eyes misted over at the memory. "They handle beautifully, Will," he added, "and the navigation was so easy. We flew in formation, so close that when we throttled back together we could almost shout across to each other. We tracked northeast from Farnborough, soon picked up the Thames and followed it straight into the City. What a way to go sightseeing! I thought Rupert might try flying through Tower Bridge, but I'm glad he let the idea go. He's a card, your cousin. When we arrived over the docks and picked up the River Lea at Limehouse Reach, he stuck his left arm out to give a hand signal just as if he was riding his motorbike. For the rest of the flight we just followed the Lea. Well under two hours start to finish." Tom stood for a moment with a faraway look on his face, reliving the flight that stood out as one of the highlights of his career.

Will tried to imagine how it must have been for Tom, looking down on the city for the first time. A practical consideration crossed his mind, "Weren't you scared there'd be no place to land if your motor quit?"

"No, that's the amazing thing, the city is just so *green*," Tom explained, "there are loads of places to put down if you have to...you just don't realize it from ground level. Some of the parks would make an ideal emergency landing ground, though you'd cop it from the park keeper I'll bet. Mind you, if this war that some people are so ruddy keen on breaks out, they'll need them as aerodromes to cope with the Zeppelins, you mark my words."

Will looked up sharply from bolting the motor into its test rig. Tom had brought up the subject that cast the only cloud on the horizon of what, for Will, promised to be a beautiful summer of aviation. "Why would anybody in their right mind want a war?" Will asked. "Sounds crazy to me."

Tom shook his head sadly, "You tell me, old chum, I had a belly full of it in South Africa. All these armchair warriors would be a damn sight less keen if they'd felt the wind from a Mauser bullet tickling their whiskers, I'll be bound." He touched the side of his face under his mustache. The white settlers of Dutch descent known as "Boers" had fought the British for control of South Africa at the turn of the century. A Boer marksman had more than tickled Tom. His bullet, fired at extreme range, had penetrated the young Lieutenant Armstrong's face just above his upper lip. Tom had staggered from the ground spitting blood, teeth and, to his comrades horror, the spent bullet. His bushy whiskers hid the scar, but when he smiled his cheerful face twisted oddly. He made light of it, claiming he could smile around corners.

"My two uncles and Mr. Walker fought in the War Between the States, an' not one of them claims there was a shred of glory in it. I think I should ship 'em all over here to go on a speakin' tour of Europe."

"I can see they made a big impression on you," Tom spoke with clear admiration. "But at least they were fighting for what they saw as a moral cause, the North fighting against slavery."

"Well...nothin's quite that simple. My Uncle Alex fought for the Confederacy, though he was an abolitionist, just like General Robert E. Lee."

Tom put down his wrench. "I say! Are you pulling my leg? The great General Lee an abolitionist?"

"Oh yeah, as soon as his father died an' he inherited the family estates he freed his slaves. He fought for Virginia an' states' rights," Will continued carefully working down the bolts.

"Well I never!" Tom shook his head in amazement. "So what about your Uncle Alex, did he free his slaves?"

Will glanced up, "He never had any. Alex is a Creek Indian, he fought against the Federal Government because of the broken treaties, but he was against slavery on moral grounds, as were many others who fought for the Confederates. There were a pile of folk with a different axe to grind who were set hard against slavery for a different reason, though you might not call it a moral stand."

The conversation had captured Tom's attention; he paused in the act of bolting the huge wooden four-bladed propeller to the business end of the motor. He peered through the V shape created by the two uppermost blades, with a hand on each one like a man parting tall grass. "Pray tell," he urged Will.

"Economics. Slave ownin' was a rich man's business. A poor farmer tryin' to compete had to work like a slave to earn any kind of livin'. The price of cotton an' all kinds of other stuff stayed low on the backs of black slaves an' dirt poor farmers."

Tom grinned at him. "Well, I do declare," he said in a fair imitation of Will's accent.

"Where does a boy of your tender years learn all this?" Tom asked, reverting back to his native King's English.

Will concentrated on snugging down the last bolt, then looked up,

"College introduced me to people with a lot of ideas an' a lot to say about them. Then we had some lively discussions after dinner at home. My pa enjoys bringin' people together with different viewpoints. There's Walter Julien who fancies himself 'Old South', Uncle Alex from the Creek Nation, Nathan who's a Yankee by birth—"

"Nathan's from the North?" Tom interrupted.

"Oh yes, Nathan was born in Boston. To give Walter his due, he's known Nathan so long, he has more of a problem with that, than the color of his skin." Will leaned back from the motor, then took a firm hold on one bank of cylinders and tried to shake the unit in its new mountings. They stood on steps to mount the motor in the test rig, high enough for the propeller to clear the ground. The steps wobbled alarmingly.

"Okay then, Will," said Tom, suddenly serious, "and please answer honestly, what is the American view on the European situation?" This conversation had convinced Tom there was more to Will than he had first thought.

Will leaned on the motor and sucked his teeth. "Dangerous," he said finally. "I think I can say that for everybody—an' foolish. To us it seems there's a real danger of war for no other reason than some powerful people want one. Lawd's sake! At least there was an argument in our war. To us France an' Germany look like two frightened men tauntin' each other with loaded guns. Sooner or later there's goin' to be an accident. An' there won't be much sympathy for Britain if she gets dragged in. Most folk back home don't hold with Empire buildin'." He paused, very aware of Tom's scarred face, "An' I hope I don't give offense, but I have to say, the South African war lost you a lot of friends."

Tom smiled his twisted smile, "No offense whatsoever, old boy, I quite agree. I have been accused of being unpatriotic for not wanting us to have a go at the Kaiser, but it is precisely because I *am* a patriot that I say it would be an unmitigated, bloody disaster if we were drawn into a land war in Europe. Let the Froggies and the Hun have a pop at each other if they want. We stayed out of the last one they had back in the '70s when France lost Alsace and Lorraine, why get involved now?" He finished bolting the propeller to the flange forming the end of the crankshaft and sighed heavily, "But, I admit, that's not a very noble point of view. If a war does break out we will bear part of the blame."

Will looked at him carefully, "I don't follow, Tom, I can't see the British doin' anythin' to start a war."

Tom flipped his wrench over in his hand and pointed it at Will, "That, my friend, is the point; we are not doing anything to stop it either. I bet you must have seen a brave man step between two coves squaring up for a fight, and push them apart. A chap with your savvy knows the two arguing are probably thoroughly relieved when that happens. That is what we have to do. Your Uncle Frank agrees with me in principle but not in the method."

"Really?" Will sounded surprised. "But Uncle is a soldier, I just kind of assumed he would be ready for a war."

Tom shook his head. "He won't mind me speaking for him on this. It's precisely because he is a soldier that he understands the mortal dangers of a modern war. He thinks we must make it plain to the Kaiser that if he attacks France we will support the French, and that way put a stop to this foolishness before it starts."

"Well, I can see that point of view."

"I can see its attraction but I disagree, I think we should say to France we *won't* support them if they find themselves in a war with Germany."

Will scratched his head, "I don't follow."

"Go back to my hypothetical scrappers outside the pub at chucking out time," Tom warmed to his theme. "They've been needling each other all night..."

"Ye-es," Will sounded doubtful.

"It's human nature. What is more likely to spark a fight: somebody saying they *will* do something, or somebody saying definitely they will *not* do something?"

"I think I take your meanin', Tom, but don't you think you're takin' this analogy too far?"

Tom gave a whoop of delight, tossed his wrench in the air and caught it deftly, "*Analogy!?* I've winkled you out, Will Turner. You're no simple country boy, you're an intellectual in disguise."

Will shrugged then laughed, "I know what you're sayin', Tom, I ain't as stupid as I look, but if I was I'd still be tryin' to ride my bike on the proper side of the road, 'stead of the left."

"And you try to tell me you know nothing about the voting rights issue," Tom laughed. "Put your arguments in order, Will, whatever they are, because you will be tested soon. Come on, enough gassing, let's see how well we've done." They wheeled the test rig to a hard standing clear of the hangar doors where they bolted it to clamps set in cement for the purpose. They ran the motor at various power settings. It moaned and howled in protest at its captive state, the big propeller flailing the air in the attempt to break free. They were so involved in their work they lost track of time.

At last Tom looked at his watch, "Time we were packing it in for the day, Will, your admirer, Maisie, will be cross with me if I keep you late and our supper gets cold." As he spoke he was looking past Will to the edge of the woods bordering the field where the track from the village emerged. "Hold up, who's this?" Tom asked.

Will followed his pointing finger, "It's Cousin Kate. Why's she in such a all-fired hurry?" They could now clearly see the cyclist furiously pumping toward them was Kate Penrose. Instead of cruising to a ladylike stop she hopped off the bike still rolling fast, in spite of her long skirts, and let it roll under its own momentum so Will had to catch it. "What's wrong, Kate?"

"Nothing," she called back over her shoulder. She ran to the steel staircase climbing up the outside of the hanger. This led to a flat wooden platform built on the apex of the roof. She took the steps two at a time and disappeared behind the wooden safety wall surrounding the platform. Her flushed face suddenly reappeared. "Where's the key, Tom?"

Tom fished a set of keys from the pocket of his overalls and tossed them up to her. "Just be careful where you point that thing, Kate Penrose," he called as she disappeared again. Will stared up at the platform then back to Tom. "After you, Will," he invited, motioning toward the stairs.

The two men clattered up the steps. Will was surprised to see Kate holding what appeared to be a pistol with a wildly exaggerated bore in one hand, while she rummaged inside a small cupboard fixed to the wall with the other. "Green," she muttered, "where's the bloody green?" Tom grinned hugely as Will's eyebrows shot up in shocked surprise to hear his cousin's profanity. "Aha! Here we are," she announced. Will stepped back in alarm as Kate broke the odd shaped weapon in the way a shotgun is loaded, then slipped a fat cartridge into the breech before snapping it shut. He reached forward to push the muzzle safely away. "Stop fussing, Will, I know what I'm doing." Kate insisted.

"You may know what you're doin'," he said dubiously. "But I don't know what you're doin' it with. Are you plannin' on a buffalo hunt with that thing?"

Kate was delighted—at an advantage for once in an area that men always seemed to want to claim as their own. "Honestly, Will! Have you never seen a Very pistol before?"

"No, ma'am, but I see why it's a 'Very' pistol, there's no chance anybody might could mistake it for an *almost* pistol. What is the caliber of that thing?" He asked, eyeing the weapon suspiciously.

"Oh Cousin!" she tried to sound exasperated. "It's named after the inventor; it's only a signal pistol to shoot flares."

Tom tapped his forehead, "See what I told you, you learn something new all the time around here." He turned to Kate, "So why the hurry, didn't you get away quickly?"

Kate was scanning the sky to the south and west anxiously and did not turn when she spoke, "I was out of the house in seconds, even then I didn't think I'd make it." She paused for effect, trying to sound nonchalant: "He's in the Bristol." For the second time she was pleased with the reaction she gained. Tom dived across to the cupboard and retrieved a pair of binoculars. He joined her sweeping the sky.

Will raised his hand to shield his eyes against the sun, "Can somebody tell me what I'm looking for?" he asked plaintively.

"I'm sorry, Will," Tom apologized. "Kate has an ongoing competition with Rupert. He telephones the house as he leaves Farnborough, and she races over on her bike to try to beat him here. We fire the flare to show she's won.

"What do you mean *try?*" Kate demanded. "He's never even come close. I usually have the tea made by the time he lands."

"You mean Rupert is flyin' here?" Will sounded incredulous, as if he thought they were joking.

Kate took the glasses from Tom and trained them at a point on the far horizon. "Of course he is," she said, surprised that Will should have considered any other way for her brother to travel home for the weekend. "When he's in the B.E.2 I have plenty of time," she continued, "but this Bristol is supposed to be at least thirty miles an hour faster. Good for over a hundred."

"Is this the machine Rupert wrote me about in February, when they were testing at Larkhill?" Will asked hopefully.

"The very same," Tom replied, "Frank Barnwell's design. He's aiming at the sporting market, I hear Lord Carberry has made an offer for it, he's hoping to enter for the London-Paris-London race in a few weeks. He'll have to wrestle it away from the Flying Corps though, they're already calling it the Scout. If Rupert had his way the Army would place an order for a hundred tomorrow." Tom was about to continue when Kate shouted.

"There he is!"

Will followed her pointing finger, "Where? I don't see him." She handed him the binoculars. He trained them on the horizon and moved the adjustment ring to bring the distant line of hills into sharp focus. For a moment he saw nothing, then a tiny movement drew his eye. He gasped. The powerful glasses revealed the sleek shape of a small biplane as it darted behind a line of trees. A few seconds later it reappeared, banking sharply in the other direction, much nearer now but still beyond hearing range.

"Come on, Will, don't hog the bins," Kate impatiently pulled the binoculars away from him. Now Will could hear the approaching airplane, sounding unlike any gasoline motor he had ever heard before. This was a high pitched, insistent, musical hum. The sound a harmonica player makes when the same note is held with a long breath.

"He won't let you see him, Kate," Tom said. "He's deliberately staying out of sight! Quick, get ready with the flare, he's coming up the valley." Tom gauged the position and track of the Bristol by the note of its engine. An instant later the biplane burst into view.

"Ohmigosh!" Will shouted. The Bristol appeared in front of them as suddenly as a genie released by magic. Rupert had held the machine down in the valley running below the airfield, using the trees on its slopes for concealment. He timed his zoom perfectly to show off the perfect plan view of the Bristol from below as he rocketed into sight in a steep climb above the wood. He leveled off, passed over their heads and used his speed to gain height. The three people in their roof top perch simultaneously craned backward to watch him, then spun around to keep him in view. Kate, taken by surprise, suddenly remembered her signal. She raised the flare pistol and held it at arm's length to shoot a fizzing green fireball arcing into the sky.

They watched Rupert roll into a slow climbing turn. Will could see the individual blades of the propeller flashing as it pulled the machine higher. The nose dropped suddenly. Kate clutched Will's arm: "He's going to...no he's not...yes...he is!" Will held his breath again. For a moment they could even see the top of the pilot's head, the dive toward them was so steep, but the nose quickly came up, and up, to the point Will thought Rupert could never cling to his space in the sky, but he kept going.

"Well, I'll be blowed—," Tom watched the Bristol pause lazily on its back for a breathless moment before plunging down to complete a perfect circle in the sky. "He's looped it!"

Will stood with his mouth open. In his wildest, and fondest, dreams

he never saw anything so complete, so natural, so wonderful. The biplane came ripping past them, exultant with the speed of the dive. "*Thrrrrriiiip, thrrrrriiiiiip,*" he heard the thrilling note of a rotary engine on the cut out button for the first time as Rupert finally curved into his approach to land, settling the machine like thistledown, running only a few yards to a complete stop as they rushed down the stairs to meet him.

Rupert Penrose had no time for the famous British reserve where his family was concerned. He sprang out of the cockpit to meet Will in his rush. They joined in a dance of greeting involving bear hugs, hand shaking and some jumping up and down.

"Hey! Do I get a kiss, Brother?" Kate joined the huddle and Rupert obliged with a smacking kiss on her cheek. Tom wondered if they might all dance in a circle like children in the game of "ring a ring o' roses."

"Can I take it you two get along then?" Tom asked.

Rupert grinned mischievously, "That's the famous ironic English humor, Will. You'll get used to it." He waved expansively at the Bristol, "Well, what do you think?"

Kate butted in, "I think that was the most shameless piece of showing off in the history of aviation, and all wasted because Sophie isn't here."

"But you are, little Sis, and you were *definitely* impressed," he planted another kiss to leave an oily mark on her other cheek. His face was black with burnt lubricant where it had not been protected by his goggles.

"Might have been," she conceded. "So what took you so long anyway?"

Rupert looked into the cockpit at the watch fixed to the instrument panel. "Hardly an hour; you must have pedaled like fun to beat me here. I bet the tires on your bike are still warm.

"Might be," she admitted, then burst out laughing as her brother mimicked her pose: hands on hips, lips pursed. Rupert seemed charged with energy even after his long flight. Not much taller than his sister he was powerfully but neatly built and rapid in his movements, as if his body matched his quick mind. His eyes, set wide apart in his broad face, were framed by the white patches where his goggles protected his face, contrasting with the blackness of his chin.

While brother and sister teased each other, Tom and Will examined the Bristol biplane. Will declared it the neatest piece of work he had ever seen. He admired the dominant feature of Frank Barnwell's little masterpiece, the perfectly circular cowling shrouding the eighty horsepower Gnome engine. This blended smoothly into the lines of the fuselage. The single cockpit located the pilot above the trailing edge of the lower wing while the forward stagger of the upper wing allowed him a good view upwards. The two sets of wings were of equal span. The machine stood on large disc wheels enhancing its tidy looks and setting it at a jaunty nose high angle when on the ground, making it appear eager for the sky. The unpainted Irish linen covering the wooden frame of the machine gave a pleasing natural finish, the color of fine old parchment.

Tom beckoned Will to the nose of the machine, "There you are." He moved the propeller a fraction. "See how the cylinders move with the propeller?"

"That is the darndest thing," said Will with admiration in his voice. "Whoever would have thought of buildin' a rotary motor where the crank stood still and everything else revolves around it?"

"A man driven to desperate solutions by overheating problems," replied Tom with feeling. He had met the designer, Laurent Seguin, in France four years previously. By then Seguin's Gnome rotary engine had been in production for two years, since 1908, and already it powered most of the successful designs in use. Light, powerful, and comparatively reliable it was the answer to the pioneer aviator's prayers.

"Seguin admitted to me the idea seemed quite batty," Tom said. "It seemed like madness to fix firmly to the mounting plate those parts of a motor that normally revolve, then allow the parts normally stationary to revolve at a furious rate with the propeller. He told me the idea had come to him over dinner in his favorite restaurant. He finished the original sketch with the first bottle of wine. The owner gave him a fresh tablecloth with the brandy so the general layout drawings could be completed."

"That sounds like a very French way of doing things," Will said.

"Maybe we should try getting plastered and see if we have any bright ideas," Tom agreed.

"Come on, chaps," Rupert urged, motioning them to start manhandling the little machine toward the hangar. "There'll be plenty of time to play with her tomorrow. I'm starving. Let's get her locked up." Will started to protest when Kate took hold of one of the grab handles fitted just forward of the horizontal stabilizer, to allow the tail to be lifted for ground handling.

She pushed him aside with a neat sideways thrust of her hips. "Oi! Find your own bit of aeroplane, Cousin, this is mine."

Will saw Rupert and Tom smiling broadly, "Just tryin' to be a gentleman, boys," he explained.

"Completely wasted on our Kate, Will," said Rupert.

Will feigned exasperation, "You're as bad as Vicky."

Kate laughed, "Runs in the family, Will. Now put your backs into it men."

"Yes, ma'am," they chorused obediently. The Bristol, with the tail raised, ran easily. They quickly stowed it in the front of the hangar. Rupert wiped the worst of the grime from his face then retrieved the bicycle he kept in the workshop for his ground transportation and joined his sister and cousin outside.

"You chaps go on," said Tom. "I'll catch you up in a few minutes, when I've locked up."

"Doubt it, Tom," Kate threw the challenge over her shoulder as she pedaled off, "we'll be home before you get that old nail of a motorbike started."

Tom looked at Rupert and Will helplessly, "Doesn't she ever give over?"

Rupert watched his departing sister for a moment, "I don't think so, she seems to have something to prove. Come on, Will, let's see if we can keep up." They pedaled across the grass, following Kate down the path that led into the woods bordering Tom's field. The track tipped steeply downhill to emerge in a farmyard. They swooped between the old thatched barns, waving to the farmer's wife who greeted them from her open kitchen window. Still rolling fast they shot through the wide open gates in time to see Kate splash through the ford that carried the road through the river running along the valley at that point. She took her feet from the pedals and spread her legs wide in front of her to avoid the spray from the few inches of water trickling over the roadway. They heard her whoop with delight.

"Have you something against the footbridge, Kate?" Rupert shouted after her.

"That's for sissies!" Kate shouted back, standing on the pedals to begin her assault on the hill rising steeply from the ford. Will and Rupert crossed the ford in a less exuberant style, pedaling slowly. Two small boys sailed a stick and paper boat in the shallow water of the ford.

"Afternoon, General," the older boy called, his hand stiffly at his cap.

"Afternoon, Admiral," Rupert replied, making his hand quiver as he returned a military salute. The boys beamed with pleasure.

"You surely do cut a dash in that uniform, Rupert," Will said. Instead of the army's modern single breasted field service jacket, worn with collar and tie and the ubiquitous leather Sam Brown belt with its diagonal cross strap running across the chest and over the shoulder, Rupert wore a double breasted tunic with an old fashioned high collar. The belt was still worn, but Will's eyes went straight to the discreet wings badge worn on the left breast.

"Oh this old thing!" Rupert adopted a high pitched voice, "Just something I had run up for the ball." He dropped the camp intonation. "Wouldn't you just know it, the first time we saw the uniform some wag christened it the 'maternity smock' and it's stuck. I'm not complaining though, because it does help keep the drafts out when we're in the air." Kate had disappeared up the hill, completely overhung by the trees on either side. The two young men dismounted by unspoken mutual consent to push their machines, and save their breath for talking. "Now come on, Will," Rupert urged, "give me the griff on this chap who's after your hide."

Will retold the Roscoe story as they eased their way to the top of the hill. He spared nothing of importance in his brief chronicle of the events leading up to the shooting incident, and after.

"So you see how I feel responsible for Roscoe?" Will concluded.

"Frankly old boy, no," Rupert said. "At worst he's a dangerous maniac, at best a complete idiot. Come on, what do you think he is, mad or bad?"

"I sincerely hope he was just intoxicated," Will said with feeling. "I never had any idea he was goin' to break bad. Booze can do funny things to people."

"You can say that again," Rupert agreed. "But you say his own brother thinks he has some kind of mental illness."

"That he does, an' I respect that. I have to say Jeff Vandersand is a very agreeable an' honest man. Nobody knows Roscoe better, an' Jeff feels his brother is so eat up with jealousy he just isn't thinkin' straight." Will paused as they remounted their bikes, "But I have to thank Roscoe for one thing."

"What's that?"

"I wouldn't be here if it wasn't for him. I don't think Pa an' me would have fallen out so bad if it wasn't for Roscoe an' all the fuss he caused."

"It's one heck of a price to pay though," Rupert said, "cut out of the will and told never to darken the family door again."

Will looked sideways at his cousin for a moment. "Who told you that?"

"Well, nobody really, I just assumed things were pretty bad at home by the way you accepted Tom's offer like a shot."

Will laughed, "I'm pleased to say things are not *that* bad. It's true I'm not to get a penny of family money while I insist on wastin' my time on flyin' machines, as Pa calls it, that's why I need the job. But he an' I have just agreed to differ, so to speak. We're gettin' along fine now. In fact he came rushin' down to Daytona with the letter offerin' me the position. Secretly, I think he's quite proud I'm workin' for the Flyin' Corps in a manner, but he still thinks I'll come to my senses an' go back to designin' railroad locomotives."

"Will you?"

"Only if I can build one with wings."

"Now that would be a sight to see!" Rupert laughed as he remounted his bike. "But what about this Roscoe character, is there any news about him? Is there any danger he might pop out of the bushes here and start blazing away with his six-gun again?" Up to speed again on his bike, Rupert relaxed and coasted along with his hands off the handlebars.

"I doubt it. His family set the Pinkerton Detective Agency lookin' for him an' they tracked him to New Orleans where he caught a train for California. Anyway, even if he does, you can shoot back bein' a soldier."

Rupert's laugh sent a bird scrambling into the air from the hedgerow. He patted his pockets. "Damn! I don't seem to be carrying my trusty cannon."

"Heck, Rupert, what sort of army sends its soldiers out without a gun?" Will asked.

Rupert eased alongside Will's bike and put a hand on his shoulder. "One that keeps its dangerous weaponry safely under lock and key at the weekend. I'm only a lieutenant, Will, you don't think they would trust me with live ammunition, do you?"

"Probably wise, Coz," Will agreed with a solemn nod, not sure if his cousin was serious.

"You have to admit," Rupert said, "this Roscoe business is thrilling stuff: six-guns, native trackers, jealous lovers. It could come straight from the pages of *Boy's Own* magazine."

"Can't say I ever thought of it that way," Will paused for a moment. "Jealous lovers! In the *Boy's Own?*"

Rupert's laugh pealed out over the fields again. "Okay, perhaps the 'Big' *Boy's Own* magazine. Now let's crack on and catch up with Kate; we'll never hear the last of it if she beats us by one of those 'country miles' you chaps are so fond of." They bent over their handlebars and sped in pursuit. The road dipped and danced through wheatfields showing the first signs of transition from dusty green to the gold of high summer. It leaped over the railway then coasted down between high hedges to the village. Try as they might the two young men only gained a few yards on Kate. "Oh, to hell with it!" Rupert gasped. "Youth has the advantage over experience this time."

"Youth and the better machine," Will panted. "Whose idea was it to buy her a lady's racin' cycle?"

"Mine," admitted Rupert between gasps, "for her last birthday. Serves me right, come on, let's walk up the hill." As they crested the hill leading from the village to the house Tom caught up on his Rudge "Multi" motorcycle. The machine Kate described so disparagingly was one of the most sophisticated motorcycles available. Tom climbed the hill easily by moving a lever providing an infinite variety of shift ratios. Rupert called to him as he chugged alongside, "Go on, Tom, a quick burst and you'll beat her."

"No fear! She'll run me off the road sooner than let me past." He chuffed through the gates of the house leading Will and Rupert.

Kate had already put her bike in the stable and waited impatiently for them to arrive. "Come on you lot! Where have you been?" she chided.

"Chokin' on your dust, Kate, you're too quick for us old men," Will conceded.

Rupert leaned close. "Crawler," he muttered, "flattery will get you everywhere." Will's Uncle Frank—Rupert and Kate's father—had already arrived by car from London. He brought Rupert's fiancé, Sophie Pellew, and his closest friend, Archie Carstairs, with him. These new arrivals were easy to find. Will, Rupert and Tom followed the sound of the guns; the double boom of a sporting shotgun leading them around to the rear of the house.

"Ah, there you are my dears," Aunt Connie greeted them, "just in time to see Archie bag a clay pigeon for supper." Archie carefully placed the gun on the table.

Frank made the introductions, "Will, meet Miss Sophie Pellew." Will took her hand and made a slight formal bow that contrasted nicely with his grubby work clothes.

"Charmed, ma'am," he looked up to catch her smile. Rupert had said little about Sophie beyond his description that she was an "absolute dear, a perfect peach." Will realized Rupert had been holding out on him. From his description Will had expected another conventionally pretty English rose. He had been misled. Sophie was a flaming redhead. Her hair really was her crowning glory. It had that rare, deep copper sheen that in the afternoon light glowed with golden streaks. She had the perfect pale complexion that went with it, but her nose and cheeks blossomed with a sprinkling of freckles that showed she spent much of her time out doors. When Will straightened up he realized she was also tall, taller than Rupert, and possessed of a figure novelists liked to describe as willowy or, as Nathan might put it, strung like whipchord. Sophie was thin, but her face somehow contrived to be broad, yet with a fine, strong jaw and high cheekbones that highlighted her gray eyes. There was nothing conventional about Sophie Pellew, and she was not English.

"My pleasure, Mr. Turner," her laughing eyes belied her formal reply.

"Like myself I guess you don't hail from these parts, Miss Pellew."

"Och, away with you, Mr. Turner, you've given away mah secret. I'm from Stirling, gateway to the Highlands."

"And Archibald Carstairs," Frank continued, "Rupert's long-time partner in crime and our cricket team's star bowler."

Will shook hands with Archie. For the first time in England he found himself literally looking up to somebody. Archie Carstairs stood a gangling six foot three inches tall. Rupert had described him to Will as a foreigner's idea of an English aristocrat: tall, sandy haired with a slightly receding chin and a face that seemed to wear a permanently good-natured but vague expression.

"Now don't run away with the idea that Archie is putting on the style of an aristocratic twit, Will," Connie said with mischief bright in her face. "He really is every bit as stupid as he looks." Will guessed Archie was a particular favorite of his Aunt.

"Delighted to meet you, old boy," Archie said, pumping Will's hand vigorously. Archie's firm grip undermined the vague air he tried to cultivate. "We're just popping off a few shots with the guns my pa gave me. Care to try a shot?"

"You bet."

Archie slipped two cartridges into the open breech of one of the pair of shotguns lying on the table, snapped the gun closed and handed it to Will, taking care to keep it pointing over the fields beside the house. "Have you ever banged away at a clay?"

"I've never even seen one," Will admitted.

"It's a baked clay disc put up by a spring loaded trap; marvelous practice outside the shootin' season," Archie said.

"I think we have somethin' similar at home, but I've never tried it."

"The great thing is the speed can be changed to suit the experience of the shooter," Archie said. "Peter, the groom, is doing the honors." He stepped away from them and bellowed across the lawn to where the young groom tended the apparatus. "Put it on the lowest setting, Peter—and stop cowering man!" He turned back to Will. "Ready?" Will raised the gun to his shoulder and nodded. "PULL!"

The two flat discs blurred across the lawn a few feet above the grass. They disappeared in puffs of dust and flying fragments with the double roar of the gun. Will peered into the breech, the ejected cartridges smoked on the gravel behind him. "Wowee! Look at this, a hammerless ejectin' action, I've never seen a gun as nice as this. Have you ever seen such a beautiful action?" He looked up, surprised to see everybody regarding him strangely. "Did I do somethin' wrong?"

"No," Archie said, "far from it. Tell me, do you do much shooting?"

"Well no," said Will, "contrary to what most folk here think—thanks to old Buffalo Bill and his Wild West show—we don't all go 'round with a Colt revolver. Fact is, I've never even fired one."

Archie clapped him on the back as everybody else smiled, "Old boy, when I said to Peter the 'lowest setting', I meant him to lob you a nice easy one. He thought I meant the lowest trajectory...those shots were damn near impossible."

"Beginners luck," Will shrugged modestly.

"We'll see...load up again." The sequence was repeated again, but this time the clays flew high and fast. Will shot them out of the sky without hesitation. He blushed as the small group of spectators, now joined by Maisie, burst into spontaneous applause.

"Come on," said Archie, "what's the secret?"

"I don't know," Will confessed, "I guess I just point the gun at where the target's goin' to be when the shot gets there. I reckon anybody can do it with a gun like this." He balanced the finely tooled weapon in his hands.

"You're too modest, Will," Frank said. "That is a Purdey and it is the best, but a good gun doesn't make a good shooter. What do you use at home? I don't recall seeing a gun at John's house."

Will placed the Purdey carefully back with its twin, "We all like to hunt quail and the wild pigs we call 'piney woods rooters', but Pa an' I borrow one of Uncle Alex's old percussion guns."

"Are you serious?" Rupert demanded. "An old muzzleloader?"

"Oh surely," Will replied. "Alex won't let Henry or me loose with a breech loader, says it's just goin' to make us waste powder. An' when we go after those old wild hogs he says it offends the spirits if we have the unfair advantage of a repeatin' arm."

"So you hunt wild boar with a muzzleloading shotgun?" Archie sounded incredulous.

"Oh no, with an old muzzleloadin' Enfield rifle, but it's fitted with a percussion lock."

"But what do you do if you miss?" Sophie asked. "Aren't wild boar dangerous?"

"Well that's Alex's point ma'am, he won't let us hunt the young or the females, we're only allowed the boar. The way he explains it, it's a fair fight with a single shot rifle. If we miss, we're in trouble, so we try not to miss."

"And if you do?" she asked.

"We are all fast tree climbers," he grinned.

"Sorry to break up the party ladies and gentlemen," said Maisie, not meaning it for a moment, "but supper's ready." The shooting party trooped indoors. There was no formal meal that evening, the village cricket club was holding a meeting in advance of the big match. Will felt honored to be part of such an intimate tradition, though he worried about his part in it. All five men set out, with Buster the family dog trotting ahead. As they walked the Englishmen tried their best to explain the intricacies of the national game: cricket.

Frank summed up, concerned that Will might be confused by terms such as "silly mid on" and "fielding in the slips". "It's easier than we make it sound Will," he said reassuringly. "When you have the bat, try to whack the ball hard without letting anybody catch it, or missing and letting it hit your stumps. When our side is fielding and their batsman hits it, you try to catch it on the fly; if it bounces before you catch it, try to knock over his stumps while the two batsmen are running."

The instant they walked into the bar of the Bull public house, Will knew he could define the word "convivial" in his own mind forevermore. The windows and door stood wide open to the warm evening air, the sound of laughter and loud conversation drifted into the street. As he stepped over the threshold his eyes were dazzled by the glint of light on polished brass and glass. The long mahogany bar gleamed with the result of polish and hours of labor.

They were greeted by a cheer and the universal welcoming words from the landlord, "What'll it be, gentlemen?" By the time they left, Will had a good understanding of the different types of ale available in a good pub—he had sampled them all. He discovered "Bitter" was a poor description for the fresh flavor of the most popular beer. He agreed that "Mild" had a softer touch and "Stout" really was a robust drink.

He was also introduced to the strangely democratic world of the cricket team. He had assumed his uncle was team captain because of his rank and assumed social standing. This was not the case. Frank Penrose was the secretary, in charge of the modest finances. Fred Harris, their gardener, held the honor of the captain's position because he was the best man for the job. Will learned that the order in which the batsmen took their turn was all important. As new man in the team he inevitably took the lowly position of "tail ender", the last man in to bat. Will was not concerned. Taking part in this very British tradition was enough for him.

Their little party set off for the walk home in high spirits. Rupert and Archie linking their arms with Will's to keep his feet moving in a straight line. "I am very impressed with the pub as an instu...instat..." Will paused, surprised to find his powers of speech impaired.

"Institution?" suggested Archie.

"That's it!" Will answered, relieved. "There's no standing on rank in the pub."

"Absolutely, old bean," Archie agreed. "In a well-run house everybody is expected to behave properly, and to leave any airs and graces outside. If you cannot abide by those rules, don't come in—simple as that."

"Another wonderful thing about a good pub, is the way I find I have agreed to do something I never would have, if I had the same discussion anywhere else." Rupert added.

"On a number nine bus for instance?" Archie queried.

"Precisely."

Frank and Tom had walked on ahead but Rupert's father was close enough to overhear their conversation. "What have you done?" Frank asked ominously.

"Nothing serious, Pa," Rupert replied lightly, "just agreed to lay on a little demonstration tomorrow."

Chapter Eleven

TOM ARMSTRONG STARED AT HIS FRIEND, "RUPERT, YOU MUST BE bloody mad. If you must kill yourself, do it somewhere else, I don't want to watch."

"I'm *not* going to kill myself, and I have to do it now," Rupert shot back. "I'll be cashiered if I try it at Farnborough."

Tom looked desperately unhappy; Will just as anxious; Archie more confused than usual. They had started early without breakfast. Before the rest of the house awoke Rupert had thrown back the curtains at dawn and seen perfect weather conditions: a clear sky with no wind. Now they stood in the soft, early morning light outside Tom's hangar while Rupert explained the experiment he meant to undertake.

"Perhaps if somebody can explain what you chaps are going on about," Archie suggested mildly, "I might at least understand why you are so steamed up."

Rupert paused for a moment then turned to Archie, "Have you read sensational stories in the newspapers about 'death spirals' and 'plucky birdmen spinning to their doom'?"

"Most certainly have," Archie confirmed. "I put two and two together and guessed it might be something to do with this 'tourbillon' dive I heard yon designer laddie talking about when I picked you up from Farnborough a few months back."

"You did?" Rupert looked at his friend with obvious surprise. "How did you work that out?"

"Well, it's obvious isn't it?" Archie looked at Will and Tom for support, "*Tourbillonner* is the French verb meaning 'to swirl around'."

"Spot on, old chum," Rupert said. "Don't let onto the regiment that you can think for yourself; they'll drum you out of the cavalry."

Archie smiled benignly, "No fear, I take my brain out when I put the uniform on. So, can I take it you want to go up and chuck yourself into a swirling death spiral?"

Rupert shuffled his feet and, it appeared to Will, lost some of his confidence under his friend's steady gaze. When he replied he sounded defensive, "Yes...more or less."

"Why?" Archie demanded.

"That's a perfectly good question," Tom chimed in.

"Because up 'til now nobody is sure what causes it, and nobody has shown how to get out of it, and most bloody important—it's killing good people needlessly." Rupert sounded downright belligerent to Will.

Tom proved just as stubborn, "But is it that much of a problem? How often have you seen a fully-developed *tourbillon* dive?"

"Once, and Wilf Parke pulled out of it—more by luck than judgment—but that's not the point."

"What is then?" Tom asked, exasperated.

"It's not so much the fully-developed dive I'm concerned with; it's all those occasions when airplanes suddenly drop a wing and smash into the ground from a few feet up, usually just after takeoff or in the final turn before landing. I think what we are seeing then is the beginning of the same phenomenon; if they were higher you would see the fully developed spiral."

"Then they smash into the ground?" An edge of sarcasm sharpened Archie's tone. Clearly he shared Will's and Tom's concern.

"If I can prove the cause, I can demonstrate the solution," Rupert's confidence bordered on enthusiasm. "I know the cause, and I'm pretty sure of the cure."

"Oh really!" Tom sounded astonished. "Don't you think that's just a little arrogant?"

"Look, I'm not trying this for entertainment, this is not some harebrained stunt. If there's a simple solution to this problem then it's my duty to find it."

"Oh well, if it's *duty* that's fine." Tom's voice smoked with barely suppressed anger. Rupert said nothing. There was a heavy silence for a moment, but when Tom spoke again he used a softer tone, "I'm sorry. That was uncalled for, but why does it have to be you?"

"Yes, why can't this Parke chap try it?" asked Archie, "He discovered whatever it is, 'finders keepers' and all."

"Because he died in the Handley Page monoplane crash last year." Rupert said quietly.

"Oh, I say!" Archie grimaced.

Will, still feeling very much the junior member of the group, spoke to ease the tension. He felt as unhappy as Tom with the plan his cousin proposed. "Could you show us what you mean, in a diagram?"

Rupert stood hunched forward, feet apart, like a rugby player preparing to charge into a scrum, then his shoulders relaxed and he smiled, "Oh, all right. You chaps are like a load of ruddy old women."

He turned to Archie and Will. "A few years ago, when I first became involved with aviation, I helped at the Military Trials on Salisbury Plain. They had me working as a timekeeper, photographer, that sort of thing—general 'dogsbody' to tell the truth. A naval chap, Wilf Parke, took that peculiar Avro biplane with the enclosed cabin and the sixty-horse Green engine for the three-hour qualifier flight. Our man, Le Breton, flew with him as observer. I waited for them to come back as we were going for breakfast together. Just after nine they came in sight from Upavon direction, everything coming along swimmingly. Wilf had her nicely set up for a landing in front of the sheds, starts into his final turn and *whoosh!* Next thing he's nose down and spinning like a top. I don't mind telling you I closed my eyes. When there was no crash I opened them to see the Avro happily beetling around at fifty feet to make a perfect landing."

"That must have put the wind up them," Archie observed.

"I'll say! It put the wind up everybody," Rupert agreed heartily. "Some people were furious—said he was stunting. Anybody who saw Wilf's face when he climbed out could see that was nonsense; he was white as the proverbial sheet. We adjourned with Geoffrey de Havilland and Mr. Short from the aircraft factory to the mess for a conference. I must say, Wilf Parke was a cool one, he remembered exactly what he had done and in what order. He believed the machine stalled when he pulled the nose up too far in the turn. The Avro rolled left as the nose pitched down and he gave it full left rudder, to catch up with the slip. At the same time he hauled back on the stick. Both controls just made matters worse. It was only when he found himself being thrown against the side of the cockpit that he had the clue to reverse the controls. He remembers ruddering against the spin and the next instant she'd stopped spinning and he pulled neatly out of the dive...easy as that!"

"That's all very well," argued Tom, "but what if that was a fluke—a one-off?"

"I don't think so," Rupert replied, his voice intense, "Geoffrey de Havilland had almost the same accident in the BS.1 last year and then

Harry Hawker did the same thing at Brooklands a few days ago in the Sopwith Scout."

"Yes! That's my point," Tom said despairingly. "They both damn well crashed!"

"I know. But Geoffrey says if he had only had a bigger rudder and more height he would have pulled out. You have to admit he does know his stuff." Geoffrey de Havilland was already considered the best designer at Farnborough and Rupert knew Tom held him in the highest esteem.

"Okay I admit that, but what does *he* think about this?"

"I don't know," Rupert confessed. "I haven't mentioned it." Tom looked sour, but Rupert pressed on, "And Harry is certain he was coming out of his spiral. Given another ten feet he would have missed that tree." He grabbed a screwdriver from the toolbox and began drawing in the dust. "Look," Rupert insisted, "this is what happens. Aeroplane in turn, wing on outside of turn traveling fast, inside wing moving slower—okay?" He looked up, seeking confirmation that his friends understood; they all nodded. "Now, pilot brings elevator up because nose starts to drop, slower inside wing stalls—drag on that wing goes off the scale—pulls wing back and down and airplane starts to spin around its axis." He looked up again to see Tom and Will nodding, "Voila! Autorotation, just like a sycamore seed. Simple cure—full opposite rudder to counter the turning moment, nose down to dive out of the stall. Goes against every instinct I know, but it makes perfect sense."

Will broke the long silence, "Yeah. That'll do it."

Tom looked at him in surprise, "You sound deuced confident! I agree it certainly makes sense, but I'm loath to see Rupert try it."

Will shrugged, "So am I. Isn't there some other way?" He looked hopefully at his cousin.

"Such as letting some other poor sap try it?" Rupert suggested.

"Yes!" His three friends chorused emphatically.

"Oh, come on chaps! That just isn't sporting is it? I've the best machine and more experience in stunting than just about anybody else. If they asked for volunteers I'd be duty bound, anyway. Would it make you feel better if I told you I'm scared out of my socks, too?"

"Much better," Tom told him with a resigned sigh. "Come on then, if you insist, let's make sure the Bristol is in tip-top condition."

Tom and Will set about checking every part of the little single-seater, while Rupert dressed in his flying gear. Tom insisted he wore a leather-covered, cork crash helmet. With his dark goggles and leather armor,

Rupert, the modern knight, dressed for battle with his own personal dragon. They wheeled the machine away from the hangar and Will swung the propeller to start the motor when Rupert called, "Contact!" It caught instantly; its ripping snarl sent startled birds scrambling into the air as a cloud of blue smoke hurried away in the blast of air from the propeller.

The rotary engine had one disadvantage: it lacked a conventional throttle. The revolutions were controlled by the careful adjustment of two levers: one lever regulated the air supply, the other metered the amount of fuel flowing through the simple carburetor.

A third control, a cut-out button, or "joystick", mounted on the pilot's control column, prevented the electrical current from flowing to the spark plugs, to stop the motor completely. This was also known as the "blip switch", because it could be used to cut the power in and out. Too much reliance on this device could be dangerous, however, as unburned fuel accumulated as the motor spun down. When the pilot released the switch to bring the still spinning motor to life, a disastrous fire frequently resulted.

A rotary engine responded well to an expert, and Rupert had the required touch. He sat for a minute warming the engine and carefully adjusting the fuel supply. He moved each flying control to its full extent, swiveling his head to ensure that every control surface moved as it should. Satisfied, he smiled reassuringly at his friends and waved the wheel chocks away. They watched the little machine start forward on its takeoff run. It swayed up on its main wheels, the tail wriggling from side-to-side as the rudder came alive in the slipstream. The Bristol bounced once and leaped into the air.

"'The Unknown Knight, who, clad in gleamin' armor, sits on a magnificent charger...,'" Will quoted quietly.

"'His cap is on, his visor down...on every tongue is the question, who can it be?'" Archie finished the familiar lines from Walter Scott for him.

"They'll know soon enough if he lands on their heads." Tom said, his voice grim.

"Typical Sapper," Archie sighed, "no bloody romance in your soul. Rupert really is like St. George don't y' know. He's off to battle with the unknown. It really is an affair of honor in a funny way."

"Well, it certainly takes guts, I'll grant him that," said Tom, "and if he has the pluck to do it, we owe it to him to have the nerve to look at what happens." They watched anxiously as the Bristol tilted at the blue morning sky, slowly circling as it gained height.

In the cockpit Rupert felt happier than the friends he had left behind on the field. The machine responded eagerly to his lightest touch on the controls. Ailerons on both upper and lower wings gave him excellent roll control, a delight compared to the cumbersome wing-warping system on many machines still in use. Generous elevators on the horizontal stabilizer and a powerful rudder combined to give him a feeling of security. He knew they were trusty weapons in his duel with the unknown aerodynamic forces he meant to confront, and defeat. The motor sang sweetly, his fingers making the delicate adjustments to compensate for the thinning air as he climbed higher. He knew height would be his greatest ally. Rupert's military training had taught him boldness alone did not guarantee success. A sound tactician always tried to stack the odds in his favor, and he intended to stack life-preserving space between himself and the unyielding earth below.

He checked his height: 5000 feet showed on the altimeter. He leaned over the left side of the cockpit, from experience he knew the slipstream battered at his face if he moved his head to the right, something to do with the rotation of the engine he suspected. The earth spreading below him seemed somehow remote, which only added to the magic of his flight. The gently trembling lower wing that Rupert could almost touch with an outstretched hand etched a line across the landscape. Climbing in a wide spiral, his view expanded each time he passed a given point. London surfaced from a night blanket of mist nearly thirty miles away. He held his course for a moment, trying to locate the dome of St. Paul's, but the distance was too great to pick out individual buildings. On the northern side of the circle distant Cambridge floated in a sea of vivid green fields, the newly risen sun glancing off the needle-like spires of the colleges. He smiled to himself. He loved this country, and this morning he surveyed it as the lord of his own very lofty manor.

A mixture of elation and anxiety had gnawed at him until the moment his wheels left the ground. He wondered when the anxiety would turn to fear and fully expected to be able to identify the point. Instead he was curious to find the anxiety subsiding, to be replaced by a new emotion as his machine clawed its way into the sky. He wondered how he could feel so calm while his nerves were stretched taut. Rupert felt detached from his life, floating in a fine roaring silence, able to observe the smallest detail: a change in the soft morning light, the tiniest vibration of the taut wires between his wings. He even thought he could smell the summer growing in the earth beneath him. He had chosen eight thousand feet as the best height for his experiment. Not so high that he could not be observed from the ground, but high enough that each and every combination of control inputs could be tried if the theory he had developed with Harry Hawker proved incorrect and the Bristol continued spinning down toward the unyielding earth. The needle of the altimeter crept past the mark. He eased the fuel supply forward, and the motor lost its even pitch, starting to choke on the rich mixture. Cutting power using the blip switch was a risk he was not prepared to take at this altitude; there could be no quick dash to the ground from this height if a fire broke out inside the cowling. The propeller started to slow; he could see the individual blades slashing the early sunlight. He allowed the nose to drop, rolled into a gliding turn to check the space below, then held the Bristol level. As the speed fell away he steadily increased back pressure on the stick to hold the nose on the reference point he had chosen on the horizon, a lake showing as a flat plate of silver in a puddle of mist.

Holding his breath, Rupert maintained a light pressure on the rudder to hold the machine straight. The machine shuddered, and he pulled the stick back hard. His airplane bucked suddenly, and the nose dropped—perfectly straight ahead. He pushed the stick forward to regain flying speed and eased back the fuel-control lever to restore life to the struggling motor. Rupert grunted with satisfaction: a normal stall with a height loss of less than two hundred feet and the Bristol flew perfectly trimmed. Now to try to duplicate the condition that had sent so many people spinning down.

Quickly climbing back to his chosen height, Rupert again choked the motor back to a rough idle. He deliberately pulled the nose high and felt the resulting tremor through his hands and feet telling him the airflow over the wings was breaking up and chattering against the movable control surfaces. The Bristol hung suspended in space. Very deliberately he pushed on full right rudder—

"Bloody hell fi—," the words were wrenched out by the violence of centrifugal force flinging Rupert against the side of the cockpit. What began as an awareness of his place in the scheme of the heavens and earth soon transformed into a growing sense of panic amid a whirling madness as the Bristol fell out of his hands and flicked into a spin.

Luckily the instinctive part of Lieutenant Rupert Penrose—born of training, study and practice—did not tumble with his machine. His eyes stayed focused straight ahead where a solitary farm revolved steadily and the surrounding fields dissolved in a blur. His feet and hands remembered the plan even though his brain hovered a hundred feet above. He slammed in full left rudder and pushed the stick forward. For less than a second the revolving farm playfully spun harder then steadied abruptly. The spin stopped as suddenly as it started. His head banged back across the cockpit. The seat belt cut into him, and he became painfully aware the propeller was acting as an airbrake, with the Bristol standing vertically nose down on it. He eased the stick back, "Whoooa," he breathed, soothing his machine as if it were a startled horse. The force of gravity pushed him hard down in his seat making his limbs heavy.

"Oh crikey!" he muttered inadequately. Rupert had strapped a notepad to his knee before taking off. He was almost surprised to find his pencil still in its clip on the side of the cockpit. He carefully noted his impressions—*rate of rotation increased for half a turn before spin stopped. Full left rudder and full down elevator together, recovered in vertical dive. Height lost: 1200 ft!!!!*—the last words he underlined for good measure. He urged the Bristol back to 8000 feet. All Rupert's anxiety had blown away in that self-induced tornado, any lingering fear replaced by curiosity.

His second attempt was smoother and more controlled. He knew what to expect this time and deliberately separated the control movements—full right rudder then stick back to neutral. "Oh yes, Josephine!" he yelled as the airplane came under control without the disconcerting jerk and in a less dramatic nose down attitude. He noted—*no increase in rotation rate, height loss: 1000 ft.* —and stowed his pencil with a flourish only he could see. Now he wanted to try every permutation of this new maneuver. He tried to tell himself this was his duty as an RFC officer, but he laughed out loud because he knew the real reason: he loved stunting.

His friends on the ground watched at first with trepidation. Tom clutched Will's arm then grinned sheepishly as the tiny gyrating speck leveled out, almost before the sun flashing off the wings told them Rupert had started his sequence. Through the binoculars Tom could see the left-hand spin develop reluctantly when Rupert attempted it, jerking through one full turn then winding into a wide spiral dive. The resulting wail of the wind in the wires only reached them after they could already see the machine restored to level flight.

They saw Rupert experiment with a spin off a right turn. Will and Tom exchanged puzzled glances when the same maneuver attempted to the left resulted in the wings flopping back level and a simple stall.

They applauded as the succession of wild gyrations ended and the airplane turned back to the field.

"Oh look at that! What a ripping show! The man's a genius!" Archie's praise for his friend was generous and heartfelt.

Tom watched the Bristol swooping back down to land, as light and precise as ever in Rupert's capable hands. He turned to Archie, "Don't tell him that, we'll never get his head through the hangar doors." Tom's voice came out balanced between laughter and hysteria from pure relief. In part for his friend but also because he had seen something sinister and unknown, a monster responsible for the death of friends, dragged into the daylight and shown up for what it was.

The little biplane rolled to a stop in front of them. "Forget your tourbillon dives and death spirals—it's a *spin,*" Rupert announced, grinning hugely, the second he stopped the motor. His friends lifted him from the cockpit, slapping him on the back. "I reckon it's the same drill as for a mountain or lake...I discovered it, so I have to name it. So there!" He was laughing as he stripped off his gloves and helmet. "No need for my spare underwear lads, it's not as bad as it looks. Now come on, get that frying pan out, and let's see breakfast started. I could eat a horse and chase the jockey!"

Over a breakfast skillfully prepared by Archie using the spirit stove and a blowtorch, Rupert told them about the behavior of his machine. "I'll warn you chaps now, and mark this well, our spin is a potentially nasty beast. What it is *not* is a spiral dive." This had been the biggest surprise for him and he expected their reaction.

"It surely looked like a twisting dive from down here," Will said.

"I know, but in a spiral dive the speed builds up. In the fully-developed spin my speed never showed above forty, and there was none of that whistling of the wind in the wires. To tell the truth it was quite unnerving: just a *swooshing* sound and a gentle creaking from the wings. I don't even think she was under any particular strain; I'll bet we'll find the trim just fine."

"We certainly heard a rare old wail when you came out of the left-hand spin," Tom pointed out. "What happened there?"

Rupert carefully dipped a finger in his tea to extract a floating leaf that he thoughtfully flicked out through the hangar door. "Blowed if I know," he admitted. "She really had to be forced to break to the left, possibly something to do with turning against the torque of that rotary. The spin felt horribly jerky, and before I knew what was going on we flicked out of the spin and into a real spiral dive. The speed built up like a greased anvil going over a cliff. There's a very real danger there. If somebody failed to distinguish between the two, they could pull the wings off by snatching back on the stick with a head of speed building up."

Tom looked at Will, "You really do look as if you are hanging on every word, old son."

"Dammit, I am," Will said with feeling. "I wish I had been up there with you, Cousin."

Rupert looked at Tom, "There you are, matey, madness must run in the family." He smiled at Will, "Don't fret, you'll have your chance. I don't think for a moment that every machine will handle as the Bristol has. Somebody will have to test every new type as it comes into service."

Archie leaned over them at their makeshift table, an upturned wooden crate. "Toast, anyone?"

Tom took a slice, "I don't think I ever saw toast prepared with a blow-torch, Archie."

"Bet you never saw it made as quick either," Archie said.

Will took a slice and spread on a slab of butter, "I'm surprised to see you so handy with a fryin' pan, Archie, I thought you aristocrats had servants to do everythin'."

Archie shrugged, "In the mess and at the stately family 'pile', yes; out in the field, junior officers are expected to muck in. The Lancers are fighting men, not decoration like the Household cavalry. My servant is the best man in the troop with the new Lewis machine gun; I'd rather he kept that clean. If he can keep the enemy off my aristocratic arse—I'll cook his breakfast."

"That's very democratic," Will said.

Archie feigned a shudder, "Oh, goodness, I hope not, can't be having with all that modern stuff. You'll be telling me it's the Twentieth Century next."

Rupert poured more tea, "While we're on the subject of the safety of your aristocratic sit-upon, if Maisie finds you've been foraging around her kitchen, helping yourself to eggs and bacon, she'll give you a good spanking."

Archie rolled his eyes and groaned theatrically, "Oh I *wish!* Do you think if I make enough noise she might catch me one morning?"

Tom shook his head in mock disgust, "Typical aristocracy: perverts to a man."

"Keeps 'em away from the livestock, Tom," Rupert pointed out mildly, then laughed as he saw the shock in Will's face. "Sorry, Coz, rough soldier talk, too much male company coarsens a chap, I'm afraid. We're only joking."

"*You* may be, chum," Archie said wistfully, "but I'm in love. Do you know how many times I've proposed to young Maisie?"

Rupert paused and pretended to count on his fingers, "'Bout fifty at the last count." He glanced at Will and winked, "Archie's serious but Maisie just giggles and dishes him up another helping of pud'."

"Y'all ain't pullin' my leg are you?" Will asked. "Wouldn't there be trouble with your family if you married, how is it you say—below stairs?"

"Mother would have a blue fit," Archie confirmed, "but dear old Pa would be over the moon. He says it's the only way to keep the aristocracy going, bring in new blood, otherwise our chins will disappear completely. He's already done his bit, I've two half brothers in addition to my official brother and sister."

"Good grief!" Will could think of no other response to this casual admission of the "goings on" in Archie's family. "What does your ma think about that?"

"Oh, she just pretends not to notice. He's a randy old goat, and she never enjoyed the old 'rumpy-pumpy' anyway."

"What you have to know about Archie," Rupert joined in, "is that he is the last of the great romantics, falls in love all the time, but never with the type of girl his mother would approve of."

Archie sighed, "The problem is, none of them take me seriously. They think I'm just after a little bit of 'naughty', then I'll go off and marry some horsey type chosen by my family."

"Can you blame them?" asked Tom reasonably.

"No, I can't," agreed Archie, "but believe me, when Archibald marries it will be for love."

"There's an easy solution to your problem in that case, Archie," Rupert told him brightly, "just let yourself fall in love with the lovely Lucy P.A. Face it my friend, that shouldn't be difficult, she's a peach."

Archie pulled a face, "I've resisted this far, the problem is that she comes as a package with her ma. I'm hoping young Will might draw the fire and let me sneak away."

"Don't you think somebody should explain what I'm bein' set up for?" Will protested.

Rupert looked from Tom to Archie, "What say, chaps, should we tell him, or save it for a surprise?"

Tom took pity on him, "Will, you must have heard tell of the formidable Marjorie Pritt-Allison."

"I have...many times. I'm kinda lookin' forward to meetin' her."

Tom grinned, "Tonight at dinner you will, and the lovely Lucy, her only daughter. Trust me, she is lovely. Her mother Marjorie, however, is the most..." he paused to find a suitable description, "spectacular, unabashed, determined social climber in the history of the county. She has raised snobbery to an art form. She has opinions on everything and has the subtlety of a cavalry charge when expressing them. I am at one and the same time appalled and lost in admiration for the woman. In short, she's absolutely ruddy infuriating."

Will struggled to take this all in, "I can't play like I understand how you could find anythin' admirable in this person. She sounds dreadful!"

Tom looked to Rupert for support. "You know what I mean, Rupert."

"Indeed I do. Tell Will about her amazing mercy drive."

"Here's a typical piece of pure Marjorie," Tom began. "Last winter we had a terrible snowstorm. One of her maids chose that night to go down with appendicitis. The doctor refused to come out so Marjorie bundled the maid up, loaded her in their big touring car and set off for the hospital with their butler along to shovel snow. The old man, Major P.A. as we call him, was conveniently stuck in town so Marjorie drove. God above only knows how she forced that big Daimler through the drifts, but she made it somehow. I had Lucy on the blower begging me to follow them because she was convinced her ma would turn the whole plot over in the ditch. I had the sidecar on the bike for the winter, so like a damn fool I set off after them. I followed the tracks and arrived at the hospital to find Ethel, the maid, already in the operating theatre and Marjorie gone. By the time I caught up with her she had motored back into Ware town itself, rousted the doc out of bed and was giving him the rollicking of all time. Poor chap, he was practically cowering on the floor. I managed to calm her down and drag her home, but she reported him to the Medical Council. It caused quite a shemozzle, I can tell you."

"How was Ethel?" asked Will.

"Oh fine...they operated just in time. It may seem strange to us, but Marjorie's staff positively adore the woman."

"I can see how that would be," said Will.

Rupert nodded in agreement, "Tonight is your chance to cross swords with our local legend."

"Cross swords?" asked Will. "Is this likely to be a difficult affair?"

"Not for us," Archie sounded almost gleeful, "but you'll probably think Marjorie is actually baiting you. She's not. What Marjorie thinks of as showing polite interest, sounds horribly like a cross-examination at the Old Bailey when you are on the receiving end. Don't worry, we'll back you up."

Rupert jumped to his feet, "Come on, chaps! Enough gassing. We've about five hours to hang that new motor on Mr. Flanders flying machine and test it if we are going to put up a decent flying show."

"What flying show?" his friends demanded.

Rupert regarded them fondly, "Goodness, you should try forming a music hall act around that. You'd be the ugliest chorus line in the West End." They glared at him. "Okay, I should have mentioned the real reason for the early start. Last night, whilst in my cups—"

"If you'd stuck to cups we'd have been all right, it was the pint pots that did the damage," Archie pointed out.

"Whilst in my pint pots," Rupert admitted, "I agreed to put on just a teensy-weensy show for the village. Two machines will make for a much better display. I've borrowed an idea from the Hendon boys, a wizard wheeze the crowds love and best of all, it's safe!"

"I'll drink to that," Tom said, draining his mug. "Let's get stuck in."

Under his expert direction they installed the new motor in less than three hours. Archie surprised Will with his practical skills. Will admitted to himself that he had fallen for the act so cleverly deployed by this gangling young man. He wondered how quickly Archie's languid demeanor might disappear in an emergency. Archie displayed an alertness, a quickness in his actions that contrasted sharply with his affected, drawling speech.

After a short break for the inevitable cup of tea, they started the motor and Tom took off for the first test flight. He stayed close to the field for ten minutes, buzzing industriously in tight circuits, then with a decisive dip of the wings in salute he disappeared over the trees. Twenty minutes later he reappeared, gliding down to a neat, three point landing. Tom quickly checked over the motor then turned to Rupert, "First class. Smooth as silk and half as much power again as the Renault motor. Mind you, I'd like to see another half an hour on her before your show. Take her up and see what you think."

"Okay, Tom," Rupert agreed. "Come on, Will, grab a warm coat, it's still chilly up there."

Will needed no urging. "I'll be with you directly," he called over his shoulder as he sprinted to the car to collect his heavy Norfolk jacket. By the time he returned to the airplane, breathlessly struggling to force his arms down the sleeves, the engine was ticking over again. Will knew his way up to his seat from practice. Instead of occupying two separate cockpits, the crew sat in what appeared to be an elongated bathtub. This had the advantage that they could easily communicate. Will settled himself in the front seat.

"Whose idea was it to fit the extra set of controls in the front cockpit?" Rupert leaned forward as he spoke.

"It was Tom's idea," Will said. "This way one of us can fly while the other records the engine performance."

Rupert advanced the throttle lever; the idling motor stirred, blasting air at them. Tom and Archie hung onto the starboard wingtip forcing the big monoplane to pirouette awkwardly into wind. Rupert pressed the throttle lever all the way forward against the stop. Tom's handiwork became immediately apparent to him, the modified RAF motor responded with a lusty, barrel-chested roar. The big four-bladed propeller thrashed at the air, scrabbling for grip, hustling the monoplane into a stiff-legged sprint. Even Rupert found himself surprised by the improved feel of their machine; after a short takeoff run it seemed to levitate rather than drag itself into the air.

Will looked over the side to see the ground falling away. He felt Rupert's quick, sure movements on the controls as they climbed steadily into a sky of the most perfect porcelain blue. The early mists had evaporated giving them unlimited visibility over a landscape that had inspired artists for centuries. It was wasted on Will. All his attention was directed to the business of managing the big machine. They had installed engine-monitoring instruments in the front cockpit: engine revolutions, oil pressure and temperature and an ingenious device to record the temperature of one of the eight separate cylinder heads. Will scribbled in a notebook as they soared over the countryside.

"Okay, Will...she's all yours," Rupert shouted above the combined roar of the slipstream and motor. "Pass me the notebook."

Will chose a point on the horizon to use as a reference while he gained a feel for the Flanders monoplane. A windmill, a pristine white mark in the distance, served him well. He glanced to his left; the wing was dropping so he quickly moved the stick to his right to pick it up. He looked forward to see the nose too low, the engine note rising as the big airplane gained speed. He eased back the stick. Now the windmill sat off to the right. He pushed the rudder bar to bring the nose around. The right wing dropped.

"Whoa! Ride 'im cowboy," Rupert yelled gleefully in his ear.

In a few seconds Will had them on an even keel as his hands and feet quickly coordinated the information his senses provided. Every part of him tuned to the task: eyes, ears, and especially the seat of his pants.

"This is fantastic," he yelled over his shoulder. "This beauty actually responds to the controls. The Wright I learned on back at Daytona just kinda flopped around the sky."

They roared back across the field and headed for Penrose Cottage. With the motor throttled back they swooped down on the house. Tiny foreshortened figures emerged from the kitchen door, waving furiously as they soared back into the sky with a surge of power.

All too soon for Will they headed back to the field. "Okay, Will, it's your landing," Rupert announced.

"You're sure about that?" Will called back.

"You'll arrive at any crash first, Will, so I don't expect you'll stuff it up," Rupert said confidently.

Will set his goggles firmly, tightened his seat belt and eased the throttle back. He let the nose tilt down into a glide and rolled into a gentle turn, carefully lining up to land into the slight breeze indicated by smoke drifting from a small bonfire lit by Tom for that purpose. He framed the field as a picture between the struts of the cabane, the skeletal structure that fixed the supporting wires for the wings just in front of his cockpit. He used this as a reference, knowing that if the picture moved up in the frame he was coming in short; if it moved down he was landing long. Satisfied that he would touch down just inside the field boundary, he pulled the motor back to idle speed. Will forced himself to relax on the controls, riding the slight turbulence in the air. He judged his height perfectly. Inches above the grass he leveled out, holding the Flanders just off the ground by steadily pulling back on the stick as the speed fell away. The wings stopped supporting the machine as the narrow tires kissed the tips of the grass. The wheels rumbled beneath them while the scraping of the metal skid under the tail told them they had landed in the perfect "three point" attitude. The Flanders trundled to a gentle stop with the propeller ticking over.

"Bravo! A perfect landing. Now come on, Will," Rupert's voice sounded unnaturally loud without the roar of the motor and wind. "I know you like it, but you'll have to give Tom his airplane back sooner or later." Will laughed out loud and advanced the throttle enough to start them rolling back to the hangar where Tom and Archie stood waiting, both feigning nonchalance. Will cut the switch to stop the motor. He sat listening to the silence, a vacant smile fixed to his face.

"Well, what do you think?" Tom demanded. "Does she sound okay to you?" Will seemed not to hear him.

"Give him a moment, Tom, I think he's still up there," Rupert said.

"Meanwhile pass me a spanner so I can unwind that silly grin."

Will shook himself, "Sorry, fellas, what was that you were sayin'?"

"I said, how does the motor sound?"

Will unbuckled his safety belt and stood up, "Beautiful, most wonderful sound I ever heard, like a symphony—no better'n that—like a choir of angels...no even—"

"Steady on, old boy!" Tom interjected, "you're 'waxing lyrical'. That'll look damn funny in my report to O'Gorman at Farnborough—'develops full revs, sounds like the choir eternal.'"

Rupert looped an arm around Tom's shoulder, "Perfect, he'll put another hundred quid on your fee. And now here's your chance to earn a few bob more." He pointed to the track that wound across the fields from the direction of the main road that ran through the nearby village of Highfield End. A procession of people on foot, on bicycles and what appeared to be a whole family perched on the back of an enormous chestnut horse were moving toward them. "I promised a show in the pub last night, word seems to have got around. Here's our audience," he turned and pointed toward his sister and fiancé cycling toward them from the other side of the field, "and here's the rest of our cast."

At a time when an airplane flying overhead brought people running into the street, Rupert gave the people of the parishes surrounding Tom Armstrong's flying field a show that could not have been bettered at Hendon or Brooklands, those famous centers for the pioneer aviators. He drew gasps of fear and admiration with his loops and spins in the Bristol, then landed to help Tom and Will take center stage.

As the Bristol rolled to a stop at the end of its display, Kate and Sophie rushed from the hangar dressed in distinctly over-the-top outfits—white dresses meant to symbolize purity and innocence. "Who will save us from wicked Sir Jasper?" They entreated the crowd. Nobody offered. Instead they cheered as Sir Jasper, otherwise known as Archie Carstairs, appeared in Uncle Frank's Vauxhall, dressed in black cloak, top hat and a large black mustache glued to his top lip.

The audience was raised on the English tradition of the Christmas pantomime. "He's behind you!" They warned the girls enthusiastically. The plot was simple. Protesting feebly, Kate and Sophie were abducted in the motorcar then paraded slowly up and down in front of the spectators, who played their part by booing and hissing the wicked Sir Jasper. This gave time for Rupert to sprint over to start the Flanders monoplane where Will and Tom sat ready for takeoff.

"Take us up, Will," Tom shouted over the rising engine note. "I've got my arms full of these blasted flour bags." Will tightened his safety belt, checked the controls for full and free movement, unconsciously set his jaw in a determined line, then pushed the throttle forward. "Don't let her jump off the ground too early," Tom shouted. "Hold the nose down until we have a safe margin of speed." That proved easier said than done. Will's previous experience in the Wright biplane had been one of coaxing a machine into the air with a steady backward pull on the stick to raise the nose. The Flanders was different. It surged forward, the wheels jolted and bounced for a few seconds, then Will felt the glorious sensation of being cradled by the swift rush of air. He found himself pushing firmly forward on the stick to keep the wings at the right angle of attack to the surging flow of air around them. He snatched a quick glance below to see they were clearing the boundary hedge by a hundred feet.

"See what I mean?" Tom yelled over the blustering slipstream. "She wants to climb like a partridge with this beauty of a motor hung on the nose." Will briefly took his hand off the throttle lever to give Tom a quick thumbs-up sign. He was concentrating hard on the turn he had to make. The audience on the ground watched the Flanders monoplane describe a wide circle that brought it neatly into line with the rope fence keeping the crowd from spilling onto the field.

Kate shielded her eyes against the sun, "Okay, Archie—now!" The Vauxhall stopped its haphazard circling and started to run down the field parallel with the audience. Her timing was perfect. Will pulled the throttle back, easing into a glide above the car. Tom took aim. "Left a bit...hold it...steady...steady." The flour bags hurtled down, to burst with satisfying clouds of dust in the path of the car. Sir Jasper dragged the brakes on and jumped down with his hands held high in surrender. Rupert appeared with a pitchfork to take his prisoner and the crowd roared with appreciation. It was a juvenile pantomime that worked because of the added excitement of the airplanes.

Archie worked the line collecting change in a bucket, "Come on, ladies and gentlemen, contributions to the poor fund or I'll come and carry off your wives and daughters." He twirled his fake mustache villainously.

"'E can come carry me off anytime 'e loikes!" A big, jolly-faced lady announced to everybody's delight.

"'Ere's Half a Crown if you will, Sir Jasper," her husband offered generously. Archie grinned and kissed the lady on the cheek to more cheers and laughter. Kate and Sophie had been equally successful with their fundraising and they counted seven pounds, four shillings and sixpence in a heap of silver and copper coins on a wooden trestle table in front of the hangar. They watched Will bring the monoplane in for his second landing. Not as smooth as the first, the machine rebounding into the air as he touched down too fast, but Will quickly settled safely on the ground. The rope fence was removed and the people were allowed to come close to the airplanes. They stood at a respectful distance, however, as Rupert explained the various parts of the machines.

The crowds reluctantly dispersed to their homes as the afternoon shadows lengthened. The vicar of the nearby church joyfully accepted the collection. There was no shortage of people needing help in his parish—agricultural wages were pitifully low in most cases, with little chance to save money against old age and sickness. Archie made his day by wrapping the change in an enormous, white Five Pound note. "God bless you my son!" the old man exclaimed. "Would there were more like you and your friends."

"Don't mention it, sir," Archie sounded embarrassed. "We'll do even better next time." The priest shook his hand and bumbled off. Archie walked back in to the hangar where the two machines were being stowed for the night. "This gives me an idea, people."

"What's that, Sir Jasper?" Will asked.

"An aerial travelling show. We could tour the country selling rides for five bob a go. You chaps could bring in the crowds with acts of aerial 'derring do', and Kate and I could collect the money."

"My ma even has a name ready for an outfit like that," Will offered.

"Oh yes, what's that?"

"A Flying Circus...that's what she called my first flight." He thought better of telling his friends Charley Turner's full description of his first effort.

"Perfect!" Archie said. "Sir Jasper's Flying Circus. I tell you, chaps, if army life carries on like this much longer, I'll resign my commission and set off for a life of adventure on the road. If I have to ponce about on one more parade I think I'll go mad. How about it?"

Will laughed, "Count me in, I'm goin' to find life awful dull after all this."

"Oh dear, Will," Rupert cautioned, "don't let Pa hear you say that, he'll worry we're leading you astray. Anyway, you'll have plenty of excitement this evening. Talking of circus acts, you might feel in need of a whip and a chair by the end of the night if Marjorie is true to form."

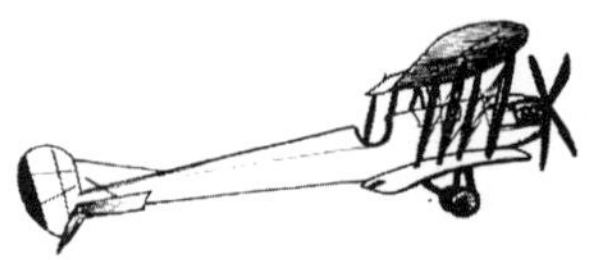

Chapter Twelve

KATE MARCHED UNANNOUNCED INTO WILL'S ROOM AND FOUND HIM before the full-length mirror, in a tangled attempt to knot his tie. "Are you decent, Will?"

"Wouldn't much matter if I wasn't, Kate. You're here anyway."

Laughing, Kate pushed a footstool into position behind her cousin and stepped up to see their joined reflection over his shoulder. "Let go, butterfingers," she said, gently slapping his hand away. She reached around his neck and neatly produced a perfect bow in seconds. "Why is it you men can cope with the mysteries of aerodynamics, but can't manage a simple job like knotting a tie?"

"Because the laws of physics are straightforward compared to this."

Kate turned him around to face her. Standing on the stool put her face level with his and, to her own surprise, she impulsively kissed him.

"Oh!" Will said.

"Oh what?" Kate grinned.

"Oh, that's nice."

"Good." She took his hand and led him to the door. "Come on, William, tonight you're being shown off. I managed to plead your case, and you're mine for the evening. I'm going in to dinner on your arm."

"That means..."

"Yes, Archie has to deal with Lucy on his own. But don't worry about him, you might find yourself feeling jealous."

He squeezed Kate's arm, "Never!"

Kate paused at the top of the stairs and held him back. She smiled and put her finger to her lips. "Marjorie always tries to make an entrance by being the last to arrive. They've just pulled up outside. Let her come in, then we'll make our grand entrance."

"Cousin Kate," he whispered, "I'm not one for tryin' to upstage people, I kinda like to blend in."

She nudged him sharply in the ribs and pushed him back into the shadows. "Just shows how much you don't understand, Will. You're doing this for Sophie and me." She looked at him and frowned. He said nothing. "Oh, all right, Will," she confessed, "mostly for me. I don't get the chance to show off very often, and I'm making the most of it."

He winked then kissed her cheek, "Good, then I'll be shown off. 'Sides, gives me a chance to weigh up the fearsome Marjorie."

"Wait 'til you see her daughter, Lucy. I have to admit she's gorgeous —I hate her." Kate giggled.

Marjorie Pritt-Allison arrived like a full-rigged sailing ship entering harbor. She was grand in entrance, voice and gesture. Her husband tagged along as if sheltering in her lee, his overall stature seemingly diminished by his wife's presence.

Her hair was piled high. She wore a fashionable but fussy blue dress emphasizing her ample bosom. A masterpiece of structural engineering in the field of corsetry squeezed her waist, which only served to draw attention to her comfortable hips and rear end; further accentuated because the dressmaker had followed the fashion for the "hobble" style, drawing the hem of the dress in at the ankles.

"Rubenesque," Kate whispered as they spied on the guests from the landing.

"I beg your pardon?"

"As in the big ladies painted by the Dutch painter, Rubens."

"Kate—you're a mind reader. I'm just tryin' to think of the word to describe her." The last member of the party entered the hall and stepped into the light. Lucy was nothing like he had imagined. He expected a pretty girl, but he saw a stunningly beautiful young lady. Delicate, perfectly formed features, a small nose, full generous lips, huge dark eyes and thick, black, lustrous hair. Her light blue gown displayed as much, if not slightly more, shoulder than was considered respectable, but it served to draw attention to the necklace glittering at her throat. The conversation in the hall dropped in volume as she turned a radiant smile on the gathering.

"You're absolutely right, Kate," Will murmured close to her ear. "She's nowhere near as pretty as you." He offered his arm with a slight bow. "Shall we make our entrance?"

Kate smiled graciously as her stomach turned a somersault. There's no justice, she thought as they descended the stairs, the man I've been looking for all my life and he's my bloody cousin! She felt a rogue tear misting her eyes but blinked it away. This was her moment, and she meant to enjoy it. All eyes turned toward them.

"Aha! This must be William." Marjorie's voice positively boomed. In pitch and volume it was clearly suited to hailing ships across storm tossed oceans.

Will smiled, took her hand and bowed. "My pleasure, ma'am, I've been lookin' forward to meetin' you." She surprised him with a firm handshake.

"This is my husband, Major Pritt-Allison." Will took his hand in turn. "And our daughter, Lucy."

Will returned Lucy's cool gaze. He politely shook her hand. If he was expected to go weak at the knees he felt the others would be disappointed. Yes, Lucy was stunningly beautiful, he thought, but no, he did not feel an instant attraction.

Frank stepped in to complete the introductions. In addition to the party assembled the previous evening, the nearest neighbor, a farmer, Douglas Finlay and his wife joined them for dinner. They greeted Will warmly. The final couple to arrive was the village postmaster and his wife. David Wells seemed an intense young man, wiry in build with sharp features. His thin black hair was parted precisely in the middle and plastered down with brilliantine. He stepped forward and shook hands quickly then stepped back to be close to his wife, Prudence, but found Aunt Connie had stepped between them to link her arms in theirs. David and Prudence smiled gratefully. Frank ushered everybody into the reception room next to the hall.

Will found himself shaking hands with one last visitor. He failed to recognize him at first, dressed as he was in a black tailcoat.

"Sherry, sir?" His uncle's driver, Joe Thorpe, smiled and offered a tray of drinks with his free hand.

"Joe! Good to see you. Are you joinin' us for dinner?"

Joe coughed discreetly, "In a manner of speaking, Mr. William, I'm standing in as butler and head waiter."

Will took a glass from the proffered tray and handed it to Kate, then took one for himself. "Who cares why you're here, Joe, it's good to see you again." Joe's sudden appearance answered a question for Will. For such a large house, his uncle and aunt employed very few staff. In addition to Peter, who also served at table, and Maisie, there was a maid, Mary, who helped in the kitchen, amongst her other duties. For a dinner party on this scale Frank called in extra help. Joe exchanged his khaki uniform for a butler's black tails. His wife, Sarah, helped Maisie in the kitchen, and Fred Harris, the gardener, also helped with the preparations for the meal.

The tall dining room windows with their arched tops looked out over the garden to the woods that bordered the property. They gave the room an airy feel complemented by Connie's decision to paint the walls white where they were not covered in mahogany panels. Several family portraits hung in heavy gilded frames, amongst them pictures of favorite departed pets. Connie had been able to put her deceased husband next to their beloved golden retriever in such a way that they looked fondly at each other as they had when they were alive.

Will marveled at the table itself, a masterpiece of the carpenter's art. Normally of a size to comfortably seat six, it extended when a crank was inserted in a discrete socket at one end and turned. A screw arrangement drove the under frame apart with the rails sliding in precisely machined grooves. When the desired length had been achieved, extra leaves slotted in place to give a glistening expanse of dark polished wood for setting the array of china and silverware needed for the twelve guests gathered that evening. The little platoons of glasses stationed at each place setting were ancient Waterford crystal. The evening sun caught the facets of the glass and sparked brilliant splinters of color from them. Connie guided David and Prudence Wells to their seats. The men drew back the chairs for the ladies before taking their own places.

Will sat with Kate on one side and Rupert's fiancé, Sophie, on the other. Marjorie sat opposite Will—in the best position to interrogate him. Joe and Peter marched in with thick vegetable soup in deep silver tureens and served methodically and quickly down each side of the table. Will saw a look of panic cross Prudence's face as her hand hovered over the cutlery beside her plate. He took his own soupspoon, raised it with a flourish and caught her eye. Prudence blushed and smiled as she picked up the correct item.

Will had hardly managed a mouthful of soup when Marjorie opened up on him.

"So how are you managing with the King's English and our quaint customs, William?"

Joe leaned over Frank's shoulder pouring wine at that precise moment. He lightly tapped the glass so it gave a discrete chime like a tiny bell.

"Seconds out..." Joe murmured.

"Round one—and let's have a good clean fight," Frank responded from the corner of his mouth, struggling to keep a straight face.

Will rose to the challenge, "Well, ma'am, I've already learned that if we need to move anythin', I put petrol in the lorry, 'stead of gas in the truck. Then I make a point of drivin' down the left side of the highway."

"Splendid!" Marjorie roared. "But what about our social structure...class?"

"Beg pardon, ma'am?"

"The class system, my dear boy...it's absolutely crucial one knows one's place in society."

Will paused, he had not expected anything so direct, "I confess I had not really given it much thought. How do you see it?" He asked innocently, playing for time. He guessed correctly that the answer could be a long one. Marjorie smiled. She put down her spoon and launched enthusiastically into her lecture on British society as she saw it.

"At the very top, of course, we have the Royal Family, and then our very own, and beloved British aristocracy," she twittered giving Archie what was intended to be a winning smile.

He leaned forward to acknowledge Marjorie with a wan smile, but as he sat back he gave Will a wicked grin and crossed his eyes.

Will struggled not to splutter in his soup. "And then, ma'am?"

Marjorie barged on, "Then we have the landed gentry which of course includes many with non-hereditary titles such as knighthoods..."

"And land?"

"Well, *of course!* And, often, senior military rank. Then we have the upper middle classes. This will include those who have reached the pinnacle of their professions, the surgeon to the King for instance and the very upper echelons of the Civil and Colonial service. It is possible, even in this class, to find some fine old families."

"Really?" He winced as he felt the heel of Kate's shoe grind onto his foot beneath the table. His fake display of interest had not fooled Kate for a second.

Marjorie then ran through the qualifications for membership of the middle, middle class and the lower middle class, looking significantly at David and Prudence Wells as she did. "And then there are the rest." She said with a barely repressed shudder.

"The rest?"

"The lower orders," her voice had dropped for the first time. She spoke in an almost conspiratorial whisper, leaning toward him across the table.

Will dropped his voice. "Oh, them." This earned him a firm kick from Kate.

"Something wrong, Katie dear?" Connie asked brightly. "Soup too hot?"

Kate's face twisted strangely and when she spoke her voice trembled an octave too high before settling down to a normal tone. "No Auntie, it's fine." She leaned toward Will using a break afforded by Marjorie summoning Peter for more wine. "You pig, Will, I'll get you for this."

He just smiled and carried on, "Am I correct in assumin' you are considered 'landed', ma'am?"

Marjorie held up both hands to him and beamed as she clapped them together, "Oh, how perceptive, my dear. Even without the benefit of royalty, you must have a similar arrangement in America."

"Er, not exactly."

"Oh, how is it different?"

"Well, apart from the obvious in that we have no Royal family," Will paused for a moment with his head on one side as if considering his reply carefully, "we simplified the class system."

Marjorie found herself drawn in, "My goodness—how?"

"We only have two classes—those who are rich, an' those who are tryin' to be rich." Marjorie looked puzzled while the rest of the table seemed to simultaneously have trouble with their soupspoons. Peter who had been standing impassively by the door executed a smart about turn and disappeared, while Joe who was in transit behind Marjorie, licked his finger and chalked a symbolic point in the air. Will immediately regretted what seemed to him a cheap crack, but Marjorie carried blithely on.

"Oh that explains so much," she said, shaking her head sorrowfully, "but how can a nation divorced from polite society by thousands of miles hope to keep pace with social progress?"

Will realized that his idea of social progress and Marjorie's, were miles apart. He also saw that his witticisms bounced off her like peas off an alligator—her hide was that thick.

"At least you haven't got flat hair," she said consolingly.

He realized everybody was suddenly studying his head. "I am sorry, ma'am, you really have lost me." Will already felt slightly self-conscious about the length of his thick blond hair and had vowed to have it cut.

"Flat hair," she said again, louder. "Young American men often have flat hair."

It dawned on him that Marjorie was referring to a craze that had gone out of fashion before he was born. Young men had indeed achieved a style where the hair was plastered to the head by wetting it and wrapping linen strips tightly around their skulls. His mother even claimed his father had once tried it. There had been a photograph to prove it, but the picture had mysteriously disappeared. Will answered gallant as ever, "I do believe that style has fallen out of favor in recent months."

"Thank goodness for that!" Marjorie trumpeted. "It looked like a patent leather skull cap, quite ridiculous; especially with those loud waistcoats and all those vulgar neckties. Tell me young man, does anybody attempt to educate your people in what is considered proper in dress and manners?"

Will saw everybody else at the table wincing. He realized they were expecting a sharp reply from him, but he kept his reply even. The woman was so lacking in manners herself she was funny instead of insulting. He remembered that Cordelia once told him that people you felt like making a fool of, invariably did it for you. He resolved not to make fun of her. "Why, Mrs. Pritt-Allison, we have a Mrs. Sherwood who writes an invaluable guide to manners. She even gives valuable advice on how to wear a mustache. I believe she is in constant correspondence with the very top people here."

"Really, William, how splendid!"

"Yes ma'am, and I am goin', with your permission, to contact her on my return to suggest she writes to you."

For an awful moment he realized his good intentions had just flown out the window. Rupert had his eyes closed and was making little choking noises, Archie seemed to be crying while Sophie and Kate had both started to chew their napkins. Aunt Connie had been taking a sip of wine and that seemed to have gone down the wrong way. Lucy glared at him with open hostility while his uncle groaned quietly. Major Pritt-Allison seemed oblivious and just carried on drinking.

Joe raised his eyes to the ceiling, "Oh my Gawd!" he muttered under his breath as he took Peter by the arm at the door. "We're not even on the main course and somebody will bust their stays if this carries on."

Marjorie, however, was clearly delighted. "Oh, William, I would be thrilled to help."

Will nodded and closed his eyes for a moment. He could not help it, he found himself liking her and determined to behave himself. "Mrs. Pritt Allison..."

"Please, William, call me Marjorie." That was it, he decided he *would* behave himself, whatever the provocation.

"Thank you, Marjorie...may I ask, how does one know when a new idea is good form? As a stranger here it is so difficult. I know if I commit some error in dressin' I won't be invited out much." He felt the highly charged atmosphere around the table ease. His uncle relaxed visibly.

"I think we can safely say, take your lead from His Majesty the King."

"I will do that ma'am,"

At that moment the heavy double doors into the dining room were pushed open. "Make way for a noble pig," Joe announced as he paraded the centerpiece of the dinner into the room. He raised the domed cover of the big silver serving tray with a flourish. A murmur of appreciation traveled around the table. The ham had been prepared over days by a traditional method involving steeping it in salt water while it lay on a bed of straw in a stone trough. The final touch was a honey and mustard glaze. The process of serving released a cheerful babble of conversation, though Marjorie's voice still dominated as she urged her daughter to eat more.

Will was pleased when Marjorie's attention was diverted away from him by a developing conversation on the subject of "breeding." He enjoyed chatting with Kate and Sophie but kept half an ear cocked to the increasingly heated conversation developing on the other side of the table. To Will's surprise Major Pritt-Allison suddenly spoke up. Will had formed the impression he was totally in awe of his wife but the view he now put forward contradicted Marjorie. Perhaps, Will guessed, the wine the major had consumed gave him courage. The rest of the table fell silent.

The major slammed down his glass and glared at his wife, "I don't know what you make such a damned fuss about, woman. People are no different from horses, dogs or cattle; if you keep breeding from the same bloodline you'll end up with weak, sickly and stupid beasts. Look at old Buster, smartest dog in the district and more of a mixture than a shepherd's pie...if ever you want to sell him, Frank, let me know."

Marjorie maintained her dignity, "Cross breeding may be acceptable for animals, but it is *not* acceptable in our family." Everybody at the table broke into energetic conversation in an effort to defuse the family row that appeared to be on the point of breaking out. The volume gave

Sophie the chance to whisper in Will's ear, "That let's you off the hook." She inclined her head toward Lucy who was talking animatedly to Archie.

"I'm not sure I take kindly to bein' compared to a prize bull, Sophie," Will quietly pointed out.

Sophie placed her hand over his, "Any more than Lucy enjoys being compared to a prize cow, Will, but that won't stop her mother trying to make a suitable marriage for her. Marjorie has her sights set on our Archie, but she is underestimating Lucy. She'll make up her own mind and it won't be Archie."

"Really? I declare I thought he would be a prize catch." Will sounded surprised.

"Now come on, Will, you sound like Marjorie," she admonished him gently. "Can't you see, the 'spark' is not there, there's no chemistry between them." The arrival of dessert muted conversation again. Between them Maisie and Sarah had produced a variety of puddings and *gateaux* to suit all tastes. The cheese board followed. Frank decided Marjorie had dominated proceedings for long enough and while he could not suppress her conversation, he could, at least, keep it focused on less controversial subjects. For the remainder of the meal he and his sister, Connie, headed her off into discussions on village matters.

According to tradition the men retired to the library for brandy and cigars while the ladies enjoyed their coffee. After a decent interval and with some relief, Frank saw the guests safely on their way before returning to the library to join his family and close friends. As Will followed him through the door he was greeted by spontaneous laughter and applause.

"Congratulations, Will," Archie roared, slapping him on the back, "you've been into the lion's den and lived."

Will mopped his brow, "An' nearly had my head bitten off. My word, that lady is some firebrand!"

Joe appeared with a fresh bottle of brandy. "I thought young Mr. Will might be in need of something strong, so I broached a bottle of the best, sir."

"I think we all are, Joe." Frank replied, "have one yourself and please join us." He passed Joe a cigar.

"Don't mind if I do, I feel in need of something to steady my nerves." Joe appeared completely at his ease. While he played the role of butler with complete assurance, Will could see Joe's relationship with his uncle and cousin went far beyond that. They settled comfortably in the old leather armchairs. Kate perched on her father's knee while Connie surprised Will by lighting up a thin, black cheroot.

"Well, Joe, what's the latest, is the wily old Hun up to any more tricks?" Rupert asked. Will looked from one to the other, his surprise obvious. Frank decided it best to explain.

"Keep this under your hat, Will; Joe is not my driver or my servant, he's a cryptographer." It was not a term Will had ever heard before and Joe explained.

"I crack codes, Mr. William, it's just a knack, but not many people seem to have it. I think it comes from all my years doing crossword puzzles."

Frank gave a short laugh. "Just a knack that comes from years of hard work, patience and more brain power than the entire General Staff can muster combined. What he is not telling you is that he is also a chess champion, writes crossword puzzles and gets paid for them, and is the best racing tipster in the business."

Joe shrugged, "That's very kind of you, sir, but don't forget, I've got the cushiest billet in the army. Warm office, all the best equipment, and some very clever people working for me."

"But—pardon me if I'm speakin' out of turn—why aren't you an officer, Joe?" Will asked.

"That's a good question, Will," Frank prompted. "I've been trying to make him take a commission for years."

Joe's smile was almost sly as he replied. "I like being a sergeant, Mr. William, it's the best rank in the army. It commands respect from private soldiers to generals; if I were to take a commission, I'd be a fifty-year-old second lieutenant: an object of pity and scorn. Plus, I'd have to take a pay cut."

Archie sided with Joe, "That's quite right, I can shout and bawl at a subaltern, but I'd never dare speak out of turn to a troop sergeant."

The niceties of military etiquette meant nothing to Will, but code cracking fascinated him. "So how do you find the messages in the first place?" He asked.

"Easier than you might imagine," Joe said, warming to his theme. "None of this is secret, far from it, in fact we are trying to make the public aware of the dangers. The stuff I would love to get my hands on, we can't touch, it comes in the diplomatic bags to the embassies concerned..."

"The German?" Will asked.

"And others," Joe replied." But then they have to pass instructions to their agents and collect intelligence from them. They can't just troop in and out of the office, so to speak, because they know we have them watched, so they have developed other techniques."

"But can't they send a letter or wire them, or telephone even?"

"They can and do," Joe conceded, "but they know they are likely to be intercepted."

"Surely that's illegal," Will sounded shocked.

"Yes," Joe said grinning, "but 'all's fair...' as they say. Because of that, one of their favorite methods is called a 'dead letter'. It's quite simple, an agent leaves a message hidden in a pre-arranged spot and somebody from the embassy collects it. We can't watch everybody all the time, and their chaps are pretty lively when it comes to shaking off a 'tail'. This is why we want to educate the public to be on the look-out for people behaving suspiciously."

"That's all very well, Joe," Connie put in, "but you know the Great British Public: nosey enough at the best of times. If you start stirring them up looking for spies, it will be difficult for decent people to do all of those things they prefer others not to know about."

"You have a very suspicious mind, Auntie," Rupert scolded gently.

Connie gave a short laugh, "Suspicious my arse! Realistic more like, young Rupert." Will had noticed his Aunt's language becoming fruitier as she grew used to having him in the house. The others were already used to it; they just smiled. "How will the farmer's boy be able to leave a note for the vicar's daughter in the graveyard if Joe's henchmen are going to come leaping out from behind the bushes?" She suddenly stopped and laid a hand on Kate's arm. "I am speaking hypothetically, my dear, I don't think Wendy Truscott has a secret beau...does she?"

"No, Auntie," Kate reassured her.

Joe tapped ash from his cigar into a brass ashtray, fashioned from the case of an old artillery shell. "I take your point, Mrs. Burnett, but we're being more subtle. We're approaching publicans, railway station staff, post office people like young David Wells; warning them to be on the lookout for strangers."

"That's one of the reasons for having my works where they are, Will," Tom added. "If a stranger shows up in the country, word goes 'round like lightning."

"The big problem though," Joe smiled as he said it, relishing the challenge, "is wireless."

"Can they transmit Morse code all the way to Germany from England?" Will asked. He had followed developments in this field for years and was surprised to hear that radio could be of any use to a spy.

"Given a transmitter powerful enough, and an aerial tall enough, possibly. We think the blighters are a sight more clever than that though. An agent could never conceal an outfit of that size. We think one of them is watching the East Coast ports and using a small portable set to send messages to ships just outside the territorial limit."

"Gol-ly," Will gasped, "this is real cloak and dagger stuff."

"Wait until you hear Archie's theory," Frank said. "Go on Archie, don't be put off just because your C.O. poured cold water on it. We're taking it seriously."

Encouraged by Frank, Archie told his story and explained his idea. "Last month my regiment traveled to Norfolk to play soldiers on the coast. Practicing rapid deployment to repel an invasion force. After all, if Germany did try to mount an invasion, the East Coast is where it is most likely to come. We had finished for the day, horses in the lines and the chaps relaxing before bedding down for the night. Some were playing footie on the beach—," he paused for a moment, seeing Will's questioning look. "Soccer," he added.

"Oh yes, of course," Will said.

Archie continued, "One of the men, Trooper Moore, is a bird watcher. He has this whacking great telescope and a book where he notes down every bird he sees: times, dates, places, quite fascinating really, though I couldn't tell a sandpiper from a seagull. Anyway, he's a really dependable type so I was quite surprised when he came rushing back, to where we were camped on the dunes, in a frightful tizzy. He shoved his telescope into my hands and pointed me out to sea. I couldn't see why he was so excited at first because I looked for a ship, but when he tilted the telescope up I saw it..." He enjoyed retelling the tale and paused to build up suspense.

Kate couldn't stand it, "Well come on, Archie, what did you see?"

"A stonking great Zeppelin."

"Good Lord, Archie, are you sure?" Connie's tone showed the alarm she felt. Kate and Sophie gasped and Will's eyes opened wide with surprise.

"As sure as I sit here," he confirmed. "The damn thing was probably twenty miles away but as big as a battleship, quite remarkable to look at. I can tell you it gave me a queer feeling seeing one in the flesh, so to speak. There it sat, calmly cruising along above a bank of clouds."

"Oh, how awful!" Sophie shuddered as she spoke. The unease generated by Archie's story was understandable. The German Imperial Navy was known to operate a number of the giant airships. In the previous months they had been seen over the British coast, one had even flown up the Thames Estuary as far as the outskirts of London itself under cover of darkness. Unlike the small blimps used by the British, which were little more than shaped balloons fitted with a small motor, the Zeppelins were built around a giant, fabric covered, aluminum skeleton. Their lift came from gas bags inside the frame. Fitted with up to six powerful motors and controlled from a wheelhouse called the gondola, they truly were ships of the air. As much as six hundred feet in length, carrying a large crew, machine guns for defense and a heavy bomb load, some strategists believed they could fly beyond the range of defending aircraft at a height where even the anti-aircraft gunners could not reach them. Their conclusion being that the cities of England could be flattened at will. The newspapers had seized on these theories and developed them with almost evangelical zeal. The writer H.G. Wells, had scored a major success, and managed to frighten the population still further with his novel *War in the Air.* In his story a fleet of German airships crossed the Atlantic to destroy New York. People were nervous, and with good reason.

Archie sought to allay some of the disquiet he had caused. "To be realistic, ladies, it is only a giant gas bag, but I want to know what it was doing there? None of our ships were on exercise at the time in those waters. Come to that, neither were anybody else's, including the Germans, but there it was, and it was still hanging around an hour later. And then, blow me, the wretched thing was there the next day, and the next!"

"He's quite correct," Frank confirmed. "Some of our ships reported seeing and hearing it. Let's hear your theory again, Archie, perhaps Will can throw some light on it, I know he's interested in any new invention."

Will nodded earnestly, "You bet! What do you think it was doin', Archie?"

"I know cavalry officers are not supposed to think, but I can't help being interested in anything new that comes my way. I found myself with some signaler chappies recently, and they told me that these radio waves, whatever they are that wireless depends on, carry especially well over water. They also told me that the higher you can raise your aerial, the further you can send your signal and, by the same principle, the higher *you* are, the more distant is the signal you can pick up. Does this make sense?"

"It certainly does...go on," Will urged. He was now sitting on the edge of his seat.

Archie seemed relieved, "Well, what if some spy, agent, whatever we call him, was lurking somewhere along the coast with a small wireless transmitter? He could send to the Zeppelin, which would act as a relay station. It could receive his message and then, using its powerful transmitters, send all the way to Germany."

"Makes perfect sense to me," Will agreed without question. "Has to be the best explanation for why it was there." He looked at his cousin.

"I'm convinced," Rupert said.

"So am I," Joe confirmed.

"So what did you do?" Will asked.

"I went straight to my C.O. and asked if we could get our wireless chaps to try to pin down where the signal might be coming from, I read somewhere they could do that, then using my chaps we could swoop down and catch the bounder red-handed. He had to be somewhere very near where we were exercising." Archie used his hands while he talked and he made an impression of an eagle falling on its victim.

"And so you caught him?" Will asked eagerly.

"No, the boss told me to stop being a silly ass and get on with the exercise."

"Oh no!" Will was as disappointed as Archie had been.

"Oh yes, unfortunately," Frank confirmed, "and we lost the opportunity to nab an agent we are convinced has been observing every move the Navy has made from the East Coast this year."

"I even managed to work out where I thought he might be..." Archie shook his head sadly, "on a boat in one of the harbors nearby."

"Why a boat?" Connie asked.

"A wireless set is quite a bulky beast, isn't that right?" he looked at Will for confirmation.

"Surely is," Will confirmed. "Smallest one I ever heard of still needs a steamer trunk to ship it around."

"Then he'd need a generator or a big set of accumulators. Then there's the aerial—*that* needs to be raised to a decent height. The ideal place would be a church tower, but he can hardly go to the jolly old vicar and say, 'Good morning, I'm Fritz the spy, can I run my aerial up your bell tower?'"

"Hardly," Frank agreed with a wry smile.

"Then again, he can hardly lug this contraption out into the woods and find a convenient tree to rig it up; he would be spotted right away. So, a boat it has to be. Room for the wireless set and accumulators, run the aerial up the jolly old mast, and there you are—Bob's your uncle—"

"And Fanny's your aunt," Connie completed the odd saying.

"Sophie looked at Archie Carstairs with affection and newfound respect. "Archie, you're supposed to be stupid, people expect you to be stupid, you're a cavalryman and an aristocrat, but at this rate they'll move you to military intelligence."

Archie threw back his head and roared with laughter, "Don't be silly, Sophie m'dear, there's no such thing!"

Chapter Thirteen

THE SKILLS REQUIRED OF A FIELDER IN CRICKET WILL FOUND TO BE much the same as in baseball: to run, catch and throw. The customs observed in playing the game, however, struck him as a bit strange. "Why are we applaudin', Rupert. Surely he's the opposition?" Will asked. The ball struck by the batsman for the other team had hummed between them, just past their outstretched fingers on its flight over the boundary for six runs.

"It was a capital stroke, Will," Rupert answered. "It had everything: style, pace, direction. It could be the best we'll see in this match."

The basic principle of the game turned out to be simpler in practice than in the explanation. Batting appeared easy to Will. The bat itself was large and flat and the ball had to pitch in front of him. He found this deceptive. When it was his turn to bat he nudged the first ball away and they took two runs. He struck the second ball squarely for four runs. He thought he had hit the third ball just as well, but it sailed up to a great height presenting the fielding side with an easy catch. Smiling and politely acknowledging the customary ripple of applause, as he walked off the field, came naturally to him, but Will was puzzled.

"Dang!" he said to Rupert as he accepted a cup of tea at the pavilion, a white painted wooden shed on the edge of the village green. "What happened there? The ball just sat up for me to hit, and it just flew off my bat."

"You were foxed by a clever 'spin' bowler, old son. The ball was spinning when you hit it." He had taken Will's bat and demonstrated how he should angle it to keep his shot low. "Never mind, six is a good score in village cricket, you'll do better in our second innings."

Now they stood in the field as the opposing team from the neighboring village of Little Hadham took their first turn to bat. Will had quickly realized cricket was a leisurely game interspersed with moments of furious activity. They found plenty of time to chat while waiting to bat, or while fielding.

"I see Marjorie nobbled you again," Rupert observed. "She's taken quite a shine to you."

"Yeah, she's decided to educate me in the ways of 'polite society'. She's tellin' me how it's possible for landed gentry to achieve promotion to the aristocracy. And all the time she's lookin' at Archie."

Rupert laughed, "Yes, she reckons our friend is her ticket to greater things. If only he'll agree to marry her Lucy."

"Will he?"

Rupert looked thoughtful and swung his arm in a wide circle to ease the cramp brought on by his spell of bowling earlier. "Personally I doubt it, but you never can tell. Marjorie's done very well already, considering. I would never underestimate her determination."

"Considerin' what?"

"Considering her background."

"But she told me her family were wealthy merchants providin' provisions for the Royal Navy. 'Trade' as she called it, but a very respectable trade."

"Absolutely," Rupert agreed. "Her dad has a fish and chip shop in Chatham; he's done very well from the naval cadets, they're always hungry."

"Well I'll be!" Will exclaimed.

"Keep it under your hat, Will, she doesn't know Archie and I called in there last year. It's a first class establishment, with a proper sit down café; or you can take your food away in newspaper in the usual way. I don't think I've ever tasted a better piece of cod."

"But why does she want to keep it quiet?" Will asked. "Where I come from folk would be proud if their family had made somethin' of a business."

"I'd have to agree with you there, Will. Marjorie's father pulled his way up by his bootstraps. He was an enlisted man in the Navy. When discharged, he plowed all his savings and a small pension into that business. As far as Marjorie's concerned though, it's lower class trade, definitely something to be hushed up."

"That seems a damn shame," Will said with feeling.

"Oh, not really, he plays along with it. The old boy is pushing eighty but still works in the shop. He's proud as punch of Marjorie and loves being promoted to 'a wealthy merchant provisioning the Royal Navy', when he and his wife are up visiting. After all, he *is* a wealthy merchant supplying sailors, in a manner of speaking."

"In that case, how did she manage to work her way up to the major?"

"You'll have to ask Aunt Connie about that, but I think she turned up with the 'fishing fleet' in India while Connie was out there with Uncle John...and my mother. I know Marjorie's father paid for the best possible education for his daughters and provided them with a foothold in 'polite society.'" (This was the first time Will had heard Rupert mention his mother, who had become ill and died in India when Kate was a young girl.) Rupert tensed as he spoke, the ball almost rolled to their feet and the batsman seemed poised to take a run. He opted for caution and Rupert scooped up the ball and tossed it back to their bowler.

"The fishin' fleet? Surely she could afford passage on a regular liner?" Will asked.

Rupert laughed, "She could—that's what they call the girls who travel out to India in search of a husband. They live there under the protection of family or friends and make the social rounds."

Will grimaced, "Sounds a mite cold blooded."

"I suppose it is, but it's the way of the world, or that world anyway," Rupert pointed out. "Anyway, Marjorie cut quite a dash from Connie's account. Strictly between you and me," Rupert lowered his voice and looked around, "she set her heart on young Lieutenant Pritt-Allison, as he was then, and just wore him down in the end.

Will shook his head, "I think we are indulgin' in what is known as 'gossip' here, Rupert."

His cousin grinned, "Quite, and we men are every bit as bad as the women. But in my case I don't pass any judgments, I like her for who she is and what she does. Though she can drive me bonkers on occasion—," Rupert stiffened. "YOURS!" he yelled.

Will had a split second to react. He dived sideways, arm outstretched, fingers groping. He felt the glorious sting of the hard leather ball as he held it, six inches above the ground.

He staggered to his feet clutching the ball. His teammates crowded around to congratulate him while applause washed across the village green. He could see the other side's batsmen clapping vigorously where they stood waiting their turn, even the man who sent the ball grinned ruefully and raised his bat in salute as he walked back to the pavilion.

"Good heavens, Will, if you never take another catch you'll be remembered in the village for that one." Rupert thumped him on the back.

"Beginner's luck I reckon, Coz." The game settled back into its steady rhythm. Will returned to their favorite topic of conversation. "So how come Marjorie is such a pal of Aunt Connie's? They would seem violently opposed in their views."

"They are, and I think Connie finds it hard to keep her temper at times, but she likes Marjorie no doubt. She may be a bit over-the-top'—"

"Just a bit," Will agreed with a smile.

"But she has a heart of gold. That woman has done more to help the poor and sick in this parish than the Poor Commissioners ever have. The nice thing is, unlike some I could mention, she doesn't trumpet it from the roof tops."

For the next half hour they had to concentrate hard on the game. The tail enders—the players at the lower end of the other side's batting list—put up a lively resistance, but it was soon time for Upper Bardfield to bat again. The opening batsmen held on for twenty-five runs between them before Rupert's stumps flew into the air. "Clean bowled" as he explained to Will. Uncle Frank came in lower down the batting order.

"Stonewalling like your General Jackson," Archie pointed out. "Hanging on but not scoring. We'll need to put some runs on soon. See what you can do." Archie patted Will on the back as the American walked out to take his place. Will could see what he needed to do, and proceeded to do it. He set about the opposing bowlers with a will, but his batting style soon caused controversy. Instead of keeping his bat down—in line with his legs and the stumps—he stood to one side, leaving the bowler a clear view of his wicket, but he held his bat in the comfortable raised style familiar from baseball. After the fourth ball had sailed over the boundary for another six runs, a halt was called. Frank, as club secretary, consulted with the umpire who was poring over a well-thumbed book.

"There you are," Frank jabbed at the page, "absolutely nothing to say how he has to hold his bat. It's his decision if he wants to throw caution to the winds." The umpire, the local miller, shrugged and snapped the rulebook shut.

"Carry on lad," his decision was final, nobody dared argue.

Frank winked, "Just keep whacking them any way you like, Will, but please don't forget where you are and go chucking your bat down and sprinting 'round the boundary looking for third base." Frank noticed Will had a trademark: his grin was definitely lopsided.

"I'll try not to forget, Uncle." Will continued, swinging at the ball with unrestrained enthusiasm. His own side and their supporters applauded wildly as he racked up his score. Little Hadham applauded politely and gritted their teeth, determined to catch him, bowl him or even lure him into spraining his ankle.

"Keep at it, Sid," their captain urged the bowler, "he's definitely tiring."

"Oh there's a surprise," Sid grated sarcastically, "must be all this running up and down we're making him do." By the time Will's last batting partner snicked an easy catch, Will's score stood at fifty-three, and he had the honor of walking off the field "not out." Excessive enthusiasm was not considered good form in cricket, but Will's reception was as warm as the summer afternoon itself. He had helped set a difficult target for their opponents to reach in their second innings. The long day belonged to the men of Upper Bardfield, they won the match with a comfortable margin of thirty runs.

Tom and Will discussed the game over tea the following morning. Rupert had left for Farnborough in the Bristol with the first light of day.

Tom made an imaginary batting stroke with an old barrel stave, "I say, Will, I thought I did well with twenty runs in the match, but a combined total of fifty-nine from your two innings—that's an outstanding debut."

"Ah...that was just beginner's luck," Will replied modestly. "Somebody will soon work out what I'm doin' and my stumps will go flyin'."

"Even so, the team is not going to want to lose you. Did you mean what you said about not wanting to go home?"

Will took a moment to consider his response, he gazed around the hangar at the two airplanes, the neatly racked tools, the sturdy workbenches. Even the smell of the place appealed to him. He felt as if he belonged.

"I miss my family an' friends, even though I've only been here just over a week, but it seems all the excitement is here in England, if you get my meanin'."

"I think I do," Rupert answered, "certainly from the aviator's point of view. There's a real sense of excitement; though some of that must come from all this war talk."

Will sighed, "There's an awful lot of that. Some folk seem to talk as if it's goin' to come off for sure. What I can't see is why they seem so all fired pleased about it."

Tom poured himself more tea and stirred it thoughtfully. Will noticed he often did that when he needed time to think, in the same way some people would make a business of lighting a cigarette. Tom spoke at last, "In the case of Rupert and Archie I think I can understand. Rupert is more aviator than soldier these days. Even so, he's looking for a chance to show the generals what our machines can do for the military. Archie is a professional soldier. Don't be taken in by that simple-minded aristocrat act of his; he's out to make a name for himself and gain promotion. A war would give him that chance."

"I thought his name would gain him the promotion anyway," Will said.

"It would have in the last century, but times are changing. The South African campaigns forced a big shake-up in the army; if Archie wants to make his way up, he'll have to do it on merit. The army is stuffed with titled junior officers—Lord this, the Honorable that, the Marquis of so and so—and they're all looking for the rank of general to go with the hereditary 'handle'. You can't blame them for wanting to prove themselves."

"Archie could prove himself on the cricket field instead of riskin' gettin' his head blown off. Did you see the way he pitched yesterday? You couldn't fault a body for throwin' himself flat on the ground when Archie starts windin' up."

Tom gave Will a shrewd look. "You're not keen on the whole idea of soldiering and the military, are you Will?"

Will swished the dregs of his tea around then pitched them onto the grass. "I'll be straight with you, Tom. I have a strong opposition to the idea of war as bein' the way to straighten out problems. Everythin' Nathan, Uncle Roy and Uncle Alex have said tells me there's no glory, just a heap of misery goes along with it. They made a big impression on me when I was growin' up. An' I certainly have no wish to join the military myself."

"Sounds like it," Tom acknowledged.

Will stretched his legs out and studied the toes of his boots, scuffed and worn. They seemed to give him inspiration, "You know why I think these folk are bad to go shootin' Germans?"

Tom had still not accustomed himself to Will's unusual choice of words, "Why are they 'bad to go off to war' then?"

"They're bored," Will stated emphatically. "They think they'll march off, have a little excitement like shootin' bunnies, might could collect a medal or two, or even a nice, polite type of wound. Nuthin' too painful or ugly, somethin' that looks good in a picture, maybe a bandage 'round the head or their arm in a sl—," his voice tailed off; he was looking straight at Tom's disfigured face. "Oh Christ, Tom, I'm sorry..."

Instead of taking offense, Tom Armstrong leaned back and roared with laughter. "Oh Lord, Will, for one so young I don't think I've ever come across such a cynic." He wiped his eyes with the sleeve of his coverall; he was laughing so much he found himself almost in tears. For the first time he had heard Will come close to bad language. He steadied himself, "The worst of it is, you're absolutely right. Oh dear, you're priceless!"

Will grinned sheepishly, "Well, you know what I mean. You heard the fellas at the game yesterday. They're all ready to go kill Germans, but I bet if one turned up at next week's match, they'd teach him to bat an' take him to the pub afterwards."

"Spot on again, my friend," Tom agreed, "though I do have to say soldiering isn't a bad life. You see the world, make good friends, even the food's not bad these days. There's just one thing I didn't like in my service days—the uniform." Will looked at him carefully, he never could tell when Tom was joking. "What's wrong with the uniform? It's not a pretty color but I guess there's worse."

"It's dangerous."

Will's eyes opened wide, "Dangerous?"

"Yeah. People keep shooting at it," Tom collapsed into laughter again, and Will joined in enthusiastically.

Tom calmed down, "Hooh—dearie me! I do enjoy a good laugh, trouble is, it's no laughing matter. It's not too bad when the other chap is running 'round in a loin cloth armed with a sharp stick and you've got a Maxim gun, but the Kaiser's lads are going to be a different proposition, I can tell you."

"Now who's being a cynic?" Will asked. "Anyway, no need to tell me, I don't need any convincin'. A friend of mine, back home, who knows 'bout these things told me the Germans have thousands of these belt-fed machine guns."

Tom's mood changed, "That confirms something I heard, but you'll never convince the top brass. The senior military mind here admires the club as a weapon for its functional simplicity"

Will stood up and waved his arm toward the Flanders monoplane standing in the doorway, ready for flight. "If our friends are so bad off for some excitement, why don't they build an airplane? I did."

"From what I hear, Will, that machine gave you as much excitement as anybody could ask for."

"Oh, that it did, Tom, it surely did," Will admitted with a broad smile.

Tom stood up and consulted a clipboard hanging on a nail driven into the wall of the hangar. "Will, the contract calls for us to put twenty hours on that motor before we send it back for fitting in a B.E.2. Are you prepared to do that for me?"

"Are you serious?"

"Of course I am."

"I'll start right away." Will picked up his helmet and goggles, but Tom put a steadying hand on his arm.

"Will, I know you are probably more experienced in the air than me, but as this is my responsibility I want you to take some advice from me."

Will caught Tom's mood. "Any advice from you is welcome, Tom, and don't forget this is *your* airplane—that's my concern."

"Okay, Will, it's simple: never, *ever,* try to turn back to the field if your motor packs up just after you leave the ground. You'll be signing your own death warrant if you do. Promise me you will never make that mistake." Tom demanded.

"I swear I won't."

"And remember, if you have to make a forced landing always keep enough speed to maintain control, better to land long and crash into the hedge at the far end of the field at twenty miles an hour, than stall and drop out of the sky like a stone. It may sound daft," Tom said, "but you must always crash the plane yourself—never let it crash you. Understood?"

"Understood," Will said, then offered his hand. They shook on the deal.

"Do a few circuits, we'll check her over, then—if you're happy—take her up again," Tom said. They moved the Flanders into position for takeoff and Will climbed aboard. Tom swung the propeller to start the engine. Will scanned his instruments, checked his fuel was switched on, deliberately moved the controls to their full extent then gave a thumbs up signal. Tom dragged the chocks from under the wheels and Will advanced the throttle. In seconds the big monoplane was soaring over the hedge; the now familiar view expanding around him.

As the big airplane soared, so did Will's heart. He found himself singing, and he made it something appropriate to the occasion. *"Mine eyes have seen the glory..."* He circled the field five times, singing and laughing to the wind. After the fifth circuit he landed, slightly fast but very acceptable. Tom appeared from inside the hangar as he taxied to a stop and cut the motor.

"Okay?" Tom inquired. Will's grin spoke for him. "Fair enough, time for a quick cuppa, then refuel and away you go again."

Tom showed Will a clipboard with a stopwatch fixed to it. "This is a testing schedule. It shows times, altitude, revs. I think I've covered about every possible form of abuse some ham-fisted army aviator can dish out."

Will gulped his tea, then checked the motor's valve clearances and oil level, the two best indicators of potential problems. He refilled the fuel tank with petrol filtered through chamois leather, as a precaution against impurities, and prepared to take off again. Tom swung the propeller, and the motor came to life. He ducked back under the wing and pulled himself up to the cockpit. "You're a sensible chap, I don't have to tell you to guard against over confidence," Will thought this was a beautiful way to warn him against growing too cocky, as they said in England. "Stay close to the field and try to fly as accurately as possible. Keep it down to an hour. Mind you, when I say 'stay close', the old family home qualifies as nearby." He was about to step down but stopped to wag a warning finger, "No buzzing the chimney pots, too many people are pushing up the daisies after pulling that stunt!"

Will gave him a thumbs up, "Right you are, boss, understood."

Tom stood back and watched as the airplane swept into the air again. He smiled to himself as Will turned toward the village and the house beyond. Tom was a very good judge of character. He knew 'sensible' did not describe Will Turner. Anybody who built their own airplane then launched it from a catapult could never be described in that way. He sensed Will was diligent, however, and that quality meant much more to him as an aviator and a businessman.

Tom was correct in that Will put a philosophy of work into practice every day—not that he would have described it as such. His approach manifested itself as diligence, but it went beyond that. Will Turner approached any task with almost religious zeal. His view was simply that having been given a job, and paid for it, it was his duty to carry out the task to the very best of his ability. He expected that of himself, and he expected the same from anybody else. The temptation was there to fool around. He had a powerful machine to himself, and he was gaining confidence in his ability to control it by the minute. But the young aviator stuck rigidly to the schedule drawn up by Tom. He gained almost as much pleasure from the growing columns of carefully pencilled data, as from the act of flight itself.

Within the confines of his self-imposed discipline, however, Will still had time to experiment. He had his first encounter with a cloud; a harmless puffball of white vapor that wandered into his path on the second day of testing. He held his breath for the silent shock of collision, shivered to its chill touch and the sudden muffling of sound, then laughed out loud as he plunged back into the world of sunlight.

❧ ♦♦♦ ☙

The weather stayed fine for the entire week, warm by English standards, but Will become painfully aware that a small increase in altitude led to a big drop in temperature."I have to admit," he had confided to Aunt Connie, "I might be a warm-blooded man. I don't think Florida is the ideal place for the aviator to acclimatize."

She laughed and disappeared into the attic, returning with a long black leather coat. "Try this on for size," she urged. "Your Uncle John had it made for riding when we were stationed in the hill country of Nepal. It should fit you. And, look here, it has these straps that fasten behind your knees to stop it flapping in the breeze." The double-breasted garment fit perfectly.

Kate made him turn all the way around in front of her. "I say, Will, you'll cut a dash in that—very sinister it looks, too!"

"Well, that was your Uncle John all over. A taste for the theatrical." Connie spoke fondly of her husband who had died a few years before the end of the last century.

◆◆◆

Cousin Kate—like Will's sister, Victoria—showed an interest in aviation and was a frequent visitor to the flying field; she made herself useful in any way she could. "Oh good heavens, Tom," she said, holding his hand firmly while carefully cleaning a gash in his thumb, "what are we going to do with you?" It was Friday morning and Will had almost completed the engine trials.

"More to the point," said Tom, wincing, "what are we going to do with you, Miss Katie?"

"Don't you worry about me, Tom Armstrong," she neatly bound his thumb with a clean dressing. "As soon as I'm old enough to take the entrance exams, I'm off to study medicine. Then you'll have to call me *Doctor* Kate."

He studied his neatly repaired thumb, "That will be a pleasure, young lady. In the meantime you can put the kettle on and stop being cheeky." She laughed and stuck her tongue out.

A soft sighing sound, accompanied by a gentle burble of exhaust, told them Will had completed the last hour of the test program and was bringing in the Flanders monoplane—directly over their heads. Kate went to the door, swinging the kettle in her hand, to watch him land.

"Nine out of ten for that landing," she announced. She watched the Flanders taxi back to the hangar then turned to Tom. "Can Will take me up before you pull the motor out?"

Tom hesitated for a moment, "Okay, but on condition he passes his tests on Monday. He might be one of the most experienced pilots in the country now, but I don't want you flying with an uncertificated pilot."

Kate's face lit up, "Oh, Tom, that's wonderful. You've arranged it!"

He took the kettle from her and placed it on the stove, "Yes, I have, but it's not all good news. The people at Hendon are quite happy for him to take the Royal Aero Club ticket there, but they are insisting he use a school machine. Mr. Beatty was quite honest with me, he admits word has gone 'round about how well the Flanders goes, and he doesn't want the people he is charging seventy-five quid to teach, demanding to know why they have to learn on something not much better than a powered kite. I'm afraid allowing Will to go whizzing around in a modern aeroplane would set the cat amongst the pigeons."

Will had walked in unnoticed, "What pigeons are those, Tom?"

"The ones you are going to be joining at eight o'clock on Monday morning, William, at Hendon."

Will grabbed Tom's arms, "Are you serious? D'you mean that? I get to take my ticket Monday?"

Tom laughed as Will led him in a little jig, "Steady on, old boy, as I was telling Kate, there's a catch. You have to fly one of their machines. I've taken the liberty of renting a Longhorn."

Will's eyebrows shot up, "A Longhorn? That's a cow!"

"It might be, but I will go up with you first to make sure it's safe." Will still looked puzzled. "It's a Maurice Farman pusher biplane," Tom explained. "They call it the Longhorn because it carries the elevator on booms in front of the nacelle. There's a sister machine from the same company they call the Shorthorn. That has a more conventional arrangement with the elevators behind. There's not much difference between them—they both fly like pregnant cows."

Tom's assessment of the flying qualities of Mr. Farman's designs did nothing to dampen Will's spirits. As far as he was concerned he was about to realize his life's ambition to become a fully qualified aviator, and he was going to fly a new type of airplane. As he cycled home with Kate later that day he felt as happy as he ever had in his life. As it was still early in the evening they stopped at the Bull. At this early hour it was considered quite respectable for Kate to sit in the garden at the rear of the building to enjoy a lemonade. Will had just brought the drinks to their table, they were alone in the garden, when young Ernie, the post office messenger boy, came clattering around the side of the pub. He wore a dark blue, military style uniform with big brass buttons and a stiff peaked cap reminiscent of an American Civil War soldier. He took his job very seriously, though tangling his feet in the pedals of his bike as he discarded it against the wall ruined the regimental effect.

He recovered and marched up to where they sat, saluting smartly, "Telegram for you, Mr.Turner, I was just on my way to the house when I saw your bike outside."

"Thank you, Ernie," Will signed the book thrust under his nose. "Won't you join us?"

"No thank you, sir, not while I'm on duty." Ernie saluted again, about-turned and promptly tripped over his pedals a second time as he mounted his bike.

Kate stifled a laugh, "Oh dear, Little Ernie wants to join the army, but they won't have him until he's old enough." She looked expectantly at Will as he tore open the envelope, Kate was still young enough not to assume a telegram automatically brought bad news.

The message inside was not in itself tragic, but it reminded Will that his life had started to collect complications. *"Pinkertons report Roscoe* ~ stop ~ *passenger manifest Kronprinzessen Cecilie* ~ stop ~ *North German Lloyd Line* ~ stop ~ *take care* ~ stop ~ *Jeff."*

"Oh, how exciting!" Kate gushed. "The star-crossed lover bent on revenge. You'd better watch out, Will."

He looked at her carefully; his cousin clearly found this thrilling news. He could not blame her for not taking it seriously, as she did not know all the facts. "Kate, my dear," he kept his voice level, "he killed a man in a similar situation." He could not have created more of an effect by throwing a bucket of icy water in her face.

"You're joking!" she said, half hoping, half demanding.

"I wish I was," he replied evenly, then went on to explain the circumstances of the incident at Yale.

"But why is he free? Why isn't he in prison?" she insisted.

Will shrugged, "Because there was not enough evidence to convict him. Because he claimed it was an accident, but mostly because his daddy has influence and can afford the best lawyers."

"That's wrong!" Kate said, stunned.

"I know," Will agreed, "and I'm glad you feel that way, but I'm 'fraid it's the way these things go."

"Then there's no justice," Kate grumbled. "But don't you worry, Will," she said brightening, "if Roscoe shows up within twenty miles of here the village grapevine will let us know."

Will studied his pint carefully, took a sip and considered for a moment. "I'm not goin' to get all steamed up 'bout this. I'm not sure, but I don't think that line sails direct to England. For whatever reason I reckon he's sailin' to Europe. Anyways, it's not my hide I'm worried about."

"Well, you should be," Kate insisted. "But what is it that worries you?"

Will tugged at his ear, "It sounds 'daft' as you would say, but it's the sheer embarrassment that man causes, wherever he goes." He could see her looking doubtful, and decided to explain further.

"You have a beautiful village here, things go on in a nice *orderly* way. The seasons come 'round, you play your cricket, make hay while the sun shines, gather in the harvest, go to church. Then everybody is polite an' friendly—" He stopped because Kate had abandoned her attempt to listen politely and was laughing openly. "What did I say?" he asked.

"Well, I'm glad we made a good impression, Will, but if that were all true, this would be the most *boring* place on earth!" She paused to sip her lemonade.

"This is a *village.* Underneath the polite exterior you'll find jealousy, pride, ignorance, drunkenness, cruelty." She stopped again, looked around carefully then lowered her voice, "We even have passion."

"What are you sayin'?"

Kate winked, "No names, no 'pack drill', as Joe says—you'll have to work that out for yourself."

Will was irritated, but decided not to press his cousin for details. "Well, that's as may be, but I'm not fixin' to inflict that idiot, Roscoe, on the people of this village. If he shows up in the area, I'll have to move on," he said, looking decidedly grim.

Kate was horrified, "Oh no! Will, you can't!" Tears appeared in her eyes.

Surprised by the force of her reaction, Will took Kate's hand. "He's libel to break bad, Kate. I daren't take the chance of somethin' like that happenin' here." He stopped and looked carefully at her, then gently pushed her chin with his knuckles, "'Specially to you."

She gulped, "Oh, Will, you're sweet, but I can take care of myself. And the village can take care of itself. What's more, I bet if you asked, everybody would say let him come. We'd teach him some manners, and knock some sense into him!"

Will's mood lifted, "Maybe that's what he needs to break himself of this foolishness. I'd like to take him aside an' try to explain I wasn't tryin' to steal his lady away. An' if that don't work, well...," he bunched his fists.

"You'll give him a good thrashing!" Kate finished for him, a note of malice in her voice.

"Cousin!" he tried to sound disapproving. "You sound like to enjoyin' the prospect."

She grinned wickedly, "I told you life can be boring in a village. Anyway, it doesn't sound as if Roscoe's coming this way, and you have more important things to worry about." The only thing that might have worried Will, apart from Roscoe, was the test he had to take on Monday, but he looked forward to it with minimal concern.

The weekend passed quietly. They worked all day Saturday, as did everybody else, but shared the custom of finishing earlier in the afternoon. The practice of attending church twice on Sunday had ended in most families by the beginning of the 20th century, leaving Sunday afternoons and evenings free for leisure pursuits. The village street usually filled with swarms of cyclists, members of the growing London cycling clubs that proliferated following the invention of the pneumatic tire. The bicycle gave a freedom to city-bound working people previously unknown. They thought nothing of covering sixty miles in a day.

Will spent his Sunday afternoon quietly with Kate, Aunt Connie and two visitors. Will's uncle and cousin had been detained by their military duties. They had attended the picturesque parish church, St. Michael's, in the morning. At the time, Will was convinced he was being shown off again by Kate. She seemed to have what could only be described as a satisfied smirk on her face as she greeted her friends.

Marjorie had invited herself and Lucy to tea at Penrose Cottage in the afternoon. This was taken in the garden at a wrought iron table set under a spreading horse chestnut tree. Will marveled at how thin Maisie could slice a sandwich, then fill it with cucumber which he identified as a form of squash cut into wafer-thin circular slices. He would have needed a truckload to satisfy his hunger. Fortunately, Maisie also baked a magnificent fruitcake. This was moist and crumbled in the mouth, loaded with raisins and sultanas and baked with a golden brown crust. It went perfectly with the tea served in delicate china cups.

He found himself grinning as he recalled Henry's dig at Nathan's acquired habit of drinking with his pinkie extended. Will found the bone china handles so small it was the only way to do it decorously.

His first meeting with Lucy, Marjorie's daughter, at dinner the previous week he felt had not gone well. Kate had pointed out to him, with uncalled for glee in his opinion, that she was bright enough to see that Will had succumbed to the temptation to, as she put it, "take the

Mickey" out of Marjorie. Will had no idea who this Mickey might be, but guessed he had been rumbled taking the rise.

He would have understood if now Lucy's attitude to him was frosty, instead she seemed at pains to be friendly. She greeted him with a warm smile and a small package.

"I hope you don't think I'm being forward, Mr. Turner, but I took the liberty of preparing a little gift for our local birdman."

He felt a rush of relief; he had no wish to make enemies. "Ma'am, I am charmed," he said, taking the package, "and please, call me Will." They all looked at him expectantly as he opened the package to reveal a strange knitted garment. He held it up; it looked like a giant sock with a hole near the top. He sensed Kate and Lucy restraining outright laughter.

"It's perfect, Will," Kate said. She took it and slipped it over his head. "It's called a Balaclava helmet. He knew he looked ridiculous but he also knew it would keep his ears warm.

He smiled graciously, "Lucy, I shall treasure this." He took it off and held it up to the light, "The stitching is masterful." He also understood the subtlety behind the gift. She had simultaneously made a lovely personal gesture and peace offering, while making him look more than a little foolish; perfect and subtle revenge on behalf of her mother. They smiled at each other, and Lucy, seeing her mother turning away, gave him a very broad and private wink of her eye.

Chapter Fourteen

THE LENGTH OF THE DAYS AS THE SUMMER SOLSTICE, MIDSUMMER Day, approached, surprised Will. The sun had not risen when Tom collected him the following morning at five, but daylight had already flushed the night away. A few mares' tails—high cirrus clouds—brushed pink by the dawn gave the sky depth. Tom scanned the heavens.

"Perfect," he announced, "the air will be like silk." Will buttoned his leather coat and reversed his cap. Tom went to start his Rudge motorcycle but paused as Kate appeared at the kitchen door, rubbing sleep from her eyes. She was barefoot and had not bothered putting a gown over her nightdress. "What ho! Who is this nymph I see?" Tom asked.

She looked at him sleepily and yawned, "Oh, shut up, Tom. Aren't you two having breakfast before you go?"

"I don't feel hungry, Kate. Too excited I guess." Will admitted. His cousin nodded.

"We'll get something on the way home," Tom reassured her. "It will only take Will a half hour or so to complete the tests. We need to hurry back."

"Why is that?" Kate asked, still half asleep.

"Because Will's taking you flying, don't you remember?"

Kate woke up. "Yes! Too right he is!" She stretched up and kissed both of them. "Aunt Connie says if you kiss somebody before they make a journey, they won't have an accident."

The bike roared into life and Will mounted the pillion. Tom gave Kate a thumbs-up sign, "You listen to your Auntie, she's a wise old bird." They shot off down the drive in a spray of gravel and a haze of blue smoke.

The roads were empty of other traffic all the way to the outskirts of the County Town, Hertford. They pushed on along country lanes until they emerged on the Great North Road near the town of Hatfield, known for the magnificent mansion simply called Hatfield House, the seat of the famous Cecil family for centuries. Tom took a shortcut across the estate to avoid the town itself. He eased off the throttle at a point where an ancient, withered oak tree stood alone in a meadow.

"See that old oak?" he called back over his shoulder. "They say Queen Elizabeth was sitting under there when they came to tell her the throne was hers." Will gazed at the historic landmark as they roared past, astonished Tom could treat it so casually.

The minor roads they had been using made do with a surface of crushed stone, but the Great North Road, the principal route between London and Scotland, boasted a hard black-top surface. The Rudge stormed along. Tom kept a wary eye out for lurking speed traps. Even at this early hour, two enthusiastic policemen armed with a stopwatch could result in a stiff fine and a lecture from a crusty old magistrate about young hooligans. Hendon Aerodrome lay in the country just to the northwest of the capital's urban sprawl. The small towns and villages that passed—Barnet, Totteridge, Mill Hill—all stretched out fingers, eager to join.

The area surrounding the flying field, however, remained comfortably free of concrete and brick. A high wooden fence surrounded the aerodrome; erected in a bid to discourage nonpaying spectators at the displays that drew thousands every weekend. Tom swung in through the gate and stopped underneath a long wooden pavilion, raised on a framework of iron beams. Despite the early hour, still well before seven, the field hummed with activity. Will heard the now familiar ripping snarl of a rotary engine being run up next to the sheds lining one side of the flying area. As he watched, a fragile monoplane hopped into the air before flopping back to the ground after a few yards.

Tom pointed. "Deperdussin: single wing design for training, 35 horsepower Anzani radial—pathetic motor—couldn't pull the skin off a rice pudding. The Deperdussin schools spend weeks teaching people how to steer the wretched things on the ground—safest place for 'em. After that, they spend weeks doing straights, that's what *he's* doing—hopping up and down like a blasted kangaroo. Complete waste of time." Will looked at his friend; it was the first time he had seen Tom show real passion.

Tom pointed at a biplane gliding toward the threshold of the field.

Its name described it perfectly. "Bristol Boxkite," he said, "actually flies better than it deserves to. Have you ever seen anything so ruddy antiquated?" Will admitted he had not, except in the illustrated pages of one of the prophetic Victorian novels about flight he had devoured as a boy. Apart from the spindly-wheeled undercarriage it hardly appeared more advanced than the original Wright Flyer. "The Bristol Company has come a long way in five years," Tom added thoughtfully. The two people on board sat completely exposed to the elements on a ladder type structure, fixed between the two wings. The motor drove a pusher propeller behind them while the tail unit dragged along fixed to spindly booms sprouting from the wings.

A cheery and very French voice interrupted Tom's systematic critique of every machine in sight. "'Allo, Tom, *Mon Brave!*" The owner appeared briefly above them on the viewing platform that ran the length of the pavilion. Will heard him bounding down the steps then stepped back in surprise as he vaulted the railing and dropped six feet to land in front of them. The little man immediately introduced Will to French customs: he kissed Tom on both cheeks, but to Will's relief shook his hand vigorously. The first impression he gave came from his intense, dark eyes. These twinkled above the biggest mustache Will had ever seen. Immense, shaggy even, it did not droop in Tom's walrus style but sprouted stiff and waxed across each side of his animated face.

"Will, allow me to introduce Monsieur Louis Calmette," Tom said, "aviateur *extraordinaire* and the man who inspired Blériot's moustache."

The Frenchman twisted one end of his whiskers, "Brave Blériot may 'ave been first across La Manche, but I, Calmette, 'ave ze bigger mustache." Calmette tempered Gallic pride with a sense of humor. He linked his arm with Will's and started to march him toward the hangars. "Now, Will, I am the official observer for the Aero Club. You understand what you must do for your certificate, *n'est-ce pas?*"

Will reeled off the requirements, "Two distance flights of at least five kilometers in a closed circuit, marked by two posts not more than five hundred meters apart, changin' direction after each post so the flight will consist of an uninterrupted series of five figures of eight."

"Bravo! You understand ze metric measures?"

"Not really," Will confessed. "I calculated it as three miles an' about two hundred yards."

"*Bien,* close enough," Calmette confirmed, "and ze altitude flight?"

"One flight reachin' at least fifty meters, that's one hundred an' sixty four feet—"

"Give or take an inch," Tom grinned.

"An' I must land from all three flights with the motor stopped before touchin' the ground and bring my machine to rest within a distance of fifty meters from a point I get to choose."

"*Exactement.* Zis makes no problem for you." Louis Calmette regarded the whole exercise as a mere formality. He knew from an earlier conversation with Tom that Will had over fifty hours solo flight to his credit. Most candidates for the Royal Aero Club Aviator's certificate were lucky to have achieved four hours, and this was often spread over months.

"Ah, there we are, Will," Tom pointed. "Looks like they've pulled Daisy out of the dairy ready for us." Hendon Flying Club had been good as their word. The Longhorn stood waiting outside its shed.

"Good grief," Will stared in amazement.

"Daisy?" asked Louis.

"Yes. Where Will hails from, a longhorn is a breed of cow," Tom explained.

"Ah, you English wiss your funny pet names. But zis one I like...she flies like a cow."

"There you are, Will," Tom said triumphantly, "told you so." He walked up to the strange contraption and pinged one of the flying wires. "Nicely rigged though." He ducked under the framework extending forward of the nacelle and looked into the cockpit, "And they've emptied the bath water, too."

Will laughed. He knew exactly what Tom meant. In the Flanders the pilots sat in a cockpit about the size of a large bath. The builders of the Maurice Farman Longhorn had taken the idea further: they appeared to have fixed the tub completely to the lower of the two wings. They had then fitted a Renault V8 motor behind it, driving an enormous two-bladed propeller that pushed the machine through the air. Not content with two sets of wings to produce a biplane, they built a biplane tail with two horizontal stabilizers kept apart by two rudders. This assembly was attached to the rest of the airplane by a spidery skeleton of booms fixed to the wings on either side of the propeller. Possibly as a result of an accidental over ordering of wood, fabric, and wire, they had then decided to mount the elevator forward of the cockpit on an extended framework, instead of on the trailing edge of the horizontal stabilizer on the tail. The whole assembly was braced up with a multitude of wires.

Tom twanged another wire. "They say if you release a sparrow inside the wires and it escapes, you've lost a wire."

Will looked over the Longhorn suspiciously, "I could almost believe that." He stood back and tried to judge the size of the propeller. It had to be nearly twelve feet from tip to tip. The top wing, longer than the lower on which the crew nacelle sat, he guessed as over fifty feet in span.

Tom had already started a thorough inspection. He heaved up and down on the lower wing tips. "Don't worry about creaks and groans from the structure, Will," he advised. "It's cracking noises that should ring alarm bells." He ducked through the wires strung between the upper and lower tail booms to gain access to the motor. He poked and prodded then ran his finger around the cylinder heads. He examined the grime on his fingertip. "No problems there. I think we can go flying. We have to hire it for a minimum of an hour, so I'll come up and check you out. Then you do the exercises and we'll have breakfast." They scrambled through the forest of wires and struts to climb into the cockpit. Will took the front place while Tom settled in behind him. Will had the only set of controls. His feet found the rudder pedals easily enough but he hesitated before firmly grabbing the control stick. It was the strangest design he could imagine. Like a giant pair of spectacles mounted on top of a robust vertical pole, it felt like holding the handlebars on his Harley. He tried to move it in the same way as in the Flanders—gently.

"No, Will, you really have to give it a heave," Tom said from behind him. Will heaved and the ailerons reluctantly moved in the correct manner, far out on the wings. "At least it has an aileron for each wing," Tom pointed out, "and it needs them. Try the elevator."

Will pushed hard on the spectacles. The control moved easier and he was pleased to see the elevator move in front of him. He shook his head, "Odd, real unusual."

Tom chuckled grimly behind him, "Just wait until we get off the ground." The cockpit boasted two instruments: a tachometer displaying the engine revolutions and an altimeter plumbed into a box about nine inches square. This was the barograph, a simple pressure-measuring device designed to record the altitude achieved for the height portion of the test. The engine controls consisted of a simple switch, clearly purchased from a domestic electrical supplier, for the magneto ignition and a throttle lever fixed to the left wall of the nacelle. Seated in the comfortable wicker chair, Will found the sides of the cockpit came to waist height. A tall narrow windshield afforded some protection.

"There's no airspeed indicator, Tom." Will searched in vain for some kind of instrument to tell him his speed through the air.

"Don't worry, matey," Tom sounded reassuring, "this thing is so bloody slow a *calendar* is all we'll need." He twisted in his seat and gave a thumbs-up to the mechanic standing behind. "Okay, Will, switch on, crack the throttle about half an inch." The mechanic threaded himself through the tail booms to reach the propeller. The motor had already been started and warmed so there was no need for the lengthy priming procedure. A single swing set the Renault purring.

The noise from the motor was pleasantly muted, but the sound of the huge propeller reminded Will of the big paddle steamers still plying the St. John's River back home in northern Florida. *Whup—whup—whup,* it thrashed the air.

"Now, Captain," Tom ordered, "full steam ahead—let her rip!"

Will could not understand why Tom laughed when he said this, but he soon found out. "Ripping" was something the Farman biplane would never do. He pushed the throttle wide open. The duet of motor and propeller increased in volume, but nothing much happened. Then, seconds later, with a gentle squeak from the undercarriage the airplane started to roll. Hendon, like every other flying field in use, did not boast runways as such. Takeoff and landing was always directly into wind on whatever part of the field was available. The windsock hung limp on its pole. All Will had to do was coax his airplane up to speed and point it straight ahead. This he found easier said, than done. "Daisy", as he had already come to think of the big biplane, imitated her namesakes by refusing to be hurried. The undercarriage creaked and groaned as she cantered across the grass. The wings flexed and shook and the whole structure wobbled alarmingly. Eventually Will's sensitive fingers felt some life in the controls.

"Wait for it, wait for it," Tom cautioned. "Now, a gentle pull." Will eased back on the control column. The rumble from beneath them ceased as the wheels left the ground. Will glanced over the side to confirm that they were climbing, at the same time pushing firmly on the throttle to make sure they had all of the limited power available.

"Hold her on this, Will," Tom instructed. He could communicate easily by leaning forward and hardly had to raise his voice as the motor, mounted behind them, barely intruded. "Don't let the nose go too high, and whatever you do—don't over bank in the turns, she'll just slip down to the ground."

They sailed majestically over the airfield hedge, still low enough that Will could return the cheery wave of the postman cycling past. He heaved the controls over and pushed the nose down to maintain speed. "Rudder, Will—give her some help." The Farman obediently swung into a left turn to parallel the road running beside the field. Tom stretched to reach the throttle to make sure it was fully forward. He pointed down to the road. "Postie's making a race of it."

Will glanced down. Sure enough the friendly postman had his head down and was pedaling furiously. "Nah—I've got the legs of him." Will said confidently. They slowly circled the field gaining height while Will absorbed the feel of the controls. "She's real sluggish, Tom, but I reckon anybody could fly this airplane. I kinda like her."

"If I bolted an engine and wings to Fred's garden shed you'd enjoy flying it. Don't be fooled though," he warned, "she'll bite like any other machine if you don't concentrate. Be especially careful in the turns. Keep the speed up and the wings as near level as you can." Tom's reservations about the lateral control were well-founded. Will found the elevator moved easily enough and gave positive control pitching the machine up or down, but even full deflection of the ailerons only gave sluggish rolling movement. It seemed to take an age for the wings to settle back to level flight after a turn.

Will held the Farman straight and level at five hundred feet, then peered out along the line of the wings. He swung the controls quickly from side to side. "I think the wings are so long they're twistin' when the ailerons deflect, so they cancel out the effect."

"Well done, Will," Tom said, "I've been telling them that for ages. You'll do better to try to pick up the wing with rudder if you hit some bumpy air." The Farman was now over the airfield boundary. "Cut the power now and bring her down," Tom directed.

"From here?" Will twisted around, his face showing his surprise.

"Trust me, she glides like a piano." Will pulled the power back and pushed the nose down. Tom had hardly exaggerated. The steady hum of the motor subsided to a low chuckle; the swish of the idling propeller became audible again. The loudest sound now was the musical whistle of the breeze in the multitude of wires. Will picked a point a hundred yards from the sheds to level out. He heaved back on the controls as the ground slowly expanded in front of them to check the dive. The big biplane hovered for a moment, then flopped to the ground. They ran for a few feet before the Farman tottered to a full stop, panting gently. "See what I mean?" Tom asked as he climbed down.

"Take your point, Tom," Will agreed. "It should be easy enough to hit the landing spot."

"Fair enough, use the same point for your three landings. Louis has set up the markers for you." He waved to Louis who stood beside a white pole topped with a red flag. "I'll be on the other marker with the photographer." Will looked to the other white pole where he could see a distant figure setting up a tripod. He grinned at Tom, it was a thoughtful gesture, he would be able to send a memorable picture to his folks. Tom struggled out from between the wires and stood clear. "Okay, Will, off you go, and don't forget what I told you about over banking."

Will gave him a thumbs up, tightened his seat belt, pulled down his goggles and pushed the throttle forward again. Will immediately felt a difference in the Farman. Relieved of Tom's weight it broke into a brisk trot and left the ground after a run of only a few hundred feet. Will quickly swung onto the course. He found that by gaining height on the short straights between the poles he could make the turns in a shallow dive. This seemed to give some life to the sluggish controls and helped keep the turns inside a respectable radius. He quickly established a rhythm as he swooped and dived through his figures of eight. Before long he burst into song as he poled his ungainly charge around the course, *"Oh, he flies through the air with the greatest of ease, that da-aring young man on the flying trapeze."* The popular ditty suited the occasion perfectly. Will completed his obligatory two landings with the engine off; the waiting mechanic sprinting out each time to restart the engine had perfected the maneuver. He dived flat on his belly to slide under the booms, then threw himself flat again as he fell back from the whirling propeller to roll neatly out of the way. Will blessed him for his skill as he urged Daisy into the air for the final part of the test: the climb to height.

Will felt relaxed about this part of the exercise; the height required was minimal, even by the standards of the day. The Longhorn was quite new, and the motor ran smooth and strong. According to the manufacturers it should have been able to reach one thousand feet in less than five minutes. Will could see no reason not to find out how well she climbed; there was no restriction on how high you could ascend for the test. He climbed in wide easy circles, always keeping the field in gliding distance. As he climbed he noted and enjoyed the landmarks as they presented themselves for his circular tour of inspection. Harrow School, grand and imposing, dominated the hill above the town of Harrow itself. To the south he could make out the silver thread of the Thames leading to the City of London itself. He calculated each circuit of the field gained him two hundred feet. The fifth circuit, he guessed, should reveal Tower Bridge and St. Paul's Cathedral to the east. There might be a chance he could make out Buckingham Palace, he thought hopefully. The bridge and cathedral came into view exactly as he planned, now all he had to do was look back down the river two or three miles.

Will hardly noticed the tremor that ran through the frame of his machine. He did notice he was twisting his head to keep the city in view: it was as if the Farman had taken a mind to turn away.

"Whooooa!" The horizon suddenly tilted at a crazy angle as a blast of air struck the side of his face. Instead of scared he found himself feeling angry and foolish. All those warnings from Tom about over banking and here he was standing on one wingtip, in full view of everyone. He threw the control over to the left to correct the bank. The machine shuddered again and the ground, now growing closer by the second started to revolve. "What is going on here!?" he demanded of nobody but his airplane. The plane seemed to be slipping and spiraling sideways into the sheds below him.

Will's mind raced. The nose had not dropped much, but everything else fitted. It was a spin—a whirling, flat spin. His left leg shot out to jam the rudders hard against the turn. He pushed forward on the stick. Nothing worked. The lazy turn continued. He had only one control left. With an effort of will—because it went against all reason—he threw the stick back to the central position. He shut his eyes; the grass was a blur over his right shoulder. He felt himself twisted again. He opened his eyes to see the wall of the shed hurtling toward him. He was level again and traveling at the highest speed the Farman had made, seeming all the faster because he was skimming the ground. He heaved back on the controls and the Farman leaped the sheds with the grace of a steeplechaser, onto the main field itself. He saw his landing mark, cut the switch, and the big biplane settled obediently to the ground, as if exhausted by its antics.

Will sat in stunned silence for a moment, humbled by the certain knowledge that luck had saved him from the consequences of his own mistake; then he became aware of the noise: cheering and applause. For the second time in his flying career an excited crowd surrounded his machine. Louis Calmette pushed his way forward. "Bravo, Will, *c'est magnifique!* It is not needed to make ze ragtime flying for ze test, but zat was superb. When you went behind ze shed ev'ry body is holding ze breaths!" Will realized he was still holding *his* breath; he let it out slowly, unbuckled his seat belt and climbed shakily to the ground. Several bystanders took turns grabbing his hand and slapping him on the back.

"Thank you, Mr. Calmette, I hope nobody thought I was grandstandin'."

"Who cares, Will?" Calmette shrugged. "Stunting brings ze crowds. Crowds mean money. Everyone is 'appy." Will looked at Tom who looked far from happy. He was white—the transparent white of a sheet of ice. Calmette carried on. He produced a document for Will to sign. "Bien! Your license comes wiss ze postman in a few days, but from now, you are an *aviateur*!" He took Will firmly by the shoulders and planted a kiss on each cheek. "Welcome to ze fellowship of ze air." The crowd cheered again. "Now let's celebrate, bacon and eggs *mes braves.*"

The little Frenchman led the way to the restaurant. As they reached the bottom of the stairs Tom grabbed Will's elbow. "If you *ever* pull a stunt like that again, I'll...I'll...," he was too furious to think what he was going to do.

Will turned to face him, "I swear, Tom, that was no stunt—that was a crash that didn't happen."

Tom glared, "Are you saying you didn't do that on purpose?"

"Swear to God, Tom, I don't know what happened, but it surely wasn't deliberate." Will looked shamefaced but Tom softened.

"Good grief, Will, that's almost worse. Come on, we'll have the inquest later, right now you buy breakfast."

The restaurant occupied much of the top of the two-floor building. The steps climbed up to a balcony that provided a view of the field, but this morning everyone was inside. Tom pushed through the door; as Will followed a burst of cheering and laughter greeted him. He grinned self-consciously. For the principle catering establishment at one of the world's leading centers for aviation Flo's Café rated as basic, but what it lacked in finery it made up for in atmosphere, service, and generous portions. For Tom, its greatest appeal was the egalitarian principles established by Flo Coppello, whose democratic style appealed to the ethos of the aviators. From the most junior apprentice mechanic to the wealthiest titled playboy, Flo subjected them all to the same cheerful abuse, in a voice honed in the streets of Whitechapel. "Whad'ya mean yer bleedin' egg's too runny, Mr. Hawker? I don't know soddin' colonials come over 'ere, tryin' to tell me 'ow to cook." Will looked over to see the world famous aviator grinning at her.

"Sorry, Flo," Hawker apologized in his rich Australian accent.

"I should think so, too." She turned her fierce gaze on a handsome young man who was suspiciously prodding at his breakfast with a fork. "Now don't you start, Mr. Beaumont, are you planning on eating that breakfast or wearing it?"

The implied threat was enough for Mr. Beaumont, "No, Flo, I'm eating it, look!" He quickly shoveled food into his mouth. Will was surprised when Flo turned to their table with a winning smile revealing false teeth that did not quite fit her mouth. She plucked a pencil from behind her ear and pushed her top teeth into position with the end.

"Now it's nice to see a real gentleman in 'ere fer once. 'Ow are you, Mr. Armstrong?"

"All the better for seeing you, my angel. That'll be two special number ones, please." Tom knew she expected her customers to be decisive. She wrote their order on her pad then shrieked in the general direction of the kitchen.

"The works...twice." She turned to Louis Calmette, pencil poised.

"I will 'ave two croissant, freshly baked to ze color of ze morning sun, some 'am, thinly sliced and *un petit morceau* of your best strawberry jam. With zis, I will 'ave some butter of Normandy and a bowl of steaming coffee—from Colombian beans of course." Louis offered his most winning smile.

Flo turned back to the kitchen, "Make that three special number ones for table four," she bellowed before stalking off to the next customers.

"Why do you do that every time, Louis?" Tom asked, "You know you really want the fry up anyway."

Calmette lit a cigarette and then fanned the smoke away from his eyes. He shrugged, "I like to live...'ow you say?...*Dangereux!*"

Will looked around. The morning sunlight streamed through picture windows looking out over the field. The customers sat at plain wooden tables with red and white checkered oilcloth covers. Framed photographs of aircraft in flight and posed outside hangars adorned the cream painted walls. Posters from air meetings in France and Germany added a splash of color. Flo felt her café had a certain status to maintain and the large sign just inside the door proved that, as far as she was concerned. "No overalls" it ordered, while a similar sign over the till at the end of the counter proclaimed, "No tick."

"What's tick?" Will asked innocently.

"Credit," Tom explained. "She might just as well hang a sign saying 'do not ask for credit as a punch in the mouth often offends'."

"Is she always so...," Will paused for a moment, "aggressive?"

"Oh Lord, no," Tom exclaimed. "She's not aggressive. She just treats us like a crowd of schoolboys. She has a lot of mouths to feed if she's going to keep her prices low. And she has told me that's her intention as otherwise we would all starve, being in the main penniless."

Louis nodded in agreement, "She is right, you know. Zis flying is like a drug for some. Zey will spend all ze monay. Take my advice, Will, if you must 'ave a passion, make it women!"

"Beggin' your pardon," Will said politely, "but you seem to have ignored your own advice." Their food arrived at that moment balanced by a waitress of middle years. As she deftly lobbed their plates down in front of them, Louis took her hand. He kissed it and gazed adoringly into her eyes.

"'Ow are you today, my leetle cabbage?" She giggled and punched him on the shoulder with her free hand. Louis winked at Will, "Zat's what you think!" They applied themselves to the serious business of eating.

When Flo said "the works", Will could see she meant it. "What's this in the fried potato?" he queried, finding what looked suspiciously like carrot and cabbage mixed in.

"That's not fried potato, Will, that's 'bubble and squeak'. What you have there is the leftovers of yesterday's dinner menu mixed with mashed potato, then fried." Tom explained.

Will shrugged, "Fine by me." He had not felt hungry at first. The excitement of his near crash left him with a hollow feeling, but Flo's homestyle cooking soon filled it. Louis ate with serious concentration, gulped his coffee then took his leave. He had another test to officiate at, and this one promised to be more of a trial, as the candidate had only amassed two hours flying time. Tom had noticed that one of the early diners at the table behind them kept looking in their direction. He was not surprised when the stranger took the opportunity of taking the seat vacated by Louis.

"Do you mind if I join you gentlemen?" Will looked up in surprise, the newcomer was an American—an intense looking dark complexioned man he guessed to be about thirty.

"Please do," they welcomed him in chorus. He shook hands with them both.

"The name's Walter Brock. Would you be *the* Will Turner, the engine tuner?"

Will looked at him in disbelief, "I am Will Turner, but I'm not sure I can get by with that description. Are you plum certain I'm the right fella?"

Tom interjected, "I'd say that's a fair reputation, Will." He turned to Brock, "How did you come to hear of our young motor wizard?"

The American explained, "I've decided to take a crack at the Aerial Derby in a week or so and bought myself one of the new Morane-Saulnier monoplanes. I'm not pulling full RPM's and the guys here tell me I should take it to Armstrong's field and have Will Turner look at it. They say he should be easy to find because he's a Yankee like me." Brock smiled graciously, "I take note they are wrong on that count."

Will laughed, "Reckon they are, but it looks like you found me." He looked at Tom, "Can we help Mr. Brock?"

"Of course! We never turn away good custom if we can help it. There'll be a delay while we wait for the new motors to come up from Farnborough. How about Wednesday, Mr. Brock?"

"You betcha! How do I find you?" he produced an Ordnance Survey map of the area north of London, and Tom carefully marked their field and drew his attention to the landmarks he would need to identify it.

"We'll expect you about nine o'clock. When we hear you nearby we will fire a green flare. We'll have some coffee brewing," Tom promised.

"Sounds good to me, I'll look forward to seeing you. Now if you will excuse me gentlemen, I must make sure I have my entry into the Aero Club by this afternoon." Brock bade them farewell, leaving Tom and Will alone.

"Okay, Will, what the hell happened up there this morning?" he demanded, at the same time pouring Will more tea.

"It wasn't over banking, Tom, it was just what Rupert is trying to tell people—a spin."

Tom sat back and took a cigarette from a silver case. He tapped it reflectively on the back of his hand before lighting it. "Go on."

"I lost concentration, I admit. She was still climbing well, but I had some rudder on and just a little bank. Now that I think about it, she kinda shook her head just before tilting over."

"It looked like far too much bank from the ground," Tom gently pointed out. "Having said that, it all looked beautifully controlled. You just spiraled down, disappeared behind the sheds, then a second later hopped over them. At no time did it seem as if the nose was dropping. From where we stood you seemed to be making a tight turning descent. No wonder everybody was fooled. And no wonder I nearly had kittens!"

Will was sincere, "I really am sorry if I gave you a fright, Tom. The nose didn't drop because I didn't let it. I banged in full opposite rudder the moment I felt her let go. Thank the Lord, Rupert made those trials an' we talked about it. I reckon I just caught the spin in time. Even so I was still goin' in. Only when I threw the aileron control back to neutral position did I get her out. I still can't work out quite what happened there."

Tom blew smoke at the ceiling, "My guess, based on Rupert's theory, is that you unstalled the down-going wing by centering the controls, and that broke the spiral. What he said about every machine behaving differently is almost certainly correct. I suspect that the framework and the elevator dangling off the bow of dear old Daisy helped stop the nose falling and probably slowed down the loss of height. Whatever, you're in one piece." He stubbed his cigarette out by twisting it firmly in the ashtray then looked at Will with a sudden grin. "My dear old dad, bless him, says that experience is being able to recognize a mistake when you make it again. Try to prove him wrong." He glanced at his wrist watch, "Come on, Will, time to push on. You can drive."

The journey home took longer, but Will enjoyed the variety of traffic he had to negotiate. The horse drawn wagons kept as far in to the side of the road as they could to allow the faster motor trucks, that the English insisted on calling "lorries", to pass. Only the cars and motorcycles they encountered ran on modern pneumatic tires. The commercial traffic all rattled along on solid rubber tired wheels, usually with the rear axle driven by massive external chains. A long gradient led into the town of Barnet. Will, who had been raised with the railroad, picked up the unmistakable round, acid scent of a coal fired steam locomotive as they started the ascent. He glanced at the tracks running beside the road but they were empty of rail traffic. The source of the mystery perfume powered up the hill ahead of them. From the rear it appeared much the same as all the other trucks they had zoomed past, but Will had to wind the handle mounted on the gas tank of their motorcycle to gain the revs to pass. A clue to the truck's nature came from the plume of steam and smoke blasting into the air above it.

"What in blue blazes—," Will stared in amazement as they drew level. The forward section of the truck where he would have expected to see the hood, was a miniature railroad locomotive complete with a round horizontal boiler and a smokestack. The pistons and valve gear shuttled energetically back and forth on top of the boiler. A firebox flared in the conventional open cab. The whole thing gleamed with polished brass and a striking green paint job contrasting with crimson wheels. The crew grinned at his astonishment, their faces blackened with coal dust.

"It's a Foden steam wagon," Tom shouted in his ear. "Pa owns a dozen of them for carting finished cloth from the mill. The most efficient wagon you can buy, it's a patent compound engine."

"Now that's a machine I've just *got* to drive before I go home!" Will gave the odd vehicle a final admiring look before waving to the crew and accelerating away.

"I'll fix it up for you," Tom promised. He held on tight to the bike's carrier as Will took them weaving through the bustling traffic of Barnet.

They were back at the field within the hour to find Kate waiting for them. "Well, how did you get on?" she asked as Will pushed up his goggles. Tom climbed stiffly off the pillion and answered for him.

"Brilliant! He gave a performance they'll never forget at Hendon." They exchanged a look but Tom did not elaborate. "He's fully qualified to take a passenger, Kate, so lend a hand and we'll have you airborne." She needed no urging. Within minutes the Flanders stood outside the hangar. Kate—to Will and Tom's surprise as the day was warm—wore a long, lightweight coat. She unbuttoned it.

"What do you think?" she asked, giving a twirl. "Rupert had it run up for me by Burberrys of London in the Haymarket." She revealed a coverall suit made of tightly woven gabardine material. The cuffs closed tightly with reinforced straps while the inside of the high neck, that she revealed by undoing the buttons for their inspection was lined with a soft almost silk like material. "They call this 'glissade.' It's very smooth and allows me to turn my head easily," she explained. To be seen in public in such an outfit would have made her the subject of village gossip. To ensure "decency" she had to wear the coat over the top of the all-enveloping garment and the lace-up boots she wore. Kate pulled her hair back, tied it, then tucked it inside her collar. She completed her preparations with a tight fitting, leather flying helmet.

"I'm ready—let's fly," she said eagerly.

Tom had checked the machine from stem to stern. They had sufficient fuel and oil, and within minutes the Flanders soared into the air. After the incident that morning Will resolved to exercise the utmost care. The awareness of his precious passenger added to his newfound sense of responsibility. As they set course for the house he felt a tug at the control stick. "Can I have a go, Captain, perleeeease?" Will laughed and glanced down, they had sufficient height, he could quickly grab control back if she did anything dangerous.

"She's all yours, Kate," Will barely had time to offer as she took control and eased them into a turn over the family house, expertly balancing the rudder against the bank. He twisted around to look at her. Her face, what he could see of it under her dark goggles, was set with concentration.

"When you said Rupert had taken you up—how many times and what did you do?" he shouted.

She leaned forward, "Six times so far, and we've covered straight and level, turns, climbing and volplaning." She used the older term for gliding, just to put him in his place.

He rested his arms on the cockpit edge and leaned back, "Take me for a ride cousin Kate, as if you haven't already." They enjoyed a gentle tour of the district with Kate confidently navigating from landmark to landmark. They swooped over the village to wave to the children in the school playground, followed the railroad tracks to the little country town of Buntingford and caused a stir in the quaintly named village of Furneaux Pelham. After a half hour of pure joyriding, and for no other purpose than the sheer pleasure of it, they turned for home. Will had noted a change in the weather. The sun had almost disappeared behind a sheet of opaque cloud. To the south and west, where previously he had been able to make out the Chiltern Hills, now all he could see was a featureless bank of dirty gray vapor. Rupert and Tom had both warned him that an Atlantic front could close the weather down in a matter of minutes rather than hours. It was time to be back on the ground; he had had enough excitement for one day. Reluctantly, Kate gave the controls back to him and they were soon coasting to stop in front of the hangar.

They walked into the office, stripping off gloves and helmets as Tom put down the telephone. "That's odd, chaps," Tom said, not bothering to differentiate between the sexes. "That was Fred the gardener. He's asking if we saw anybody hanging around when we left this morning. He found the padlock—that should be on the shed door—missing."

"Aw hell, how much has been stolen?" Will asked.

"That's the peculiar thing. Nothing, just the lock."

"Maybe we disturbed them when we left so early," Will suggested.

Tom shrugged, "Oh well, no harm done."

Chapter Fifteen

FOR THE FIRST TIME SINCE HE HAD ARRIVED IN ENGLAND, WILL DID not enjoy the cycle ride home. The weather had broken. A fine drizzle had settled over the fields and the light, filtered through a mass of dense cloud, had acquired an odd, uneasy gleam. Despite the season he felt chilled.

"Good Lord, Kate, how can it be so cold in the summertime?" He could see his hands turning red on the handlebars of his bike.

She looked at him surprised, "You really are cold aren't you? And there's me thinking it's quite muggy. Never mind, I'll make you some hot cocoa when we get home." She picked up the pace and the hard work pedaling his bike warmed him. As soon as they arrived she disappeared into the kitchen, so Will took the call when he heard the telephone ring. When Kate returned with two steaming mugs of hot cocoa she realized immediately that something was wrong. Her cousin looked decidedly pale.

"What is it, Will?" she put the drinks down on a table in the hall.

"That was your father. It's Aunt Connie."

Kate's eyes opened wide, beseeching, "Oh no, she went up to town this morning. Tell me she's not been hurt."

"No, far from it," he said looking bewildered. "She's, she's... "

Kate's expression changed in an instant from fear to anticipation. "Auntie's done it!" she shrieked. "She's chained herself to the railings outside Number 10 Downing Street, hasn't she?"

Will shook his head slowly, he could hardly believe what he was about to say. "No," he spoke quietly, "she's chained herself to the goddamn Prime Minister."

Understanding dawned when he saw Kate's reaction to the news. For a moment she said nothing, then she jumped in the air with a whoop of delight, fell on him and embraced him fiercely. He felt stiff as a board to her.

"Oh come on, Will! Don't stand there like a great stuffed booby. Isn't this wonderful?"

He held her at arm's length. "You knew about this. You never said a word when you heard about the padlock."

"Of course I bloody well knew about it," she looked at him pityingly. "It was me who pinched it. Why did you think I was up so early?"

"I thought it was to see me off," he replied with just a touch of hurt in his voice.

"Oh, well, that as well." She looked at Will earnestly. "Does this mean you don't approve?" Kate asked. "I thought you were a modern thinker."

"It's not whether I approve or not, Kate," he answered truthfully, "I'm worried about Aunt Connie; she's in big trouble. They've locked her up at Scotland Yard, and Uncle Frank is furious."

"Oh, well, I suppose Pa will be a little bit upset."

"Kate, he's a senior army man, what will this do to his career?"

"Oh, honestly, Will, you sound like a real stuffed shirt. It won't make a ha'porth of difference because he wants to retire anyway. He'll get over it."

"But won't he punish you?"

"Only if he finds out, and the only way that will happen is if you tell him," she glared at him, challenging.

"D'you mean you won't tell him you had a part in this?"

"Too bloody right I won't!"

"Kate!"

"Is it my language or my views that you find so objectionable?" Will felt the chill in the air extending to her voice. For the first time since he arrived in England he suddenly felt like an outsider, almost as if she expected him to choose sides.

"As it happens, I know squat about your views, and yes, you are too goddamn free with your cussin'—for a lady."

She glared at him, hands on hips. "So you're trying to tell me there's too much bloody swearing going on, but it's all right for you because you're a man?" Will realized what he had just said; he went to open his mouth to speak but realized he would only be sinking deeper. Kate's spirits flew too high to keep her amusement in check. She was teasing him and he knew it.

"Oh, take your pompous hat off, Will. You're not the only one in the family who can cause a shemozzle."

"Point taken," he conceded, "but let me keep my worried hat on. Our aunt is in a police cell for God's sake!"

"Oh, it's not the first time she's been banged up," Kate said, intending to be reassuring.

"Banged up!? What the hell—"

"Nicked, chucked in the slammer, thrown in clink, had her collar felt. We know all the slang you know. What did you think I meant?"

"Oh is that all," Will said heavily. "It means something quite different where I come from. At least this is not serious." He looked at his cousin wearily.

"D'you know, Will, that's almost ironic. I'll make an Englishman of you yet." Kate smirked at him and handed him his cocoa. "So, what's to do?"

"We're to take the car and meet Joe at Scotland Yard and arrange to bail her out, but Uncle Frank says not to hurry, he wants her to stew for a while." He sounded doubtful, "I don't want to go against his orders, Kate, but I'm fixin' to head on out now. I can't stand the thought of her locked up in some dark cell."

Kate sat down on the stairs, "You old softie! Don't go worrying about Aunt Connie, she won't be in a cell, and *she* won't want us to go dashing down there."

Her eyebrow arched in response to Will's questioning look. "She wants time for the press to gather, that's the whole point of it."

Kate was proven right on the first point. When they arrived at Scotland Yard three hours later they found Aunt Connie drinking tea with Joe in a sparsely furnished office. The newsworthy side of her exploit, however, had proved a sad disappointment.

"Done up like a kipper, Kate," Connie announced sourly. "The only people who know about it are the old fool himself and this shower."

She jerked a thumb over her shoulder at the grinning group of policemen pretending not to stare from the door of the adjoining room.

"But how, Auntie? Nobody has ever pulled off anything like this." Kate was near to tears.

Connie shrugged, "For an old boy Herbert Asquith is too damn light on his feet. I suppose I have to give him credit. Everything had gone swimmingly. I had sneaked along Downing Street...nobody even guessed that an old bird like me had a length of chain in her bag, they're wise to us these days you know."

Joe explained for Will's benefit, "The suffragette movement have raised chaining themselves to notable monuments to the level of a sport."

Connie gave him a withering stare, "If I'd pulled this off properly, Joe, I'd be the W.G. Grace of chaining," she paused, "famous cricketer, Will, best all rounder the ga—"

"Ooooh, what happened then?" Kate whined with frustration.

"Patience, child," Connie admonished gently. "I gave the copper on the door my best little-old-lady smile. I had the chain 'round my waist under my shawl, all ready to go, when who should come breezing out of the door but dear old Herbert. I was on him in a flash. I flipped the chain 'round him and snapped the padlock on; the timing was pure chance but perfect." She smiled happily at the memory.

"So what went wrong?" Kate asked.

"Him. The old fool moved as fast as me. He dragged me back into Number 10 and slammed the door behind him—bugger it!" Connie banged the desk with the flat of her hand in frustration, making Joe pick up his cup protectively. "Can you imagine what a chump I felt? There I sat, chained to the P.M. with all his smirking cronies gathered 'round. Oh, they couldn't resist crowing, could they—'Would you like a cup of tea, Mrs. Burnett? Are you sitting comfortably, Mrs. Burnett?'"

"What happened then?" Will listened to the story with growing admiration.

"Mr. Plod the policeman turned up, cut him free and carted me off. So here we are."

A voice cut in from behind them. "Not for much longer, Burnett, I want you out of here—*now!*" Kate and Will spun around to look at the newcomer. He was a small man in his early forties. The first thing Will noticed, was the disconcerting way he seemed to look sideways past his long, thin nose. It made him look devious despite his conservative brown tweed suit.

Neither Connie nor Joe seemed surprised at his abrupt manner. "That's *Mrs.* Burnett to you, Inspector Reece," Joe corrected him mildly.

"You can shut up, Thorpe, I don't want any trouble from you," Reece snapped.

"Very wise, Teddy, my boy, you must have learned your lesson last time." Joe's tone did not change, but Will recognized the menace carried in his soft words.

Reece backed down from the confrontation. He slapped a sheet of paper down on the desk in front of Connie. "Sign there. You're free to go."

"Don't be ridiculous man," she protested, "you haven't charged me yet."

"And I'm not going to because nothing happened. So come on, clear off." He sounded triumphant, his problem solved for him by higher authority. Connie's one-woman demonstration had not been observed, and they had enough wit to realize that no witnesses meant no publicity. The newspapers would have had a field day if they found out the Metropolitan Police had allowed a suffragette, an elderly suffragette at that, to chain herself to the Prime Minister. "And don't get any silly ruddy ideas about causing a fuss in here. I'll just charge you with drunk and disorderly and that won't do your precious cause any good." He smirked, whipped the top off his fountain pen and offered it to her. She glared at him for a moment, snatched it and signed her name.

"Come on, children, let's see if we can find some more honest company down the East End." Connie had no intention of leaving without a farewell insult. She stood up, pushed Reece out of the way with the tip of her umbrella and went to sweep out of the door. He grabbed her arm.

"Oh no! Not that way, you might have some of your newspaper chums waiting for you. It's the tradesman's entrance for you." Connie glowered at him but led the way down a long, echoing corridor. Will thought it strange his aunt seemed to know her way around New Scotland Yard.

Reece escorted them to a heavy oak door that led out into a courtyard. "Now push off—the lot of you." He had no use for pleasantries. "And, Thorpe, tell your boss that if that troublemaking old cow ever ends up in here ag—," he stopped abruptly, winded as Will's finger poked him in the ribs.

"I think you had best apologize for that unguarded remark, Mr. Reece." His voice was calm, yet Nathan Walker's employees in Florida would have recognized the authoritative tone in Will's voice.

Reece snarled back at him, "Do that once more and I'll 'ave you for assaulting a police officer."

Will seized him firmly by the throat with his left hand and drew back his fist, "Then I'd better make it worth my while." His arm started to swing but jerked to a stop, seized in an iron grip.

"Not a good idea, Will," Joe said, holding him firmly. "Mr. Reece here has a bit of a glass jaw, he can't win a fight with an old lady, even when he gets the first punch in." They stood locked in their little tableau for a long moment before Will reluctantly relaxed his grip and lowered his arm. Reece, badly shaken, squirmed free.

"You 'aven't 'eard the last of this, Yank, 'owever well connected you are."

Joe pushed his face into Reece's. "Just behave yourself, and your little secret stays between us."

The inspector said nothing, but glanced furtively around to make sure they were still alone and nobody had witnessed his humiliation. He wagged a finger at Will, "Just...just watch it, *you.*" He stalked back into the building, slamming the door behind him.

Kate stood clutching Connie's arm, "Gosh, Will, what a temper you have!"

Will adjusted his tie and smoothed down the lapels of his jacket. "Ma'am, that was not a fit of temper, that was deliberate. That was the most outrageous thing to say about a lady." He turned to Joe. "I am obliged for your concern, Joe, to keep me out of trouble. But I regret not givin' him a thrashin'."

Joe shook his head, "He's not worth the trouble, William. Anyway, your aunt is quite capable of looking after herself."

Connie laughed, "Joe's quite right, Will. I'm grateful to you for your honorable intentions, but poor old Reece has already had his 'thrashin' and I don't think we should add more injury."

Will made the connection with an earlier conversation with Tom Armstrong, and Joe's remarks. "Is that the man—?"

Connie nodded, "Don't mention balloons to him, he'll come over all faint." She made a swinging motion with the big leather bag she carried everywhere and smiled. "Biff," she said softly.

Will scratched his chin, "Gosh!" was all he had to say. They walked through an imposing set of gates guarded by a uniformed policeman in a wooden box similar to those used by military sentries. He touched the short peak of his distinctively tall helmet with two fingers.

"Evenin', Mrs. Burnett, Miss Kate, fine performance this afternoon if I might say."

"Thank you, Alf, you know I always try to give a good account of myself." He laughed as they passed through.

"Good grief, Aunt Connie, do you know every policeman in London?"

Joe answered for her, "Oh yes, William, your aunt is, as they say, 'known to the police.'"

"I do my best for dear Emmeline, but the powers that be are reluctant to throw a batty old bird, like me, into clink." Connie sounded full of regret.

"Auntie!" Will protested. "You aren't batty. 'Sides, who's Emmeline?"

Connie and Kate began to explain enthusiastically, but Joe interrupted. "Ladies, you've made me miss my supper, so I've laid something on at the private dining rooms above the Bunch of Grapes just around the corner. It's a perfectly respectable house."

"Oh bother! Will they allow a criminal like me on the premises?" Connie inquired sweetly.

"Criminals like you, Mrs. Burnett, should be welcomed everywhere," Joe said gallantly, holding the door of the big Renault sedan open for her. Will and Kate had taken the unusual step of bringing the family car into town. Will had been glad of Kate's surprising knowledge of the route, but she assured him finding the way was easy. New Scotland Yard stood on the Thames Embankment so, even if they did lose themselves in the busy streets, simply driving south to the river would put them on the right track. The Renault with its coach-built, closed bodywork needed concentration to drive well. Kate's prompt and accurate directions kept them on course.

The pub Joe took them to was located a short drive from the Yard. The second floor of the Bunch of Grapes provided an extensive dining area, entered from a separate door at the bottom of a narrow flight of stairs. The waitress smiled at Joe as they entered, "Evenin', Mr. Thorpe, your usual table?"

Connie gave him a knowing look, "Your usual table? Come here often, Joe?"

"I'm a regular. I thought William and Miss Kate might enjoy the atmosphere," he remarked over his shoulder as he lead them to a table in the corner. "Very popular for what you might call *assignations.*" He inclined his head slightly toward a nearby table where a middle-aged man entertained a young woman perhaps half his age.

"Probably his niece," suggested Connie in a whisper.

"Of course," Joe agreed with a slight smile, "there's other types of meeting as well, being so handy for the Yard." He nodded a discrete greeting to two men at the other corner table; one just winked at him.

"Oh how exciting!" Kate kept her voice low, catching the prevailing air. "You mean copper's narks meet up with detectives here?"

"How do you find out about these things, Miss Kate?" Joe asked.

"Spend time with Aunt Constance and you find out all sorts of things," Kate explained.

Connie smiled modestly but could see that her nephew had lost track of their conversation, "I think you call them 'snitches', Will."

There was nothing discrete about the food served for supper. Will went straight for the steak and kidney pie served in rich gravy with slightly overcooked vegetables. He and Kate decided they could manage dessert but Joe and Connie excused themselves to take coffee in an adjoining lounge. Joe had been looking for an opportunity to speak to her alone. "The colonel's not happy, Mrs. Burnett."

"I don't suppose he is, Joe, but he has his battles to fight and I have mine."

"Nicely put, but we both know that's not really how it is, don't we?" Joe replied evenly.

She looked at him hard through a haze of cigarette smoke. "I suppose you might say I'm over simplifying things."

"I would."

"Did he ask you to speak to me, Joe?"

"Good Lord, no! I'm asking you to go easy on him—as a friend. He's got a lot on his plate."

She leaned across to him and took his hand, "Joe Thorpe, you're the best friend a man could ever want. I don't know how he would have coped without you after his darling Georgina passed away."

"So you'll stop getting nicked?" Joe asked hopefully.

Connie shrugged, "I'm getting a little past it for all this direct action. Emmeline has told me to give it up, she thinks I'm too old."

"So why do you do it?"

She grinned, "Because I love it! You know I can't sit around growing old gracefully." She sat quietly for a moment, "Oh, all right, Joe, I'll behave myself until this European rumpus dies down. It's hard to see how I could top this last little escapade anyway."

He sat back with a sigh of relief. The waitress arrived with two brandies and Connie raised a traditional toast, "Confusion to our enemies, whomever they might be."

Joe raised his glass. "I'll drink to that." He took a sip and closed his eyes in appreciation. "Talking of confusion, our young American friend left old Reece in a bit of a tizz."

"He certainly takes the old fashioned gallantry thing to heart," Connie said. "What did you make of what he said to Kate afterward?"

"He meant it," Joe said flatly. "I saw the look in his eyes. That was no flare up of temper. That was a cold-blooded decision. If I hadn't stopped him, Inspector Reece would be back in St. Thomas's Hospital."

"Will's just like his father from what I hear. John Turner is the kindest, most honest chap you could wish to meet. A real gentleman, with the emphasis on the *gentle*, but he can't abide a bully and he won't stand by and watch wrongdoing."

"Sounds like a decent chap."

"He certainly is, Joe," Connie paused, "much like yourself. Come on drink up, those children have been up since very early this morning."

The last gleam of light had finally left the evening sky when they came out to the car. Will blessed his uncle for upgrading to electric lights from the acetylene gas lamps the Renault had been fitted with at the factory. Joe took his leave when they dropped him at Baker Street Station. He stepped down from the car, but Connie stopped him with a hand on his arm. "What is this little secret between you and Reece?"

Joe looked quickly around him before leaning close to whisper in her ear, "Married police inspectors should know better than to lean on working girls for a free one." He winked.

"The dirty little sod!" Connie roared with delight.

"Dirty, tight-fisted little—," Joe grinned. "If he'd paid up like a toff she never would have told my Sarah."

"What was that all about Auntie?" Kate called back over her shoulder as Will pulled away.

"Nothing that need concern you my dear." Her aunt replied, primly pursing her lips. In Will's skilled hands the Renault performed smoothly. The late brandy had its effect on Connie, and she snored peacefully in the big, leather seat that stretched across the rear of the passenger compartment. Kate showed no sign of tiredness, to Will's relief as he feared he might doze off at the wheel. She took the chance to explain about Emmeline Pankhurst and the Women's Social and Political Union, or the "WSPU" as it was commonly known. Kate's devotion was absolute. She spoke breathlessly of Mrs. Pankhurst's career: of her arrests and subsequent imprisonment, and her hunger strikes while in prison.

"So she's your hero?" he asked when he could finally get a word in.

"I suppose she is." Kate replied, "Is there anything wrong with that?"

"No, nothing at all, so long as you don't end up in prison with her," Will added.

"I would if I had to."

Will glanced across at his cousin as he made a particularly slick change in the crash gear box. Her face was set in a fierce glare. "Oh no, Kate, please don't do that."

"Why should you care, you don't approve anyway?" She folded her arms and sat stiffly next to him.

"Well, that just shows how much you know. I care because I'm the one who would have to come an' bust you out of jail with dynamite. That's how we do things back home. Surely you've heard of the James Gang, and the Younger Brothers? Family takes care of its own." He paused while he advanced into a higher gear. "I s'pose that Inspector Reece might act in a manner upset if I blow up his police station."

Kate completely forgot how annoyed she felt, "Oh yes! And then we could go on the run together, robbing trains and banks."

"That's right, and then, when we've stolen enough money, we could run for the border and live down in Mexico." Will adjusted the hand throttle as he extended the fantasy.

"Then again," Kate suggested, "you could build aeroplanes, be the first man to fly the Atlantic and the most famous aviator in the world, and I could study medicine and become a great doctor."

"Now who's bein' a stuffed shirt? Where's your sense of adventure?" Will asked with a smile.

"You know, Will, I have a feeling that this might be as much adventure as anyone might need."

Chapter Sixteen

WILL HAD NO COMPLAINTS WHEN THEY FINALLY ARRIVED HOME and he found a message from Tom telling him not to rush to work in the morning. Word had spread, in the village at least, about Connie's exploit, and Tom had been party to the arguments that raged in the "Bull" that evening. Traditionalists predicted the downfall of the Empire, if not the end of civilization, if women won the vote. Others, less fixed in their views, admired her spirit if not all of her aims. A few forward thinkers gave their full support.

Tom regaled Will with a full report on the debate when he arrived at the hangar in the morning. "The old farts are fighting a rearguard action, Will, and a hard one at that. But they might as well give in, after all, the ladies have had the vote in local elections for years."

"I met one of the old guard last night," Will sounded grim. "Inspector Reece kinda swung me onto the ladies' side."

"From what I hear you nearly did some swinging of the other kind."

Will looked surprised, "Word travels fast. I don't break bad of a habit. I think even David Wells might have acted the same way." Will had learned the young postmaster was a Quaker with firmly pacifist beliefs. "What that sorry excuse for a lawman said was inexcusable. Our sheriff back home would have shot him on the spot for dishonoring the law an' insultin' a lady."

"Drastic, Will, but tempting," Tom mused. "Anyway, on to more mundane matters. I am about to reveal to you the mysteries of...the rotary engine."

Will bent down, plucked his cycle clips off and flipped them neatly onto a nail above the bench. "Lead me to it," he said eagerly.

For the rest of the day Tom demonstrated the techniques for servicing and repairing the tricky Gnome motors. The weather stayed cool with sagging low cloud and intermittent drizzling rain. At times they could hardly see across the field.

"Is summer often like this, Tom?" Will asked, buttoning his overalls to his neck.

"Oh yes, this isn't too bad. I've seen it snow in May; it's the penalty for living on the edge of a very large ocean. I hope it improves, otherwise Mr. Brock will never make it here tomorrow."

Tom's hopes were dashed. The following morning the weather had deteriorated. The drizzle had given way to a steady penetrating rain, falling from a smothering blanket of sodden gray cloud that only reluctantly allowed daylight to seep through. It was midsummer.

Will and Tom stood at the entrance to the hangar with their tea, watching the rain draping itself in sheets over the nearby woods. "He'll never make it in this, Will. Never mind, we have to modify the engine mountings on the Flanders to take the rotary Farnborough are sending up." He turned to walk back into the workshop, but Will stayed him with a hand on his arm.

"No, listen!" They stood stock still, straining to catch the faint hum Will had heard. They stared at each other. The unmistakable sound of a rotary droned nearer. "Holy mackerel, Tom, the man must be able to fly under water an' find his way!"

"Quick, the flare pistol, he'll need help to find the field." Tom urged. Will thundered up the stairs to the viewing platform. He fumbled a cartridge into the Very pistol, raised his arm and fired. At the top of its arc the flare disappeared into the cloud, an eerie green glow marking its path. A blurred shape appeared through the rain, sharpening into a tidy shoulder wing monoplane that banked steeply around the edge of their field and plonked down in a sudden spray of water and mud. The pilot kept the motor running in bursts, using the "blip" switch to taxi right up to the hangar door. Tom and Will splashed through the mud to grab the tail.

"Don't get out," Tom called to the muffled figure in the cockpit. "We'll have you in the dry in a jiffy." They lifted the tail and swung the frail machine until they could run it backwards into the hangar. They found it even lighter than the Bristol to wheel around. In seconds the Morane–Saulnier monoplane stood dripping inside the door.

Walter Brock unwound his scarf, took off his mud-spattered goggles and slapped his cap against the side of the fuselage to knock off the worst of the moisture. He grinned at his hosts. "I would say, 'nice weather for ducks', but they're all walking today." He jumped down from his machine.

Tom shook his hand warmly, "Well done, old boy. How on earth did you manage to find us in this muck?"

"Mainly thanks to these marvelous Ordnance Survey maps everybody uses here, but I've added my own refinement. What do you think of this?" He reached back into the cockpit and unclipped a device attached to the side. It consisted of two rollers set in a frame. A continuous strip of paper stretched between them. By cranking a handle the paper wound between the rollers. "I make notes for the whole trip on this: landmarks, hazards, distances, likely times between turning points and cross refer to the map. As I move along the route I wind the handle and it keeps me up to date."

"Clever!" Will said, examining it carefully. He grinned, "Good old American 'know how', as my pa would say."

"With a good old British map," Brock replied diplomatically.

Tom was already examining the machine. "Is this one of the three Moranes built by the Grahame–White Company under license at Hendon?"

"Sure is," Brock replied. "The problem is they could not lay hands on a brand new motor, but they fitted this one they salvaged from a wreck. They warned me it might be a little 'tired' but they took off a big sum from the price of the machine. That leaves me plenty for an overhaul, Mr. Armstrong, so please don't feel obliged to find ways to cut the cost. I want this brought up to scratch if you can."

Tom opened his tool box, "Mr. Brock, you're my kind of customer."

Walter Brock proved to be not only a good customer but a good mechanic, too. With Tom, Will and Walter working on the Gnome they were able to complete the tear down and rebuild in one long workday. As Tom predicted, all valves and the piston rings needed changing. They replaced the brushes in the magneto and the fragile high tension leads to the spark plugs for good measure. The weather cleared allowing Walter to test his machine by the early evening. He came back beaming with pleasure.

"It feels like a different machine, gentlemen," he announced, climbing down and accepting a cup of coffee from Tom. "I do believe I can enter the Derby with at least a chance of not making a damn fool of myself."

The sight of his Morane flying over the house had brought Katie pedaling quickly to the field. Will made the introduction. "Miss Kate Penrose, my cousin."

"Walter Brock, ma'am. Say, do you have family by the name of Rupert?"

"Why, yes, my brother."

"Well, maybe we'll all meet again. I overheard Mr. Sopwith saying he was going to ask a Lieutenant Rupert Penrose to fly his spare Tabloid in the race. I sure hope we're talking about the same fellow."

"Oh yes! I do hope so," Kate said with feeling. "That would be absolutely ripping."

The airplane designer and builder T.O.M. Sopwith, known universally as "Tom", had indeed asked Rupert to fly one of his tiny Tabloid biplanes in the Third Aerial Derby, a circuit race around the south-eastern counties of England starting and finishing at Hendon. Rupert telephoned Tom Armstrong's shop to confirm the good news, while the hum of Walter Brock's overhauled motor could still be heard receding in the distance as he flew back to Hendon in pale, watery sunshine.

For Tom, races meant an opportunity to fill all the gaps in his work schedule—a welcome chance to improve the cash flow of his business. He blessed the fates that had sent Will Turner in his direction. When they were not busy working on projects for the Royal Aircraft Factory, they were fettling the Sopwith for the racing season. Two more prestigious races were due to run later in the summer: The London–Manchester–London and finally, the most ambitious, London–Paris–London.

The Third Aerial Derby, early in June, proved Brock's fears groundless. He did not make a fool of himself—he won it easily, against some of the best aviators in Europe. The weather had closed in again, the visibility was so bad that only eleven of the twenty-one machines entered actually started the race, but Rupert Penrose was one of the eleven. None of the pilots had much idea of where they stood in the race as they flew. At West Thurrock in Essex the competitors plunged into thick fog and the observers had great difficulty identifying the machines as they flashed past. By the last turn at Hertford only five machines were left in the race, the others having retired with mechanical failures or after becoming hopelessly lost.

Ironically it was here, on his home ground, that Rupert, as he put it, "came unstuck." The local brewery, a good landmark, provided the turning point. Wiping moisture and castor oil thrown out by his rotary motor from his goggles, Rupert was immensely relieved to see the distinctive red brick tower, surmounted by a flag pole with the biggest Union flag the townspeople could muster for the event, looming out of the mist. He relaxed for a moment as he rounded the mark, then felt his bowels contract involuntarily as he saw his mistake. Disorientated for only a second by the poor visibility, he turned the wrong way, toward a wooded ridge known locally as the "Warren." Rabbits dived back into their holes as they saw the little Sopwith Tabloid hurtling toward them. Desperately he hauled back on the stick and kicked the rudder. His vision filled with branches and leaves towering above him. He braced himself for the crash. It came with a sound like a buzz saw and a momentary check in forward motion. When he opened his eyes, the Sopwith still hung in the air. He thrust the stick forward and slid back down the side of the slope, missing the tower of a tiny Norman church by inches.

He regained his bearings and set course for Hatfield. At first he thought the vibration he could feel had something to do with his heart rate, but a few more miles confirmed he had a serious problem. The vibration grew to a continuous shudder. He put down in a field next to the Great North Road and climbed stiffly to the ground. The source of the vibration was obvious: two inches had disappeared from the end of one propeller blade. "Bugger!" he swore with feeling. "That'll teach me to go chopping wood with the propeller."

Meanwhile Louis Noel, the Frenchman, had crossed the finish line but had missed the last turn at Hertford. Walter Brock was the first man to cross the line having completed the full ninety-four mile course. Carr and Verrier followed him home in their Henry Farman biplanes. These three were the only competitors to complete the course.

Will covered the short distance back to Hatfield in the Renault with a replacement propeller for the Sopwith, allowing Rupert to arrive back at Hendon for the celebratory dinner in a nearby hotel. There they discovered Walter Brock was modest to the point of shyness. Accepting the *Daily Mail* Gold Cup and two hundred sovereigns, plus the "Shell Petroleum Trophy" and a further one hundred sovereigns, he attributed his success to luck, his machine and the superb work done by his new friends, Tom Armstrong and Will Turner.

"Are all Americans as sweet as you and Mr. Brock?" Katie asked Will with a twinkling smile.

"All the aviators, definitely," he assured her.

The London to Manchester race confirmed what many had already guessed. Walter Brock made his own luck. Again he flew a brilliant race. The weather had improved two weeks later, on Saturday June 20th, when the competitors took off from Hendon again, visibility had increased to half a mile. Lord Carberry had succeeded in purchasing the Bristol Scout and had clocked a speed over one hundred miles per hour with it. Harry Hawker and Rupert, however, were expected to give him a run for his money with their Sopwith Tabloids. The race did not go as anyone expected.

Hawker retired due to illness. Carberry collapsed the undercarriage of the Bristol at Birmingham while Louis Noel damaged his Morane landing on Birmingham racecourse instead of Castle Bromwich sports fields. It was Louis Strange, the tall, handsome son of a Sussex farmer who led the remaining field into Manchester in his Bleriot monoplane. Walter Brock had lost himself for the first time and landed short of Birmingham to ask directions from a startled farmer.

"Have you flown all the way from America in that thing?" the farmer demanded.

"No, sir, just from London, and now I'm trying to find my way to Birmingham."

"That's all right then," the farmer sounded relieved, "I can direct you to Birmingham, but I'm not too sure about the way to America. Now here's what you do. When you take off, fly over them trees, and when you see the church, turn right. Just past the post office you'll see a pub called the Rose and Crown, turn left there and follow that road all the way into Birmingham."

Walter raised his cap politely and thanked him. He took off and followed the excellent directions straight to the checkpoint.

By the time he arrived at Manchester there were only five planes left in the race. He had overtaken Carr again and nearly caught Rupert, who was, in turn, only two minutes behind the leader, Louis Strange. He saw the crowd gathered around Strange's Bleriot as he set his machine down. The competitors were sent off strictly by the intervals they landed, this meant that nobody was penalized by delays on the ground caused by over enthusiastic spectators so he thought nothing of it. The three aircraft were refueled and after a quick sandwich and coffee, the pilots lined up to take off in order. Rupert was nearer the take off point, so he sat with the Sopwith's engine running waiting for Louis Strange to taxi past and take off. Walter Brock's Morane–Saulnier monoplane was next in line behind Rupert, and this put him in the perfect position to see what happened next. He could hardly believe his eyes.

Louis waved to Rupert as he taxied past. Suddenly the air was full of flying debris and Strange's Bleriot lurched to a stop. In the same instant, Rupert's Sopwith rocked violently and when Walter saw him throw up his arms he was out of his plane and running across to the Sopwith in an instant.

"What in thundering tarnation happened?" he yelled. He reached into Rupert's cockpit and cut the motor.

Louis Strange had raced across to join him, "Are you all right, Rupert?" He sounded close to panic but Rupert maintained his *sang-froid*.

One question at a time please, Chaps," he touched his gloved finger to his cheek where a thin trickle of blood showed. "I believe I am, but don't ask me what happened, I don't know."

"I'm sorry, Rupert, I do." Louis Strange's voice sounded heavy with disappointment. "That bloody fool of a Lord Mayor used my flying wires as a ladder when he climbed up to shake hands. I didn't realize he had done any damage, but when I started moving a wire bust, wrapped itself 'round my propeller, and smashed it to bits. I'm afraid some of it has gone through your wing." A gaping hole in the fabric of the upper wing showed pieces of splintered rib. Smaller fragments of propeller, flung out at terrific speed had peppered the fuselage and Rupert, luckily not causing any serious injury. "Goodness, I'm so sorry," Louis sounded wretched.

"Don't be ridiculous, old boy, hardly your fault." Rupert twisted in his seat to see where a line of policemen held back the curious crowd. "Tell you what, Louis, if we do go to war I want the Mayor of Manchester given to the other side—two machines out of commission in one go. He'd make one hell of a secret weapon."

They both suddenly looked at Brock, "Well, come on, Walter. Carr's only just behind you, you'd better get your skates on." Louis advised.

"Gee, fellas, are you sure, are you both okay?" Brock asked anxiously.

Rupert answered for them both, "Of course we are, there's nothing to do here, get moving. Quick, we'll start you." A group of officials had clustered around them but Rupert and Louis pushed them aside and ran to Brock's plane. He had already lost two minutes, and they rushed to start him. Thankfully the motor caught on the first swing.

Walter leaned from his cockpit to yell to Rupert, "I'm real sorry to be taking the lead this way."

"Don't fret over it, if it makes you feel better, you can treat us to dinner at the Ritz from your winnings," Rupert suggested.

Walter grinned, "That's a deal! See you in London." He revved the engine and bounced across the grass.

Rupert and Louis watched him soar into the air. "Oh well," sighed Louis, "*c'est la vie.*"

Rupert took his arm and they walked off the field, "Thoroughly decent chap though, if we have to be beaten I can't think of a nicer fellow to lose to."

Rupert phoned Will back in Hendon, "Bring fabric and some ribs made up ready with all your woodworking kit, Will. And pop over to the Grahame–White chaps and pick up a propeller and a set of flying wires for the Bleriot."

"Lordy, Rupert, what happened...did you an' Louis collide?" Will suggested.

"No, not exactly, it'll take too long to explain on the telephone. Walter Brock will be back in an hour or so, God willing, he'll tell you all about it. There's no rush, we're staying here for the night, believe it or not they've laid on a civic reception for us."

"Oh, well," Will said consolingly, "I expect you'll have a good time."

Rupert laughed, "We damn well intend to. See you tomorrow."

His prediction proved accurate. Walter won again, finishing over an hour ahead of his nearest rival. This time he won the *Daily Mail* Gold Trophy and cash prizes amounting to six hundred and fifty pounds. By now he was attracting huge attention from the press who wanted to know all about him. At the same time he felt himself being overwhelmed by back-slapping *bonhomie.* His quiet charm did not desert him, but when Will told him he was setting off at first light for Manchester in the Renault, Walter offered his help on the spot. He had found the ideal opportunity to escape from the spotlight. The discovery that he was not at Hendon the next morning caused consternation amongst the race organizers and the press, but when they discovered the reason, his reputation as a sportsman soared to an even higher level.

He confided to Will on the long journey, "It's downright embarrassing, Will, all this fuss. And some of those ladies! I thought English women were supposed to be cold, but some of the offers I had last night were downright hot! Seems like a little fame does something funny to 'em."

Will laughed, "I've heard that, but managed to keep my head down."

"Keep it that way," Walter urged. "I find it downright disturbing."

The journey north was a revelation for Will. Walter's offer had allowed Tom to stay behind to prepare for the next week's work, but his directions were clear. They followed a map provided by the Royal Automobile Club. This took them through the towns of Bedford and Leicester, prosperous towns but still sleeping at this hour on a Sunday morning. They made excellent time on the deserted roads, traveling at thirty miles per hour for much of the time. They stopped at an inn for breakfast where their unusual accents attracted almost as much interest as the propeller tied to a rack on the roof of the car. North of the town of Derby, the scenery changed dramatically. The road climbed through rocky gorges. The stone shining almost black with the water cascading down from the hills above. Moss and fern glowed green in the light from the thin strip of sky showing at the top of the ravine. When they finally emerged on the hills above the town of Macclesfield, they were greeted with a stunning view over ancient hills. Will blessed the excellent brakes fitted to their car as he spent much of the time steering around sheep wandering in the road.

"Mighty pretty country, Will," Walter exclaimed. "I didn't see any of this yesterday; it was covered in fog."

"How high were you flying?" Will asked.

Walter sat quietly for a moment, surveying the peaks surrounding them. "Not as high as this. Boy, am I glad I managed to stick to the route," he said with feeling.

They arrived in Manchester in time for lunch at the hotel where Rupert and Louis had been staying. The repairs to the aircraft took all afternoon. Even though the damage to the Sopwith proved less serious than expected, time had to be allowed for glue and dope to dry overnight. The following morning was a Monday, but a huge crowd gathered to see the two airplanes takeoff. They lifted off together, then circled the field once before dipping their wings in salute and setting course for London. Will arrived home late that evening. He had dropped Walter off at Hendon but, even with that detour, he was pleased to have made the journey in twelve hours.

Walter was good as his word and an invitation arrived to join him at the Ritz on Saturday evening. Kate persuaded Marjorie to allow Lucy to join them and Rupert collected Sophie from her family home in Guildford. The band had embraced the craze for "ragtime" and the dancers stepped out with abandon. Among friends Walter relaxed; he proved as accomplished on the dance floor as he was in the air. Eventually he slumped in a chair next to Rupert and Will.

"You know boys," he confided, "I'd planned to see 'Gay *Paree*' before heading home. I can't imagine my luck will last with the racing. When we set off on the London–Paris race in a couple of weeks, I'm taking my dancing shoes and a few clothes with me. If I get there and I'm nowhere in the running, I'll retire from the race and take myself off sightseeing for a few days."

"I really would appreciate that, Walter," Rupert said with a laugh. "Give the rest of us a chance."

"Believe me, those two wins were a fluke," Walter insisted.

"No such thing in this game," Rupert said. "Luck does come into it, but without a lot of skill, luck is worth nothing. I'll say one thing though, I'm going to finish this race if I have to carry the bloody Sopwith the last few miles."

"Okay," Walter conceded, "a degree of skill, but without good preparation skill won't get you anywhere, and my motor has been purring like a kitten since these guys gave it their attention. It hasn't missed a beat, even flying through rain. I have you guys to thank for that."

"That's our pleasure," Will said. "But I wouldn't bother takin' your French language primer, somethin' tells me you won't be in France long enough to need it."

Rupert said later that Will could add the gift of prophecy to that of engine tuning. Walter Brock took off on schedule from Hendon. He arrived first in Paris, gazed longingly at the Eiffel Tower as he took off again, refueled at Boulogne before crossing the Channel and arrived back at Hendon at 4:48 P.M. having averaged 71 m.p.h. for the whole race. Meanwhile, Lord Carberry had ditched the Bristol in the Channel when his motor suddenly stopped. Fortunately, the sea was calm and he put his machine down with such skill next to a small steamer that they were able to pick up him *and* the Bristol. He even managed to keep his feet dry.

Rupert fulfilled his ambition. The visibility had been poor again but he had navigated to Paris successfully. He had lost time when he made a precautionary landing on the beach near Calais to find his bearings; he was certain he had strayed off course over the Channel. A delighted crowd had rushed to his plane and carried him shoulder high to a nearby bandstand where the mayor launched into a long speech welcoming the "hero of the air" to France. Rupert explained to his friends later that the French were all so pleased to see him, he couldn't bring himself to be rude. He had endured the mayor's speech, made one himself in very acceptable French, and toasted the *entente cordiale* with several glasses of champagne, before he was able to escape.

"I felt quite squiffy by the time I reached Paris," Rupert admitted, "must be something to do with altitude and alcohol, it definitely has an effect."

He had taken off from Paris late in the afternoon. Overtaken by darkness at Boulogne he decided not to be the first person to attempt the Channel at night. He took off the next morning, having slept with his machine, and arrived at Hendon just as his team was sitting down to lunch. They were not concerned, as the newspapers had been following his progress with intense interest. First place had gone to an American, second and third to Frenchmen. Rupert had salvaged national pride. Much to Walter's relief, Rupert's late arrival took most of the attention away from him for a time. A special award of fifty pounds for determination and "pluck" rewarded Rupert for his efforts.

Walter Brock's respite did not last. That evening, as the debris from the awards ceremony was cleared away, he was almost dragged into Lord Northcliffe's Rolls Royce to be taken back to London for more celebration and exposure. As the imposing car rolled grandly to the gate, Will heard Walter shouting to the driver.

"Whoa! Hold up there," he called, leaning out of the window and motioning to Will. "I'm sorry, Will, I forgot to mention. While I was refueling in Boulogne, a guy pushed through the crowd. He asked me if I knew of an American guy called Will Turner, working with airplanes in England." A look of alarm on Will's face quickly showed Walter he had done the right thing.

"To tell the truth, Will, I didn't much care for the look of him, guessed he might be one of these newspaper hounds, but from his accent, I think he was American. Anyway, I told him I thought there might be somebody like that working at Brooklands. That way, if you want to meet him, you can always leave a message down there."

"Thanks, Walter, you're a pal," Will said with feeling. "What did he look like?"

"In his twenties I guess, black hair, blue eyes, kinda sharp dresser." Walter rattled off the description as the car started to draw away. "You take care now, Will, see you back in the States."

Will waved to him as the big car purred away. He watched it turn toward London, deep in thought about the last few weeks.

Chapter Seventeen

THE ONLY LOGICAL CONCLUSION WILL COULD DRAW FROM WALTER Brock's information was that Roscoe Vandersand had been en route to England from Europe, with only one aim in mind—to find him. He confided as much to Tom but begged him to keep the news to himself; he did not want to alarm his family. Tom went through his tea-preparing ritual as he thought about the situation, then he spoke, "What you must not do is overreact. It's quite possible he's come to his senses and for all you know is hoping to meet with you with every intention of apologizing like a gentleman."

"Lord knows I hope so, Tom, but if he's still eat up with jealousy I fear he's bad to cause trouble." Will replied.

Tom sipped his tea and screwed up his face, "Don't think I'm not taking this seriously, Will, because I am. I can't afford to have my chief pilot and engine tuner killed by some bloody nutcase. Even so, I say let him come."

"D'you mean that, Tom?"

"Of course I do," Tom answered firmly. "If he shows up in the district we'll be first to know. What I suggest is that we use you as bait." Will's eyebrows shot up in surprise.

"Very expressive face you have, Will," Tom said with a wicked grin.

Will scratched his head, "Very interestin' ideas you have, Tom."

"Trust me, this will work." Tom said, serious again. "We'll spread the word that we think German agents are snooping around. He won't get within five miles before the jungle drums start beating. Let him take a swing at you, challenge you to a duel, whatever...they are criminal acts. Then the coppers feel his collar, and he'll be deported before his patent leather boots touch the ground. End of problem."

Will smiled slowly, "I'm grateful to you, Tom, I hope the plan works."

"It *has* to work, if the worst comes we'll be busier than you could ever imagine and we'll have no time to fool with Roscoe Vandersand, " Tom said with feeling.

Will knew Tom referred to the worsening European situation. "Now, Tom, can you explain to me why this Archie Duke fella gettin' himself murdered in Serbia, wherever the hell that is, has anythin' to do with us?"

Tom looked sideways at Will, "Don't come your simple country boy act with me, Will Turner. You know damn well where Sarajevo is, and you know the archduke was the equivalent of our Prince of Wales, next in line of the Hapsburg dynasty."

"Yeah, but that's the Austrian Empire," Will pointed out. "What's that got to do with the British, or the French for that matter?"

"Nothing directly," Tom admitted, "but Europe is a tangle of alliances." Taking a steel rod from the bench, Tom drew a map of Europe in the dust at their feet; the sun had returned and dried their field.

"The Austrians, here," he prodded at his crude map, "have always claimed *that* part of the Balkans, here, as their own. They've been itching for an excuse to teach the Serbs a lesson, and the assassination of the archduke has given them that. The Serbs have an alliance with the Russians, who have an alliance with the French in turn. The Austrians, however, have an alliance with—"

"Germany," Will said flatly, filling in the last piece of the puzzle. "An' they're itchin' to have a pop at the French. But I still don't see where the British come in; there's no formal alliance with France."

"No, but we do have a treaty to protect Belgian neutrality, and if your uncle is correct, *that's* how we will be dragged in," Tom explained.

"Aw, come on, Tom, you're not tellin' me the Germans are like to just march into Belgium? What harm did they ever do anybody?"

"None, but they stand in the way of the Kaiser's master strategy, the Schlieffen Plan."

"The what?"

"The Schlieffen Plan. Frank must have mentioned it, he's been banging on about it for years, it's hardly a secret, perhaps that's its strength, nobody believes the Germans will dare try it. The French certainly don't take it seriously."

"Who is Schlieffen?" Will asked.

"Was," Tom corrected him. "He died last year, no loss to the civilized world. He was the German field marshall who drew the plan up. The intelligence boys don't know the details, but they've a damn good idea of the general plan. Of all people it was the Kaiser himself who let the cat out of the bag a few years ago. He only asked Leopold, the Belgian king, if he would be prepared to allow German troops to cross his territory—can you imagine that?"

"Hardly diplomatic," Will agreed.

"Hardly, and you don't need to be a military strategist to work out that it isn't so his boys can have a paddle on the beach at Ostend. It's so his army can attack France through its unprotected border while the French Army is busy defending the obvious eastern frontier. If it works, they'll be in Paris in days.

"What's to stop them?" Will asked.

Tom sighed, "The British Army...*my* army in a manner of speaking, I'm still on the reserve list."

"The hell you are!" Will said, surprised by the news.

"The hell I am," Tom replied reasonably. "Once a sapper, always a sapper, at least for another three years." He used the nickname given to British military engineers.

"Does that mean they'll order you back to the colors?"

"I doubt it," Tom said. "But it will mean I'll be under orders one way or another. I have to warn you, it might cause some big changes."

"It makes my little Roscoe problem seem trivial," Will said apologetically.

"No!" Tom said, looking Will squarely in the eye. "Of all the 'ifs' flying around these days, that is the most likely to need dealing with. We'll all keep our eyes open, and *if,* or when, he shows up, we'll settle this business once and for all." He took Will's empty cup, "For the moment, though, let's worry about this new hundred horsepower Gnome, we've work to do."

Without ever becoming aware of it, Will had, in a few short weeks, joined the exclusive little band who could, if they had ever considered it important, have called themselves "aviation professionals." He had brought with him a wealth of practical engineering experience. Just as important, from Tom's point of view, Will possessed a scientific turn of mind that rejoiced in the theory of flight. He had a sound training in math and physics and the diligence to apply it. Above all he had the touch of a born aviator coupled with a strong desire to see any project through to its finish, as Tom had seen when Will presented him with the full results of the test flights he had flown in the Flanders. Will had gone far beyond the bare figures and analyzed them in detail for Tom's inspection.

Tom's instincts told him that Will might have a reckless streak that, combined with his curiosity, could lead to problems. He knew all about Will's first flight in the *Flyer* and Will had admitted himself that his eagerness to fly had overwhelmed his sense of caution on that occasion. Tom had been reassured, however, when Will arrived at work one day with a letter from Henry containing detailed accounts, press cuttings, and photographs of the exploits of Lincoln Beachey, the stunt pilot creating a storm across America with his aerobatic exhibitions.

"Ever fancy trying a loop?" Tom asked, gently probing.

"Lord no!" Will replied, shocked at the suggestion. "I'm not about to go cuttin' the fool in the Flanders, Tom, it's not my airplane. What would you say if I carried her back here all mommocked up?"

"I'd be more worried about you being mommocked up," Tom laughed as he replied, the phrase amused him.

"Now, in my *own* airplane!" Will said enthusiastically. "Just you watch. I'll make it fly backward an' upside down."

"Just let me know when you pull that stunt, Will, I'll take care not to be behind you."

Will demonstrated his professional approach a few days later. He preferred to limit his test flights to the area between the field and the City of Cambridge twenty miles to the north. The dramatic architecture of King's College made a perfect navigation mark, and numerous wide open meadows between the city and his home base made perfect emergency landing grounds, and he had cause to try them on several occasions. The rotary motors they worked on lived up to their reputation for unreliability, leaving him without power. His knowledge of the area grew intimate.

One warm afternoon late in July, as he flew above Cambridge, he mentally thanked Kate for insisting that he joined her on one of his rare days off. She had taken him for an afternoon poling a punt on the River Cam running behind the colleges. He had noted the surface and approaches of one particular meadow a mile or so outside the town as being excellent for a landing. Nevertheless, he was surprised as he flew over that afternoon, to see an airplane in the field he had seen a few weeks earlier. He checked the wind direction from smoke rising from a small bonfire in a neighboring farmyard, and circled the field twice as low as he could. A small crowd stood gathered by the machine standing in the corner of the field but one figure moved away from it with both arms raised making a thumbs-up gesture. Will cut the throttle and curved down to land.

"Good mornin', sir, can I help?" Will asked, having stilled the whirling rotary fitted to the Flanders that day.

The figure he had seen from the air strode up to the Flanders. "If ye happen to have a spare magneto with you, yes." He said with a smile, as if knowing what an outlandish suggestion he made.

Will studied the grounded biplane from the cockpit of his own machine, "I declare that's one of Mr. de Havilland's B.E.2's with a Renault motor."

"It is," the aviator replied.

"Then it's your lucky day, I'm carrying a spare from the time we were testing our own eight-cylinder model." Will jumped down from the cockpit of his machine and reached back inside. He suddenly stopped and turned around. "Sir, I am forgettin' my manners, Will Turner, at your service." He shook hands with the stranded flyer who still seemed taken aback at this turn of events.

"And I'm forgetting mine. Liam Power, late of the 'DLI', now attached to the Flying Corps." He was a big man, as tall as Will. He would have had the classical looks of one of the Greek heroes whose sculpted heads stood in Cambridge's Fitzwilliam Museum just beyond the meadow, but the sculptor had apparently been called away before he could finish the job. Liam Power's face was all flat planes and angles behind a large broken nose. An army barber had cut his thick, straight hair quickly and severely. He wore the coarse high-wasted khaki trousers of an enlisted soldier with the puttees Will had seen Joe Thorpe wearing the morning he picked him up from his uncle's club. His flying kit and tunic were draped over the tail of his machine. His face wore a look of good-natured surprise. "Would I be right in guessin' you're not from these parts, Mr. Turner?" he asked.

"You certainly would," Will confirmed with a smile. "You're not exactly a Cambridge man yourself, I'd hazard a guess."

"From Waterford town, itself," Power said with pride.

"Tallahassee in the State of Florida is my home, Mr. Power. Are you one of these Anglo Irishmen I keep hearing about?"

Liam Power roared with laughter, "Bless you no. I'm a real Irish Irishman."

"Pardon my ignorance, Mr. Power, but what is the DLI?" Will asked.

"The Durham Light Infantry."

"So why's an Irishman servin' in a regiment from the north of England?" Will asked in his forthright way. "Seems a long way from home."

Power smiled, "His regiment is home for a soldier, Mr. Turner, but I take your point. It all dates back to my great great granddad. He was in the 68th, one of the first rifle regiments. His son followed him and was promoted from the ranks by the Duke of Wellington himself, they was the DLI by then. The tradition seems to have carried on. Where I come from the first son inherits, and the rest go for a priest or a soldier."

"An' you didn't care for the priesthood?"

Power grimaced, "All that piety? No thanks. 'Sides I've not much of a head for the drink—terrible disadvantage for a man of the cloth."

Will laughed, "Sometimes seems to be the case in my hometown." He retrieved a small wooden box from a locker behind his seat. He opened the box carefully to reveal the precious Bosch magneto. An instruction booklet lay beside it.

Liam Power opened the pages, his brow furrowed, "Now there's a thing! It's all in German." He held it up for Will who had his hands full with the magneto. He studied it briefly.

"It's just the standard instructions 'bout polarity an' servicin', there's nothin' unusual here." Will reassured him.

Power looked at him with respect. "Do you speak the German then?"

"I can certainly read it fine," Will said with no false modesty, "but a German gent on the boat over here said I speak with a strong Bavarian accent."

"Now how does a lad from America pick up the language, let alone an accent?"

Will placed the magneto carefully on the grass next to the B.E.2, "My ma tried to civilize me. She had me takin' piano lessons from the age of five. My teacher was a lovely old gal from Munich, Fraulein Ziepke. I can bash out a tune but I'll never reach concert standard, she gave up on that, years ago. I kinda picked up on what she was sayin' an' by the time I was in high school it just seemed nat'rel to use German with her."

"Could be useful," Power pointed out.

"If I thought I could talk Kaiser Bill outta this foolishness I'd fly that machine to Berlin right now," Will said.

"Not much chance of that...did ye hear the Austrians have invaded

Serbia?" Power asked.

Will answered from underneath the cowling of the B.E.2 biplane, "I did, it looks bad from where I stand."

Power bent down and peered up into the space behind the motor where Will was trying to undo the bolts holding the faulty part to the back of the crankcase. "It sure looks dark anyway, Mr. Turner." He straightened up to address the small crowd standing around the machine at a respectful distance, "Could any of ye good people oblige us with a torch?" A middle-aged man cheerfully trotted off to find a flashlight. With the aid of the beam Will quickly removed the offending component. He held it up and shook it, a rattle of loose parts telling its own story.

"You made a good diagnosis, Mr. Power." Will congratulated him.

"Ah, it didn't need a genius," he admitted, "the bloody thing just stopped, no 'by your leave', coughin' or spittin' like we have with a fuel problem. It had to be ignition."

Will wriggled his way back up under the cowling with the new magneto so he could not look up when Power suddenly said, "Jaysus Christ, it's the boss himself."

The new arrival could be clearly heard even inside the engine cowling, his voice boomed, "Good day to you, Mr. Power, I see you have some assistance."

Power's reply sounded respectful, but he was clearly on good terms with the new arrival, "That I have, sir, it's Mr. Turner from Tom Armstrong's aeroplane works."

Will could only see a pair of smart blue, pinstriped trousers from the knees down, and a pair of highly polished black boots. He was jammed up in the confined space behind the motor. The trousers and boots addressed him, "Would that be Mr. Will Turner, Frank Penrose's nephew?"

"It would, sir," Will had to shout, his voice muffled by the sheet metal of the cowling.

"How is it going under there?"

"Almost right, but with airplanes 'almost' is never good enough, I'll be out in a moment."

"No, no, take your time," the detached voice insisted.

Will tightened the last bolt and scrambled out from under the nose of the aircraft. He went to shake hands but noticed the grime on his fingers. The newcomer ignored it and seized his hand, shaking it firmly.

"Trenchard, RFC, I'd been hoping to run into you, Mr. Turner."

Will felt himself being studied, carefully. He guessed Trenchard's age at about forty. He stood taller than Will, but stooped slightly, as if trying to peer inside him. His deep-set eyes held Will. Trenchard wore civilian clothes but his brusque manner suggested a man used to command. There was nothing intimidating about him, however, Will responded politely.

"May I ask why, sir?"

"Of course," the big man's voice reverberated against the metal cowling of the airplane, "I want to offer you a commission in the RFC." Liam Power looked from his senior officer to Will. He folded his arms, his head cocked to one side, as interested as Trenchard to hear Will's reply.

"I'm honored, sir," Will replied after a short pause, "but I don't think I can do that, me bein' a United States citizen."

"Your uncle said that would be your answer," Trenchard replied amiably, "but I hope you don't mind me asking. I was motoring back to London when I heard Lieutenant Power was down near Cambridge, it's very lucky finding you here. Can I appeal to your family loyalties, your mother being English? We're in desperate straits and an engineer and pilot of your caliber would be a very welcome recruit to the corps."

Will felt Trenchard was not a man given to flattery, his manner came across as straightforward and Will knew he expected a direct reply. "With the greatest respect, my father is an American, I was born in America and I consider myself an American."

"That is a very fair and honorable answer, Mr. Turner, but if you change your mind you could enlist as a Canadian and we would make up your papers as such. In that way, if you did fall into enemy hands, your government would not be compromised. We already have three of your chaps signed up."

"Goodness, sir, you move fast."

"No choice, old boy. Here's my card. Think about it, just call this chap," he scribbled a name on the back of his card, "if a soldier's life suddenly appeals." Trenchard looked up to see a beaming, silver-haired lady bearing a tray toward them, "Ah! Splendid, madam, the cup that cheers." He did not try to persuade Will again. They stood beside Liam Power's airplane drinking tea, chatting about the weather and flying, while, without Will realizing it, the French and German armies stirred ponderously into motion a few hundred miles away. Trenchard did not continue his journey by car; he sent his driver on his way and joined Liam Power in his B.E.2. after starting both aircraft with a powerful swing.

Will mentioned his meeting to his Uncle Frank that evening. Frank was pleased to see him, the old soldier appeared tired but he brightened up when Will told him about Trenchard's offer.

"So you met Boom, did you, Will?"

"Boom, sir?"

"Yes. That's what the lads call him. On account of his way of speaking. Between you and me I wonder if he might be a little deaf." Frank added.

"He sure has a powerful voice, I wouldn't like to be in the same room if he an' Marjorie fell to arguin'."

A smile spread across Frank's leathery face at the thought. "Well put. Anyway, what did you say?"

"I had to say no, sir, but I thanked him for his offer of course. He said some very kind things 'bout my abilities."

"He only said what everybody else is saying, Will, you've made quite a name for yourself in the time you've been here. Well, you may blush—"

"Indeed!" Kate said, joining them in the kitchen where they enjoyed a supper of cold meat and cheese. "All of the girls are asking about him, but I tell them he's only interested in his smelly old aeroplanes—no time for poor village maidens." She bent over the table and stole a pickled onion from his plate. Will flushed scarlet.

"Kate!" Frank tried to sound severe. "Can't you see you're embarrassing Will?"

"Sorry, Coz," she grinned at him, not meaning it for a moment.

Frank steered the conversation back to Will's meeting that afternoon. "I'm glad you said that, Will. My sister would have a fit if you joined up. She would blame me, of course."

"Uncle, I would never let Ma do that, it would be my decision." Will said. He went on, "They wrote in their last letter they feel I am old enough to decide for myself what to do if war does come, and they understand I have a duty toward Tom, him havin' been so good to me."

"That *does* surprise me," Frank said.

"There is another reason," Will admitted. "They think crossin' the Atlantic will be too dangerous with all this talk of submarines an' such. They think everythin's blown up so quick, I've left it too late. I'll be safer if I stay put until it's all over, one way or another."

"They may very well be right. I can honestly say from a personal, *and* an official point of view, I'm glad you're staying. The corps needs all the technical help it can get."

"Thank you, sir." Will replied.

"And who was the airman you rescued with your mechanical wizadry," Frank asked.

"An Irish gentleman, Lieutenant Liam Power. He's a real nice fella, he invited me to come fishin' with him at his home in Ireland, as soon as he and the other guys in the corps have sorted out the Kaiser."

"Oh, I know young Liam, thoroughly decent chap and underneath that easygoing exterior a real hard charger. He's seen action on the Northwest Frontier and covered himself with glory already. He'll make a general one day, you just see." Frank scraped his chair back from the table. "Well, I'm off to bed, your aunt will be back later, she's rabble rousing in Bishops Stortford this evening."

"Oh, Father!" Kate protested. "She's giving her photographic slide show of the flowers of India to the Townswomen's Guild."

Frank laughed, "That's what I said, dangerous bunch of anarchists if you ask me." He disappeared upstairs, still chuckling to himself. Kate gathered the plates, rolled up her sleeves and started washing up; it was Mary's night off.

Kate threw a cloth at Will, "I'll wash, you dry."

"So what happened between Uncle Frank an' Aunt Connie about her little exploit?" Will asked.

Kate whistled through her teeth, "Phew! Maisie tells me there was the very dickens of a row. She could hear it even though they were in the study."

"An' she was at the keyhole?" Will suggested.

"Probably," Kate admitted. "Anyway, it cleared the air."

"So Uncle gave her a good tellin' off," Will sounded satisfied.

"You smug so-and-so!" Kate answered sharply, flicking soapy water at him. "Just what I would expect of you. No, *she* tore into him."

"What? Even though he sprang her from jail?" Will could not understand why his aunt should feel justified in her anger toward his uncle.

"*That* is precisely why she's so steamed, William." Kate patiently explained, "She *wanted* to end up in court, that's the whole point of the exercise. She found out Father had 'leaned' on Scotland Yard not to press charges." Will felt uncomfortable with the thought of disharmony in his family, and very uncomfortable with the idea that his uncle should use his influence for personal, or family ends. He said as much to Kate.

She posed him a difficult question. "Can you tell me, honestly, that if Vicky were in the same position one day, you wouldn't do the same thing?"

"Oh hell, Kate, that's not fair," he protested.

"Oh yes it is," she gave no quarter.

Will slowly rubbed a plate with his drying cloth while he thought. "Dammit, I probably would."

"Thank goodness for that, Will, otherwise I would have to mark you down for a pompous prig." She grinned and flicked more water at him.

Will tried to steer the conversation away from himself. "Can you tell me why Aunt Connie has such a poor opinion of military men? What she said about Lord Kitchener was pretty outrageous." Kate fell into fits of giggles at the memory. "I thought the bishop was goin' to have some kinda seizure." Will added, trying not to laugh himself. At Sunday tea a few weeks before, in front of several worthy local figures including a visiting churchman, Connie had suggested how Rupert might create an impression at a fancy dress party he and Sophie had been invited to.

"Take out half your brain, stick a ramrod up your arse and go as

Field Marshall Kitchener, dear," she said brightly. The bishop had made his apologies and left shortly afterward.

"In Kitchener's case it all goes back to South Africa. Haven't you heard the story?" Kate asked.

"I recall my ma an' pa gettin' involved at our end. They put pressure on people in Washin'ton to protest to the British government. But I never understood what it was all about, I was just a child at the time."

Kate told the story, her mood serious again. "To try to bring the Boer farmers they were fighting under control during the war in South Africa, the army rounded up their women and children and placed them in what they called 'concentration camps.' They were just cities of tents out on the veldt. Pa says it is the most shameful episode in the history of the army, he very nearly resigned his commission over it. He says there was no deliberate policy of cruelty, but the men they put in charge were either idiots, or swine, probably both. The result was no proper sanitation in the camps, no decent water supply and before long disease running through the camps like wildfire. Hundreds, if not thousands of these innocent women and children died."

"Good grief, Kate, was it that bad?"

She shrugged, "It's hard to believe, I know, it was probably worse. That fool Simmons, the officer in charge, had influence and managed to cover up his incompetence, but we know the truth. Aunt Connie was on her way back from India after Uncle John died, and she got wind of these camps. They tried to stop her, but she managed to get into them. As it turned out Marjorie was on a boat that docked in Cape Town a week after Connie arrived, and she enlisted her help. While Marjorie steamed into the authorities there and organized what amounted to a rescue, Connie made all possible haste back to London to confront Kitchener and make sure the press here had the story. The army had managed to keep them away up to that point.

"So Marjorie an' Aunt Connie go back a long time?" Will asked.

"Oh yes, 'partners in crime' as Pa says," Kate confirmed. "Aunt Connie managed to bring the scandal to public attention with a vengeance."

"Ah, yes," Will said, "the famous challenge."

"Goodness, Will, I would have loved to have been there that day. Just imagine, in front of all those people." There was awe in her voice.

"Just what did she do?" he asked.

Kate told the story with evident relish. "Kitchener was attending the unveiling of a new portrait of Wellington at the National Gallery. There he stood, in all his finery, surrounded by black frock coats and silk toppers when Aunt Connie swept up to him, still in mourning black for Uncle John, all the better for the drama. She slapped him across the face with her glove then threw it down, 'If I were a man, I would challenge you to a duel.' She didn't need to raise her voice, they said afterward you could have heard a pin drop on the other side of Trafalgar Square."

"What did he do?" Will asked.

"Oh, she hadn't finished with him: 'You're a disgrace to that uniform and the civilized world,' she told him before stalking off. Well, you can imagine, the newspapers went wild. They clamored around her to find out what this was all about. To give Kitchener his due, he moved fast to sort the mess out, but it was too late for many poor souls in those horrible camps."

"I can see why Kitchener might be wary of Aunt Connie; what I can't understand is why it hasn't affected Uncle Frank's career," Will asked the question most on his mind.

"Whatever Aunt Connie might say about him, Lord Kitchener's no fool. He soon found out where the blame lay and Simmons's career ended for all intents and purposes. He sent Pa, who was a major then, to organize the relief. It was not by way of a punishment, he was the best man for the job," Kate finished proudly.

"Okay," Will said slowly, "I can understand why she may not hold a good opinion of military men, but it seems to go deeper than that."

Kate looked at him carefully, "They've never told you about the mutiny?" She stood with her arms in the sink.

"I know about the Indian Mutiny, an' I guess she would have been there at the time, as a young girl, but how did it affect her?"

Kate's eyes opened wide. She took off the apron she had put on for washing the dishes and dried her hands on it. Without saying a word she motioned Will to sit down at the table while she retrieved an old, bound album from the top shelf of the kitchen dresser. She opened it to reveal a mass of press clippings pasted to the pages. Carefully flipping through them until she found the page she wanted, she then turned the album to face Will. "There. Who do you think that is supposed to be?" The picture that accompanied the newspaper report was the type of artist's impression only the Victorian press could have produced. In the foreground, turbaned men fled terrified from a goddess-like figure standing on a balcony brandishing a pistol. At her feet, on the stairs, a figure lay sprawling with a neat bullet hole drilled in the forehead.

"Calamity Jane?" Will suggested flippantly.

Kate frowned at him, "For all the resemblance it might as well be. That's Aunt Connie."

Will looked at the picture again in disbelief, "What's she supposed to be doing?"

"Oh, she *did* it all right. She's saving Pa from the mutineers; he was only three years old at the time. That's him." Kate pointed to a bundle being cradled by a robed figure disappearing through a door in the background."

"What on earth happened?" Will asked.

"What father would call a 'classic cockup', made worse on this occasion by cowardice. The British garrison commander in the small town where Gran'pa was stationed as District Officer panicked when the mutineers came marching in his direction. He was sure his own Indian soldiers would either revolt or refuse to fight and decided to march the whole garrison to the nearest fortified town, fifty miles away. Unfortunately, in his hurry he conveniently forgot that Aunt Connie and father were in the house with only their native servants. Gran'pa was out in the field trying to organize the locals against the mutineers. Obviously he would never have left if he knew what was about to happen."

"Obviously," Will agreed.

"The mutineers did arrive a few hours later, but Connie, who was sixteen at the time, had already started to make her own arrangements with their servants to hide them. She never was one to expect others to sort things out."

"'God helps those—'," Will quoted his aunt's favorite saying.

"Who help themselves," Kate completed it. "When I say *only* the native servants, I'm not being fair. Their Ayah, that's the Indian word for a nursemaid, would have given her life for them. The head of the household they called the Havildar, he was a retired Indian Army NCO with a reputation for chopping off heads with his giant sword as easily as you or I would sharpen a pencil."

"Lordy! Not a man to cross."

"You can say that again," Kate agreed, "and by great good fortune, one of the British soldiers disobeyed orders, bless him, and came back to find Connie."

"I bet there's a story there, some dashin' young cavalry officer, I guess?"

Will thought Kate looked sad when she replied, "There is a long story there. It was a sixteen-year-old bugler who came to their aid, a lad from the slums of Sheffield." Will waited for her to elaborate but she pressed on with the story.

"They were not quick enough getting away from the house. They had just reached the top of the stairs when the mutineers burst through the front door. There was a pitched battle in the hall of the house and Connie was in the thick of it. Gran'pa had left her his presentation set of Adams patent revolvers, and they said afterwards she killed several men. The bugler had rifles loaded ready, and he and the Havildar cut the mutineers down. They escaped through the back way and into the jungle where the local people sheltered them, but not before they shot and bayoneted three more mutineers trying to get in through the garden."

Will sat speechless for a moment. When he could speak, all he said was, "Good Lord!"

He nearly jumped out of his skin when Connie, who had walked in unheard behind him, said, "He was good that day, I can tell you." She leaned over Will and looked at the yellowing paper. "I hate that picture, bloody stuff n' nonsense. For one thing, within seconds you couldn't see a thing for smoke and for another I was not waving father's revolver around like a fairy. I wouldn't be here today if I had. I held it in both hands just as he showed me and waited until he," she jabbed at the fallen man in the picture, "was practically touching it with his face...then I blew his brains out. The ball passed through his head and killed the man behind him!" She looked at the picture again as if seeing it for the first time. "And it doesn't show the Havildar and Bugler Harris shooting down the mutineers as they came through the door until they blocked it with their bodies. Neither does it show the house burning when the wadding from our cartridges set fire to the curtains, and it doesn't show me bringing up my breakfast all down that silly dress as we ran away."

There was an uncomfortable silence in the kitchen for a moment before Connie spoke again. "I learned three things that day that have stood me in good stead all my life: Never take it for granted that those in a position of responsibility will live up to it. You will find out who your friends are when the going gets tough, and never, never, ever, give up."

She shook her head sadly, "Desperate days, children, I hope you never have to see anything like that, but I fear you might." She brightened suddenly. "Has my brother gone to bed?"

"Yes, Auntie," Kate and Will said together.

"Good," she said, walking over to the Welsh dresser and retrieving a bottle from the cupboard in its base. She held it by the neck and showed it to them. "After a blood-and-guts story like that I think we deserve a tot of rum."

Chapter Eighteen

THE PREVIOUS EVENING'S STORY LEFT WILL IN A SOMBER MOOD THAT even the now-glorious summer weather could not shake. The newspaper headline Tom showed him when he arrived at the shop did nothing to lift his spirits.

"Oh, hellfire, Tom, I guess that's it then." Russia had mobilized her armies.

"I'm afraid so, Will. You can expect the Germans and the French to do the same today." Tom shook his head sadly. "It's still not too late for them to pull back from the brink, if they want to, but I don't think they do."

Will studied the details again, "I just can't believe how quick this all blew up! If we're dragged in, won't we be totally unprepared?"

"We?" Tom queried, with the suggestion of a smile.

Will realized what he had said and shrugged, "I'm here, an' if the Zeppelins come, they won't be sayin' 'Don't drop the bombs, Will Turner's down there an' he's neutral.'"

"Good for you, Will. Dear old Blighty is going to need all the help she can get." Tom sounded relieved. "As for your question: no, we're not unprepared. Now is when we find out if your Uncle Frank's brainchild is going to work."

"What on earth is that?"

"They call it the War Book, and it's been years in the planning. It's a general plan for mobilization, but this time it covers everybody, not just the military. Police headquarters, post offices, town halls, shipping companies, even the railway stationmasters have their own instructions under lock and key. In theory, everybody will know what to do if the telegrams go out. Nobody called to the colors will have to scratch up the money for his fare, he'll be issued with a travel warrant and five bob for expenses. Local magistrates will be able to requisition billets, the town hall will be able to make payments to reservists' families until the first army pay comes through, even the post office will have special powers to make sure the mail gets to the troops. They've even done a census of all horses and commercial vehicles, to make sure enough transport is available. It should work like clockwork—"

Tom broke off at the sound of a sharp rap on the door of the hangar. They both looked up as Frank strode in. The tired old man of the previous evening had gone. He bounced through the door; his wiry frame strung with energy. His uniform almost crackled. "*Should!*" he laughed. "Then again it might be the most glorious cockup, but nobody can say we haven't tried. The trouble is, in my experience, the more you try to put things in order with forms and schedules, the more opportunities it gives for the thick in head and dim in spirit to jam things up. It gives them something to hide behind instead of using their initiative. Is that kettle on? I've just time for a quick cup of char before we declare war on Germany."

Will smiled, one thing he had learned was that the British did nothing without the obligatory cup of tea. He wondered if it had the same power as the ceremonies practiced by Creek families at home, before momentous occasions. "So you think it's war then, Uncle?" Will asked.

"I'm afraid so, Will. It's not official, but the Fleet has been ordered to its war station. I'm off to the office and I don't know when I'll be back. That's why I'm here. You're man of the house for all intents and purposes. Your Aunt Connie wants you to sign some papers as soon as you arrive home this evening. She's worried that I'll be killed, Rupert will be killed and she'll be left with no executor for her will. Humor her please and sign them." He drained his cup, slapped Will on the back and shook hands with Tom. "Good luck, chaps." With that he winked, touched the peak of his cap with his silver tipped cane and marched out to the car waiting outside.

The full import of recent events began to sink in. The matter-of-fact way in which his uncle talked of the destruction of the male side of the family struck Will as chilling. "He's not jokin', is he, Tom?"

Tom slowly shook his head, "Not about this, Will. If the army is going in to action he will expect to be in the thick of it, even at his age. And Rupert...," he left the thought hanging.

Will filled in for him, "He'll be *over* the thick of it, sittin' in a wood an' wire flyin' machine." He suddenly felt a moment of helpless panic and a desire to do as he had suggested to Liam Power, fly to Berlin and Paris and tell the warmongers to stop their foolishness. The moment passed and he said sadly, "So what do *we* do?"

"*We*," Tom said firmly, "crack on with the job until somebody tells us different." He did not have long to wait. The telephone in his tiny office jangled in the early afternoon. He put down the receiver and leaned around the door to shout to Will who was filing the rough edges from a weld at the bench. "We're summoned to a conference at Farnborough tomorrow at midday."

"Me as well?" Will sounded incredulous.

"Most definitely, the major was very specific about that. Nice to know nobody is panicking, that it's such a civilized hour we'll have time for a pint in the Bull tonight. He also wanted to know if you had reconsidered Trenchard's offer?" Tom added as an afterthought.

"What did you say?"

"That I couldn't afford to lose you, but it's up to you. He did say they would release you immediately if hostilities don't break out."

"Ha!" Will said, with what sounded like disgust. "That's damn decent of 'em." He was silent for a moment. "I will be able to carry on workin' for you, won't I?"

Tom came over to the bench and put his arm around Will's shoulders, "I'm sorry old chum, I can't promise that. If it's up to me, of course, but it might not be up to me. As I told you, I'm still on the active reserve and they might insist on me taking up my commission again, but in the RFC instead of the sappers. Then again, they might retain my services at the Royal Aircraft Factory as a civilian. Either way, you might be out on a limb as they will regard you as an alien and might not be happy about you having access to what will amount to military secrets in a time of war."

"Oh," Will said heavily, "I s'pose it's a case of 'you're either for us or agin' us.'"

"That about sums it up, I'm afraid. So you might have to make a decision. Anyway, we'll find out tomorrow."

Will returned to the house that evening and, sure enough, Connie was waiting anxiously for him to appear. He felt the weight of responsibility on his shoulders as he signed the papers she put before him, solemnly witnessed by Douglas Finlay, the farmer Connie had asked to the house for that purpose. The mood lightened when he arrived at the Bull. The handsome old inn was packed and the mood, that he had expected to be somber, turned out to be almost feverish with expectation and opinion. It would have been a brave man who contradicted the generally held view that the British Army would lick the Kaiser and send him and his army packing, in time to allow the troops home for Christmas, at the very latest.

A Union flag appeared in the bar later in the evening and this provoked an outburst of patriotic singing. Mrs. Haines, the landlord's wife, brought an emotional hush to the pub with her rendition of a plaintiff song from an earlier war. She sang *The Boers Have Got My Daddy*, with such passion that Will saw several men surreptitiously wiping a tear away with their sleeve.

Will leaned close to Tom, where they sat squashed into the corner, "They're really ready for this, aren't they?"

Tom replied from the corner of his mouth, "Ain't they just, and the further away from military age they are, the keener they seem to be."

Even with this mildly cynical streak, they found themselves carried along with the general mood and were soon singing the martial songs increasingly popular in pubs throughout the land. Mr. Haines always said the local brewery sold him good "singing beer." Tom had wisely accepted Connie's offer of a bed for the night, he had rooms in a village on the main road to Cambridge, conveniently close to the flying field but inconveniently far from the Bull, which he considered his "local." As they rolled across the road outside the pub to start the walk to Penrose Cottage, Will's mood had lightened. He happily concentrated on placing one foot in front of the other and really thought he had failed in this simple exercise when he found himself flying bodily into the ditch.

The next few moments would have been confusing in any case. A great weight crashed down on top of him, and he was vaguely aware of shouting. Then he felt an elbow in his ribs and the weight eased. A great commotion washed above him. A shout of "Bastard!" rang out amid a clatter of running feet, a bottle smashed some ways away as a car motor suddenly roared into life.

"What the bloody hell—?" Tom said from the ditch next to him. Hands grabbed them both and dragged them out. Concerned faces crowded around, shining dimly in the light from the pub.

"What's going on?" The landlord, Bob Haines, demanded from the door. He would tolerate no fighting even *near* his premises and he had jumped to that conclusion.

"Some bloody maniac nearly ran Mr. Tom and young Will down with a motorcar," an unidentified voice explained.

It was not until he heard this that Will realized what had happened. The great weight he had felt was his friend and cricket teammate, Jack, who had spotted the unlit car bearing down on them as they crossed the road. With the surprising speed and agility sometimes possessed by those with great size and strength, he had hurled himself across the road and charged them both out of harm's way.

"By God, Jack, you saved our lives!" Tom said, seizing the big man by the hand and shaking it.

"Never mind that, Mr. Tom, we better have Mr. Haines telephone the Constable. I 'eaved a bottle after that motor and I reckon I clipped him. That be a German spy out to murder thee, I'll bet." An angry murmur swelled in the crowd. Bob Haines rushed back to the pub to telephone the police while the crowd gathered solicitously around Tom and Will. The concern for their well being increased when Mrs. Haines declared this a special occasion and opened the bar again. Neither Will nor Tom had suffered more than a few scratches, but the car was summoned, against their will, from the house. Peter, who had only just learned to drive the Renault, brought it gingerly down the hill to the pub.

Connie and Kate, who had been roused from her bed, greeted them with great relief and a barrage of questions when they finally arrived at the house. "Do you really think it was a German spy, Tom?" Connie asked.

"It seems pretty unlikely, to be honest," Tom replied. He had regained his usual good humor. "Why pick on me?"

"Because you're an aeroplane expert, of course, just like Will." Kate replied. "Just imagine what a coup that would be for the swine. The two leading aviation experts in the country wiped out before the fighting even begins."

Tom looked at her carefully and then took her hands, "That's a good point, Kate, we are not at war with Germany, not yet, anyway. It was probably just some drunk too feeble to notice he had no lights on his motor. It won't do for people to start running around in a panic."

"I'm not panicking," Kate protested, "I'm just worried about you both."

Will spoke, almost for the first time since the incident, "We're obliged, Kate, but don't worry, we'll be okay."

The following morning Tom and Will set off for Farnborough by train. With quick connections in London they had plenty of time in hand.

Will seemed unusually quiet to his friend. He seemed lost in thought as he gazed from the window at the countryside rolling past.

Tom looked up from his paper and studied Will carefully. "Penny for them, old chum," he prompted.

Will shook himself from his reverie, "That was no drunk, and it wasn't a German agent either, I think we both know that."

Tom shrugged, "Your friend, Roscoe, had crossed my mind, but we can't go jumping to conclusions, there's no proof. My money's still on a drunk."

"You don't know Roscoe, Tom, I'm sorry to disagree with you, but there's no doubt in my mind. That was deliberate, and it had all the hallmarks of his way of actin'."

"What makes you say that, I thought he tried to shoot you before?" Tom pointed out.

"I don't think he's too choosy about his methods," Will said.

"Okay, just say you're right, what can we do about him?" Tom asked.

"I'm the only one who can do anythin', Tom, though I really do appreciate your concern. It's not the first time a Turner has found himself in this position. I don't like what I have to do, but I'm doin' it."

"Really!" Tom said. "You have a plan, what is it?"

For the first time that morning Tom saw Will's characteristic lopsided smile. "You'll have to wait, but I think it's for the best."

Tom respected Will's wish to keep the idea to himself, and the rest of the journey was spent discussing likely outcomes of the meeting they had to attend. The moment they arrived at the guardroom at the entrance to the Royal Flying Corps barracks, it seemed to Will he was caught in the working of a great machine. They were ushered politely down a long corridor painted in what Tom described as army brown, in all its attractive shades. A door opened as they neared the end of the corridor.

"Come in, Tom, simply lovely to see you again, old boy," the man behind the plain desk greeted him as a long lost friend, as indeed he was. "And Mr. Turner, so good of you to come along at short notice." Will had never met anybody quite like the officer standing before him. Tom had warned him that Sefton Brancker might appear a "bit of a fop", and this was a good description. Like Trenchard, he was a tall man, but without the other man's pugnacious stance. Instead he seemed almost delicate. His tightly trimmed military mustache did nothing to confer a more warlike countenance on a long sensitive face. Without the uniform Will might have guessed him to be a poet, not knowing that it was a passion of this literate and cultured man. He enhanced his vaguely eccentric air by wearing a monocle in his right eye.

As Tom had said, appearances in this case were deceptive. The man was all business, direct and to the point. The inevitable tea arrived, but Brancker had no time for small talk. "I have been asked to organize procurement of machines and materials at this end, working from the War Office. Geoffrey de Havilland has asked specifically for you, Tom, to work with him here at Farnborough. You will be given anything you need to develop new machines and organize the production of existing types. You will be given the reserve rank of captain with the pay, and seniority that goes with it, but we do not expect you to wear uniform or work as part of the military establishment. It is in recognition of your previous service and gives you authority and mess privileges if you have to visit other military establishments or the front."

"Goodness!" Tom said, clearly pleased. "The best of both worlds."

Brancker smiled, "You might think otherwise at the end of a twenty-hour work day."

"Point taken," Tom acknowledged.

Brancker turned his attention to Will. "Mr. Turner, I have a problem, and I hope you can solve it."

"I'll do my best, sir," Will replied evenly.

Brancker explained, "You have earned a reputation as an expert pilot and an engineer of great ability."

"Adequate, sir, just about."

Brancker brushed aside his modest protest. "My problem is we need your services. Unfortunately, though a welcome guest, you are classified as an alien, and will have to register as such. You will not be allowed to work in any occupation involving aviation. All civilian flying will cease if and when war is declared. There is a simple solution..."

"Mr. Trenchard's," Will completed the sentence for him.

"Precisely." Brancker put his long hands together on the desk in front of him to form a steeple. "We would issue papers showing you as William Turner, Canadian, a subject of His Majesty, and commission you as a first lieutenant in the Royal Flying Corps. We have a very particular and valuable task we want you to undertake, and we feel it advisable that you at least appear to have some seniority to give you the authority to carry it out."

Tom explained. "The first rung on the ladder is second lieutenant, or *subaltern*, the lowest of the low I'm afraid. This way you will be able to throw your weight around a bit if you have to. It's not uncommon for people with particular skills to enter at a certain rank. Doctors, for example, are usually commissioned as captains in the Medical Corps."

"But isn't it against international law to just change somebody's nationality?" Will asked.

"Yes," Brancker said, matter-of-factly, "and so is invading another sovereign state. But you won't be changing your nationality, just borrowing another one."

"Fine. I'll do it," Will said, equally straightforward. Brancker had started to say more in an effort to persuade him, but he stopped with his mouth open. His monocle popped out and swung gently at the end of the chord fixed to his breast pocket.

Tom turned in his seat and looked at him, hardly believing what he had just heard. "Don't you want some time to think about this, Will? You could still make your way home."

"I've done nothing *but* think about it, Tom. Thanks for your concern but it's either the French Foreign Legion, the Texas Rangers, or this. And the other two don't have an aviation section." Tom looked baffled. "I'll tell you about Uncle Roy some time, it might make more sense then." Will added.

Brancker had no reservations. He stood and leaned across the desk with his hand outstretched, "Top hole, old chap! Welcome aboard."

Will shook his hand, "Thank you, sir, I'll try not to let you down." Brancker sat down and took a checkbook from a desk drawer. He added his signature, ripped out a check and handed it to Will who stared at it uncomprehendingly, "Seventy-five pounds? Sir, I don't understand."

"I am authorized to reimburse every officer who paid for his own flying tuition." Brancker explained.

"I can't possibly accept that, sir," Will protested. "It cost me nowhere near that much to learn." He tried to hand the check back, but Brancker pointedly folded his arms.

"Explain, if you will please, Tom." Brancker smiled.

"That's not how the army works, Will. The regulations say you *will* be paid. That's an order."

Will shrugged, folded the check and put it in his pocket. "Guess if that's the worst order I ever have to follow, I'll be doin' okay."

"That's the ticket, old boy," Brancker enthused. "Now let me explain what we want you to do for us. We will set up a depot well behind any battle lines in France or Belgium to repair aircraft too seriously damaged to be repaired at the 'sharp end', so to speak. Your job in the first instance will be to assess each incident and make the decision as to whether a machine can be repaired by the squadron, or must return to the depot. We want you to prepare a categorization system, you know the sort of thing: 'A' for minor damage, 'B' for repair at squadron level. We'll see how things go, but once we're settled over there you will be expected to train the squadron's own fitters in the system. You will never be able to manage on your own once we start to build up."

"Sounds like you're expectin' this to last more than a few weeks, sir." Will said.

"Hope for the best—prepare for the worst," Brancker replied briskly. "I'm sorry to say you won't see any action." He gave Tom a significant look before continuing, "It may even seem boring work to you, but believe me, you will be doing your mother's country an enormous service."

Will gulped, "I'll do my best, sir." He was about to ask when he would be expected to report, when the door burst open. The man who strode into the office was the negative to Brancker's positive. His build was heavyset to the point of fat; Will found himself looking at the way his tight collar rolled a fold of flesh into the bristles of his close-cropped hair. The man's face glowed red with indignation; his mustache bristled under a lumpish nose.

"Ah, good afternoon, Major Matrett," Brancker began evenly. "May I introduce Captain Armstrong and—"

"Never mind that," Matrett did not exactly bark—his voice was strangely high for a big man—he snapped like a terrier. "What's this I hear about you commissioning people, willy-nilly?"

Brancker showed no sign of emotion beyond an obvious weariness. "Nothing willy-nilly about it, I only choose the best."

Matrett glared at him, "First you take three bloody hobbledyhoy instructors and turn them into officers—"

"Supply and demand," Brancker pointed out. "The Navy offered them commissions. I offered them commissions *and* more money."

"And now I hear you've taken on some damn foreign chappy!" Matrett ignored Brancker's explanation.

Brancker smiled sweetly, "Yes, Major, this is Mr. Turner. He's kindly agreed to become a Canadian and help us beat the Kaiser."

Recognizing his own gaffe took the wind out of Matrett's sails, but he had gone too far to back down without losing face. "Damn it all, Brancker, what on earth do you think you're doing? You can't just take anybody who can fly, off the street and commission them," he insisted angrily.

Brancker shrugged, "Actually, I can."

"But what about breeding, man? What about class? You don't just make an officer with a stroke of a pen."

Brancker turned to Will, "Did you go to public school, Mr. Turner?"

"I did, sir." Will answered truthfully.

"Can you ride?"

"Yes, sir," Will answered cheerfully, "horse, jackass or motorcycle... I'll get on anythin'."

"And your family?"

"My uncle is Colonel Frank Penrose."

The last answer deflated Matrett, Tom detected a hint of alarm in his eyes, but the bullish Major would not give up. "I tell you, Brancker," he paused, seeking a suitable rejoinder but gave up, "it's just not cricket!"

"Cricket, sir?" Will said brightly. "I scored a half century, not out, in my first game." Tom stifled a laugh, and Brancker smiled as he bowed slightly to Matrett.

"There you are, Major, he's perfectly qualified."

Matrett started for the door, then stopped in his tracks. "Marching—these instant officers of yours can't even bloody well march."

Brancker decided he had wasted enough time, he raised his voice to carry through the door to the adjoining office. "Sergeant Major Cattle!"

"Yessir." The door snapped open. This man, unlike Joe Thorpe, *did* fit Will's idea of a military man. His frame filled his uniform at every point, particularly around his chest that jutted forward like a pigeon. Will guessed his hair color as gray, what was left of it after the severest haircut he had seen. The same treatment had been used for his mustache, a thin bristling line over his thin top lip. His glittering little eyes swept over Will.

"Sergeant Major, I want you to make a parade ground soldier out of Mr. Turner. Major Matrett is concerned that he might not be able to march."

"Yessir."

"Can you do it in two hours?"

The sergeant major allowed himself a smile, "Yessir, with pleasure, sir." Will felt uneasy at his tone.

"Right. Off you go, Mr. Turner, the sergeant major will look after you." Brancker dismissed him pleasantly. The sergeant major snatched his cap from a hook behind the office door, jammed it on, stuck a cane under his arm, threw Brancker a salute that quivered a regulation amount then ushered Will through the door.

They emerged from the hut onto the path outside. Cattle fell into step behind Will and immediately began bellowing in his ear. "Marching lesson begins now! Straighten up—sir. Get those bleedin' shoulders back—sir. Let's see those arms swingin' high...higher, up to the shoulder of the man in front of you."

"But there's nobody in front—" Will started to protest.

"Did I ask for your fuckin' opinion—sir?" The sergeant major's voice rose to a scream that made Will wince, *and* straighten up, pull his shoulders back and start swinging his arms high. They marched quickly down the path toward two single story buildings standing apart from the others. Cattle was so close behind he nearly trod on Will's ankles. From the office window they looked like some form of bizarre mechanical toy.

"Do you think we'll make a soldier of young Mr. Turner, Tom?" Brancker asked.

"No, but we have plenty of soldiers. He's a brilliant pilot and engineer."

"That's what I'm banking on," Brancker said. "Don't worry about that little performance, that's for Matrett's benefit. Cattle has been briefed to sort something out far more important than drill."

Will and the sergeant major progressed quickly around the back of the isolated sheds. The instant they were out of sight of the office, Cattle screamed new orders, "Lef' turn! Right turn! HALT!" Will staggered on a few paces before turning to look suspiciously at the soldier. "Stand easy, sir," Cattle said in a reasonable conversational tone. "Sorry about that, sir. All for the benefit of any spectators." He winked and put his hand on the door of the nearest building.

"What? You mean you're not teachin' me drill, sir?"

"Ah, let's get something straight, Mr. Turner. *You're* sir, I'm Sergeant Major to you."

"But shouldn't I know how to drill?" Cattle smiled. Will thought he almost looked human.

"Can you dance, sir?" Cattle asked.

"Beg pardon?"

"Dance, sir. You know, waltz—quick step—fox trot."

"Why yes, but what has that got to do with drill?"

"Everything, Mr. Turner. It's all a question of steps and rhythm. If you have any sense of rhythm, you can march in step. The maneuvers are all about easy steps...I'll show you." With quick neat movements, punctuated by the smack of his brilliant, polished hobnail boots, Cattle showed Will the left and right turn and the about turn. "Think you can remember that, sir?"

"No problem."

"Show me then."

Will copied the movements he had been shown.

"Excellent, sir. Now show me how you would salute."

Will raised his hand to his forehead as he had seen soldiers at home do when they saluted the flag. Cattle stepped forward and twisted his wrist so his palm faced outward. "That's how we do it. You're a knight of old raising the visor on your helmet. The other way is how the sailors do it—they're scanning the horizon for the next tot of rum." Cattle grinned but continued in a serious tone, "Remember, the men are saluting the king through your uniform, they are not saluting *you.* You respond with a smart salute, not by touching your cap with your walking-out cane." The sergeant major smiled again. "Don't worry, sir, you can always have your sergeants show you the finer points of drill in time for the victory parade. That's part one of your basic training out of the way, now let's press on with the important part." He pushed open the door to the building.

Will followed him into the long, low room. A long counter with a lift-up flap like a saloon ran the length of the room. Hundreds of rifles, connected by endless chains passing through the trigger guards, stood like tight packed sentinels in racks against the back wall. Cattle called out, "Stan, are you here?"

"In the back, Eric." A voice replied from an adjoining room. The door opened and a gray hared man beckoned them in. He wore a brown warehouseman's dustcoat over his uniform. "Cuppa?" he asked.

"Yes please, Stan, I'm gaspin' and I expect Mr. Turner is, too." To Will's surprise, Cattle divested himself of cap and belt and undid the top button of his tunic. Army life was proving complicated. He had gone from screaming military discipline to a tea party in one minute. "It's all a big show, Mr. Turner," Cattle said simply. "As an officer you'll come to understand that."

"I'm sorry, Sergeant Major, I don't really follow," Will's bafflement showed.

"It's all part of the scheme. All that shoutin' and 'ollerin we do out there, all the chasing the men 'round and putting them on charges and fatigues. That's to get 'em used to the idea that life ain't fair. If they don't understand that, they'll stand rooted to the spot the first time some 'airy great Prussian Guard comes charging toward them. Getting 'em used to obeying orders without question might save their lives."

"I can see your point," Will said.

"Then again," Cattle continued, apparently serious, "we 'ave to instill discipline because if we didn't, what's to stop all those men from shooting their officers and NCO's and chopping off the king's head like them Frenchies in *their* revolution? That would never do."

Will suspected his leg was being pulled but replied seriously, "No, Sergeant Major, that would be a very poor show indeed." The tea arrived and Cattle, who clearly knew a great deal about Will, took the opportunity to explain something of the organization of the Royal Flying Corps. Like most of the men Will had met, he had volunteered for the new service, every inch a career soldier—he was also a fanatical believer in military aviation. His grasp of the situation was clear.

"The basic problem is, sir, that the Germans have already put hundreds of machines into service and we can only muster a few dozen. That's why it's so important we look after the ones we have."

"I hope to help in that," Will offered.

"And there's the other thing, sir, we don't have enough skilled men, officers or fitters. And that's why we can't afford to lose a one, killed or captured. That's why I've been told to bring you in here."

Will looked around, they sat in a small workshop where parts of rifles and some other unidentifiable weapons lay on benches. He could see where Cattle's conversation might be leading. "I'm told I won't see any action, they said things might be a little borin' from that point of view. I'll be goin' back an' forth twixt the squadrons an' headquarters." He paused for a moment. He did not want to seem lacking the right spirit in front of these professional soldiers. "Mind, it would be a shame to go home without seein' a little excitement."

Cattle and the armorer laughed, Will had the unpleasant feeling they knew something he did not. "Whatever *they* say, begging your pardon, sir, I won't be at all surprised if Kaiser Bill don't lay on some fun for you." Cattle sounded almost apologetic. "Just in case things don't go to plan and you find the German army knocking on your workshop door, what kind of a weapon did you have in mind for persuading them to keep their distance?"

Will shrugged and looked around the workshop, "I suppose I'll be expected to carry a pistol, bein' in a manner an officer."

The armorer slid off the bench where he had perched his backside and went back through the door. He returned with a rifle and passed it to Cattle who addressed Will seriously, "You will be issued with a pistol, but to be honest with you, sir, it's more a badge of office than any use. If they're close enough to hit with a service revolver then you should have run away a long time before."

"Isn't runnin' away frowned on in military circles?" Will asked.

"Oh dear no, sir, providing we all run away together it's called a 'tactical retreat' and the newspapers will say how cunning we are. Of course, if you run away on your own it's called 'cowardice' and they'll court martial you and shoot you."

"I'll bear that in mind, Sergeant Major."

"Best to," Cattle advised. "Anyway, when we're all running away together, everybody would really appreciate it if you can use one of these properly." He pulled the bolt back and tossed the rifle forcefully at Will who snatched it deftly from the air, pointed the muzzle at the ceiling and peered into the breech to make sure the exposed chamber was empty. The two old soldiers looked at each other and nodded approvingly. "The basic rules, sir: It is the accepted etiquette that you never pass a weapon with the breech closed, that's good manners and good sense. You treat any weapon as if it is loaded even when you know it's not. You only put one up the spout if action is imminent, and you never, ever point your rifle at somebody unless you are going to shoot him."

"Understood, Mr. Cattle," Will said, balancing the rifle in his hands. "This is a very well made piece for a soldier's weapon."

"It is, sir. That's the standard version of the short, magazine Lee–Enfield. The 'short' applies to the overall length of the rifle, not the magazine. There were earlier versions with longer barrels but this is the standard model now. They've been making them in this form since 1907, but there are a few of the earlier ones drifting around that have been modified to this Mark three standard. They're okay, but try to lay hands on one of these if you can. Try the action, sir," he urged. Will worked the bolt forward and down to lock the breech then squeezed the trigger. There was a satisfying click from the mechanism. He pulled the bolt up and back, on each movement it felt as if he initiated the movement, the slick action then seemed to complete it for him.

"Does this work as fast with cartridges in the magazine?" he asked, the engineer in him thrilled by the smooth precision of the action.

"Oh yes, sir," the armorer took the rifle from him and produced a clip with five white painted rounds. He placed them above the open breech and stripped them down into the magazine with an easy pressure of his thumb. He passed the weapon back to Will, "Drill purpose dummy rounds, sir, always painted white." Will worked the bolt quickly back and forth, the ejected cartridges springing clear to the side. Cattle caught them.

"I'm only sorry there's no time to take you out on the range. There's a hefty kick, as you'd expect, no more than a twelve-bore shotgun though," Cattle said reassuringly.

"Twelve *gauge* I think Mr. Turner might call it, Eric," the armorer pointed out.

"That I might," Will said with a smile. "Is it accurate as well as rapid?"

"Yes, to a thousand yards in very skilled hands," the armorer said. "But realistically, it's deadly up to five hundred. You probably know our lads are expected to get fifteen *aimed* shots off in a minute and that includes reloading."

"And the magazine holds ten rounds?" Will queried.

"Yes, sir. It's not only rapid and accurate but reliable as well. There's a lot of thought gone into this. See how the furniture extends right to the muzzle? That protects it from knocks." Will examined the business end of the rifle. The muzzle protruded barely a fraction of an inch from the wooden stock.

Will handed the Lee–Enfield back to the armorer who took it from him carefully and cradled it in his arms. "So why do some folk write critical things about it? I read an article in the *Countryman* magazine where some fellow reckoned everything about it was wrong."

Cattle snorted with disgust. "That would be the so-called expert Mr. Blanch. His real beef is that it is not a Mauser. Everybody goes on about that rifle because of South Africa, where the Boers used it. I don't deny the Model 98 is very accurate, but it's heavy, slow to operate and only holds five rounds in the magazine. It's a good target rifle," he paused and grinned maliciously, "but the Enfield is a good killin' rifle, and that's what we're going to need. If it ever comes to that, sir, remember to aim low, at their knees. Try to count your shots as you fire and any time you think you've let go five rounds make sure you take any opportunity to slip another clip in. That could save your life.

Will thanked the armorer for his time and advice. He found to his surprise that he marched in step with the Sergeant Major back to the office where he joined Tom and Sefton Brancker. "Has Sergeant Major Cattle made a soldier of you then, Mr. Turner?" Brancker asked with a smile.

"No, sir," Will answered truthfully, "but I can march well enough now to look like a soldier from a distance."

Brancker laughed, "Splendid. That'll do. To be honest we don't set much store by marching, the only reason we do it is to make sure we don't lose anybody when we're on the move." He was suddenly serious again, "You'll have to put together whatever kind of uniform you can from stores. Perhaps Tom and your family can sort you out something until you can make arrangements with a good tailor. I must admit," he said showing a trace of weariness, "appearing 'regimental' is the least of our worries at the moment."

Chapter Nineteen

THE ARRIVAL OF WILL'S LETTERS AT HIS HOME IN TALLAHASSEE HAD become a social event over the course of the summer of 1914. An excellent correspondent, Will adopted the policy of sending his letters alternately to the individual recipients, his family, the Walkers, and Marie Julien, in the hope they might be shared to some extent.

The custom had grown for the two families and Marie to meet on the Saturday afternoon following receipt of the letters. Charlie Turner had grown particularly sensitive to Marie's feelings. To Charlie's surprise, Marie seemed to have lost her interest in other boys, at least for the time being. Cordelia's intuition had not failed her; this was the "real thing."

Three Saturdays after the fateful weekend that saw Europe pitched into war, Charlie Turner read her son's letter explaining his new situation for the tenth time. "Please tell me what you said about army support again, Nathan."

Nathan understood her need to hear what he had to say on the subject, "It's exactly as I said," he rumbled, "fo' every man in the line, there's five supportin' him. You've supplies people, clerks, headquarters staff, cooks, armorers an' engineers. An' that's what Will's doin', he's an engineer, an' his Royal Flyin' Corps is goin' to need five engineers alone, to keep every machine in the air—ain't that right son?"

Henry nodded earnestly, "More!" he said quickly, doing his part to reassure Charlie. She shook her head slowly, John could see she was biting her lip.

"I suppose that must be true," Charlie said, "and after all, he says they are keeping him and the other mechanics well back from the battle areas." John Turner could read his wife's brave face. The previous

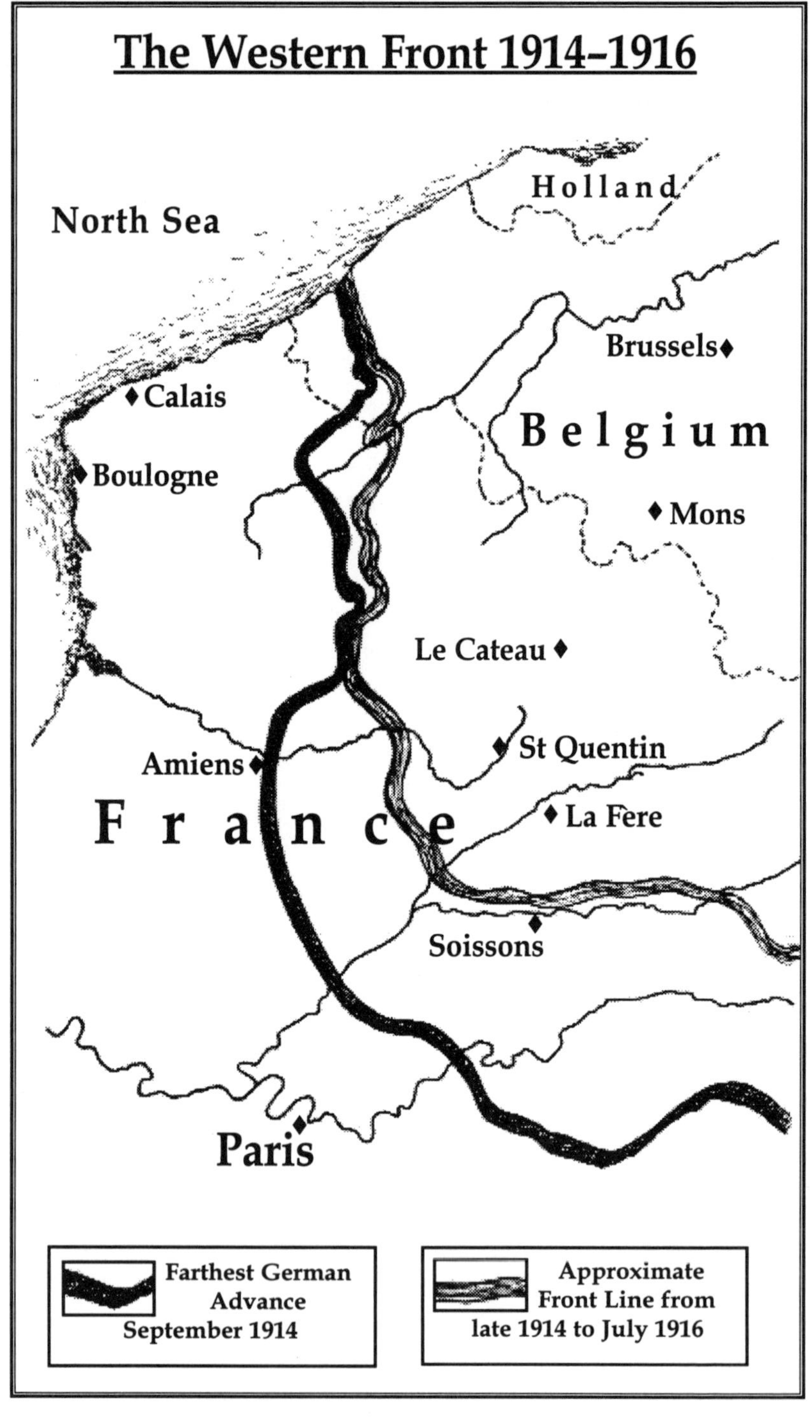
The Western Front 1914–1916
North Sea
Holland
Brussels
Calais
Belgium
Boulogne
Mons
Le Cateau
St Quentin
Amiens
France
La Fere
Soissons
Paris
Farthest German Advance September 1914
Approximate Front Line from late 1914 to July 1916

evening she had broken down, sobbing, blaming herself for encouraging Will's journey to England. "If I thought it would bring him home, I'd have Marie write and propose now," she wept in his arms.

Vicky, for her part, had complete confidence in her brother's ability to find his way out of any scrape. His sudden leap to commissioned rank, in what people already perceived as a glamorous corps, gave her a certain reflected glory among her friends. She knew she would have to wait for a photograph, he had sent his only picture taken in England to Marie. In the meantime, she enjoyed the words of his commission that he had copied out for her.

George, by the Grace of God, of the United Kingdom of Great Britain and Ireland, and of the British Dominions beyond the Seas, King, Defender of the Faith, Emperor of India, etc.
To Our Trusty and well beloved William Turner
Greeting.
We reposing especial Trust and Confidence in your Loyalty, Courage and good Conduct, do by these Presents Constitute and Appoint you to be an Officer in Our Special Reserve of Officers...

The King went on to describe Will's rank and what he expected of him and signed the document as *"Given at our Court at Saint James's."* Vicky was very impressed, but Will had pointed out in his letter that the King might be less enthusiastic if he knew that his "Trusty and well beloved" William Turner was not a resident of any of the long list of territories claimed by His Majesty. In strict legal terms Will Turner sailed under false colors. He was, to all intents and purposes, a mercenary. His status, however, was of no interest to the men with whom he now served. If anything it would have enhanced their already high regard for him, because unlike the armies of the other belligerent nations, the British Expeditionary Force that sailed for France in August 1914 was made up of professional soldiers. They did not fight for patriotic or philosophical ideals; they fought because they were paid to.

The letters read in Tallahassee that hot summer afternoon had been hastily written and dispatched after Will's interview and token basic training. He did not go off to war with the good wishes of his entire family following him. His Aunt Connie had reacted with disbelief rapidly followed by anger on his return from Farnborough following his unconventional enlistment. "You have done what!?" she demanded when he joined her and his cousin Kate in the drawing room at Penrose Cottage.

"I've joined the Flyin' Corps." He was taken back by her reaction to the news.

"You've joined the bloody army!? I don't believe it! After all your fine words about not wanting to be part of the military and thinking war is stupid! I'm, I'm, ooooh..." Connie's voice tailed off.

"But I've no choice," Will tried to explain.

"What do you mean no choice? You could stay and work with Tom, you could stay here..."

"I can't. He's been called up from the reserve an' they won't let me near an airplane because I'm an alien, an—"

"But they don't mind having you in the army?" Connie's voice rose in disbelief. "For goodness sake, William, you could bugger off home..."

Will took a pace back. "Aunt Constance, I need the damn job," his voice rose to match hers.

"Oh for Godsake, that makes you no better than a mercenary."

"If that were true I'd be findin' out how much the goddamn Germans are payin'" he lashed back. She stared at him for a moment, her mouth working. No reply came; instead she turned on her heel and flounced from the room. Will turned to Kate who had remained silent throughout the exchange. "Lordy, Kate," he breathed, "I had no idea she'd take this so hard."

Kate stood up and took his hand. "Will, she's scared for you and for us. This has come like a bolt out of the blue. She expected to have at least you safe and sound while her brother and one nephew are away fighting. You've snatched that security away from her. Come on, you have to go to her."

Will found his aunt in the kitchen. As he entered she made a feeble flapping gesture with her hands as if to send him away. He ignored it and sat down next to her. He took her hand and was surprised when she clutched it fiercely. She was sobbing. "Aunt Connie, I'm so very sorry you feel this way...," he struggled for words.

"I know, it's your 'duty', you're 'honor bound', etcetera, etcetera..."

He put an arm around her shoulders. "Well, I suppose there's some of that, but I confess I'm not thinkin' of it that way. Aunt Connie, I *do* need the job. Otherwise, I'd just have to go home with my tail between my legs."

Connie sniffed, "Well I suppose it's better than being taken in by all that silly jingoistic flag waving and drum beating. At least you are not going into this with high ideals."

He drew back slightly to look at her. "You prefer that idea?"

She sniffed again and looked at him with red rimmed eyes, then suddenly hugged him desperately. He felt her heaving with sobs again. He held her until her sobbing quieted. At last she released him and looked at him steadily. Will handed his aunt a handkerchief and she blew her nose noisily. "Yes," she said. The ghost of a smile appeared. "Because young men with high patriotic ideals are prone to earn themselves posthumous gallantry medals. Mercenaries are more likely to keep their heads down."

"Aunt Constance," he looked at her seriously, "I will never, ever, try to earn any medals. I promise."

"Promise?" she was much brighter. "Cross your heart and hope *not* to die?"

He laughed, "Absolutely."

"Good! I'll hold you to that. I still think you're a bloody young fool." She stood abruptly and took him by the hand back into the drawing room, "I need a dr—" Her face lit up when she saw Kate with the decanter, "Kate, dear, you read my mind."

❧ ◆◆◆ ❧

The airplanes of the Royal Flying Corps converged on Swingate Downs above the Kent coastal town of Dover to prepare for the flight to France. Will and Tom had both been dispatched by Brancker to assist, and they worked ceaselessly to repair machines damaged on incoming flights and to prepare all planes for crossing the twenty-mile stretch of water that separates England from France.

Will felt woefully unprepared for the military duties that went with his new position. He did not feel like an army officer and was painfully conscious of his inexperience. Most of the pilots were junior officers but were all established in their careers. Only a few, like himself, were enlisted in the RFC special reserve. The others were drawn from over forty different regiments. Among them he found Rupert.

"What ho! Lieutenant Turner, how do you like the life of a soldier?" Rupert greeted him with a slap on the back. He had landed in tandem with another Avro biplane. Will straightened up from beneath the wing of the machine he was tending. He wore oil-stained coveralls and one of the soft-peaked caps favored by the enlisted soldiers for their comfort.

"So far it's not much different from workin' for Nathan Walker at home," he said with a grin. "Everythin' needin' to be done just so—an' polished."

Rupert became serious, "How are you finding the military side of things? You've hardly had any time to acclimatize to the bull."

Will wiped his hands on a rag, "I'm really glad Tom is here; I take my lead from him. But it's the damnedest thing, I don't believe I've given an order yet. Still, folk just keep runnin' up an' askin' for advice, an' I give it when I can."

"I'm not surprised, Will," Rupert said. "You know, Trenchard has managed to recruit the very best craftsmen in the country. Our chaps are paid far more than the average Tommy, but by God, they're worth every penny."

Rupert appreciated the effort the RFC had made in finding the men to maintain and repair the aircraft. Many came from outside the airplane industry, their experience gained with trucks or automobiles. Some were skilled wood workers from the furniture trade, others brought obscure but vital skills such as coppersmithing. They all quickly came to rely on the young officer with the odd accent for an accurate diagnosis of an engine or rigging problem.

"They're a fine bunch of fellows, Rupert, you couldn't ask for a more willin' crew. One day I might even work out what all the badges an' ranks stand for."

"Don't worry too much about that for the moment, old boy. Just remember, when we get to France: brown uniforms—our side, gray uniforms—the other side." Rupert studied Will carefully, "You look knackered. Try to get some sleep tonight; our orders are for takeoff at six."

Will managed to snatch a few hours rest under the wing of a Farman Longhorn. He woke to the first pastel light of a beautiful summer morning with most of the Royal Flying Corps.

All the aircraft setting off that morning were two-place machines, crewed by a pilot and an air mechanic. No formal sea rescue system had been set up. When Will realized this he sent men into the town to buy all the tire inner tubes they could find. They would be better than nothing as life preservers if a crew came down in the waters of the channel. Will remembered that the last time he had floated in a tube was on the river at home, the only thing he had to worry about there was the curious alligator, Jackson. He guessed the cold of the English Channel might be more deadly.

In spite of the early hour, the townsfolk of Dover turned out to cheer them on their way. As each fragile machine, overloaded with tools and equipment, staggered into the air a great roar rose from the crowd lifting the aviators as they fluttered overhead. The scene appeared to Will like a patriotic carnival instead of an army going to war. The majestic bulk of Dover Castle overlooked Swingate Downs where the spectators had brought along every flag they could find to wave for the benefit of the airmen.

Rupert leaned down from the cockpit of his Avro to bid Will farewell. "Looks like the circus has come to town, Coz," he said, gesturing toward the crowd waiting to boost him on his way.

"Please don't give 'em too much of a show, Rupert, make it nice an' steady," Will said anxiously.

Rupert pulled down his goggles, "Do I know any other way to fly?" Will could hear him laughing as the Avro revved to full power and began its extended takeoff run. One by one the airplanes disappeared into the light mist over the channel. The field fell silent. Tom appeared at Will's side as he watched the departing flock of airplanes through powerful field glasses.

"How are they doing?" Tom asked.

Will passed him the binoculars. "Hard to tell, but I think they're over safe. I can see the French coast clear enough an' everybody has turned right. Except one." Tom laughed and a murmur of appreciation came from the watching mechanics.

Tom raised the glasses again and trained them on the distant sky. "Harvey-Kelly, I'll put money on it."

"You already did, sir," a mechanic pointed out. "Two bob on Mr. Harvey-Kelly to win." They were running a "book" on the order of arrival at Amiens, the intended destination.

"My money's safe," Tom said with a satisfied smile. He handed the binoculars back to Will. "The stragglers are on their way. Louis Strange won't be here for a day or so, but Dick Thomas with the prototype Vickers fighting biplane expects to be here before lunch. Is your kit ready?"

"You bet, Tom—I mean, Captain. Do you know anythin' about this new machine?"

"It's a pusher but a much tidier machine than a Farman. The idea is that one of the Vickers company's own machine guns is mounted in the front cockpit. Dick said not to worry, though, they can't spare one so it's unarmed and there'll be plenty of room for your toolkit."

"What'll we do if we meet a Zeppelin over the Channel?" Will asked. The possibility seemed real enough.

"Land on top, then unbolt their engines, that'll teach 'em." Tom suspected that Will might try, "Then again, just give 'em two fingers as you motor past." He advised.

Dick Thomas arrived in the Vickers on schedule. Will had been scanning the sky to the west anxiously. His kit was packed and ready: flying gear, spare goggles, revolver, a water bottle, and a haversack with a few rations. It stood next to his precious toolbox. The Vickers landed neatly and puttered to a stop next to the tent being used as a temporary headquarters. Lieutenant Dick Thomas jumped down. Will's short acquaintance with the RFC had convinced him that the new corps acted as a magnet for every eccentric in the British army. Thomas was no exception. He was a tiny man, fragile in appearance, but the most striking thing about him was that his head appeared too big for his body. It seemed to wobble precariously on his neck and usually settled in a lopsided attitude giving him a permanent quizzical look.

"Will Turner, I presume. Delighted to meet you." He also possessed a smile that Will saw could charm the birds from the trees. "Sorry for the delay, the chaps at the factory were still building her this morning, *capital* airplane, though."

"Nice trip?" Tom asked.

"Absolutely smashing. I managed to take some snaps of that Roman villa just back up the road toward Canterbury. Do you think you could get the plates back to Mama at the old family pile? She'll develop them for me."

Will looked at the cockpit of the new airplane, a compact camera sat fixed in a mounting bolted to the side. Thomas saw Will looking at it.

"What do you think, any use for observation?"

"That surely is a nice piece of work there, Mr. Thomas." Will replied, examining the mounting carefully.

Thomas looked at Will and smiled politely. "They told me I'm going across with a Canadian. If you're from Canada, I'm the Emperor of China."

"I'm a Canadian of convenience, Mr. Thomas," Will said as they shook hands. "Will Turner, out of Tallahassee, Florida."

Thomas's eyes opened wide with surprise, "I say, how absolutely fascinating, I'm very interested in the indigenous people of your region.

I'm developing a theory about migration in the New World."

Tom explained, "Dick is a rare thing in the army—an intellectual."

"Oh, I wouldn't say that, old boy," Thomas protested, "just have an interest in antiquities, and the army gives me plenty of opportunities to see things I would never have the chance to otherwise. Now take that Roman Villa just up the road, if it wasn't for the use of this fine machine, nobody would know it was there."

For a moment all thoughts of the war drifted away. "But why ever not," Will asked. "How could people not spot a pile of ruins?"

Thomas smiled happily, "Because it's buried under ground, probably as much as three feet down. You see, it's under a standing crop of wheat that is just now ripe for harvesting. All those lines of buried stone have the effect of retarding the way the crop grows above it. The wheat is stunted and shows up as a pattern in the field. A perfect plan of the building." He sighed blissfully, "Fascinating, absolutely fascinating, and now I have some photographs to prove my theory."

Tom broke in, "I hate to interrupt this fascinating lecture on Roman Britain, but I think the Kaiser is rather anxious to make your acquaintance."

"Oh yes, of course, I knew there was something I was supposed to be doing," Thomas shook his head like an old lady remembering she had to go to the post office. "Attacking the German Army—that was it. Lay on MacDuff!"

While Dick Thomas ate a sandwich and gulped down some tea, Will checked over the brand new machine. To his surprise he found everything in good adjustment and working well; his experience showed that new airplanes usually needed more attention than those in service. Will loaded his kit and tools and climbed up to the front cockpit. Dick mounted into the rear seat. This machine, as its designation suggested, had been designed for hostile action rather than observation. Only a gun was lacking.

The motor started on the first swing, coughing a cloud of blue smoke that whipped away with the whirlwind created by the propeller. Tom climbed up on the landing skid to bring himself level with Will as Dick carefully checked the controls. "Good luck, Will, I'm going to try to have you posted back to Farnborough when things settle down. I'm working on a new design and I'll need your help. Keep your head down and your feet dry." He gripped Will's hand briefly in both his own, then stepped down, walked clear, and watched as the Vickers climbed away and began circling to gain height. Will waved as they set course and headed out boldly over the water.

From his lofty viewpoint Will could see the famous White Cliffs of Dover falling behind. He twisted in his seat to see Dick Thomas smiling serenely, his lips moving as he sang to himself. Will gave him a thumbs up sign, "Nice day for it."

Dick Thomas leaned forward and shouted above the roar of the wind. "It's the only way for a gentleman to go to war—sitting down." Will laughed and settled back in his seat, his feet propped comfortably on his toolbox. He resolved to enjoy the ride. Like Harvey-Kelly, Dick Thomas ignored the instructions to follow the coast until he could track the River Somme to Amiens. He knew this part of France from extended cycle tours and struck out confidently across country. A small compass helped to guide him.

The aerodrome proved easy to find when they arrived overhead late in the afternoon. Thirty airplanes were already lined up, but as they came whispering out of a perfect summer sky it became obvious that the orderly atmosphere of a British aerodrome was not waiting for them. Dick had to cut the motor as soon as the wheels touched because a crowd of excited people surged around the Vickers. Amiens was *en fete.* They found themselves mobbed: hugged and kissed enthusiastically by both sexes. They both carried flowers and several bottles of wine by the time they struggled to the tent serving as headquarters.

Will attempted a smart salute, "Lieutenants Thomas and Turner, reporting, sir." Major Josh Higgins waved his hand vaguely then adjusted his monocle.

"Well done, lads, that's nearly everybody accounted for." He stopped, leaned forward and examined Will's face, "You've rouge on your cheek, Turner." Will flushed scarlet and attempted to juggle the wine bottles as he struggled to wipe the makeup away with a grubby handkerchief. Higgins smiled, "Don't worry, the French are so glad to see us, anybody who hasn't drunk himself senseless on all this plonk will probably be shagged senseless before we even arrive at Maubeuge."

The supreme commander of the British forces, Kitchener, had warned against the temptations of drunkenness and fornication in a famous notice to the men of the British Expeditionary Force before they sailed. This had provoked huge mirth from the French and a determination on the part of Kitchener's men to succumb to temptation whenever the opportunity arose.

In spite of this the army moved to its designated position to protect the French left flank. Under the direct command of Sir John French in the field, the "BEF" comprised two army corps, a cavalry division and a cavalry brigade: a total of 80,000 men with 250 artillery pieces. They faced the First German Army under von Kluck. The British were heavily outnumbered and outgunned. The German Kaiser described it as a "contemptibly small army", and joked about sending his police force to arrest it. The British, perhaps deliberately, translated this as "that contemptible little army", a description they turned to an accolade with what Will now knew was typical perversity. He and his comrades waiting at Maubeuge near the frontier with Belgium a few days later had become members of a select band; they were "Contemptibles", those who met the German advance at Mons. They would earn the right to carry that name with pride.

To Will and the rest of the advance party waiting by their field outside Maubeuge, the army striving to catch up with them looked like a brave and large enough force. The Royal Flying Corps had landed the previous afternoon and felt decidedly exposed, knowing that nothing stood between them and the Germans. The pilots stood beside the road watching the long column of British soldiers marching toward the town. Their relief flavored the exchange of banter.

"Nice of you chaps to show up," Dick Thomas called.

"Couldn't you give us a lift?" a voice called from the ranks. The army came into focus as it neared them. Rifles were unslung and smartly shouldered, the long files straightened, regimental colors unfurled and the bands struck up. As the men came swinging past, fatigue from their long march from the coast disappeared. They sang lustily.

"Ah, the old marching songs," Dick said wistfully as a band thumped out the tune of *The Girl I Left Behind Me.* Will grinned as he caught the words his infantry comrades bellowed happily:

"Oh we don't give a fuck, for old von Kluck,
and all his bleedin' army..."

Dick looked embarrassed, "Oh! They changed the words." Will laughed out loud at his surprise. He had learned many things in his few short weeks of service—one being that he had enlisted in the most profane army in the world. The language of the troops was shocking to his ears. He was also having to learn the strangely exotic army slang that had absorbed words from so many distant parts of the British Empire.

Char was tea from Hindi. *Imshi* from Arabic meant either go away or hurry up. The word *blighty*, used to loosely describe the British Isles, came from the Urdu word *bilati* meaning away. The opportunities for misunderstanding were many, not just in language but in terms of military procedure. Luckily he could rely on the enlisted men who made up the teams of mechanics. They possessed a fund of knowledge on army traditions and practices. Many were "old sweats", men who had been members of the Royal Engineer unit that formed the nucleus of the new corps. These men enjoyed passing on their knowledge to the easy-going young officer suddenly pushed into service with them.

Will had no serious problem adapting to his new role. He benefited from the very nature of the RFC. The British army was rigidly hierarchical; the gulf between enlisted men and the commissioned officers as wide as ever. The officers of the RFC, however, found themselves having to adapt to new circumstances. The men under their command possessed technical skills that usually exceeded their own. The mechanics were often well educated and highly literate. The success of the RFC depended, to a large extent, on their abilities. The pilots found themselves in a position of dependency demanding respect on both sides.

The circumstances prevailing aided rather than hindered Will's acceptance as an officer. Common sense, adaptability, and leadership were the qualities needed to make the new corps function in the field. Conventional notions of parade-ground soldiering were of little use.

To everybody's surprise, including his own, Will demonstrated a talent for field soldiering the evening following their arrival at Maubeuge. With no one sure of the disposition of the German forces, a small detachment of infantry under the command of a young second lieutenant stayed behind to guard the flying field against a surprise attack from roaming cavalry. The young officer chafed at being left behind the main force, still marching toward the Belgian town of Mons. He made no attempt to hide his irritation, for he clearly felt the Royal Flying Corps to be an irrelevant novelty, a view shared by many.

Will, taking a short break from urgent repairs to one of the Avro biplanes, stood scratching his head. He looked around the field again. On three sides small parties of soldiers stood concealed behind hedges. The remaining side of the field bordered the extensive gardens and orchards of an elegant country house. It struck Will that if he had been planning a raid on their field, *that* would be where he would sneak up.

The open fields on the other three sides offered no cover. He could see no sign of pickets on the vulnerable side.

"I see you've hidden your men in the trees inside the garden...damn well camouflaged, I can't see nary a one," Will observed.

The lieutenant looked down his nose at Will, he couldn't see any badges of rank under the coveralls and deduced from Will's accent that he was being addressed by some form of "Damn Colonial." "That's because there aren't any," he explained in a bored voice.

"Beg pardon?" Will thought he had misheard. "None! You mean that side of the field is unguarded?"

"Well, of course," the lieutenant sneered. "They're hardly going to come that way—it's private property." He spoke as if explaining himself to a child.

Will said nothing, he took off his cap again, scratched his head and jammed the cap back on. "Sarn't Major Cattle!" he bellowed suddenly in a way that alarmed the young officer. The strange colonial had that easy confidence in his voice that the young lieutenant tried so hard to muster.

The Sergeant Major stepped out of one of the tents, marched up to them and saluted, his uniform as immaculate as if he were on parade at Aldershot.

"Yes, Mr. Turner?"

"Sergeant Major," Will drawled, "I'm none too sure of the protocol here, bein' new to this business."

"I'm here to help, sir," Sergeant Major Cattle assured him, "What can I do for you?" He stood stiffly to attention and looked straight ahead.

"The lieutenant here," Will gestured vaguely with an oil-grimed hand, "tells me the Germans won't attack us through the gardens of the ole' plantation house here, because it's private property. Is it in order for me to shoot him for stupidity?"

The Sergeant Major made a small sound that Will knew was a stifled laugh. Cattle opened his eyes again; he had squeezed them shut for a moment while he controlled himself. "No, sir. Strictly against regulations. Only the major can do that. Would you like me to fetch him?"

There was no need. Josh Higgins had listened to the exchange with mounting disbelief from inside his tent. He hurried up to them, "Lieutenant Turner, Sergeant Major Cattle, carry on. I'll deal with this."

Will and Cattle both saluted and marched away as Higgins explained to the infantry officer the basic flaw in his tactical reasoning. Will spoke out of the corner of his mouth as the tirade continued behind them, "Not only is the lieutenant a very silly fellow—"

"He ain't got no mummy or daddy either, sir, according to Major Higgins," Cattle finished for him. The story went around the squadrons like wildfire, enhancing Will's reputation.

Rupert tackled him on the subject the following morning. "I don't know how the hell you've done it, Will. There's young officers strive for years to gain the respect of their men—officers from fine old military families, trained at Sandhurst. Then you show up, a complete outsider, an amateur if you don't mind the word, and you have them eating out of your hand."

Will blushed, "I don't know, they're a great bunch of fellows, I know some of them from Hendon an' I guess they put 'round the word I know somethin' about airplanes. But you're right, I'm a complete beginner when it comes to soldierin'."

"There's more to it than that," Rupert argued. "There's a balance to be struck between being too familiar with your men, and being standoffish and not getting the best from them. It usually takes years to learn that, but you just do it."

Will shrugged, "Maybe I'm not such a complete beginner. Nathan had me in charge of workin' parties makin' repairs to track an' bridges an' such, soon as my voice broke. Someone has to be in charge. There's folk like to be killed on jobs like that if ever'body falls to arguin' about how to tackle it. I don't see this as bein' much different."

Rupert laughed, "I can see you making colonel if you carry on like this." He looked across to where his machine was being readied for flight. "I'm off in ten minutes, Joubert and Mapplebeck found the Germans yesterday, but those idiots at headquarters just gave them a drink, listened politely and told them to toddle off home. Joubert is absolutely livid. The brass don't think we can count, and all they found was a small diversion force."

Will held the spark plug, he had been cleaning, up to the light and squinted at it. "You don't think the French might have it c'rect after all and it really is just a feint attack?"

"No," Rupert said with conviction. "The Froggie generals still think the main attack is coming from the east because the German force in Belgium is making slow progress. From what we are picking up from our intelligence people, the reason for that is the Belgians are putting up one hell of a fight, but old von Kluck is on his way, you can count on it."

Will smiled, "Do we give a fuck, for old von Kluck?"

Rupert laughed, a short explosive sound that always cheered people around him. "I really think we should. The problem is, convincing the brass hats that our information is reliable."

Lieutenant Rupert Penrose was correct in his reasoning. The Belgians were putting up a desperate, furious resistance to the invading German army, and the French commanders were reluctant to admit the danger. They were mistaken. Von Kluck and his men were on their way from the north.

Lieutenant Will Turner was also quite right in his assessment of the men he commanded. They were outstandingly competent. In the short time he had been in France he had been able to complete the task he had originally been entrusted with by Major Sefton Brancker. His system for categorizing damage, worked out with the aid of the Technical Sergeant Majors and the other engineering officers, had already been sent back in a detailed report to RFC headquarters. It was a model of clarity and practicality, a testimony to the dynamic nature of the new organization. Because, instead of being filed away and forgotten, Will's report became the basis on which damaged aircraft would be repaired. The task he had been given was complete.

Will looked thoughtfully at the Vickers biplane he was working on. It was the new machine in which he had crossed to France. Dick Thomas, the regular pilot, was flying a Bleriot at this moment while the Vickers received attention to the motor. Thomas had left his camera attached to the side. Will came to a decision. He replaced the spark plug, checked over his work, then collected his flying coat and helmet from the requisitioned bright red Bovril beef drink truck that had become his mobile workshop and home. He called to one of the mechanics as he strode toward the Vickers, "Give me a start, Patterson. I'm goin' to test this machine an' make sure it's safe to fly." He climbed into the pilot's seat but looked down in surprise as Sergeant Major Cattle came trotting up.

Cattle saluted. "Beggin' your pardon, Mr. Turner, but where the 'ell do you think you're going?"

"Why, an air test of course, Sergeant Major," he smiled down from his perch.

"Bollocks, sir, you're going off looking for Germans."

Will frowned, "Have you been appointed my personal nursemaid, Sergeant Major?"

"In a manner of speaking, sir. If you come to any harm Colonel Trenchard will have my guts for garters."

Will looked down at Cattle. He smiled. "So you've been told to keep an eye on me?"

"Yessir." He knew there was no point in denying it.

"So you'd rather be where you can see me?"

"Yessir."

"Saddle up, Sergeant Major. I know you've been tryin' to wangle your way onto a patrol for days. Do you know how to use Mr. Thomas's camera?"

"Yes, sir!" The big NCO scrambled up into the front cockpit with surprising agility. He pulled on the flying coat and helmet left in the position by the regular observer as Will urged the Vickers into position with blasts of power.

"You don't have a problem with disobeyin' orders then, Sergeant Major?" Will shouted above the calico-tearing snarl of the rotary as he blipped it in and out on the cut-out switch. It seemed to Will a younger man twisted in his seat to grin back at him.

"I'm not disobeying orders, sir...you are. I'm following yours. And if you go getting us killed, Colonel Trenchard will never be able to find us where we're going." He pulled a face and jabbed his thumb down, then threw back his head and roared.

"That's *very* reassurin', Sergeant Major, very reassurin'," Will grinned as he pushed the stick forward to raise the tail as they tore across the field.

Chapter Twenty

WILL STARED OVER THE SIDE OF THE COCKPIT IN DISBELIEF. Beneath them the German First Army surged along the road to Mons like mercury squeezing up the tube of a thermometer. From where they circled over the head of the column they could not see the tail. Squadrons of cavalry capered through the fields on either side of the marching files. Even from two thousand feet they could make out massive artillery pieces hauled by motor tractors. A pall of dust drifted away from the road, kicked up by thousands of pounding boots.

"I think we found 'em," Will shouted, banking the Vickers to line up with the road. He leaned forward. "Better start taking notes. If we give exact figures the brass hats are more likely to believe us." He throttled back and eased downwards. Something pinged against a steel undercarriage fitting. Will flinched, "Nice to be shot at by the enemy for a change." They had quickly learned that all soldiers—French, Belgian, German and British—worked on the principle that all aircraft were hostile. As they flew over encamped British troops they were always greeted by a volley of musketry. Not only was this galling, it was worrying. The Tommies had a well earned reputation for their shooting skills. Will slipped to one side to increase the distance from the German marksmen and worked slowly down the lines.

They finally found the end of the column miles behind the vanguard, an untidy concentration of horse drawn supply wagons bringing up the rear. Sergeant Major Cattle made a circling motion above his head. "Take us back down the line, sir, I'll try to take some pictures with the camera, they'll have to believe us if Corporal Smith can develop them." Will nodded and hauled their machine around in a tight turn. His determination to produce photographic evidence made sense.

Information collected by patrols the previous day had been largely disregarded by the staff officers. A combination of distrust of this new form of reconnaissance—many of the "old school" officers believing this was a job for the cavalry—and an unwillingness to believe the size of the force confronting them, had made them receive the RFC pilots politely but patronizingly. Liam Power had offered to take a particularly snooty Colonel in his airplane to see for himself, but the senior officer had declined and offered Liam a drink instead. When the Irishman arrived back at the field seething, Will learned a few more words for his dictionary of army invective.

Will held the Vickers steady as they tracked above the massed columns. The sergeant major manipulated the separate photographic plates as best he could, each photograph requiring a new plate. He used the last one and stowed it in the issued wooden box as they passed over the leading regiments. They had both been aware of an occasional ticking sound. Will craned his head around to look at the motor mounted behind them to see if it showed any obvious sign of distress, but quickly ducked back when the real source of the noise revealed itself. Three holes appeared in the lower wing as if punched by an invisible finger, a fourth bullet ricocheted off a steel strut fitting with an angry whine, audible even above the roar of the engine churning around a few feet behind them. Will cursed and booted the rudder hard to spoil the gunners aim. "The bastards are machine gunnin' us," he shouted unnecessarily. "Shouldn't we take some sort of offensive action?"

Cattle grimaced as he stared down at the massed troops, "Hold her steady, sir, then I'll stand up and piddle on 'em. That'll be pretty bloody offensive."

Will turned the Vickers back toward Maubeuge. The sweating German soldiers glanced up at the fragile little machine and cursed as it droned away. They plodded steadily in pursuit. The field was in sight when Cattle suddenly pointed to their right. Another airplane floated alongside. They were quickly learning that other machines seemed to pop up from nowhere. To their relief they saw it was a Number 2 Squadron machine. The pilot waved to them, pointing at his observer who lay crumpled in his cockpit and then at the ground.

"He wants to land first," Will shouted. "I think the observer's been hit." They followed the other airplane down and landed close behind. Will and Cattle leaped from the cockpit and ran to help. The wounded observer moved feebly but his face beneath his goggles showed a ghastly white. Will looked inside the cockpit. "Oh Christ!" he muttered, fighting not to retch. Startling white fragments of bone shone in the dark mess of the wound in the man's thigh. Blood covered the cockpit and the pilot, who was trying to release the wounded man's safety belt. Will recovered himself, "Stretcher bearers!" he roared to the group running toward them. Between them they eased the observer onto the ground. Will tore off his scarf and tied it quickly around the gaping wound. Blood, warm and viscous, ran up Will's arm as he tied the makeshift dressing. Other willing hands loosened the man's collar.

Major Josh Higgins held a silver hip flask to the observer's lips. "Sergeant Major Jillings," he said with an encouraging pat on the wounded man's arm, "to you falls the singular honor of being the first British soldier wounded in an aeroplane."

Jillings, slightly revived by the brandy, smiled weakly through his pain, "I'll treasure that, sir." A ripple of laughter ran through the crowd, relieved to see their comrade not dangerously wounded. The medical team quickly loaded him into an ambulance.

Higgins adjusted his monocle and turned to the pilot, "What happened, Robson?"

The blood-soaked pilot pulled off his helmet wearily. "We were at two thousand feet, sir, over the whole German army. They were sniping at us all the time, but I thought we were out of range."

Higgins put his hand on Robson's arm, "Never mind, lad, it was just bad luck. You've done a good job, I can see that. Damn nuisance losing an experienced observer though." He turned to Cattle, "Do you have anything to report, Sergeant Major, after your *air test*?" He gave Will a withering look.

Cattle snapped to attention. "It's all in here, sir," he opened his notebook. "Infantry by regiment, cavalry by squadron, plus guns, lorries and horse-drawn wagons."

Higgins took the book from him and adjusted his monocle. His lips moved soundlessly as he totted up the figures. Robson had retrieved Jillings's notebook. The pages were stuck together with blood but Higgins patiently pulled them apart. He compared the figures; they matched nearly enough. "Good Lord Almighty!" he breathed. "This must be the bulk of the German army."

"We took photographs as well," Will offered.

Higgins thought for a moment, then started to snap orders. "Corporal Smith, take Mr. Turner's plates and develop them. Sergeant Major, go with the dispatch rider to GHQ find Colonel Page and tell him we have found the German force—and it's four times the size we thought."

Cattle saluted, took the notebooks and ran to the waiting motorcycle. Joubert leaned close to Will and spoke quietly. "Well done, old boy. That was a brilliant wheeze taking old thunderguts with you. He was with Page all through the South African campaigns, and he'll accept Cattle's figures without question. If you or I went to him with those numbers he'd think we were behaving like hysterical schoolgirls."

The pilots gathered around Higgins as he addressed them again. "Gentlemen, extra orders. HQ are taking us seriously now. They've lost the bloody French Fifth Army—"

"How awfully careless," a lanky, sandy-haired officer drawled.

"Precisely, Shuttleworth," Higgins agreed. "You and Power with Joubert and Allen can see if you can find them. We want to know what they're doing. And while you're about it, see if you can see any sign of Waterfall and Bayly, they're overdue."

"What the hell is going to happen when that flaming great army we saw meets our chaps at Mons?" Robson asked, his face anxious.

Higgins slapped him on the back, "Von Kluck might surrender, but let's not count on it, eh chaps?" He turned to Will, "Turner, I want you to...," he stopped in mid-sentence and turned to watch a B.E.2 approaching the field. Everybody froze as it swooped lower, almost touching the ground, then recoiled into the air before dipping again like somebody testing the temperature of water with his toe before diving in. One wing tilted perilously low. Again the biplane skimmed the earth before staggering briefly into the air. Finally, as if tired of its antics the B.E.2 nosed decisively down, and this time it did not pull up. With a loud crunch the landing skid gave way as it hit the ground. The machine ran forward a few yards then tilted on its nose. "Sort out that mess," Higgins concluded wearily.

Will watched Higgins strutting quickly back to his tent; he reminded him of a turkey. His rear end stuck out and he walked with a strange knock kneed gait that accentuated his unusual anatomy. Dermott Allen, a tall, thin Irishman with startling blue eyes, paused in buckling up his flying coat and nodded after Higgins. "You see why we call him 'Old B-B-Bum and Eyeglass'?"

Will nodded, "Seems like a decent man."

Allen had a slight speech impediment that appeared at odd moments. "One of the b-b-b-best," he agreed with a quick smile.

Will wished him luck with his mission and hurried across the field to deal with the upended B.E.2. By the time he reached the machine the pilot had been helped out by the mechanics. They now stood rigidly to attention while the new arrival berated them. Will could hardly believe what he heard.

"Of all the cockeyed crews I have ever set eyes on you lot take the prize," the new pilot glared at them, then started pacing up and down. He slapped his leather gauntlets against his leg. "You leave a damn great hole in the landing area, and if that's not bad enough, you don't even mark it!" He stopped again. The four mechanics who had rushed to his aid stood bewildered. "Well?"

"Well what, sir?" a young Air Mechanic queried nervously.

The stranger's voice rose to a querulous scream, "Well, what have you got to say for yourselves?"

"*I'd* say everybody else has managed," Will spoke quietly from behind him. The new pilot whirled around, his face coloring. He had big features. An odd, almost square face with thick lips now twisted back in a sneer. His left cheek supported an angry red boil. Before he could say anything else, Will gave orders: "Wells, Nichol, grab a rope an' haul this machine back on the level. Find some extra men an' don't let the tail crash down, then haul her off the field. We need the room." The stranger went to speak but Will cut across him again. "Have you fellas eaten yet?"

"No, sir," the mechanics spoke eagerly and in chorus.

"Well, grab some food, an' while you're there fetch me a bully beef doorstep an' some tea, we're gonna be up all night fixin' this." They stood still, uncertain. "Well go on—*Imshi!*" Will urged. They ran off grinning.

The new officer moved suddenly, he grabbed Will's arm and tried to drag him behind the upended B.E.2, out of view of the other mechanics working in the tent sheltering the temporary workshop. They all pretended not to watch. Will shook his hand off angrily but let him speak.

"I don't know who the hell you are, but if you ever try to undermine my authority like that again, I'll—," he had to stop because he was not sure what he could do.

"Report me to the CO?" Will asked quietly. "Well let's do that now, because I do believe it's considered polite in this army to report on arrival—however you turn up." Pointing out the breach of etiquette had the effect he needed; it took the wind out of the new man's sails. Will kept the initiative, extending a hand he introduced himself, "Will Turner, pleased to make your acquaintance." The other man hesitated for a moment, then took Will's outstretched hand.

"Hubert Matrett, at your service," he said grudgingly.

"Hey, are you related to Major Matrett? I met him at Farnborough." Lieutenant Matrett smiled for the first time. "Yes," he sounded enormously pleased, "he's my uncle."

"Well, I be darned," Will said with a forced smile. "It's a small army."

At that moment, five thousand feet above him, the crew of a German reconnaissance airplane looked down on the BEF in its positions around Mons and reached the same conclusion. Whatever his skills as a pilot, Lieutenant Matrett had sharp hearing. He looked up suddenly and pointed at the German airplane, "What type is *that?*"

Will followed his outstretched arm. "That's an Etrich Taube, unless my eyes deceive me." Even at that height, the distinctive bird shaped wings of the German monoplane were clearly visible. The designer had modeled his wings on those of a dove and named his machine after it. In seconds the airfield resembled a disturbed ants' nest as everybody spotted the Taube sailing into view. Men ran to drag airplanes into position to takeoff in pursuit. Two B.E.2's were hastily armed with boxes of hand grenades and rifles and set off.

Will second-guessed the situation and ran straight to Louis Strange's Farman biplane, calling for help from the mechanics to start it. He knew this was the only machine that might be capable of bringing the intruder down, for Strange had had the foresight to mount a Lewis machine gun in the front cockpit. Strange and Penn-Gaskell rushed to mount their machine. In less than a minute they were roaring across the field. Will stood with his mechanics, a tin mug of hot sweet tea in one hand, a "doorstep" sandwich in the other, watching the pursuit from the ground. He still had a feeling of unreality, as if he were an interested spectator at some bizarre aviation meeting, even though for the second time in his life he had been shot at that morning. The three British machines achieved nothing. The German circled unmolested above them for several minutes as they thrashed back and forth below, like sailboats tacking in a gale, struggling to reach him. Finally, either having made all the notes they needed or simply bored with their sport, the German crew turned for home with a cheery wave to Strange and Penn-Gaskell, still floundering along a thousand feet below.

"Sorry, lads," Higgins informed them when they landed, "your artillery will have to go. That Lewis weighs too much, no wonder you couldn't come to grips with him. You'll have to make do with a rifle in the future."

"But, sir," Louis Strange protested, "the B.E.2's didn't get any closer." Higgins would not be moved, and Strange reluctantly unshipped the odd-shaped weapon. He removed the flat, circular magazine, worked the cocking lever then pointed the muzzle into the air and pulled the trigger.

Satisfied the gun was safe he handed the lethal device down to Will who examined it curiously. At first glance it appeared to have a three-inch bore, but closer inspection showed this to be a sleeve around the rifle caliber barrel. A conventional butt fitted against the user's shoulder. "Why have they fixed this old drain pipe 'round the barrel, Louis? It must make it damn difficult to use in the air, with the slipstream pushin' against it."

Strange swung himself to the ground. "The theory is that the blast from the muzzle draws air in through the back of the sleeve where it attaches to the breech, then this travels up the tube and carries heat away from the barrel." Louis looked at Will, expecting an opinion.

"Horse shit," Will grinned, "that won't make any difference, might as well throw it away an' save the weight."

Louis was not disappointed, he knew Will could be relied on to express his views in a forthright way. "Still, it won't make much difference if the boss won't let us carry it," Louis pointed out.

"From what I see of the German army this mornin' he'll have us carryin' a damn field piece this time next week, just you wait an' see." Will ventured.

Louis Strange nodded, "I think I'll give it a good clean, just in case." He shouldered his machine gun and gave Will a mock salute. He nodded toward his Farman airplane, "You can take the jolly old chariot and put her in the mews garage, I won't be needing her again today."

Will grinned and tugged his forelock, "Right you are, m'lord."

"And when you've oiled and greased her—you can give her ladyship a good service." Louis marched off to his tent laughing. Will watched him go, his face thoughtful. A few miles away he knew an immense army bore down on them. The feeling that he might be a spectator as history was made was being rapidly replaced by the knowledge that for all his fine words, he was going to be a part of that history. Will knew by rights he should be scared witless, but he found the high spirits of his new friends hugely reassuring. They clearly had no illusions about what they were up against, but he knew he was not seeing the famous British stiff upper lip, only confidence and determination. The men of the RFC were going to show the world what they could achieve with their flimsy machines, or die trying. That message was hammered home by the end of the afternoon. Lieutenants Waterfall and Bayly of 5 Squadron had been shot down in their Avro biplane while observing the progress of German infantry. Will's face showed his confusion when Liam Power brought him the news. "But how can they be missing?" Will asked, "I was only talkin' with them an hour or so back."

Liam said nothing; he had soldiered for ten years. Time enough to lose many friends to wounds and disease. "Sure, Will, 'tis not maneuvers," he said gently, "we're in trouble here. They won't be the last."

How much trouble soon became apparent to them all. Joubert and Allen found the French army falling back around the town of Charleroi, leaving the British force hopelessly exposed. The commander of the French Fifth Army had asked Sir John French to carry out a local offensive action at Mons to relieve pressure on his men, before joining them in a strategic withdrawal. They were overtaken by events. The British could only shoot their way out. The following day the British Expeditionary Force fought a short and bitter engagement at Mons, delaying the German advance enough to allow them to begin an orderly withdrawal at daybreak on the 24th of August. Less than three weeks after the declaration of war the British army fell back in full retreat.

Two days later Will looked on in disbelief as the soldiers streamed back past the field. Most were wounded. All were dejected, tired and hungry. The fortunate rode on gun limbers, the unlucky limped along as best they could. Will rushed to hold a man as his knees buckled. The soldier supported himself on his rifle for a few seconds, gray faced, his breath rasping. The last strength ebbed from him and he collapsed into Will's arms as Will tried to drag him to the verge. His comrades paused briefly in their slow march.

"He's finished, sir, he can't march another step."

"Then he'll have to ride." Will threw up his hand to stop one of the squadron transports as it lurched through the gate. "Nichol, make room for these men."

The driver gestured at the open back of the two ton truck. "I'm sorry, sir, we've no room."

Will lowered the soldier gently to the ground and stalked to the back of the truck. He stopped and stared. "What the hell is that?" he pointed at several large pieces of highly polished furniture lashed down with rope.

"It's Mr. Matrett's stuff, sir. His 'field furniture' he calls it. It came up with a supply truck yesterday."

Will stared for a moment then took his knife from his pocket. He snapped the blade open and without saying a word slashed through the ropes. They parted with a satisfying *twang*. He turned, white-faced, to the driver. His voice was low at first. "We are not a fuckin' movin' company," he heard himself say, as if he stood apart from his own body. He recognized the voice as it rose in a parade ground scream, for a moment he sounded like Sergeant Major Cattle, "Get it OFF!" Nichol and Wells obeyed instantly with huge grins on their faces. They heaved the furniture over the tailboard. It fell with a splintering crash.

The infantrymen dragged their stricken friend into the truck and collapsed gratefully among the airplane parts that were left. One wearily extended a hand in salute to Will. "Bless you, sir."

"On your way, boys," Will answered quickly, "look after your pal an' my airplane parts. They tell me there's German cavalry everywhere. You might could have to fight for your ride." He turned to the driver. "Nichol, make sure these men get some rations when you reach the next landin' field, the adjutant will know where they can find an assembly point."

Nichol saluted. "Right you are, sir." He pointed over Will's head, "I think Mr. Matrett wants a word." He let in the clutch and the overloaded truck heaved away down the dusty road.

Matrett had jumped from the cockpit of his B.E.2 as he saw his furniture being dumped. Now he stood surveying the wreckage. He pointed and stared at Will. His eyes bulged. His face flushed a livid red. Will could have sworn he saw foam at his mouth. Matrett managed to speak at last but his words came in short truncated bursts. "Turner, you unspeakable—a family heirloom—bastard colonial shit—"

"Heck, Matrett, no need to get yourself so worked up," Will answered reasonably. "I'm not stoppin' you takin' your things. Just you're not takin' them on my transport." He turned to walk away, then froze as a familiar voice bellowed across the field.

"Matrett...Turner...What the hell is going on here?" Higgins strutted toward them.

Matrett answered quickly. "I want Turner court martialed, sir. Willful destruction of a brother officer's property. Disobeying orders. Conduct unbecoming an officer and a gentleman."

"Matrett!" Higgins voice cracked like a whip.

"Yessir."

"Shut up or I'll have you shot."

"Yessir." Matrett was a professional. He knew when to back down.

"We've enough problems without you idiots arguing amongst yourselves. We'll sort this out later. Matrett, take anything valuable you can load in your aircraft. I'll speak to you later about unauthorized use of corps transport. Turner?"

"Yessir."

"Have your men removed the motor from the wrecked Farman?"

"They have, sir."

"Burn the rest of the machine. Have Dick Thomas stand by your Vickers. Take this." Higgins thrust an old brass-bound telescope at him, "Take yourself to the top of that rise and watch the wood to the north. Air Mechanic Barr is coming with you. At the first sign of movement in the wood, send him back with a report: numbers, composition, what they're up to. Stay put until we're all away then leg it back to your machine and you and Thomas can follow on."

Will looked at the telescope in his hands, "Shouldn't I shoot at them first, sir?" he realized he sounded stupid even as he said it.

"No, you bloodthirsty young fool, not unless you fancy taking on the Hun on your own. We're running away laddie, all of us, together. So when you see 'em coming, run like hell. See you at Le Cateau."

Will set off for the ridge. It was little more than a bump in the rolling farmland of the frontier area but it commanded a fine view of the open country south of the border with Belgium. The young mechanic, Alf Barr, fell into step beside him. He whistled cheerfully as he strode along. Will looked at him curiously. "Aren't you just a little concerned, Barr?"

The mechanic looked surprised, "No, sir, why should I be?" Will went to answer but thought better of it. He realized the boy, younger than himself, had complete faith in him. As far as he was concerned he was with an officer, and no harm could come to him. Barr carried a knapsack, which he opened. "Cookie did us proud, sir. He's done us some hard-boiled eggs, some bully beef sarnies with the last of the bread and a canteen of tea."

They reached the ridge and settled under a hedge. Will pulled out the tubes of the telescope and focused it on the line of trees he could see in the middle distance. The incessant tapping he had been hearing for the last twenty-four hours, like demented woodpeckers, had ceased. "I can't hear the machine guns anymore." he said. Then suddenly turned to Barr, "You didn't think to bring a gun of some kind, did you?"

"No, sir, I thought you might have one," Barr stopped and rummaged in the knapsack, he held up a twist of paper. "I did remember to bring some salt though."

Will grunted, "To be honest, that's more use to us. I left my revolver with my kit."

Barr passed him an egg, "Don't worry, sir, the junior officer's servant, Adams, packed your stuff and put it on the lorry. It'll be waiting for you at Le Cateau." Will suddenly felt very glad to have Barr with him. He wondered if Higgins might have detailed him for this duty because he set such a good example of complete unflappability. "What do you make of them, sir?" Barr indicated the fields away to their left with a wave of the tea canteen.

"Jumpin—!" Will cut short his exclamation as his telescope focused. "They're *our* fellas," he said with real relief. The two lines of men were not staggering and stumbling like the men on the road. The first line moved purposefully forward across the field while through the lens he could see the second line actually walking backwards. He heard a distant *pop,* nothing more, but the hundred men he watched reacted instantly. The front rank dropped from sight, the rear rank knelt and brought their rifles to the aim. There was a brief pause. Then he saw a glint of light reflect off metal at the edge of the wood behind them and a flurry of movement. Through the telescope he saw light flashing on ejected cartridges and the rapid arm movements of the kneeling men working the bolts of their weapons, before the rippling crackle of rapid rifle fire reached his ears. The movement at the edge of the wood stopped. The distant figures resumed their unhurried progress across the fields.

"They do shoot well, don't they? I think that must be part of the rearguard. I reckon them Uhlans are probably in the wood but they don't care to get too close." Barr's phlegmatic attitude had an effect on Will. He poured tea into a mug and passed it to his companion who thanked him politely.

"Mr. Barr," Will could not come to grips with the military ranks, "if they're the rearguard, and they've now passed out of sight to our left to catch up with the army, doesn't that make *us* the rearguard now?"

"Well, I'm not too much up on soldiering terms, sir, but I suppose it does." He rolled over and pointed to the field behind them. A pall of smoke rose from the wreck of the Farman biplane they had been forced to abandon. The last trucks waited for the final pieces of equipment. One serviceable airplane remained. "They're nearly ready anyway, sir."

Will focused on the wood again. He could see movement in the shadows but could not make out who or what was in there. "I don't see any point in you hangin' around, Mr. Barr. Cut along back to the field an' tell Major Higgins there are definitely enemy soldiers in the wood two thousand yards to the north."

"Aren't you coming, sir?"

"Directly." Barr still did not move. "Go on," Will ordered firmly, "they'll be waitin' on you now."

Barr nodded, "Right you are, Mr. Turner." He groped around in the knapsack and handed Will the last sandwich. "Good luck, sir." He wormed his way back through the hedge; his heavy boots could be heard thudding on the sunbaked earth as he ran back to the field. The thought crossed Will's mind that he was alone for the first time since he joined the corps. The idea did not trouble him. Time alone with his thoughts now seemed a luxury seen in the light of this strange situation. He trained his telescope on the flying field. The last truck swayed out through the gate. He turned the lens on the remaining machine, the Vickers that he and Dick Thomas flew across the Channel. It was his ride away from danger now. He smiled to himself when he recognized Dick leaning on the lower wing, turning the pages of a book propped against a strut while casually smoking a cigarette; a man apparently without a care in the world.

Will rolled over and studied the wood from where he expected the German army to advance. Nothing showed. After the violent action and movement of the preceding twenty-four hours he found himself in a pocket of calm, like the eye of a hurricane. He studied a peaceful rural scene, a good subject for an artist. The harvest had already been gathered, leaving the fields covered in a golden stubble. The trees in the distant wood had lost the bite of early summer color and now presented softened shades. In some places the leaves had already started to show a russet tint. The lens of the telescope picked up the dusty haze in the air and swarms of midges danced at some indeterminate distance between him and the wood. Will had to admit he had no good reason to stay at this post, it was curiosity pure and simple. He wanted a good look at the men who so brazenly marched into other people's countries, and fields, and backyards—and homes. "Dammit," he thought to himself, "it's one hell of a way to carry on." He idly cleaned the big objective lens of the telescope. He turned the handsome old instrument over in his hands and read the inscription engraved on a brass plate fixed to the main body:

Presented to Captain James Trevarthen,
by the grateful survivors of the S.S. Edward Price.

He wondered who James Trevarthen might have been. A right sound, seafaring man, Will reckoned, with a fine set of whiskers and a stout heart, perhaps even with a parrot perched on his shoulder, ready to risk life and limb to go to the aid of those in peril. He put the telescope to his eye again and swept the horizon.

"Holy Moses," he said aloud. "Where in hell have they come from?" In the time he had spent admiring Captain Trevarthen's telescope a full squadron of horse soldiers had drawn up at the edge of the trees for his inspection. These were the dreaded German *Uhlans,* light cavalry armed with long lances, easily recognized by their peculiar headgear: shaped like a British police helmet with the top cut off and a flower vase fixed where it should come to a point. Will was not impressed. "You boys are best suited to light opera," he muttered. "No place for you in a shootin' war like this." He snapped the telescope shut and pushed it safely in the big flap pocket of his tunic. "Time to go, William," he said to himself. He slid through the hedge then thrust his hand back to retrieve his sandwich wrapper. "Nobody's goin' to say *my* army left the place untidy." He sprinted across the field. As he ran he made a wild circling motion with his hand. "Wind her up, Dick," he yelled. "They're comin'!"

Dick looked up calmly, marked the page in his book and ground out his cigarette with the heel of his boot. "Who might that be, William?"

"Who d'you think? Damn *Uhlans,* hundreds of 'em," Will yelled, pointing vaguely over his shoulder.

"So they are," Dick said casually. The sunlight flashed on lance points and lit up gaily colored pennants fluttering from the shafts as the horsemen trotted over the fields toward them. "And I do believe they've spotted us." The leading troop had urged their mounts to a canter rather than a full-blooded gallop, thinking the airplane they could see might be one of their own. Will said nothing, he swung under the tail booms and grabbed the propeller as Dick clambered into the pilot's seat.

"Ready?" he yelled.

"Switch on." Dick replied evenly.

"Contact," Will swung the propeller with all his strength. He knew instantly they were in trouble. An experienced mechanic could feel instinctively when a motor was ready to run. This one was not. "Jesus Christ!" he swore. "It's not primed!" His voice rose, part in disbelief and part in growing panic.

"Switch off, petrol on," Dick called back. "Sorry old chap, didn't expect you to hang around to shake hands with the buggers."

"Sucking in!" Will bellowed. He rapidly heaved the blades around. He knew it might need six or seven turns to prime the motor but he could hear hoof beats pounding toward him. He did not dare look over his shoulder. Four...five, he forced himself to throw the blade over one more time. "Contact!" he screamed. The motor spun to life. Will staggered back, then threw himself under the booms to roll clear. "Go, go, go!" He looked up as he stumbled to his feet. He caught a fleeting glimpse of rearing horses and angry faces. The Vickers started to roll.

Will flung himself at the front cockpit but missed his footing. His desperate hands grabbed the cockpit rim as his feet tangled in the long curved landing skid projecting forward from the undercarriage. He lost grip with one hand and swayed back. He found himself looking straight at one of his "comic opera" opponents. There was nothing funny about him now. He had thrown away his long lance and struggled to draw a carbine from a holster fixed to his saddle. His face contorted with rage as he tried to control his mount, shying from the roaring airplane.

The forward motion of the plane saved Will. That and Dick Thomas's surprising strength. Somehow he managed to control the Vickers and reach out to grab Will's flailing hand. With strength and agility borne of desperation Will regained his grip on the cockpit rim, found a foothold on the landing skid and dragged himself over the side as the wheels left the ground. He tumbled headfirst into the cockpit. He found his nose grinding against the floorboards as his legs waved in the air.

"Do stop arsing around, Will," Dick complained from the pilot's cockpit behind him. "I can't see where we're going."

Will managed to pull his legs inside the cockpit and twist himself around so that he found himself kneeling on the seat facing Dick behind him. Will glared at him. "Don't you *ever* lose your bloody *sang-froid?*"

Dick banked the airplane; they were already at three hundred feet. "Yes, there's one thing guaranteed to make me wild." He had to lean forward to shout above the wind noise. "Cruelty to animals. Did you see the way that brute was handling his mount? A bloody disgrace. If we had time I'd go back and horsewhip the swine!"

Will shook his head in weary surrender, "I do believe you would."

"And when I'd finished with him, Mama would deal him out a sound thrashing as well," Dick shouted. "She's the area secretary for the RSPCA."

Will twisted around and flopped into his seat. "If somebody can't stop them, she might have to." He suddenly felt very tired. Perhaps, he thought, they might form a royal society for prevention of cruelty to airmen as well as animals. Without protection of goggles or flying helmet the wind whipped at his eyes making them stream. He crouched behind the rudimentary windscreen but the slipstream now scoured the side of his face as the Vickers sideslipped. He turned, questioning the violent maneuver. The ground slid toward them, but Dick leaned out of his seat staring in the direction of the developing turn. He shouted to Will while concentrating hard as he deliberately cross controlled, thrusting the stick to the left while holding full right rudder, a wild piece of flying in the awkward biplane.

"Trying to make us a hard target!" Dick bawled. "Those boys can shoot!" As if to prove his point a bullet ricocheted past with a metallic howl. "Damn and blast! They've hit a cylinder." The vibration from the rattling engine sent tremors through the structure.

"Ease the air supply and give her a little more gas," Will undid his seat belt and leaned back.

Dick made the adjustment, like everybody else he believed Will could work miracles with a rotary engine. He gave Will a relieved grin. "That's better, but I think we should fly direct to Le Cateau." The vibration eased but it was obvious that they could not stay in the air long. The Vickers wallowed around a turn. "How far?" Dick asked anxiously.

"'Bout twenty miles, say twenty-five at the most."

In level flight Dick found he could coax the Vickers into a shallow climb. The loss of power meant their speed relative to the ground slowed, and he had no desire to give the German gunners a chance for glory. If no bullets found their mark, and if the engine kept running, they had a journey of nearly half an hour to endure. The altimeter in

Dick's cockpit crept toward a thousand feet. Will realized he had hunched forward in his seat to urge their machine on. His chest felt as if somebody was squeezing it. His throat was parched and he felt the taste of cordite on his lips from the smoke that drifted around them even at this height. He pulled on his helmet and pulled down his goggles.

Stut–stut–stut...The Gnome engine faltered. Will lunged awkwardly for the controls, stretching between the two cockpits. His sensitive fingers increased the air supply. The motor picked up again. Dick eased the stick forward as the Vickers sagged on the edge of a stall. Will slowly let his breath out and slipped back into his own cockpit. He stared over the side; watching others suffer below did nothing to ease the tension. If they could not nurse the Vickers home, they were of no use to the men struggling to form a line in the fields around Le Cateau.

Open country lay beneath them with no sign of enemy forces. At least they could land and make an emergency repair if the motor died on them. Before Will could relax he felt Dick slapping urgently on his shoulder. He turned and followed his friend's pointing finger. The wing obscured his view, but as it dipped gently he saw the reason for Dick's concern. A mile behind and slightly above to their right, a strange biplane tracked their course. Will pushed up his goggles and stared intently. The color told him nothing: a pale yellowish cream, the natural color of the linen covering common to every machine serving in France, and it carried no markings signifying national identity. It had two sets of wings, a biplane, with a tractor propeller dragging it through the air.

"Could be a B.E.2," Will said. Dick looked hopeful. "Aw shoot!" Will said with his next breath. The strange machine flew into a pool of sunlight; he recognized the solid lines from photographs he had studied. "It's a Hun. Albatros two-seater I guess." He looked ahead and then back at the German plane. "He's got the legs of us, Dick. There's no way in hell we're gonna make the field before he catches up."

"Maybe he's just curious," Dick suggested hopefully. There had already been several encounters between British and German machines, characterized by a lack of hostility. There seemed to exist a common bond between flyers on both sides. A feeling shared by some that aviation had enough hazards without adding to them.

"I hope so, Dick, I really don't want to have to shoot him," Will meant it, with all his heart. These were fellow flyers—men to whom, in a crowd, they would be instantly drawn. In other, better, circumstances, probably instant friends. Will took the field glasses they carried for observation from their case and trained them on the other machine. The closer view, even though the image danced with the vibration imparted by the sick engine, did nothing to reassure him.

"Damn it, Dick, I don't know what to make of that. Looks like the pilot an' observer's positions are reversed." The conventional layout on most machines had the pilot's seat in the rear cockpit, with the observer tucked away in the forward cockpit, hemmed in by the wings on a tractor biplane. This machine reversed that arrangement. Whether it left the factory this way, or had been modified in the field, Will neither knew nor cared. What concerned him was that the black-coated figure in the rear cockpit clearly stood behind a machine gun. "An' he's packin' a damn big self loader of some kind."

Dick grunted, "Looks like Louis Strange isn't the only one with that idea."

Will leaned forward to check the distance to Le Cateau. It seemed as far as ever. He turned and looked carefully at what they could now see clearly was an Albatros two-seater; the first German airplane he had seen. It's appearance struck him as downright intimidating. As he half expected, the design struck a Gothic theme. Will could easily imagine Wagner's Valkyrie riding in this machine. The long wings were trussed like a bridge. The Mercedes engine mounted in the nose stood too tall to be enclosed by a cowling. The cylinders reared up proudly, girdled by brass pipes carrying cooling fluid from the radiator. The exhaust pipes twisted together to be carried as one into a smokestack ejecting foul engine fumes over the top wing. The fuselage was slab sided, like the hull of a battleship. A simple and sturdy triangular tail added to the solid impression. "There's only one reason he's carrying that machine gun, Will. He's up for a fight and we're obliged to tackle him."

Will studied the Albatros, weighing the possibilities. He still hoped the German airmen might sheer off, but knew it was unlikely. They had patiently pursued the Vickers for over twenty minutes and flew miles from anywhere they might be employed on observation. They were squaring off for a duel, whether Will wanted it or not.

He undid his safety belt and knelt on his seat, the better to talk to Dick. "To bring that gun to bear, he has to fly in front, or alongside of us. He can't shoot through his propeller. I guess he's goin' to try to edge us 'round an' push us back toward his army." Will suddenly realized he did not feel scared, he felt completely calm. He knew exactly what he had to do, and how to do it. He stared at the enemy plane, now only a

few hundred yards away, through the field glasses again. "That machine gun sits on some kind of a pillar mountin' this side, an' I can just make out one on t'other side of his cockpit. If he wants to fire off the other beam, he's gonna have to carry that thing over an' fix it again."

Dick leaned forward to shout in Will's ear. "I'm with you. I'll wait until he's alongside, give him the idea I'm sheering off, then shove the nose down, duck underneath and come up on his other side. Then you shoot him."

Will nodded grimly, tugged the rifle out of the bracket holding it to the fuselage side and cranked a round into the breech, "Then I'll shoot him."

The action, when it came, lasted a few seconds. There was an awful inevitability to it. The Albatros used its height to swoop down and gain the last few yards. The gunner opened fire. Will heard bullets crack past his head. Dick eased off to the left, a perfect feint: then pushed the nose down to gain enough speed to zoom up on the other side of the German machine, the range shockingly close. Will stared at his opponent from a few yards distant. The man moved fast. He almost had the machine gun re-fixed in the mounting facing them when Will, carefully, shot him. He watched in sickened fascination as the man's goggles flew up and away, caught by the slipstream.

"Damn you, sir," he muttered. The gunner disappeared down into his cockpit. His weapon swung vertical spewing bullets harmlessly into the sky, a dead man's finger on the trigger. Will saw the frightened face of the pilot staring at him as he worked the bolt of his rifle. Will fired again. The pilot flinched away from a stream of scalding steam bursting from the hole Will drilled in the radiator, mounted just ahead of his cockpit. The Vickers lurched, making Will grab the cockpit side as they staggered on the edge of another stall. Dick pushed the nose firmly down. By the time they recovered, the Albatros showed as a distant speck, drifting away toward the German lines.

Their glide took them to the field. The Gnome sputtered to a full stop a few feet above the ground leaving the Vickers to arrive with a grateful thump. They scraped to a halt, the silence palpable. Will sat for a moment then swung his leg over the side of the cockpit and climbed quickly to the ground. Without a word he disappeared from sight. The sound of violent vomiting came from behind their machine. At last Dick spoke. "Thanks, Will," he said simply, "you saved our bacon."

Will reappeared. Wiping his mouth with a handkerchief, his face pale. "Mebbe," he acknowledged, then he swung a kick at a raised lump of turf. "Damn fool!" he spat. "I declare! Why the hell he couldn't have just left us alone I do not know."

Dick still sat in the cockpit, looking down on his friend. "Will," he said firmly, "I know it sounds trite, but it really was him or us. Do you think for a moment that old Fritz would have given a monkey's toss about us? He was a professional soldier, he knew the risks, and if he'd filled us full of holes he would have gone back to his mess and celebrated. They would have given him a medal and he would have said 'ta very much.' But you shot faster and straighter. End of story. You'll have to become hardened to the idea." Dick's voice had an edge of impatience.

Will nodded and straightened up. He unloaded the rifle and slipped the unused cartridges into his pocket. "You're right. But God help me if ever I get used to it."

Their moment of privacy ended. The squadron tender—a Crossley pickup truck—rolled up, crowded with pilots and mechanics. They bombarded Dick and Will with questions. The action had taken place in full view of the field. The labored pursuit with its violent conclusion had been watched almost from start to finish. Dick explained what happened, sparing nothing of Will's part. He stood smiling politely in a flurry of backslapping and handshaking.

Captain Harvey-Kelly punched the air with his fist. "Bravo! Turner, first blood to the Flying Corps."

"What I want to know," a familiar voice cut in, "is why you aimed at the radiator and not the pilot's head? We could have claimed the first enemy aircraft shot down if you had." All eyes turned toward Hubert Matrett. "Not got the stomach for it, Turner?"

The silence lasted only a second before an indignant chorus of "I says" and "That's a bit strong" stopped him from saying anything else.

The group fell silent as Will replied, "The range was increasin' when I fired again, an' the radiator was the bigger target. I need some practice before I could hit a man's head movin' fast." He paused and looked at the rifle in his hands, "Maybe you'd care to oblige, Matrett. Trot across the field an' I'll have a crack." Will smiled. The way he spoke drew a nervous laugh from the audience. Liam Power leaned toward Matrett and whispered something in his ear. Matrett turned on his heel and walked quickly away.

"Well, come on lads," Will said, "give us a hand now. Let's have this old girl over to the workshop wagon. She deserves some attention. Willing hands hoisted the tail and wheeled the stricken machine across the turf.

Dick found himself pushing on one of the interplane struts with Liam Power, "What did you say to Matrett?"

Power chuckled, "Gave him a word of friendly advice. Told him not to push his luck. Between you and me, I shudder to think what our 'Canadian' friend might be capable of. I met a fella like him once before. Sure he couldn't abide violence an' killin', so he used to get it over with quick—and he was powerful good at it."

Dick gasped from the exertion, "I can vouch for that in Turner's case, I've never seen shooting like it. I swear he shot the man straight between the eyes."

They heaved the Vickers to a spot beside the workshop and Will quickly started work on the motor. His movements seemed quick and intense. Dick peered over his shoulder. After a few moments Will grunted with satisfaction. "Look at that. Just as I thought, they shot away a high-tension lead to a plug. This will take five minutes to fix."

"What the hell have you two been playing at?" Higgins demanded from behind them. He stood bent over, his mighty rear end thrust out, examining the rudder of their machine. He had his finger pushed into a hole in the fabric.

Dick and Will looked at each other. "They shot at us as we took off, sir," Will suggested.

Higgins pulled back a flap of loose material and pointed accusingly.

"No bullet made that hole. Looks like a sword cut of all things."

"Oh no," Dick protested, "they came close, but not *that* close." Higgins grunted and screwed his monocle firmly in. In his case it was not an affectation. He looked again.

"Never mind." He stood up, "Take your lunch on the hoof. I need this machine in the air in half an hour. Collect your orders from the adjutant. He's set up his office in the cab of the furniture lorry. There's no point in unpacking, we'll be on the move in the morning."

Dick looked horrified, "Aren't we making a stand in the fortress at Maubeuge?" They had been immensely cheered by the sight of the old fortifications and had seen extensive preparations going on to defend it.

"No," Higgins replied shortly, "orders from HQ. They're not going to risk ending up penned in like rats in a trap. Von Kluck captured heavy guns from the Belgians and he would just pound us to pieces. The retreat goes on." He strutted quickly away.

Will looked at Dick and raised an eyebrow quizzically. "Didn't get close enough to do that with a sword?" he pointed at the slashed fabric.

"No. I never tell a lie to the CO. A lance did that. He was, oh, ten feet away. When the engine started the horses all panicked and gave us the few seconds we needed. You missed that while you were demonstrating your acrobatic routine."

Will looked Dick straight in the eye. "How long is this retreat goin' to go on do you think?"

Dick shrugged, "Until we link up with the French outside Paris, I expect. Then it's do or die. Come on, let's prepare our chariot for the next round." They refueled the Vickers from the tins of gasoline that somehow always appeared when needed. Will slapped a patch on the rent in the fabric of their tail feathers while Dick stood in line at the field kitchen for hot food for them both. A strange democracy had descended now that they were in action, the automatic preference accorded to officers replaced by a single line for rations. They considered themselves lucky. The infantrymen streaming down the roads and across the fields in tired disarray had not eaten for two days. From the air Will and his comrades could see the full extent of the situation. In a few places lines of khaki clad British soldiers marched in good order but everywhere there were small groups and individuals staggering along. Many supported injured comrades, some even carrying wounded on makeshift stretchers. In some places officers stood in prominent positions trying to sort groups into a form of military order.

They flew back toward Mons and found isolated groups still holding strategic points. They realized that in some cases these men had not received orders to withdraw, and swept low over their heads dropping messages telling them to pull back. Others were fighting hopeless actions with no hope of relief or escape. The roads were littered with abandoned equipment, but Dick was gratified to see that almost every man they saw still carried his rifle. The news they carried back to their temporary refuge at Le Cateau, while grim, had one shred of comfort. The German army had not advanced in strength far beyond Bavais to the north and their probing cavalry seemed reluctant to press too close on the heels of the retreating army.

The last patrols came sighing down from the evening sky. The mechanics worked feverishly to repair the day's wear and tear on the precious airplanes. Though dead on his feet from the events of the long day, Will, along with the other pilots and observers, took his place in turn on the airfield perimeter to guard against surprise attack from fast moving Uhlans. Their nerves stretched as the night filled with the sound of low voices and trudging feet and the exhausted survivors of the battles around Mons moved south. Will regretted his lack of experience. His fellow flyers were nearly all regular army officers with a good knowledge of the units the stragglers belonged to: Royal Fusiliers, Suffolk Regiment, Rifle Brigade, Oxfordshire and Buckinghamshire Light Infantry. To Will they were names from history books, to men like Rupert Penrose they meant people and faces. Will could hear his cousin at the crossroads a few yards from where he stood, leaning against a gatepost staring nervously out into the dark fields. Rupert had set himself up, as he put it, like the Salvation Army. He had requisitioned a large can of rum and several boxes of ration issue cigarettes. He dispensed these with words of encouragement, directions and a tot of rum.

"Chin up, lads, you're nearly there—Fusiliers?" he asked of shadowy figures. "Some of your lot are in the orchard two hundred yards down here." He pointed along the road and the figures shuffled off mumbling their thanks. Pinpoints of light glowed as they sucked greedily on their first cigarettes for hours. Silence fell. "Will?" he called softly. "You still there?"

"Of course, Rupert. It's so damn dark I ain't leavin' here in case I wander into the Germans."

"Good lad. Look, I'm running low on fags for the boys, and I think we should be hanging onto some of these stragglers to stand guard with us. I'm popping back to stock up and have a word with the Boss. If the Kaiser shows up—shoot the old bastard."

"Right you are, Coz." Rupert disappeared into the night leaving Will feeling as lonely as he ever had in his life. For all he knew the Kaiser and all his court could be creeping across the field toward him. Tiredness played tricks on his eyes and his imagination. He fantasized that all he needed was a gramophone and a recording of *Deutschland Uber Alles.* All he would have to do would be to play the German national anthem and the well disciplined Prussians would have to stand to attention, and he could just pop them off. He grinned at the thought, but the smile froze in place. He could not see them, but his senses told him men were moving in the fields he faced. He sank onto one knee. He held his mouth slightly open and slowly turned his head from side to side, a trick his uncle had taught him to help catch the slightest sound when they hunted the woods around his home. Something was moving. He fixed his eyes to one side of where he detected solid shapes in the blackness. His right hand dropped to the bolt of his rifle. Its cold, solid feel reassured him but he decided against cocking the weapon. The click of the mechanism would sound like a thunderclap in the stillness and give his position away. He waited.

He heard a low murmur. That was enough, he pushed the first round into the breech and bellowed into the night, "Halt! Who goes where? Fiend or froe? There was silence for a moment, then a burst of mocking laughter.

"Eh up Lad! Make oop tha mind." The voice was pure Yorkshire. Will decided there and then the man had the most wonderful accent he had ever heard. "The reet challenge is *friend* or *foe.*"

"Gee, sorry fellas, this is all new to me," Will apologized to the men now stepping confidently forward. "Who are you?" Hugely relieved he slipped the safety catch on his rifle and leaned it against the gate.

"KOYLIs, King's Own Yorkshire Light Infantry, mostly, and a few odds and sods," the stocky Sergeant leading the group answered. "And where do thee come from? Tha's a reet queer accent."

"Canada," Will replied promptly, then remembered the proper military response. "Royal Flying Corps," he added. He peered into the darkness. "How many of you are there?"

"Twenty-three," the Sergeant answered briskly, then stopped. "By 'eck! Sorry, sir, didn't take you for an officer in the dark," he was about to go on but another voice came from behind them.

"I'm not surprised."

Will recognized the sneer in the man's voice even though he could not see his face in the dark. "Good evening, Mr. Matrett, I'm taking this guard turn."

Hubert Matrett shone a flashlight into the face of the Yorkshire Sergeant. The man cursed under his breath and shielded his eyes. "And where were you and your men off to, Sergeant?"

"T' find fuckin' army—sir." Will was astonished at the venom in the man's reply, he had never heard an NCO speak to an officer that way. He had not realized the inference in Matrett's question. Another voice spoke from the darkness, this one pure London but the hostility just the same.

"Bleedin' cheek." Will's throat tightened as he heard a rifle bolt worked in the group. Will knew he should do something but before he could act he heard his cousin's voice behind him.

"That's enough, Mr. Matrett." Rupert stalked up. "Sergeant, your rifle if you please." The soldier snatched the bolt back and presented arms smartly. Rupert took the Lee-Enfield, sniffed the open breech then whirled around and thrust it to Matrett's face. "Just for the experience, Lieutenant Matrett," his tone icily polite, "*that* is how a rifle smells when it has been fired until it glows hot but hasn't been cleaned." He handed it back to the soldier. A murmur of approval came from the ranks behind him. "You're needed by the Adjutant, Lieutenant. Cut along." Matrett said nothing. He turned on his heel and walked quickly away. Rupert turned back to the soldiers now gathered in a group, some leaning heavily on their companions. "How much ammunition do you have, men?"

"Down to two rounds per man, and twenty in the Lewis we found, sir," the Sergeant replied crisp as ever.

"You've a Lewis! Well done, lads," Rupert congratulated them on their find. "How about rations?"

"Nothing since yesterday morning, sir."

"Windy Gale's got a bag of bull's eyes in his pack that he thinks we don't know about, sir," the same London voice offered. The small joke about the secret hoard of mint candy raised a tired laugh and erased the tension generated by the confrontation with Matrett.

"I can do better than that, lads," Rupert told them. "You're drafted in to defend our field as of now and that means we feed you. Cookie's burning a stew down there you could choke a horse on, and he's brewing tea by the bucket. Make your way over to the light you can see in the far corner of the field, then sort yourselves out for a guard rota so you can all get some kip." The exhausted group came to life and started gratefully across the field.

"What the hell was that all about?" Will demanded when they had disappeared.

"That bloody fool Matrett. He was more or less accusing them of deserting in the face of the enemy. He was damn lucky they didn't shoot him. If you hadn't been here they probably would have."

"Oh, come on, Coz, it wasn't that serious," Will protested.

"Will, the situation *is* that serious. I have never been this close to it, but I have heard enough anecdotes in the mess to know that discipline hangs by a thread in a beaten army, mutiny is never far below the surface. A bad decision, obvious cowardice on the part of officers, a wrong word...," he left the idea hanging.

"But they ain't beaten, Rupert. They've *taken* a beatin', but they've handed one out as well."

"Well, there you have it, Will. They've been killing Germans for two days—slaughtering them from what I'm hearing—men they don't even know and have no reason to hate. Then along comes Matrett and his big mouth. It's very easy in the dark, no witnesses, confusion, and there you have one dead pain in the arse. Believe me, it's happened many times."

Will laughed softly, "Rupert, I've never heard you with a bad word for anyone, but I declare you don't care for young Hubert Matrett."

Rupert grunted, "No, I don't. He's a dangerous piece of work with connections. His father's bought himself a life peerage and wields a fearsome amount of influence and money. His elder brother's an up-and-coming MP and his uncle will wangle his way onto the general staff, just you wait and see."

"Would that be Major Matrett who I met at Farnborough?"

"The same," Rupert confirmed.

"At least he's a Royal Flying Corps man," Will pointed out.

"Where did you get that idea?" Rupert asked, surprised.

"He was at Farnborough when I had my interview with Mr. Sefton Brancker," Will explained. "He marched into the office, bold as you please."

"Pure coincidence, old chum. He happened to be there at a meeting where he was trying to do us down by arguing the case for having us made part of the cavalry, of all things. If he came into Brancker's office it would be because he was trying to score a point. Sefton Brancker can't stand the man, but Matrett has made the mistake of underestimating him. He thinks that just because Brancker reads poetry and cultivates a windowbox outside his office, he must be some kind of a fairy," Rupert chuckled. "Our Sefton's done more real soldiering in a week than Matrett has managed in a career."

"Well, you live and learn," Will said.

"That's the idea, Will, m'boy," Rupert slapped him heartily on the back. "Keep learning—and you'll keep living. Don't forget that." He picked up the supplies he had dumped at their feet and strode off down the road to his self-appointed aid post. In the dim light his shadow appeared enormous, distorted by the barrel of rum under one arm and the big box of cigarettes under the other.

A few moments later reinforcements arrived in the shape of the young Londoner who Will suspected of being the man contemplating murder. He grinned at Will, "Evening, sir, lovely night." Will relaxed. The force defending their side of the field had now doubled.

"Er, sorry 'bout that little misunderstandin' earlier," Will knew as an officer he should not be apologizing for Matrett, but the army had not had him long enough to suppress his good manners.

The young fusilier laughed. "Not to worry, sir. Wasn't your doing. Bit hoity-toity that other bloke—," he stopped, worried that he might have gone too far. The orderliness of the RFC field had restored some of his faith in the army.

Will just grinned. "A bit, he's been under a lot of strain...crashed three machines since he got here."

"Cor, blimey, how long's that?"

Will had to stop and think hard. "Since the day before yesterday."

"That must be some sort of a record," the lad spoke with awe in his voice. "You'd never get me up in one of those things. Beggin' your pardon, sir, but they look really dangerous to me."

"Not as dangerous as what you have been in. Did you see what happened at Mons?"

"See it, sir? I was right in the thick of it," he spoke with pride and a sense of wonder at what he had been through and survived. Will let him talk. "We was standing to, on this side of the canal when we first saw 'em. Bleeding thousands of 'em. It was like a big gray wall moving at us. Well, our officers were cool as you like, calling out the range: 'At five hundred yards, four fifty...' We just mowed 'em down wiv our rapid fire. Everybody firing their fifteen aimed shots a minute, steady as you like. Of course we were losing men, especially when they started that shrapnel shelling, but we kept chucking 'em back."

He paused to take a drink from his canteen. "It's a funny thing. You don't have time to feel scared; you don't feel much of anything. See, all your mates are there. Anyway, you can't help admiring them Germans. They've got some pluck, I'll grant 'em that," he fell silent, deep in thought.

"So have *you*, fusilier, so have you." Will could just see the boy's grin in the thin starlight.

"Yeah. We did all right. Do you want to go back now, sir? I can take care of this sentry go, and Chalky's relieving me in an hour." Will gratefully accepted the offer, picked up his rifle and made his way back to where the aircraft were picketed. He wrapped himself in a blanket and lay down under the wing of the Vickers. He was asleep before his head touched the ground.

Chapter Twenty-One

FOR A FEW MOMENTS WILL THOUGHT SLEEP STILL CLUNG TO HIM, AS if in that state where he knew he was dreaming but could not surface to the real world. Above the ground a theatrical mist shifted uneasily. Indistinct figures moved in the gloom. He struggled onto one elbow and tried to recall where he was. He slumped back to the ground. Le Cateau he remembered, the events of the previous day crowding in on him.

"Tea up, sir!"

"Are you always this goddamn cheerful, Nichol?" Will grumbled, kicking away the damp blanket tangled around his legs. There was no doubt he lived in the real world now; Air Mechanic Nichol was too ugly to be in the dream he had been enjoying. He gratefully took the steaming mug of strong sweet tea.

"Usually, sir," Nichol replied, "especially on a lovely summer's morn'."

Will stared into the mist. "Lovely morn'?"

"We did have a couple of showers during the night, sir, but they'll lay the dust. Mind you, there was a bleedin' noisy battle going on just up the road, surprised it didn't wake you."

Will managed a tight smile, "Thanks for the tea, Mr. Nichol, I'm much obliged. It sounds pretty quiet now."

"Calm before the storm, sir. They say there's going to be a real set to, this morning."

Will swished the tea around in his mouth and spat it out. "I'll stay awake, wouldn't want to miss it." Nichol laughed, saluted and marched off. Will looked around the field. In the half-light he could see men preparing the machines for the first patrols of the day. The sky above was an indistinct shifting gray, sodden with moisture from the summer storms that had hammered the field while he lay deeply asleep. He shivered, apprehension driving the chill deeper into his bones.

"Morning, Will," Louis Strange strolled past in his shirtsleeves, suspenders dangling, a towel casually draped over his shoulder. "There's hot water for a wash and shave if you hurry, might be the last chance we get for a while."

Will shook his head, they could be on a camping trip for all the concern Strange showed, but he grabbed his shaving kit and followed him anyway. There's something to be said for keeping up appearances, Will admitted to himself, even if it's only for my own benefit. He joined Louis Strange at the rear of a truck where the tailboard had become a temporary washstand.

Louis explained the situation as they shared a piece of broken mirror. He carefully stroked his cut-throat razor over his chin. "The situation is grim, Will. The town itself is a hopeless bottleneck. We've reinforcements coming up who have met the refugees struggling south and jammed the place solid. But it's the only way out for our chaps."

Will worked up a lather with his brush. "Can't we just make our way across the fields and bypass the town?"

"Some can; certainly the cavalry. But the guns and transport have to go through the town on the roads. And without artillery and supplies we're finished. What the army has to do is hammer Von Kluck and his boys to a stop. Dish out such a bloody nose they won't want to follow."

"Seein' as how we seem to be outnumbered five to one, that strikes me as a tall order," Will said.

Louis Strange twisted his mouth from side to side to check the closeness of his shave in the mirror. Satisfied, he towelled his face vigorously. "It is," he agreed, emerging from the cloth, "but they have their problems. I made the last patrol yesterday and it was pretty obvious they are having trouble bringing all their men along. They're dog tired as well, they've had to fight hard through Belgium, then our musketry came as a very nasty surprise to them at Mons. My guess is they don't want to mix it with our infantry again. They appear to be bringing up more heavy artillery. This could well be a gunner's battle, William." He paused while he trimmed his neat moustache with a pair of delicate silver scissors. "The essence of it is, General Smith—Dorrien is going to have to fight them to a standstill then disengage in broad daylight."

Will's blade stopped drawing a track through the foam on his cheek.

"Can that be done?"

Strange poured the remaining hot water into Will's bowl. "It has to be done, William." He casually slung his towel over his shoulder, "Anyway, more important than all this tactical business, our inestimable cook has found a very nice piece of pig from somewhere and has made up a batch of bacon sandwiches for breakfast. I'll save you some." Will watched him stroll away, whistling. He shrugged, but smiled inwardly as he finished shaving. He noted with satisfaction that his hand did not shake anymore. As he dried his face the first rays of the rising sun pierced the mist hanging over the field.

The early morning swelled into a sultry, sweating day. One by one the airplanes of the Royal Flying Corps launched into a sky top-heavy with overbearing cumulus, intent on gathering vital information. Will glanced at Wells, who worked with him to repair a B.E.2 motor, when a low rumble rolled across the field.

Wells shrugged, "Thunder, sir?"

A battery of heavy guns roared a reply from a sunken road behind the field. "Yeah," Will said, " a rare old storm's brewin'. Crack on, Mr. Wells, this is goin' to be a busy day." A sour taste bit into the back of his throat.

For the moment, every serviceable machine was in the air, leaving only the biplane they were repairing. The mechanics hoped for a brief respite, but they saw a dispatch rider skid up to the big furniture van that served as their headquarters. Will did not wait for the inevitable command, he pointed at the trucks. "Load up, men, we're gettin' out of here."

Captain Tyler, the adjutant, stuck his arm out of the cab with his thumb raised to acknowledge Will's order. "St. Quentin, Mr. Turner, you have your maps. The road through the town is clearing." They worked to the routine already established. The heavy transport and headquarters trucks rolled first, leaving three light vehicles behind with enough fuel, oil and spares to service each of the returning aircraft and send it on its way to the new field. It never occurred to Will to be anything other than the last man to leave. The fear of failure seemed more real to him than the threat of the German army.

"Like the captain of a sinking ship, sir?" Nichol suggested.

"Exactly," Will confirmed, "an' just like the captain of a ship, I need a ship's boy to hold my telescope an' pass on my signals—I've just volunteered you for the job."

"Thank you, sir! I'll be proud to serve you in that honorable tradition."

"Nichol?"

"Yes, sir?"

"Are you takin' the piss?"

"Yes, sir."

"Thank God for that," Will said with feeling. "Can you ride a motorcycle?" Will jabbed his thumb at the Chater-Lea machine propped against one of the remaining trucks.

Nichol's face broke into a wide smile, "Just about, sir."

Will saw Nichol's friend, Wells, grinning. "Is there something I'm missin' here?"

"Artie here was placed ninth in the Senior Tourist Trophy race on the Isle of Man, sir," Wells explained.

Will looked up sharply from the magneto he had finished reassembling. "Well, I'll be damned! That's some achievement, Mr. Nichol. That decides it, you drive—I'll ride the pillion. That machine is our ticket out of here."

The rumble of artillery, intermittent at first, grew continuous—and nearer—as the morning wore on. He did his best to ignore it. The airplanes returned singly and in pairs. Will and his team of mechanics worked feverishly to send them off again. He gave no orders; there was no need. Each man knew exactly what had to be done. The returning crews updated them on the developing situation. None of the news was good.

Liam Power pulled off his helmet and ran his fingers through his hair. "Jesus, lads, it's grim. I've just seen two teams shot to pieces trying to pull a battery out. Horses and men going down, right, left and center. You've never seen anything like these horse artillery fellas, mad as hatters. A third team managed to pull it off and galloped the guns away."

"Yes, but only thanks to you, Liam. What were you two daft buggers trying to do?" Rupert Penrose had landed and joined the queue for fuel.

"Oh, you saw that, then?"

"I certainly did," Rupert said. "You must have had your wheels touching the ground when you charged that squadron of Uhlans." Will looked to his cousin for more details. "These two," Rupert indicated Power and Shuttleworth who had been acting as Liam's observer, "saw a squadron of German cavalry riding to cut off the teams that had pulled that stunt off. They dived down on the deck and flew straight at the huns and broke up their charge. Were you firing flares at them, Shufflebum?"

Andrew Shuttleworth grinned, "We keep being accused of frightening the horses so I thought I would see if we really could. That Very pistol and its fireworks caused more chaos than a drunk on a skating rink."

"Looked like it to me," Rupert said. "They were scattered from here to bedtime by the time you finished."

The two machines were quickly refueled and back in the air. As Rupert and Liam Power roared over the hedge surrounding the field, Louis Strange's Farman biplane swished overhead and landed neatly as always. He swung around with a burst of power and brought the biplane rocking across the rough ground to where the mechanics waited with the cans of fuel. He switched off. "Fill her up, chaps, and check the oil." He walked quickly around his machine. He stopped and poked a finger through a hole in the wing fabric. "That's about the only damage; otherwise she's fine." He patted the Farman affectionately.

Will ran his eye over the rigging. "I wouldn't expect anything else, Mr. Strange. You seem to keep your machine in first-class shape."

"The airman must think of his aeroplane in the same way a cavalryman thinks of his horse. Look after it and it's bound to look after you." Strange took Will by the arm and led him away from the others. "The situation is bad, but not hopeless by a long chalk. We are retreating in good order. The cavalry is doing an incredible job, dashing around, chivvying our people into fighting formations and directing stragglers. Most of the infantry are well away now. God above only knows how Smith-Dorrien has pulled this off, but I think he has. The Germans are in the town, but they seem to be jammed up on the far side. We've been dropping petrol bombs and grenades on them, and one of our batteries has ranged them and done fearful damage."

Strange glanced quickly around the field. "I don't want to raise any false hopes, but it looks as if the French have come up with batteries of their seventy-fives to cover the left flank and driven the Germans well back from this side of town." The vicious crack of the rapid-firing French 75 millimeter field guns had reached the airfield.

Will looked over his diminished team—a dozen mechanics, three trucks and a motorcycle. "I only need a half hour to see Dick Thomas safely away."

Strange shook his head. "No, Will, it's too much of a risk. We can't afford to lose one of these men—killed or captured—especially you. The road you have to take is safe for now, but I can't say for how long. Send the men on their way in the lorries."

Will scanned the sky to the north and west. "We can't just leave Dick to fend for himself, and what about the B.E?" he pointed to the biplane they had repaired.

Strange thought for no more than a second. "Okay, send the men on their way with the wagons and the motorbike. Keep one man behind. Have the engine on the B.E. running and both of you in the cockpit. At the very first sign of trouble, push off out of here. If Dick arrives, refuel him at the double, don't even let him stop the engine and then away—sharpish. Got that?" His tone brooked no argument.

Will saluted, "You're the boss, Louis. That's how we'll play it."

Strange laughed and slapped him on the back. "Don't be an ass, Will, there's no need to salute me."

"There is, Louis...there is." He felt reassured at Louis Strange's presence, the situation called for a soldier. Will turned back to the airplanes and raised his voice. "Okay, you fellas, everybody into the trucks. Nichol, you take the bike. Leave enough petrol for Mr. Thomas in the Vickers. I need one volunteer to stay with me an' fly back to St. Quentin in the B.E." Depending on what he was doing, every mechanic either raised his hand or stepped forward. Will made a quick decision. "Barr, you're the lightest, you come with me."

Strange nudged Will in the ribs, "From that reaction, I think I should be saluting you." He extended his hand, "Good luck, old chum, and don't take any risks." He scrambled back into his cockpit high above them. He raised his hand like a priest giving a benediction from the pulpit. "Good luck, chaps, don't dilly dally on the way, I'll have the kettle on for tea when you reach St. Quentin." The mechanics cheered him as the Farman rumbled away on its creaking undercarriage.

"Okay, you fellas," Will urged them, "you heard Mr. Strange—on your way." The sound of a rotary being blipped made Will look up. His relief turned to irritation when he saw the missing Vickers side-slipping to a flashy landing; the propeller stood rigid. "Aw hell, Dick," he greeted Thomas, as the Vickers skidded to a silent stop. "I didn't even want you to stop the engine, we've to be away from here—pronto."

Dick Thomas pushed his goggles up onto his head. "Sorry, Will, no can do," he waved a lever with a length of cable attached. "We're either up or down, running or stopped, the buggers have shot my engine controls away. I flew her back on the blip switch."

His observer, Lieutenant Charles Rabagliati, twisted around to look at his pilot. "Oh, bloody marvelous—now he tells me!"

"Didn't want to worry you, old chap," Dick said.

Will thought quickly. He held up his hand and stopped the last truck, rummaging in a box for spare parts before sending the crew on their way. "Plan C, gentlemen," he announced. "I can fix this." He pointed to the B.E.2. "Mr. Rabagliati, you take Barr in the BE, I'll fix the Vickers and Lieutenant Thomas and I will fly out in that. If you would be so good as to refuel us before you go."

Rabagliati jumped down from the front cockpit of the Vickers. "My pleasure, Mr. Turner," he pointed to a pile of bottles with rags stuffed in them as stoppers lying on the ground near the BE. "Barr, are they what I think they are? "

"Yes, sir, they're petrol bombs."

"Good, are you up for some mischief?"

"Always ready for that, Mr. Rab."

"Excellent. We'll refuel the Vickers and then see if we can create a diversion for the column of motor lorries heading this way."

Will looked quickly from the darkly handsome Rabagliati to the fragile-appearing Thomas. "Tell me he's jokin', Dick."

"Wish I could, old boy, but there is a column heading this way. Still I wouldn't worry about *them.*"

"Why not?"

"Because the troop of cavalry are much closer."

"How much closer, dammit?" Will knew an edge of hysteria showed in his voice.

Dick stood up in the cockpit and shaded his eyes as he peered into the distance. "At least two miles away, and they're not moving, so I wouldn't be too worried."

Will cursed under his breath as he punched a new bolt through the bracket holding the engine controls. "Ever get a feeling of *déjà vu?*"

Dick Thomas climbed down from the cockpit and looked over Will's shoulder to see how the job progressed. "After a few narrow scrapes they won't seem so narrow. Can I help?"

"Yes, stand by to pass me the tools as I need them." Will's forehead was furrowed in concentration; he tried not to think about the consequences of not finishing the repair quickly enough. He moved fast, but deliberately.

Dick remained his usual, unflustered, self. He took a flat tin from his pocket and started to roll himself a cigarette. With deft fingers he flattened a "Rizla" paper from its packet, then formed a groove in it, he sprinkled the black French tobacco he had discovered into the part folded cigarette paper. "This is the dam'dest experience, Will..."

"What, havin' your machine give trouble?"

"No, flying over the battlefield. It's at one and the same time horrible, but fascinating. You have the oddest feeling of somehow being remote. The noise of the motor and the wind masks most of the sound from the ground." He paused to lick the edge of the paper and roll his cigarette into a tube. "You see men dying, from only a few hundred feet away, but it's like some ghastly play, rather like one of those new moving picture shows." Will nodded, intent on his work. "I almost feel guilty, like some kind of voyeur," Dick said, "safe in my flying machine while men struggle for their lives."

Will glanced up. "Not that safe, Dick. I don't want to worry you, but the bullet that carried this away," he nodded at the shattered bracket he had discarded, "could have taken you with it."

Thomas lit his cigarette with a flick of his silver lighter, blowing a thin stream of smoke into the still air. "I suppose you're right. They've brought up high angle guns and are chucking shrapnel shells at us, it was a burst from one of those that did this." He turned to wave to Rabagliati and Barr as they taxied past. The pair had finished refueling the Vickers and were now taking off in the B.E. The oppressive late afternoon heat squeezed a heavy silence on the field as their engine noise faded.

An occasional heavy gun thumped in the distance, but the song of a skylark drifting down to them registered more on their conscious hearing. Its clear, high voice mocked the sickening manmade din and made Will's heart lurch. He climbed up on the wheel and leaned over into the cockpit, his voice came from inside, strangely muffled. "I think I know what you're talkin' about. I know our friends are fightin' for their lives just a mile or so away, and here we are safe an' peaceful, carryin' on as if we were at a race meet at Hendon... There! That should hold it." He straightened up and stared, amazed, at Dick Thomas who now crouched under the wing with his revolver drawn, aiming at the gap in the hedge surrounding the field.

Dick spoke in a low, urgent whisper, "Quick, Will, get her started. Men are moving down the road. Throw me the rifle."

Will snatched the Lee–Enfield from the bracket on the side of the cockpit but ignored Dick's plea. He threw it to his shoulder, resting his elbow on the top wing to steady his aim. He sighted quickly on the field gateway. Then sighed with relief. The crouched figure sprinting past the opening wore British army khaki. "Hold it, Dick, they're our fellas."

"Flying Corps!" Dick bellowed. "What regiment?"

A face appeared behind the rifle barrel that had been thrust around the gatepost. "Rifle Brigade, sir." A group of men materialized, some, to Will's alarm, from his side of the hedge where they had worked their way along a shallow ditch. He had not seen the potential ambush developing.

"Thank goodness for that," Dick called back, half laughing with relief.

The man who had appeared marched quickly to the airplane, slammed to attention, and saluted. "Sorry about that, sir. We thought you could be the enemy."

"Are you planning to fight the Germans on your own, Sergeant?" Dick asked. "The rest of the infantry pulled back hours ago."

"We were at the quarry north of here, sir. We were cut off from the rest of the brigade and didn't get the order to retire. Lucky for us the cavalry gent took an awful chance and galloped up to tell us to get out."

"Cavalry gent?"

"Him, sir." The sergeant gestured to a figure on a stretcher now being laid carefully in the shade of the hedge. "That's why we've been a bit longer than we should have been. I'm afraid he's slowing us down, sir."

"Good grief, Sergeant, how bad is he?"

"Bad enough, he's hit in the leg. He just reached us and the bastards shot him off his horse—the bloody thing ran off before we had a chance to catch it." Dick ran across to the wounded man.

Will jumped down from the Vickers and followed him. "Ohmigod! It's Archie Carstairs."

Dick turned to Will, "You know him?"

Will dropped to his knees. "Know him! He's my friend." He anxiously pushed up Archie's eyelids. Only the whites of his eyes showed. His face was a sickly gray. Mud caked his uniform except where the blood soaking his left leg had dried to an ugly brown. A rough field dressing bound his leg below the knee. Will forced himself to raise the edge of the loose bandage. Broken ends of shattered bone shone a bright, mocking white among the unrecognizable parts of human leg revealed by the prying bullet. He swallowed hard then looked at the man tenderly wiping Archie's forehead with a cloth soaked in water from his canteen. "This is bad, isn't it." It was a statement, not a question.

"Yes, sir. That leg will have to come off, and soon, or gas gangrene will set in, and that'll be curtains for him."

"Gas gangrene?"

"Yes, sir. It's this fucking French dirt, you see. They cover it with shit to make things grow, and it brews up all these microbes. Not like the clean dirt we had in Africa, hardly ever had a problem with gangrene there." The soldier sniffed the air. "You can smell it starting already."

Dick took the sergeant's arm and pulled him away. "You'll have to leave him, you'll all end up in the bag and he will die anyway. His best chance is for the Germans to find him. They have better medical facilities than we do."

"Can't do that, sir," the sergeant said stubbornly. "He didn't leave us, and we can't leave him."

Will joined them a few paces from where Archie showed signs of regaining consciousness. "No need, Sergeant, lend me your bayonet." They stared at him. Dick's jaw dropped open. Will saw what had gone through their minds, but held out his hand. "Your bayonet. Quickly now, man." With a questioning look at Dick, the sergeant handed the long blade to Will who strode quickly to the nose of the Vickers. He methodically punched holes through the plywood and fabric covered nacelle. "Get his leg splinted. I'm makin' a hole so we can push it through when we strap him in the front seat."

"Hang on, Will," Dick laid a hand on his arm. "You can't just make big holes in an aeroplane."

"Who says I can't?" Will started to hack away at the remaining material between the holes he had made. "It won't make any difference to the way she flies and we'll just slap a patch on later. Can you think of a better way of gettin' Archie to the hospital?"

"No. But how are you going to make it back?"

"I'll walk. *I* can do that—*he* can't." He ripped away a section of the nose cone and threw it away. "I'm sure the sergeant won't mind me tagging along, will you?"

"No, sir, very pleased to have you in my platoon."

"Good, then that's settled."

"Hold on!" Dick protested. "I'm the senior officer here, I should be giving the orders."

Will gave a short laugh, more of a snort. "As you English say, 'bollocks'—put me on a charge if you like, but only after you carry Archie to the hospital."

Dick gave in graciously. He clapped Will on the back. "You win, you daft sod. The boss is going to have my guts for garters for leaving you, so I'll have to come back and get you later. I'll sort out a rendezvous point with Sergeant Coppin here, and he'll deliver you there. You sort my patient out."

The soldiers carefully hoisted Archie into the front cockpit. They threaded his leg through the hole Will had created, then fixed it in position with bundled great coats. The sudden movement dragged Archie through layers of pain to consciousness. He grabbed Will's arm when he realized what was happening. "I told them to leave me," he gasped. "Lovely little waitress in a restaurant back there called the *Chapeau Rouge*—the Red Hat. She would have looked after me until this was all over." He winced as Will strapped the safety belt around him and pulled a flying helmet over his head. Archie ground on through clenched teeth. "You know what they say, Will, red hat...no draw...," his voice faded as he drifted into unconsciousness again.

Will fondly patted him on the head and pulled the goggles down over his closed eyes. "Archie, m'boy. I think you're goin' to make it." He jumped down and swung himself between the tail booms. "Fuel on?"

"Fuel on, switches on," Dick responded from the cockpit.

"Contact!" Will swung the propeller and the Gnome spun into life. He rolled out from under the booms and joined the riflemen who had stood clear. They watched the machine roll into a short take off run and bound into the air. The wings dipped in salute as it circled the field once and headed off to the south.

"Is the other gentleman a good pilot, sir?" Sergeant Coppin asked, "I mean, like, does he make gentle landings?"

"Indeed he does, Sergeant; he's the best. Lieutenant Carstairs will think he's in a featherbed."

"Good. Because *he's* one of the best, that Mr. Carstairs, a real toff." He looked Will up and down. "Your own boots, sir?"

"Yes, Sergeant, I brought them from home with me, they're not army issue."

"Excellent, sir, because we've a hard march in front of us if we're going to catch up with the rest of the army, we're right out on a limb here, and we'll have to cut across the angle. Mind if I make a suggestion?"

"Go ahead, Sarge, I'm no soldier, I'm a mechanic. Let's just make that clear from the get go. You give the orders, I do what I'm told."

"That's very irregular, sir."

"Well, that may be, but I prefer to be irregular an' alive. What's your suggestion?"

Sergeant Coppin seemed to have lost his train of thought for a moment, "Oh, right you are, I was just going to say it would be worth cutting those pips off your shoulder straps. That way you'll look exactly like the rest of us, seeing as how you're not wearing officers togs, and if there are any snipers around they won't single you out to shoot first. They can make those badges out from hundreds of yards through those fancy telescopic sights they use."

Will dressed in the standard issue infantryman's jacket, puttees, and their soft-peaked cap because he found them most comfortable when working in his main role as a mechanic. He carried a pack for emergencies—slung using the same webbing belts and cross straps—and the rifle Dick had handed down from the Vickers. But Adams, the junior officer's servant, had been horrified at Will's lack of respect for regulation uniform codes and had sewn his lieutenant's rank badges, or "pips" as they were known, onto his jacket. Will presented his shoulder to Coppin. "Cut 'em off, quick, you never know who's watchin'." Coppin complied with a grim smile.

Will knew he had to reinforce the sergeant's position as leader. He did it in the most obvious way. As the group of twenty men moved quickly out of the field and made their way down the narrow road between high grass banks, he fell in place at the rear of the column. He found the other stranger in the group there. Corporal Jeffrey Jones was not from England, his sing-song accent was the voice of the valleys of Wales. He was a great bull of a man. To Will it looked as if his upper body was a massive barrel propelled along by short, powerful legs working like locomotive pistons. He had a big, round innocent face topped by thinning red hair revealed when he took his cap off to mop the sweat streaming down his forehead. He carried a Lewis machine gun on his shoulder with no more effort than if he had been sporting a walking cane. Spare magazines, strung on thick chord, were festooned around him like a bizarre collection of circular cake tins. Will could see little to laugh about in the situation he found himself, but Jones's surprisingly high-pitched giggle had Will grinning in spite of himself. "See, I reckon they're so bloody fast because they're used to running away from policemen," the big Welshman confided to Will waving a contemptuous hand at the men in front of them. "Bloody riflemen, look at 'em." They broke into a trot for a few paces to keep up. "It's history, see, this is their special light infantry pace, sort of a quick, quick march, then running a few steps. They made a name for themselves in

Wellington's army, tear arsing around Spain and Portugal," Jones explained. "Damn good job I'm fit—play rugby, of course, being Welsh."

"Will glanced at Jones's cap badge. "You're not from their outfit, then?"

"Oh no, sir. I'm in a proper regiment, South Wales Borderers, me," he raised his voice slightly so it carried to the men in front. He was rewarded with a low ruffle of laughter and muted curses. "*Strictly* between you and me, sir, this lot did all right back at the quarry—with a little help from me and Mr. Lewis here." He patted the tubular casing of the machine gun on his shoulder and laid his cheek against it like a lover. "Beautiful bit of kit, sir. Killed dozens of the bastards, we did."

"Why were you with the Rifle Brigade?"

"On loan to instruct on this machine gun, sir."

"Is it hard to shoot?"

Jones uncorked his canteen and took a sip without breaking his stride. "No, it's easy to shoot, but it's hard to *keep* it shooting, and it's far too easy to waste all your ammunition even if you don't get a stoppage. The secret is to use it like a self-loading rifle, semi-automatic I suppose you'd say. It stands to reason when you think about it. It only rests on these tiddly little legs," he gestured at the simple stand folded back against the barrel, "so the only shot that's aimed is the first one. The vibration must throw the next one out. Maybe you'll get lucky, but anymore than three rounds in a burst is like piddling in the wind. Here, tell you what, sir, if we can find some Germans you can have a go."

Will looked at Jones and could see he was not joking. He was giving him the chance to spray bullets with the insouciance of a boy offering a ride on his new bicycle. "Tell you what, Mr. Jones, if we meet the enemy I'll let you do the shootin', an' give me a demonstration. I'll have a try on the range when the consequences of missin' are not so serious."

"Right you are, sir. But mind you watch carefully, there'll be a test on it afterwards."

Will counted the magazines strung from the Welshman's belt. "How much ammunition do you have, Mr. Jones?"

"Nearly three hundred rounds, sir. But I'm more worried about water."

"Water?"

"Yes, sir. How much you got in your canteen?"

"It's about half full. Why, are you worried we'll all die of thirst, Mr.

Jones? It's hardly a desert is it?" Will gestured vaguely at the countryside, lush from the overnight rain.

"You'd be surprised, sir. Lads haven't had a chance to fill their canteens all day, and finding clean water is always bloody hard. Go easy on that if I were you."

A few hours later, well into the night and their forced march, Will grew painfully aware that Jones, the old campaigner, knew what he was talking about. The blistering pace had carried them miles from the landing field in a direction slightly west of south by midnight. The summer nights were longer now, in late August, but there was no relief from the sticky heat of the day. At midnight Coppin allowed a break of half an hour. They slumped gratefully to the ground. Will swallowed the last drops in his canteen. The warm water tasted as good as anything he had ever drunk. He consulted with the sergeant over a map illuminated with the shielded bulb of a small flashlight.

"I reckon we are here, sir," Coppin stabbed a finger at a point half way toward but slightly south of the town of Bapaume.

"But we need to be here," Will indicated the town of St. Quentin well to the south.

"That's right, sir. We've put distance between us and the Germans if they're following our boys, now we can strike slightly east of south and we'll pick up the trail then."

"How will we know? If we overshoot we could end up blundering into the enemy."

The dim light exaggerated the twist in Coppin's smile. "Stiffs, sir." He sensed Will's incomprehension. "Corpses, sir. Our blokes who've dropped down dead or died in the ambulances. They won't stop to bury them. We'll know by the smell if nothing else."

The sergeant's words seemed to pull the breath from Will's lungs. He tried to say something but all he could manage was, "Oh."

The older man sensed Will's dismay and continued cheerfully, "But there'll be other kit as well: equipment, broken down wagons and motors I expect. If we're really lucky maybe some rations or even a water carrier."

"Oh yes, Mr. Coppin, please let there be a water wagon."

"A little dry, sir?"

"A lot dry, Sergeant."

They pressed on. Will's feet ached despite the friendly familiarity of his non-regulation boots. His knees ached. His back ached. His breath rasped in his throat and sweat stung his eyes as they stumbled forward in the night. His rifle weighed heavily on whichever shoulder he slung it. But only one image throbbed in his head. Water. A desperate need for water. Visions of the smooth flowing rivers and the crystal clear, cold springs around his home teased him. All he and his hard marching companions could think of was liquid. In low voices they discussed drinks they now lusted for. The ales of their hometowns, the ciders of the west of England, lemonade pressed for village fetes and sweet concoctions like dandelion and burdock, they were all discussed in reverent tones. They asked him to tell them again about the sinkholes and mysterious rivers of North Florida and, as they passed the night in these fantasies, the clinging darkness began to ease. In the dim glow of the pre-dawn, they slumped in the trees at the edge of a forest bordering a long rectangular field, shorn of its crop of summer wheat and reduced to stubble.

"Right, Mr. Turner, this is where you pick up your lift."

"Beg pardon, Sergeant, I don't follow." Will wondered if his tongue was beginning to swell, his voice sounded unnatural in his ears.

"Your ride, sir. Mr. Thomas agreed we would rendezvous here, next to the farm." He looked out at the field anxiously, "It will be big enough, won't it, sir?"

"Oh, yes, but Mr. Coppin, I can't just leave you fellas." The thought struck Will as treasonable.

"Why ever not, sir?" Coppin looked at him as if trying to explain something to a very old and recalcitrant relative. "And I don't see as you have any choice in the matter, sir. That was an order from Lieutenant Thomas."

Will frowned. "Yes, the field's big enough, but it doesn't seem right leavin' you here."

Jones moved forward and crouched next to them. "Right doesn't come into it, sir. We're infantry, we get paid to walk. The King, bless him, pays you to fix his aeroplanes, and I don't see many around here."

"Take your point, gentlemen, but how about we see to some water for the men."

Coppin indicated the far side of the field. It dipped slightly at the southern edge, and beyond it they could make out a low wall in the gathering light. "There's a farm there, they'll have a pump or a well. The boys can hang on for a few more minutes until you're safe away." The sergeant looked at the lightening sky. "He'll be here any minute. In the meantime we better sort these lads out, Corporal Jones. Divide them up into two sections and send that grubby little poacher, Rigsby, down here." Jones winked and slid back into the trees, moving with surprising stealth for a man of his size.

Will sat against the edge of the bank, his feet extended into the field, his back against his pack now propped behind him. All the weight fell away from his aching limbs. If only somebody would bring him a glass of cold water, he thought, he would be glad to spend the rest of his life on this very spot, not moving. He watched idly as Rigsby, a skinny man older than most of the men in the company, consulted with his sergeant. After a few words he slipped into the trees, vanishing instantly.

Coppin moved back, "Just being on the safe side. Rigsby's going to work his was 'round and do a quick recce of the farm to make sure it's peaceful in there." He looked into the sky, head cocked slightly to one side. "I do believe they've sent your cab, sir."

The drone of an approaching airplane could now be heard clearly. The light had flooded into the sky as the blazing disc of the sun prized back the darkness from the eastern horizon. Will suddenly realized how tired he felt. He staggered to his feet, leaning on his rifle. He could make out the shape of the approaching machine. It looked like a B.E.2, flying in from the south. Will signaled his comrades back into the wood. "Rest easy, boys, he'll see me okay. Thanks for your comp—," he never finished the sentence. His voice drowned by the roar of gunfire from the farm. For a second he stood rooted to the spot, then instinct took over. He hit the dirt, literally. He tasted it in his mouth as he tried to burrow a trench with his body.

"Fucking hell!" somebody screamed. Will heard bellowed orders. He wondered if he was hit—how could they have missed with all those rifles aimed at him. Perhaps I'm dead, he thought, but why can I still hear everything and taste this muck? The shooting died away to a few sporadic shots. Will cautiously raised his head an inch, expecting to see spurts of dust kicked up by the bullets that would surely creep closer and thud into his cringing body. The voice that had screamed earlier now spoke in urgent tones from a few feet away, "Quick, sir, before they see you, get back in here."

Will scrambled to his knees and launched himself back into the wood. He lay on his back, gasping for breath, "Did they hit him?" He suddenly felt ashamed at the delight he felt when he understood the fusillade had been aimed at the B.E.2 and not him.

"Missed him by miles. But he's buggered off, sir." A young rifleman knelt behind a tree branch and watched the rapidly retreating B.E.2 through binoculars.

Will sat up. "Good for him, there's nothin' he can do here. That farm must be full of Germans. Looks like you're stuck with me after all, Sergeant Coppin."

"I'm sorry you lost your ride, Mr. Turner. This is looking bad." He turned to the soldier with the field glasses, "Can you see anything, Chalky?"

"Cavalry, Sarge, Uhlans, and some sort of motor. I can't see straight into the farmyard from here, but I'd guess about fifty men and horses."

"Oh, sod it." Coppin rubbed his chin. "Sorry, lads, we're going to have to find another watering hole. There's too many to tackle, even for Corporal Taff and his Lewis. We'll work our way 'round and pick up Rigsby on the way."

The riflemen dragged themselves to their feet, but as they started to move Will saw a change come over them. The tiredness disappeared. They moved on the balls of their feet, crouched, tense, their rifles held at the ready. Through the fringe of trees he could see the farm—sturdy wooden outbuildings with heavy thatch in good repair, longer lower sheds he guessed to house livestock. The red tiles of the house itself glistened with dew. He knew the enemy horsemen were close enough to hear them and he tried to hold his breath. A low outer wall separated the farm from the field. It was less than fifty yards distant.

"Where's bloody Rigsby?" Coppin muttered under his breath. A single rifle shot cracked an answer.

Chapter Twenty-Two

WILL TURNER'S AUNT CONSTANCE AND HIS COUSIN, KATE, SAT together in the soft dawn light that crept into the kitchen at Penrose Cottage. They were little more than two hundred miles to the west of him, but the difference was enough that the sun had not risen over the woods separating the Penrose paddock from Mr. Findlay's fields.

Connie pointed to Kate's plate. "Aren't you going to eat that toast?"

"No, you have it, Auntie, I don't seem to have any appetite since the fighting started. It's as if I have this horrible knot in my stomach."

Connie spread marmalade thick on the slice. "That won't do anybody any good. You are entitled to be worried, but that's no reason for mooning around like some feeble girl." She crunched hard on her toast.

"Perhaps I am a feeble girl, Auntie, I just don't know what to do. I would feel better if I could be out there with father, Rupert and Will."

Connie laughed and threw herself back in her chair, striking a pose with the back of her hand against her forehead, her long white nightgown adding to the effect. "'Oh, what shall I do? I think I'll faint if I can't bayonet a German.' Listen to yourself, Kate, you're talking nonsense. How can you be feeble, if in the next breath you want to join the army in the field?"

Kate smiled for the first time since she had padded barefoot into the kitchen, wrapped in her old blue flannel dressing gown. "You know what I mean. It's the sitting around waiting for news that's so awful. I want to do something—something positive, useful."

"And so you shall, Kate Penrose. I have made a decision. I'm declaring a truce on the male of the species and soldiers in particular until this business is over. If we're to win this war, it's we women who will do it." Constance spread the last slice of toast and thrust it back at Kate. "Eat up, my dear, somebody has to organize the Volunteer Aid Detachment for this district and *we* are going to do it—you'll need all your energy."

Kate sat back and stared at her aunt, "You mean us? *We're* going to organize VAD nurses?"

"Of course we are—you, me, and Marjorie—who else? There's no official organization. The hospitals will never be able to cope when the wounded start pouring in so we have to start straight away. Today."

A slow smile spread over Kate's face. She bit into the toast and poured herself more tea, "I feel hungry all of a sudden."

"That's the spirit, my girl. Now stop worrying about those men. Your father is a staff officer, and the biggest danger he faces is being hit in the eye by a flying champagne cork. Rupert is the finest pilot in any air force and will be flying high above the shot and shell, and Will is miles from the enemy, happy as Larry up to his elbows in oil and grease." It was a whopping lie and Connie knew it. Her carefree attitude was a brilliant act for the benefit of her niece and Maisie, whose brother fought with the Suffolk Regiment. Connie knew exactly how Kate felt, the only difference was she knew that sick and empty sensation only too well. It came back like a veteran from a dozen campaigns that her brother, Frank Penrose, had fought through in a forty-year career. The stiff upper lip cost her dear, but she saw no alternative. She knew her throwaway description of the disposition of her nearest and dearest menfolk was probably inaccurate, but she could never have guessed how far she was from the facts.

At that very moment she would never have recognized her brother. Colonel Frank Penrose wore a rough canvas smock over his uniform, an enlisted soldier's cap with no badges and his face was disfigured by diagonal black stripes applied with burnt cork—*that* was, at least, from a champagne bottle. Joe Thorpe, camouflaged in similar fashion, crouched next to him. At the exact moment she was trying to reassure her niece, Connie's brother was no more than one hundred yards from Von Kluck's army.

Frank passed his field glasses to Joe. "What do you think?"

Joe moved slowly, parting the grass in front of his face to push the glasses through. He studied the scene before him, then compared the map in his hand with the compass Frank held in front of him. A slow smile spread across his face. It was as much as he could do not to laugh, "The silly sods are going the wrong way. They think we're falling back to the coast." He focused again on the lines of troops plodding past, marching doggedly on a line angled forty-five degrees from the real direction of the British withdrawal. "And I'll tell you something else—we're getting too bloody old for this." The two men wriggled back into the trees. Safely in the shadows they stood, and as they did three more figures materialized to join them. Slowly they crept away to where a Rolls Royce armored car waited to whisk them back to rejoin the retreating British army.

Connie's real concern lay with her nephew—Frank Penrose's son—Rupert. The thought of him fluttering over the German army in his fragile biplane, with only a thin covering of canvas and wood between him and their massed weapons, gave her nightmares. As she spoke of him above the fighting, and suffered a pang of anxiety on his behalf, she would have felt conflicting emotions of relief and irritation if she had known where he really was in the early morning of August 27.

Rupert sat propped up in a four-poster bed in one of the finest hotels in Paris, enjoying a breakfast of croissants and coffee brought to him by a liveried servant. He felt some guilt at being away from the action but had decided to make the most of his present situation. On landing at St. Quentin he had immediately been ordered to Paris by road to collect a replacement machine. The journey in the sidecar of a French motorcycle had given him the opportunity to see the preparations being made to defend the city. As they approached the capital, they were waved through numerous barricades and motored past long lines of trenches where the blades of pick axes only appeared above ground at the top of each swing. At the racetrack where he was supposed to collect a brand new Farman biplane, he was told that regrettably his machine would not be ready until the morning, but was assured accommodation and dinner had been arranged for him at the Imperial Hotel. "Oh, bother," Rupert said with a smile he could not conceal.

Connie felt no real concern for Will. As far as she was concerned he was the least likely to look for trouble and *should* be miles from the British Expeditionary Force. By a bitter irony she was correct on both counts. Will Turner had not gone looking for trouble, it had found him, and he *was* miles from the British army, but in the wrong direction. He was, however, very close to the German army and sprinting closer as she spoke.

"Now! Down!" Corporal Jones bellowed from behind him. Will flung himself onto his stomach in the dirt, his rifle in front of him. "Now, rapid fire, fast as you can," Jones urged, thumping down beside him.

"Fire? What at fer Chrissakes?" Will demanded.

"Anything that bloody moves—just make a lot of noise. Cover *them*." The other section rushed forward.

Jones led by example. The Lewis gun crashed a few inches from Will's ear, making him jerk his first shot. He frantically worked the bolt on his rifle, the stuttering blast of rapid firing around him making him miss the sound of his own shooting. Only when his rifle butt stopped slamming back into his shoulder when he pressed the trigger did he realize he had shot off ten rounds. "Oh, fuck! Fuck! " he cursed as he fumbled another clip into position.

"Up!" Jones screamed in his ear. Will dimly heard a whistle shrill and Coppin shouting. The big Welshman seized Will's pack and hoisted him to his feet with it. He stumbled forward. The wall at the edge of the farm was only yards away. They dived behind it. Will finished reloading and knelt up to rest his elbows on the top of the wall to take aim. Before he could fire he felt himself dragged down and thrust to the end of the brickwork where a gateway formed a gap. Jones lectured Will between short blasts with his machine gun. "Never shoot over cover if you can shoot 'round it, sir. You're exposing your head and upper body. Shoot 'round a corner and you only expose your hand and half your face."

Will followed the advice and fired again at a window in one of the cattle sheds. A rush of feet, more shouts and Jones pushed him forward again. Something cracked past his head. They stormed headlong at a gap leading into the farmyard. The world moved in slow motion with startling clarity. A man appeared briefly, facing him. Will saw a blue uniform and heavy black mustache. His mouth was open. A dark spot appeared in his forehead and the man crumpled like a puppet that had had its strings cut. More men appeared, but they were running away from him. Will raised his rifle and soon realized it was his own voice he heard screaming. A group of horsemen wheeled and reared in the barnyard. He charged at them with his rifle held high even though he had no bayonet. They thundered away, some leaping the wall between them and the road. A truck rattled around the corner of the barn, quickly gathering speed. Will aimed at the driver, "STOP!" To his amazement the truck stopped.

The driver stood up in the roofless cab and meekly raised his hands.

"*Kamerad,*" he said quickly. "*Kamerad.*"

Jones rushed to Will's side, his hob nailed boots skidding on the wet cobbles. "Comrade? What's all this bloody comrade business they're all coming out with? Fine time to want to make friends."

Will slowly lowered his rifle and looked around him. A dozen men in blue uniforms, some with the distinctive Uhlan helmets, stood with their hands high in the air. "No, it's *Kamerad* they're saying. It means they've surrendered."

Jones took off his cap and scratched his head. "Well I'll be buggered!" He opened his mouth to speak again but the sound of rapid hoof beats stopped the words. Before any one of them could do anything to stop him, a solitary horseman clattered from behind the barn. Hatless and with no weapons he dashed through the gap between the buildings and cleared the wall into the field they had just charged across. It was a magnificent leap. Coppin raised his rifle, then lowered it without firing.

Rigsby spoke from behind Will, "After the war I'm going to put money on him if enters the Grand National."

Coppin glared at Rigsby, "Just what the fuck do you think you were doing? This had better be good." The sergeant looked around the farmyard. Will could see he was counting heads. He had already done it himself. Their own men were all present and apparently unwounded. Apart from the nervous German cavalrymen, another group were gathered in front of the barn next to the house. This building had an open door twenty feet above the ground. A simple block and tackle hung from a beam extending over the cobbles to allow bales to be swung into the hayloft. Will guessed these people were the family who lived at the farm. They crouched around a man lying beneath the beam. An old woman dressed in black held a heavy glass against his lips; a younger woman caressed his face. They ignored the body of a German cavalryman lying next to them, facedown in a thin stream of dirty water flowing through the yard. Blood joined the stream where it flowed under his head.

Rigsby checked his rifle and slipped the safety catch on before slinging it over his shoulder. "Well Sarge," his eyebrows furrowed in concentration.

"I'm waiting."

"Well, I couldn't let them top him, could I? That's been a sport for toffs for years, and I decided to put a stop to this one."

Coppin glared at him. "What are you rambling on about?"

The wiry little soldier pointed to the farmer being tended by his family. "The bastards were going to string him up. The Huns had some sort of an argument, one of the officers seemed to be trying to stop it, but then they slung a rope up on the crane there and had that big git pulling on the other end. They'd got the froggie's feet off the ground when the airyplane came over and they took the time to take pot shots at that, then they went back to hanging him. It was horrible Sarge, I'm surprised you didn't hear the women carrying on from where you were—screaming and crying, they were. Anyway, it gave me time to get into a good firing position, and I shot the one pulling on the rope."

"Where from?"

"Corner of the orchard there, easy shot, about a hundred yards."

Coppin shrugged grudgingly, "You did all right Rigsby, but if you'd missed I would have had you court-martialed. What would you have done if we'd buggered off?"

"I knew you wouldn't, Sarge."

"It's all very well for you to say that, but I've been charged with getting Mr. Turner safe back to headquarters. Now, thanks to you, he ends up taking part in a demonstration of me putting a platoon in the attack."

Rigsby grinned at Will, "Sorry about that, sir, at least you can say you've been in a skirmish."

One of the men had taken Will's canteen and filled it at the pump in the corner of the yard. He drank gratefully. His brain hammered at the inside of his skull but the water instantly calmed it. He wiped his mouth with the back of his sleeve then squinted at Coppin. "Only a skirmish, Sergeant? I can't say I've been in a battle then?"

The sergeant relaxed, "Not really, sir, all over in two minutes, but you did bloody well if I may say so. But didn't you hear me when I told you to stay back?"

"Gee, sorry, Mr. Coppin. I kinda lost my head, I thought you shouted 'Mr. Turner, attack.' So I did."

"You certainly did that. That yell you gave as we came into the yard fair curdled the blood. It certainly panicked the horse soldiers. What was that about?"

"My uncle fought with the Confederacy in the late unpleasantness in my own country. He told me they always did that yell, and it unsettled the other side."

"It works," Coppin said. He called across to one of his soldiers who bent over the French farmer still laying in front of his house. "Byrne, is your French good enough to find out what happened here?" Byrne conversed in rapid French with the young woman. Will and Coppin walked across the yard to join them. Will felt as if his legs moved in an awkward fashion, as if they belonged to somebody else. He tried not to look at the corpse lying next to them, but his eyes were drawn to it. A wisp of smoke curled from the small hole in the base of the man's skull. Will suppressed a heave in his stomach.

Byrne straightened up, "The cavalry turned up just as it was getting light. They were foraging, that's why they have the lorry with them. They dragged the family outside shouting about *Francs Tireurs.* They claimed somebody took a pot shot at them and blamed the farmer here. They were going to string him up, but one of the German officers tried to stop them. The others dragged the officer off behind the barn, and they would have hung this fella—"

"But Rigsby spoiled their fun," Coppin said.

"That's about the strength of it, Sarge. And a grand job he did, too," Byrne spoke with a strong Irish accent.

"You speak damn good French, Mr. Byrne," Will said.

"Benefit of a good Catholic school, sir. The nuns beat an education into me, but I'm grateful they did."

A shout drew their attention. Two riflemen appeared from behind the barn supporting a German soldier who slumped between them. "Found him behind the barn, Sarge, looks like somebody belted him over the head."

Coppin looked at Will. "Beats me, Sergeant," he shrugged, "maybe the same person who shot at them, you can hardly blame the locals for trying to defend their land."

"The young lady says her brother is missing and so's her dad's shotgun," Byrne put in.

"Makes sense," Coppin said. "But tell her they must find her brother and get the whole family out of here, and quick. We gave that lot a fright and chased them away, but they'll be back, and they'll probably hang everybody next time."

Byrne talked again with the two women and the farmer who was now sitting up. An ugly welt ran around his throat and up behind his ear. When he spoke his voice came as a croak. Byrne explained, "They thought we might be part of a counter attack and be driving the Germans away, but I've put them straight. They have family about thirty miles away to the west, beyond somewhere called Arras. They have good horses and a big cart; they're getting out with what they can."

"Good," Coppin said, "tell them not to waste a minute. And that goes double for us."

"The old lady wants us to stand the prisoners against the wall and lend her a rifle so she can shoot them," Byrne added with a grin.

"Tell her she's a stupid old cow," Coppin said. He turned to his men. "Be ready to march in ten minutes, have your canteens filled. Cut the braces and buttons off those bugger's trousers, take the bolts out of their carbines and toss them down the well, then tell them to clear off, we can't drag prisoners with us."

Will laid a hand on Coppin's arm, "Sergeant, you may enjoy walkin', but I'm takin' a ride home in that." He jabbed his thumb over his shoulder at the truck he had captured.

The sergeant's face lit up, "Blimey, sir, can you drive?"

"Of course I can, can't you?"

"No, sir, nobody here can, they'd be in the transport corps if they could." He turned to his troops; a cheer greeted the news.

Will quickly checked over the truck. The maker's plate said Daimler and underneath Marienfelde in a curly script. Will grunted with satisfaction, "It's a good make." He opened the hood. "Four cylinders," he said to nobody in particular, then glanced underneath the chassis. "Fully enclosed gear drive—this is the ticket boys. Now let's just hope she's got some gas." He unscrewed the cap on the tank and peered inside. "Oh glory be! No more marchin', there's enough to take us all the way back to Piccadilly." He climbed up to the driver's seat and worked his way around the controls. "Okay, Sergeant Coppin, get the boys aboard, there's plenty of room for everybody."

"Room to take one of them as a prisoner, sir? It'll be a rare old feather in our caps." He pointed to the dismounted cavalrymen who now looked anything but grand. Their strange headgear and polished high boots made them look like extras in a musical comedy. The effect increased as they all struggled to maintain their dignity and their trousers while the old woman berated them, pausing only to spit on their tunics.

"Yeah, I guess that's what we're supposed to do," Will said. The idea had not occurred to him. He pointed to the two bodies still lying where they fell. "Shouldn't we do something about them?"

Coppin walked quickly over to the man Rigsby had assassinated.

Before Will could look away, the sergeant rolled him over. His lower jaw had disappeared leaving a gaping, bloody maw, but his face above the top lip was completely unmarked. His stiff waxed moustache still bristled indignantly. Coppin was indifferent to the sight. He felt around in the man's pockets and looked up. "Senior NCO, sir, he's got nothing of any military value on him, just his paybook." A photograph dropped out of the book and fell in the mud at the sergeant's feet. He quickly retrieved it, glanced at it, and then carefully wiped it clean before folding it back into the stiff-covered book. He put the document back in the dead man's pocket and buttoned it down. He straightened up, "They'll find them soon enough and give them a proper burial." He looked down the line of prisoners, then pointed. "That one, with the extra scrambled egg on his sleeve, we'll take him. The rest of you—fuck off back to Germany. You're not wanted here." He gestured angrily.

The cavalrymen did not understand the words, but they understood the tone of voice. They shambled off through the gate to the road. Jones watched them for a moment then cocked the Lewis and fired a short burst over their heads. The awkward trot turned into a gallop. They disappeared from sight with the jeers of Coppin's men and the curses of the French in their ears. It was a small victory, but it meant a lot to the exhausted riflemen. They piled gratefully into the back of the truck. The young Frenchwoman reappeared from the kitchen, long loaves and a round wheel of cheese in her arms. She thrust them at the men in the back of the truck. The farmer staggered after her with a clutch of bottles in each hand. Rigsby took them from him. "Thanks, mate, much appreciated."

The Frenchman took Rigsby's head in his big rough hands. "*Merci,* Tommy—*Vive la France.*" He planted a smacking kiss on each of Rigsby's cheeks and stood back saluting as Will let in the clutch and took the truck lurching toward the gate. Will paused in the entrance to the farmyard, pushing the gear lever in every direction.

Coppin sat beside him in the open cab. "And you can really drive this thing, sir?" he said with open admiration.

Will grimaced as he ground the gears, "Sarge, if it's got wheels, I can drive it." He let the clutch in and the truck jerked backwards to ribald cheers from the back. He found the right gear and turned out of the farm, "Badly, but I can drive it." Will indicated the family watching them go with a jerk of his chin, "Do you think they'll be okay?"

"As long as they just get out and go west they should be fine, sir.

There's no reason for Von Kluck to go that way, he should be following us toward St. Quentin." He turned in his seat to talk to his men. They had bound their prisoner's wrists and ankles and thrust him to the front of the load bed behind the driver's seat. "Go easy on that wine, lads, we're still not out of the woods. But give laughing boy here a bottle, it might loosen his tongue. Mr. Turner here speaks his lingo, and he might let something go."

The morning was still only an hour old as Will drove steadily down the narrow lane. They came to a crossroads and gratefully followed a signpost pointing them toward St. Quentin. Coppin opened his map then held it up for Will to view. "This road runs alongside the one our boys have taken until just before we reach St. Quentin when it joins it here," he jabbed at the map with a dirty finger, "and that's no bad thing."

"Why's that?" Will asked.

"Because they will have barricaded and booby trapped it any way they can as they go. One of the best tricks is a big howitzer shell planted in a ditch with thin wire strung across the road holding a spring loaded hammer clamped to the detonator. First man, horse or motor to come down the road breaks the wire and the shell goes off."

"Nasty," Will said.

"And effective," Coppin pointed out, "there's advantages to being on the losing side if you have engineers with a vicious streak."

"And ours do?"

"Oh yes, sir, a mile wide and very inventive too."

"It's a comfort to know they're on our side. How far do you think we have to run?"

"Twenty miles at the most, how fast will this go, sir?"

Will looked at the countryside rolling past for a moment—there was no speed indicator on the dashboard. "We're making a good ten miles per hour I guess. Two hours and we should be safely back in the bosom of the army."

"I'd rather be in the bosom of that French lass, sir," Rigsby called from the back. "Just my luck to have her *dad* kiss me." The others laughed and cheered at his discomfort, but within a few minutes the excited chatter died away.

Coppin suddenly spun around in his seat, "Chapman, stay awake and keep an eye on our friend here." The rest of the men were already dozing, slumped on their packs and each other.

The soldier sat up straight, shaking his head, "Sorry, Sarge." He pointed his rifle at the prisoner, "No funny stuff, chum, *comprendo?*" The German just glared at him. Rigsby shook himself awake and passed Coppin a chunk of cheese and a loaf. He sliced it roughly in half with a clasp knife and made a crude sandwich for Will. The food helped dispel the lightheaded sensation that made him concerned he might put them in the ditch. The big Daimler rolled along on solid rubber tires—its lusty motor chugging steadily.

Will glanced at Coppin who sat upright in his seat, constantly scanning the fields behind and to their left. "Do you think you might relax, Sergeant? I'd guess we've put enough distance between us and them."

"Beggin' your pardon, sir, but no. Cavalry can move twice as fast as this and cross-country at that. While they're on horseback we've no problem, we can shoot 'em. It's if they have the sense to get ahead of us and set up an ambush I'm worried about."

"Pah! Sense—from our officers?" the words, heavily accented and bitter came from behind them. Will ignored the road and twisted in his seat to confirm that the German prisoner had spoken in English. Half of the riflemen had jerked awake and were staring at the stranger in their midst.

"*Sie sprechen Englisch?*" Will demanded.

"*Ja, ein wenig*—a little." He held up a finger and thumb close together.

"Well, my lad!" Coppin said. "You've some explaining to do."

"I will give only my name, rank, and service number."

"Bollocks," Coppin spat, "I couldn't give a stuff about that, Fritz, what I want to know is what do you think you were doing back there with that froggie. We've been hearing stories about atrocities against civilians in Belgium, but we didn't believe them; now it looks as if we should."

The German said nothing for a few moments, he looked warily at the accusing faces, when he spoke it was slowly and carefully, "This is the policy of our high command, *Schrecklichkeit*. They stared at him blankly. "'Frightfulness' is the nearest word in English," he explained. "We are to punish severely any attempts at resistance by the civilian population of conquered territories. In this way there will be no need for large garrisons to control the population, leaving all forces available to fight at the front. These orders come from the great Hindenburg himself."

Byrne glared at the prisoner, "So, you go along with it, you gobshite."

The German seemed to struggle to understand the Irishman's accent. But his reply when it eventually came made it clear he not only understood, but spoke English very well. "I am a soldier, I have to follow orders, as do you. At least I take my orders from my own countrymen, not from a foreign power."

Byrne lunged forward, but his comrades hauled him back, "You arrogant little bastard!"

The German held up his hands awkwardly as his wrists were still tied. "I am sorry, I am speaking out of turns, as you say," he paused for a moment. They waited for him to speak again, he was clearly struggling to find the right words. "No," he finally said, "I do not, how you say? 'Go along with it.' I did not join the army to make war on women and children. I was raised a good Christian in the Catholic Church and this goes against all I ever learned."

Byrne's face lit up; it was like the sun coming out after a storm. "Why the fuck didn't you say so in the first place? Here, have a fag."

The prisoner accepted with a smile and changed the subject. "Gentlemen, it does not matter now, the war is finished for me, but I want you to know we did not panic when you attacked."

"Oh really," Will called back over his shoulder, "what did happen then?"

"The *verdammte* horses panicked," he smiled at their laughter but stuck to his explanation. He shook his head sadly, "They are stupid creatures, when you attacked the horses were not tied up. Those without riders ran away and the ones with men on ran after them. Most of us were left with nothing to fight you with because our *Gewehr*—"

"Rifles," Will translated.

"—were on our saddles. They are herd animals and have no place in this war, I fear. The days of glorious charges are over, this war will be won with these infernal machines." He banged his boot heel on the bed of the truck.

"You can walk if you prefer," Coppin offered.

"No thank you. If I am going to hell, I will ride."

"Hold up!" Coppin stopped the chat with a wave of his hand.

Will followed the sergeant's pointing finger and started to brake, "They're ours, Sergeant. But they don't know who we are." Will could see the troop of cavalry trotting toward them wore khaki and flat caps. They showed no lack of dash despite their drab uniforms. The formation fanned out across the field where they had first appeared next to the road and accelerated to a gallop to cut them off as Will hauled the truck to a shuddering stop. He waited, tense, to see how Coppin dealt with the situation. He relaxed when he saw the officer leading the charge raise his hand to slow his men to a trot. They formed a single line behind him as he urged his mount up the low embankment onto the road.

Coppin stood up and saluted, correct as ever, "Rifle Brigade, sir, plus one Welshman and a prisoner."

The officer returned his salute, "Fourth Dragoon Guards." He looked into the back of the truck, "A prisoner you say! Jolly good show, *and* you've captured a charabanc." He opened a notebook, "Rifle Brigade, let's see, your chaps went through hours ago. You'll find them to the south of the town. They may already be on the march."

"We're not making a stand here, sir?"

"Oh dear me no, Sergeant, we're falling back to link up with the French. Even as we speak the wounded are being evacuated by train. I'm afraid there's a long way for you to march yet."

Coppin shrugged, "We're used to it, sir. At least the wounded are being got away."

"That's the spirit." The young officer had somehow contrived to shave and keep his uniform immaculate, and the sight of him on his prancing horse made Will feel distinctly shabby.

"Have your driver take you to the station where you can hand over your prisoner, then follow the signposts for the town of Ham. You will find your people on that road."

"Right you are, sir. But this is not my driver, this is Lieutenant Turner of the Flying Corps."

Will had taken no part in the conversation, feeling it was about military matters that were not his business. He smiled and touched the peak of his cap, "How do."

"Oh, I say! Beg pardon and all that but I didn't realize," the cavalry officer sounded genuinely apologetic. He saluted, "Bingham-Carter, Second Lieutenant."

Will suddenly recognized that he outranked this smart young soldier. "No reason why you should," he pointed out reasonably. "These fellas cut off my pips so the Germans wouldn't single me out to shoot first."

Bingham-Carter thought about this for a moment. "What a splendid wheeze," he said. "That might be why bullets keep whizzing past my head all the time. Do you know, I'm the last subaltern still in the saddle in my regiment?"

Will kept his face straight, "You don't say!"

"Might be as well to stick them back on now, Mr. Turner," he advised, "if you want to hang onto this motor, otherwise somebody might try to requisition it. You captured it so it's finders keepers in my books." He had a high braying laugh, "Oh well, can't stand about chatting all day, must press on." He called to the men in the back of the truck, "Well done, you chaps, keep it up—toodle pip!" He waved his men forward and they trotted past in single file. The troop sergeant at the rear of the column winked at Coppin as he passed.

The soldier they called Sammy offered to restore Will to his rank, so Will threw him his jacket. The day was warming as the sun rose higher. A thin rain had fallen during the night, enough to lay the dust at least, but by the time they rolled into the town the air hung heavy and oppressive again. Will threaded the Daimler through groups of exhausted soldiers who walked in a trance, blindly following the man in front, oblivious to the shouts from Coppin to clear the way. In the square by the railway station Will found himself easing his way around men asleep where they had fallen.

"Jeez, Sergeant, have you ever seen anything like this?" Will eased forward again as two of the riflemen remounted the truck after lifting two prone figures from their path.

"No, sir, I haven't, and I hope I never do again. Some of these men are drunk," he broke off to shout at a soldier urinating against the wall of the station. "That man there, where do you think you are!"

The soldier, his face red under a cap sitting side ways on his head turned half toward them, "Fuck off."

Will put a hand on Coppin's arm to restrain him, "Leave it." His firmness surprised the men in the truck.

Coppin glared, then reluctantly sat down. "Discipline's going, sir, there's going to be trouble. Let's get shot of Fritz and get out of here. I want to be back with our mob."

The German prisoner attracted mild curiosity from the soldiers draped over the seats in front of the station. Coppin had untied him before they reached the town as he showed no sign of trying to escape. The riflemen sent him on his way with as many cigarettes as they could spare, two squares of chocolates and their best wishes.

"Good luck, Fritz," Byrne called after him as two military policemen marched him off. "If you ever make it to Dublin when this is over, I'll buy you a drink."

"Thanks, Paddy," he called back over his shoulder, "keep your head down."

Coppin climbed back to his seat and handed Will a slip of paper. Will studied it. "What's this for?" he asked.

"Receipt for your prisoner, sir. You get the credit for him in your record, it all goes toward promotion and the dishing out of medals."

"That's crazy, Mr. Coppin," Will protested, "he was your prisoner, I had nothin' to do with it."

"That's not how it works, sir. You were the officer present at the time so he's your property. Of course if you want to say how the Rifles performed in your report, we would appreciate that."

"Too damn right I will," Will replied. "Anyway, did you learn anything while you were in the station?" He slipped the truck into gear and moved out of the square.

Coppin kept his voice low, "It doesn't look good. They were loading all the headquarters stuff into wagons in the siding. The general staff are clearing out. They have taken the wounded away, but there's nowhere near enough wagons and carriages to take all the men in the town now. And if you ask me they've had it, they can't march another step, even if they wanted to, and you saw for yourself some have lost the stomach for it." He turned and looked over his men in the back of the truck—most were dozing again. "I saw an old mate of mine in the station, a sergeant with General French's staff, he told me we've taken over fifty percent casualties since it started at Mons."

Will drove on in silence for a moment while the words sunk in. "Oh my God, half our men," was all he could say. He heaved on the wheel and set them rumbling out of town. Even the effort of driving the heavy truck was enough to make his muscles protest. He could not imagine walking another step, but knew the men behind them in the town must feel far worse. Yet their only hope lay in stepping out down this road to the south where a defensive line would be formed behind the River Somme. They had no food, no orders and no sleep for days. Will knew he had not seen outright mutiny, but he guessed it was something close. If only, he thought, we could find a few more trucks like this, we could shuttle back and forth and ride the men away. His thoughts were interrupted by Sergeant Coppin.

"There they are, sir! That's our Mr. Osborn." As he shouted a young officer staggered to his feet at the roadside where he rested on the verge with a dozen men. Will pulled the truck to a stop.

Osborn stepped forward and stared up at Coppin and the men grinning at him from the back of the truck. He looked to Will to be barely out of his teens, with fair hair, smooth cheeks and even a trace of youthful acne, but his eyes were those of a man who had seen too much in a long lifetime. "Sergeant Alf Coppin, is that you?" Coppin saluted. Osborn turned to look at the others, "Sammy Cohen, Pat Byrne, Bill Rigsby—you're alive." Will could see how far things had gone in a few days, now he witnessed a minor break down of discipline of a benign nature. Osborn greeted his men as friends and comrades, the barrier between officer and men temporarily dropped in his relief at seeing them. The soldiers on the roadside stirred as the others dropped off the tailboard. Will watched a scene of reunion and jubilation, the first display of emotion he had witnessed. In the midst of the backslapping and handshaking he saw tears running down grimy, unshaven cheeks.

"So where's the rest of B Company, Mr. Osborn?" Coppin asked.

Osborn waved wearily at the dozen men with him. "This *is* B Company, Sergeant, what's left of it. You, me, us...we happy band, we band...," he started to quote Shakespeare but gave up, his lips compressed. "Twenty lads left from the other companies asleep in the field yonder—we are the Regiment." His shoulders drooped.

For the first time in their brief acquaintance, Will thought Coppin might show his feelings. For a few seconds he stood saying nothing, but when he spoke Will could see he was taking command, putting heart into the tired boy who had given his all for the men who depended on him. "No, sir, it's not that bad," he spoke firmly. "There are thousands more coming down the road, but they're all mixed and muddled. There's bound to be hundreds more RBs with them. We'll give these lads another half hour, then my lot can carry an extra pack or two between them, we've done nothing but sit on our arses half the day, thanks to Mr. Turner's taxi, and then we'll press on—okay lads?" The others nodded. He turned to Will, "I don't know what we would have done without you, Mr. Turner. Me and the lads want you to know we appreciate what you did." The others joined him in a chorus of thanks and good wishes.

Will sat partly slumped over the steering wheel. He raised himself and pointed down the highway. "You can thank me by getting safe down that road and stayin' alive, boys. Then next time we meet you'll be comin' the other way and whuppin' Kaiser Bill's ass, okay?" As he drove away to find the flying field he was amazed to hear their cheers following him. He drove with a pain in every joint of his body, and a lump in his throat. The field was easy to find, he followed a B.E.2 gliding down to land. He took the truck rocking and lurching into the field to see a familiar scene. The RFC were packing and leaving. Oh heck, he thought, the circus is back on the road again. As he rolled to a stop next to what had become the headquarters van, he became dimly aware that faces were staring at him. He slumped back wearily in his seat and let the noise wash over him—shouts, cheers, laughter. He felt the truck rock as a big man joined him. He opened his eyes—Major Higgins knelt on the wooden bench seat.

"Turner? It *is* you." He adjusted his monocle, "Look at the state of you." Will thought Higgins sounded like his father.

Liam Power came bounding over to the truck and leaped onto the running board. He slapped Will on the back, "Ah, the proverbial bad penny, always turns up. That's grand to see you, Willy m'boy—where the hell have you been?"

"Takin' a stroll in the country." He looked over the sea of excited faces and suddenly came awake. "Where's Dick? Did he make it back?" He saw Higgins exchange a quick glance with Liam Power.

"He made it back with your friend, Carstairs, but I'm afraid they were both carted off to hospital."

Will came wide awake. "What happened? Is he...is...?" he could not bring himself to say the word.

Higgins patted him on the shoulder, "Last time we saw him he was doing well, but I'm afraid he won't be coming back to us, he's lost an arm. Somewhere between here and Le Cateau he was hit by ground fire. The bullet smashed his left elbow to pieces."

"For such a little fella, Dick's a tough bastard," Liam said. "He brought the old Vickers in smooth as you like and made us pull Carstairs out and load him in the ambulance before he'd let us attend to him. They went off together joking about being put together as a team so they'd have a full set of arms and legs between them."

Will put his head in his hands. What drives these people? he asked himself. He pulled his fingers down his cheeks, forcing his eyes open. Weariness had settled like a blanket over his shoulders but he knew he had to press on. He looked at Higgins who still regarded him solicitously. "Major Higgins, sir, I want permission to take this truck back into the town and start ferrying the men there to the next rendezvous point. There's hundreds of men too tired to move."

Higgins snorted and climbed down. "Mr. Turner, you're in no fit state to drive anybody anywhere, you'll fall asleep at the wheel and have 'em in the ditch. Apart from that we need this lorry. I don't know how the hell you won it, but it's a gift from above as far as I'm concerned."

"But, sir," Will started to protest.

Higgins, for once, was conciliatory, "We're moving down the road to La Fere. When we've unloaded, we'll see what we can do to help. You," he pointed firmly at Will, "get your head down for a few hours. You're no use to us like that."

Will nodded dumbly. He went to climb down from his perch but stumbled. Willing hands caught him and hoisted him shoulder high and bore him away in triumph. Before his mechanics laid him gently on the grass, he was asleep. He woke, briefly, but decided it was a dream. He had a sensation of being rocked and a vision of trees passing slowly by with an enormous pair of boots forming the bottom of the picture. They must be my boots, he decided, bloody good boots, and drifted back to sleep.

Chapter Twenty-Three

WILL AWOKE WITH A GUILTY START. HE STRUGGLED TO PLACE where he lay. It was dry, he felt warm, and the familiar aroma of oil and doped fabric filled the air. A dim light showed through an open window. Forcing his eyes to focus, he saw that it was not a window. He could see the lightening sky as he looked through the open doors of one of the moving vans used to carry spare parts. Will threw the blanket that was covering him aside and found his boots. He went to drag them on but stopped, staring aghast at his feet—they were blistered, bloody and raw. He eased himself down from the truck, the cool grass of the unfamiliar flying field was balm to his feet.

A voice shattered the stillness of the morning, "Mr. Turner, sir! Get yourself some breakfast, sir! Then tidy yourself up, sir! You look like a ruddy tramp, sir!"

Ah, thought Will, Disciplinary Sergeant Major Cattle's dulcet tones—I'm home. He turned to Cattle with a grin, "Mornin' Sergeant Major. Good to see you again."

Cattle stamped to attention, saluted, and thrust the now-familiar mug of tea at Will. His eyes twinkled beneath the peak of his cap. "Marvellous to see you, sir. You're our second stray to make it back. Mr Smith-Barry, was in hospital in St. Quentin with two busted legs, but he commandeered a cab and got himself away."

"Oh, good show!" Will realized how British he sometimes sounded.

"And you've done very well if you don't mind my saying, Mr. Turner. We heard about you driving the riflemen safe to the fold, and the fight at the farm."

"Lordy, Sergeant Major, word travels fast in a small army. But there's no credit owin' to me, it was Sergeant Coppin who did all the work."

"That's not what he said, sir."

"You met him?"

"Mr. Strange did, sir. Volunteers moved hundreds of men in your lorry last night, shuttling back and forwards, and his lot was among them. Wells and Nichol carried out a little modification, hope you don't mind." He indicated the Daimler truck parked next to them. Will laughed. During the night it had grown wider. Down each side of the body a row of benches had been skilfully strapped, allowing a line of men to ride on the outside with their feet dangling.

"Are those the seats that were outside the station in St. Quentin?"

"Yes, sir. We can carry twice as many now. Not what you might call luxurious, but a bad ride beats a good walk any day, as my old mum says."

Will looked down at his battered feet, "You can say that again."

"You're excused boots, sir. I'll have one of the lads cut a pair of Wellingtons, and you can wear them stuffed with paper until those go down." Cattle pointed at Will's feet, "Bathe them in salt water as often as you can. They'll soon harden."

"I hope so, Mr. Cattle, but I don't plan on any more strolls in the countryside." Will looked over the field to the road running outside. "So everybody got away from St. Quentin okay?"

Cattle gave his familiar snort of disgust, "Yes, sir, but not before we had a very shameful incident."

"That doesn't surprise me." Will recalled the scene in the town square the previous day. "Did the men refuse to follow orders?"

"Not exactly, sir. They followed the wrong orders, at least until Major Bridges sorted things out."

Will sipped his tea, "Pray tell, Mr. Cattle."

"I am ashamed to have to admit to you, sir, that two senior British officers surrendered nearly a thousand men without a fight."

"Good Lord, Sergeant Major, that don't sound like this army."

"No, sir, it's not. But yesterday afternoon, even while those too sick and weak were being hauled away in carts and whatever else we could lay hands on, Colonel Ellington and Colonel Mainwaring surrendered the Warwicks and the Dublin Fusiliers."

"Great Scott!"

"Did it all proper they did—signed the documents and handed them to the mayor so the Germans wouldn't destroy the town." Cattle's moustache twitched indignantly as he told the story.

"So who's Major Bridges, and how did he sort it out?"

"That's Major Tom Bridges of the Fourth Dragoons, sir, a cavalry gent. Seems he was another straggler who had escaped going in the bag back at Mons. He managed to rejoin his men, and when they rode into St. Quentin he found out what had happened. They say he was bleedin' furious," Cattle chortled at the idea.

"I bet he was."

"They say he nearly throttled the mayor, snatched the surrender documents back and put Ellington and Mainwaring under arrest."

"Can a major do that to a colonel?" Will asked.

"When the colonel's a cowardly shit he can, sir." Will could see Cattle would expect him to have done the same thing without a second thought. "Anyway," the Sergeant Major continued, "having straightened that out and *un*-surrendered them in a manner of speaking, he had the problem of stirring up the men lying around in the square. At first they wouldn't obey his orders, saying they didn't want any interference from the bleedin' cavalry, and they wouldn't budge. Said they were taking orders from their old man only."

"So how the hell did he make them march?"

"Shamed 'em into it, sir. He broke into a toyshop and grabbed a tin whistle and a drum. He had his trumpeter march 'round and 'round playing *British Grenadiers* on the whistle while he followed banging on the drum. He got them all on their feet and then led them out like the bloomin' Pied Piper. *And* he had his horse led and marched at their head all the way down past here to Ham. They came through yesterday evening, and I lined the men up, and we cheered them on their way. That Mr. Bridges deserves to be made a general."

"He surely does. What about the two colonels?"

Cattle looked as if he might spit but restrained himself, "Arrested and to be tried by court-martial, sir. I hope they'll be shot. I'll volunteer to command the firing party."

Under the circumstances Will found Cattle's uncompromising attitude understandable, but he had one more question, "Sergeant Major, where the hell are we?"

"La Fere, sir. The patrols will be leaving as soon as it's light, and as soon as they're gone, we move onto Compiegne. Major Higgins is making sure we don't risk losing anybody again. The aircraft will go straight there, so we need to move the Bovril van smartish if you don't mind, sir. The gentlemen have come to rely on it for finding the new field—it being bright red."

Will gulped the last of his tea, "Then we better crack on, Sergeant Major." Cattle saluted, and Will hobbled off to find some breakfast. He knew he had a hard day in front of him, a day of nonstop work followed by another, then another. The RFC moved steadily south, leapfrogging ahead of the retreating army, helping when they could by carrying footsore, exhausted men on their already overloaded transport. The dreadful journey continued day-after-day. The names of the towns and villages were entered into squadron records—Senlis, Juilly, Serris—but the details of each field merged into a blur for the pilots and mechanics as they fought their own battle to keep the battered planes in the air. The beautiful summer weather had given way to low cloud, mist and often a thin driving rain that swept across the field chilling them to the bone as they worked on the battered airplanes.

Will looked up from the wing spar he was inspecting as Higgins bustled up. A small, hairy dog of doubtful pedigree now trotted with him, one of the many strays abandoned by the refugees making their own way to safety. Will pressed his thumb into the wood, "Look at that, sir." Moisture squeezed out.

Higgins adjusted his monocle and bent closer. "Good Lord! We're in danger of sinking. Will it fly?"

Will grimaced, "*Just*, sir. Providing the engine will run long enough, the curvature of the earth will make the ground fall away—I can't promise a climb."

"Bad as that?"

"Bad as that, sir."

"Well, I have some good news. We're here, and this is where we stay for a while." It had been ten long days since Will had caught up with the RFC at St. Quentin.

"Beg pardon, sir," Will asked, "but where exactly is *here*."

"A place called Melun. We're nearly thirty miles south and east of Paris. We've stayed one step ahead of Von Kluck since Le Cateau. Lord above only knows why he set off in the wrong direction; he must have thought we were beaten and heading back to the coast. It would never surprise me if the officer in charge of the cavalry unit you chased out of that farm reported that he had been attacked by a full brigade and that experience convinced Von Kluck we had a strong force to the west."

Will looked askance at Higgins, "It would be kinda good to think so, but do you think that's likely, sir?"

"Put yourself in Captain Fritz von Frankfurter's place. Would you go back to headquarters and admit you had been bested by a dozen ragamuffin riflemen and a flightless RFC man?"

Will grinned, "Not if I wanted to stay a captain."

"Precisely. So it's quite likely the thought followed the wish. They wanted to believe we were beaten, and a fierce action west of Le Cateau convinced them. If Von Kluck hadn't been so eager to believe we were finished, he would have realized that he had very few prisoners. Beaten armies yield up thousands of prisoners. All they have are the wounded we couldn't move—who are now a burden on their medical service."

"Do you think they are being cared for, sir?"

"I believe they are. In fact, they are making propaganda capital out of it. Pictures have appeared in the papers of our boys in hospital in Germany, and there was an article boasting how they had saved one poor chap's life by pulling a bullet out of his head." Higgins pulled a piece of paper from his pocket. "Anyway, the situation is changing by the minute. We have joined up with the French and the retreat is over. This is where we turn the Germans back."

"You sound very confident, sir."

Higgins grunted. "I'll forgive you that remark, Turner, seeing as you're not experienced," he glared. "Of course I'm bloody confident—I'm paid to be."

"Sorry, sir."

Higgins smiled again, "And I've seen the reinforcements coming up, thousands of them from Paris itself. An extraordinary sight, all rolling along in taxis and buses as if they were off on an outing. But it would be a damn sight easier if we knew what Von Kluck is up to. We are certain the Germans are making a wheeling movement to the southeast instead of encircling Paris. Biffy Borton and Furse are sure they saw formations moving that way. But it's back to the old story, HQ won't believe them."

Will carefully fixed the repair patch to the wing as he spoke, "Why ever not? Surely we've shown what we can do."

"I'm sure we have," Higgins agreed, "but on this occasion I can understand why they're doubtful."

"Why's that, sir?"

"Because it's madness. It means the Germans abandoning their precious Schlieffen Plan to try to outflank the French, ignoring the fact that we are here threatening their right flank as they cross from west to east in front of us along the line of the River Marne. It means Von Kluck really does think we have ceased to exist as a force. It is, to put it bluntly, too bloody good to be true. But if it is," Higgins balled his fists and looked to the sky, "we'll give them such a good hiding." He looked hard at Will. "And that's why I'm here."

"You want me to go searchin' for Germans, sir?" he sounded hopeful. It had been weeks since he had felt the soaring rush into the sky.

"Do you mind, Turner?" It seemed to Will a strange way to order him into the air. Higgins continued, "I know I gave you a rollicking for taking Sergeant Major Cattle on that unauthorized recce at Mons, but I need every machine, and this is the only one left. It needs more than a pilot and an observer—it needs a man who can keep it in the air and get it back up again if it packs up and has to force land."

Will slammed his toolbox shut. "I'm your man, sir, I've no trainin' as an observer, but I can see an' write notes. I'll grab my gear. She's as ready as she ever will be." He nodded at the big Farman Shorthorn he had patched up.

"No, Turner, you will fly her—Lieutenant Matrett will be your observer."

"But this is Mr. Matrett's machine, sir, he'll be awful put out," Will offered politely.

"Correction, Mr. Turner, this is Lieutenant Matrett's *fifth* machine. Despite your best efforts, he has written off four others," his irritation showed, "I must remind you that *I* decide who flies."

Will saluted, "Thank you, sir."

Higgins gave a grim smile, "I'm probably saving your life. Now, Captain Tyler has your orders, on your way, quick as you can." He clicked his fingers to the dog, "Come on Hindenburg."

Matrett accepted his role with bad grace. Will tried to ease the atmosphere between them as they strapped into the Farman. "I've no experience as an observer, Matrett. That's why the boss has put you in the hot seat."

Matrett sat in the front seat of the nacelle. "Just shut up and drive, Turner, and make sure you take us where I tell you."

Will looked at Nichol the mechanic and shrugged. He made a circular motion in the air with his finger, and the motor started. Louis Strange had helped him grind the valves on the engine of Matrett's machine the previous evening, and the big Renault responded well, though it was clearly at a disadvantage due to age and hard use. Will opened the throttle. He patiently urged the Farman into a trot. As soon as he could, he pushed hard on the controls to raise the tailskid. Freed from the dragging friction of the mud, the ungainly biplane picked up its skirts and started to canter. Will pushed hard on the throttle to gain the last ounce of power. The wings were flexing now, taking the weight, but he resisted the urge to lift off too early. They were galloping across the field, but the hedge grew closer and seemingly higher by the second. With a spark of malicious glee he saw that Matrett's hands were gripping the edge of the cockpit. He pulled firmly back on the controls, a fraction later than he needed. The wheels left the ground cleanly and cleared the hedge by inches.

Matrett had sunk lower into his seat as the hedge loomed, but he would not give Will the satisfaction of seeing him rattled. Will thought he heard the word "bastard" from the front seat. He leaned forward pretending to misunderstand. "Yes," he yelled, "I had to pull hard."

Will sat back with a smile and concentrated on gaining height. He found it hard work. He tried every trick he knew, but after twenty minutes they had barely struggled to one thousand feet. The machine sagged in his hands. The left wing tended to drop unless he held the stick permanently to one side. The drag on that wing forced him to compensate with right rudder. He knew this meant they were flying in what Will called an unbalanced condition. He felt acutely aware that allowing the Farman to stall would provoke a spin similar to the one that nearly put him into the ground at Hendon, and this time there would be no pulling out. Nevertheless, a stall seemed imminent as he patiently balanced available power against the angle at which he allowed the wings to meet the flow of air.

In spite of the reluctance of their machine, Will felt surging elation. The weather had cleared at last, and they staggered through a sky studded with hurrying clouds in a background of washed blue. The visibility seemed limitless in all directions. A broad river snaked across the landscape in their path, sliding off to their left where they could see a city, now quite clear on the horizon. Will peered at it then slapped Matrett on the shoulder, "I be damned, Matrett, look...you can just make out the Eiffel Tower."

Matrett glanced in the direction will pointed. "We're not on a sightseeing tour, Turner, just concentrate on what you're doing."

Will leaned forward and shouted in good humor, "Matrett, I think it's important you should know, just in case we're killed, that you are a complete and utter asshole. You should know that before you die."

To Will's surprise, Matrett ignored his provocation. He just pointed, "Take us down and follow the line of that river."

Will shrugged. Perhaps he knows, he thought. He eased the throttle a fraction and the Farman sagged gratefully into a shallow dive. Will held them at seven hundred feet. Matrett pointed down with another angry jab of his finger. "If we go lower we'll be in range of every rifle an' machine gun in the German army—if they are down there," Will shouted.

Matrett twisted in his seat. He pushed up his goggles. "That's the idea—if they start shooting at us we'll see the flashes. Scared, Turner?" he sneered.

Without replying, Will pushed firmly on the stick and felt the weightless sensation as the Farman pitched into a dive. At four hundred feet they trundled steadily across the plains to the east of Paris in search of the elusive German army. After half an hour, which put them almost to the northwest of the capital, Matrett turned to him again.

"This is where they should be if they are trying to surround Paris," he called back. It was the first civil thing he had said during the flight. Will hoped that they could conclude their patrol in a professional, if not cordial, manner. "Go lower still and work back toward Meux. I know where the missing cavalry corps might be, and they'll be in the vanguard." Will had to admire Matrett's determination and respect his experience—more so ten minutes later.

"Bloody hell, Turner! There they are!" Will banked the Farman to give them a better view. He looked straight down the line of his wings at a concentration of streams and river backwaters where dozens of horses drank their fill while the riders lounged nearby. Long lines of tethered mounts stood gathered in farmyards. Will rolled the Farman level and eased into a turn toward the south. "Where the hell are you going, Turner?"

"Back to the field, of course. We've found them an' this old bird is not goin' to stay in the air much longer." Will had picked up an irregular beat in the motor, and subtle vibrations through his hands and feet told him they could not rely on staying airborne.

Matrett pointed north, "That way, Turner—do as you're told."

"Okay, Mr. Matrett, if that's what you want." He heaved the controls over and sent the Farman wheeling over the heads of the cavalry.

"Take us over that wood," Matrett indicated a forest north of the river. They crawled toward it at three hundred feet. Will looked in disbelief as hundreds of gray-clad figures rushed from the edge of the trees. Even at that height he could see the flashes from hundreds of rifles aimed at them. Simultaneously, he felt the controls jerk in his hands as bullets crashed through the wings and tail surfaces. Matrett turned to him, a look of fierce triumph in his eyes. "Found 'em, by gad! The top brass will have to be—," he paused for a second and turned to look down as Will forced the controls over, trading height for speed to take them away, "—lieve us now."

Will stared at him, horrified. As Matrett spoke the last words, bright blood burst through his lips to blow back over Will's shoulder. "You damn fool, Matrett, you're hit."

Matrett looked at him stupidly, "Oh blast." He put his hand to his chest where Will could see two smoking holes in the fabric of his flying coat. Strangely, no blood came from them. Matrett smiled weakly, "Better go home then."

Will cursed and pushed the throttle wide. The protesting engine shuddered. They could barely maintain height and Will could see they now faced a headwind. He looked right and left. If he flew back toward Paris he would be flying over the massed formations that must surely be pushing from that direction. The cavalry units were between him and safety. Will made a quick decision. He would angle to the east, try to pass ahead of the Germans and then back to the RFC field—*if* the Farman would fly long enough.

Matrett had collapsed in his seat, moving feebly. Will tried to gauge how far they needed to fly. It had to be twenty miles to the British lines, but he could put down as soon as he saw friendly troops. He looked longingly to the south, but even as he did the motor coughed, hesitated and then ran on. It might as well be twenty thousand miles, he thought bitterly. Why the hell had he allowed Matrett to taunt him into such a stupid stunt once they knew the position of the cavalry? He struggled on, coaxing the Farman through the air.

Looking ahead, Will saw another enemy formation camped by the edge of a field. From two hundred feet he could easily see vehicles and horses and even upturned faces. He flinched, expecting another fusillade of bullets, and tried to ease the biplane away. What insignia is that? he thought dumbly—a big red cross on a white circle.

Matrett stirred himself to look at Will as he heard him cut the switches to stop the motor. "What the hell are you doing?"

Will could not hear the words, he just saw Matrett's lips moving in pooled blood. "Saving your fool life," he bellowed. He concentrated on an inevitable crash landing. The Farman, once so reluctant to fly, now seemed bent on prolonging its life. They were in danger of overshooting the field. Will thrust his right foot hard against the rudder and pushed the stick to the left while pulling back. The big machine staggered in a sideslip, hanging for a moment almost stationary before subsiding gracefully to the ground. Will let go of the controls as they hit, and put his arms over his head. He expected an impact, but there was none—just a splintering, shattering, screeching crash that went on for what seemed like minutes. The noise stopped. He looked around. He almost laughed. They sat, still strapped in their seats, on the ground in what looked like the makings of a bonfire. "Christ!" he swore. "A bonfire." He unbuckled his seat belt and then tugged his observer clear of the wreck.

Matrett was still conscious. Glaring at Will, he found enough strength for words, "You treacherous bastard...you cowardly swine. You've surrendered."

Will looked in the direction of the massive tent he had seen from the air. A dozen men were hurrying toward them, but two individuals, one wearing a white coat, were sprinting ahead of the others. Matrett suddenly moved against his legs where Will had propped him. Will looked down in disbelief as Matrett struggled to draw his service revolver. Will bent down, snatched it from Matrett's hand and threw it away from them. He straightened up and raised both his hands high in the air. "*Kamerad,*" he shouted.

The two Germans in the lead ignored him and skidded to a halt. The one in the white coat dropped to his knees and tore Matrett's coat open. He looked up at Will who suddenly felt foolish. "Where is he hit, just in the chest?"

Will dropped his hands and squatted down, "I think so, Doctor." The man's profession was obvious, not just from his attitude but also from the stethoscope that he now pressed to Matrett's chest.

"Ah," he said with that mixture of determination and triumph familiar when a first diagnosis is confirmed. "One or two bullets through the lung, but just one lung I think." He put his hand on Matrett's back, "Yes, a sucking wound." The orderly with him, an older man, had a large, compressed dressing ready and handed it to the doctor who put it in place and listened to the stethoscope again. "*Ja, gut. Sehr gut.*" He looked at Will and smiled reassuringly. "I think we can save your friend."

"Thank you, Doctor...for getting here so quickly, I mean."

"Thank you, *Herr Leutnant,* for delivering the patient to my hospital, and so soon after he was wounded. I wish it was always the case." He was a small man with tiny, steel-rimmed glasses and a goatee.

"You speak English very well, sir."

"Thank you, I should. I studied at Oxford and worked at the London Hospital in Whitechapel. Rosenthal is the name." He turned to direct the team loading Matrett onto a stretcher.

Will noticed none of the men who had rushed across the field, and who now studied the wreck of the Farman with undisguised curiosity, were armed. He turned back to the doctor, "I declare, I have no idea of the correct military procedure, I suppose I am your prisoner."

The doctor regarded him carefully. " I suppose you are," he said. Then added, "You're not British are you?"

"No, sir, Canadian," Will answered quickly, feeling a sudden chill.

Dr. Rosenthal smiled and raised his eyebrows, "Really?" Then he pointed to the hospital tent. "Come, I must work quickly on your friend, my operating theatre is free at the moment. You, too, must be checked for injury."

"I'm okay, sir, just a few bruises I think."

"Even so, there will be after-effects that will surprise you after an experience like this."

Will found, to his surprise, that the doctor was absolutely right. They sat him in a tent to wait for an escort to take him away. Within ten minutes his whole body started to shake. His teeth chattered, and he watched his hands shuddering as if they belonged to someone else. An orderly looked him over sympathetically. The spasm passed, and the orderly soon returned with a clear liquid in a glass. "*Trinken Sie,*" he ordered.

Will took the glass. "Medicine?" he asked in English.

The orderly nodded eagerly and laughed. "*Ja, Medizin—Prost!*"

Will drank it down in one gulp, the fiery spirit burning his throat but creating a warm glow in his belly. He held the glass away from him and studied it. "Schnapps?" he asked.

"*Ja, Schnapps.*"

Will thanked the orderly. He looked around—nobody seemed to be taking much interest in him. He knew his duty was to escape, but these people have just been so damn kind, he thought. He knew it was ridiculous, but he feared his hosts would get into fearful trouble if he escaped. Not only that, but they were not even acting like the military despite the uniforms. Maybe it was the effect of the Schnapps, he thought, but he resolved to make his escape from *real* soldiers. He did not have long to wait before they arrived. A car pulled up at the entrance to the field hospital. Dr. Rosenthal appeared with blood on his apron.

"I am pleased to report your friend has survived the operation to remove one bullet from his body. The other passed through him. I think his chances are excellent. I am afraid we must part, however. Your escort is here to take you to headquarters."

Will ignored the blood and shook the doctor's hand warmly. "I appreciate all you have done for Mr. Matrett. I hope we will meet again under better circumstances."

"So do I, Mr. Turner." As Will turned to follow the escort to the car, Dr. Rosenthal called after him. "Oh, and give my regards to Toronto when you get home. I spent a semester there as well."

Will smiled and waved a hand as he climbed into the car. Damn, he thought, just my luck to meet the only man in the German army who can recognize a Canadian. He soon found he was wrong. His interview at the local headquarters of this part of the German First Army was conducted in a magnificent study, clearly just vacated by the owner, in a beautiful country house. Not quite a chateau, but impressive as far as Will was concerned. The officer questioning him spoke perfect English. He was a tall, blond-haired man with the flowing moustache that seemed to be fashionable with cavalry men. He was cordial, but by no means friendly; not that Will expected him to be. After five minutes of questioning, in which Will steadfastly refused to divulge any more than name, rank and serial number, the German officer turned to his aide and announced, in German, that the British airman in front of them was no more a Canadian than he was. Something unpleasant took hold of Will's stomach as he heard the officer go on to tell his assistant that he would bet a horse's arse to a bottle of champagne that Lieutenant Turner was an American from the southern states. He even came perilously close by guessing Georgia as Will's home.

Will said nothing, just smiled. He had one trump card. There was no reason they should know he spoke German. He had not used it while at the hospital because he had only spoken with the doctor in English. He knew he had to escape, and now thoroughly regretted not slipping away from the hospital. This headquarters was run on strictly military lines, and he wondered how he would manage his getaway. He needed a plan, but then Nathan had always advised "running with your luck." Will wondered if his luck might be running out.

The officer shuffled the papers in front of him, placed them on the table, then took out a tiny penknife and slowly sharpened his pencil. He leaned forward suddenly, "Lieutenant Turner, I put it to you that —," he broke off as there was a knock on the door and an NCO put his head into the room. "Yes, what is it?"

"The messenger is on his way from GHQ, sir. We need your signature for the orders."

The officer broke off the interview, ordering Will placed in an anteroom next to the main entrance of the house. He examined the room. A small chaise lounge was set against the wall and an ornate writing desk received the light from a high window looking out over the garden. He guessed it was a lady's study. He heard the key turn in the lock. No escape that way, he thought, as he paced quickly to the window. A complete troop of cavalry had their horses picketed on the lawn. For the first time a wave of despair swept over him. Will Turner, you are in for it now, he thought miserably.

Will sat on the chaise lounge and gazed longingly at the blue sky through the window. Thoughts of home flooded him. He wondered what his family would be doing now. He glanced at his wristwatch. It would be breakfast. He tried to recall the exact details of the kitchen where they often ate. It was strangely comforting to try to remember the exact number of plates on the dresser, the sun streaming through the window past the gingko tree in the yard. But as he sat there another more urgent feeling came over him.

Damn, I need to pee, he thought. He tapped on the door. "Excuse me, soldier, I need to use the bathroom." He stood back as the door opened. Will pointed to a door on the other side of the big hallway that showed a discreet WC sign.

The soldier grinned, "*Ja, naturlich,*" he motioned Will through the door. The bathroom was remarkably spacious and ornate but very much in keeping with the nature of the house, tasteful but with all modern conveniences. He had heard much about French plumbing, but this was as good as any he had seen in England. A row of urinals with gleaming brass pipework stood against a tiled wall. Behind them two cubicles with heavy, carved oak doors offered relief to the hard-pressed occupant. He selected a urinal and stood before it.

In midstream the door from the hall burst open and a man rushed in. Bringing with him the scent of fresh air and burnt castor oil. "*Entschuldigung!*" he called breezily as he excused his abrupt entry.

He dived into the nearest cubicle, and Will heard the unmistakable sounds of a man relieving himself of severe intestinal distress.

"I'm sorry," Will called over the top of the stall as he buttoned his fly, "I don't speak German." He was determined to stick with that line.

"Oh, sorry, old chap," the reply came back in perfect but slightly-accented English. "Are you British?"

"Canadian—shot down this mornin' an' taken prisoner."

"Oh dear, what rotten luck."

"Are you another Oxford man?" Will asked, amused despite himself.

"Goodness, no! Cambridge. Look, pardon me if I don't shake hands, I think I might be here some time."

"No you carry on," Will urged.

"Flyer, eh?" the disembodied voice continued. "Have you ever flown behind one of these damn rotaries?"

"Only for short hops, but I've heard the stories."

"Well, they're all true! I've never known anything like it. We've all got the shits from breathing all those castor oil fumes. My pilot, Feldwebel Bergmann, only just made it to the bogs back at HQ, but I am an officer—I made it this far." He chuckled. "Well, good luck my Canadian friend, I hope we can meet again one day when this is over."

"So do I," Will called as he opened the door to the hall. He meant it. He liked the sound of the distressed but jolly Cambridge man.

As Will stepped out into the hallway, a different soldier from the one who had released him snapped to attention and saluted.

"I am sorry, sir, your car has been called away on another urgent mission. But we have a motorcycle with a sidecar to take you back to HQ." Will nodded, surprised that the man should address him with such a long, complex sentence in German. The soldier thrust a folder at him and a black, bound book that Will could see had columns filled with numbers against which signatures had been penned. The soldier pointed at a space and handed him a pen. Will signed with a flourish. You have to hand it to these fellas, he thought, they certainly are organized, they've made up a file on me already.

Will put the folder under his arm. The soldier saluted with a click of his heels, and Will returned it, impressing himself with how well he made the click. The soldier motioned to the main door and Will stepped back into the fresh air, buttoning his flying coat to the collar and pulling on his helmet in preparation for the ride in the sidecar.

The motorcycle chuffed gently, the rider standing to attention alongside. He saluted and waited until Will climbed into the sidecar. They moved off smartly, a spray of gravel spurting from the back wheel. Will looked around carefully. It must be some kind of trap, he thought, perhaps they want me to try to escape, then they can shoot me. The driver of the motorcycle wasn't even armed, and he seemed so polite. He leaned over to speak to Will. "I'm sorry your car was called away, *Herr Leutnant.* After it brought you here there was an order for him to return immediately to the railway station."

Will digested the information for a moment. What the hell was the man talking about? he asked himself, and why do they all keep using German as if they know I understand. It's as if they think I *am* a German officer. He sat bolt upright. Without saying a word he carefully eased the folder open. It contained maps and typed orders. Will caught his breath. Holy shit! he muttered under his breath. It suddenly fit. The shift had changed. If the man who had handed him the file had not been there when the German flyer rushed in and went straight to the men's room he would not have known that there were *two* aviators in the building. Unlike most British airmen who wore a light brown leather flying coat, Will's was black, just like his German counterparts, and he had fastened it almost to the top, covering his khaki tunic, when he came out of the bathroom. The soldier had been ordered to release the folder to the aviator, and that is just what he had done. Breathing slowly he replied to his driver. "*Kein Problem.*"

The driver smiled and whipped them through a bend. Having been so slow to catch onto his good fortune, Will thought fast. He could be in even more trouble if he was caught with the information in the folder. They already knew he was not who he claimed to be. With this information in his possession they could shoot him as a spy.

Perhaps that was the trap, he thought, they had planted the evidence. Then he admonished himself. This was not one of his crime novels. This was war, and what was that his uncle had said about paperwork and procedures? Something about it being an excuse for people not to think for themselves. He would ride his luck for all it was worth.

Will pushed himself up in his seat to speak to the driver. He prayed his German was good enough to pass himself off, "Did you come from HQ?"

"Yes, sir."

"Is my aircraft in the same position? Feldwebel Bergmann has not moved it?"

"No, sir, it is still behind the house in the meadow."

"Good," Will said, while thinking, thank you, Lord. A plan was forming in his mind as the journey came quickly to an end. They could not have travelled more than two miles when a magnificent chateau came in sight. This was the real thing, glistening white in the afternoon sun, ornamental turrets at either end of the façade and an entrance drive between ornamental gates leading past formal gardens to an imposing entrance. A circular courtyard with a fountain in the center of the circle allowed carriages to deposit their occupants at the foot of the stone stairs and continue with ease. Will prayed the sheer size of this palatial residence would work to his benefit. He had to play this role for all it was worth.

He hopped out of the sidecar, saluted the driver and trotted up the stairs. Two soldiers guarding the door presented arms as he reached the top step, slightly breathless. He marched confidently inside. A desk had been set up in the hall. Will gasped—the place was magnificent. The floor was laid with black and white marble and massive pillars supported the roof lost in the shadows above. Heavily carved screens separated galleries from the drop into the hall on each floor. He did not pause. He caught the eye of the orderly at the desk and mouthed the word "*Klosett?*" pointing into the depths of the building. The man smiled politely and said, "Down the hall, right to the end, sir."

Will marched on. Toilets were featuring heavily in his day. He nodded curtly to a soldier leaving a room deep inside the hall. He turned a corner and nearly walked into an elderly officer carrying a sheaf of papers. His heart leaped into his mouth but he stepped smartly to one side, clicked his heels and bowed his head sharply as he had seen others do inside buildings. This seemed to replace a salute while indoors. The old man ignored him.

Will fought the urge to run. He turned another corner. A gallery ran along the rear of the chateau, looking over the gardens. He guessed at one time it may have been open to the elements, but now tall windows ran along its length. Damn, he thought, the gardens were at a lower level at the rear of the house. It would look too obvious if he opened a window and dropped to the ground. He walked quickly to the door at the far end. It was open, revealing a short flight of steps. He took them two at a time, and, finding another door at the bottom, he opened it. He was out, in the garden. He breathed again; just being in the open air was a relief.

Will glanced around. The direct approach had worked every time. He strode purposefully straight down the path between the lawns to a tiled area at the end. This had a stone balustrade protecting strollers from falling twenty feet to the meadow beyond. He leaned on the stonework. The plane was there. And so, obviously, was Sergeant Bergmann, the pilot, recovered from the effects of the rotary engine. He stood leaning casually against the wing chatting with a group of curious soldiers. Will smiled through his disappointment. It was asking too much to get away with stealing an airplane to fly home. With the real pilot there he had no chance of passing himself off as the authentic observer. He had to think—and fast. Could I walk back? he asked himself, or maybe just hole up in some wood and wait for our side to advance. He suddenly realized he was in full view of the chateau and marched quickly to the corner of the lawn. In a few quick paces he moved into the shrubs bordering the gardens. He needed time to catch his breath, and think. The cover provided him with that time; he was hidden from the view of anybody looking from the chateau, or from the meadow. Speed had worked for him so far, it could not be much more than ten minutes since he climbed into the sidecar. It was even possible his unseen friend might still be cloistered in the men's room, but he doubted it. The hue and cry must have started. They would know the motorcyclist had delivered him to the chateau. He had to move fast.

A steady noise had been in his ears since he had been in the garden and now it impinged on his conscious hearing. He peered cautiously from his hiding place. It was heavy transport moving down a major highway bordering the grounds. The sound he had heard was the muttering of gasoline engines and the clatter of driving chains and solid-tire wheels on the road. He straightened up. Where is the last place, he asked himself, I would look for an escaped prisoner? He sprinted through the shrubs and crouched to avoid detection from the house. He slid through the hedge, glanced up and down the road, then stepped boldly out in a gap between the convoys of trucks heading south. A solitary vehicle approached. He stepped out with his hand held high. "Driver, you must take me to our advanced landing ground. My plane is down in this field, and I must go for help." He jerked a thumb at the airplane standing in the meadow behind the chateau. It made for a beautifully plausible explanation and the driver responded as he hoped. He stood up in his cab to get a better view of the machine.

"Of course, sir. Where is the landing ground?"

"Where our advanced landing ground always is, soldier, as close to the damned British as we can be." He spoke harshly but instantly regretted it. Liam Power often spoke of "over-egging the pudden" and he feared he might have just done it. But he need not have worried.

"Of course, sir. I will take you as close as possible. Here, let me move these lazy swine." Two men sagged on the seat next to him, snoring with mouths open.

"No!" Will realized he had spoken too loudly. He had no wish to ride in the front of the truck, clearly visible. He needed to be safely hidden under the canvas top covering the back. He softened his tone, "You infantry have earned a few moments rest, leave them, I will ride with the others in the back." Will could not be sure if it was surprise or gratitude in the man's face, but he moved quickly to the rear of the truck where eager hands hauled him in. He was aware of a general straightening up in the two rows of men facing each other on the long wooden seats running the length of the load bed. They shuffled up to make room for him. He knew he had to keep up his pretense. "What regiment men? I am a flier, not one of your regular army types." He prayed they were not Bavarians who would recognize his accent and ask questions about their assumed shared home.

"Brandenburg Grenadiers, sir," the soldier facing him replied politely. Will breathed a silent prayer of relief. "Did you have trouble with your machine?"

"Yes, damned ignition system, too much for me to repair I'm afraid." He did not volunteer too much for fear of saying something contradictory.

Will knew he must prompt the soldiers into talking to him. From experience he was certain that would not be too difficult. "Have you boys seen any action?" It was enough. Before long he was being regaled with stories of their exploits. He prompted from time-to-time, recognizing snippets of information that could be useful. He quickly found he was heading toward the "enemy", the tense atmosphere in the truck told him that anyway, but he also learned from the sergeant that all reserves were fully committed. He revealed that when he bemoaned the fact that he had not had more time to "lick these farm boys into shape."

The sargeant jerked a thumb at the two soldiers sitting next to Will. They looked no more than schoolboys, "Wouldn't wonder if they didn't lie about their ages, sir." The two lads smiled shyly and looked at their boots. The convoy made good time on the empty roads. There were no refugees to impede the progress of the conquering army. Will calculated he must have put a good fifteen miles between him and the chateau. He made the calculation again in his head. Hell's teeth, he thought to himself, unless the BEF has pulled back even further we must be nearly at the battle lines. He saw the countryside they were driving through was the same he had moved past a few days before in his own transport. He pondered the difficulty of extracting himself from his present company, congenial though it was, when the solution came screaming toward them. The truck slammed to a stop, sending them sprawling in the back. A whistle shrilled, drowned by a steadily gathering howl.

"Out! Out! Everybody out!" the sergeant screamed. "Into the ditch!" Will tumbled from the truck, a rush of bodies flew past him. A bright flower of flame blossomed on the road behind them, a geyser of smoke and dust erupting above it. Another closer. Then another. A thousand screaming banshees howled above them. He saw the two young recruits standing rooted to the spot. He acted instinctively. He spread his arms, charged them down and hurled them into the ditch, covering their bodies with his own. Something hit him on the back. The noise stopped as suddenly as it started.

Will hauled himself out of the ditch. A large clod of earth had struck him between the shoulders. The sergeant brushed him down. "What the hell was that?" he stopped, had he said that in English? He looked anxiously at the faces around him, if he had, nobody had noticed, their ears were probably ringing like his.

"British horse artillery, sir, probably eighteen pounders," the sergeant said confidently. "They dash out, fire a salvo or two, and then run away."

"Cowardly swine," Will said, determined to keep in character.

"Nearly caught us though, sir. No casualties, thanks to you." He beckoned to the two soldiers saved by Will's quick reflexes. "You two, come here and thank this officer for saving your miserable lives."

They stood to attention and saluted. "Thank you, sir."

Will decided he could afford to play the benevolent leader. "Any time, men. Now remember, next time your NCO says take cover—take cover!"

"*Ja, Herr Leutnant.*"

Will looked around, searching for an excuse. "Quick, men, get moving. My comrades are this way," he pointed vaguely over the fields. "I think it is safer if I walk from here."

The sergeant stood to attention. "As you wish, sir, and thank you again."

"On your way, and good luck. See you in Paris." Will waved to the departing truck. "In peacetime with one of Mr. Cook's tourist plans I hope," he added under his breath. He slipped off the road and worked his way along a hedge until he was sure he was out of sight. More transport moved down the road, but he made another quick calculation. One of the pilots in Two Squadron had been an artillery officer. Will remembered listening to him extolling the virtues of the eighteen pounder. If the German Grenadier sergeant was correct, the maximum those shells could have been fired from would be six-and-a-half thousand yards, a little over three-and-a-half miles. Will decided he must be in some sort of no man's land between the two sides where they were jockeying for position.

A dense wood stood between him and the British. Will moved forward cautiously. In ten minutes he had plunged into the darkness of the trees. He had never in his life felt so good being in a forest. He laid down and checked his watch. It was still only early afternoon. Will was tempted to wait for darkness to escape, but he reluctantly opened the folder and looked inside, then groaned. There were pages documenting intended troop movements for the next three days, with maps covered in arrows annotated with numbers. "Shit!" he swore out loud. "This stuff is important."

The forest was deliciously cool, full of the sweet scents of damp wood and growth. It would be so good to just curl up here and wait for the whole damn thing to turn around and let the war roll past him. As far as the RFC were concerned he was either dead or captured. As far as the Germans were concerned he had escaped. They were too busy trying to conquer France to worry much about him, though he guessed they would be fuming over the loss of these papers.

A movement nearby made him jump. A squirrel clung to a tree trunk, staring at him. "What should I do?" he asked. The squirrel glared, chattered, then scampered up the tree. "Damn, you're right, my duty—they do pay me, after all." He moved off through the trees, treading as quietly as he could and keeping his senses tuned for any signs of human activity. The wood proved to be more vast than Will expected, but the going was relatively easy. Deep paths criss-crossed under the canopy of oak and ash. Will surmised this might be some big landowner's private hunting ground. He laughed at the memory of the young subaltern who only guarded three sides of their first field at Maubeuge because one side was private property. He tried to work out how long ago that had been. It felt like a lifetime but could only have been three weeks before, at the most.

His woodsman's instincts guided him well. By late afternoon he found the trees thinning, a well-made road ran through the very edge of the forest. He debated which direction to take and had just decided to cross and keep moving south when a movement in the distance caught his eye. A small party of men marched along the road. He shrank back into the trees and lay flat. They were still a mile away, too far to distinguish uniforms. After five minutes he was sure they were not wearing the spiked helmet he had seen on many of the German troops, but, still, some of them wore a flat peakless cap like a sailor's hat. In another five minutes he was confident the men coming toward him wore khaki like his own. They were British infantry. He sat back against a tree and waited. His only problem now was to join up with them without getting shot by mistake.

He thought he had solved the problem. He waited until they were opposite where he waited. He called from behind the security of a tree trunk for cover, "Hey, army! Don't shoot." He was amazed and impressed at the reaction. The squad seemed to evaporate. They dropped flat in the undergrowth on the far side of the road. All he could see was a dozen rifle muzzles pointing in his general direction. "Hell, fellas, I don't blame you bein' nervous, but I'm a British officer, RFC, shot down on the other side."

"Show yourself," The peremptory order came back. There was something in the man's tone that made Will hang back.

"Now hold on there, soldier, let's be careful here." There was a silence for a moment. Then another voice called.

"Step out where we can see you, with your hands up." They didn't leave Will much choice. He unbuttoned his coat to reveal his uniform and stepped into the light with his hands held high above his head. The soldiers slowly stood up from their cover, and the corporal in charge advanced cautiously on Will.

"Don't you think you might be oversteppin' the mark, Corporal?" Before Will had a chance to even lower his hands the corporal stepped forward and with a lightning movement reversed his rifle and slammed the butt into Will's stomach. He collapsed, too winded to even protest. Will tried to suck air, but before he could the corporal's boot slammed into his ribs. Will curled into a ball to protect himself.

"You're no British officer with an accent like that," he snarled. "I don't know what you're trying to pull, but I'll bloody soon find out." He lashed out again with his boot. This time it caught Will on the shoulder and he groaned.

"Hold on," one of the others protested, "there's all types in the Flying Corps, he might be an Australian or something."

The corporal rounded on him, "When I want your opinion, I'll bleedin' well ask for it Huggins. In the meantime I'll deal with this bloody spy my way." He lifted his foot to lash out again but this time he found himself propelled up and back. Will had seized his boot, twisting and pushing viciously. Before the corporal could do anything about it, he was flat on his back with Will's knee on his chest and the point of his own bayonet in his right nostril. Will's face was inches from his own and his hand was around his throat.

Will's voice was surprisingly level. The more experienced men in the squad knew it was dangerously level. "Let me explain again, *Private*, because that's sure as hell what you're goin' to be tomorrow. I am Lieutenant William Turner, Royal Flying Corps. *Who am I*?"

"Lieutenant William Turner, sir, Royal Flying Corps," the corporal tried to focus on his nose.

"I've had a very tryin' day, Corporal. I've been shot at, shot down, captured by the enemy—who I might add are a damned sight more polite than you—and shelled by our own artillery. And now I've been assaulted by one of my own men. What do you think I should do about that?" He pushed the bayonet a fraction further.

"Accept an apology, sir?" The corporal was in no doubt of the magnitude of his error, but he sounded hopeful. Before Will could consider clemency, a voice lashed out.

"What the bloody hell is going on here?" Will looked up, an officer glared down at them from the back of his horse. The squad that had been watching proceedings on the ground sprang to attention.

Will climbed to his feet and dragged the corporal up with him, by the collar of his tunic. "A little misunderstandin' between the corporal and myself."

"And who the devil are you?"

"Lieutenant William Turner, Royal Flying Corps." He had frightened the corporal so efficiently he said the words with him. Will glared at him.

"And why are you trying to throttle the corporal, Turner?"

"As I said, sir, a misunderstanding. The corporal thought I was a spy an' knocked me flat. I was just explainin' the difference."

The major glowered down at them. "Is that correct, Corporal?"

"Yes, sir, the gentleman has a funny accent and I thought he was a German spy."

The major took off his cap and wiped his brow, "Good grief, man, have you ever *heard* a German accent?"

"No, sir."

"Well it's nothing like Mr. Turner's here." He relaxed slightly in the saddle. "Do you wish to take any further action, Lieutenant Turner?"

Will considered for a moment, he had seen the contents of the corporal's pack spill onto the ground. A brand new, circular tin of fifty cigarettes had rolled out. Will quickly counted the horsemen drawn up behind the major. "If the corporal would care to pass his cigarettes around, I'm sure I would see that as a friendly gesture that would make me forget all about it." The major laughed. The corporal smiled weakly and opened the tin. It passed around his own squad and rapidly through the cavalry squadron. It came back with two remaining. Will took one and passed the other to the corporal, he lit it for him.

"Thank you, sir."

Will winked, "No hard feelings, Corporal?"

"No, sir." He dragged on his cigarette. "Do you mind my asking where you learned the trick that put me down like that?"

Will thought for a moment, "My little sister, actually."

"Blimey, sir, they breed 'em tough in your part of the world."

"They do indeed."

The major sent the squad on its way and turned to Will. "Thank you, Mr. Turner, you handled that well. Those men have a thankless task patrolling this sector, and they're entitled to be jumpy. Now what are you doing exactly?" Will explained his movements of the day and concluded by showing the major the file he had brought back with him. "Good grief, man! Do you have any idea what this is?"

"I speak German, sir, I've a fair idea. It needs to be carried to headquarters as fast as possible."

"Do you ride?"

"Yes, sir."

A trooper came forward leading a remount. "Gaylor, take Mr. Turner to HQ, by the most direct route possible."

Will mounted. It had been years since he had ridden with any sort of saddle, let alone an English style, but the horse felt solid yet docile.

"Well done, Mr. Turner. But please note that you still needed a horse to finish your recce." Will laughed and shook the major's hand. Gaylor led him down the road at a trot. When he saw that Will did not fall off he increased the gait to a canter. They came to a crossroads.

Gaylor pointed down the road. "It's five miles that way, sir, or two this way, as the crow flies."

"Or as the horse jumps?"

Gaylor raised an eyebrow questioningly, "Are you up for it, sir?

"Lead on, Trooper." It was an easy and exhilarating ride. They thundered over open fields, clearing low gates in easy strides. Will almost felt regret when they clattered into the courtyard of the house taken over as the British HQ. He patted his mount's neck as he handed the reins back to Gaylor. "Thanks, Gaylor, that sure beat walking. But, I quite forgot my manners, what's the major's name?"

"That was Major Bridges, sir."

"*The* Tom Bridges?"

"The very one, sir. He's made something of a name for himself."

"You can say that again, Gaylor. Thanks for the riding lesson. Good luck."

Will watched the trooper ride away in the direction they came from, then found the entrance to the building. He expected to be ignored and shunted into a side room by the busy staff officers as so many of his friends had been previously. He was surprised, therefore, when three staff officers came to greet him the moment he stepped through the door. At first he thought it might be his dramatic style of arrival that attracted attention but he soon realized that while that had alerted them, it was the fact he was Flying Corps that brought them running. What a change from two weeks ago, he thought.

"Where's your report, man, what can you tell us?" an older man with a flowing, white moustache and bright, blue eyes demanded.

Will struggled to work out the man's rank. My God, he thought, this is my first general. He stood to attention. "I haven't brought a written report, sir. I was shot down on the other side and escaped. But I have brought this." He held out the precious folder, now torn and stained.

The general studied the contents for a few moments. "Good God Almighty, man, how in heaven's name did you lay hands on this?"

"Well, actually, sir, they gave it to me."

"They what?"

"They handed it to me, sir, by mistake."

The general studied it a little longer, then to Will's amazement did a little jig, right there, in the hall of the headquarters. "Do you know what this is, Lieutenant?"

Will went through the litany again. "I speak German, sir, it's orders for troop movements an' such."

The general beamed at him, "Yes, but it's more than that, it's *proof*, now General Joffre has to seize his chance. He cannot deny Von Kluck has changed direction now."

He turned to a sergeant who hovered nearby. "Randall, bring my car 'round, we're away to see General Joffre." He turned back to Will. "Well done, my boy—bloody well done!" As he strode through the door he called over his shoulder, "Biddulph, make sure the Lieutenant gets a decent drink, not that horse piss you give the French."

One of the two colonels who had greeted Will ushered him into a side room. "Show me on the map, as far as possible, what you saw this morning." As he pointed to the positions on the wall map where he had been fired on during his ill-fated patrol, a servant appeared at his elbow with a glass and decanter. The colonel looked up from his notebook where he scribbled as Will gave details. "That is the good stuff, not the horse piss."

Will had to agree it was as fine a scotch as he had ever tasted. He gave as many details as he could and at last the colonel seemed satisfied. "Is there any chance of a lift back to my airfield, sir?"

The colonel looked uncomfortable, "Sorry, old chap, nothing to spare." He thought for a second, "Smith?"

"Yes, sir?" the servant had not left the room.

"Are those bikes still around the back where the French left them?"

"They are, sir."

"Good. There you go, Mr. Turner. That should take you home. Go with Smith and he'll sort you out."

Will pedaled slowly through the gathering dusk. He weaved through lines of marching men and around lumbering carts. He knew the road well enough and soon gratefully rolled into the flying field. As he freewheeled past the workshop truck he rang the little bell on his handlebars. "Is the tea on, lads? I'm gaspin'." The effect on the activity of the field was completely out of proportion. It stopped. Every mechanic, every pilot, every driver and cook, froze, and gaped at him.

"Bleedin' 'ell!" Cattle said quietly. "It's 'im, 'e's done it again."

Will rode a strange steed for a conquering hero, but that was the reception he earned. Elation, release from anxiety, grief not called for and the grim satisfaction of death defied were some of the emotions in the throng that swarmed around him. Most of all, in a time when expectations had been cruely shattered, the men of the RFC needed something to celebrate.

Higgins pushed his way through the crowd and confronted Will with a look of mock severity. "Turner, you're slipping—you've only captured a bike this time."

Will dismounted. He put his hands in the capacious pockets on each side of his black flying coat and produced two bottles of whisky. "Not *just* a bike, sir."

Chapter Twenty-Four

WILL STOOD WITH THE ASSEMBLED PILOTS OF THE RFC SQUADRONS watching Major Josh Higgins complete a complex diagram on the blackboard set up against one wall of the tent. They stood on what the British called duckboards to keep their feet out of the mud, listening to a fitful wind tugging at the canvas. The tent approached the size of a circus big top but was square in shape. Although a temporary structure, the tent reflected the established nature of this field, St. Omer. For nearly two months they had lived from the back of their trucks, living the peripatetic life of a traveling theatre company: actors in a grim drama. He tried to count the number of moves that had brought them to this point. He gave up at twelve.

Higgins tapped his pointer against the blackboard. "Gentlemen! May I have your attention please." The hum of conversation died away. "As you know, after we trounced the Hun at The Battle of the Marne, we pushed him back over forty miles to the River Aisne. But he's formed a defensive line there and all attempts to budge him have failed." Higgins swept his pointer over the bottom of the map he had carefully created: "Then, we beat him to the Channel Ports, and thanks to our work—and you can all pat each other on the back—we knocked him back from Ypres." His pointer jabbed at a kink in the line, a feature already known as the Ypres Salient. "This leaves us with a line running north-south from the Belgian Coast, here, at Nieuport, to roughly Compiegne where the line turns east to follow the Aisne." The map was familiar enough to Will and his comrades, but they made polite noises of comprehension. Higgins continued, "To all intents and purposes it has been decided that we will be responsible for most of the north–south axis of the line, from Nieuport to just beyond the Somme at about Montdidier. The French will take care of the rest."

"Bloody good job, they're welcome to it." Shuttleworth shouted from the back to general laughter.

Higgins allowed himself a smile, "My sentiments entirely. There is just one tiny bone of contention and it's not with the French."

"Would the Germans be disputing our ownership then, sir?"

"I think they might, Power."

"Ah, that's grand."

Will smiled at the scuffle as somebody pushed Liam off the duckboard. Still carrying on like overgrown schoolboys, he thought.

Higgins rapped on the blackboard. "Believe it or not," order returned as they waited for his revelation, "it's our friends from the RNAS."

"The Rather Nice Aerial Sailors!" Louis Strange scoffed.

Higgins laughed out loud, "Indeed, Mr. Strange, The Royal Naval Air Service is laying claim to the part of the line nearest the coast and the right to shoot down any Zeppelins they find. Hopefully they'll leave some for us. But we won't concern ourselves with them. If our patrols overlap, so much the better." He bent over the table set up with the blackboard and studied his notes. "The important thing, as far as you men are concerned, is that, starting from this evening and proceeding over the next few weeks, you will be sent home in batches—some to form the new squadrons as part of Colonel Trenchard's drive to expand the corps, others to train new pilots, and a few men to specialist posts to develop new machines and equipment." Will saw Higgins look straight at him when he spoke. "With that in mind I would like to see Lieutenants Strange, Power, Shuttleworth and Turner in my office immediately after this meeting. The rest of you gentlemen—thank you and dismissed."

Liam leaned against the fuselage of the new Avro biplane when Will emerged from his interview. "Did Chalky have it right, what he told you then, Will?"

"Indeed he did, Liam, though I'm damned if I know how the mess corporal seems to know more than the CO. I'm reclaimed by Tom Armstrong to help him set up a new field near Ipswich to test new types."

"Now *that* is grand, Will. You'll be close enough to pop home for the weekend."

"And you're posted to Hendon to instruct?"

"That's right, the fleshpots of London on my doorstep. The army's been kind to us for once, Will. This is our last patrol together, let's make it a good one—toss you for who drives." Will lost the flip of the coin and climbed into the observer's position in the front cockpit. The new Avro started with an eagerness to the familiar ripping sound of its rotary that promised good performance. Will's only regret was that he was not at the controls as they leaped into the air. They headed in the direction of Loos at the southern end of their patrol sector. Liam leveled the Avro under a sagging layer of threatening dark cloud, stretching to the horizon. It looked so solid Will felt he could rip it apart like an old mattress if he held a knife blade above the wing, and let sunlight through. How he longed to see the sun.

"What's our height?" Will shouted back over his shoulder.

"Two thousand feet."

Will sat up in the cockpit. He had grown used to the fine mist of castor oil thrown back from the spinning motor a few feet in front of him. He felt some warmth from the cylinders in the turbulent rush of air as he took his notebook and pencil and scanned the earth before him. He wondered again at the dead line carved in the living earth before him. A jagged, festering wound gouged in the skin of France. He tried to think of words to adequately convey his horror and disgust at the hellish vision the trench lines had so recently formed below. He gave up and leaned back to Liam, "What a goddamn awful mess we've gotten into."

Liam grimaced under his goggles. "And I hate flying just under this cloud layer like this, we're a perfect target for the gunners." It was as if the men crouched over their range finders had heard him. A dirty white cloud appeared as if conjured by a malevolent genie. Then another. He skidded the Avro sideways and throttled back, dodging through and under the exploding anti-aircraft shells. "I hope the German gunners are no better than ours today." He waved a fist at the invisible idiot below who had fired on his own side.

Will pointed to the north, and the Avro curved over the trench line. The motor sang sweetly and the gunners left them alone as Will made careful notes and sketched quickly on a separate pad. He undid his seat belt and turned to talk to Liam again, kneeling on his seat. He pointed to the west. "That's enough, we're on our way home, look the sun's breakin' through...," he was still gazing longingly at the shaft of sunlight when his head hit the underside of the wing. Then he had the briefest vision of Liam's horrified face inches from his own and heard a strange splintering sound in his ears.

Will's confusion was absolute, he groped for the edge of the cockpit but his hands seemed pinned. The noise of the motor and wind had gone, replaced by a terrible, gut-wrenching groan, an animal sound of pain. In an instant of comprehension he knew the groans were his own. Pain wracked his entire being. He clenched his jaws shut. A voice called from near him, "Nurse..." He felt himself falling. Liam's face was in front of him again, and there was another Irishman with him. Will shut his eyes.

The stranger spoke, "Is this man a Catholic, Mr. Power?"

"For goodness sake, Father, I don't know and I don't care. I'm not asking you to give him absolution, but he has to hear my confession as well."

Will opened his eyes. He lay on his side, neatly tucked in a bed set in a row against the wall of a long room. A severe looking man with a long, aquiline face stood next to his bed. He wore an army uniform but also a dog collar at his throat. Liam stood next to him. "This is highly irregular, Lieutenant, but get on with it."

"Bless me, Father, for I have sinned..."

"Yes, yes, get to the point."

Liam abandoned the pretense of being in the confessional box. He smiled shyly and passed the priest a coin. "I cheated, Father, and because of it my friend received a painful wound."

The priest turned the coin over in his hand, then laughed loudly. "You wicked little gobshite, Liam," he abandoned the army formality, "a double-headed coin." He took Liam's hand and pressed the penny into his palm. "You, my son, need to ask Mr. Turner's forgiveness, not God's." He patted Will's shoulder. "Glad to have you back with us Mr. Turner. Would dinner at the finest restaurant in London compensate for Liam's wickedness?"

"It would, Father."

"Good man. As for you Liam Power, a hundred Hail Marys and a drink next time I see you."

Liam bowed his head, "Thanks, Father Driscoll, I'll keep you to that."

Will struggled to raise himself, but pain seared through his body. He gave up and lay back. "He seems a good type."

Liam watched the priest as he moved down the ward, chatting to every patient regardless of the religion shown in the notes hung on the bed frame. "He is that. He looks a dry old stick but he's a real sport." Liam rearranged Will's pillow. "I really am sorry, Will, I shouldn't have pulled that trick with my lucky coin. It's that I wanted, just once, to fly a decent machine before I ended up back at Hendon instructing on those dreadful old Rumpetys. Because of that you were in the front cockpit instead of me when that shell burst underneath us."

Will sighed. "Don't be ridiculous, Liam, it's the luck of the draw." He stopped to gather his thoughts. "So *that's* what happened."

"'Fraid so, Will. Just as you leaned back to speak to me, a shell went off directly underneath us. A bloody great splinter came through the floor, hit you in the arse and smashed you up into the top wing. You weren't strapped in—you fell toward me and bust my windshield with your face. I grabbed you and pushed you back into your cockpit, stuffed the nose down and made for home all out."

"So where am I?"

"The new hospital near Hazebrouck—they've converted a girls' boarding school."

"Cripes! Liam, what time is it?"

"Thursday."

"What do you mean, Thursday? It's Tuesday."

"No it's not, you've been in and out of consciousness for two days. Every time you started to come 'round you made everybody's stomach turn with your moaning and groaning so they sedated you again."

"How did you know that?"

Liam shrugged. "I've been here most of the time."

Will sank back in the bed. "Daft bugger."

Liam stood up to leave. He looked at his watch. "I have to go, Will. I'm glad to see you back in the land of the living. The tender is picking me up in five minutes to take me to Calais. I'll see you back in Blighty."

Will shook his hand, "You *will*, count on it. You owe me that dinner." The big Irishman grinned, squeezed Will's hand hard and turned to go. "And don't forget your penance."

Will found the company in his hospital ward very pleasant. None of the patients were seriously wounded. His was one of the worst. After Liam left he carefully explored under the covers. He found out immediately why the nurses had virtually imprisoned him on his side. A heavy dressing covered part of his backside and extended down his leg. In addition to that he could hardly see from his right eye because it was partly covered by the dressings on his face.

A cheerful doctor gave him the good news. "The funny thing is, Lieutenant Turner, you used to have a slightly wonky nose, but now the swelling is going down, we can see you bashed it almost straight again."

"Oh, good oh!" Will replied, his sarcasm lost on the doctor.

A steady stream of visitors soon cheered him. As the pilots and observers were shipped out they all called on their way to the boat. On Will's fifth day in the hospital he looked up to see Wells and Nichol standing shyly at the door, obviously intimidated to be in the officers' ward.

"Hey!" Will called. "Come on in." They advanced to his bed. "Fer Chrissake stop standing to attention and give me the gossip, boys."

They quickly relaxed and filled him in on the progress of the corps and the various personalities. They had come ostensibly with paperwork for him to sign, but Will knew that Higgins had arranged for them to visit on behalf of the mechanics. They chatted about technical matters and local news. Anything but the fighting going on a few miles away. It was a throwaway remark from Nichol that made Will jerk upright in bed.

"They say your friend Major Matrett is a happy bunny now, sir."

"Ha! That would take some doing," Will grunted. "I hear he's blamin' me personally for handin' over his nephew to the Germans."

"Yes, sir," Wells confirmed, "he wanted you court-martialed but Colonel Trenchard had already put you forward for the Military Cross."

Will groaned, "Oh no! I'll have to put a stop to that. My ma will have a fit if she hears I've been anywhere near the front. So what's cheered old misery guts?"

"Didn't you hear, sir? They've made him the town major because this whole area is under martial law. He's caught himself a spy, and he's going to have him shot with all the full ceremonial. The best part as far as he's concerned is that this poor bugger is trying to claim he's an American journalist, and that's why he was wandering around the district asking questions. That's almost as good as shooting you as far as he's concerned. He had a letter in German on him, and a Luger in his pocket when they picked him up. Worse still for him, Matrett says he has a German name, but it sounds more Dutch if you ask me."

Will lay back in bed, the strength suddenly knocked from him. He breathed a name "Vandersand?"

"That sounds like it, sir," Wells replied. "How did you know that?"

"Never mind, when's this execution supposed to take place—dawn?"

"Oh no, sir, this afternoon. Matrett wants plenty of spectators to make a big example, he says."

"Get my clothes."

"Beg pardon, sir?"

"My clothes dammit. And a car, quickly, men."

They stared at him uncomprehendingly. "We've the squadron Crossley tender outside, sir, but you can't move..."

"Watch me." He heaved himself over the edge of the bed. Pain shot the length of his body as his right foot touched the floor—he almost fell. Wells caught him and put him back on the bed.

"You're too ill to move, sir."

Will glared at him. "My clothes, now!" The two mechanics looked at each other, shrugged and started to help him dress. He forced himself into his trousers, tears springing in his eyes. His tunic proved easier. He put on his cap, straightened it and took the crutches Nichol had found in the corridor. They headed for the door to find it blocked by the hospital matron, the chief of the nursing staff.

"Where do you think you're going, Mr. Turner. Return to your bed immediately!"

Will looked her in the eye. "Ma'am, stand aside, that is a direct order." Her mouth dropped open. Her authority was absolute, even generals cowered under her steely gaze. Mere lieutenants she treated as children and expected to behave as such. This one scribbled and tore a page from his notebook. He thrust it at her. "Telephone GHQ, ask for this gentleman and read my message to him word for word. Thank you."

She looked at the note and stood back. "Yes, sir."

Will and his supporters lurched through the oak doors at the entrance to the building. The mechanics lifted Will into the passenger seat. His urgency had communicated itself to them. He scribbled in his book again and ripped out the page. "Wells, find some transport, anything, steal it if you have to, and go to this address. Find this gentleman, and bring him to the town major's office. Go!" Wells saluted and ran to a bicycle leaning against the gates of the hospital. "Nichol, drive like the wind."

Nichol drove at a furious pace. Will hung on desperately. Trading pain for every jolt and lurch. The rain had returned, soaking the streets of the town and the miserable soldiers who cluttered the streets. Nichol needed both hands for the wheel so Will pumped the bulb horn frantically. They turned onto the highway at the edge of the town that led to the mansion Matrett had taken over as his headquarters. Nichol swung off the road to the side of the building. He dodged past a line of cars and an army truck parked at the front of the building. The occupants of the cars wore various uniforms of differing nationalities. They stared dully at Will and Nichol as the tender skidded to a halt. A high, red brick wall ran from the end of the house. Will heaved himself from the cab, clinging to the door for support.

"In there I expect, sir." Nichol pointed to a gate in the wall.

To confirm his words, a voice rang clear from beyond it. "Ready—aim—fire!"

Will staggered as if the ragged volley had hit him. He moved forward, awkwardly hauling himself on his crutches. His lips moved soundlessly. He turned the handle of the gate and forced it open. He made himself look at the wall at the end of the enclosed courtyard now revealed. Brick dust hung in the damp air. A wide pattern of bullet holes scarred the brickwork. The man who had given the order to fire was berating the thoroughly miserable soldiers who stood in an uneasy line in front of him. "Now look, you cack-handed-bastards, I know you can shoot better than that. Whatever is the prisoner going to think if you miss him? Now for fuck's sake let's try again."

"Sergeant!" The authority in Will's voice made the man spin around and snap to attention in an automatic response. His face gave nothing away.

"Yes, sir."

"What the hell are you doing?"

"Rehearsing these men for the execution, sir. They're Territorials you see, but I know they can shoot if they put their minds to it."

"Dismiss these men and send them to lunch. There's not going to be an execution."

"Beg pardon, sir? Major Matrett will be here any minute with the prisoner."

"Are you disobeyin' an order, Sergeant?"

"Er, no, sir." He turned to order the firing party to stand easy, but they were already streaming past him in their relief.

"Where is Major Matrett?"

"Through there, sir." He pointed to a door in the side of the main building. Will hauled himself across the yard and stabbed the door open with the end of his crutch. It crashed back. Major Matrett stepped back smartly to avoid catching it in his face. He was directing a small party down the corridor leading to the outside.

For a moment he failed to recognize the apparition blocking the doorway. Then his face set like stone. "You!"

Will knew only one maxim in military tactics—attack is the best means of defense. He pointed at the NCO immediately behind Matrett. "Sergeant, arrest this officer."

The man was surprisingly unflustered. "Which officer, sir?"

"Major Matrett."

"Why, sir?"

"You're not paid to ask questions, Sergeant. Obey my order!" The bewildered sergeant paused. Matrett *was* a disagreeable little swine, yet this strange officer looked terrifying, with his face swollen and bruised, one good eye fixed on him, and standing inches taller than anybody else there—but Matrett was the superior officer.

The major saved him from a decision. "You've gone too far this time, Turner. As soon as I've dealt with the prisoner I'll deal with you."

"Call me, sir and stand to attention when you address me, Private Matrett." Will's bellow filled the corridor and brought startled faces peering around doors.

Matrett found himself completely at a loss. His orderly world worked on a system of rank and regulation. This was outside his experience. He struggled to ground himself. "What the hell are you blithering about, man?"

"I believe that's the procedure, Matrett. They strip you of your rank before they execute you." The mention of the word procedure struck home.

"You've taken leave of your senses, Turner. Execute *me*—for what?"

"Murder, Mr. Matrett, pure and simple—if you shoot *that* man." He pointed to Roscoe Vandersand who stood looking at him blankly, sandwiched between the sergeant and a corporal behind him carrying a rifle with fixed bayonet. "The American ambassador in Paris will insist on your arrest and extradition to the United States, where you will be tried for murder in the first degree. However, to avoid the United States entering the war on the German side I imagine the British authorities will charge you, try you and execute you—to placate American public opinion."

"Why in God's name should the American public take any interest in a German spy?"

"He's not a spy. He is who he says he is."

"Rubbish, man," Matrett had gathered himself. "Stand out of my way."

Will thrust one of his crutches across the corridor, barring Matrett's progress. "Roscoe, tell the major who your pa is." Roscoe was dumbstruck, in a state of shock.

"Okay, *I'll* tell him. Mr. Vandersand's father is a United States senator—do you know what that is?" Matrett shook his head. He did not know, but it sounded important and Matrett respected a title above anything. "It's like one of your English Lords, but elected, by a democratic vote. A very, very important man, Matrett, and a vindictive one."

Matrett did not give up easily, Will had to admit that. He waved a piece of paper under Will's nose. "He *claims* to be a journalist," Matrett said, "but he has no credentials, and he *does* have *this*!" Will snatched the paper, opened it and started to laugh. "What's so damn funny, Turner?"

"Do you speak German?"

"Of course I don't speak their Hunnish language."

"So this is your evidence? The evidence that convinced you to execute a man without trial?"

"Of course," Matrett puffed himself up, "this area is under martial law and I have the authority to shoot spies and saboteurs on sight."

"This is a love letter, you damn fool."

"It's in German—damn you."

"Germans fall in love as well, I guess."

Matrett was losing the battle, but he had one last try. "What about the

Luger pistol, how do you explain *that?*"

"All the proof you need that he's an American, Major. We can't resist a souvenir, isn't that right, Roscoe?" Vandersand nodded. Will could see he looked deathly pale.

Matrett jabbed a finger into Will's chest, "Turner, I am going—"

An orderly interrupted him by thrusting a telephone receiver toward him. "General Sir John French for you, sir."

Matrett blanched visibly, he took the phone and stood to attention. A voice could be heard on the other end of the line. Will thought he caught the words "bloody fool." Matrett only said two words in the entire conversation. "Yes, sir." But he repeated them several times. There was an audible click, followed by a long silence. Matrett handed the phone back to the orderly and spoke quickly to Will. "The prisoner is to be released under parole into your charge, Turner. My clerk will prepare the paperwork." He turned on his heel and stalked away without another word.

Will smiled at the corporal. "We won't be needing that," he motioned at the rifle. The papers appeared and Will signed for Roscoe Vandersand who still had not said a word. An orderly handed Roscoe his jacket, hat and a leather Gladstone bag. Will hopped outside, he was gaining confidence on his crutches. Nichol waited at the front of the building with a huge smile on his face. The cars and truck had disappeared carrying the witnesses and now redundant firing party. A tall officer with the red tabs of a staff officer stood with him.

"Hi there, Uncle Frank, sorry to drag you away but we nearly had a very serious misunderstandin' over Roscoe here."

"Ah, the infamous Mr. Vandersand, delighted to meet you, old chap." Frank Penrose shook Roscoe by the hand. He looked at him carefully. "I think you could do with a stiff drink. Follow me chaps." They drove to a small restaurant that still contrived to maintain its elegance. Will dismissed his mechanics and Frank slipped some bank notes into Nichol's hand. "Well done chaps, no medals as I'm afraid this has to be kept under your hats, but have a few on me." They saluted and disappeared.

Frank sat Roscoe at a table and Will eased himself painfully into the seat opposite. He studied the man who had caused him so much trouble. The good looks seemed to have deserted him, though his hair was as thick as ever. "I think you owe me an explanation, Roscoe."

Frank returned with three glasses and a bottle. He poured for Roscoe.

"Knock that back, Mr. Vandersand." The brandy worked. Roscoe started to talk, and once he started he could not stop. Frank had seen it before when people had survived against the odds. They had to talk it out. They listened to how he had fled after the shooting in Tallahassee, bribing two bootleggers to take him away down the river to the Gulf of Mexico. Then he had taken a ship to New Orleans, cleaned out his accounts and headed for New York. Once there he had sailed for Europe aboard a German liner and headed for his old university town of Heidelberg to join old friends. He had found many of them training in the reserve regiments they belonged to. They arranged for him to join them in the campaign in France. The authorities had been surprisingly eager for him to accompany the army, keen to show off the prowess of the German military machine to an influential American. At first he had enjoyed the mad dashes across the fields of Belgium and had even sent some dispatches to a Washington newspaper, but as the evidence of the atrocities against civilians mounted his attitude changed. He believed for a while that he might be able to intercede, but it soon became apparent he could not. He became an embarrassment to his hosts.

"And then one day we came across this farm after the terrible battle at Le Cateau. We heard a shot when we approached, though nobody was hit." Roscoe shook his head in disgust, "The Captain, a real bastard, had his Uhlans drag the family out of bed, read some ridiculous declaration and tried to string the farmer up from his own barn. I couldn't stand for that and tried to stop it. They lost patience with me and dragged me around the back of the barn, but just then an aeroplane came over and they took time out to shoot at it, then went back to trying to hang the poor farmer. I turned away but just at that moment there was a single shot and the sergeant carrying out the hanging fell with a bullet through the head. Then all hell broke loose. The farm was attacked by what must have been a brigade of Tommies. You have never seen anything like it, a positive hurricane of bullets, they must have all had machine guns—," Roscoe stopped. "Why are you laughing, Will?"

"There were twenty-two of us." Roscoe stopped talking for the first time in ten minutes and stared at Will. "We drove the German cavalry off and you took the chance to escape. You damn near ran me down as you went for the field."

Roscoe sat back and smiled for the first time. "I'll be damned! You were there?"

"Indeed I was. I had been forced to march back with a company of riflemen, or what was left of them, after I had to give up my ride in our one remaining plane. We captured the truck your cavalry friends had with them and drove back in that."

Roscoe shuddered, "They're no friends of *mine.*"

"That's not what Matrett thought," Will pointed out. "Honestly, Roscoe! What the hell did you think you were playing at?"

"It never crossed my mind I was doing anything wrong. I crossed back into Belgium, handed the horse back to the Germans, bought some civilian clothes and just made my way to Holland." He felt in his pocket and showed them his documents, "I still have my passport, it was easy, we're neutral. I thought I would gather some information from this side, talk to some refugees and get their story, then head back to the states and maybe try to do something to help these poor civilians by writing for the papers. On the way I hoped I could track you down in England, Will, and apologize like a gentleman for my actions back home." He looked hopefully at Will. "My only excuse is, I was drunk."

Will smiled and extended his hand, "Apology accepted. So you were never in France then?"

"Not until now."

Will sat back with a curse. "Damn, that guy really was a journalist. And here's me thinkin' you were tryin' to do me in."

"Good Lord no! Will, I've been trying to pluck up the courage to confront you all this time."

Frank poured them all more brandy. "It seems there have been more than enough misunderstandings this year. When they go too far you end up with a war like this one. Mr. Vandersand, I have a proposition for you. I want you to go with one of my officers and visit the refugee camps that have been set up, to speak to the French and Belgian civilians as you planned, but to do it officially this time, in the proper manner. Then go back to the United States and tell their story."

"Sir, it would be an honor." An ornate clock chimed gently above the bar. Roscoe looked at it and his face paled. "Good Lord, gentlemen, this is the time they set for my execution."

Frank smiled and placed a fatherly hand on Roscoe's arm. "The grim reaper has been cheated. Don't fret, he has plenty more work in front of him."

Chapter Twenty-Five

KATE SAT AT THE KITCHEN TABLE IN PENROSE COTTAGE AND ADMIRED her cousin. Will sat opposite her. The scar above his right eye had healed well and his hair had grown longer. He wore an old sweater with leather patches on the sleeve. It was Christmas Eve, over two months since he had been shipped back to England to convalesce. "That's a charming Christmas present, Will. What should we do with it?"

Will picked up Roscoe's souvenir Luger and, with what was now an automatic reflex, checked to make sure it was unloaded. "Maybe give it to the museum in Hertford and they can charge to see it to raise money for the widows and orphans fund."

Kate looked quickly away so he could not see the tears start in her eyes. She looked back at him. "Is it true the BEF suffered nearly three-quarters casualties?"

"I'm afraid so, Kate, whatever the papers say. How's Maisie now?"

"Putting a brave face on it, but she'll never be the same since her brother Eric was killed at Le Cateau."

Will pushed the pistol away from him. "Well Roscoe was glad to see the back of this. Can't say I blame him." He stood up and opened a draw in the dresser and threw the Luger into it.

Kate recovered some of her good humor. She was dressed in the plain gray uniform with the long, dragging skirt of a VAD nurse. "I must say, he's awfully handsome and a real charmer."

Will laughed, "Isn't he just! My big worry is that he has said he is coming straight back to France after his planned lecture tour for the refugees—to join the French Foreign Legion, of all things."

"Oh, how romantic!"

Will grunted, "How incredibly stupid. They're being shoved into every weak point in the French line and takin' desperate casualties.

Hopefully his family will stop him."

Connie bustled into the room bringing a scent of wood smoke with her. "Your family are not having much luck stopping you, are they, William?"

"I've started the job, Aunt Connie, can't stop 'til it's finished. I will have to go back one day, the sooner the better."

She shook her head, "You're just as bad as Rupert, he's trying to fix a posting back to the front."

"It's probably safer than instructin'." Will said.

Connie sniffed. "Anyway, the postman brought a package for you." She put a heavy envelope on the table. It bore a postmark from the military postal service and the marks to show it had been opened by the censor.

Kate looked at it eagerly, "Go on, open it."

Will tore the packet open and shook something heavy into his hand. There was a note from Nichol:

> *Dear Mr. Turner,*
>
> *One of the nurses at the hospital gave me this, she said it was with your notes and you might like it for a souvenir. It was extracted from your wound.*
>
> *With respectful best Wishes for the Season,*
> *Air Mechanic A. Nichol*

It was a small piece of brass, not much bigger than the top joint of his thumb. Will held it up to the light. "Looks like a piece of fuse mechanism for an artillery shell. He turned it around. "Damn!" He stared hard at the fragment. Connie and Kate looked at him expectantly. He tossed it to Connie who adjusted her glasses to see it better. She started to laugh, and laugh, until she was helpless. Tears of merriment coursed down her cheeks. Will started to chuckle with her.

Kate looked from one to the other, "What's so funny?"

Connie passed her the fragment. "It's so tragic—it has to make you laugh." She pointed to the broad arrow mark of the British War Department stamped in the metal. "Poor old Will came four thousand miles to serve his mother country, and all the thanks he gets is to be shot in the bum." He sat shaking his head ruefully. Connie calmed down, "Come on, Will, we appreciate you, let's break out the sherry to celebrate being alive."

The Adventure Continues!

Turn the page for an excerpt from

Turner's Flight:

Will Turner's Flight Logs

Part Two

by

Chris Davey

The second book in the series takes place from the autumn of 1915 to the spring of 1916, during the period historians refer to as the "Fokker Scourge." During this short period, the German airforce gained what we now call Air Superiority with Fokker monoplanes and forward-firing machine guns.

Turner's Flight focuses on the commanding officer of an aggressive British squadron, outstanding for its effective tactics.

Turner's Flight

10TH. AUGUST 1915. PULLING-PALMER. SER. 1611 ORFORD - ORFORD. FLIGHT DURATION 15 SECS.

LIEUTENANT WILLIAM TURNER, RFC, UNFASTENED HIS SAFETY BELT and forced himself to stand against the blast of air battering the cockpit of his machine. The slipstream tugged at his long black coat flapping unrestrained by any parachute straps. He fell back on the decking behind his seat, made a despairing grab for a strut, and missed. The onlookers gasped as he half somersaulted and fell from the airplane.

"Steady on old chap," Tom Armstrong cautioned as he rushed to help Will Turner now sprawled on the grass next to the Pulling-Palmer Quadriplane. It sat shuddering to the beat of its motor where Will had dragged it to a standstill.

Will let Tom pull him to his feet then shouted in his ear above the blatter of the thick four-bladed propeller, "It won't stop."

"What do you mean?" Tom yelled back.

"The damn thing won't fly, but the motor won't quit...have somebody shoot it." The motor abruptly stopped before anybody could carry out his order. A relieved laugh rippled through the crowd of mechanics who had stood watching, horrified, as Will had forced the quadriplane to stumble briefly into the air.

"It heard you," Tom said, now able to speak at a normal level in the welcome silence.

"The ground wire in the magneto has probably shaken loose leaving it permanently hot," Will explained. "I had to turn off the gas. Expect to find everythin' else shaken apart as well. I have never felt vibration like it."

"A high frequency buzz?" Tom hazarded a guess.

"Buzz my ass!" Will laughed. "It's like ridin' a bicycle in an earthquake." He stepped back a few paces to study the machine. "Whatever possessed me to think I could make it fly?"

"Well, the fact it has four sets of wings would suggest it has some chance to drag itself off the ground," Tom said mildly. "In theory it should be twice as eager compared to a conventional biplane."

Will rubbed his chin and turned to look at his friend thoughtfully. "I have the greatest respect for theory, especially when somebody else has to try it in practice, but I have a naggin' doubt that neither Mr. Pullin' nor Mr. Palmer placed the aerodynamics of their machine under the spotlight of applied math before sending it to us—by truck. That should have given us a clue. Those guys might be stupid, but they're not dumb."

Tom laughed and clapped a hand on Will's shoulder. "Now you're sounding like a scientist and not a *devil-may-care* young birdman of the gallant RFC."

"Now *you're* soundin' like a hack journalist."

"Well, in the finest traditions of British newspapermen, I suggest we repair to the Hope and Anchor, you look as if you could do with a drink."

Will shook his head ruefully, "I could do with lockin' up for my own protection." He waved his hand dismissively at the quadriplane and called to the mechanics. "Put it away at the back of the hangar, fellas: and hope everyone forgets it's there."

He turned to follow his friend now striding away toward the low wooden hut at the edge of the field. Will cast his eyes over the landscape as he walked, trying to imprint the scene on his memory. He knew this would be his last day on the east coast of England, among the dunes backing the wide sand and shingle beaches over which the North Sea spilled an endless succession of slick, shining waves against the county of Suffolk—not Suffolk*shire* as the local people patiently explained to him, just Suffolk, the old Saxon name, the land of the South folk. It was one of the counties that make up that part of England known as East Anglia.

The picture before him was benign enough, but it had been very different when he had arrived in February of that year, 1915. The flat landscape had then cowered under a vast churning vault of threatening black and gray clouds that pressed a savage cold wind on land and sea, goading the waves into a fragmented turmoil while flattening the sparse grasses and reads that covered the field and the surrounding dunes. For many days, flying had been impossible and Will and Tom huddled around a potbellied stove in the office drinking tea and proposing war-winning schemes and inventions, watching rivulets of rain harassed by the wind on their way down the windowpane. But today the sun blessed the fields and beaches.

Tom paused for a moment, narrowed his eyes and peered into the distance. "Do you hear what I hear?" The hum of a rotary engine teased their ears for a moment, then faded to nothing. They stood still, shoulders slightly hunched, heads forward, straining to catch the sound. "There it is," Tom shaded his eyes with his hand and pointed again with his cane. A speck had appeared high in the sky to the south. As they watched, the sound of the airplane's motor swelled. Their well-accustomed ears told them it was a rotary-powered machine. Will guessed at one of the 100-hp *Monosoupape* engines now being churned out under license by British factories. The machine itself was not familiar. As it droned closer the bright sunlight drew out the biplane wings, and picked out details. It was a "pusher" design. A nacelle, the shape and size of a bathtub, was fixed to the lower of the two main planes carrying the single occupant in a position ahead of the leading edge of the wings. The motor was bolted to the back of the nacelle driving a propeller pushing the machine through the air. The tail unit was carried on a framework of booms and struts so spidery that, as the strange machine banked away from them, it appeared as if the horizontal stabilizer and rudder were a separate structure following eagerly behind the main body of the machine.

The new arrival circled the field once, the rotary engine humming busily. Will nodded approvingly as the pilot slipped off a little height, dropped to a neat three-point landing and rolled to a halt, the tail-skid rasping on the dry grass, a few yards from where they stood. The pilot unfastened his seat belt and stood up in the cockpit. He saluted, "Captain Armstrong?"

"Guilty," Tom replied with a quick smile. "No need for formality here, Lieutenant, you're among friends."

The young flier laughed and vaulted from the cockpit. "Glad to hear it, sir." He introduced himself, "Robson, attached to the Farnborough establishment."

Will shook Robson's hand, "Turner, attached to Armstrong's experimental department. My name's Will, do you have a name they use at home?"

Robson grinned, "Edward, though everybody calls me Ned."

Will made a sweeping gesture toward the little biplane. "Well, Ned, what have you brought us? Would this be Geoffrey de Havilland's latest design?"

"It certainly is," Robson confirmed. "The DH2 single-seat scout. Guaranteed to sweep the Hun from the sky."

Will looked at him, a questioning eyebrow raised. "Guaranteed?"

Robson shrugged, "Providing we have plenty of them. It's not a bad little machine and of course you have a clear field of fire for the Lewis machine gun in the nose."

Will stepped up to the nacelle of the DH2. The designer had achieved protection against the slipstream with the minimum of structure. The sides of the cockpit reached to shoulder height. The pilot's feet extended into the smooth curve of the front panel which sloped back to a small rectangular windscreen. "Where's the Lewis to be fitted?"

Robson stretched up and traced an imaginary slot beneath the windscreen with his finger, "The plan is to cut a rectangle from here and mount the gun on a free swinging mounting inside the cockpit, with the barrel sticking out through the hole." He turned to Will who still wore his flying helmet with his goggles perched on top of his head. "I say, do you fancy taking her up now? I re-fuelled at Goldhanger so there's plenty of juice aboard."

Will patted Tom on the arm. "I've been waitin' to get my hands on this little beast for weeks, ever since Geoffrey told us about it. You'll just have to wait for that pint."

Tom shrugged, "Off you go then, you might as well do the first flight. Mr. Robson has some paperwork for me I expect. I don't imagine Farnborough will let it go without signatures in triplicate. We can do that while you're enjoying yourself."

Will was not surprised to see the mechanics clustered around the biplane. He had learned they had a gift for materializing from thin air whenever anything new or interesting appeared at the field. Whether it was Tom Armstrong's Rudge motorcycle or a new airplane, a curious crowd gathered to examine it in detail. "What do you think, Chiefy?" Will called to the sergeant who crouched under the wing, carefully examining the landing gear.

"Serviceable I'd say, sir, very serviceable," Sergeant Childs replied.

"Leaving the engine without cowlings is going to make it easier to work on and you won't get the build up of unburnt fuel when hamfisted...beggin' your pardon, sir...young gentlemen rely too much on the cut-out button." Will nodded in agreement, very aware of the temptation to control the speed of a rotary by "blipping" the ignition. Most rotaries were either running full on, or off. Some adjustment of engine speed could be achieved with the two separate levers for air and fuel supply through the crude carburetor, but pressing the button that switched the ignition off to allow the engine to run down, then releasing it to restore full power, was always tempting. This resulted in unburned fuel collecting inside any cowlings fitted, often resulting in a fierce and frequently fatal gasoline fire.

Will followed the sergeant mechanic around the machine. Starting at the cockpit where he checked the magneto switch was off, he worked methodically, inspecting the rigging wires stretched between the wings to make sure they were taught and unbroken. He heaved up and down on the lower wing tips, listening for unusual creaks and groans that might betray a broken spar or wing rib, invisible under the taught linen covering of each wing. He waggled each flying control and checked the hinges. He scrambled under the steel tube booms that carried the tail unit and carefully turned the engine over by moving the big mahogany propeller. He ran an experienced eye over each exposed cylinder as it revolved. Finally, satisfied the machine was airworthy, he accepted the unspoken offer made by two of the mechanics as they cupped their hands to accept his boot, and boost him into the narrow cockpit as if he was mounting a horse.

The thin seat creaked under his weight; he beckoned to Robson, "Any tips on handlin'?"

Robson put one foot on a wheel and hauled himself up by grabbing the rim of the cockpit. He pointed out the various controls, "Everything where you would expect to find it, the usual instruments, pretty straightforward really. She tends to fly a little tail heavy but responds very well to the controls, quite sensitive really." Robson glanced around and lowered his voice, "And she stunts beautifully." He winked as he jumped down to the ground.

Will smiled then twisted in his seat to see Sergeant Childs already stationed by the propeller. "I think she's warm enough not to need suckin' in, Chiefy, let's give it a whirl."

Childs gave him a thumbs-up sign. "Right you are, sir."

Will selected the fuel tap to on, flipped the magneto switch and called over his shoulder, "Petrol on, switches on...contact!"

Childs replied, "Contact," paused for a second, then swung the propeller with an easy, graceful swing, stepping away as far as he could within the confines of the tail booms that formed a cage around him. The propeller seemed to pause for a moment then blurred into a spinning disc. A cloud of aromatic blue smoke scurried away, carried on the blast of air. The sergeant ducked under the tail booms with surprising agility for a man of his age and size. Will sat for a moment testing the flight controls and adjusting the fuel and air mixture, before pressing the cutout switch to blip the motor. He raised both hands in front of his face then crossed them in a sweeping gesture. The two mechanics standing either side of the cockpit pulled the wheel chocks away and the DH2 started to roll. There had been no need to reposition for take off. Will had nearly a mile of flat, sandy field in front of him. The biplane accelerated rapidly, skittering across the scrubby grass. He pushed forward firmly on the stick to raise the tail, mindful of Robson's advice, but was surprised to feel the machine already buoyant beneath him. He grinned. This, he thought, is going to be interesting.

He eased the forward pressure on the stick and the DH2 fairly leaped into the air after a run of barely one hundred yards. The boundary of the field passed beneath him as he eased the stick to his right and fed in a touch of rudder. "Whoa!" he laughed, surprised but pleased by the lightness of the controls. He eased left to line up with the beach, looking for a clear datum to measure the degree of responsiveness in the turns. His experienced hands quickly adapted to the sensitive feel of the new machine. He glanced at the altimeter to see one thousand feet already registering. Not bad, he thought, checking his watch, up to a thousand in barely a minute. Will looked around carefully. The cockpit was snug but adequate even for his six-foot frame. He glanced down at the town of Aldeburgh as it slipped beneath him, marveling as to why he should have no fear of the dizzy height when he would be the first to admit he hated going to the top of a ladder. One of life's mysteries he told himself, twisting the DH2 into a violent turn.

The horizon tilted to the vertical as he sent the compact little machine racketing through a complete circle. He felt the reassuring press of gravity pinning him in his seat. A rapid reversal of the controls: stick hard to the right then check back to the central position, a touch of rudder and a firm pull. The machine, with its wings now at an angle of ninety degrees to the horizon, responded to the upward deflection of the elevators by hauling around in a tight, vertical bank in the opposite direction. Will held the turn until the beach gave him his line then flipped his mount back to straight and level flight. "Lawdy!" he shouted out loud, "You're a lively little devil an' no mistake." He adjusted the fuel mixture again for maximum revs and allowed the nose to rise, glancing at his watch to note the time to climb.

At five thousand feet he leveled the machine. For a few moments he allowed himself the joy of the panoramic view afforded by his altitude. The fields over his left shoulder had assumed the patchwork appearance characteristic of the English countryside: the different crops separated by ancient hedgerows and winding lanes. Tidy villages, each with their different style of church tower: jaunty spires or squat miniature fortresses, dotted the countryside. White dots, like tiny angels he thought, moved in a corner of a village green. He studied them for a moment then smiled, he recognized cricketers practicing for the weekend's matches. War or no war, the rhythm of the English countryside would not be disturbed by the Kaiser. Will looked forward to Sunday when he would take his turn with bat and ball in the Upper Bardfield team. A precious day away from his duties.

To his right the North Sea shone like polished metal. A single warship, long and lean, trailed a bright wake over which the smoke from its four slender funnels lingered in the still summer air. Will smiled to himself. A view like this and they pay me too, he thought with grim satisfaction. He pulled back to the task he had set himself. A slow turn allowed him to carefully scan the air beneath. Few machines patroled at this height but he had no wish to find himself crowded by one of the Royal Naval Air Service seaplanes operating from Felixstowe. He lined up on the beach again then quickly cut the fuel supply. The cheerful roar of the rotary behind him faded to a dull rumble, he squeezed the rudder bar to correct for a slight swing as the finely balanced little machine reacted to the sudden change in thrust and torque from the spinning mass of the motor. He felt the speed fall away and the nose dropping to try to restore it. Left to its own devices, Will knew the DH2 would react like any other well designed airplane, falling into a gentle glide. Its natural stability would accelerate it to a speed sufficient to maintain a safe flow of air over the wings. He took charge, pulling back steadily on the stick to keep the nose firmly placed on the horizon. For a few seconds the little machine hung poised in space, then with a shudder the nose fell and the controls went slack. It felt to Will as if the airplane had fallen out of his hands as it stalled. He allowed the speed to build in the resulting dive and then pushed the fuel supply open. The motor responded with a sudden, eager surge of power. He leveled out and glanced at the altimeter. *Not bad*—he noted on the pad strapped to his knee—*height loss under three hundred feet, no significant wing drop*—he scribbled with the stub of pencil he kept tucked under the strap of his goggles. He allowed the nose to rise again and scrambled back to five thousand feet.

He circled slowly as he allowed his mind to wander over the possibilities this new machine presented. Just imagine, he thought, I were some inexperienced young child, fresh out of Eton School an' believin' everythin' some old fool told me about flyin' bein' like ridin' a horse: maybe with only two or three hours on this machine after trainin' on some gentle old crock. Then just imagine I arrive back over my field after a first jaunt over the line, an' I'm tired an' cold, an' scared as well as not over bright. Will lined up for an imaginary landing and then deliberately stabbed the cut out button. The motor quickly spun down behind him. "Then I might could be subject to ignorin' everythin' Rupert told me at trainin' school, an use the blip switch to cut the power, " Will muttered to himself. "Then realize I've let the speed fall too low..." He pulled back deliberately on the stick to haul the nose above the horizon, "panic an' let go the switch." His gloved thumb came off the cut out button.

"HOLY CRIPES..." he gasped as the docks of Felixstowe suddenly appeared above his head then disappeared in a spinning blur as the nose lurched sickeningly down. The DH2 had reacted, to the rotary engine flinging itself back into life, by trying to revolve around it in the opposite direction. Poised at the point of the stall with no air flowing over the controls, Will was powerless to prevent the little scout from hurling itself into a vicious tailspin. His hands and feet moved quickly, automatically, training taking over when sense and reason temporarily deserted him. He pulled back the mixture to quiet the engine again, stamped on the rudder bar against the direction of the spin, paused briefly then pushed the stick firmly forward. The spin stopped with a jerk, as sudden as it started. Will found himself hanging against his seat belt looking straight down.

"Dayum!" he shouted, then laughed as he eased the machine back to level flight. He heard himself and recognized the accent in his own voice. "Only takes a little excitement an' the cracker in me jumps right out," he confided out loud to his machine. "But you are goin' to need watchin'—you little minx." He glanced at the altimeter, his eyes opening wide behind the triplex glass of his goggles. The spin had cost over a thousand feet of height in a few seconds. Oh well, he thought, a shame to waste the air I have left. He pushed the nose down and let the speed build, the hiss of air flowing through the rigging wires sharpened to a hum, to a whistle, to a scream, to a howl. Will pulled firmly on the stick, now taut with the pressure of the slipstream rushing over the control surfaces at over a hundred miles an hour. The horizon flashed beneath him as the DH2 reared into a loop. Bright blue sky filled his vision. He leaned back comfortably in his seat, held positively in place by the effects of gravity. Almost lazily he turned his head from side to side, checking that his wingtips performed a perfect circle, telling him his loop would appear accurate and precise to those watching critically from the ground. He threw his head back to search for the horizon. The fields swapped places with the sky as he soared over the top, his left hand automatically throttling the motor back. Will Turner smiled happily to himself. He was now enjoying that perfect harmony that comes to a natural pilot when he achieves union with his machine. He talked to the airplane. It sang to him.

What he saw as he looked up at the ground, briefly hanging inverted over the East Anglian countryside, ruined the moment. Across his field of view, between himself and the ground something flew. Something so alien it could not have surprised him more if one of his native Florida pelicans had followed him to England. This was never so benign. On long, gray, black crossed wings a German seaplane sailed over the fields and villages of rural Suffolk. Will shut his eyes and shook his head as he let the DH2 plunge down the back side of the loop. He half hoped it was some illusion, perhaps a trick of the light playing on the wings of a British machine. He felt the pressure build, gravity forcing his chin toward his chest, his arms growing heavy as he tugged his machine back to level flight. The apparition had been flying across the line of his loop, toward the sea. Will peeled into another vertical turn, his movements automatic now, sending his airplane howling in pursuit. It was no apparition. A mile away and still a thousand feet below him the big gray machine forged steadily on its way.

"Bloody impertinence!" he spoke sharply to his airplane. Sometimes he sounded very British. "These Huns have the nerve of the devil—I'll have to do somethin' about it." In an unarmed, untried, experimental fighting biplane, Will Turner set off in gamely pursuit. Unsure of what he would do when he caught up with the German machine, he pressed hard on the stick and wound his motor to full revs. His height gave him the speed he needed as he dived into the chase. The details of the seaplane grew distinct as it expanded in his windscreen. He surprised himself. While his body seemed to tense with his airplane, taut with an emotion he had come to know, a cocktail of fear and excitement, a part of him stayed calm and analytical. It was this part of his brain that examined the machine he was swooping toward. He judged it a big machine, with a wingspan over fifty feet. For its size it was a handsome airplane. The wings showed a slight sweep back reflected in the shape of the long horizontal stabilizer. The vertical stabilizer extended underneath the thin square fuselage to lend the appearance of an underfin to the tail unit. From his position above and behind he could see a tall exhaust stack ejecting fumes over the leading edge of the top wing. A puff of black smoke blossomed briefly.

"Go on. Pour on the coal, you bastard, you're not gettin' away from me," Will muttered through a tight, mirthless smile." With odd detachment he watched the observer in the rear cockpit calmly checking the free-swinging machine gun he was bringing to bear against him. There was no chance of approaching unobserved. Will's gaze fixed on that gun. The sleeve surrounding the barrel fretted with slots to allow cooling air to flow. The ammunition belt, contained in a circular drum, was clipped at one side. The observer had pressed the rifle-like stock against his shoulder as he calmly took aim—the sudden flash visible at the muzzle even in the bright afternoon sun.

"Christ!" Will swore as something stung his cheek. He jabbed at the rudder bar to skid sideways. In the last seconds of his dive the seaplane suddenly seemed to jerk backwards toward him. As his path crossed directly behind his opponents he smelt the stench of exhaust fumes and hot oil, felt the bump of the slipstream and heard the crack of bullets as the determined gunner blasted at him with short accurate bursts.

He dived underneath, safe for a second, shielded from the field of defensive fire. The speed of his dive carried him quickly beneath the seaplane, so close he felt he could reach up and touch the long pontoon floats. He jerked back on the stick to hurtle up in the path of the German machine, hoping his sudden appearance might unnerve the crew. Instead he found himself bracketed by gunfire again as the observer fired forward over his own top wing. Will allowed his climbing turn to continue, crouched in his seat expecting the hammer blow of a bullet at any instant, but now the relative speed of the two machines as he hurtled back past the seaplane saved him. He continued in a wide circle, gathering his wits and trying to decide on some course of action. Christ on a bike, Fritz! Will admitted to himself. You're good. Clearly these were not men who could be intimidated into landing. He glanced over his shoulder at the shoreline receding in the distance. I'll have to do something, and quick, before I end up swimming home, he thought.

A desperate plan formed in his mind. If only I can stay beneath him, out of range of that damned gun, he thought. I might be able to take his rudder off by ramming it, without killing myself. He pushed the power on again and tried to close the gap. But now the distance between the two machines hardly seemed to close. The big seaplane seemed to be gaining speed. It was pitching forward in a dive toward the sea. Will realized his idea was ridiculous. The German pilot was an old hand at this game. Skimming just above the surface he would keep Will in the field of fire of his sharp-shooting observer, while still heading for home. The DH2 did not have sufficient speed to overhaul him in a tail chase, and what could he do about it, he acknowledged, even if he did catch him? Will pressed on regardless, forcing the nose down in pursuit, kicking the rudder bar to make his little machine skip from side to side to spoil the gunner's aim. He winced as the stick twitched with the impact of a bullet gouging through an aileron. "Oh hell! Now what?" he shouted out loud in alarm as a dirty white cloud blossomed between him and the German. Cordite stung his nostrils as he hurtled through the smoke from a bursting anti-aircraft shell. For one awful moment he thought the German gunner had an artillery piece aboard, but the source of the extra gunfire appeared between the wings of the seaplane. The warship he had seen a few minutes earlier was directly ahead. In an instant he realized the reason for the seaplane's dive. He was not diving to escape. He was diving to attack.

The next few seconds felt like an eternity. Will watched in horror as a single bomb fell from a rack under the belly of the German airplane. He watched it fall, seemingly in slow motion, toward the British light cruiser. He breathed again as he saw it would miss by at least a hundred feet. A vertical geyser of water plumed upward, the sun catching the droplets and spinning a fleeting rainbow from the spray. Will had no time to admire it. The sailors below let fly with everything they had—at him. He twisted and turned through a maelstrom of tracer bullets and exploding shells. He had followed the Germans in their dive and paid the price for his recklessness. With a final desperate skidding turn he fled the scene, looked up, and saw to his horror he was flying in close formation, no more than thirty feet from and alongside the German seaplane. Intent on escaping the British gunfire he had made a terrible blunder. He froze as he stared at the crew. They were laughing. The gunner was actually holding his sides.

Will gaped at them. They revealed the reason for their hilarity. The man standing in the rear cockpit spun the now silent machine gun and pointed it at the sky. He pointed at the cocking lever and tried to jerk it back, then turned to Will, shrugging with his palms turned outward. "Jammed solid," Will breathed to himself. The German pointed at the front of the little DH2, still laughing. He had obviously seen, possibly on that first pass, that Will's machine was unarmed. He pointed at Will then cocked his thumb, and mouthed "bang," like a child playing cowboys and indians. Despite himself Will started to laugh with them. The pilot turned in his seat and pointed behind him. Will glanced back. The shoreline was already a distant blur. The pilot made a jabbing gesture at the land. Will saw his lips move, he could have sworn he was shouting "go back" in English.

Will raised a hand in salute. "Safe home—you sons of bitches!" he shouted across the narrow gap between the two machines. He hauled around and headed for the distant coast, easing warily away from the cruiser now making a fine cloud of black smoke as it headed for port. He endured anxious minutes as the land seemed to stay far in the distance. He felt sure the rotary was misfiring, even though the rev counter showed his rpm's to be fine. Automatic rough, he smiled to himself, always happens over water. His fuel level gave cause for concern. He had no way of judging how much he had left. No fuel gauge told him and he did not even know how much the DH2 carried. He cursed himself for his poor airmanship. With enormous relief he saw the shingle beach slip beneath him. In a few more minutes he slipped the biplane in to a perfect three point landing. He cut the motor and allowed Geoffrey de Havilland's little fighter to coast to a curving stop. It had proved itself. He suddenly felt very tired, his limbs like jelly. Wearily he pushed up his goggles then pulled his helmet off. He looked down at the excited crowd that had appeared at the field. Mechanics happily pointed out the holes in the aileron, and another group in the rudder, their voices full of admiration.

Tom pushed his way to the front. "Are you all right, Will? What's that on your cheek?"

Will pulled off his glove and touched his fingers to the side of his face. They came away with a smear of blood. He grinned down at his friend. "I'm just fine, Tom. But I think I need that drink now."